THE WORLD OF MR. MULLINER

The World of
MR. MULLINER

by P. G. WODEHOUSE

 AVON
PUBLISHERS OF BARD, CAMELOT AND DISCUS BOOKS

CONTENTS

PREFACE

As I sit down to begin this Preface to "The World Of Mr. Mulliner", it is not the thought of how heavy the book is going to be for the customers to hold that causes me concern; it is the question so many authors have asked themselves when preparing their material for the printer, "How about this stuff? Is it all right?"

It is so easy for a writer of humorous stories to go wrong, as Oliver Wendell Holmes, the Autocrat At the Breakfast Table man, once did. He wrote what he knew to be his masterpiece, and in genial mood gave it to his butler to read before taking it down to the editorial office. The butler first giggled a little, then started shaking like a jelly, and finally fell to the floor in convulsions. Holmes had made the mixture too rich. He concludes the poem in which he recorded the incident with the words:

Week after week, both day and night, I nursed that wretched man.
So now I never dare to write as funny as I can.

I must warn my public that in "The World Of Mr. Mulliner" I am writing as funny as I can, and I can only hope that there will be no ill results.

It was some time, several years in fact, before I made Mr. Mulliner's acquaintance, and during those years, though I was getting along all right, I had my dark moods when I would ask myself "Where do I go from here?" "Off to a nice start," I would say to myself, "but what of the shape of things to come?" As a littérateur I was in the position of a cricket captain with two bowlers he can rely on. Jeeves held down the pavilion end while at the other was the Drones Club, and both were doing well. I knew, however, that sooner or later I would need a change.

But where to find one?

All this time I had been getting ideas for stories and shoving them down in the old notebook, but it seemed to me that they were all too bizarre for editorial consumption. Editors like a laugh, but would George Horace Lorimer of the *Saturday Evening Post*, who had been lavish with his hospitality up till now, like one enough to pay *Saturday Evening Post* prices for something about a man who cured himself of stammering by getting chased across country by an angry mob armed with pitchforks? I could not but feel that the odds a level-headed turf accountant would have given against were in the neighbourhood of a hundred to eight. So for a while the plots remained where they were, filed for future reference.

Oddly enough, it was while reading a magazine story of a type I particularly dislike that I was enabled to solve the problem and get over the crux or impasse or whatever you call it. You know the sort of thing I mean; you must have read them by the dozens. We were sitting round the fire at the club that winter night—old General Frobisher, Lucas the barrister, Jukes the surgeon and a few more—and the conversation had turned to narrow escapes. Jukes had just told us of a delicate operation in his younger days when, having allowed his attention to wander, he had been on the point of removing a patient's left lung when it ought to have been his right hip bone and had collected himself just in time, and there was a silence.

It was broken by Lionel Popjoy, the big-game hunter and explorer, a bronzed taciturn man who until now had not spoken.

"I don't know if I have ever told you fellows about the close shave I had some years ago when I was in East Africa trying to steal the ruby which was the eye of the idol of the 'Mgumbi tribe'."

And then you get the story.

I was skimming my way through it, I think I had come to the part about the sacred crocodile, when suddenly a thought came like a full-blown rose, flushing my brow, as the fellow said. Why not have those stories of mine told by a fisherman, whose veracity would be automatically suspect? And at the same moment the name Mr. Mulliner occurred to me. Flinging the magazine from me, I went to my desk, took typewriter in hand, and hitting the wrong key once or twice in my agitation wrote.

THE TRFTH ABOUT GEORGE

BY

P. G. W%DEHOUSE

The results were magical. From then on it was like finding money in the street. Lorimer liked the story and suggested a series, and a series, of course, was what I had nothing else but. The plots of at least half a dozen more were down in my notebook. I took Jeeves off, transfering him to novels, and put Mr. Mulliner on at the pavilion end, where he has remained ever since.

One of the great attractions of these stories (to me) is that they came out so easily. Authors as a class are not men who like work. Just as, according to Shakespeare, snails creep unwillingly to school, so do writers of wholesome fiction slow up as they approach their desks. I myself have probably sharpened as many pencils and cleaned out as many pipes before getting down to it as any man in the business. But with the Mulliner stories there was none of this reluctance to start giving English Literature a shot in the arm. I flew to the task like the Polish gentleman in the ballad who sang "Ding dong, ding dong, I hurry along, for it is my wedding morning". The stuff came pouring out as if somebody had turned a tap. I am, as a rule, a thousand-words-at-a-sitting man, but with Mulliner it was more like half a story before lunch.

A word of warning. As regards the medium dose for an adult, I would recommend, as I did in my Preface to "The World Of Jeeves," not more than two or perhaps three stories a day, taken at breakfast or before retiring. Don't try to read the whole book straight through just so as to say you've done it. Nervous people and invalids will of course be guided by their doctor's advice.

P. G. WODEHOUSE.

1
THE TRUTH ABOUT GEORGE

Two men were sitting in the bar-parlour of the Anglers' Rest as I entered it; and one of them, I gathered from his low, excited voice and wide gestures, was telling the other a story. I could hear nothing but an occasional "Biggest I ever saw in my life!" and "Fully as large as that!" but in such a place it was not difficult to imagine the rest; and when the second man, catching my eye, winked at me with a sort of humorous misery, I smiled sympathetically back at him.

The action had the effect of establishing a bond between us; and when the story-teller finished his tale and left, he came over to my table as if answering a formal invitation.

"Dreadful liars some men are," he said genially.

"Fishermen," I suggested, "are traditionally careless of the truth."

"He wasn't a fisherman," said my companion. "That was our local doctor. He was telling me about his latest case of dropsy. Besides"— he tapped me earnestly on the knee—"you must not fall into the popular error about fishermen. Tradition has maligned them. I am a fisherman myself, and I have never told a lie in my life."

I could well believe it. He was a short, stout, comfortable man of middle age, and the thing that struck me first about him was the extraordinarily childlike candour of his eyes. They were large and round and honest. I would have bought oil stock from him without a tremor.

The door leading into the white dusty road opened, and a small man with rimless pince-nez and an anxious expression shot in like a rabbit and had consumed a gin and ginger-beer almost before we knew he was there. Having thus refreshed himself, he stood looking as us, seemingly ill at ease.

"N-n-n-n-n-n——" he said.

We looked at him inquiringly.

"N-n-n-n-n-n-ice d-d-d-d——"

His nerve appeared to fail him, and he vanished as abruptly as he had come.

"I think he was leading up to telling us that it was a nice day," hazarded my companion.

"It must be very embarrassing," I said, "for a man with such a painful impediment in his speech to open conversation with strangers."

"Probably trying to cure himself. Like my nephew George. Have I ever told you about my nephew George?"

I reminded him that we had only just met, and that this was the first time I had learned that he had a nephew George.

"Young George Mulliner. My name is Mulliner. I will tell you about George's case—in many ways a rather remarkable one."

My nephew George (said Mr. Mulliner) was as nice a young fellow as you would ever wish to meet, but from childhood up he had been cursed with a terrible stammer. If he had had to earn his living, he would undoubtedly have found this affliction a great handicap, but fortunately his father had left him a comfortable income; and George spent a not unhappy life, residing in the village where he had been born and passing his days in the usual country sports and his evenings in doing crossword puzzles. By the time he was thirty he knew more about Eli, the prophet, Ra, the Sun God, and the bird Emu than anybody else in the county except Susan Blake, the vicar's daughter, who had also taken up the solving of crossword puzzles and was the first girl in Worcestershire to find out the meaning of "stearine" and "crepuscular".

It was his association with Miss Blake that first turned George's thoughts to a serious endeavour to cure himself of his stammer. Naturally, with this hobby in common, the young people saw a great deal of one another: for George was always looking in at the vicarage to ask her if she knew a word of seven letters meaning "appertaining to the profession of plumbing", and Susan was just as constant a caller at George's cosy little cottage being frequently stumped, as girls will be, by words of eight letters signifying "largely used in the manufacture of poppet-valves". The consequence was that one evening, just after she had helped him out of a tight place with the word "disestablishmentarianism," the boy suddenly awoke to the truth and realised that she was all the world to him—or, as he put it to himself from force of habit, precious, beloved, darling, much-loved, highly esteemed or valued.

And yet, every time he tried to tell her so, he could get no further than a sibilant gurgle which was no more practical use than a hiccup.

Something obviously had to be done, and George went to London to see a specialist.

"Yes?" said the specialist.

"I-I-I-I-I-I-I——" said George.

"You were saying——?"

"Woo-woo-woo-woo-woo-woo——"

"Sing it," said the specialist.

"S-s-s-s-s-s-s——?" said George, puzzled.

The specialist explained. He was a kindly man with moth-eaten whiskers and an eye like a meditative cod-fish.

"Many people," he said, "who are unable to articulate clearly in ordinary speech find themselves lucid and bell-like when they burst into song."

It seemed a good idea to George. He thought for a moment; then threw his head back, shut his eyes, and let it go in a musical baritone.

"I love a lassie, a bonny, bonny lassie," sang George. "She's as pure as the lily in the dell."

"No doubt," said the specialist, wincing a little.

"She's as sweet as the heather, the bonny purple heather—Susan, my Worcestershire bluebell."

"Ah!" said the specialist. "Sounds a nice girl. Is this she?" he asked, adjusting his glasses and peering at the photograph which George had extracted from the interior of the left side of his under-vest.

George nodded, and drew in breath.

"Yes, sir," he carolled, "that's my baby. No, sir, don't mean maybe. Yes, sir, that's my baby now. And, by the way, by the way, when I meet that preacher I shall say—'Yes, sir, that's my——'."

"Quite," said the specialist, hurriedly. He had a sensitive ear. "Quite, quite."

"If you knew Susie like I know Susie," George was beginning, but the other stopped him.

"Quite. Exactly. I shouldn't wonder. And now," said the specialist, "what precisely is the trouble? No," he added, hastily, as George inflated his lungs, "don't sing it. Write the particulars on this piece of paper."

George did so.

"H'm!" said the specialist, examining the screed. "You wish to woo, court, and become betrothed, engaged, affianced to this girl, but you find yourself unable, incapable, incompetent, impotent, and powerless. Every time you attempt it, your vocal cords fail, fall short, are insufficient, wanting, deficient, and go blooey."

George nodded.

"A not unusual case. I have had to deal with this sort of thing before. The effect of love on the vocal cords of even a normally eloquent subject is frequently deleterious. As regards the habitual stammerer, tests have shown that in ninety-seven point five six nine recurring of cases the divine passion reduces him to a condition where he sounds like a soda-water siphon trying to recite Gunga Din. There is only one cure."

"W-w-w-w-w——?" asked George.

"I will tell you. Stammering," proceeded the specialist, putting the tips of his fingers together and eyeing George benevolently, "is mainly mental and is caused by shyness, which is caused by the inferiority complex, which in its turn is caused by suppressed desires or introverted inhibitions or something. The advice I give to all young men who come in here behaving like soda-water siphons is to go out and make a point of speaking to at least three perfect strangers every day. Engage these strangers in conversation, persevering no matter how priceless a chump you may feel, and before many weeks are out you will find that the little daily dose has had its effect. Shyness will wear off, and with it the stammer."

And, having requested the young man—in a voice of the clearest timbre, free from all trace of impediment—to hand over a fee of five guineas, the specialist sent George out into the world.

The more George thought about the advice he had been given, the less he liked it. He shivered in the cab that took him to the station to catch the train back to East Wobsley. Like all shy young men, he had never hitherto looked upon himself as shy—preferring to attribute his distaste for the society of his fellows to some subtle rareness of soul. But now that the thing had been put squarely up to him, he was compelled to realise that in all essentials he was a perfect rabbit. The thought of accosting perfect strangers and forcing his conversation upon them sickened him.

But no Mulliner has ever shirked an unpleasant duty. As he reached the platform and strode along it to the train, his teeth were set, his eyes shone with an almost fanatical light of determination, and he intended before his journey was over to conduct three heart-to-heart chats if he had to sing every bar of them.

The compartment into which he had made his way was empty at the moment, but just before the train started a very large, fierce-looking man got in. George would have preferred somebody a little less formidable for his first subject, but he braced himself and bent forward. And, as he did so, the man spoke.

"The wur-wur-wur-wur-weather," he said, "sus-sus-seems to be ter-ter-taking a tur-tur-turn for the ber-ber-better, der-doesn't it?"

George sank back as if he had been hit between the eyes. The train had moved out of the dimness of the station by now, and the sun was shining brightly on the speaker, illuminating his knobbly shoulders, his craggy jaw, and, above all, the shockingly choleric look in his eyes. To reply "Y-y-y-y-y-y-y-yes" to such a man would obviously be madness.

But to abstain from speech did not seem to be much better as a policy. George's silence appeared to arouse this man's worst passions. His face had turned purple and he glared painfully.

"I uk-uk-asked you a sus-sus-civil quk-quk-quk," he said, irascibly. "Are you d-d-d-d-deaf?"

All we Mulliners have been noted for our prescence of mind. To open his mouth, point to his tonsils, and utter a strangled gurgle was with George the work of a moment.

The tension relaxed. The man's annoyance abated.

"D-d-d-dumb?" he said, commiseratingly. "I beg your p-p-p-p-pup. I t-t-trust I have not caused you p-p-p-p-pup. It m-must be tut-tut-tut-tut-tut not to be able to sus-sus-speak fuf-fuf-fuf-fuf-fluently."

He then buried himself in his paper, and George sank back in his corner, quivering in every limb.

To get to East Wobsley, as you doubtless know, you have to change at Ippleton and take the branch-line. By the time the train reached this junction, George's composure was somewhat restored. He deposited his belongings in a compartment of the East Wobsley train, which was waiting in a glued manner on the other side of the platform, and, finding that it would not start for some ten minutes, decided to pass the time by strolling up and down in the pleasant air.

It was a lovely afternoon. The sun was gilding the platform with its rays, and a gentle breeze blew from the west. A little brook ran tinkling at the side of the road; birds were singing in the hedgerows; and through the trees could be discerned dimly the noble facade of the County Lunatic Asylum. Soothed by his surroundings, George began to feel so refreshed that he regretted that in this wayside station there was no one present whom he could engage in talk.

It was at this moment that the distinguished-looking stranger entered the platform.

The newcomer was a man of imposing physique, simply dressed in pyjamas, brown boots, and a mackintosh. In his hand he carried a top-hat, and into this he was dipping his fingers, taking them out, and then waving them in a curious manner to right and left. He nodded so affably to George that the latter, though a little surprised at the other's costume, decided to speak. After all, he reflected, clothes do not make the man, and, judging from the other's smile, a warm heart appeared to beat beneath that orange-and-mauve striped pyjama jacket.

"N-n-n-n-nice weather," he said.

"Glad you like it," said the stranger. "I ordered it specially."

George was a little puzzled by this remark, but he persevered.

"M-might I ask wur-wur-what you are dud-doing?"

"Doing?"

"With that her-her-her-her-hat?"

"Oh, with this hat? I see what you mean. Just scattering largesse to the multitude," replied the stranger, dipping his fingers once more and waving them with a generous gesture. "Devil of a bore, but it's expected of a man in my position. The fact is," he said, linking his arm in George's and speaking in a confidential undertone, "I'm the Emperor of Abyssinia. That's my palace over there," he said, pointing through the trees. "Don't let it go any further. It's not supposed to be generally known."

It was with a rather sickly smile that George now endeavoured to withdraw his arm from that of his companion, but the other would have none of this aloofness. He seemed to be in complete agreement with Shakespeare's dictum that a friend, when found, should be grappled to you with hooks of steel. He held George in a vice-like grip and drew him into a recess of the platform. He looked about him, and seemed satisfied.

"We are alone at last," he said.

This fact had already impressed itself with sickening clearness on the young man. There are few spots in the civilised world more deserted than the platform of a small country station. The sun shone on the smooth asphalt, on the gleaming rails, and on the machine which, in exchange for a penny placed in the slot marked "Matches", would supply a package of wholesome butter-scotch—but on nothing else.

What George could have done with at the moment was a posse of police armed with stout clubs, and there was not even a dog in sight.

"I've been wanting to talk to you for a long time," said the stranger, genially.

"Huh-huh-have you?" said George.

"Yes. I want your opinion of human sacrifices."

George said he didn't like them.

"Why not?" asked the other, surprised.

George said it was hard to explain. He just didn't.

"Well, I think you're wrong," said the Emperor. "I know there's a school of thought growing up that holds your views, but I disapprove of it. I hate all this modern advanced thought. Human sacrifices have always been good enough for the Emperors of Abyssinia, and they're good enough for me. Kindly step in here, if you please."

He indicated the lamp-and-mop room, at which they had now arrived. It was a dark and sinister apartment, smelling strongly of oil and porters, and was probably the last place on earth in which George would have wished to be closeted with a man of such peculiar views. He shrank back.

"You go in first," he said.

"No larks," said the other, suspiciously.

"L-l-l-l-larks?"

"Yes. No pushing a fellow in and locking the door and squirting water at him through the window. I've had that happen to me before."

"Sus-certainly not."

"Right!" said the Emperor. "You're a gentleman and I'm a gentleman. Both gentlemen. Have you a knife, by the way? We shall need a knife."

"No. No knife."

"Ah, well," said the Emperor, "then we'll have to look about for something else. No doubt we shall manage somehow."

And with the debonair manner which so became him, he scattered another handful of largesse and walked into the lamproom.

It was not the fact that he had given his word as a gentleman that kept George from locking the door. There is probably no family on earth more nicely scrupulous as regards keeping its promises than the Mulliners, but I am compelled to admit that, had George been able to find the key, he would have locked that door without hesitation. Not being able to find the key, he had to be satisfied with banging it. This done, he leaped back and raced away down the platform. A confused noise within seemed to indicate that the Emperor had become involved with some lamps.

George made the best of the respite. Covering the ground at a high rate of speed, he flung himself into the train and took refuge under the seat.

There he remained, quaking. At one time he thought that his uncongenial acquaintance had got upon his track, for the door of the compartment opened and a cool wind blew in upon him. Then, glancing along the floor, he perceived feminine ankles. The relief was enormous, but even in his relief George, who was the soul of modesty, did not forget his manners. He closed his eyes.

A voice spoke.

"Porter!"

"Yes, ma'am?"

"What was all that disturbance as I came into the station?"

"Patient escaped from the asylum, ma'am."

"Good gracious!"

The voice would undoubtedly have spoken further, but at this moment the train began to move. There came the sound of a body descending upon a cushioned seat, and some little time later the rustling of a paper. The train gathered speed and jolted on.

George had never before travelled under the seat of a railway-carriage; and, though he belonged to the younger generation, which is supposed to be so avid of new experiences, he had no desire to do so now. He decided to emerge, and if possible, to emerge with the minimum of ostentation. Little as he knew of women, he was aware that as a sex they are apt to be startled by the sight of men crawling out from under the seats of compartments. He began his manœuvres by poking out his head and surveying the terrain.

All was well. The woman, in her seat across the way, was engrossed in her paper. Moving in a series of noiseless wriggles, George extricated himself from his hiding-place and, with a twist which would have been impossible to a man not in the habit of doing Swedish exercises daily before breakfast, heaved himself into the corner seat. The woman continued reading her paper.

The events of the past quarter of an hour had tended rather to drive from George's mind the mission which he had undertaken on leaving the specialist's office. But now, having leisure for reflection, he realised that, if he meant to complete his first day of the cure, he was allowing himself to run sadly behind schedule. Speak to three strangers, the specialist had told him, and up to the present he had spoken to only one. True, this one had been a pretty considerable stranger, and a less conscientious young man than George Mulliner might have considered himself justified in chalking him up on the score-board as one and a half or even two. But George had the dogged, honest Mulliner streak in him, and he refused to quibble.

He nerved himself for action, and cleared his throat.

'Ah-h'rm!" said George.

And, having opened the ball, he smiled a winning smile and waited for his companion to make the next move.

The move which his companion made was in an upwards direction, and measured from six to eight inches. She dropped her paper and regarded George with a pale-eyed horror. One pictures her a little in the position of Robinson Crusoe when he saw the footprint in the sand. She had been convinced that she was completely alone, and lo! out of space a voice had spoken to her. Her face worked, but she made no remark.

George, on his side, was also feeling a little ill at ease. Women always increased his natural shyness. He never knew what to say to them.

Then a happy thought struck him. He had just glanced at his watch and found the hour to be nearly four-thirty. Women, he knew, loved a drop of tea at about this time, and fortunately there was in his suit-case a full thermos-flask.

"Pardon me, but I wonder if you would care for a cup of tea?" was what he wanted to say, but, as so often happened with him when in the presence of the opposite sex, he could get no further than a sort of sizzling sound like a cockroach calling to its young.

The woman continued to stare at him. Her eyes were now about the size of regulation standard golf-balls, and her breathing suggested the last stages of asthma. And it was at this point that George, struggling for speech, had one of those inspirations which frequently come to Mulliners. There flashed into his mind what the specialist had told him about singing. Say it with music—that was the thing to do.

He delayed no longer.

"Tea for two and two for tea and me for you and you for me ——"

He was shocked to observe his companion turning Nile-green. He decided to make his meaning clearer.

"I have a nice thermos. I have a full thermos. Won't you share my thermos, too? When skies are grey and you feel you are blue, tea sends the sun smiling through. I have a nice thermos. I have a full thermos. May I pour out some for you?"

You will agree with me, I think, that no invitation could have been more happily put, but his companion was not responsive. With one last agonised look at him, she closed her eyes and sank back in her seat. Her lips had now turned a curious grey-blue colour, and they were moving feebly. She reminded George, who, like myself, was a keen fisherman, of a newly-gaffed salmon.

George sat back in his corner, brooding. Rack his brain as he might, he could think of no topic which could be guaranteed to interest, elevate, and amuse. He looked out of the window with a sigh.

The train was now approaching the dear old familiar East Wobsley country. He began to recognise landmarks. A wave of sentiment poured over George as he thought of Susan, and he reached for the bag of buns which he had bought at the refreshment room at Ippleton. Sentiment always made him hungry.

He took his thermos out of the suit-case, and, unscrewing the top, poured himself out a cup of tea. Then, placing the thermos on the seat, he drank.

He looked across at his companion. Her eyes were still closed, and she uttered little sighing noises. George was half inclined to renew his offer of tea, but the only tune he could remember was "Hard-Hearted Hannah, the Vamp from Savannah," and it was difficult to fit suitable words to it. He ate his bun and gazed out at the familiar scenery.

Now, as you approach East Wobsley, the train, I must mention, has to pass over some points; and so violent is the sudden jerking that strong men have been known to spill their beer. George, forgetting this in his preoccupation, had placed the thermos only a few inches from the edge of the seat. The result was that, as the train reached the points, the flask leaped like a live thing, dived to the floor, and exploded.

Even George was distinctly upset by the sudden sharpness of the report. His bun sprang from his hand and was dashed to fragments. He blinked thrice in rapid succession. His heart tried to jump out of his mouth and loosened a front tooth.

But on the woman opposite the effect of the untoward occurrence was still more marked. With a single piercing shriek, she rose from her seat straight into the air like a rocketing pheasant; and, having clutched the communication-cord, fell back again. Impressive as her previous leap had been, she excelled it now by several inches. I do not know what the existing record for the Sitting High-Jump is, but she undoubtedly lowered it; and if George had been a member of the Olympic Games Selection Committee, he would have signed this woman up immediately.

It is a curious thing that, in spite of the railway companies' sporting willingness to let their patrons have a tug at the extremely moderate price of five pounds a go, very few people have ever either pulled a communication-cord or seen one pulled. There is, thus, a widespread ignorance as to what precisely happens on such occasions.

The procedure, George tells me, is as follows: First there comes a grinding noise, as the brakes are applied. Then the train stops. And finally, from every point of the compass, a seething mob of interested onlookers begins to appear.

It was about a mile and a half from East Wobsley that the affair had taken place, and as far as the eye could reach the countryside was totally devoid of humanity. A moment before nothing had been visible but smiling cornfields and broad pasture-lands; but now from east, west, north, and south running figures began to appear. We must remember that George at the time was in a somewhat overwrought frame of mind, and his statements should therefore be accepted with caution; but he tells me that out of the middle of a single empty meadow, entirely devoid of cover, no fewer than twenty-seven distinct rustics suddenly appeared, having undoubtedly shot up through the ground.

The rails, which had been completely unoccupied, were now thronged with so dense a crowd of navvies that it seemed to George absurd to pretend that there was any unemployment in England. Every member of the labouring classes throughout the country was so palpably present. Moreover, the train, which at Ippleton had seemed sparsely occupied, was disgorging passengers from every door. It was the sort of mob-scene which would have made David W. Griffith scream with delight; and it looked, George says, like Guest Night at the Royal Automobile Club. But, as I say, we must remember that he was overwrought.

It is difficult to say what precisely would have been the correct behaviour of your polished man of the world in such a situation. I think myself that a great deal of sang-froid and address would be required even by the most self-possessed in order to pass off such a contretemps. To George, I may say at once, the crisis revealed itself immediately as one which he was totally incapable of handling. The one clear thought that stood out from the welter of his emotions was the reflection that it was advisable to remove himself, and to do so without delay. Drawing a deep breath, he shot swiftly off the mark.

All we Mulliners have been athletes; and George, when at the University, had been noted for his speed of foot. He ran now as he had never run before. His statement, however, that as he sprinted across the first field he distinctly saw a rabbit shoot an envious glance at him as he passed and shrug its shoulders hopelessly, I am inclined to discount. George, As I have said before, was a little over-excited.

Nevertheless, it is not to be questioned that he made good going. And he had need to, for after the first instant of surprise, which had enabled him to secure a lead, the whole mob was pouring across country after him; and dimly, as he ran, he could hear voices in the throng informally discussing the advisability of lynching him. Moreover, the field through which he was running, a moment before a bare expanse of green, was now black with figures, headed by a man with a beard who carried a pitchfork. George swerved sharply to the right, casting a swift glance over his shoulder at his pursuers. He disliked them all, but especially the man with the pitchfork.

It is impossible for one who was not an eye-witness to say how long the chase continued and how much ground was covered by the interested parties. I know the East Wobsley country well, and I have checked George's statements; and, if it is true that he travelled east as far as Little Wigmarsh-in-the-Dell and as far west as Higgleford-cum-Wortlebury-beneath-the-Hill, he must undoubtedly have done a lot of running.

But a point which must not be forgotten is that, to a man not in a condition to observe closely, the village of Higgleford-cum-Wortlebury-beneath-the-Hill might easily not have been Higgleford-cum-Wortlebury-beneath-the-Hill at all, but another hamlet which in many respects closely resembles it. I need scarcely say that I allude to Lesser-Snodsbury-in-the-Vale.

Let us assume, therefore, that George, having touched Little-Wigmarsh-in-the-Dell, shot off at a tangent and reached Lesser-Snodsbury-in-the-Vale. This would be a considerable run. And, as he remembers flitting past Farmer Higgins's pigsty and the Dog and Duck at Pondlebury Parva and splashing through the brook Wipple at the point where it joins the River Wopple, we can safely assume that, wherever else he went, he got plenty of exercise.

But the pleasantest of functions must end, and, just as the setting sun was gilding the spire of the ivy-covered church of St. Barnabas the Resilient, where George as a child had sat so often, enlivening the tedium of the sermon by making faces at the choir-boys, a damp and bedraggled figure might have been observed crawling painfully along the High Street of East Wobsley in the direction of the cosy little cottage known to its builder as Chatsworth and to the village tradesmen as "Mulliner's".

It was George, home from the hunting-field.

Slowly George Mulliner made his way to the familiar door, and, passing through it, flung himself into his favourite chair. But a moment later a more imperious need than the desire to rest forced itself upon his attention. Rising stiffly, he tottered to the kitchen and mixed himself a revivifying whisky-and-soda. Then, refilling his glass, he returned to the sitting-room, to find that it was no longer empty. A slim, fair girl, tastefully attired in tailor-made tweeds, was leaning over the desk on which he kept his Dictionary of English Synonyms.

She looked up as he entered, startled.

"Why, Mr. Mulliner!" she exclaimed. "What has been happening? Your clothes are torn, rent, ragged, tattered, and your hair is all dishevelled, untrimmed, hanging loose or negligently, at loose ends!"

George smiled a wan smile.

"You are right," he said. "And what is more, I am suffering from extreme fatigue, weariness, lassitude, exhaustion, prostration and languor."

The girl gazed at him, a divine pity in her soft eyes.

"I'm so sorry," she murmured. "So very sorry, grieved, distressed, afflicted, pained, mortified, dejected, and upset."

George took her hand. Her sweet sympathy had effected the cure for which he had been seeking so long. Coming on top of the violent emotions through which he had been passing all day, it seemed to work on him like some healing spell, charm, or incantation. Suddenly, in a flash, he realised that he was no longer a stammerer. Had he wished at that moment to say "Peter Piper picked a peck of pickled peppers," he could have done it without a second thought.

But he had better things to say than that.

"Miss Blake—Susan—Susie." He took her other hand in his. His voice rang out clear and unimpeded. It seemed to him incredible that he had ever yammered at this girl like an overheated steam-radiator. "It cannot have escaped your notice that I have long entertained towards you sentiments warmer and deeper than those of ordinary friendship. It is love, Susan, that has been animating my bosom. Love, first a tiny seed, has burgeoned in my heart till, blazing into flame, it has swept away on the crest of its wave my diffidence, my doubt, my fears, and my fore-boding, and now, like the topmost topaz of some ancient tower, it cries to all the world in a voice of thunder: 'You are mine! My mate! Predestined to me since Time first began!' As the star guides the mariner when, battered by boiling billows, he hies him home to the haven of hope and happiness, so do you gleam upon me along life's rough road and seem to say, 'Have courage, George! I am here!' Susan, I am not an eloquent man—I cannot speak fluently as I could wish —but these simple words which you have just heard come from the heart, from the unspotted heart of an English gentleman. Susan, I love you. Will you be my wife, married woman, matron, spouse, help-meet, consort, partner or better half?"

"Oh, George!" said Susan. "Yes, yea, ay, aye! Decidedly, unquestionably, in-dubitably, incontrovertibly, and past all dispute!"

He folded her in his arms. And, as he did so, there came from the street outside —faintly, as from a distance—the sound of feet and voices. George leaped to the window. Rounding the corner, just by the Cow and Wheelbarrow public-house, licensed to sell ales, wines, and spirits, was the man with the pitchfork, and be-hind him followed a vast crowd.

"My darling," said George, "for purely personal and private reasons, into which I need not enter, I must now leave you. Will you join me later?"

"I will follow you to the ends of the earth," replied Susan, passionately.

"It will not be necessary," said George. "I am only going down to the coal-cellar. I shall spend the next half-hour or so there. If anybody calls and asks for me, perhaps you would not mind telling them that I am out."

"I will, I will," said Susan. "And, George, by the way. What I really came here for was to ask you if you knew a hyphenated word of nine letters, ending in k and signifying an implement employed in the pursuit of agriculture."

"Pitchfork, sweetheart," said George. "But you may take it from me, as one who knows, that agriculture isn't the only thing it is used in pursuit of."

And since that day (concluded Mr. Mulliner) George, believe me or believe me not, has not had the slightest trace of an impediment in his speech. He is now the chosen orator at all political rallies for miles around; and so offensively self-con-fident has his manner become that only last Friday he had his eye blacked by a hay-corn-and-feed merchant of the name of Stubbs. It just shows you, doesn't it?

2
A SLICE OF LIFE

THE conversation in the bar-parlour of the Anglers' Rest had drifted round to the subject of the Arts: and somebody asked if that film-serial, "The Vicissitudes of Vera", which they were showing down at the Bijou Dream, was worth seeing.

"It's very good," said Miss Postlethwaite, our courteous and efficient barmaid, who is a prominent first-nighter. "It's about this mad professor who gets this girl into his toils and tries to turn her into a lobster."

"Tries to turn her into a lobster?" echoed we, surprised.

"Yes, sir. Into a lobster. It seems he collected thousands and thousands of lobsters and mashed them up and boiled down the juice from their glands and was just going to inject it into this Vera Dalrymple's spinal column when Jack Frobisher broke into the house and stopped him."

"Why did he do that?"

"Because he didn't want the girl he loved to be turned into a lobster."

"What we mean," said we, "is why did the professor want to turn the girl into a lobster?"

"He had a grudge against her."

This seemed plausible, and we thought it over for a while. Then one of the company shook his head disapprovingly.

"I don't like stories like that," he said. "They aren't true to life."

"Pardon me, sir," said a voice. And we were aware of Mr. Mulliner in our midst.

"Excuse me interrupting what may be a private discussion," said Mr. Mulliner, "but I chanced to overhear the recent remarks, and you, sir, have opened up a subject on which I happen to hold strong views—to wit, the question of what is and what is not true to life. How can we, with our limited experience, answer that question? For all we know, at this very moment hundreds of young women all over the country may be in the process of being turned into lobsters. Forgive my warmth, but I have suffered a good deal from this sceptical attitude of mind which is so prevalent nowadays. I have even met people who refused to believe my story about my brother Wilfred, purely because it was a little out of the ordinary run of the average man's experience."

Considerably moved, Mr. Mulliner ordered a hot Scotch with a slice of lemon.

"What happened to your brother Wilfred? Was he turned into a lobster?"

"No," said Mr. Mulliner, fixing his honest blue eyes on the speaker, "he was not. It would be perfectly easy for me to pretend that he was turned into a lobster; but I have always made it a practice—and I always shall make it a practice—to speak nothing but the bare truth. My brother Wilfred simply had rather a curious adventure."

My brother Wilfred (said Mr. Mulliner) is the clever one of the family. Even as a boy he was always messing about with chemicals, and at the University he devoted his time entirely to research. The result was that while still quite a young man he had won an established reputation as the inventor of what are known to the trade as Mulliner's Magic Marvels—a general term embracing the Raven Gipsy Face-Cream, the Snow of the Mountains Lotion, and many other preparations, some designed exclusively for the toilet, others of a curative nature, intended to alleviate the many ills to which the flesh is heir.

Naturally, he was a very busy man: and it is to this absorption in his work that I attribute the fact that, though—like all the Mulliners—a man of striking personal charm, he had reached his thirty-first year without ever having been involved in an affair of the heart. I remember him telling me once that he simply had no time for girls.

But we all fall sooner or later, and these strong concentrated men harder than any. While taking a brief holiday one year at Cannes, he met a Miss Angela Purdue, who was staying at his hotel, and she bowled him over completely.

She was one of these jolly, outdoor girls; and Wilfred had told me that what attracted him first about her was her wholesome, sunburned complexion. In fact, he told Miss Purdue the same thing when, shortly after he had proposed and been accepted, she asked him in her girlish way what it was that had first made him begin to love her.

"It's such a pity," said Miss Purdue, "that the sunburn fades so soon. I do wish I knew some way of keeping it."

Even in his moments of holiest emotion Wilfred never forgot that he was a business man.

"You should try Mulliner's Raven Gipsy Face-Cream," he said. "It comes in two sizes—the small (or half-crown) jar and the large jar at seven shillings and sixpence. The large jar contains three and a half times as much as the small jar. It is applied nightly with a small sponge before retiring to rest. Testimonials have been received from numerous members of the aristocracy and may be examined at the office by any bona-fide inquirer."

"Is is really good?"

"I invented it," said Wilfred, simply.

She looked at him adoringly.

"How clever you are! Any girl ought to be proud to marry you."

"Oh, well," said Wilfred, with a modest wave of his hand.

"All the same, my guardian is going to be terribly angry when I tell him we're engaged."

"Why?"

"I inherited the Purdue millions when my uncle died, you see, and my guardian has always wanted me to marry his son, Percy."

Wilfred kissed her fondly, and laughed a defiant laugh.

"Jer mong feesh der selar," he said lightly.

But, some days after his return to London, whither the girl had preceded him, he had occasion to recall her words. As he sat in his study, musing on a preparation to cure the pip in canaries, a card was brought to him.

"Sir Jasper ffinch-ffarrowmere, Bart.," he read. The name was strange to him.

"Show the gentleman in," he said. And presently there entered a very stout man with a broad, pink face. It was a face whose natural expression should, Wilfred felt, have been jovial, but at the moment it was grave.

"Sir Jasper Finch-Farrowmere?" said Wilfred.

"ffinch-ffarrowmere," corrected the visitor, his sensitive ear detecting the capital letters.

"Ah yes. You spell it with two small f's."

"Four small f's."

"And to what do I owe the honour——"

"I am Angela Purdue's guardian."

"How do you do? A whisky-and-soda?"

"I thank you, no. I am a total abstainer. I found that alcohol had a tendency to increase my weight, so I gave it up. I have also given up butter, potatoes, soups of all kinds and——However," he broke off, the fanatic gleam which comes into the eyes of all fat men who are describing their system of diet fading away, "this is not a social call, and I must not take up your time with idle talk. I have a message for you, Mr. Mulliner. From Angela."

"Bless her!" said Wilfred. "Sir Jasper, I love that girl with a fervour which increases daily."

"Is that so?" said the baronet. "Well, what I came to say was, it's all off."

"What?"

"All off. She sent me to say that she had thought it over and wanted to break the engagement."

Wilfred's eyes narrowed. He had not forgotten what Angela had said about this man wanting her to marry his son. He gazed piercingly at his visitor, no longer deceived by the superficial geniality of his appearance. He had read too many detective stories where the fat, jolly, red-faced man turns out a fiend in human shape to be a ready victim to appearances.

"Indeed?" he said, coldly. "I should prefer to have this information from Miss Purdue's own lips."

"She won't see you. But, anticipating this attitude on your part, I brought a letter from her. You recognize the writing?"

Wilfred took the letter. Certainly, the hand was Angela's, and the meaning of the words he read unmistakable. Nevertheless, as he handed the missive back, there was a hard smile on his face.

"There is such a thing as writing a letter under compulsion," he said.

The baronet's pink face turned mauve.

"What do you mean, sir?"

"What I say."

"Are you insinuating——"

"Yes, I am."

"Pooh, sir!"

"Pooh to you!" said Wilfred. "And, if you want to know what I think, you poor ffish, I believe your name is spelled with a capital F, like anybody else's."

Stung to the quick, the baronet turned on his heel and left the room without another word.

Although he had given up his life to chemical research, Wilfred Mulliner was no mere dreamer. He could be the man of action when necessity demanded. Scarcely had his visitor left when he was on his way to the Senior Test-Tubes, the famous chemists' club in St. James's. There, consulting Kelly's "County Families", he learnt that Sir Jasper's address was ffinch Hall in Yorkshire. He had found out all he wanted to know. It was at ffinch Hall, he decided, that Angela must now be immured.

For that she was being immured somewhere he had no doubt. That letter, he was positive, had been written by her under stress of threats. The writing was Angela's, but he declined to believe that she was responsible for the phraseology and sentiments. He remembered reading a story where the heroine was forced into courses which she would not otherwise have contemplated by the fact that somebody was standing over her with a flask of vitriol. Possibly this was what that bounder of a baronet had done to Angela.

Considering this possibility, he did not blame her for what she had said about him, Wilfred, in the second paragraph of her note. Nor did he reproach her for signing herself "Yrs truly, A. Purdue." Naturally, when baronets are threatening to pour vitriol down her neck, a refined and sensitive young girl cannot pick her words. This sort of thing must of necessity interfere with the selection of the *mot juste*.

That afternoon, Wilfred was in a train on his way to Yorkshire. That evening, he was in the ffinch Arms in the village of which Sir Jasper was the squire. That night, he was in the gardens of ffinch Hall, prowling softly round the house, listening.

And presently, as he prowled, there came to his ears from an upper window a sound that made him stiffen like a statue and clench his hands till the knuckles stood out white under the strain.

It was the sound of a woman sobbing.

Wilfred spent a sleepless night, but by morning he had formed his plan of action. I will not weary you with a description of the slow and tedious steps by which he first made the acquaintance of Sir Jasper's valet, who was an *habitué* of the village inn, and then by careful stages won the man's confidence with friendly words and beer. Suffice it to say that, about a week later, Wilfred had induced this man with bribes to leave suddenly on the plea of an aunt's illness, supplying—so as to cause his employer no inconvenience—a cousin to take his place.

This cousin, as you will have guessed, was Wilfred himself. But a very different Wilfred from the dark-haired, clean-cut young scientist who had revolutionised the world of chemistry a few months before by proving that $H_2O + b3g4z7 - m9z8 = g6f5p3x$. Before leaving London on what he knew would be a dark and dangerous enterprise, Wilfred had taken the precaution of calling in at a well-known costumier's and buying a red wig. He had also purchased a pair of blue spectacles: but for the role which he had now undertaken these were, of course, useless. A blue-spectacled valet could not but have aroused suspicion in the most guileless baronet. All that Wilfred did, therefore, in the way of preparation, was to don the wig, shave off his moustache, and treat his face to a light coating of the Raven Gipsy Face-Cream. This done, he set out for ffinch Hall.

Externally, ffinch Hall was one of those gloomy, sombre country-houses which seem to exist only for the purpose of having horrid crimes committed in them. Even in his brief visit to the grounds, Wilfred had noticed fully half a dozen places which seemed incomplete without a cross indicating the spot where body was found by the police. It was the sort of house where ravens croak in the front garden just before the death of the heir, and shrieks ring out from behind barred windows in the night.

Nor was its interior more cheerful. And, as for the personnel of the domestic staff, that was less exhilarating than anything else about the place. It consisted of an aged cook who, as she bent over her cauldrons, looked like something out of a travelling company of "Macbeth", touring the smaller towns of the North, and Murgatroyd, the butler, a huge, sinister man with a cast in one eye and an evil light in the other.

Many men, under these conditions, would have been daunted. But not Wilfred Mulliner. Apart from the fact that, like all the Mulliners, he was as brave as a lion, he had come expecting something of this nature. He settled down to his duties and kept his eyes open, and before long his vigilance was rewarded.

One day, as he lurked about the dim-lit passage-ways, he saw Sir Jasper coming up the stairs with a laden tray in his hands. It contained a toast-rack, a half bot. of white wine, pepper, salt, veg., and in a covered dish something which Wilfred, sniffing cautiously, decided was a cutlet.

Lurking in the shadows, he followed the baronet to the top of the house. Sir

Jasper paused at a door on the second floor. He knocked. The door opened, a hand was stretched forth, the tray vanished, the door closed, and the baronet moved away.

So did Wilfred. He had seen what he had wanted to see, discovered what he had wanted to discover. He returned to the servants' hall, and under the gloomy eyes of Murgatroyd began to shape his plans.

"Where you been?" demanded the butler, suspiciously.

"Oh, hither and thither," said Wilfred, with a well-assumed airiness.

Murgatroyd directed a menacing glance at him.

"You'd better stay where you belong," he said, in his thick, growling voice. "There's things in this house that don't want seeing."

"Ah!" agreed the cook, dropping an onion in the cauldron.

Wilfred could not repress a shudder.

But, even as he shuddered, he was conscious of a certain relief. At least, he reflected, they were not starving his darling. That cutlet had smelt uncommonly good: and, if the bill of fare was always maintained at this level, she had nothing to complain of in the catering.

But his relief was short-lived. What, after all, he asked himself, are cutlets to a girl who is imprisoned in a locked room of a sinister country-house and is being forced to marry a man she does not love? Practically nothing. When the heart is sick, cutlets merely alleviate, they do not cure. Fiercely Wilfred told himself that, come what might, few days should pass before he found the key to that locked door and bore away his love to freedom and happiness.

The only obstacle in the way of this scheme was that it was plainly going to be a matter of the greatest difficulty to find the key. That night, when his employer dined, Wilfred searched his room thoroughly. He found nothing. The key, he was forced to conclude, was kept on the baronet's person.

Then how to secure it?

It is not too much to say that Wilfred Mulliner was non-plussed. The brain which had electrified the world of Science by discovering that if you mixed a stiffish oxygen and potassium and added a splash of trinitrotoluol and a spot of old brandy you got something that could be sold in America as champagne at a hundred and fifty dollars the case had to confess itself baffled.

To attempt to analyse the young man's emotions, as the next week dragged itself by, would be merely morbid. Life cannot, of course, be all sunshine: and in relating a story like this, which is a slice of life, one must pay as much attention to shade as to light: nevertheless, it would be tedious were I to describe to you in detail the soul-torments which afflicted Wilfred Mulliner as day followed day and no solution to the problem presented itself. You are all intelligent men, and you can picture to yourselves how a high-spirited young fellow, deeply in love, must have felt; knowing that the girl he loved was languishing in what practically amounted to a dungeon, though situated on an upper floor, and chafing at his inability to set her free.

His eyes became sunken. His cheek-bones stood out. He lost weight. And so noticeable was this change in his physique that Sir Jasper ffinch-ffarrowmere commented on it one evening in tones of unconcealed envy.

"How the devil, Straker," he said—for this was the pseudonym under which Wilfred was passing, "do you manage to keep so thin? Judging by the weekly books, you eat like a starving Esquimaux, and yet you don't put on weight. Now I, in addition to knocking off butter and potatoes, have started drinking hot unsweetened lemon-juice each night before retiring: and yet, damme," he said—for, like all baronets, he was careless in his language—"I weighed myself this morning, and I was up another six ounces. What's the explanation?"

"Yes, Sir Jasper," said Wilfred, mechanically.

"What the devil do you mean, Yes, Sir Jasper?"

"No, Sir Jasper."

The baronet wheezed plaintively.

"I've been studying this matter closely," he said, "and it's one of the seven wonders of the world. Have you ever seen a fat valet? Of course not. Nor has anybody else. There is no such thing as a fat valet. And yet there is scarcely a moment during the day when a valet is not eating. He rises at six-thirty, and at seven is having coffee and buttered toast. At eight, he breakfasts off porridge, cream, eggs, bacon, jam, bread, butter, more eggs, more bacon, more jam, more tea, and more butter, finishing up with a slice of cold ham and a sardine. At eleven o'clock he has his "elevenses", consisting of coffee, cream, more bread and more butter. At one, luncheon—a hearty meal, replete with every form of starchy food and lots of beer. If he can get at the port, he has port. At three, a snack. At four, another snack. At five, tea and buttered toast. At seven—dinner, probably with floury potatoes, and certainly with lots more beer. At nine, another snack. And at ten-thirty he retires to bed, taking with him a glass of milk and a plate of biscuits to keep himself from getting hungry in the night. And yet he remains as slender as a string-bean, while I, who have been dieting for years, tip the beam at two hundred and seventeen pounds, and am growing a third and supplementary chin. These are mysteries, Straker."

"Yes, Sir Jasper."

"Well, I'll tell you one thing," said the baronet, "I'm getting down one of those indoor Turkish Bath cabinet-affairs from London; and if that doesn't do the trick, I give up the struggle."

The indoor Turkish Bath duly arrived and was unpacked; and it was some three nights later that Wilfred, brooding in the servants' hall, was aroused from his reverie by Murgatroyd.

"Here," said Murgatroyd, "wake up. Sir Jasper's calling you."

"Calling me what?" asked Wilfred, coming to himself with a start.

"Calling you very loud," growled the butler.

It was indeed so. From the upper regions of the house there was proceeding a series of sharp yelps, evidently those of a man in mortal stress. Wilfred was reluctant to interfere in any way if, as seemed probable, his employer was dying in agony; but he was a conscientious man, and it was his duty, while in this sinister house, to perform the work for which he was paid. He hurried up the stairs; and, entering Sir Jasper's bedroom, perceived the baronet's crimson face protruding from the top of the indoor Turkish Bath.

"So you've come at last!" cried Sir Jasper. "Look here, when you put me into this infernal contrivance just now, what did you do to the dashed thing?"

"Nothing beyond what was indicated in the printed pamphlet accompanying the machine, Sir Jasper. Following the instructions, I slid Rod A into Groove B, fastening with Catch C——"

"Well, you must have made a mess of it, somehow. The thing's stuck. I can't get out."

"You can't?" cried Wilfred.

"No. And the bally apparatus is getting considerably hotter than the hinges of the Inferno." I must apologize for Sir Jasper's language, but you know what baronets are. "I'm being cooked to a crisp."

A sudden flash of light seemed to blaze upon Wilfred Mulliner.

"I will release you, Sir Jasper——"

"Well, hurry up, then."

"On one condition." Wilfred fixed him with a piercing gaze. "First, I must have the key."

"There isn't a key, you idiot. It doesn't lock. It just clicks when you slide Gadget D into Thingummybob E."

"The key I require is that of the room in which you are holding Angela Purdue a prisoner."

"What the devil do you mean? Ouch!"

"I will tell you what I mean, Sir Jasper ffinch-ffarrowmere. I am Wilfred Mulliner!"

"Don't be an ass. Wilfred Mulliner has black hair. Yours is red. You must be thinking of someone else."

"This is a wig," said Wilfred. "By Clarkson." He shook a menacing finger at the baronet. "You little thought, Sir Jasper ffinch-ffarrowmere, when you embarked on this dastardly scheme, that Wilfred Mulliner was watching your every move. I guessed your plans from the start. And now is the moment when I checkmate them. Give me that key, you Fiend."

"ffiend," corrected Sir Jasper, automatically.

"I am going to release my darling, to take her away from this dreadful house, to marry her by special licence as soon as it can legally be done."

In spite of his sufferings, a ghastly laugh escaped Sir Jasper's lips.

"You are, are you?"

"I am."

"Yes, you are!"

"Give me the key."

"I haven't got it, you chump. It's in the door."

"Ha, ha!"

"It's no good saying 'Ha, ha!' It is in the door. On Angela's side of the door."

"A likely story! But I cannot stay here wasting time. If you will not give me the key, I shall go up and break in the door."

"Do!" Once more the baronet laughed like a tortured soul. "And see what she'll say."

Wilfred could make nothing of this last remark. He could, he thought, imagine very clearly what Angela would say. He could picture her sobbing on his chest, murmuring that she knew he would come, that she had never doubted him for an instant. He leapt for the door.

"Here! Hi! Aren't you going to let me out?"

"Presently," said Wilfred. "Keep cool." He raced up the stairs.

"Angela," he cried, pressing his lips against the panel. "Angela!"

"Who's that?" answered a well-remembered voice from within.

"It is I—Wilfred. I am going to burst open the door. Stand clear of the gates."

He drew back a few paces, and hurled himself at the woodwork. There was a grinding crash, as the lock gave. And Wilfred, staggering on, found himself in a room so dark that he could see nothing.

"Angela, where are you?"

"I'm here. And I'd like to know why you are, after that letter I wrote you. Some men," continued the strangely cold voice, "do not seem to know how to take a hint."

Wilfred staggered, and would have fallen had he not clutched at his forehead.

"That letter?" he stammered. "You surely didn't mean what you wrote in that letter?"

"I meant every word and I wish I had put in more."

"But—but—but—— But don't you love me, Angela?"

A hard, mocking laugh rang through the room.

"Love you? Love the man who recommended me to try Mulliner's Raven Gipsy Face-Cream!"

"What do you mean?"

"I will tell you what I mean. Wilfred Mulliner, look on you handiwork!"

The room became suddenly flooded with light. And there, standing with her hand on the switch, stood Angela—a queenly, lovely figure, in whose radiant beauty the sternest critic would have noted but one flaw—the fact that she was piebald.

Wilfred gazed at her with adoring eyes. Her face was partly brown and partly white, and on her snowy neck were patches of sepia that looked like the thumb-prints you find on the pages of books in the Free Library: but he thought her the most beautiful creature he had ever seen. He longed to fold her in his arms: and but for the fact that her eyes told him that she would undoubtedly land an upper-cut on him if he tried it he would have done so.

"Yes," she went on, "this is what you have made of me, Wilfred Mulliner—you and that awful stuff you call the Raven Gipsy Face-Cream. This is the skin you loved to touch! I took your advice and bought one of the large jars at seven and six, and see the result! Barely twenty-four hours after the first application, I could have walked into any circus and named my own terms as the Spotted Princess of the Fiji Islands. I fled here to my childhood home, to hide myself. And the first thing that happened"—her voice broke—"was that my favourite hunter shied at me and tried to bite pieces out of his manger: while Ponto, my little dog, whom I have reared from a puppy, caught one sight of my face and is now in the hands of the vet, and unlikely to recover. And it was you, Wilfred Mulliner, who brought this curse upon me!"

Many men would have wilted beneath these searing words, but Wilfred Mulliner merely smiled with infinite compassion and understanding.

"It is quite all right," he said. "I should have warned you, sweetheart, that this occasionally happens in cases where the skin is exceptionally delicate and finely-textured. It can be speedily remedied by an application of the Mulliner Snow of the Mountains Lotion, four shillings the medium-sized bottle."

"Wilfred! Is this true?"

"Perfectly true, dearest. And is this all that stands between us?"

"No!" shouted a voice of thunder.

Wilfred wheeled sharply. In the doorway stood Sir Jasper ffinch-ffarrowmere. He was swathed in a bath-towel, what was visible of his person being a bright crimson. Behind him, toying with a horse-whip, stood Murgatroyd, the butler.

"You didn't expect to see me, did you?"

"I certainly," replied Wilfred, severely, "did not expect to see you in a lady's presence in a costume like that."

"Never mind my costume," Sir Jasper turned. "Murgatroyd, do your duty!"

The butler, scowling horribly, advanced into the room.

"Stop!" screamed Angela.

"I haven't begun yet, miss," said the butler, deferentially.

"You shan't touch Wilfred. I love him."

"What!" cried Sir Jasper. "After all that has happened?"

"Yes. He has explained everything."

A grim frown appeared on the baronet's vermilion face.

"I'll bet he hasn't explained why he left me to be cooked in that infernal Turkish Bath. I was beginning to throw out clouds of smoke when Murgatroyd, faithful fellow, heard my cries and came and released me."

"Though not my work," added the butler.

Wilfred eyed him steadily.

"If," he said, "you used Mulliner's Reduc-o, the recognised specific for obesity, whether in the tabloid form at three shillings the tin, or as a liquid at five and six the flask, you would have no need to stew in Turkish Baths. Mulliner's Reduc-o, which contains no injurious chemicals, but is compounded purely of health-giving herbs, is guaranteed to remove excess weight, steadily and without weakening after-effects, at the rate of two pounds a week. As used by the nobility."

The glare of hatred faded from the baronet's eyes.

"Is that a fact?" he whispered.

"It is."

"You guarantee it?"

"All the Mulliner preparations are fully guaranteed."

"My boy!" cried the baronet. He shook Wilfred by the hand. "Take her," he said, brokenly. "And with her my b-blessing."

A discreet cough sounded in the background.

"You haven't anything, by any chance, sir," asked Murgatroyd, "that's good for lumbago?"

"Mulliner's Ease-o will cure the most stubborn case in six days."

"Bless you, sir, bless you," sobbed Murgatroyd. "Where can I get it?"

"At all chemists."

"It catches me in the small of the back principally, sir."

"It need catch you no longer," said Wilfred.

There is little to add. Murgatroyd is now the most lissom butler in Yorkshire. Sir Jasper's weight is down under the fifteen stone and he is thinking of taking up hunting again. Wilfred and Angela are man and wife; and never, I am informed, have the wedding-bells of the old church at ffinch village rung out a blither peal than they did on that June morning when Angela, raising to her love a face on which the brown was as evenly distributed as on an antique walnut table, replied to the clergyman's question, "Wilt thou, Angela, take this Wilfred?" with a shy, "I will". They now have two bonny bairns—the small, or Percival, at a preparatory school in Sussex, and the large, or Ferdinand, at Eton.

Here Mr. Mulliner, having finished his hot Scotch, bade us farewell and took his departure.

A silence followed his exit. The company seemed plunged in deep thought. Then somebody rose.

"Well, good night all," he said.

It seemed to sum up the situation.

3
MULLINER'S BUCK-U-UPPO

THE village Choral Society had been giving a performance of Gilbert and Sullivan's "Sorcerer" in aid of the Church Organ Fund; and, as we sat in the window of the Anglers' Rest, smoking our pipes, the audience came streaming past us down the little street. Snatches of song floated to our ears, and Mr. Mulliner began to croon in unison.

"'Ah me! I was a pa-ale you-oung curate then!'" chanted Mr. Mulliner in the rather snuffling voice in which the amateur singers seems to find it necessary to render the old songs.

"Remarkable," he said, resuming his natural tones, "how fashions change, even in clergymen. There are very few pale young curates nowadays."

"True," I agreed. "Most of them are beefy young fellows who rowed for their colleges. I don't believe I have ever seen a pale young curate."

"You never met my nephew Augustine, I think?"

"Never."

"The description in the song would have fitted him perfectly. You will want to hear all about my nephew Augustine."

At the time of which I am speaking (said Mr. Mulliner) my nephew Augustine was a curate, and very young and extremely pale. As a boy he had completely out-grown his strength, and I rather think at his Theological College some of the wilder spirits must have bullied him; for when he went to Lower Briskett-in-the-Midden to assist the vicar, the Rev. Stanley Brandon, in his cure of souls, he was as meek and mild a young man as you could meet in a day's journey. He had flaxen hair, weak blue eyes, and the general demeanour of a saintly but timid cod-fish. Precisely, in short, the sort of young curate who seems to have been so common in the 'eighties, or whenever it was that Gilbert wrote "The Sorcerer".

The personality of his immediate superior did little or nothing to help him to overcome his native diffidence. The Rev. Stanley Brandon was a huge and sinewy man of violent temper, whose red face and glittering eyes might well have intimi-dated the toughest curate. The Rev. Stanley had been a heavy-weight boxer at Cambridge, and I gather from Augustine that he seemed to be always on the point of introducing into debates on parish matters the methods which had made him so successful in the roped ring. I remember Augustine telling me that once, on the occasion when he had ventured to oppose the other's views in the matter of decorating the church for the Harvest Festival, he thought for a moment that the vicar was going to drop him with a right hook to the chin. It was some quite trivial point that had come up—a question as to whether the pumpkin would look better in the apse or the clerestory, if I recollect rightly—but for several seconds it seemed as if blood was about to be shed.

Such was the Rev. Stanley Brandon. And yet it was to the daughter of this formidable man that Augustine Mulliner had permitted himself to lose his heart. Truly, Cupid makes heroes of us all.

Jane was a very nice girl, and just as fond of Augustine as he was of her. But, as each lacked the nerve to go to the girl's father and put him abreast of the position of affairs, they were forced to meet surreptitiously. This jarred upon Augustine who, like all the Mulliners, loved the truth and hated any form of deception. And one evening, as they paced beside the laurels at the bottom of the vicarage garden, he rebelled.

"My dearest," said Augustine, "I can no longer brook this secrecy. I shall go into the house immediately and ask your father for your hand."

Jane paled and clung to his arm. She knew so well that it was not her hand but her father's foot which he would receive if he carried out this mad scheme.

"No, no, Augustine! You must not!"

"But, darling, it is the only straightforward course."

"But not tonight. I beg of you, not tonight."

"Why not?"

"Because father is in a very bad temper. He has just had a letter from the bishop, rebuking him for wearing too many orphreys on his chasuble, and it has upset him terribly. You see, he and the bishop were at school together, and father can never forget it. He said at dinner that if old Boko Bickerton thought he was going to order him about he would jolly well show him."

"And the bishop comes here tomorrow for the Confirmation services!" gasped Augustine.

"Yes. And I'm so afraid they will quarrel. It's such a pity father hasn't some other bishop over him. He always remembers that he once hit this one in the eye for pouring ink on his collar, and this lowers his respect for his spiritual authority. So you won't go in and tell him tonight will you?"

"I will not," Augustine assured her with a slight shiver.

"And you will be sure to put your feet in hot mustard and water when you get home? The dew has made the grass so wet."

"I will indeed, dearest."

"You are not strong, you know."

"No, I am not strong."

"You ought to take some really good tonic."

"Perhaps I ought. Good night, Jane."

"Good night, Augustine."

The lovers parted. Jane slipped back into the vicarage, and Augustine made his way to his cosy rooms in the High Street. And the first thing he noticed on entering was a parcel on the table, and beside it a letter.

He opened it listlessly, his thoughts far away.

"*My dear Augustine.*"

He turned to the last page and glanced at the signature. The letter was from his Aunt Angela, the wife of my brother, Wilfred Mulliner. You may remember that I once told you the story of how these two came together. If so, you will recall that my brother Wilfred was the eminent chemical researcher who had invented, among other specifics, such world-famous preparations as Mulliner's Raven Gipsy Face-Cream and the Mulliner Snow of the Mountains Lotion. He and Augustine had never been particularly intimate, but between Augustine and his aunt there had always existed a warm friendship.

My dear Augustine (wrote Angela Mulliner),

I have been thinking so much about you lately, and I cannot forget that, when I saw you last, you seemed very fragile and deficient in vitamins. I do hope you take care of yourself.

I have been feeling for some time that you ought to take a tonic, and by a lucky chance Wilfred has just invented one which he tells me is the finest thing he has ever done. It is called Buck-U-Uppo, and acts directly on the red corpuscles. It is not yet on the market, but I have managed to smuggle a sample bottle from Wilfred's laboratory, and I want y u to try it at once. I am sure it is just what you need.

> *Your affectionate aunt,*
> *Angela Mulliner.*

P.S.—You take a tablespoonful before going to bed, and another just before breakfast.

Augustine was not an unduly superstitious young man, but the coincidence of this tonic arriving so soon after Jane had told him that a tonic was what he needed affected him deeply. It seemed to him that this thing must have been meant. He shook the bottle, uncorked it, and, pouring out a liberal tablespoonful, shut his eyes and swallowed it.

The medicine, he was glad to find, was not unpleasant to the taste. It had a slightly pungent flavour, rather like old boot-soles beaten up in sherry. Having taken the dose, he read for a while in a book of theological essays, and then went to bed.

And as his feet slipped between the sheets, he was annoyed to find that Mrs. Wardle, his housekeeper, had once more forgotten his hot-water bottle.

"Oh, dash!" said Augustine.

He was thoroughly upset. He had told the woman over and over again that he suffered from cold feet and could not get to sleep unless the dogs were properly warmed up. He sprang out of bed and went to the head of the stairs.

"Mrs. Wardle!" he cried.

There was no reply.

"Mrs. Wardle!" bellowed Augustine in a voice that rattled the window-panes like a strong nor'-easter. Until tonight he had always been very much afraid of his housekeeper and had both walked and talked softly in her presence. But now he was conscious of a strange new fortitude. His head was singing a little, and he felt equal to a dozen Mrs. Wardles.

Shuffling footsteps made themselves heard.

"Well, what is it now?" asked a querulous voice.

Augustine snorted.

"I'll tell you what it is now," he roared. "How many times have I told you always to put a hot-water bottle in my bed? You've forgotten it again, you old cloth-head!"

Mrs. Wardle peered up, astounded and militant.

"Mr. Mulliner, I am not accustomed——"

"Shut up!" thundered Augustine. "What I want from you is less back-chat and more hot-water bottles. Bring it up at once, or I leave tomorrow. Let me endeavour to get it into your concrete skull that you aren't the only person letting rooms in this village. Any more lip and I walk straight round the corner, where I'll be appreciated. Hot-water bottle ho! And look slippy about it."

"Yes, Mr. Mulliner. Certainly, Mr. Mulliner. In one moment, Mr. Mulliner."

"Action! Action!" boomed Augustine. "Show some speed. Put a little snap into it."

"Yes, yes, most decidedly, Mr. Mulliner," replied the chastened voice from below.

An hour later, as he was dropping off to sleep, a thought crept into Augustine's mind. Had he not been a little brusque with Mrs. Wardle? Had there not been in his manner something a shade abrupt—almost rude? Yes, he decided regretfully, there had. He lit a candle and reached for the diary which lay on the table at his bedside.

He made an entry.

The meek shall inherit the earth. Am I sufficiently meek? I wonder. This evening, when reproaching Mrs. Wardle, my worthy housekeeper, for omitting to place a hot-water bottle in my bed, I spoke quite crossly. The provocation was severe, but still I was surely to blame for allowing my passions to run riot. Mem: Must guard agst. this.

But when he woke next morning, different feelings prevailed. He took his ante-breakfast dose of Buck-U-Uppo: and looking at the entry in the diary, could

scarcely believe that it was he who had written it. "Quite cross?" Of course he had
been quite cross. Wouldn't anybody be quite cross who was for ever being perse-
cuted by beetle-wits who forgot hot-water bottles?

Erasing the words with one strong dash of a thick-leaded pencil, he scribbled in
the margin a hasty "Mashed potatoes! Served the old idiot right!" and went down
to breakfast.

He felt amazingly fit. Undoubtedly, in asserting that this tonic of his acted
forcefully upon the red corpuscles, his Uncle Wilfred had been right. Until that
moment Augustine had never supposed that he had any red corpuscles; but now,
as he sat waiting for Mrs. Wardle to bring him his fried egg, he could feel them
dancing about all over him. They seemed to be forming rowdy parties and sliding
down his spine. His eyes sparkled, and from sheer joy of living he sang a few bars
from the hymn for those of riper years at sea.

He was still singing when Mrs. Wardle entered with a dish.

"What's this?" demanded Augustine, eyeing it dangerously.

"A nice fried egg, sir."

"And what, pray, do you mean by nice? It may be an amiable egg. It may be a
civil, well-meaning egg. But if you think it is fit for human consumption, adjust
that impression. Go back to your kitchen, woman; select another; and remember
this time that you are a cook, not an incinerating machine. Between an egg that is
fried and an egg that is cremated there is a wide and substantial difference. This
difference, if you wish to retain me as a lodger in these far too expensive rooms,
you will endeavour to appreciate."

The glowing sense of well-being with which Augustine had begun the day did
not diminish with the passage of time. It seemed, indeed, to increase. So full of
effervescing energy did the young man feel that, departing from his usual custom
of spending the morning crouched over the fire, he picked up his hat, stuck it at
a rakish angle on his head, and sallied out for a healthy tramp across the fields.

It was while he was returning, flushed and rosy, that he observed a sight which
is rare in the country districts of England—the spectacle of a bishop running. It is
not often in a place like Lower Briskett-in-the-Midden that you see a bishop at all;
and when you do he is either riding in a stately car or pacing at a dignified walk.
This one was sprinting like a Derby winner, and Augustine paused to drink in the
sight.

The bishop was a large, burly bishop, built for endurance rather than speed;
but he was making excellent going. He flashed past Augustine in a whirl of flying
gaiters: and then, proving himself thereby no mere specialist but a versatile all-
round athlete, suddenly dived for a tree and climbed rapidly into its branches. His
motive, Augustine readily divined, was to elude a rough, hairy dog which was
toiling in his wake. The dog reached the tree a moment after his quarry had
climbed it, and stood there, barking.

Augustine strolled up.

"Having a little trouble with the dumb friend, bish?" he asked, genially.

The bishop peered down from his eyrie.

"Young man," he said, "save me!"

"Right most indubitably ho!" replied Augustine. "Leave it to me."

Until today he had always been terrified of dogs, but now he did not hesitate. Almost quicker than words can tell, he picked up a stone, discharged it at the animal, and whooped cheerily as it got home with a thud. The dog, knowing when he had had enough, removed himself at some forty-five m.p.h.; and the bishop, descending cautiously, clasped Augustine's hand in his.

"My preserver!" said the bishop.

"Don't give it another thought," said Augustine, cheerily "Always glad to do a pal a good turn. We clergymen must stick together."

"I thought he had me for a minute."

"Quite a nasty customer. Full of rude energy."

The bishop nodded.

"His eye was not dim, nor his natural force abated. Deuteronomy xxxiv. 7," he agreed. "I wonder if you can direct me to the vicarage? I fear I have come a little out of my way."

"I'll take you there."

"Thank you. Perhaps it would be as well if you did not come in. I have a serious matter to discuss with old Pieface—I mean, with the Rev. Stanley Brandon."

"I have a serious matter to discuss with his daughter. I'll just hang about the garden."

"You are a very excellent young man," said the bishop, as they walked along. "You are a curate, eh?"

"At present. But," said Augustine, tapping his companion on the chest, "just watch my smoke. That's all I ask you to do—just watch my smoke."

"I will. You should rise to great heights—to the very top of the tree."

"Like you did just now, eh? Ha, ha!"

"Ha, ha!" said the bishop. "You young rogue!"

He poked Augustine in the ribs.

"Ha, ha, ha!" said Augustine.

He slapped the bishop on the back.

"But all joking aside," said the bishop as they entered the vicarage grounds, "I really shall keep my eye on you and see that you receive the swift preferment which your talents and character deserve. I say to you, my dear young friend, speaking seriously and weighing my words, that the way you picked that dog off with that stone was the smoothest thing I ever saw. And I am a man who always tells the strict truth."

"Great is truth and mighty above all things. Esdras iv. 41," said Augustine.

He turned away and strolled towards the laurel bushes, which were his customary meeting-place with Jane. The bishop went on to the front door and rang the bell.

Although they had made no definite appointment, Augustine was surprised when the minutes passed and no Jane appeared. He did not know that she had been told off by her father to entertain the bishop's wife that morning, and show her the sights of Lower Briskett-in-the-Midden. He waited some quarter of an hour with growing impatience, and was about to leave when suddenly from the house there came to his ears the sound of voices raised angrily.

He stopped. The voices appeared to proceed from a room on the ground floor facing the garden.

Running lightly over the turf, Augustine paused outside the window and listened. The window was open at the bottom, and he could hear quite distinctly.

The vicar was speaking in a voice that vibrated through the room.

"Is that so?" said the vicar.

"Yes, it is!" said the bishop.

"Ha, ha!"

"Ha, ha! to you, and see how you like it!" rejoined the bishop with spirit.

Augustine drew a step closer. It was plain that Jane's fears had been justified and that there was serious trouble afoot between these two old schoolfellows. He peeped in. The vicar, his hands behind his coat-tails, was striding up and down the carpet, while the bishop, his back to the fireplace, glared defiance at him from the hearth-rug.

"Who ever told you you were an authority on chasubles?" demanded the vicar.

"That's all right who told me," rejoined the bishop.

"I don't believe you know what a chasuble is."

"Is that so?"

"Well, what is it, then?"

"It's a circular cloak hanging from the shoulders, elaborately embroidered with a pattern and with orphreys. And you can argue as much as you like, young Pieface, but you can't get away from the fact that there are too many orphreys on yours. And what I'm telling you is that you've jolly well got to switch off a few of these orphreys or you'll get it in the neck."

The vicar's eyes glittered furiously.

"Is that so?" he said. "Well, I just won't, so there! And it's like your cheek coming here and trying to high-hat me. You seem to have forgotten that I knew you when you were an inky-faced kid at school, and that, if I liked, I could tell the world one or two things about you which would probably amuse it."

"My past is an open book."

"Is it?" The vicar laughed malevolently. "Who put the white mouse in the French master's desk?"

The bishop started.

"Who put jam in the dormitory prefect's bed?" he retorted.

"Who couldn't keep his collar clean?"

"Who used to wear a dickey?" The bishop's wonderful organ-like voice, whose softest whisper could be heard throughout a vast cathedral, rang out in tones of thunder. "Who was sick at the house supper?"

The vicar quivered from head to foot. His rubicund face turned a deeper crimson.

"You know jolly well," he said, in shaking accents, "that there was something wrong with the turkey. Might have upset anyone."

"The only thing wrong with the turkey was that you ate too much of it. If you had paid as much attention to developing your soul as you did to developing your tummy, you might by now," said the bishop, "have risen to my own eminence."

"Oh, might I?"

"No, perhaps I am wrong. You never had the brain."

The vicar uttered another discordant laugh.

"Brain is good! We know all about your eminence, as you call it, and how you rose to that eminence."

"What do you mean?"

"You are a bishop. How you became one we will not inquire."

"What do you mean?"

"What I say. We will not inquire."

"Why don't you inquire?"

"Because," said the vicar, "it is better not!"

The bishop's self-control left him. His face contorted with fury, he took a step forward. And simultaneously Augustine sprang lightly into the room.

"Now, now, now!" said Augustine. " Now, now, now, now, now!"

The two men stood transfixed. They stared at the intruder dumbly.

"Come, come!" said Augustine.

The vicar was the first to recover. He glowered at Augustine.

"What do you mean by jumping through my window?" he thundered. "Are you a curate or a harlequin?"

Augustine met his gaze with an unfaltering eye.

"I am a curate," he replied, with a diginity that well became him. "And, as a curate, I cannot stand by and see two superiors of the cloth, who are moreover old schoolfellows, forgetting themselves. It isn't right. Absolutely not right, my old superiors of the cloth."

The vicar bit his lip. The bishop bowed his head.

"Listen," proceeded Augustine, placing a hand on the shoulder of each. "I hate to see you two dear good chaps quarrelling like this."

"He started it," said the vicar, sullenly.

"Never mind who started it." Augustine silenced the bishop with a curt gesture as he made to speak. "Be sensible, my dear fellows. Respect the decencies of debate. Exercise a little good-humoured give-and-take. You say," he went on, turning to the bishop, "that our good friend here has too many orphreys on his chasuble?"

"I do. And I stick to it."

"Yes, yes, yes. But what," said Augustine, soothingly, "are a few orphreys between friends? Reflect! You and our worthy vicar here were at school together. You are bound by the sacred ties of the old Alma Mater. With him you sported on the green. With him you shared a crib and threw inked darts in the hour supposed to be devoted to the study of French. Do these things mean nothing to you? Do these memories touch no chord?" He turned appealingly from one to the other. "Vicar! Bish!"

The vicar had moved away and was wiping his eyes. The bishop fumbled for a pocket-handkerchief. There was a silence.

"Sorry, Pieface," said the bishop, in a choking voice.

"Shouldn't have spoken as I did, Boko," mumbled the vicar.

"If you want to know what I think," said the bishop, "you are right in attributing your indisposition at the house supper to something wrong with the turkey. I recollect saying at the time that the bird should never have been served in such a condition."

"And when you put that white mouse in the French master's desk," said the vicar, "you performed one of the noblest services to humanity of which there is any record. They ought to have made you a bishop on the spot."

"Pieface!"

"Boko!"

The two men clasped hands.

"Splendid!" said Augustine. "Everything hotsy-totsy now?"

"Quite, quite," said the vicar.

"As far as I am concerned, completely hotsy-totsy," said the bishop. He turned to his old friend solicitously. "You will continue to wear all the orphreys you want —will you not, Pieface?"

"No, no. I see now that I was wrong. From now on, Boko, I abandon orphreys altogether."

"But, Pieface——"

"It's all right," the vicar assured him. "I can take them or leave them alone."

"Splendid fellow!" The bishop coughed to hide his emotion, and there was another silence. "I think, perhaps," he went on, after a pause, "I should be leaving you now, my dear chap, and going in search of my wife. She is with your daughter, I believe, somewhere in the village."

"They are coming up the drive now."

"Ah, yes, I see them. A charming girl, your daughter."

Augustine clapped him on the shoulder.

"Bish," he exclaimed, "you said a mouthful. She is the dearest, sweetest girl in the whole world. And I should be glad, vicar, if you would give your consent to our immediate union. I love Jane with a good man's fervour, and I am happy to inform you that my sentiments are returned. Assure us, therefore, of your approval, and I will go at once and have the banns put up."

The vicar leaped as though he had been stung. Like so many vicars, he had a
poor opinion of curates, and he had always regarded Augustine as rather below
than above the general norm or level of the despised class.

"What!" he cried.

"A most excellent idea," said the bishop, beaming. "A very happy notion, I call
it."

"My daughter!" The vicar seemed dazed. "My daughter marry a curate."

"You were a curate once yourself, Pieface."

"Yes, but not a curate like that."

"No!" said the bishop. "You were not. Nor was I. Better for us both had we
been. This young man, I would have you know, is the most outstandingly excellent
young man I have ever encountered. Are you aware that scarcely an hour ago he
saved me with the most consummate address from a large shaggy dog with black
spots and a kink in his tail? I was sorely pressed, Pieface, when this young man
came up and, with a readiness of resource and an accuracy of aim which it would
be impossible to over-praise, got that dog in the short ribs with a rock and sent
him flying."

The vicar seemed to be struggling with some powerful emotion. His eyes had
widened.

"A dog with black spots?"

"Very black spots. But no blacker, I fear, than the heart they hid."

"And he really plugged him in the short ribs?"

"As far as I could see, squarely in the short ribs."

The vicar held out his hand.

"Mulliner," he said, "I was not aware of this. In the light of the facts which
have just been drawn to my attention, I have no hesitation in saying that my
objections are removed. I have had it in for that dog since the second Sunday
before Septuagesima, when he pinned me by the ankle as I paced beside the river
composing a sermon on Certain Alarming Manifestations of the So-called Modern
Spirit. Take Jane. I give my consent freely. And may she be as happy as any girl
with such a husband ought to be."

A few more affecting words were exchanged, and then the bishop and Augustine
left the house. The bishop was silent and thoughtful.

"I owe you a great deal, Mulliner," he said at length.

"Oh, I don't know," said Augustine. "Would you say that?"

"A very great deal. You saved me from a terrible disaster. Had you not leaped
through that window at that precise juncture and intervened, I really believe I
should have pasted my dear old friend Brandon in the eye. I was sorely
exasperated."

"Our good vicar can be trying at times," agreed Augustine.

"My fist was already clenched, and I was just hauling off for the swing when you checked me. What the result would have been, had you not exhibited a tact and discretion beyond your years, I do not like to think. I might have been unfrocked." He shivered at the thought, though the weather was mild. "I could never have shown my face at the Athenæum again. But, tut, tut!" went on the bishop, patting Augustine on the shoulder, "let us not dwell on what might have been. Speak to me of yourself. The vicar's charming daughter—you really love her?"

"I do, indeed."

The bishop's face had grown grave.

"Think well, Mulliner," he said. "Marriage is a serious affair. Do not plunge into it without due reflection. I myself am a husband, and, though singularly blessed in the possession of a devoted helpmeet, cannot but feel sometimes that a man is better off as a bachelor. Women, Mulliner, are odd."

"True," said Augustine.

"My own dear wife is the best of women. And, as I never weary of saying, a good woman is a wondrous creature, cleaving to the right and the good under all change; lovely in youthful comeliness, lovely all her life in comeliness of heart. And yet——"

"And yet?" said Augustine.

The bishop mused for a moment. He wriggled a little with an expression of pain, and scratched himself between the shoulder-blades.

"Well, I'll tell you," said the bishop. "It is a warm and pleasant day today, is it not?"

"Exceptionally clement," said Augustine.

"A fair, sunny day, made gracious by a temperate westerly breeze. And yet, Mulliner, if you will credit my statement, my wife insisted on my putting on my thick winter woollies this morning. Truly," sighed the bishop, "as a jewel of gold in a swine's snout, so is a fair woman which is without discretion. Proverbs xi. 21."

"Twenty-two," corrected Augustine.

"I should have said twenty-two. They are made of thick flannel, and I have an exceptionally sensitive skin. Oblige me, my dear fellow, by rubbing me in the small of the back with the ferrule of your stick. I think it will ease the irritation."

"But, my poor dear old bish," said Augustine, sympathetically, "this must not be."

The bishop shook his head ruefully.

"You would not speak so hardily, Mulliner, if you knew my wife. There is no appeal from her decrees."

"Nonesense," cried Augustine, cheerily. He looked through the trees to where the lady bishopess, escorted by Jane, was examining a lobelia through her lorgnette with just the right blend of cordiality and condescension. "I'll fix that for you in a second."

The bishop clutched at his arm.

"My boy! What are you going to do?"

"I'm just going to have a word with your wife and put the matter up to her as a reasonable woman. Thick winter woollies on a day like this! Absurd!" said Augustine. "Preposterous! I never heard such rot."

The bishop gazed after him with a laden heart. Already he had come to love this young man like a son: and to see him charging so light-heartedly into the very jaws of destruction afflicted him with a deep and poignant sadness. He knew what his wife was like when even the highest in the land attempted to thwart her; and this brave lad was but a curate. In another moment she would be looking at him through her lorgnette: and England was littered with the shrivelled remains of curates at whom the lady bishopess had looked through her lorgnette. He had seen them wilt like salted slugs at the episcopal breakfast-table.

He held his breath. Augustine had reached the lady bishopess, and the lady bishopess was even now raising her lorgnette.

The bishop shut his eyes and turned away. And then—years afterwards, it seemed to him—a cheery voice hailed him: and, turning, he perceived Augustine bounding back through the trees.

"It's all right, bish," said Augustine.

"All—all right?" faltered the bishop.

"Yes. She says you can go and change into the thin cashmere."

The bishop reeled.

"But—but—but what did you say to her? What arguments did you employ?"

"Oh, I just pointed out what a warm day it was and jollied her along a bit——"

"Jollied her along a bit!"

"And she agreed in the most friendly and cordial manner. She has asked me to call at the Palace one of these days."

The bishop seized Augustine's hand.

"My boy," he said in a broken voice, "you shall do more than call at the Palace. You shall come and live at the Palace. Become my secretary, Mulliner, and name your own salary. If you intend to marry, you will require an increased stipend. Become my secretary, boy, and never leave my side. I have needed somebody like you for years."

It was late in the afternoon when Augustine returned to his rooms, for he had been invited to lunch at the vicarage and had been the life and soul of the cheery little party.

"A letter for you, sir," said Mrs. Wardle, obsequiously.

Augustine took the letter.

"I am sorry to say I shall be leaving you shortly, Mrs. Wardle."

"Oh, sir! If there's anything I can do——"

"Oh, it's not that. The fact is, the bishop has made me his secretary, and I shall have to shift my toothbrush and spats to the Palace, you see."

"Well, fancy that, sir! Why, you'll be a bishop yourself one of these days."

"Possibly," said Augustine. "Possibly. And now let me read this."

He opened the letter. A thoughtful frown appeared on his face as he read.

My dear Augustine,

I am writing in some haste to tell you that the impulsiveness of your aunt has led to a rather serious mistake.

She tells me that she dispatched to you yesterday by parcels post a sample bottle of my new Buck-U-Uppo, which she obtained without my knowledge from my laboratory. Had she mentioned what she was intending to do, I could have prevented a very unfortunate occurrence.

Mulliner's Buck-U-Uppo is of two grades or qualities—the A and the B. The A is a mild, but strengthening, tonic designed for human invalids. The B, on the other hand, is purely for circulation in the animal kingdom, and was invented to fill a long-felt want throughout our Indian possessions.

As you are doubtless aware, the favourite pastime of the Indian Maharajahs is the hunting of the tiger of the jungle from the backs of elephants; and it has happened frequently in the past that hunts have been spoiled by the failure of the elephant to see eye to eye with its owner in the matter of what constitutes sport.

Too often elephants, on sighting the tiger, have turned and galloped home: and it was to correct this tendency on their part that I invented Mulliner's Buck-U-Uppo "B". One teaspoonful of the Buck-U-Uppo "B" administered in its morning bran-mash will cause the most timid elephant to trumpet loudly and charge the fiercest tiger without a qualm.

Abstain, therefore, from taking any of the contents of the bottle you now possess,

And believe me,

Your affectionate uncle,

Wilfred Mulliner.

Augustine remained for some time in deep thought after perusing this communication. Then, rising, he whistled a few bars of the psalm appointed for the twenty-sixth of June and left the room.

Half an hour later a telegraphic message was speeding over the wires.

It ran as follows:

Wilfred Mulliner,
The Gables,
Lesser Lossingham,
Salop.

Letter received. Send immediately, C.O.D., three cases of the "B". "Blessed shall be thy basket and thy store" Deuteronomy xxviii 5.

Augustine.

4
THE BISHOP'S MOVE

ANOTHER Sunday was drawing to a close, and Mr. Mulliner had come into the bar-parlour of the Anglers' Rest wearing on his head, in place of the seedy old wideawake which usually adorned it, a glistening top-hat. From this, combined with the sober black of his costume and the rather devout voice in which he ordered hot Scotch and lemon, I deduced that he had been attending Evensong.

"Good sermon?" I asked.

"Quite good. The new curate preached. He seems a nice young fellow."

"Speaking of curates," I said, "I have often wondered what became of your nephew—the one you were telling me about the other day."

"Augustine?"

"The fellow who took the Buck-U-Uppo."

"That was Augustine. And I am pleased and not a little touched," said Mr. Mulliner, beaming, "that you should have remembered the trivial anecdote which I related. In this self-centred world one does not always find such a sympathetic listener to one's stories. Let me see, where did we leave Augustine?"

"He had just become the bishop's secretary and gone to live at the Palace."

"Ah, yes. We will take up his career, then, some six months after the date which you have indicated."

It was the custom of the good Bishop of Stortford—for, like all the prelates of our Church, he loved his labours—to embark upon the duties of the day (said Mr. Mulliner) in a cheerful and jocund spirit. Usually, as he entered his study to dispatch such business as might have arisen from the correspondence which had reached the Palace by the first post, there was a smile upon his face and possibly upon his lips a snatch of some gay psalm. But on the morning on which this story begins an observer would have noted that he wore a preoccupied, even a sombre, look. Reaching the study door, he hesitated as if reluctant to enter; then, pulling himself together with a visible effort, he turned the handle.

"Good morning, Mulliner, my boy," he said. His manner was noticeably embarrassed.

Augustine glanced brightly up from the pile of letters which he was opening.

"Cheerio, Bish. How's the lumbago today?"

"I find the pain sensibly diminished, thank you, Mulliner—in fact, almost non-existent. This pleasant weather seems to do me good. For lo! the winter is past, the rain is over and gone; the flowers appear on the earth; the time of the singing birds is come, and the voice of the turtle is heard in the land. Song of Solomon ii. 11, 12."

"Good work," said Augustine. "Well, there's nothing much of interest in these letters so far. The Vicar of St. Beowulf's in the West wants to know, How about incense?"

"Tell him he mustn't."

"Right ho."

The bishop stroked his chin uneasily. He seemed to be nerving himself for some unpleasant task.

"Mulliner," he said.

"Hullo?"

"Your mention of the word 'vicar' provides a cue, which I must not ignore, for alluding to a matter which you and I had under advisement yesterday—the matter of the vacant living of Steeple Mummery."

"Yes?" said Augustine eagerly. "Do I click?"

A spasm of pain passed across the bishop's face. He shook his head sadly.

"Mulliner, my boy," he said. "You know that I look upon you as a son and that, left to my own initiative, I would bestow this vacant living on you without a moment's hesitation. But an unforeseen complication has arisen. Unhappy lad, my wife has instructed me to give the post to a cousin of hers. A fellow," said the bishop bitterly, "who bleats like a sheep and doesn't know an alb from a reredos."

Augustine, as was only natural, was conscious of a momentary pang of disappointment. But he was a Mulliner and a sportsman.

"Don't give it another thought, Bish," he said cordially. "I quite understand. I don't say I hadn't hopes, but no doubt there will be another along in a minute."

"You know how it is," said the bishop, looking cautiously round to see that the door was closed. "It is better to dwell in a corner of the housetop than with a brawling woman in a wide house. Proverbs xxi. 9."

"A continual dropping in a very rainy day and a contentious woman are alike. Proverbs xxvii. 15," agreed Augustine.

"Exactly. How well you understand me, Mulliner."

"Meanwhile," said Augustine, holding up a letter, "here's something that calls for attention. It's from a bird of the name of Trevor Entwhistle."

"Indeed? An old schoolfellow of mine. He is now Headmaster of Harchester, the foundation at which we both received our early education. What does he say?"

"He wants to know if you will run down for a few days and unveil a statue which they have just put up to Lord Hemel of Hempstead."

"Another old schoolfellow. We called him Fatty."

"There's a postscript over the page. He says he still has a dozen of the '87 port."

The bishop pursed his lips.

"These earthly considerations do not weigh with me so much as old Catsmeat—
as the Reverend Trevor Entwhistle seems to suppose. However, one must not
neglect the call of the dear old school. We will certainly go."

"We?"

"I shall require your company. I think you will like Harchester, Mulliner. A
noble pile, founded by the seventh Henry."

"I know it well. A young brother of mine is there."

"Indeed? Dear me," mused the bishop, "it must be twenty years and more
since I last visited Harchester. I shall enjoy seeing the old, familiar scenes once
again. After all, Mulliner, to whatever eminence we may soar, howsoever great may
be the prizes which life has bestowed upon us, we never wholly lose our sentiment,
for the dear old school. It is our Alma Mater, Mulliner, the gentle mother that
has set our hesitating footsteps on the——"

"Absolutely," said Augustine.

"And, as we grow older, we see that never can we recapture the old, careless
gaiety of our school days. Life was not complex then, Mulliner. Life in that halcyon
period was free from problems. We were not faced with the necessity of disap-
pointing our friends."

"Now listen, Bish," said Augustine cheerily, "if you're still worrying about that
living, forget it. Look at me. I'm quite chirpy, aren't I?"

The bishop sighed.

"I wish I had your sunny resilience, Mulliner. How do you manage it?"

"Oh, I keep smiling, and take the Buck-U-Uppo daily."

"The Buck-U-Uppo?"

"It's a tonic my uncle Wilfred invented. Works like magic."

"I must ask you to let me try it one of these days. For somehow, Mulliner, I am
finding life a little grey. What on earth," said the bishop, half to himself and
speaking peevishly, "they wanted to put up a statue to old Fatty for, I can't
imagine. A fellow who used to throw inked darts at people. However," he continued, abruptly abandoning this train of thought, "that is neither here nor there.
If the Board of Governors of Harchester College have decided that Lord Hemel
of Hempstead has by his services in the public weal earned a statue, it is not for
us to cavil. Write to Mr. Entwhistle, Mulliner, and say that I shall be delighted."

Although, as he had told Augustine, fully twenty years had passed since his last
visit to Harchester, the bishop found, somewhat to his surprise, that little or
no alteration had taken place in the grounds, buildings and personnel of the
school. It seemed to him almost precisely the same as it had been on the day,
forty-three years before, when he had first come there as a new boy.

There was the tuck-shop where, a lissom stripling with bony elbows, he had
shoved and pushed so often in order to get near the counter and snaffle a jam-
sandwich in the eleven o'clock recess. There were the baths, and fives courts, the

football fields, the library, the gymnasium, the gravel, the chestnut trees, all just as they had been when the only thing he knew about bishops was that they wore boot-laces in their hats.

The sole change that he could see was that on the triangle of turf in front of the library there had been erected a granite pedestal surmounted by a shapeless something swathed in a large sheet—the statue to Lord Hemel of Hempstead which he had come down to unveil.

And gradually, as his visit proceeded, there began to steal over him an emotion which defied analysis.

At first he supposed it to be a natural sentimentality. But, had it been that, would it not have been a more pleasurable emotion? For his feelings had begun to be far from unmixedly agreeable. Once, when rounding a corner, he same upon the captain of football in all his majesty, and there had swept over him a hideous blend of fear and shame which had made his gaitered legs wobble like jellies. The captain of football doffed his cap respectfully, and the feeling passed as quickly as it had come: but not so soon that the bishop had not recognized it. It was exactly the feeling he had been wont to have forty-odd years ago when, sneaking softly away from football practice, he had encountered one in authority.

The bishop was puzzled. It was as if some fairy had touched him with her wand, sweeping away the years and making him an inky-faced boy again. Day by day this illusion grew, the constant society of the Rev. Trevor Entwhistle doing much to foster it. For young Catsmeat Entwhistle had been the bishop's particular crony at Harchester, and he seemed to have altered his appearance since those days in no way whatsoever. The bishop had had a nasty shock when, entering the headmaster's study on the third morning of his visit, he found him sitting in the headmaster's chair with the headmaster's cap and gown on. It seemed to him that young Catsmeat, in order to indulge his distorted sense of humour, was taking the most frightful risk. Suppose the Old Man were to come in and cop him!

Altogether, it was a relief to the bishop when the day of the unveiling arrived.

The actual ceremony, however, he found both tedious and irritating. Lord Hemel of Hempstead had not been a favourite of his in their school days, and there was something extremely disagreeable to him in being obliged to roll out sonorous periods in his praise.

In addition to this, he had suffered from the very start of the proceedings from a bad attack of stage fright. He could not help thinking that he must look the most awful chump standing up there in front of all those people and spouting. He half expected one of the prefects in the audience to step up and clout his head and tell him not to be a funny young swine.

However, no disaster of this nature occurred. Indeed, his speech was notably successful.

"My dear Bishop," said old General Bloodenough, the Chairman of the College

Board of Governors, shaking his hand at the conclusion of the unveiling, "your magnificent oration put my own feeble efforts to shame, put them to shame, to shame. You were astounding!"

"Thanks awfully," mumbled the bishop, blushing and shuffling his feet.

The weariness which had come upon the bishop as the result of the prolonged ceremony seemed to grow as the day wore on. By the time he was seated in the headmaster's study after dinner he was in the grip of a severe headache.

The Rev. Trevor Entwhistle also appeared jaded.

"These affairs are somewhat fatiguing, bishop," he said, stifling a yawn.

"They are, indeed, Headmaster."

"Even the '87 port seems an inefficient restorative."

"Markedly inefficient. I wonder," said the bishop, struck with an idea, "if a little Buck-U-Uppo might not alleviate our exhaustion. It is a tonic of some kind which my secretary is in the habit of taking. It certainly appears to do him good. A livelier, more vigorous young fellow I have never seen. Suppose we ask your butler to go to his room and borrow the bottle? I am sure he will be delighted to give it to us."

"By all means."

The butler, dispatched to Augustine's room, returned with a bottle half full of a thick, dark coloured liquid. The bishop examined it thoughtfully.

"I see there are no directions given as to the requisite dose," he said. "However, I do not like to keep disturbing your butler, who has now doubtless returned to his pantry and is once more settling down to the enjoyment of a well-earned rest after a day more than ordinarily fraught with toil and anxiety. Suppose we use our own judgment?"

"Certainly. Is it nasty?"

The bishop licked the cork warily.

"No. I should not call it nasty. The taste, while individual and distinctive and even striking, is by no means disagreeable."

"Then let us take a glassful apiece."

The bishop filled two portly wine-glasses with the fluid, and they sat sipping gravely.

"It's rather good," said the bishop.

"Distinctly good," said the headmaster.

"It sort of sends a kind of glow over you."

"A noticeable glow."

"A little more, Headmaster?"

"No, I thank you."

"Oh, come."

"Well, just a spot, bishop, if you insist."

"It's rather good," said the bishop.

"Distinctly good," said the headmaster.

Now you, who have listened to the story of Augustine's previous adventures with the Buck-U-Uppo, are aware that my brother Wilfred invented it primarily with the object of providing Indian Rajahs with a specific which would encourage their elephants to face the tiger of the jungle with a jaunty sang-froid: and he had advocated as a medium dose for an adult elephant a teaspoonful stirred up with its morning bran-mash. It is not surprising, therefore, that after they had drunk two wine-glassfuls apiece of the mixture the outlook on life of both the bishop and the headmaster began to undergo a marked change.

Their fatigue had left them, and with it the depression which a few moments before had been weighing on them so heavily. Both were conscious of an extraordinary feeling of good cheer, and the odd illusion of extreme youth which had been upon the bishop since his arrival at Harchester was now more pronounced than ever. He felt a youngish and rather rowdy fifteen.

"Where does your butler sleep, Catsmeat?" he asked, after a thoughtful pause.

"I don't know. Why?"

"I was only thinking that it would be a lark to go and put a booby-trap on his door."

The headmaster's eyes glistened.

"Yes, wouldn't it!" he said.

They mused for a while. Then the headmaster uttered a deep chuckle.

"What are you giggling about?" asked the bishop.

"I was only thinking what a priceless ass you looked this afternoon, talking all that rot about old Fatty."

In spite of his cheerfulness, a frown passed over the bishop's fine forehead.

"It went very much against the grain to speak in terms of eulogy—yes, fulsome eulogy—of one whom we both know to have been a blighter of the worst description. Where does Fatty get off, having statues put up to him?"

"Oh well, he's an Empire builder, I suppose," said the headmaster, who was a fair-minded man.

"Just the sort of thing he would be," grumbled the bishop. "Shoving himself forward! If ever there was a chap I barred, it was Fatty."

"Me, too," agreed the headmaster. "Beastly laugh he'd got. Like glue pouring out of a jug."

"Greedy little beast, if you remember. A fellow in his house told me he once ate three slices of brown boot-polish spread on bread after he had finished the potted meat."

"Between you and me, I always suspected him of swiping buns at the school shop. I don't wish to make rash charges unsupported by true evidence, but it always seemed to me extremely odd that, whatever time of the term it was, and however hard up everybody else might be, you never saw Fatty without his bun."

"Catsmeat," said the bishop, "I'll tell you something about Fatty that isn't generally known. In a scrum in the final House Match in the year 1888 he deliberately hoofed me on the shin."

"You don't mean that?"

"I do."

"Great Scott!"

"An ordinary hack on the shin," said the bishop coldly, "no fellow minds. It is part of the give and take of normal social life. But when a bounder deliberately hauls off and lets drive at you with the sole intention of laying you out, it—well, it's a bit thick."

"And those chumps of Governors have put up a statue to him!"

The bishop leaned forward and lowered his voice.

"Catsmeat."

"What?"

"Do you know what?"

"No, what?"

"What we ought to do is to wait till twelve o'clock or so, till there's no one about, and then beetle out and paint that statue blue."

"Why not pink?"

"Pink, if you prefer it."

"Pink's a nice colour."

"It is. Very nice."

"Besides, I know where I can lay my hands on some pink paint."

"You do?"

"Gobs of it."

"Peace be on thy walls, Catsmeat, and prosperity within thy palaces," said the bishop. "Proverbs cxxxi. 6."

It seemed to the bishop, as he closed the front door noiselessly behind him two hours later, that providence, always on the side of the just, was extending itself in its efforts to make this little enterprise of his a success. All the conditions were admirable for statue-painting. The rain which had been falling during the evening had stopped: and a moon, which might have proved an embarrassment, was conveniently hidden behind a bank of clouds.

As regarded human interference, they had nothing to alarm them. No place in the world is so deserted as the ground of a school after midnight. Fatty's statue might have been in the middle of the Sahara. They climbed the pedestal, and, taking turns fairly with the brush, soon accomplished the task which their sense of duty had indicated to them. It was only when, treading warily lest their steps should be heard on the gravel drive, they again reached the front door that anything occurred to mar the harmony of the proceedings.

"What are you waiting for?" whispered the bishop, as his companion lingered on the top step.

"Half a second," said the headmaster in a muffled voice. "It may be in another pocket."

"What?"

"My key."

"Have you lost your key?"

"I believe I have."

"Catsmeat," said the bishop, with grave censure, "this is the last time I come out painting statues with you."

"I must have dropped it somewhere."

"What shall we do?"

"There's just a chance the scullery window may be open."

But the scullery window was not open. Careful, vigilant, and faithful to his trust, the butler, on retiring to rest, had fastened it and closed the shutters. They were locked out.

But it has been well said that it is the lessons which we learn in our boyhood days at school that prepare us for the problems of life in the larger world outside. Stealing back from the mists of the past, there came to the bishop a sudden memory.

"Catsmeat!"

"Hullo?"

"If you haven't been mucking the place up with alterations and improvements, there should be a water-pipe round at the back, leading to one of the upstairs windows."

Memory had not played him false. There, nestling in the ivy, was the pipe up and down which he had been wont to climb when, a pie-faced lad in the summer of '86, he had broken out of this house in order to take nocturnal swims in the river.

"Up you go," he said briefly.

The headmaster required no further urging. And presently the two were making good time up the side of the house.

It was just as they reached the window and just after the bishop had informed his old friend that, if he kicked him on the head again, he'd hear of it, that the window was suddenly flung open.

"Who's that?" said a clear young voice.

The headmaster was frankly taken aback. Dim though the light was, he could see that the man leaning out of the window was poising in readiness a very nasty-looking golf-club: and his first impulse was to reveal his identity and so clear himself of the suspicion of being the marauder for whom he gathered the other had mistaken him. Then there presented themselves to him certain objections to revealing his identity, and he hung there in silence, unable to think of a suitable next move.

The bishop was a man of readier resource.

"Tell him we're a couple of cats belonging to the cook," he whispered.

It was painful for one of the headmaster's scrupulous rectitude and honesty to stoop to such a falsehood, but it seemed the only course to pursue.

"It's all right," he said, forcing a note of easy geniality into his voice. "We're a couple of cats."

"Cat-burglars?"

"No. Just ordinary cats."

"Belonging to the cook," prompted the bishop from below.

"Belonging to the cook," added the headmaster.

"I see," said the man at the window. "Well, in that case, right ho!"

He stood aside to allow them to enter. The bishop, an artist at heart, mewed gratefully as he passed, to add verisimilitude to the deception: and then made for his bedroom, accompanied by the headmaster. The episode was apparently closed.

Nevertheless, the headmaster was disturbed by a certain uneasiness.

"Do you suppose he thought we really were cats?" he asked anxiously.

"I am not sure," said the bishop. "But I think we deceived him by the nonchalance of our demeanour."

"Yes, I think we did. Who was he?"

"My secretary. The young fellow I was speaking of, who lent us that capital tonic."

"Oh, then that's all right. He wouldn't give you away."

"No. And there is nothing else that can possibly lead to our being suspected. We left no clue whatsoever."

"All the same," said the headmaster thoughtfully, "I'm beginning to wonder whether it was in the best sense of the word judicious to have painted that statue."

"Somebody had to," said the bishop stoutly.

"Yes, that's true," said the headmaster, brightening.

The bishop slept late on the following morning, and partook of his frugal breakfast in bed. The day, which so often brings remorse, brought none to him. Something attempted, something done had earned a night's repose: and he had no regrets—except that, now that it was all over, he was not sure that blue paint would not have been more effective. However, his old friend had pleaded so strongly for the pink that it would have been difficult for himself, as a guest, to override the wishes of his host. Still, blue would undoubtedly have been very striking.

There was a knock on the door, and Augustine entered.

"Morning Bish."

"Good morning, Mulliner," said the bishop affably. "I have lain somewhat late today."

"I say, Bish" asked Augustine, a little anxiously. "Did you take a very big dose of the Buck-U-Uppo last night?"

"Big? No. As I recollect, quite small. Barely two ordinary wine-glasses full."

"Great Scott!"

"Why do you ask, my dear fellow?"

"Oh, nothing. No particular reason. I just thought your manner seemed a little strange on the water-pipe, that's all."

The bishop was conscious of a touch of chagrin.

"Then you saw through our—er—innocent deception?"

"Yes."

"I had been taking a little stroll with the headmaster," explained the bishop, "and he had mislaid his key. How beautiful is Nature at night, Mulliner! The dark, fathomless skies, the little winds that seem to whisper secrets in one's ear, the scent of growing things."

"Yes," said Augustine. He paused. "Rather a row on this morning. Somebody appears to have painted Lord Hemel of Hempstead's statue last night."

"Indeed?"

"Yes."

"Ah, well," said the bishop tolerantly, "boys will be boys."

"It's a most mysterious business."

"No doubt, no doubt. But, after all, Mulliner, is not all Life a mystery?"

"And what makes it still more mysterious is that they found your shovel-hat on the statue's head."

The bishop started up.

"What!"

"Absolutely."

"Mulliner," said the bishop, "leave me. I have one or two matters on which I wish to meditate."

He dressed hastily, his numbed fingers fumbling with his gaiters. It all came back to him now. Yes, he could remember putting the hat on the statue's head. It had seemed a good thing to do at the time, and he had done it. How little we guess at the moment how far-reaching our most trivial actions may be!

The headmaster was over at the school, instructing the Sixth Form in Greek Composition: and he was obliged to wait, chafing, until twelve-thirty, when the bell rang for the half-way halt in the day's work. He stood at the study window, watching with ill-controlled impatience, and presently the headmaster appeared, walking heavily like one on whose mind there is a weight.

"Well?" cried the bishop, as he entered the study.

The headmaster doffed his cap and gown, and sank limply into a chair.

"I cannot conceive," he groaned, "what madness had me in its grip last night."

The bishop was shaken, but he could not countenance such an attitude as this.

"I do not understand you, Headmaster," he said stiffly. "It was our simple duty, as a protest against the undue exaltation of one whom we both know to have been a most unpleasant school-mate, to paint that statue."

"And I suppose it was your duty to leave your hat on its head?"

"Now there," said the bishop, "I may possibly have gone a little too far." He coughed. "Has that perhaps somewhat ill-considered action led to the harbouring of suspicions by those in authority?"

"They don't know what to think."

"What is the view of the Board of Governors?"

"They insist on my finding the culprit. Should I fail to do so they hint at the gravest consequences."

"You mean they will deprive you of your headmastership?"

"That is what they imply. I shall be asked to hand in my resignation. And, if that happens, bim goes my chance of ever being a bishop."

"Well, it's not all jam being a bishop. You wouldn't enjoy it, Catsmeat."

"All very well for you to talk, Boko. You got me into this, you silly ass."

"I like that! You were just as keen on it as I was."

"You suggested it."

"Well, you jumped at the suggestion."

The two men had faced each other heatedly, and for a moment it seemed as if there was to be a serious falling-out. Then the bishop recovered himself.

"Catsmeat," he said, with that wonderful smile of his, taking the other's hand, "this is unworthy of us. We must not quarrel. We must put our heads together and see if there is not some avenue of escape from the unfortunate position in which, however creditable our motives, we appear to have placed ourselves. How would it be——?"

"I thought of that," said the headmaster. "It wouldn't do a bit of good. Of course, we might——"

"No, that's no use, either," said the bishop.

They sat for a while in meditative silence. And, as they sat, the door opened.

"General Bloodenough," announced the butler.

"Oh, that I had wings like a dove. Psalm xlv. 6," muttered the bishop.

His desire to be wafted from that spot with all available speed could hardly be considered unreasonable. General Sir Hector Bloodenough, V.C., K.C.I.E., M.V.O., on retiring from the army, had been for many years, until his final return to England, in charge of the Secret Service in Western Africa, where his unerring acumen had won for him from the natives the soubriquet of Wah-nah-B'gosh-B'jingo—which, freely translated, means Big Chief Who Can See Through The Hole In A Doughnut.

A man impossible to deceive. The last man the bishop would have wished to be conducting the present investigations.

The general stalked into the room. He had keen blue eyes, topped by bushy white eyebrows: and the bishop found his gaze far too piercing to be agreeable.

"Bad business, this," he said. "Bad business. Bad business."

"It is, indeed," faltered the bishop.

"Shocking bad business. Shocking. Shocking. Do you know what we found on the head of that statue, eh? that statue, that statue? Your hat, bishop. Your hat. Your hat."

The bishop made an attempt to rally. His mind was in a whirl, for the general's habit of repeating everything three times had the effect on him of making his last night's escapade seem three times as bad. He now saw himself on the verge of standing convicted of having painted three satues with three pots of pink paint, and of having placed on the head of each one of a trio of shovel-hats. But he was a strong man, and he did his best.

"You say my hat?" he retorted with spirit. "How do you know it was my hat? There may have been hundreds of bishops dodging about the school grounds last night."

"Got your name in it. Your name. Your name."

The bishop clutched at the arm of the chair in which he sat. The general's eyes were piercing him through and through, and every moment he felt more like a sheep that has had the misfortune to encounter a potted meat manufacturer. He was on the point of protesting that the writing in the hat was probably a forgery, when there was a tap at the door.

"Come in," cried the headmaster, who had been cowering in his seat.

There entered a small boy in an Eton suit, whose face seemed to the bishop vaguely familiar. It was a face that closely resembled a ripe tomato with a nose stuck on it, but that was not what had struck the bishop. It was of something other than tomatoes that this lad reminded him.

"Sir, please, sir," said the boy.

"Yes, yes, yes," said General Bloodenough testily. "Run away, my boy, run away, run away. Can't you see we're busy?"

"But sir, please, sir, it's about the statue."

"What about the statue? What about it? What about it?"

"Sir, please, sir, it was me."

"What! What! What! What! What!"

The bishop, the general, and the headmaster had spoken simultaneously: and the "What's" had been distributed as follows:

The Bishop	.	.	.	.	.	.	.	1
The General	.	.	.	.	.	.	.	3
The Headmaster	.	.	.	.	.	.	.	1

making five in all. Having uttered these ejaculations, they sat staring at the boy, who turned a brighter vermilion.

"What are you saying?" cried the headmaster. "You painted that statue?"

"Sir, yes, sir."

"You?" said the bishop.

"Sir, yes, sir."

"You? You? You?" said the general.

"Sir, yes, sir."

There was a quivering pause. The bishop looked at the headmaster. The head-master looked at the bishop. The general looked at the boy. The boy looked at the floor.

The general was the first to speak.

"Monstrous!" he exclaimed. "Monstrous. Monstrous. Never heard of such a thing. This boy must be expelled, Headmaster. Expelled. Ex——"

"No!" said the headmaster in a ringing voice.

"Then flogged within an inch of his life. Within an inch. An inch."

"No!" A strange, new dignity seemed to have descended upon the Rev. Trevor Entwhistle. He was breathing a little quickly through his nose, and his eyes had assumed a somewhat prawnlike aspect. "In matters of school discipline, general, I must with all deference claim to be paramount. I will deal with this case as I think best. In my opinion this is not an occasion for severity. You agree with me, bishop?"

The bishop came to himself with a start. He had been thinking of an article which he had just completed for a leading review on the subject of Miracles, and was regretting that the tone he had taken, though in keeping with the trend of Modern Thought, had been tinged with something approaching scepticism.

"Oh, entirely," he said.

"Then all I can say," fumed the general, "is that I wash my hands of the whole business, the whole business, the whole business. And if this is the way our boys are being brought up nowadays, no wonder the country is going to the dogs, the dogs, going to the dogs."

The door slammed behind him. The headmaster turned to the boy, a kindly, winning smile upon his face.

"No doubt," he said, "you now regret this rash act?"

"Sir, yes, sir."

"And you would not do it again?"

"Sir, no, sir."

"Then I think," said the headmaster cheerily, "that we may deal leniently with what, after all, was but a boyish prank, eh, bishop?"

"Oh, decidedly, Headmaster."

"Quite the sort of thing—ha, ha!—that you or I might have done—er—at his age?"

"Oh, quite."

"Then you shall write me twenty lines of Virgil, Mulliner, and we will say no more about it."

The bishop sprang from his chair.

"Mulliner! Did you say Mulliner?"

"Yes."

"I have a secretary of that name. Are you, by any chance, a relation of his, my lad?"

"Sir, yes, sir. Brother."

"Oh!" said the bishop.

The bishop found Augustine in the garden, squirting whale-oil solution on the rose-bushes, for he was an enthusiastic horticulturist. He placed an affectionate hand on his shoulder.

"Mulliner," he said, "do not think that I have not detected your hidden hand behind this astonishing occurrence."

"Eh?" said Augustine. "What astonishing occurrence?"

"As you are aware, Mulliner, last night, from motives which I can assure you were honourable and in accord with the truest spirit of sound Churchmanship, the Rev. Trevor Entwhistle and I were compelled to go out and paint old Fatty Hemel's statue pink. Just now, in the headmaster's study, a boy confessed that he had done it. That boy, Mulliner, was your brother."

"Oh yes?"

"It was you who, in order to save me, inspired him to that confession. Do not deny it, Mulliner."

Augustine smiled an embarrassed smile.

"It was nothing, Bish, nothing at all."

"I trust the matter did not involve you in any too great expense. From what I know of brothers, the lad was scarcely likely to have carried through this benevolent ruse for nothing."

"Oh, just a couple of quid. He wanted three, but I beat him down. Preposterous, I mean to say," said Augustine warmly. "Three quid for a perfectly simple, easy job like that? And so I told him."

"It shall be returned to you, Mulliner."

"No, no, Bish."

"Yes, Mulliner, it shall be returned to you. I have not the sum on my person, but I will forward you a cheque to your new address, The Vicarage, Steeple Mummery, Hants."

Augustine's eyes filled with sudden tears. He grasped the other's hand.

"Bish," he said in a chocking voice, "I don't know how to thank you. But— have you considered?"

"Considered?"

"The wife of thy bosom. Deuteronomy xiii. 6. What will she say when you tell her?"

The bishop's eyes gleamed with a resolute light.

"Mulliner," he said, "the point you raise had not escaped me. But I have the situation well in hand. A bird of the air shall carry the voice, and that which hath wings shall tell the matter. Ecclesiastes x. 20. I shall inform her of my decision on the long-distance telephone."

5

CAME THE DAWN

THE man in the corner took a sip of stout-and-mild, and proceeded to point the moral of the story which he had just told us.

"Yes, gentlemen," he said, "Shakespeare was right. There's a divinity that shapes our ends, rough-hew them how we will."

We nodded. He had been speaking of a favourite dog of his which, entered recently by some error in a local cat show, had taken first prize in the class for short-haired tortoiseshells; and we all thought the quotation well-chosen and apposite.

"There is, indeed," said Mr. Mulliner. "A rather similar thing happened to my nephew Lancelot."

In the nightly reunions in the bar-parlour of the Anglers' Rest we have been trained to believe almost anything of Mr. Mulliner's relatives, but this, we felt, was a little too much.

"You mean to say your nephew Lancelot took a prize at a cat show?"

"No, no," said Mr. Mulliner hastily. "Certainly not. I have never deviated from the truth in my life, and I hope I never shall. No Mulliner has ever taken a prize at a cat show. No Mulliner, indeed, to the best of my knowledge, has ever been entered for such a competition. What I meant was that the fact that we never know what the future holds in store for us was well exemplified in the case of my nephew Lancelot, just at it was in the case of this gentleman's dog which suddenly found itself transformed for all practical purposes into a short-haired tortoiseshell cat. It is rather a curious story, and provides a good illustration of the adage that you never can tell and that it is always darkest before the dawn."

At the time at which my story opens (said Mr. Mulliner) Lancelot, then twenty-four years of age and recently come down from Oxford, was spending a few days with old Jeremiah Briggs, the founder and proprietor of the famous Briggs's Breakfast Pickles, on the latter's yacht at Cowes.

This Jeremiah Briggs was Lancelot's uncle on the mother's side, and he had always interested himself in the boy. It was he who had sent him to the University; and it was the great wish of his heart that his nephew, on completing his education, should join him in the business. It was consequently a shock to the poor old gentleman when, as they sat together on deck on the first morning of the visit,

Lancelot, while expressing the greatest respect for pickles as a class, firmly refused to start in and learn the business from the bottom up.

"The fact is, uncle," he said, "I have mapped out a career for myself on far different lines. I am a poet."

"A poet? When did you feel this coming on?"

"Shortly after my twenty-second birthday."

"Well," said the old man, overcoming his first natural feeling of repulsion, "I don't see why that should stop us getting together. I use quite a lot of poetry in my business."

"I fear I could not bring myself to commercialise my Muse."

"Young man," said Mr. Briggs, "if an onion with a head like yours came into my factory, I would refuse to pickle it."

He stumped below, thoroughly incensed. But Lancelot merely uttered a light laugh. He was young; it was summer; the sky was blue; the sun was shining; and the things in the world that really mattered were not cucumbers and vinegar but Romance and Love. Oh, he felt, for some delightful girl to come along on whom he might lavish all the pent-up fervour which had been sizzling inside him for weeks!

And at this moment he saw her.

She was leaning against the rail of a yacht that lay at its moorings some forty yards away; and, as he beheld her, Lancelot's heart leaped like a young gherkin in the boiling-vat. In her face, it seemed to him, was concentrated all the beauty of all the ages. Confronted with this girl, Cleopatra would have looked like Nellie Wallace, and Helen of Troy might have been her plain sister. He was still gazing at her in a sort of trance, when the bell sounded for luncheon and he had to go below.

All through the meal, while his uncle spoke of pickled walnuts he had known, Lancelot remained in a reverie. He was counting the minutes until he could get on deck and start goggling again. Judge, therefore, of his dismay when, on bounding up the companionway, he found that the other yacht had disappeared. He recalled now having heard a sort of harsh, grating noise towards the end of luncheon; but at the time he had merely thought it was his uncle eating celery. Too late he realised that it must have been the raising of the anchor-chain.

Although at heart a dreamer, Lancelot Mulliner was not without a certain practical streak. Thinking the matter over, he soon hit upon a rough plan of action for getting on the track of the fair unknown who had flashed in and out of his life with such tragic abruptness. A girl like that—beautiful, lissom, and— as far as he had been able to tell at such long range—gimp, was sure to be fond of dancing. The chances were, therefore, that sooner or later he would find her at some night club or other.

He started, accordingly, to make the round of the night clubs. As soon as one was raided, he went on to another. Within a month he had visited the Mauve Mouse, the Scarlet Centipede, the Vicious Cheese, the Gay Fritter, the Placid Prune, the Café de Bologna, Billy's, Milly's, Ike's, Spike's, Mike's, and the Ham and Beef. And it was at the Ham and Beef that at last he found her.

He had gone there one evening for the fifth time, principally because at that establishment there were a couple of speciality dancers to whom he had taken a dislike shared by virtually every thinking man in London. It had always seemed to him that one of these nights the male member of the team, while whirling his partner round in a circle by her outstretched arms, might let her go and break her neck; and though constant disappointment had to some extent blunted the first fine enthusiasm of his early visits, he still hoped.

On this occasion the speciality dancers came and went unscathed as usual, but Lancelot hardly noticed them. His whole attention was concentrated on the girl seated across the room immediately opposite him. It was beyond a question she.

Well, you know what poets are. When their emotions are stirred, they are not like us dull, diffident fellows. They breathe quickly through their noses and get off to a flying start. In one bound Lancelot was across the room, his heart beating till it sounded like a by-request from the trap-drummer.

"Shall we dance?" he said.

"Can you dance?" said the girl.

Lancelot gave a short, amused laugh. He had had a good University education, and had not failed to profit by it. He was a man who never let his left hip know what his right hip was doing.

"I am old Colonel Charleston's favourite son," he said, simply.

A sound like the sudden descent of an iron girder on a sheet of tin, followed by a jangling of bells, a wailing of tortured cats, and the noise of a few steam-riveters at work, announced to their trained ears that the music had begun. Sweeping her to him with a violence which, attempted in any other place, would have earned him a sentence of thirty days coupled with some strong remarks from the Bench, Lancelot began to push her yielding form through the sea of humanity till they reached the centre of the whirlpool. There, unable to move in any direction, they surrendered themselves to the ecstasy of the dance, wiping their feet on the polished flooring and occasionally pushing an elbow into some stranger's encroaching rib.

"This," murmured the girl with closed eyes, "is divine."

"What?" bellowed Lancelot, for the orchestra, in addition to ringing bells, had now begun to howl like wolves at dinner-time.

"Divine," roared the girl. "You certainly are a beautiful dancer."

"A beautiful what?"

"Dancer."

"Who is?"

"You are."

"Good egg!" shrieked Lancelot, rather wishing, though he was fond of music, that the orchestra would stop beating the floor with hammers.

"What did you say?"

"I said, 'Good egg'."

"Why?"

"Because the idea crossed my mind that, if you felt like that, you might care to marry me."

There was a sudden lull in the storm. It was as if the audacity of his words had stricken the orchestra into a sort of paralysis. Dark-complexioned men who had been exploding bombs and touching off automobile hooters became abruptly immobile and sat rolling their eyeballs. One or two people left the floor, and plaster stopped falling from the ceiling.

"Marry you?" said the girl.

"I love you as no man has ever loved a woman before."

"Well, that's always something. What would the name be?"

"Mulliner. Lancelot Mulliner."

"It might be worse." She looked at him with pensive eyes. "Well, why not?" she said. "It would be a crime to let a dancer like you go out of the family. On the other hand, my father will kick like a mule. Father is an Earl."

"What Earl?"

"The Earl of Biddlecombe."

"Well, earls aren't everything," said Lancelot with a touch of pique. "The Mulliners are an old and honourable family. A Sieur de Moulinières came over with the Conqueror."

"Ah, but did a Sieur de Moulinières ever do down the common people for a few hundred thousand and salt it away in gilt-edged securities? That's what's going to count with the aged parent. What with taxes and super-taxes and death duties and falling land-values, there has of recent years been very, very little of the right stuff in the Biddlecombe sock. Shake the family money-box and you will hear but the faintest rattle. And I ought to tell you that at the Junior Lipstick Club seven to two is being freely offered on my marrying Slingsby Purvis of Purvis's Liquid Dinner Glue. Nothing is definitely decided yet, but you can take it as coming straight from the stable that, unless something happens to upset current form, she whom you now see before you is the future Ma Purvis."

Lancelot stamped his foot defiantly, eliciting a howl of agony from a passing reveller.

"This shall not be," he muttered.

"If you care to bet against it," said the girl, producing a small notebook, "I can accommodate you at the current odds."

"Purvis, forsooth!"

"I'm not saying it's a pretty name. All I'm trying to point out is that at the present moment he heads the 'All the above have arrived' list. He is Our New-market Correspondent's Five-Pound Special and Captain Coe's final selection.

What makes you think you can nose him out? Are you rich?"

"At present, only in love. But tomorrow I go to my uncle, who is immensely wealthy——"

"And touch him?"

"Not quite that. Nobody has touched Uncle Jeremiah since the early winter of 1885. But I shall get him to give me a job, and then we shall see."

"Do," said the girl, warmly. "And if you can stick the gaff into Purvis and work the Young Lochinvar business, I shall be the first to touch off red fire. On the other hand, it is only fair to inform you that at the Junior Lipstick all the girls look on the race as a walk-over. None of the big punters will touch it."

Lancelot returned to his rooms that night undiscouraged. He intended to sink his former prejudices and write a poem in praise of Briggs's Breakfast Pickles which would mark a new era in commercial verse. This he would submit to his uncle; and, having stunned him with it, would agree to join the firm as chief poetry-writer. He tentatively pencilled down five thousand pounds a year as the salary which he would demand. With a long-term contract for five thousand a year in his pocket, he could approach Lord Biddlecombe and jerk a father's blessing out of him in no time. It would be humiliating, of course, to lower his genius by writing poetry about pickles; but a lover must make sacrifices. He bought a quire of the best foolscap, brewed a quart of the strongest coffee, locked his door, disconnected his telephone, and sat down at his desk.

Genial old Jeremiah Briggs received him, when he called next day at his palatial house, the Villa Chutney, at Putney, with a bluff good-humour which showed that he still had a warm spot in his heart for the young rascal.

"Sit down, boy, and have a pickled onion," said he, cheerily, slapping Lancelot on the shoulder. "You've come to tell me you've reconsidered your idiotic decision about not joining the business, eh? No doubt we thought it a little beneath our dignity to start at the bottom and work our way up? But, consider, my dear lad. We must learn to walk before we can run, and you could hardly expect me to make you chief cucumber-buyer, or head of the vinegar-bottling department, before you have acquired hard-won experience."

"If you will allow me to explain, uncle——"

"Eh?" Mr. Briggs's geniality faded somewhat. "Am I to understand that you don't want to come into the business?"

"Yes and no," said Lancelot. "I still consider that slicing up cucumbers and dipping them in vinegar is a poor life-work for a man with the Promethean fire within him; but I propose to place at the disposal of the Briggs Breakfast Pickle my poetic gifts."

"Well, that's better than nothing. I've just been correcting the proofs of the last thing our man turned in. It's really excellent. Listen:

> *"Soon, soon all human joys must end:*
> *Grim Death approaches with his sickle:*
> *Courage! There is still time, my friend,*
> *To eat a Briggs's Breakfast Pickle."*

"If you could give us something like that——"
Lancelot raised eyebrows. His lip curled.
"The little thing I have dashed off is not quite like that."
"Oh, you've written something, eh?"
"A mere *morceau*. You would care to hear it?"
"Fire away, my boy."
Lancelot produced his manuscript and cleared his throat. He began to read in a low, musical voice.

"DARKLING (A Threnody).
BY L. BASSINGTON MULLINER.
(*Copyright in all languages, including the Scandinavian.*)

(*The dramatic, musical comedy, and motion picture rights of this Threnody are strictly reserved. Applications for these should be made to the author.*)"

"What is a Threnody?" asked Mr. Briggs.
"This is," said Lancelot.
He cleared his throat again and resumed.

"Black branches,
Like a corpse's withered hands,
Waving against the blacker sky:
Chill winds,
Bitter like the tang of half-remembered sins;
Bats wheeling mournfully through the air,
And on the ground
Worms,
Toads,
Frogs,
And nameless creeping things;
And all around
Desolation,
Doom,
Dyspepsia,
And Despair.
I am a bat that wheels through the air of Fate;

I am a worm that wriggles in a swamp of Disillusionment;
I am a despairing toad;
I have got dyspepsia."

He paused. His uncle's eyes were protruding rather like those of a nameless creeping frog.

"What's all this?" said Mr. Briggs.

It seemed almost incredible to Lancelot that his poem should present any aspect of obscurity to even the meanest intellect; but he explained.

"The thing," he said, "is symbolic. It essays to depict the state of mind of the man who has not yet tried Briggs's Breakfast Pickles. I shall require it to be printed in hand-set type on deep cream-coloured paper."

"Yes?" said Mr. Briggs, touching the bell.

"With bevelled edges. It must be published, of course, bound in limp leather, preferably of a violet shade, in a limited edition, confined to one hundred and five copies. Each of these copies I will sign——"

"You rang, sir?" said the butler, appearing in the doorway.

Mr. Briggs nodded curtly.

"Bewstridge," said he, "throw Mr. Lancelot out."

"Very good, sir."

"And see," added Mr. Briggs, superintending the subsequent proceedings from his library window, "that he never darkens my doors again. When you have finished, Bewstridge, ring up my lawyers on the telephone: I wish to alter my will."

Youth is a resilient period. With all his worldly prospects swept away and a large bruise on his person which made it uncomfortable for him to assume a sitting posture, you might have supposed that the return of Lancelot Mulliner from Putney would have resembled that of the late Napoleon from Moscow. Such, however, was not the case. What, Lancelot asked himself as he rode back to civilization on top of an omnibus, did money matter? Love, true love was all. He would go to Lord Biddlecombe and tell him so in a few neatly-chosen words. And his lordship, moved by his eloquence, would doubtless drop a well-bred tear and at once see that the arrangements for his wedding to Angela—for such, he had learned, was her name—were hastened along with all possible speed. So uplifted was he by this picture that he began to sing, and would have continued for the remainder of the journey had not the conductor in a rather brusque manner ordered him to desist. He was obliged to content himself until the bus reached Hyde Park Corner by singing in dumb show.

The Earl of Biddlecombe's town residence was in Berkeley Square. Lancelot rang the bell and a massive butler appeared.

"No hawkers, street criers, or circulars," said the butler.

"I wish to see Lord Biddlecombe."

"Is his lordship expecting you?"

"Yes," said Lancelot, feeling sure that the girl would have spoken to her father over the morning toast and marmalade of a possible visit from him.

A voice made itself heard through an open door on the left of the long hall.

"Fotheringay"

"Your lordship?"

"Is that the feller?"

"Yes, your lordship."

"Then bung him in, Fotheringay"

"Very good, your lordship."

Lancelot found himself in a small, comfortably-furnished room, confronting a dignified-looking old man with a patrician nose and small side-whiskers, who looked like something that long ago had come out of an egg.

"Afternoon," said this individual.

"Good afternoon, Lord Biddlecombe," said Lancelot.

"Now, about these trousers."

"I beg your pardon?"

"These trousers," said the other, extending a shapely leg. "Do they fit? Aren't they a bit baggy round the ankles? Won't they jeopardize my social prestige if I am seen in them in the Park?"

Lancelot was charmed with his affability. It gave him the feeling of having been made one of the family straight away.

"You really want my opinion?"

"I do. I want your candid opinion as a God-fearing man and a member of a West-end tailoring firm."

"But I'm not."

"Not a God-fearing man?"

"Not a member of a West-end tailoring firm."

"Come, come," said his lordship, testily. "You represent Gusset and Mainprice, of Cork Street."

"No, I don't."

"Then who the devil are you?"

"My name is Mulliner."

Lord Biddlecombe rang the bell furiously.

"Fotheringay!"

"Your lordship?"

"You told me this man was the feller I was expecting from Gusset and Main-price."

"He certainly led me to suppose so, your lordship."

"Well, he isn't. His name is Mulliner. And—this is the point, Fotheringay. This is the core and centre of the thing—what the blazes does he want?"

"I could not say, your lordship."

"I came here, Lord Biddlecombe," said Lancelot, "to ask your consent to my immediate marriage with your daughter."

"My daughter?"

"Your daughter?"

"Which daughter?"

"Angela."

"My daughter Angela?"

"Yes."

"You want to marry my daughter Angela?"

"I do."

"Oh? Well, be that as it may," said Lord Biddlecombe, "can I interest you in an ingenious little combination mousetrap and pencil-sharpener?"

Lancelot was for a moment a little taken aback by the question. Then, remembering what Angela had said of the state of the family finances, he recovered his poise. He thought no worse of this Grecian-beaked old man for ekeing out a slender income by acting as agent for the curious little object which he was now holding out to him. Many of the aristocracy, he was aware, had been forced into similar commercial enterprises by recent legislation of a harsh and Socialistic trend.

"I should like it above all things," he said, courteously. "I was thinking only this morning that it was just what I needed."

"Highly educational. Not a toy. Fotheringay, book one Mouso-Penso."

"Very good, your lordship."

"Are you troubled at all with headaches, Mr. Mulliner?"

"Very seldom."

"Then what you want is Clark's Cure for Corns. Shall we say one of the large bottles?"

"Certainly."

"Then that—with a year's subscription to 'Our Tots'—will come to precisely one pound three shillings and sixpence. Thank you. Will there be anything further?"

"No, thank you. Now, touching the matter of——"

"You wouldn't care for a scarf-pin? Any ties, collars, shirts? No? Then goodbye, Mr. Mulliner."

"But——"

"Fotheringay," said Lord Biddlecombe, "throw Mr. Mulliner out."

As Lancelot scrambled to his feet from the hard pavement of Berkeley Square, he was conscious of a rush of violent anger which deprived him momentarily of speech. He stood there, glaring at the house from which he had been ejected, his face working hideously. So absorbed was he that it was some time before he became aware that somebody was plucking at his coat-sleeve.

"Pardon me, sir."

Lancelot looked round. A stout smooth-faced man with horn-rimmed spectacles was standing beside him.

"If you could spare me a moment——"

Lancelot shook him off impatiently. He had no desire at a time like this to chatter with strangers. The man was babbling something, but the words made no impression upon his mind. With a savage scowl, Lancelot snatched the fellow's umbrella from him and, poising it for an instant, flung it with a sure aim through Lord Biddlecombe's study window. Then, striding away, he made for Berkeley Street. Glancing over his shoulder as he turned the corner, he saw that Fotheringay, the butler, had come out of the house and was standing over the spectacled man with a certain quiet menace in his demeanour. He was rolling up his sleeves, and his fingers were twitching a little.

Lancelot dismissed the man from his thoughts. His whole mind now was concentrated on the coming interview with Angela. For he had decided that the only thing to do was to seek her out at her club, where she would doubtless be spending the afternoon, and plead with her to follow the dictates of her heart and, abandoning parents and wealthy suitors, come with her true mate to a life of honest poverty sweetened by love and *vers libre*.

Arriving at the Junior Lipstick, he inquired for her, and the hall-porter dispatched a boy in buttons to fetch her from the billiard-room, where she was refereeing the finals of the Débutantes' Shove-Ha'penny Tournament. And presently his heart leaped as he saw her coming towards him, looking more like a vision of Springtime than anything human and earthly. She was smoking a cigarette in a long holder, and as she approached she inserted a monocle inquiringly in her right eye.

"Hullo, laddie!" she said. "You here? What's on the mind besides hair? Talk quick. I've only got a minute."

"Angela," said Lancelot, "I have to report a slight hitch in the programme which I sketched out at our last meeting. I have just been to see my uncle and he has washed his hands of me and cut me out of his will."

"Nothing doing in that quarter, you mean?" said the girl, chewing her lower lip thoughtfully.

"Nothing. But what of it? What matters it so long as we have each other? Money is dross. Love is everything. Yes, love indeed is light from heaven, a spark of that immortal fire with angels shared, by Allah given to lift from earth our low desire. Give me to live with Love alone, and let the world go dine and dress. If life's a flower, I choose my own. 'Tis Love in Idleness. When beauty fires the blood, how love exalts the mind! Come, Angela, let us read together in a book more moving than the Koran, more eloquent than Shakespeare, the book of books, the crown of all literature—Bradshaw's Railway Guide. We will turn up a page and you shall put your finger down, and wherever it rests there we will go, to live for ever with our happiness. Oh, Angela, let us——"

"Sorry," said the girl. "Purvis wins. The race goes by the form-book after all. There was a time when I thought you might be going to crowd him on the rails and get your nose first under the wire with a quick last-minute dash, but apparently it is not to be. Deepest sympathy, old crocus, but that's that."

Lancelot staggered.

"You mean you intend to marry this Purvis?"

"Pop in about a month from now at St. George's, Hanover Square, and see for yourself."

"You would allow this man to buy you with his gold?"

"Don't overlook his diamonds."

"Does love count for nothing? Surely you love me?"

"Of course I do, my desert king. When you do that flat-footed Black Bottom step with the sort of wiggly twiggle at the end, I feel as if I were eating plovers' eggs in a new dress to the accompaniment of heavenly music." She sighed. "Yes, I love you, Lancelot. And women are not like men. They do not love lightly. When a woman gives her heart, it is for ever. The years will pass, and you will turn to another. But I shall not forget. However, as you haven't a bob in the world——" She beckoned to the hall-porter. "Margerison."

"Your ladyship?"

"Is it raining?"

"No, your ladyship."

"Are the front steps clean?"

"Yes, your ladyship."

"Then throw Mr. Mulliner out."

Lancelot leaned against the railings of the Junior Lipstick, and looked out through a black mist upon a world that heaved and rocked and seemed on the point of disintegrating into ruin and chaos. And a lot he would care, he told himself bitterly, if it did. If Seamore Place from the west and Charles Street from the east had taken a running jump and landed on the back of his neck, it would have added little or nothing to the turmoil of his mind. In fact, he would rather have preferred it.

Fury, as it had done on the pavement of Berkeley Square, robbed him of speech. But his hands, his shoulders, his brows, his lips, his nose, and even his eyelashes seemed to be charged with a silent eloquence. He twitched his eyebrows in agony. He twiddled his fingers in despair. Nothing was left now, he felt, as he shifted the lobe of his left ear in a nor'-nor'-easterly direction, but suicide. Yes, he told, himself, tightening and relaxing the muscles of his cheeks, all that remained now was death.

But, even as he reached this awful decision, a kindly voice spoke in his ear.

"Oh, come now, I wouldn't say that," said the kindly voice.

And Lancelot, turning, perceived the smooth-faced man who had tried to engage him in conversation in Berkeley Square.

"Say, listen," said the smooth-faced man, sympathy in each lens of his horn-rimmed spectacles. "Tempests may lower and a strong man stand face to face with his soul, but hope, like a healing herb, will show the silver lining where beckons joy and life and happiness."

Lancelot eyed him haughtily.

"I am not aware——" he began.

"Say, listen," said the other, laying a soothing hand on his shoulder. "I know just what has happened. Mammon has conquered Cupid, and once more youth has had to learn the old, old lesson that though the face be fair the heart may be cold and callous."

"What——?"

The smooth-faced man raised his hand.

"That afternoon. Her apartment. 'No. It can never be. I shall wed a wealthier wooer.' "

Lancelot's fury began to dissolve into awe. There seemed something uncanny in the way this total stranger had diagnosed the situation. He stared at him, bewildered.

"How did you know?" he gasped.

"You told me."

"I?"

"Your face did. I could read every word. I've been watching you for the last two minutes, and, say, boy, it was a wow!"

"Who are you?" asked Lancelot.

The smooth-faced man produced from his waistcoat pocket a fountain-pen, two cigars, a packet of chewing-gum, a small button bearing the legend, "Boost for Hollywood," and a visiting-card—in the order named. Replacing the other articles, he handed the card to Lancelot.

"I'm Isadore Zinzinheimer, kid," he said. "I represent the Bigger, Better, and Brighter Motion-Picture Company of Hollywood, Cal., incorporated last July for sixteen hundred million dollars. And if you're thinking of asking me what I want, I want you. Yes, sir! Say, listen. A fellow that can register the way you can is needed in my business; and, if you think money can stop me getting him, name the biggest salary you can think of and hear me laugh. Boy, I use bank-notes for summer underclothing, and I don't care how bad you've got the gimme's if only you'll sign on the dotted line. Say, listen. A bozo that with a mere twitch of the upper lip can make it plain to one and all that he loves a haughty aristocrat and that she has given him the air because his rich uncle, who is a pickle manufacturer living in Putney, won't have anything more to do with him, is required out at Hollywood by the next boat if the movies are ever to become an educational force in the truest and deepest sense of the words."

Lancelot stared at him.

"You want me to come to Hollywood?"

"I want you, and I'm going to get you. And if you think you're going to prevent me, you're trying to stop Niagara with a tennis racket. Boy, you're great! When you register, you register. Your face is as chatty as a board of directors. Say, listen. You know the great thing we folks in the motion-picture industry have got to contend with? The curse of the motion-picture industry is that in every audience there are from six to seven young women with adenoids who will insist on reading out the titles as they are flashed on the screen, filling the rest of the customers with harsh thoughts and dreams of murder. What we're trying to collect is stars that can register so well that titles won't be needed. And, boy, you're the king of them. I know you're feeling good and sore just now because that beazle in there spurned your honest love; but forget it. Think of your Art. Think of your Public. Come now, what shall we say to start with? Five thousand a week? Ten thousand? You call the shots, and I'll provide the blank contract and fountain-pen."

Lancelot needed no further urging. Already love had turned to hate, and he no longer wished to marry Angela. Instead, he wanted to make her burn with anguish and vain regrets; and it seemed to him that Fate was pointing the way. Pretty silly the future Lady Angela Purvis would feel when she discovered that she had rejected the love of a man with a salary of ten thousand dollars a week. And fairly foolish her old father would feel when news reached him of the good thing he had allowed to get away. And racking would be the remorse, when he returned to London as Civilised Girlhood's Sweetheart and they saw him addressing mobs from a hotel balcony, of his Uncle Jeremiah, of Fotheringay, of Bewstridge, and of Margerison.

A light gleamed in Lancelot's eye, and he rolled the tip of his nose in a circular movement.

"You consent?" said Mr. Zinzinheimer, delighted. " 'At-a-boy! Here's the pen and here's the contract."

"Gimme!" said Lancelot.

A benevolent glow irradiated the other's spectacles.

"Came the Dawn!" he murmured. "Came the Dawn!"

THE STORY OF WILLIAM

Miss Postlethwaite, our able and vigilant barmaid, had whispered to us that the gentleman sitting over there in the corner was an American gentleman.

"Comes from America," added Miss Postlethwaite, making her meaning clearer.

"From America?" echoed we.

"From America," said Miss Postlethwaite. "He's an American."

Mr. Mulliner rose with an old-world grace. We do not often get Americans in the bar-parlour of the Anglers' Rest. When we do, we welcome them. We make them realise that Hands Across the Sea is no mere phrase.

"Good evening, sir," said Mr. Mulliner. "I wonder if you would care to join my friend and myself in a little refreshment?"

"Very kind of you, sir."

"Miss Postlethwaite, the usual. I understand you are from the other side, sir. Do you find our English country-side pleasant?"

"Delightful. Though, of course, if I may say so, scarcely to be compared with the scenery of my home State."

"What State is that?"

"California," replied the other, baring his head. "California, the Jewel State of the Union. With its azure sea, its noble hills, its eternal sunshine, and its fragrant flowers, California stands alone. Peopled by stalwart men and womanly women . . ."

"California would be all right," said Mr. Mulliner, "if it wasn't for the earth-quakes."

Our guest started as though some venomous snake had bitten him.

"Earthquakes are absolutely unknown in California," he said, hoarsely.

"What about the one in 1906?"

"That was not an earthquake. It was a fire."

"An earthquake, I always understood," said Mr. Mulliner. "My Uncle William was out there during it, and many a time has he said to me, 'My boy, it was the San Francisco earthquake that won me a bride'."

"Couldn't have been the earthquake. May have been the fire."

"Well, I will tell you the story, and you shall judge for yourself."

"I shall be glad to hear your story about the San Francisco fire," said the Californian, courteously.

My Uncle William (said Mr. Mulliner) was returning from the East at the time. The commercial interests of the Mulliners have always been far-flung: and he had been over in China looking into the workings of a tea-exporting business in which he held a number of shares. It was his intention to get off the boat at San Francisco and cross the continent by rail. He particularly wanted to see the Grand Canyon of Arizona. And when he found that Myrtle Banks had for years cherished the same desire, it seemed to him so plain a proof that they were twin souls that he decided to offer her his hand and heart without delay.

This Miss Banks had been a fellow-traveller on the boat all the way from Hong Kong; and day by day William Mulliner had fallen more and more deeply in love with her. So on the last day of the voyage, as they were steaming in at the Golden Gate, he proposed.

I have never been informed of the exact words which he employed, but no doubt they were eloquent. All the Mulliners have been able speakers, and on such an occasion he would, of course, have extended himself. When at length he finished, it seemed to him that the girl's attitude was distinctly promising. She stood gazing over the rail into the water below in a sort of rapt way. Then she turned.

"Mr. Mulliner," she said, "I am greatly flattered and honoured by what you have just told me." These things happened, you will remember, in the days when girls talked like that. "You have paid me the greatest compliment a man can bestow on a woman. And yet . . ."

William Mulliner's heart stood still. He did not like that "And yet——"

"Is there another?" he muttered.

"Well, yes, there is. Mr. Franklyn proposed to me this morning. I told him I would think it over."

There was a silence. William was telling himself that he had been afraid of that bounder Franklyn all along. He might have known, he felt, that Desmond Franklyn would be a menace. The man was one of those lean, keen, hawk-faced, Empire-building sort of chaps you find out East—the kind of fellow who stands on deck chewing his moustache with a far-away look in his eyes, and then, when the girl asks him what he is thinking about, draws a short, quick breath and says he is sorry to be so absent-minded, but a sunset like that always reminds him of the day when he killed the four pirates with his bare hands and saved dear old Tuppy Smithers in the nick of time.

"There is a great glamour about Mr. Franklyn," said Myrtle Banks. "We women admire men who do things. A girl cannot help but respect a man who once killed three sharks with a Boy Scout pocket-knife."

"So he says," growled William.

"He showed me the pocket-knife," said the girl, simply. "And on another occasion he brought down two lions with one shot."

William Mulliner's heart was heavy, but he struggled on.

"Very possibly he may have done these things," he said, "but surely marriage means more than this. Personally, if I were a girl, I would go rather for a certain steadiness and stability of character. To illustrate what I mean, did you happen to see me win the Egg-and-Spoon race at the ship's sports? Now there, it seems to me, in what I might call microcosm, was an exhibition of all the qualities a married man most requires—intense coolness, iron resolution, and a quiet, unassuming courage. The man who under test conditions has carried an egg once and a half times round a deck in a small spoon is a man who can be trusted."

She seemed to waver, but only for a moment.

"I must think," she said. "I must think."

"Certainly," said William. "You will let me see something of you at the hotel, after we have landed?"

"Of course. And if—I mean to say, whatever happens, I shall always look on you as a dear, dear friend."

"M'yes," said William Mulliner.

For three days my Uncle William's stay in San Francisco was as pleasant as could reasonably be expected, considering that Desmond Franklyn was also stopping at his and Miss Banks's hotel. He contrived to get the girl to himself to quite a satisfactory extent; and they spent many happy hours together in the Golden Gate Park and at the Cliff House, watching the seals basking on the rocks. But on the evening of the third day the blow fell.

"Mr. Mulliner," said Myrtle Banks, "I want to tell you something."

"Anything," breathed William tenderly, "except that you are going to marry that perisher Franklyn."

"But that is exactly what I was going to tell you, and I must not let you call him a perisher, for he is a very brave, intrepid man."

"When did you decide on this rash act?" asked William dully.

"Scarcely an hour ago. We were talking in the garden, and somehow or other we got on to the subject of rhinoceroses. He then told me how he had once been chased up a tree by a rhinoceros in Africa and escaped by thowing pepper in the brute's eyes. He most fortunately chanced to be eating his lunch when the animal arrived, and he had a hard-boiled egg and the pepper-pot in his hands. When I heard this story, like Desdemona, I loved him for the dangers he had passed, and he loved me that I did pity them. The wedding is to be in June."

William Mulliner ground his teeth in a sudden access of jealous rage.

"Personally," he said, "I consider that the story you have just related reveals this man Franklyn in a very dubious—I might almost say sinister—light. On his own showing, the leading trait in his character appears to be cruelty to animals. The fellow seems totally incapable of meeting a shark or a rhinoceros or any other of our dumb friends without instantly going out of his way to inflict bodily injury on it. The last thing I would wish is to be indelicate, but I cannot refrain from pointing out that, if your union is blessed, your children will probably be the sort of children who kick cats and tie tin cans to dogs' tails. If you take my advice, you will write the man a little note, saying that you are sorry but you have changed your mind."

The girl rose in a marked manner.

"I do not require your advice, Mr. Mulliner," she said, coldly. "And I have not changed my mind."

Instantly William Mulliner was all contrition. There is a certain stage in the progress of a man's love when he feels like curling up in a ball and making little bleating noises if the object of his affections so much as looks squiggle-eyed at him; and this stage my Uncle William had reached. He followed her as she paced proudly away through the hotel lobby, and stammered incoherent apologies. But Myrtle Banks was adamant.

"Leave me, Mr. Mulliner," she said, pointing at the revolving door that led into the street. "You have maligned a better man than yourself, and I wish to have nothing more to do with you. Go!"

William went, as directed. And so great was the confusion of his mind that he got stuck in the revolving door and had gone round in it no fewer than eleven times before the hall-porter came to extricate him.

"I would have removed you from the machinery earlier, sir," said the hall-porter deferentially, having deposited him safely in the street, "but my bet with my mate in there called for ten laps. I waited till you had completed eleven so that there should be no argument."

William looked at him dazedly.

"Hall-porter," he said.

"Sir?"

"Tell me, hall-porter," said William, "suppose the only girl you have ever loved had gone and got engaged to another, what would you do?"

The hall-porter considered.

"Let me get this right," he said. "The proposition is, if I have followed you correctly, what would I do supposing the Jane on whom I had always looked as a steady mamma had handed me the old skimmer and told me to take all the air I needed because she had gotten another sweetie?"

"Precisely."

"Your question is easily answered," said the hall-porter. "I would go around the corner and get me a nice stiff drink at Mike's Place."

"A drink?"

"Yes, sir. A nice stiff one."

"At where did you say?"

"Mike's Place, sir. Just round the corner. You can't miss it."

William thanked him and walked away. The man's words had started a new, and in many ways interesting, train of thought. A drink? And a nice stiff one? There might be something in it.

William Mulliner had never tasted alcohol in his life. He had promised his late mother that he would not do so until he was either twenty-one or forty-one—he could never remember which. He was at present twenty-nine; but wishing to be on the safe side in case he had got his figures wrong, he had remained a teetotaller. But now, as he walked listlessly along the street towards the corner, it seemed to him that his mother in the special circumstances could not reasonably object if he took a slight snort. He raised his eyes to heaven, as though to ask her if a couple of quick ones might not be permitted; and he fancied that a faint, far-off voice whispered, "Go to it!"

And at this moment he found himself standing outside a brightly-lighted saloon.

For an instant he hesitated. Then, as a twinge of anguish in the region of his broken heart reminded him of the necessity for immediate remedies, he pushed open the swing doors and went in.

The principal feature of the cheerful, brightly-lit room in which he found himself was a long counter, at which were standing a number of the citizenry, each with an elbow on the woodwork and a foot upon the neat brass rail which ran below. Behind the counter appeared the upper section of one of the most benevolent and kindly-looking men that William had ever seen. He had a large smooth face, and he wore a white coat, and he eyed William, as he advanced, with a sort of reverent joy.

"Is this Mike's Place?" asked William.

"Yes, sir," replied the white-coated man.

"Are you Mike?"

"No, sir. But I am his representative, and have full authority to act on his behalf. What can I have the pleasure of doing for you?"

The man's whole attitude made him seem so like a large-hearted elder brother that William felt no diffidence about confiding in him. He placed an elbow on the counter and a foot on the rail, and spoke with a sob in his voice.

"Suppose the only girl you had ever loved had gone and got engaged to another, what in your view would best meet the case?"

The gentlemanly bar-tender pondered for some moments.

"Well," he replied at length, "I advance it, you understand, as a purely personal opinion, and I shall not be in the least offended if you decide not to act upon it; but my suggestion—for what it is worth—is that you try a Dynamite Dew-Drop."

One of the crowd that had gathered sympathetically round shook his head. He was a charming man with a black eye, who had shaved on the preceding Thursday.

"Much better give him a Dreamland Special."

A second man, in a sweater and a cloth cap, had yet another theory.

"You can't beat an Undertaker's Joy."

They were all so perfectly delightful and appeared to have his interests so unselfishly at heart that William could not bring himself to choose between them. He solved the problem in diplomatic fashion by playing no favourites and ordering all three of the beverages recommended.

The effect was instantaneous and gratifying. As he drained the first glass, it seemed to him that a torchlight procession, of whose existence he had hitherto not been aware, had begun to march down his throat and explore the recesses of his stomach. The second glass, though slightly too heavily charged with molten lava, was extremely palatable. It helped the torchlight procession along by adding to it a brass band of singular power and sweetness of tone. And with the third somebody began to touch off fireworks inside his head.

William felt better—not only spiritually but physically. He seemed to himself to be a bigger, finer man, and the loss of Myrtle Banks had somehow in a flash lost nearly all its importance. After all, as he said to the man with the black eye, Myrtle Banks wasn't everybody.

"Now what do you recommend?" he asked the man with the sweater, having turned the last glass upside down.

The other mused, one forefinger thoughtfully pressed against the side of his face.

"Well, I'll tell you," he said. "When my brother Elmer lost his girl, he drank straight rye. Yes, sir. That's what he drank—straight rye. 'I've lost my girl,' he said. 'and I'm going to drink straight rye.' That's what he said. Yes, sir, straight rye."

"And was your brother Elmer," asked William, anxiously, "a man whose example in your opinion should be followed? Was he a man you could trust?"

"He owned the biggest duck-farm in the southern half of Illinois."

"That settles it," said William. "What was good enough for a duck who owned half Illinois is good enough for me. Oblige me," he said to the gentlemanly bartender, "by asking these gentlemen what they will have, and start pouring."

The bar-tender obeyed, and William, having tried a pint or two of the strange liquid just to see if he liked it, found that he did, and ordered some. He then began to move about among his new friends, patting one on the shoulder, slapping another affably on the back, and asking a third what his Christian name was.

"I want you all," he said, climbing on to the counter so that his voice should carry better, "to come and stay with me in England. Never in my life have I met men whose faces I liked so much. More like brothers than anything is the way I regard you. So just you pack up a few things and come along and put up at my little place for as long as you can manage. You particularly, my dear old chap," he added, beaming at the man in the sweater.

"Thanks," said the man with the sweater.

"What did you say?" said William.

"I said, 'Thanks'."

William slowly removed his coat and rolled up his shirt-sleeves.

"I call you gentlemen to witness," he said, quietly, "that I have been grossly insulted by this gentleman who has just grossly insulted me. I am not a quarrelsome man, but if anybody wants a row they can have it. And when it comes to being cursed and sworn at by an ugly bounder in a sweater and a cloth cap, it is time to take steps."

And with these spirited words William Mulliner sprang from the counter, grasped the other by the throat, and bit him sharply on the right ear. There was a confused interval, during which somebody attached himself to the collar of William's waistcoat and the seat of William's trousers, and then a sense of swift movement and rush of cool air.

Willam discovered that he was seated on the pavement outside the saloon. A hand emerged from the swing door and threw his hat out. And he was alone with the night and his meditations.

These were, as you may suppose, of a singularly bitter nature. Sorrow and disillusionment racked William Mulliner like a physical pain. That his friends inside there, in spite of the fact that he had been all sweetness and light and had not done a thing to them, should have thrown him out into the hard street was the saddest thing he had ever heard of; and for some minutes he sat there, weeping silently.

Presently he heaved himself to his feet and, placing one foot with infinite delicacy in front of the other, and then drawing the other one up and placing it with infinite delicacy in front of that, be began to walk back to his hotel.

At the corner he paused. There were some railings on his right. He clung to them and rested awhile.

The railing to which William Mulliner had attached himself belonged to a brownstone house of the kind that seems destined from the first moment of its building to receive guests, both resident and transient, at a moderate weekly rental. It was, in fact, as he would have discovered had he been clear-sighted enough to read the card over the door, Mrs. Beulah O'Brien's Theatrical Boarding-House ("A Home From Home—No Cheques Cashed—This Means You").

But William was not in the best of shape for reading cards. A sort of mist had obscured the world, and he was finding it difficult to keep his eyes open. And presently, his chin wedged into the railings, he fell into a dreamless sleep.

He was awakened by light flashing in his eyes; and, opening them, saw that a window opposite where he was standing had become brightly illuminated. His slumbers had cleared his vision; and he was able to observe that the room into which he was looking was a dining-room. The long table was set for the evening meal; and to William, as he gazed, the sight of that cosy apartment, with the gaslight falling on the knives and forks and spoons, seemed the most pathetic and poignant that he had ever beheld.

A mood of the most extreme sentimentality now had him in its grip. The thought that he would never own a little home like that racked him from stem to stern with an almost unbearable torment. What, argued William, clinging to the railings and crying weakly, could compare, when you came right down to it, with a little home? A man with a little home is all right, whereas a man without a little

home is just a bit of flotsam on the ocean of life. If Myrtle Banks had only consented to marry him, he would have had a little home. But she had refused to
marry him, so he would never have a little home. What Myrtle Banks wanted,
felt William, was a good swift clout on the side of the head.

The thought pleased him. He was feeling physically perfect again now, and
seemed to have shaken off completely the slight indisposition from which he had
been suffering. His legs had lost their tendency to act independently of the rest
of his body. His head felt clearer, and he had a sense of overwhelming strength.
If ever, in short, there was a moment when he could administer that clout on the
side of the head to Myrtle Banks as it should be administered, that moment was
now.

He was on the point of moving off to find her and teach her what it meant to
stop a man like himself from having a little home, when someone entered the room
into which he was looking, and he paused to make further inspection.

The new arrival was a coloured maid-servant. She staggered to the head of the
table beneath the weight of a large tureen containing, so William suspected, hash.
A moment later a stout woman with bright golden hair came in and sat down
opposite the tureen.

The instinct to watch other people eat is one of the most deeply implanted in
the human bosom, and William lingered, intent. There was, he told himself, no
need to hurry. He knew which was Myrtle's room in the hotel. It was just across
the corridor from his own. He could pop in any time, during the night, and give
her that clout. Meanwhile, he wanted to watch these people eat hash.

And then the door opened again, and there filed into the room a little procession. And William, clutching the railings, watched it with bulging eyes.

The procession was headed by an elderly man in a check suit with a carnation in
his buttonhole. He was about three feet six in height, though the military jaunti-
ness with which he carried himself made him seem fully three feet seven. He was
followed by a younger man who wore spectacles and whose height was perhaps
three feet four. And behind these two came, in single file, six others, scaling down
by degrees until, bringing up the rear of the procession, there entered a rather
stout man in tweeds and bedroom slippers who could not have measured more
than two feet eight.

They took their places at the table. Hash was distributed to all. And the man in
tweeds, having inspected his plate with obvious relish, removed his slippers and,
picking up his knife and fork with his toes, fell to with a keen appetite.

William Mulliner uttered a soft moan, and tottered away.

It was a black moment for my Uncle William. Only an instant before he had
been congratulating himself on having shaken off the effects of his first indulgence
in alcohol after an abstinence of twenty-nine years; but now he perceived that he
was still intoxicated.

Intoxicated? The word did not express it by a mile. He was oiled, boiled, fried, plastered, whiffled, sozzled, and blotto. Only by the exercise of the most consummate caution and address could he hope to get back to his hotel and reach his bedroom without causing an open scandal.

Of course, if his walk that night had taken him a few yards farther down the street than the door of Mike's Place, he would have seen that there was a very simple explanation of the spectacle which he had just witnessed. A walk so extended would have brought him to the San Francisco Palace of Varieties, outside which large posters proclaimed the exclusive engagement for two weeks of

MURPHY'S MIDGETS.

BIGGER AND BETTER THAN EVER.

But of the existence of these posters he was not aware; and it is not too much to say that the iron entered into William Mulliner's soul.

That his legs should have become temporarily unscrewed at the joints was a phenomenon which he had been able to bear with fortitude. That his head should be feeling as if a good many bees had decided to use it as a hive was unpleasant, but not unbearably so. But that his brain should have gone off its castors and be causing him to see visions was the end of all things.

William had always prided himself on the keenness of his mental powers. All through the long voyage on the ship, when Desmond Franklyn had related anecdotes illustrative of his prowess as a man of Action, William Mulliner had always consoled himself by feeling that in the matter of brain he could give Franklyn three bisques and a beating any time he chose to start. And now, it seemed, he had lost even this advantage over his rival. For Franklyn, dull-witted clod though he might be, was not such an absolute minus quantity that he would imagine he had seen a man of two feet eight cutting up hash with his toes. That hideous depth of mental decay had been reserved for William Mulliner.

Moodily he made his way back to his hotel. In a corner of the Palm Room he saw Myrtle Banks deep in conversation with Franklyn, but all desire to give her a clout on the side of the head had now left him. With his chin sunk on his breast, he entered the elevator and was carried up to his room.

Here as rapidly as his quivering fingers would permit, he undressed; and, climbing into the bed as it came round for the second time, lay for a space with wide-open eyes. He had been too shaken to switch his light off, and the rays of the lamp shone on the handsome ceiling which undulated above him. He gave himself up to thought once more.

No doubt, he felt, thinking it over now, his mother had had some very urgent reason for withholding him from alcoholic drink. She must have known of some family secret, sedulously guarded from his infant ears—some dark tale of a fatal Mulliner taint. "William must never learn of this!" she had probably said when they told her the old legend of how every Mulliner for centuries back had died a maniac, victim at last to the fatal fluid. And tonight, despite her gentle care, he had found out for himself.

He saw now that this derangement of his eyesight was only the first step in the gradual dissolution which was the Mulliner Curse. Soon his sense of hearing would go, then his sense of touch.

He sat up in bed. It seemed to him that, as he gazed at the ceiling, a considerable section of it had parted from the parent body and fallen with a crash to the floor.

William Mulliner stared dumbly. He knew, of course, that it was an illusion. But what a perfect illusion! If he had not had the special knowledge which he possessed, he would have stated without fear of contradiction that there was a gap six feet wide above him and a mass of dust and plaster on the carpet below.

And even as his eyes deceived him, so did his ears. He seemed to be conscious of a babel of screams and shouts. The corridor, he could have sworn, was full of flying feet. The world appeared to be all bangs and crashes and thuds. A cold fear gripped at William's heart. His sense of hearing was playing tricks with him already.

His whole being recoiled from making the final experiment, but he forced himself out of bed. He reached a finger towards the nearest heap of plaster and drew it back with a groan. Yes, it was as he feared, his sense of touch had gone wrong too. That heap of plaster, though purely a figment of his disordered brain, had felt solid.

So there it was. One little moderately festive evening at Mike's Place, and the Curse of the Mulliner's had got him. Within an hour of absorbing the first drink of his life, it had deprived him of his sight, his hearing, and his sense of touch. Quick service, felt William Mulliner.

As he climbed back into bed, it appeared to him that two of the walls fell out. He shut his eyes, and presently sleep, which has been well called Tired Nature's Sweet Restorer, brought oblivion. His last waking thought was that he imagined he had heard another wall go.

William Mulliner was a sound sleeper, and it was many hours before consciousness returned to him. When he awoke, he looked about him in astonishment. The haunting horror of the night had passed; and now, though conscious of a rather severe headache, he knew that he was seeing things as they were.

And yet it seemed odd to think that what he beheld was not the remains of some nightmare. Not only was the world slightly yellow and a bit blurred about the edges, but it had changed in its very essentials overnight. Where eight hours before there had been a wall, only an open space appeared, with bright sunlight streaming through it. The ceiling was on the floor, and almost the only thing remaining of what had been an expensive bedroom in a first-class hotel was the bed. Very strange, he thought, and very irregular.

A voice broke in upon his meditations.

"Why, Mr. Mulliner!"

William turned, and being, like all the Mulliners, the soul of modesty, dived abruptly beneath the bed-clothes. For the voice was the voice of Myrtle Banks. And she was in his room!

"Mr. Mulliner!"

William poked his head out cautiously. And then he perceived that the proprieties had not been outraged as he had imagined. Miss Banks was not in his room, but in the corridor. The intervening wall had disappeared. Shaken, but relieved, he sat up in bed, the sheet drawn round his shoulders.

"You don't mean to say you're still in bed?" gasped the girl.

"Why, is it awfully late?" said William.

"Did you actually stay up here all through it?"

"Through what?"

"The earthquake."

"What earthquake?"

"The earthquake last night."

"Oh, that earthquake?" said William, carelessly. "I did notice some sort of an earthquake. I remember seeing the ceiling come down and saying to myself, 'I shouldn't wonder if that wasn't an earthquake.' And then the walls fell out, and I said, 'Yes. I believe it *is* an earthquake.' And then I turned over and went to sleep."

Myrtle Banks was staring at him with eyes that reminded him partly of twin stars and partly of a snail's.

"You must be the bravest man in the world!"

William gave a curt laugh.

"Oh, well," he said, "I may not spend my whole life persecuting unfortunate sharks with pocket-knives, but I find I generally manage to keep my head fairly well in a crisis. We Mulliners are like that. We do not say much, but we have the right stuff in us."

He clutched his head. A sharp spasm had reminded him how much of the right stuff he had in him at that moment.

"My hero!" breathed the girl, almost inaudibly.

"And how is your fiancé this bright, sunny morning?" asked William, nonchalantly. It was torture to refer to the man, but he must show her that a Mulliner knew how to take his medicine.

She gave a little shudder.

"I have no fiancé," she said.

"But I thought you told me you and Franklyn . . ."

"I am no longer engaged to Mr. Franklyn. Last night, when the earthquake started, I cried to him to help me; and he with a hasty 'Some other time!' over his shoulder, disappeared into the open like something shot out of a gun. I never saw a man run so fast. This morning I broke off the engagement." She uttered a scornful laugh.

"Sharks and pocket-knives! I don't believe he ever killed a shark in his life."

"And even if he did," said William, "what of it? I mean to say, how infrequently in married life must the necessity for killing sharks with pocket-knives arise! What a husband needs is not some purely adventitious gift like that—a parlour trick you might almost call it—but a steady character, a warm and generous disposition, and a loving heart."

"How true!" she murmured, dreamily.

"Myrtle," said William, "I would be a husband like that. The steady character, the warm and generous disposition, and the loving heart to which I have alluded are at your disposal. Will you accept them?"

"I will," said Myrtle Banks.

And that (concluded Mr. Mulliner) is the story of my Uncle William's romance. And you will readily understand, having heard it, how his eldest son, my cousin, J. S. F. E. Mulliner, got his name.

"J. S. F. E.?" I said.

"John San Francisco Earthquake Mulliner," explained my friend.

"There never was a San Francisco earthquake," said the Californian. "Only a fire."

7
PORTRAIT OF A DISCIPLINARIAN

It was with something of the relief of fog-bound city-dwellers who at last behold the sun that we perceived, on entering the bar-parlour of the Anglers' Rest, that Mr. Mulliner was seated once more in the familiar chair. For some days he had been away, paying a visit to an old nurse of his down in Devonshire: and there was no doubt that in his absence the tide of intellectual conversation had run very low.

"No," said Mr. Mulliner, in answer to a question as to whether he had enjoyed himself, "I cannot pretend that it was an altogether agreeable experience. I was conscious throughout of a sense of strain. The poor old thing is almost completely deaf, and her memory is not what it was. Moreover, it is a moot point whether a man of sensibility can ever be entirely at his ease in the presence of a woman who has frequently spanked him with the flat side of a hair-brush."

Mr. Mulliner winced slightly, as if the old wound still troubled him.

"It is curious," he went on, after a thoughtful pause, "how little change the years bring about in the attitude of a real, genuine, crusted old family nurse towards one who in the early knickerbocker stage of his career has been a charge of hers. He may grow grey or bald and be looked up to by the rest of his world as a warm performer on the Stock Exchange or a devil of a fellow in the sphere of Politics or the Arts, but to his old Nanna he will still be the Master James or Master Percival who had to be hounded by threats to keep his face clean. Shakespeare would have cringed before his old nurse. So would Herbert Spencer, Attila the Hun, and the Emperor Nero. My nephew Frederick . . . but I must not bore you with my family gossip."

We reassured him.

"Oh well, if you wish to hear the story. There is nothing much in it as a story, but it bears out the truth of what I have just been saying."

I will begin (said Mr. Mulliner) at the moment when Frederick, having come down from London in response to an urgent summons from his brother, Doctor George Mulliner, stood in the latter's consulting-room, looking out upon the Esplanade of that quiet little watering-place, Bingley-on-Sea.

George's consulting-room, facing west, had the advantage of getting the afternoon sun: and this afternoon it needed all the sun it could get, to counteract

Frederick's extraordinary gloom. The young man's expression, as he confronted his brother, was that which a miasmic pool in some dismal swamp in the Bad Lands might have worn if it had had a face.

"Then the position, as I see it," he said in a low, toneless voice, "is this. On the pretext of wishing to discuss urgent business with me, you have dragged me down to this foul spot—seventy miles by rail in a compartment containing three distinct infants sucking sweets—merely to have tea with a nurse whom I have disliked since I was a child."

"You have contributed to her support for many years," George reminded him.

"Naturally, when the family were clubbing together to pension off the old blister, I chipped in with my little bit," said Frederick. "Noblesse oblige."

"Well, noblesse obliges you to go and have tea with her when she invites you. Wilks must be humoured. She is not so young as she was."

"She must be a hundred."

"Eighty-five."

"Good heavens! And it seems only yesterday that she shut me up in a cup-board for stealing jam."

"She was a great disciplinarian," agreed George. "You may find her a little on the autocratic side still. And I want to impress upon you, as her medical man, that you must not thwart her slightest whim. She will probably offer you boiled eggs and home-made cake. Eat them."

"I will not eat boiled eggs at five o'clock in the afternoon," said Frederick, with a strong man's menacing calm, "for any woman on earth."

"You will. And with relish. Her heart is weak. If you don't humour her, I won't answer for the consequences."

"If I eat boiled eggs at five in the afternoon, I won't answer for the conse-quences. And why boiled eggs, dash it? I'm not a schoolboy."

"To her you are. She looks on all of us as children still. Last Christmas she gave me a copy of *Eric, or Little by Little*."

Frederick turned to the window, and scowled down upon the noxious and de-pressing scene below. Sparing neither age nor sex in his detestation, he regarded the old ladies reading their library novels on the seats with precisely the same dislike and contempt which he bestowed on the boys' school clattering past on its way to the bathing-houses.

"Then, checking up your statements," he said, "I find that I am expected to go to tea with a woman who, in addition, apparently, to being a blend of Lucretia Borgia and a Prussian sergeant-major, is a physical wreck and practically potty. Why? That is what I ask. Why? As a child, I objected strongly to Nurse Wilks: and now, grown to riper years, the thought of meeting her again gives me the heeby-jeebies. Why should I be victimised? Why me particularly?"

"It isn't you particularly. We've all been to see her at intervals, and so have the Oliphants."

"The Oliphants!"

The name seemed to affect Frederick oddly. He winced, as if his brother had been a dentist instead of a general practitioner and had just drawn one of his back teeth.

"She was their nurse after she left us. You can't have forgotten the Oliphants. I remember you at the age of twelve climbing that old elm at the bottom of the paddock to get Jane Oliphant a rook's egg."

Frederick laughed bitterly.

"I must have been a perfect ass. Fancy risking my life for a girl like that! Not," he went on, "that life's worth much. An absolute wash-out, that's what life is. However, it will soon be over. And then the silence and peace of the grave. That," said Frederick, "is the thought that sustains me."

"A pretty kid, Jane. Someone told me she had grown up quite a beauty."

"Without a heart."

"What do you know about it?"

"Merely this. She pretended to love me, and then a few months ago she went off to the country to stay with some people named Ponderby and wrote me a letter breaking off the engagement. She gave no reasons, and I have not seen her since. She is now engaged to a man named Dillingwater, and I hope it chokes her."

"I never heard about this. I'm sorry."

"I'm not. Merciful release is the way I look at it."

"Would he be one of the Sussex Dillingwaters?"

"I don't know what county the family infests. If I did, I would avoid it."

"Well, I'm sorry. No wonder you're depressed."

"Depressed?" said Frederick, outraged. "Me? You don't suppose I'm worrying myself about a girl like that, do you? I've never been so happy in my life. I'm just bubbling over with cheerfulness."

"Oh, is that what it is?" George looked at his watch. "Well, you'd better be pushing along. It'll take you about ten minutes to get to Marazion Road."

"How do I find the blasted house?"

"The name's on the door."

"What is the name?"

"Wee Holme."

"My God!" said Frederick Mulliner. "It only needed that!"

The view which he had had of it from his brother's window should, no doubt, have prepared Frederick for the hideous loathsomeness of Bingley-on-Sea: but, as he walked along, he found it coming on him as a complete surprise. Until now he had never imagined that a small town could possess so many soulsearing features. He passed little boys, and thought how repulsive little boys were. He met tradesmen's carts, and his gorge rose at the sight of them. He hated the houses. And, most of all, he objected to the sun. It shone down with a cheeriness which was not only offensive but, it seemed to Frederick Mulliner, deliberately offensive. What he wanted was wailing winds and driving rain: not a beastly expanse of vivid blue. It was not that the perfidy of Jane Oliphant had affected him in any way: it was simply that he disliked blue skies and sunshine. He had a temperamental antipathy for them, just as he had a temperamental fondness for tombs and sleet and hurricanes and earthquakes and famines and pestilences and . . .

He found that he had arrived in Marazion Road.

Marazion Road was made up of two spotless pavements stretching into the middle distance and flanked by two rows of neat little red-brick villas. It smote Frederick like a blow. He felt as he looked at those houses, with their little brass knockers and little white curtains, that they were occupied by people who knew nothing of Frederick Mulliner and were content to know nothing; people who were simply not caring a whoop that only a few short months before the girl to whom he had been engaged had sent back his letters and gone and madly got herself betrothed to a man named Dillingwater.

He found Wee Holme, and hit it a nasty slap with its knocker. Footsteps sounded in the passage, and the door opened.

"Why, Master Frederick!" said Nurse Wilks. "I should hardly have known you."

Frederick, in spite of the natural gloom caused by the blue sky and the warm sunshine, found his mood lightening somewhat. Something that might almost have been a spasm of tenderness passed through him. He was not a bad-hearted young man—he ranked in that respect, he supposed, somewhere mid-way between his brother George, who had a heart of gold, and people like the future Mrs. Dillingwater, who had no heart at all—and there was a fragility about Nurse Wilks that first astonished and then touched him.

The images which we form in childhood are slow to fade: and Frederick had been under the impression that Nurse Wilks was fully six feet tall, with the shoulders of a weight-lifter and eyes that glittered cruelly beneath beetling brows. What he saw now was a little old woman with a wrinkled face, who looked as it a puff of wind would blow her away.

He was oddly stirred. He felt large and protective. He saw his brother's point now. Most certainly this frail old thing must be humoured. Only a brute would refuse to humour her—yes, felt Frederick Mulliner, even if it meant boiled eggs at five o'clock in the afternoon.

"Well, you are getting a big boy!" said Nurse Wilks, beaming.

"Do you think so?" said Frederick, with equal amiability.

"Quite the little man! And all dressed up. Go into the parlour, dear, and sit down. I'm getting the tea."

"Thanks."

"WIPE YOUR BOOTS!"

The voice, thundering from a quarter whence hitherto only soft cooings had proceeded, affected Frederick Mulliner a little like the touching off of a mine beneath his feet. Spinning round he perceived a different person altogether from the mild and kindly hostess of a moment back. It was plain that there yet lingered in Nurse Wilks not a little of the ancient fire. Her mouth was tightly compressed and her eyes gleamed dangerously.

"Theideaofyourbringingyournastydirtybootsintomynicecleanhousewithoutwiping them!" said Nurse Wilks.

"Sorry!" said Frederick humbly.

He burnished the criticised shoes on the mat, and tottered to the parlour. He felt much smaller, much younger and much feebler than he had felt a minute ago. His morale had been shattered into fragments.

And it was not pieced together by the sight, as he entered the parlour, of Miss Jane Oliphant sitting in an arm-chair by the window.

It is hardly to be supposed that the reader will be interested in the appearance of a girl of the stamp of Jane Oliphant—a girl capable of wantonly returning a good man's letters and going off and getting engaged to a Dillingwater: but one may as well describe her and get it over. She had golden-brown hair; golden-brown eyes; golden-brown eyebrows; a nice nose with one freckle on the tip; a mouth which, when it parted in a smile, disclosed pretty teeth; and a resolute little chin.

At the present moment, the mouth was not parted in a smile. It was closed up tight, and the chin was more than resolute. It looked like the ram of a very small battleship. She gazed at Frederick as if he were the smell of onions, and she did not say a word.

Nor did Frederick say very much. Nothing is more difficult for a young man than to find exactly the right remark with which to open conversation with a girl who has recently returned his letters. (Darned good letters, too. Reading them over after opening the package, he had been amazed at their charm and eloquence.)

Frederick, then, confined his observations to the single word "Guk!" Having uttered this, he sank into a chair and stared at the carpet. The girl stared out of the window: and complete silence reigned in the room till from the interior of a clock which was ticking on the mantlepiece a small wooden bird suddenly emerged, said "Cuckoo", and withdrew.

The abruptness of this bird's appearance and the oddly staccato nature of its diction could not but have their effect on a man whose nerves were not what they had been. Frederick Mulliner, rising some eighteen inches from his chair, uttered a hasty exclamation.

"I beg your pardon?" said Jane Oliphant, raising her eyebrows.

"Well, how was I to know it was going to do that?" said Frederick defensively.

Jane Oliphant shrugged her shoulders. The gesture seemed to imply supreme indifference to what the sweepings of the Underworld knew or did not know.

But Frederick, the ice being now in a manner broken, refused to return to the silence.

"What are you doing here?" he said.

"I have come to have tea with Nanna."

"I didn't know you were going to be here."

"Oh?"

"If I'd known that you were going to be here . . ."

"You've got a large smut on your nose."

Frederick gritted his teeth and reached for his handkerchief.

"Perhaps I'd better go," he said.

"You will do nothing of the kind," said Miss Oliphant sharply. "She is looking forward to seeing you. Though why . . ."

"Why?" prompted Frederick coldly.

"Oh, nothing."

In the unpleasant silence which followed, broken only by the deep breathing of a man who was trying to choose the rudest out of the three retorts which had presented themselves to him, Nurse Wilks entered.

"It's just a suggestion," said Miss Oliphant aloofly, "but don't you think you might help Nanna with that heavy tray?"

Frederick, roused from his preoccupation, sprang to his feet, blushing the blush of shame.

"You might have strained yourself, Nanna," the girl went on, in a voice dripping with indignant sympathy.

"I was going to help her," mumbled Frederick.

"Yes, after she had put the tray down on the table. Poor Nanna! How very heavy it must have been."

Not for the first time since their acquaintance had begun, Frederick felt a sort of wistful wonder at his erstwhile fiancée's uncanny ability to put him in the wrong. His emotions now were rather what they would have been if he had been detected striking his hostess with some blunt instrument.

"He always was a thoughtless boy," said Nurse Wilks tolerantly. "Do sit down, Master Frederick, and have your tea. I've boiled some eggs for you. I know what a boy you always are for eggs."

Frederick, starting, directed a swift glance at the tray. Yes, his worst fears had been realised. Eggs—and large ones. A stomach which he had fallen rather into the habit of pampering of late years gave a little whimper of apprehension.

"Yes," proceeded Nurse Wilks, pursuing the subject, "you never could have enough eggs. Nor cake. Dear me, how sick you made yourself with cake that day at Miss Jane's birthday party."

"Please!" said Miss Oliphant, with a slight shiver.

She looked coldly at her fermenting fellow-guest, as he sat plumbing the deepest abysses of self-loathing.

"No eggs for me, thank you," he said.

"Master Frederick, you will eat your nice boiled eggs," said Nurse Wilks. Her voice was still amiable, but there was a hint of dynamite behind it.

"I don't want any eggs."

"Master Frederick!" The dynamite exploded. Once again that amazing transformation had taken place, and a frail little old woman had become an intimidating force with which only a Napoleon could have reckoned. "I will not have this sulking."

Frederick gulped.

"I'm sorry," he said, meekly. "I should enjoy an egg."

"Two eggs," corrected Nurse Wilks.

"Two eggs," said Frederick.

Miss Oliphant twisted the knife in the wound.

"There seems to be plenty of cake, too. How nice for you! Still, I should be careful, if I were you. It looks rather rich. I never could understand," she went on, addressing Nurse Wilks in a voice which Frederick, who was now about seven years old, considered insufferably grown-up and affected, "why people should find any enjoyment in stuffing and gorging and making pigs of themselves."

"Boys will be boys," argued Nurse Wilks.

"I suppose so," sighed Miss Oliphant. "Still, it's all rather unpleasant."

A slight but well-defined glitter appeared in Nurse Wilks's eyes. She detected a tendency to hoighy-toightiness in her young guests' manner, and hoighty-toightiness was a thing to be checked.

"Girls," she said, "are by no means perfect."

"Ah!" breathed Frederick, in rapturous adhesion to the sentiment.

"Girls have their little faults. Girls are sometimes inclined to be vain. I know a little girl not a hundred miles from this room who was so proud of her new panties that she ran out in the street in them."

"Nanna!" cried Miss Oliphant pinkly.

"Disgusting!" said Frederick.

He uttered a short laugh: and so full was this laugh, though short, of scorn, disdain, and a certain hideous masculine superiority, that Jane Oliphant's proud spirit writhed beneath the infliction. She turned on him with blazing eyes.

"What did you say?"

"I said 'Disgusting!' "

"Indeed?"

"I cannot," said Frederick judicially, "imagine a more deplorable exhibition, and I hope you were sent to bed without any supper."

"If you ever had to go without your supper," said Miss Oliphant, who believed in attack as the best form of defence, "it would kill you."

"Is that so?" said Frederick.

"You're a beast, and I hate you," said Miss Oliphant.

"Is that so?"

"Yes, that is so."

"Now, now, now," said Nurse Wilks. "Come, come, come!"

She eyed the two with that comfortable look of power and capability which comes naturally to women who have spent half a century in dealing with the young and fractious.

"We will have no quarrelling," she said. "Make it up at once. Master Frederick, give Miss Jane a nice kiss."

The room rocked before Frederick's bulging eyes.

"A what?" he gasped.

"Give her a nice big kiss and tell her you're sorry you quarrelled with her."

"She quarrelled with me."

"Never mind. A little gentleman must always take the blame."

Frederick, working desperately, dragged to the surface a sketchy smile.

"I apologise," he said.

"Don't mention it," said Miss Oliphant.

"Kiss her," said Nurse Wilks.

"I won't!" said Frederick.

"What!"

"I won't."

"Master Frederick," said Nurse Wilks, rising and pointing a menacing finger, "you march straight into that cupboard in the passage and stay there till you are good."

Frederick hestitated. He came of a proud family. A Mulliner had once received the thanks of his Sovereign for services rendered on the field of Crecy. But the recollection of what his brother George had said decided him. Infra dig as it might be to allow himself to be shoved away in cupboards, it was better than being responsible for a woman's heart-failure. With bowed head he passed through the door, and a key clicked behind him.

All alone in a dark world that smelt of mice, Frederick Mulliner gave himself up to gloomy reflection. He had just put in about two minutes' intense thought of a kind which would have made the meditations of Schopenhauer on one of his bad mornings seem like the day-dreams of Polyanna, when a voice spoke through the crack in the door.

"Freddie. I mean Mr. Mulliner."

"Well?"

"She's gone into the kitchen to get the jam," proceeded the voice rapidly. "Shall I let you out?"

"Pray do not trouble," said Frederick coldly. "I am perfectly comfortable."

Silence followed. Frederick returned to his reverie. About now, he thought, but for his brother George's treachery in luring him down to this plague-spot by a misleading telegram, he would have been on the twelfth green at Squashy Hollow, trying out that new putter. Instead of which . . .

The door opened abruptly, and as abruptly closed again. And Frederick Mulliner, who had been looking forward to an unbroken solitude, discovered with a good deal of astonishment that he had started taking in lodgers.

"What are you doing here?" he demanded, with a touch of proprietorial disapproval.

The girl did not answer. But presently muffled sounds came to him through the darkness. In spite of himself, a certain tenderness crept upon Frederick.

"I say," he said awkwardly. "There's nothing to cry about."

"I'm not crying. I'm laughing."

"Oh?" The tenderness waned. "You think it's amusing, do you, being shut up in this damned cupboard . . ."

"There is no need to use bad language."

"I entirely disagree with you. There is every need to use bad language. It's ghastly enough being at Bingley-on-Sea at all, but when it comes to being shut up in Bingley cupboards . . ."

". . . with a girl you hate?"

"We will not go into that aspect of the matter," said Frederick with dignity. "The important point is that here I am in a cupboard at Bingley-on-Sea when, if there were any justice or right-thinking in the world, I should be out at Squashy Hollow . . ."

"Oh? Do you still play golf?"

"Certainly I still play golf. Why not?"

"I don't know why not. I'm glad you are still able to amuse yourself."

"How do you mean, still? Do you think that just because . . .?"

"I don't think anything."

"I suppose you imagined I would be creeping about the place a broken-hearted wreck?"

"Oh no. I knew you would find it very easy to console yourself."

"What do you mean by that?"

"Never mind."

"Are you insinuating that I am the sort of man who turns lightly from one woman to another—a mere butterfly who flits from flower to flower, sipping . . .?"

"Yes, if you want to know, I think you are a born sipper."

Frederick started. The charge was monstrous.

"I have never sipped. And, what's more, I have never flitted."

"That's funny."

"What's funny?"

"What you said."

"You appear to have a very keen sense of humour," said Frederick weightily. "It amuses you to be shut up in cupboards. It amuses you to hear me say . . ."

"Well, it's nice to be able to get some amusement out of life, isn't it? Do you want to know why she shut me up in here?"

"I haven't the slightest curiosity. Why?"

"I forgot where I was and lighted a cigarette. Oh, my goodness!"

"Now what?"

"I thought I heard a mouse. Do you think there are mice in this cupboard?"

"Certainly," said Frederick. "Dozens of them."

He would have gone on to specify the kind of mice—large, fat, slithery, active mice: but at this juncture something hard and sharp took him agonizingly on the ankle.

"Ouch!" cried Frederick.

"Oh, I'm sorry. Was that you?"

"It was."

"I was kicking about to discourage the mice."

"I see."

"Did it hurt much?"

"Only a trifle more than blazes, thank you for inquiring."

"I'm sorry."

"So am I."

"Anyway, it would have given a mouse a nasty jar, if it had been one, wouldn't it?"

"The shock, I should imagine, of a lifetime."

"Well, I'm sorry."

"Don't mention it. Why should I worry about a broken ankle, when . . ."

"When what?"

"I forgot what I was going to say."

"When your heart is broken?"

"My heart is not broken." It was a point which Frederick wished to make luminously clear. "I am gay . . . happy . . . Who the devil is this man Dillingwater?" he concluded abruptly.

There was a momentary pause.

"Oh, just a man."

"Where did you meet him?"

"At the Ponderbys'."

"Where did you get engaged to him?"

"At the Ponderbys'."

"Did you pay another visit to the Ponderbys', then?"

"No."

Frederick choked.

"When you went to stay with the Ponderbys, you were engaged to me. Do you mean to say you broke off your engagement to me, met this Dillingwater, and got engaged to him all in the course of a single visit lasting barely two weeks?"

"Yes."

Frederick said nothing. It struck him later that he should have said "Oh,

Woman, Woman!" but at the moment it did not occur to him.

"I don't see what right you have to criticize me," said Jane.

"Who criticized you?"

"You did."

"When?"

"Just then."

"I call Heaven to witness," cried Frederick Mulliner, "that not by so much as a single word have I hinted at my opinion that your conduct is the vilest and most revolting that has ever been drawn to my attention. I never so much as suggested that your revelation had shocked me to the depths of my soul."

"Yes, you did. You sniffed."

"If Bingley-on-Sea is not open for being sniffed in at this season," said Frederick coldly, "I should have been informed earlier."

"I had a perfect right to get engaged to anyone I liked and as quick as I liked, after the abominable way you behaved."

"Abominable way I behaved? What do you mean?"

"You know."

"Pardon me, I do not know. If you are alluding to my refusal to wear the tie you bought for me on my last birthday, I can but repeat my statement, made to you at the time, that, apart from being the sort of tie no upright man would be seen dead in a ditch with, its colours were those of a Cycling, Angling, and Dart-Throwing club of which I am not a member."

"I am not alluding to that. I mean the day I was going to the Ponderbys' and you promised to see me off at Paddington, and then you phoned and said you couldn't as you were detained by important business, and I thought, well, I think I'll go by the later train after all because that will give me time to lunch quietly at the Berkeley, and I went and lunched quietly at the Berkeley, and when I was there who should I see but you at a table at the other end of the room gorging yourself in the company of a beastly creature in a pink frock and henna'd hair. That's what I mean."

Frederick clutched at his forehead.

"Repeat that," he exclaimed.

Jane did so.

"Ye gods!" said Frederick.

"It was like a blow over the head. Something seemed to snap inside me, and . . ."

"I can explain all," said Frederick.

Jane's voice in the darkness was cold.

"Explain?" she said.

"Explain," said Frederick.

"All?"

"All."

Jane coughed.

"Before beginning," she said, "do not forget that I know every one of your female relatives by sight."

"I don't want to talk about my female relatives."

"I thought you were going to say that she was one of them—an aunt or something."

"Nothing of the kind. She was a revue star. You probably saw her in a piece called 'Toot-Toot'."

"And that is your idea of an explanation!"

Frederick raised his hand for silence. Realising that she could not see it, he lowered it again.

"Jane," he said in a low, throbbing voice, "can you cast your mind back to a morning in the spring when we walked, you and I, in Kensington Gardens? The sun shone brightly, the sky was a limpid blue flecked with fleecy clouds, and from the west there blew a gentle breeze . . ."

"If you think you can melt me with that sort of . . ."

"Nothing of the kind. What I was leading up to was this. As we walked, you and I, there came snuffling up to us a small Pekingese dog. It left me, I admit, quite cold, but you went into ecstasies: and from that moment I had but one mission in life to discover who that Peke belonged to and buy it for you. And after the most exhaustive inquiries, I tracked the animal down. It was the property of the lady in whose company you saw me lunching—lightly, not gorging—at the Berkeley that day. I managed to get an introduction to her, and immediately began to make offers to her for the dog. Money was no object to me. All I wished was to put the little beast in your arms and see your face light up. It was to be a surprise. That morning the woman phoned, and said that she had practically decided to close with my latest bid, and would I take her to lunch and discuss the matter? It was agony to have to ring you up and tell you that I could not see you off at Paddington, but it had to be done. It was anguish having to sit for two hours listening to that highly-coloured female telling me how the comedian had ruined her big number in her last show by standing up-stage and pretending to drink ink, but that had to be done too. I bit the bullet and saw it through and I got the dog that afternoon. And next morning I received your letter breaking off the engagement."

There was a long silence.

"Is this true?" said Jane.

"Quite true."

"It sounds too—how shall I put it?—too frightfully probable. Look me in the face!"

"What's the good of looking you in the face when I can't see an inch in front of me?"

"Well, is it true?"

"Certainly it is true."

"Can you produce the Peke?"

"I have not got it on my person," said Frederick stiffly. "But it is at my flat, probably chewing up a valuable rug. I will give it you for a wedding present."

"Oh, Freddie!"

"A wedding present," repeated Frederick, though the words stuck in his throat like patent American health-cereal.

"But I'm not going to be married."

"You're—what did you say?"

"I'm not going to be married."

"But what of Dillingwater?"

"That's off."

"Off?"

"Off," said Jane firmly. "I only got engaged to him out of pique. I thought I could go through with it, buoying myself up by thinking what a score it would be off you, but one morning I saw him eating a peach and I began to waver. He splashed himself to the eyebrows. And just after that I found that he had a trick of making a sort of funny noise when he drank coffee. I would sit on the other side of the breakfast table, looking at him and saying to myself 'Now comes the funny noise!' and when I thought of doing that all the rest of my life I saw that the scheme was impossible. So I broke off the engagement.

Frederick gasped.

"Jane!"

He groped out, found her, and drew her into his arms.

"Freddie!"

"Jane!"

"Freddie!"

"Jane!"

"Freddie!"

"Jane!"

On the panel of the door there sounded an authoritative rap. Through it there spoke an authoritative voice, slightly cracked by age but full, nevertheless, of the spirit that will stand no nonsense.

"Master Frederick."

"Hullo?"

"Are you good now?"

"You bet I'm good."

"Will you give Miss Jane a nice kiss?"

"I will do," said Frederick Mulliner, enthusiasm ringing in every syllable, "just that little thing!"

"Then you may come out," said Nurse Wilks. "I have boiled you two more eggs."

Frederick paled, but only for an instant. What did anything matter now? His lips were set in a firm line, and his voice, when he spoke, was calm and steady.

"Lead me to them," he said.

8
THE ROMANCE OF A BULB-SQUEEZER

SOMEBODY had left a copy of an illustrated weekly paper in the bar-parlour of the Anglers' Rest; and, glancing through it, I came upon the ninth full-page photograph of a celebrated musical comedy actress that I had seen since the preceding Wednesday. This one showed her looking archly over her shoulder with a rose between her teeth, and I flung the periodical from me with a stifled cry.

"Tut, tut!" said Mr. Mulliner, reprovingly. "You must not allow these things to affect you so deeply. Remember, it is not actresses' photographs that matter, but the courage which we bring to them."

He sipped his hot Scotch.

I wonder if you have ever reflected (he said gravely) what life must be like for the men whose trade it is to make these pictures? Statistics show that the two classes of the community which least often marry are milkmen and fashionable photographers—milkmen because they see women too early in the morning, and fashionable photographers because their days are spent in an atmosphere of feminine loveliness so monotonous that they become surfeited and morose. I know of none of the world's workers whom I pity more sincerely than the fashionable photographer; and yet—by one of those strokes of irony which make the thoughtful man waver between sardonic laughter and sympathetic tears—it is the ambition of every youngster who enters the profession some day to become one.

At the outset of his career, you see, a young photographer is sorely oppressed by human gargoyles: and gradually this begins to prey upon his nerves.

"Why is it," I remember my cousin Clarence saying, after he had been about a year in the business, "that all these misfits want to be photographed? Why do men with faces which you would have thought they would be anxious to hush up wish to be strewn about the country on whatnots and in albums? I started out full of ardour and enthusiasm, and my eager soul is being crushed. This morning the Mayor of Tooting East came to make an appointment. He is coming tomorrow afternoon to be taken in his cocked hat and robes of office; and there is absolutely no excuse for a man with a face like that perpetuating his features. I wish to goodness I was one of those fellows who only take camera-portraits of beautiful women."

His dream was to come true sooner than he had imagined. Within a week the great test-case of Biggs *v.* Mulliner had raised my cousin Clarence from an obscure studio in West Kensington to the position of London's most famous photographer.

You possibly remember the case? The events that led up to it were, briefly, as follows:

Jno. Horatio Biggs, O.B.E., the newly-elected Mayor of Tooting East, alighted from a cab at the door of Clarence Mulliner's studio at four-ten on the afternoon of June the seventeenth. At four-eleven he went in. And at four-sixteen and a half he was observed shooting out of a first-floor, window, vigorously assisted by my cousin, who was prodding him in the seat of the trousers with the sharp end of a photographic tripod. Those who were in a position to see stated that Clarence's face was distorted by a fury scarcely human.

Naturally the matter could not be expected to rest there. A week later the case of Biggs *v.* Mulliner had begun, the plaintiff claiming damages to the extent of ten thousand pounds and a new pair of trousers. And at first things looked very black for Clarence.

It was the speech of Sir Joseph Bodger, K.C., briefed for the defence, that turned the scale.

"I do not," said Sir Joseph, addressing the jury on the second day, "propose to deny the charges which have been brought against my client. We freely admit that on the seventeenth inst. we did jab the defendant with our tripod in a manner calculated to cause alarm and dependency. But, gentlemen, we plead justification. The whole case turns upon one question. Is a photographer entitled to assault— either with or, as the case may be, without a tripod—a sitter who, after being warned that his face is not up to the minimum standard requirements, insists upon remaining in the chair and moistening the lips with the tip of the tongue? Gentlemen, I say Yes!

"Unless you decide in favour of my client, gentlemen of the jury, photographers —debarred by law from the privilege of rejecting sitters—will be at the mercy of anyone who comes along with the price of a dozen photographs in his pocket. You have seen the plaintiff, Biggs. You have noted his broad, slab-like face, intolerable to any man of refinement and sensibility. You have observed his walrus moustache, his double chin, his protruding eyes. Take another look at him, and then tell me if my client was not justified in chasing him with a tripod out of that sacred temple of Art and Beauty, his studio.

"Gentlemen, I have finished. I leave my client's fate in your hands with every confidence that you will return the only verdict that can conceivably issue from twelve men of your obvious intelligence, your manifest sympathy, and your superb breadth of vision."

Of course, after that there was nothing to it. The jury decided in Clarence's favour without leaving the box; and the crowd waiting outside to hear the verdict carried him shoulder-high to his house, refusing to disperse until he had made a speech and sung Photographers never, never, never shall be slaves. And next morning every paper in England came out with a leading article commending him for having so courageously established, as it had not been established since the days of Magna Charta, the fundamental principle of the Liberty of the Subject.

The effect of this publicity on Clarence's fortunes was naturally stupendous. He had become in a flash the best-known photographer in the United Kingdom, and was now in a position to realise that vision which he had of taking the pictures of none but the beaming and the beautiful. Every day the loveliest ornaments of Society and the Stage flocked to his studio; and it was with the utmost astonishment, therefore, that, calling upon him one morning on my return to England after an absence of two years in the East, I learned that Fame and Wealth had not brought him happiness.

I found him sitting moodily in his studio, staring with dull eyes at a camera-portrait of a well-known actress in a bathing-suit. He looked up listlessly as I entered.

"Clarence!" I cried, shocked at his appearance, for there were hard lines about his mouth and wrinkles on a forehead that once had been smooth as alabaster. "What is wrong?"

"Everything," he replied, "I'm fed up."

"What with?"

"Life. Beautiful women. This beastly photography business."

I was amazed. Even in the East rumours of his success had reached me, and on my return to London I found that they had not been exaggerated. In every photographers' club in the Metropolis, from the Negative and Solution in Pall Mall to the humble public-houses frequented by the men who do your pictures while you wait on the sands at seaside resorts, he was being freely spoken of as the logical successor to the Presidency of the Amalgamated Guild of Bulb-Squeezers.

"I can't stick it much longer," said Clarence, tearing the camera-portrait into a dozen pieces with a dry sob and burying his face in his hands. "Actresses nursing their dolls! Countesses simpering over kittens! Film stars among their books! In ten minutes I go to catch a train at Waterloo. I have been sent for by the Duchess of Hampshire to take some studies of Lady Monica Southbourne in the castle grounds."

A shudder ran through him. I patted him on the shoulder. I understood now.

"She has the most brilliant smile in England," he whispered.

"Come, come!"

"Coy yet roguish, they tell me."

"It may not be true."

"And I bet she will want to be taken offering a lump of sugar to her dog, and the picture will appear in *The Sketch* and *Tatler* as 'Lady Monica Southbourne and Friend'."

"Clarence, this is morbid."

He was silent for a moment.

"Ah, well," he said, pulling himself together with a visible effort, "I have made my sodium sulphite, and I must lie in it."

I saw him off in a cab. The last view I had of him was of his pale, drawn profile. He looked, I thought, like an aristocrat of the French Revolution being borne off to his doom on a tumbril. How little he guessed that the only girl in the world lay waiting for him round the corner.

No, you are wrong. Lady Monica did not turn out to be the only girl in the world. If what I said caused you to expect that, I misled you. Lady Monica proved to be all his fancy had pictured her. In fact, even more. Not only was her smile coy yet roguish, but she had a sort of coquettish droop of the left eyelid of which no one had warned him. And, in addition to her two dogs, which she was portrayed in the act of feeding with two lumps of sugar, she possessed a totally unforeseen pet monkey, of which he was compelled to take no fewer than eleven studies.

No, it was not Lady Monica who captured Clarence's heart, but a girl in a taxi whom he met on his way to the station.

It was in a traffic jam at the top of Whitehall that he first observed this girl. His cab had become becalmed in a sea of omnibuses, and, chancing to look to the right, he perceived within a few feet of him another taxi, which had been heading for Trafalgar Square. There was a face at its window. It turned towards him, and their eyes met.

To most men it would have seemed an unattractive face. To Clarence, surfeited with the coy, the beaming, and the delicately-chiselled, it was the most wonderful thing he had ever looked at. All his life, he felt, he had been searching for something on these lines. That snub-nose—those freckles—that breadth of cheek-bone —the squareness of that chin. And not a dimple in sight. He told me afterwards that his only feeling at first was one of incredulity. He had not believed that the world contained women like this. And then the traffic jam loosened up and he was carried away.

It was as he was passing the Houses of Parliament that the realisation came to him that the strange bubbly sensation that seemed to start from just above the lower left side-pocket of his waistcoat was not, as he had at first supposed, dyspepsia, but love. Yes, love had come at long last to Clarence Mulliner; and for all the good it was likely to do him, he reflected bitterly, it might just as well have been the dyspepsia for which he had mistaken it. He loved a girl whom he would probably never see again. He did not know her name or where she lived or anything about her. All he knew was that he would cherish her image in his heart for ever, and that the thought of going on with the old dreary round of photographing lovely women with coy yet roguish smiles was almost more than he could bear.

However, custom is strong; and a man who has once allowed the bulb-squeezing habit to get a grip on him cannot cast it off in a moment. Next day Clarence was back in his studio, diving into the velvet nose-bag as of yore and telling peeresses to watch the little birdie just as if nothing had happened. And if there was now a strange, haunting look of pain in his eyes, nobody objected to that. Indeed, inasmuch as the grief which gnawed at his heart had the effect of deepening and mellowing his camera-side manner to an almost sacerdotal unctuousness, his private sorrows actually helped his professional prestige. Women told one another that being photographed by Clarence Mulliner was like undergoing some wonderful spiritual experience in a noble cathedral; and his appointment-book became fuller than ever.

So great now was his reputation that to anyone who had had the privilege of being taken by him, either full face or in profile, the doors of Society opened automatically. It was whispered that his name was to appear in the next Birthday Honours List; and at the annual banquet of the Amalgamated Bulb-Squeezers, when Sir Godfrey Stooge, the retiring President, in proposing his health, concluded a glowingly eulogistic speech with the words, "Gentlemen, I give you my destined successor, Mulliner the Liberator!" five hundred frantic photographers almost shivered the glasses on the table with their applause.

And yet he was not happy. He had lost the only girl he had ever loved, and without her what was Fame? What was Affluence? What were the Highest Honours in the Land?

These were the questions he was asking himself one night as he sat in his library, sombrely sipping a final whisky-and-soda before retiring. He had asked them once and was going to ask them again, when he was interrupted by the sound of someone ringing at the front-door bell.

He rose, surprised. It was late for callers. The domestic staff had gone to bed, so he went to the door and opened it. A shadowy figure was standing on the steps.

"Mr. Mulliner?"

"I am Mr. Mulliner."

The man stepped past him into the hall. And, as he did so, Clarence saw that he was wearing over the upper half of his face a black velvet mask.

"I must apologise for hiding my face, Mr. Mulliner," the visitor said, as Clarence led him to the library.

"Not at all," replied Clarence, courteously. "No doubt it is all for the best."

"Indeed?" said the other, with a touch of asperity. "If you really want to know, I am probably as handsome a man as there is in London. But my mission is one of such extraordinary secrecy that I dare not run the risk of being recognised." He paused, and Clarence saw his eyes glint through the holes in the mask as he directed a rapid gaze into each corner of the library. "Mr. Mulliner, have you any acquaintance with the ramifications of international secret politics?"

"I have."

"And you are a patriot?"

"I am."

"Then I can speak freely. No doubt you are aware, Mr. Mulliner, that for some time past this country and a certain rival Power have been competing for the friendship and alliance of a certain other Power?"

"No," said Clarence, "they didn't tell me that."

"Such is the case. And the President of this Power——"

"Which one?"

"The second one."

"Call it B."

"The President of Power B. is now in London. He arrived incognito, travelling under the assumed name of J. J. Shubert: and the representatives of Power A., to the best of our knowledge, are not yet aware of his presence. This gives us just the few hours necessary to clinch this treaty with Power B. before Power A. can interfere. I ought to tell you, Mr. Mulliner, that if Power B. forms an alliance with this country, the supremacy of the Anglo-Saxon race will be secured for hundreds of years. Whereas if Power A. gets hold of Power B., civilisation will be thrown into the melting-pot. In the eyes of all Europe—and when I say all Europe I refer particularly to Powers C., D., and E.—this nation would sink to the rank of a fourth-class Power."

"Call it Power F.," said Clarence.

"It rests with you, Mr. Mulliner, to save England."

"Great Britain," corrected Clarence. He was half Scotch on his mother's side. "But how? What can I do about it?"

"The position is this. The President of Power B. has an overwhelming desire to have his photograph taken by Clarence Mulliner. Consent to take it, and our difficulties will be at an end. Overcome with gratitude, he will sign the treaty, and the Anglo-Saxon race will be safe."

Clarence did not hesitate. Apart from the natural gratification of feeling that he was doing the Anglo-Saxon race a bit of good, business was business; and if the President took a dozen of the large size finished in silver wash it would mean a nice profit.

"I shall be delighted," he said.

"Your patriotism," said the visitor, "will not go unrewarded. It will be gratefully noted in the Very Highest Circles."

Clarence reached for his appointment-book.

"Now, let me see. Wednesday?—No, I'm full up Wednesday. Thursday?—No. Suppose the President looks in at my studio between four and five on Friday?"

The visitor uttered a gasp.

"Good heavens, Mr. Mulliner," he exclaimed, "surely you do not imagine that, with the vast issues at stake, these things can be done openly and in daylight? If the devils in the pay of Power A. were to learn that President intended to have his photograph taken by you, I would not give a straw for your chances of living an hour."

"Then what do you suggest?"

"You must accompany me now to the President's suite at the Milan Hotel. We shall travel in a closed car, and God send that these fiends did not recognise me as I came here. If they did, we shall never reach that car alive. Have you, by any chance, while we have been talking, heard the hoot of an owl?"

"No," said Clarence. "No owls."

"Then perhaps they are nowhere near. The fiends always imitate the hoot of an owl."

"A thing," said Clarence, "which I tried to do when I was a small boy and never seemed able to manage. The popular idea that owls say 'Tu-whit, tu-whoo' is all wrong. The actual noise they make is something far more difficult and complex, and it was beyond me."

"Quite so." The visitor looked at his watch. "However, absorbing as these reminiscences of your boyhood days are, time is flying. Shall we be making a start?"

"Certainly."

"Then follow me."

It appeared to be holiday-time for fiends, or else the nightshift had not yet come on, for they reached the car without being molested. Clarence stepped in, and his masked visitor, after a keen look up and down the street, followed him.

"Talking of my boyhood——" began Clarence.

The sentence was never completed. A soft wet pad was pressed over his nostrils: the air became a-reek with the sickly fumes of chloroform: and Clarence knew no more.

When he came to, he was no longer in the car. He found himself lying on a bed in a room in a strange house. It was a medium-sized room with scarlet wallpaper, simply furnished with a wash-hand stand, a chest of drawers, two cane-bottomed chairs, and a "God Bless Our Home" motto framed in oak. He was conscious of a severe headache, and was about to rise and make for the water-bottle on the wash-stand when, to his consternation, he discovered that his arms and legs were shackled with stout cord.

As a family, the Mulliners have always been noted for their reckless courage; and Clarence was no exception to the rule. But for an instant his heart undeniably beat a little faster. He saw now that his masked visitor had tricked him. Instead of being a representative of His Majesty's Diplomatic Service (a most respectable class of men), he had really been all along a fiend in the pay of Power A.

No doubt he and his vile associates were even now chuckling at the ease with which their victim had been duped. Clarence gritted his teeth and struggled vainly to loose the knots which secured his wrists. He had fallen back exhausted when he heard the sound of a key turning and the door opened. Somebody crossed the room and stood by the bed, looking down on him.

The newcomer was a stout man with a complexion that matched the wall-paper. He was puffing slightly, as if he had found the stairs trying. He had broad, slab-like features; and his face was split in the middle by a walrus moustache. Somewhere and in some place, Clarence was convinced, he had seen this man before.

And then it all came back to him. An open window with a pleasant summer breeze blowing in; a stout man in a cocked hat trying to climb through this window; and he, Clarence, doing his best to help him with the sharp end of a tripod. It was Jno. Horatio Biggs, the Mayor of Tooting East.

A shudder of loathing ran through Clarence.

"Traitor!" he cried.

"Eh?" said the Mayor.

"If anybody had told me that a son of Tooting, nursed in the keen air of freedom which blows across the Common, would sell himself for gold to the enemies of his country, I would never have believed it. Well, you may tell your employers——"

"What employers?"

"Power A."

"Oh, that?" said the Mayor. "I am afraid my secretary, whom I instructed to bring you to this house, was obliged to romance a little in order to ensure your accompanying him, Mr. Mulliner. All that about Power A. and Power B. was just his little joke. If you want to know why you were brought here——"

Clarence uttered a low groan.

"I have guessed your ghastly object, you ghastly object," he said quietly. "You want me to photograph you."

The Mayor shook his head.

"Not myself. I realize that that can never be. My daughter."

"Your daughter?"

"My daughter."

"Does she take after you?"

"People tell me there is a resemblance."

"I refuse," said Clarence.

"Think well, Mr. Mulliner."

"I have done all the thinking that is necessary. England—or, rather, Great Britain—looks to me to photograph only her fairest and loveliest; and though, as a man, I admit that I loathe beautiful women, as a photographer I have a duty to consider that is higher than any personal feelings. History has yet to record an instance of a photographer playing his country false, and Clarence Mulliner is not the man to supply the first one. I decline your offer."

"I wasn't looking on it exactly as an offer," said the Mayor, thoughtfully. "More as a command, if you get my meaning."

"You imagine that you can bend a lens-artist to your will and make him false to his professional reputation?"

"I was thinking of having a try."

"Do you realise that, if my incarceration here were known, ten thousand photographers would tear this house brick from brick and you limb from limb?"

"But it isn't," the Mayor pointed out. "And that, if you follow me, is the whole point. You came here by night in a closed car. You could stay here for the rest of your life, and no one would be any the wiser. I really think you had better reconsider, Mr. Mulliner."

"You have had my answer."

"Well, I'll leave you to think it over. Dinner will be served at seven-thirty. Don't bother to dress."

At half-past seven precisely the door opened again and the Mayor reappeared, followed by a butler bearing on a silver salver a glass of water and a small slice of bread. Pride urged Clarence to reject the refreshment, but hunger overcame pride. He swallowed the bread which the butler offered him in small bits in a spoon, and drank the water.

"At what hour would the gentleman desire breakfast, sir?" asked the butler.

"Now," said Clarence, for his appetite, always healthy, seemed to have been sharpened by the trials which he had undergone.

"Let us say nine o'clock," suggested the Mayor. "Put aside another slice of that bread, Meadows. And no doubt Mr. Mulliner would enjoy a glass of this excellent water."

For perhaps half an hour after his host had left him, Clarence's mind was obsessed to the exclusion of all other thoughts by a vision of the dinner he would have liked to be enjoying. All we Mulliners have been good trenchermen, and to put a bit of bread into it after it had been unoccupied for a whole day was to offer to Clarence's stomach an insult which it resented with an indescribable bitterness. Clarence's only emotion for some considerable time, then, was that of hunger. His thoughts centred themselves on food. And it was to this fact, oddly enough, that he owed his release.

For, as he lay there in a sort of delirium, picturing himself getting outside a medium-cooked steak smothered in onions, with grilled tomatoes and floury potatoes on the side, it was suddenly borne in upon him that this steak did not taste quite so good as other steaks which he had eaten in the past. It was tough and lacked juiciness. It tasted just like rope.

And then, his mind clearing, he saw that it actually was rope. Carried away by the anguish of hunger, he had been chewing the cord which bound his hands; and now discovered that he had bitten into it quite deeply.

A sudden flood of hope poured over Clarence Mulliner. Carrying on at this rate, he perceived, he would be able ere long to free himself. It only needed a little imagination. After a brief interval to rest his aching jaws, he put himself deliberately into that state of relaxation which is recommended by the apostles of Suggestion.

"I am entering the dining-room of my club," murmured Clarence. "I am sitting down. The waiter is handing me the bill of fare. I have selected roast duck with green peas and new potatoes, lamb cutlets with Brussels sprouts, fricassee of chicken, porterhouse steak, boiled beef and carrots, leg of mutton, haunch of mutton, mutton chops, curried mutton, veal, kidneys, sauté, spaghetti Caruso, and eggs and bacon, fried on both sides. The waiter is now bringing my order. I have taken up my knife and fork. I am beginning to eat."

And, murmuring a brief grace, Clarence flung himself on the rope and set to.

Twenty minutes later he was hobbling about the room, restoring the circulation to his cramped limbs.

Just as he had succeeded in getting himself nicely limbered up, he heard the key turning in the door.

Clarence crouched for the spring. The room was quite dark now, and he was glad of it, for darkness well fitted the work which lay before him. His plans, conceived on the spur of the moment, were necessarily sketchy, but they included jumping on the Mayor's shoulders and pulling his head off. After that, no doubt, other modes of self-expression would suggest themselves.

The door opened. Clarence made his leap. And he was just about to start on the programme as arranged, when he discovered with a shock of horror that this was no O.B.E. that he was being rough with, but a woman. And no photographer worthy of the name will ever lay a hand upon a woman, save to raise her chin and tilt it a little more to the left.

"I beg your pardon!" he cried.

"Don't mention it," said his visitor, in a low voice. "I hope I didn't disturb you."

"Not at all," said Clarence.

There was a pause.

"Rotten weather," said Clarence, feeling that it was for him, as the male member of the sketch, to keep the conversation going.

"Yes, isn't it?"

"A lot of rain we've had this summer."

"Yes. It seems to get worse every year."

"Doesn't it?"

"So bad for tennis."

"And cricket."

"And polo."

"And garden parties."

"I hate rain."

"So do I."

"Of course, we may have a fine August."

"Yes, there's always that."

The ice was broken, and the girl seemed to become more at her ease.

"I came to let you out," she said. "I must apologise for my father. He loves me foolishly and has no scruples where my happiness is concerned. He has always yearned to have me photographed by you, but I cannot consent to allow a photographer to be coerced into abandoning his principles. If you will follow me, I will let you out by the front door."

"It's awfully good of you," said Clarence, awkwardly. As any man of nice sentiment would have been, he was embarrassed. He wished that he could have obliged this kind-hearted girl by taking her picture, but a natural delicacy restrained him from touching on this subject. They went down the stairs in silence.

On the first landing a hand was placed on his in the darkness and the girl's voice whispered in his ear.

"We are just outside father's study," he heard her say. "We must be as quiet as mice."

"As what?" said Clarence.

"Mice."

"Oh, rather," said Clarence, and immediately bumped into what appeared to be a pedestal of some sort.

These pedestals usually have vases on top of them, and it was revealed to Clarence a moment later that this one was no exception. There was a noise like ten simultaneous dinner-services coming apart in the hands of ten simultaneous parlour-maids; and then the door was flung open, the landing became flooded with light, and the Mayor of Tooting East stood before them. He was carrying a revolver and his face was dark with menace.

"Ha!" said the Mayor.

But Clarence was paying no attention to him. He was staring open-mouthed at the girl. She had shrunk back against the wall, and the light fell full upon her.

"You!" cried Clarence.

"This——" began the Mayor.

"You! At last!"

"This is a pretty——"

"Am I dreaming?"

"This is a pretty state of af——"

"Ever since that day I saw you in the cab I have been scouring London for you. To think that I have found you at last!"

"This is a pretty state of affairs," said the Mayor, breathing on the barrel of his revolver and polishing it on the sleeve of his coat. "My daughter helping the foe of her family to fly——"

"Flee, father," corrected the girl, faintly

"Flea or fly—this is no time for arguing about insects. Let me tell you——"
Clarence interrupted him indignantly.

"What do you mean," he cried, "by saying that she took after you?"

"She does."

"She does not. She is the loveliest girl in the world, while you look like Lon
Chaney made up for something. See for yourself." Clarence led them to the large
mirror at the head of the stairs. "Your face—if you can call it that—is one of those
beastly blobby squashy sort of faces——"

"Here!" said the Mayor.

"——whereas hers is simply divine. Your eyes are bulbous and goofy——"

"Hey!" said the Mayor.

"——while hers are sweet and soft and intelligent. Your ears——"

"Yes, yes," said the Mayor, petulantly. "Some other time, some other time.
Then am I to take it, Mr. Mulliner——"

"Call me Clarence."

"I refuse to call you Clarence."

"You will have to very shortly, when I am your son-in-law."

The girl uttered a cry. The Mayor uttered a louder cry.

"My son-in-law."

"That," said Clarence, firmly, "is what I intend to be—and speedily." He
turned to the girl. "I am a man of volcanic passions, and now that love has come
to me there is no power in heaven or earth that can keep me from the object of my
love. It will be my never-ceasing task—er——"

"Gladys," prompted the girl.

"Thank you. It will be my never-ceasing task, Gladys, to strive daily to make
you return that love——"

"You need not strive, Clarence," she whispered, softly. "It is already returned."
Clarence reeled.

"Already?" he gasped.

"I have loved you since I saw you in that cab. When we were torn asunder, I
felt quite faint."

"So did I. I was in a daze. I tipped my cabman at Waterloo three half-crowns.
I was aflame with love."

"I can hardly believe it."

"Nor could I, when I found out. I thought it was threepence. And ever since
that day——"

The Mayor coughed.

"Then am I to take it—er—Clarence," he said, "that your objections to photographing my daughter are removed?"

Clarence laughed happily.

"Listen," he said, "and I'll show you the sort of son-in-law I am. Ruin my professional reputation though it may, I will take a photograph of you too!"

"Me!"

"Absolutely. Standing beside her with the tips of your fingers on her shoulder. And what's more, you can wear your cocked hat."

Tears had begun to trickle down the Mayor's cheeks.

"My boy!" he sobbed, brokenly. "My boy!"

And so happiness came to Clarence Mulliner at last. He never became President of the Bulb-Squeezers, for he retired from business the next day, declaring that the hand that had snapped the shutter when taking the photograph of his dear wife should never snap it again for sordid profit. The wedding, which took place some six weeks later, was attended by almost everybody of any note in Society or on the Stage; and was the first occasion on which a bride and bridegroom had ever walked out of church beneath an arch of crossed tripods.

9

HONEYSUCKLE COTTAGE

"Do you believe in ghosts?" asked Mr. Mulliner abruptly. I weighed the question thoughtfully. I was a little surprised, for nothing in our previous conversation had suggested the topic.

"Well," I replied, "I don't like them, if that's what you mean. I was once butted by one as a child."

"Ghosts. Not goats."

"Oh, ghosts? Do I believe in ghosts?"

"Exactly."

"Well, yes—and no."

"Let me put it another way," said Mr. Mulliner, patiently. "Do you believe in haunted houses? Do you believe that it is possible for a malign influence to envelop a place and work a spell on all who come within its radius?"

I hesitated.

"Well, no—and yes."

Mr. Mulliner sighed a little. He seemed to be wondering if I was always as bright as this.

"Of course," I went on, "one has read stories. Henry James's *Turn of The Screw* . . ."

"I am not talking about fiction."

"Well, in real life——Well, look here, I once, as a matter of fact, did meet a man who knew a fellow . . ."

"My distant cousin James Rodman spent some weeks in a haunted house," said Mr. Mulliner, who, if he has a fault, is not a very good listener. "It cost him five thousand pounds. That is to say, he sacrificed five thousand pounds by not remaining there. Did you ever," he asked, wandering, it seemed to me, from the subject, "hear of Leila J. Pinckney?"

Naturally I had heard of Leila J. Pinckney. Her death some years ago has diminished her vogue, but at one time it was impossible to pass a book-shop or a railway bookstall without seeing a long row of her novels. I have never myself actually read any of them, but I knew that in her particular line of literature, the Squashily Sentimental, she had always been regarded by those entitled to judge as pre-eminent. The critics usually headed their reviews of her stories with the words:

ANOTHER PINCKNEY

or sometimes, more offensively:

ANOTHER PINCKNEY ! ! !

And once, dealing with, I think, *The Love Which Prevails*, the literary expert of the *Scrutinizer* had compressed his entire critique into the single phrase "Oh, God!"

"Of course," I said. "But what about her?"

"She was James Rodman's aunt."

"Yes?"

"And when she died James found that she had left him five thousand pounds and the house in the country where she had lived for the last twenty years of her life."

"A very nice little legacy."

"Twenty years," repeated Mr. Mulliner. "Grasp that, for it has a vital bearing on what follows. Twenty years, mind you, and Miss Pinckney turned out two novels and twelve short stories regularly every year besides a monthly page of Advice to Young Girls in one of the magazines. That is to say, forty of her novels and no fewer than two hundred and forty of her short stories were written under the roof of Honeysuckle Cottage."

"A pretty name."

"A nasty, sloppy name," said Mr. Mulliner severely, "which should have warned my distant cousin James from the start. Have you a pencil and a piece of paper?" He scribbled for a while, poring frowningly over columns of figures. "Yes," he said, looking up, "if my calculations are correct, Leila J. Pinckney wrote in all a matter of nine million one hundred and forty thousand words of glutinous sentimentality at Honeysuckle Cottage, and it was a condition of her will that James should reside there for six months in every year. Failing to do this, he was to forfeit the five thousand pounds."

"It must be great fun making a freak will," I mused. "I often wish I was rich enough to do it."

"This was not a freak will. The conditions are perfectly understandable. James Rodman was a writer of sensational mystery stories, and his aunt Leila had always disapproved of his work. She was a great believer in the influence of environment, and the reason why she inserted that clause in her will was that she wished to compel James to move from London to the country. She considered that living in London hardened him and made his outlook on life sordid. She often asked him if he thought it quite nice to harp so much on sudden death and blackmailers with squints. Surely, she said, there were enough squinting blackmailers in the world without writing about them.

"The fact that Literature meant such different things to these two had, I believe, caused something of a coolness between them, and James had never dreamed that he would be remembered in his aunt's will. For he had never concealed his opinion that Leila J. Pinckney's style of writing revolted him, however dear it might be to her enormous public. He held rigid views on the art of the novel, and always maintained that an artist with a true reverence for his craft should not descend to gooey love stories, but should stick austerely to revolvers, cries in the night, missing papers, mysterious Chinamen and dead bodies—with or without gash in throat. And not even the thought that his aunt had dandled him on her knee as a baby could induce him to stifle his literary conscience to the extent of pretending to enjoy her work. First, last and all the time, James Rodman had held the opinion—and voiced it fearlessly—that Leila J. Pinckney wrote bilge.

"It was a surprise to him, therefore, to find that he had been left this legacy. A pleasant surprise, of course. James was making quite a decent income out of the three novels and eighteen short stories which he produced annually, but an author can always find a use for five thousand pounds. And, as for the cottage, he had actually been looking about for a little place in the country at the very moment when he received the lawyer's letter. In less than a week he was installed at his new residence."

James's first impressions of Honeysuckle Cottage were, he tells me, wholly favourable. He was delighted with the place. It was a low, rambling, picturesque old house with funny little chimneys and a red roof, placed in the middle of the most charming country. With its oak beams, its trim garden, its trilling birds and its rose-hung porch, it was the ideal spot for a writer. It was just the sort of place, he reflected whimsically, which his aunt had loved to write about in her books. Even the apple-cheeked old housekeeper who attended to his needs might have stepped straight out of one of them.

It seemed to James that his lot had been cast in pleasant places. He had brought down his books, his pipes and his golf-clubs, and was hard at work finishing the best thing he had ever done. *The Secret Nine* was the title of it; and on the beautiful summer afternoon on which this story opens he was in the study, hammering away at his typewriter, at peace with the world. The machine was running sweetly, the new tobacco he had bought the day before was proving admirable, and he was moving on all six cylinders to the end of a chapter.

He shoved in a fresh sheet of paper, chewed his pipe thoughtfully for a moment, then wrote rapidly:

"For an instant Lester Gage thought that he must have been mistaken. Then the noise came again, faint but unmistakable—a soft scratching on the outer panel.

"His mouth set in a grim line. Silently, like a panther, he made one quick step to the desk, noiselessly opened a drawer, drew out his automatic. After that affair of the poisoned needle, he was taking no chances. Still in dead silence, he tiptoed to the door; then, flinging it suddenly open, he stood there, his weapon poised.

"On the mat stood the most beautiful girl he had ever beheld. A veritable child of Faërie. She eyed him for a moment with a saucy smile; then with a pretty, roguish look of reproof shook a dainty forefinger at him.

"I believe you've forgotten me, Mr. Gage!" she fluted with a mock severity which her eyes belied."

James stared at the paper dumbly. He was utterly perplexed. He had not had the slightest intention of writing anything like this. To begin with, it was a rule with him, and one which he never broke, to allow no girls to appear in his stories. Sinister landladies, yes, and naturally any amount of adventuresses with foreign accents, but never under any pretext what may be broadly described as girls. A detective story, he maintained, should have no heroine. Heroines only held up the action and tried to flirt with the hero when he should have been busy looking for clues, and then went and let the villain kidnap them by some childishly simple trick. In his writing, James was positively monastic.

And yet here was this creature with her saucy smile and her dainty forefinger horning in at the most important point in the story. It was uncanny.

He looked once more at his scenario. No, the scenario was all right.

In perfectly plain words it stated that what happened when the door opened was that a dying man fell in and after gasping, "The beetle! Tell Scotland Yard that the blue beetle is——" expired on the hearth-rug, leaving Lester Gage not unnaturally somewhat mystified. Nothing whatever about any beautiful girls.

In a curious mood of irritation, James scratched out the offending passage, wrote in the necessary corrections and put the cover on the machine. It was at this point that he heard William whining.

The only blot on this paradise which James had so far been able discover was the infernal dog, William. Belonging nominally to the gardener, on the very first morning he had adopted James by acclamation, and he maddened and infuriated James. He had a habit of coming and whining under the window when James was at work. The latter would ignore this as long as he could; then, when the thing became insupportable, would bound out of his chair, to see the animal standing on the gravel, gazing expectantly up at him with a stone in his mouth. William had a weak-minded passion for chasing stones; and on the first day James, in a rash spirit of camaraderie, had flung one for him. Since then James had thrown no more stones; but he had thrown any number of other solids, and the garden was littered with objects ranging from match boxes to a plaster statuette of the young Joseph prophesying before Pharaoh. And still William came and whined, an optimist to the last.

The whining, coming now at a moment when he felt irritable and unsettled, acted on James much as the scratching on the door had acted on Lester Gage. Silently, like a panther, he made one quick step to the mantelpiece, removed from it a china mug bearing the legend A Present From Clacton-on-Sea, and crept to the window.

And as he did so a voice outside said, "Go away, sir, go away!" and there followed a short, high-pitched bark which was certainly not William's. William was a mixture of Airedale, setter, bull-terrier, and mastiff; and when in vocal mood, favoured the mastiff side of his family.

James peered out. There on the porch stood a girl in blue. She held in her arms a small fluffy white dog, and she was endeavouring to foil the upward movement toward this of the blackguard William. William's mentality had been arrested some years before at the point where he imagined that everything in the world had been created for him to eat. A bone, a boot, a steak, the back wheel of a bicycle— it was all one to William. If it was there he tried to eat it. He had even made a plucky attempt to devour the remains of the young Joseph prophesying before Pharaoh. And it was perfectly plain now that he regarded the curious wriggling object in the girl's arms purely in the light of a snack to keep body and soul together till dinner-time.

"William!" bellowed James.

William looked courteously over his shoulder with eyes that beamed with the pure light of a life's devotion, wagged the whiplike tail which he had inherited from his bull-terrier ancestor and resumed his intent scrutiny of the fluffy dog.

"Oh, please!" cried the girl. "This great rough dog is frightening poor Toto."

The man of letters and the man of action do not always go hand in hand, but practice had made James perfect in handling with a swift efficiency any situation that involved William. A moment later that canine moron, having received the present from Clacton in the short ribs, was scuttling round the corner of the house, and James had jumped through the window and was facing the girl.

She was an extraordinarily pretty girl. Very sweet and fragile she looked as she stood there under the honeysuckle with the breeze ruffling a tendril of golden hair that strayed from beneath her coquettish little hat. Her eyes were very big and very blue, her rose-tinted face becomingly flushed. All wasted on James, though. He disliked all girls, and particularly the sweet, droopy type.

"Did you want to see somebody?" he asked stiffly.

"Just the house," said the girl, "if it wouldn't be giving any trouble. I do so want to see the room where Miss Pinckney wrote her books. This is where Leila J. Pinckney used to live, isn't it?"

"Yes; I am her nephew. My name is James Rodman."

"Mine is Rose Maynard."

James led the way into the house, and she stopped with a cry of delight on the threshold of the morning-room.

"Oh, how too perfect!" she cried. "So this was her study?"

"Yes."

"What a wonderful place it would be for you to think in if you were a writer too."

James held no high opinion of women's literary taste, but nevertheless he was conscious of an unpleasant shock.

"I am a writer," he said coldly. "I write detective stories."

"I—I'm afraid"—she blushed—"I'm afraid I don't often read detective stories."

"You no doubt prefer," said James, still more coldly, "the sort of thing my aunt used to write."

"Oh, I love her stories!" cried the girl, clasping her hands ecstatically. "Don't you?"

"I cannot say that I do."

"What?"

"They are pure apple sauce," said James sternly; "just nasty blobs of sentimentality, thoroughly untrue to life."

The girl stared.

"Why, that's just what's so wonderful about them, their trueness to life! You feel they might all have happened. I don't understand what you mean."

They were walking down the garden now. James held the gate open for her and she passed through into the road.

"Well, for one thing," he said, "I decline to believe that a marriage between two young people is invariably preceded by some violent and sensational experience in which they both share."

"Are you thinking of *Scent o' the Blossom,* where Edgar saves Maud from drowning?"

"I am thinking of every single one of my aunt's books." He looked at her curiously. He had just got the solution of a mystery which had been puzzling him for some time. Almost from the moment he had set eyes on her she had seemed somehow strangely familiar. It now suddenly came to him why it was that he disliked her so much. "Do you know," he said, "you might be one of my aunt's heroines yourself? You're just the sort of girl she used to love to write about."

Her face lit up.

"Oh, do you really think so?" She hesitated. "Do you know what I have been feeling ever since I came here? I've been feeling that you are exactly like one of Miss Pinckney's heroes."

"No, I say, really!" said James, revolted.

"Oh, but you are! When you jumped through that window it gave me quite a start. You were so exactly like Claude Masterton in *Heather o' the Hills.*"

"I have not read *Heather o' the Hills,*" said James with a shudder.

"He was very strong and quiet, with deep, dark, sad eyes."

James did not explain that his eyes were sad because her society gave him a pain in the neck. He merely laughed scornfully.

"So now, I suppose," he said, "a car will come and knock you down and I shall carry you gently into the house and lay you——Look out!" he cried.

It was too late. She was lying in a little huddled heap at his feet. Round the corner a large automobile had come bowling, keeping with an almost affected precision to the wrong side of the road. It was now receding into the distance, the occupant of the tonneau, a stout red-faced gentleman in a fur coat, leaning out over the back. He had bared his head—not, one fears, as a pretty gesture of respect and regret, but because he was using his hat to hide the number plate.

The dog Toto was unfortunately uninjured.

James carried the girl gently into the house and laid her on the sofa in the morning-room. He rang the bell and the apple-cheeked housekeeper appeared.

"Send for the doctor," said James. "There has been an accident."

The housekeeper bent over the girl.

"Eh, dearie, dearie!" she said. "Bless her sweet pretty face!"

The gardener, he who technically owned William, was routed out from among the young lettuces and told to fetch Doctor Brady. He separated his bicycle from William, who was making a light meal off the left pedal, and departed on his mission. Doctor Brady arrived and in due course he made his report.

"No bones broken, but a number of nasty bruises. And, of course, the shock. She will have to stay here for some time, Rodman. Can't be moved."

"Stay here! But she can't! It isn't proper."

"Your housekeeper will act as a chaperon."

The doctor sighed. He was a stolid-looking man of middle age with side whiskers.

"A beautiful girl, that, Rodman," he said.

"I suppose so," said James.

"A sweet, beautiful girl. An elfin child."

"A what?" cried James, starting.

This imagery was very foreign to Doctor Brady as he knew him. On the only previous occasion on which they had had any extended conversation, the doctor had talked exclusively about the effect of too much protein on the gastric juices.

"An elfin child; a tender, fairy creature. When I was looking at her just now, Rodman, I nearly broke down. Her little hand lay on the coverlet like some white lily floating on the surface of a still pool, and her dear, trusting eyes gazed up at me."

He pottered off down the garden, still babbling, and James stood staring after him blankly. And slowly, like some cloud athwart a summer sky, there crept over James's heart the chill shadow of a nameless fear.

It was about a week later that Mr. Andrew McKinnon, the senior partner in the well-known firm of literary agents, McKinnon & Gooch, sat in his office in Chancery Lane, frowning thoughtfully over a telegram. He rang the bell.

"Ask Mr. Gooch to step in here." He resumed his study of the telegram. "Oh,

Gooch," he said when his partner appeared, "I've just had a curious wire from young Rodman. He seems to want to see me very urgently."

Mr. Gooch read the telegram.

"Written under the influence of some strong mental excitement," he agreed. "I wonder why he doesn't come to the office if he wants to see you so badly."

"He's working very hard, finishing that novel for Prodder & Wiggs. Can't leave it, I suppose. Well, it's a nice day. If you will look after things here I think I'll motor down and let him give me lunch."

As Mr. McKinnon's car reached the crossroads a mile from Honeysuckle Cottage, he was aware of a gesticulating figure by the hedge. He stopped the car.

"Morning, Rodman."

"Thank God you've come!" said James. It seemed to Mr. McKinnon that the young man looked paler and thinner. "Would you mind walking the rest of the way? There's something I want to speak to you about."

Mr. McKinnon alighted; and James, as he glanced at him, felt cheered and encouraged by the very sight of the man. The literary agent was a grim, hard-bitten person, to whom, when he called at their offices to arrange terms, editors kept their faces turned so that they might at least retain their back collar studs. There was no sentiment in Andrew McKinnon. Editresses of society papers practised their blandishments on him in vain, and many a publisher had waked screaming in the night, dreaming that he was signing a McKinnon contract.

"Well, Rodman," he said, "Prodder & Wiggs have agreed to our terms. I was writing to tell you so when your wire arrived. I had a lot of trouble with them, but it's fixed at twenty per cent., rising to twenty-five, and two hundred pounds advance royalties on day of publication."

"Good!" said James absently. "Good! McKinnon, do you remember my aunt, Leila J. Pinckney?"

"Remember her? Why, I was her agent all her life."

"Of course. Then you know the sort of tripe she wrote."

"No author," said Mr. McKinnon reprovingly, "who pulls down a steady twenty thousand pounds a year writes tripe."

"Well anyway, you know her stuff."

"Who better?"

"When she died she left me five thousand pounds and her house, Honeysuckle Cottage. I'm living there now. McKinnon, do you believe in haunted houses?"

"No."

"Yet I tell you solemnly that Honeysuckle Cottage is haunted!"

"By your aunt?" said Mr. McKinnon, surprised.

"By her influence. There's a malignant spell over the place; a sort of miasma of sentimentalism. Everybody who enters it succumbs.

"Tut-tut! You musn't have these fancies."

"They aren't fancies."

"You aren't seriously meaning to tell me——"

"Well, how do you account for this? That book you were speaking about, which Prodder & Wiggs are to publish—*The Secret Nine*. Every time I sit down to write it a girl keeps trying to sneak in."

"Into the room?"

"Into the story."

"You don't want a love interest in your sort of book," said Mr. McKinnon, shaking his head. "It delays the action."

"I know it does. And every day I have to keep shooing this infernal female out. An awful girl, McKinnon. A soppy, soupy, treacly, drooping girl with a roguish smile. This morning she tried to butt in on the scene where Lester Gage is trapped in the den of the mysterious leper."

"No!"

"She did, I assure you. I had to rewrite three pages before I could get her out of it. And that's not the worst. Do you know, McKinnon, that at this moment I am actually living the plot of a typical Leila J. Pinckney novel in just the setting she always used! And I can see the happy ending coming nearer every day! A week ago a girl was knocked down by a car at my door and I've had to put her up, and every day I realise more clearly that sooner or later I shall ask her to marry me."

"Don't do it," said Mr. McKinnon, a stout bachelor. "You're too young to marry."

"So was Methuselah," said James, a stouter. "But all the same I know I'm going to do it. It's the influence of this awful house weighing upon me. I feel like an eggshell in a maelstrom. I am being sucked in by a force too strong for me to resist. This morning I found myself kissing her dog!"

"No!"

"I did! And I loathe the little beast. Yesterday I got up at dawn and plucked a nosegay of flowers for her, wet with the dew."

"Rodman!"

"It's a fact. I laid them at her door and went downstairs kicking myself all the way. And there in the hall was the apple-cheeked housekeeper regarding me archly. If she didn't murmur 'Bless their sweet young hearts!' my ears deceived me."

"Why don't you pack up and leave?"

"If I do I lose the five thousand pounds."

"Ah!" said Mr. McKinnon.

"I can understand what has happened. It's the same with all haunted houses. My aunt's subliminal ether vibrations have woven themselves into the texture of the place, creating an atmosphere which forces the ego of all who come in contact with it to attune themselves to it. It's either that or something to do with the fourth dimension."

Mr. McKinnon laughed scornfully.

"Tut-tut!" he said again. "This is pure imagination. What has happened is that you've been working too hard. You'll see this precious atmosphere of yours will have no effect on me."

"That's exactly why I asked you to come down. I hoped you might break the spell."

"I will that," said Mr. McKinnon jovially.

The fact that the literary agent spoke little at lunch caused James no apprehension. Mr. McKinnon was ever a silent trencherman. From time to time James caught him stealing a glance at the girl, who was well enough to come down to meals now, limping pathetically; but he could read nothing in his face. And yet the mere look of his face was a consolation. It was so solid, so matter of fact, so exactly like an unemotional coconut.

"You've done me good," said James with a sigh of relief, as he escorted the agent down the garden to his car after lunch. "I felt all along that I could rely on your rugged common sense. The whole atmosphere of the place seems different now."

Mr. McKinnon did not speak for a moment. He seemed to be plunged in thought.

"Rodman," he said, as he got into his car, "I've been thinking over that suggestion of yours of putting a love interest into *The Secret Nine*. I think you're wise. The story needs it. After all, what is there greater in the world than love? Love—love—aye, it's the sweetest word in the language. Put in a heroine and let her marry Lester Gage."

"If," said James grimly, "she does succeed in worming her way in she'll jolly well marry the mysterious leper. But look here, I don't understand——"

"It was seeing that girl that changed me," proceeded Mr. McKinnon. And as James stared at him aghast, tears suddenly filled his hard-boiled eyes. He openly snuffled. "Aye, seeing her sitting there under the roses, with all that smell of honeysuckle and all. And the birdies singing so sweet in the garden and the sun lighting up her bonny face. The puir wee lass!" he muttered, dabbing at his eyes. "The puir bonny wee lass! Rodman," he said, his voice quivering, "I've decided that we're being hard on Prodder & Wiggs. Wiggs has had sickness in his home lately. We mustn't be hard on a man who's had sickness in his home, hey, laddie? No, no! I'm going to take back that contract and alter it to a flat twelve per cent and no advance royalties."

"What!"

"But you shan't lose by it, Rodman. No, no, you shan't lose by it, my manny. I am going to waive my commission. The puir bonny wee lass!"

The car rolled off down the road. Mr. McKinnon, seated in the back, was blowing his nose violently.

"This is the end!" said James.

It is necessary at this point to pause and examine James Rodman's position with an unbiased eye. The average man, unless he puts himself in James's place, will be unable to appreciate it. James, he will feel, was making a lot of fuss about nothing. Here he was, drawing daily closer and closer to a charming girl with big blue eyes, and surely rather to be envied than pitied.

But we must remember that James was one of Nature's bachelors. And no ordinary man, looking forward dreamily to a little home of his own with a loving wife putting out his slippers and changing the gramophone records, can realise the intensity of the instinct for self-preservation which animates Nature's bachelors in times of peril.

James Rodman had a congenital horror of matrimony. Though a young man, he had allowed himself to develop a great many habits which were as the breath of life to him; and these habits, he knew instinctively, a wife would shoot to pieces within a week of the end of the honeymoon.

James liked to breakfast in bed; and, having breakfasted, to smoke in bed and knock the ashes out on the carpet. What wife would tolerate this practice?

James liked to pass his days in a tennis shirt, grey flannel trousers and slippers. What wife ever rests until she has inclosed her husband in a stiff collar, tight boots and a morning suit and taken him with her to *thés musicales*?

These and a thousand other thoughts of the same kind flashed through the unfortunate young man's mind as the days went by, and every day that passed seemed to draw him nearer to the brink of the chasm. Fate appeared to be taking a malicious pleasure in making things as difficult for him as possible. Now that the girl was well enough to leave her bed, she spent her time sitting in a chair on the sun-sprinkled porch, and James had to read to her—and poetry, at that; and not the jolly, wholesome sort of poetry the boys are turning out nowadays, either—good, honest stuff about sin and gas-works and decaying corpses—but the old-fashioned kind with rhymes in it, dealing almost exclusively with love. The weather, moreover, continued superb. The honeysuckle cast its sweet scent on the gentle breeze; the roses over the porch stirred and nodded; the flowers in the garden were lovelier than ever; the birds sang their little throats sore. And every evening there was a magnificent sunset. It was almost as if Nature were doing it on purpose.

At last James intercepted Doctor Brady as he was leaving after one of his visits and put the thing to him squarely:

"When is that girl going?"

The doctor patted him on the arm.

"Not yet, Rodman," he said in a low, understanding voice. "No need to worry yourself about that. Mustn't be moved for days and days and days—I might almost say weeks and weeks and weeks."

"Weeks and weeks!" cried James.

"And weeks," said Doctor Brady. He prodded James roguishly in the abdomen.

"Good luck to you, my boy, good luck to you," he said.

It was some small consolation to James that the mushy physician immediately afterward tripped over William on his way down the path and broke his stethoscope. When a man is up against it like James every little helps.

He was walking dismally back to the house after this conversation when he was met by the apple-cheeked housekeeper.

"The little lady would like to speak to you, sir," said the apple-cheeked exhibit, rubbing her hands.

"Would she?" said James hollowly.

"So sweet and pretty she looks, sir—oh, sir, you wouldn't believe! Like a blessed angel sitting there with her dear eyes all a-shining."

"Don't do it!" cried James with extraordinary vehemence. "Don't do it!"

He found the girl propped up on the cushions and thought once again how singularly he disliked her. And yet, even as he thought this, some force against which he had to fight madly was whispering to him, "Go to her and take that little hand! Breathe into that little ear the burning words that will make that little face turn away crimsoned with blushes!" He wiped a bead of perspiration from his forehead and sat down.

"Mrs. Stick-in-the-Mud—what's her name?—says you want to see me."

The girl nodded.

"I've had a letter from Uncle Henry. I wrote to him as soon as I was better and told him what had happened, and he is coming here tomorrow morning."

"Uncle Henry?"

"That's what I call him, but he's really no relation. He is my guardian. He and daddy were officers in the same regiment, and when daddy was killed, fighting on the Afghan frontier, he died in Uncle Henry's arms and with his last breath begged him to take care of me."

James started. A sudden wild hope had waked in his heart. Years ago, he remembered, he had read a book of his aunt's entitled *Rupert's Legacy*, and in that book—

"I'm engaged to marry him," said the girl quietly.

"Wow!" shouted James.

"What?" asked the girl, startled.

"Touch of cramp," said James. He was thrilling all over. That wild hope had been realised.

"It was daddy's dying wish that we should marry," said the girl.

"And dashed sensible of him, too; dashed sensible," said James warmly.

"And yet," she went on, a little wistfully, "I sometimes wonder——"

"Don't!" said James. "Don't! You must respect daddy's dying wish. There's nothing like daddy's dying wish; you can't beat it. So he's coming here tomorrow, is he? Capital, capital. To lunch, I suppose? Excellent! I'll run down and tell

Mrs. Who-Is-It to lay in another chop."

It was with a gay and uplifted heart that James strolled the garden and smoked his pipe next morning. A great cloud seemed to have rolled itself away from him. Everything was for the best in the best of all possible worlds. He had finished *The Secret Nine* and shipped it off to Mr. McKinnon, and now as he strolled there was shaping itself in his mind a corking plot about a man with only half a face who lived in a secret den and terrorised London with a series of shocking murders. And what made them so shocking was the fact that each of the victims, when discovered, was found to have only half a face too. The rest had been chipped off, presumably by some blunt instrument.

The thing was coming out magnificently, when suddenly his attention was diverted by a piercing scream. Out of the bushes fringing the river that ran beside the garden burst the apple-cheeked housekeeper.

"Oh, sir! Oh, sir! Oh, sir!"

"What is it?" demanded James irritably.

"Oh, sir! Oh, sir! Oh, sir!"

"Yes, and then what?"

"The little dog, sir! He's in the river!"

"Well, whistle him to come out."

"Oh, sir, do come quick! He'll be drowned!"

James followed her through the bushes, taking off his coat as he went. He was saying to himself, "I will not rescue this dog. I do not like the dog. It is high time he had a bath, and in any case it would be much simpler to stand on the bank and fish for him with a rake. Only an ass out of a Leila J. Pinckney book would dive into a beastly river to save——"

At this point he dived. Toto, alarmed by the splash, swam rapidly for the bank, but James was too quick for him. Grasping him firmly by the neck, he scrambled ashore and ran for the house, followed by the housekeeper.

The girl was seated on the porch. Over her there bent the tall soldierly figure of a man with keen eyes and greying hair. The housekeeper raced up.

"Oh, miss! Toto! In the river! He saved him! He plunged in and saved him!"

The girl drew a quick breath.

"Gallant, damme! By Jove! By gad! Yes, gallant, by George!" exclaimed the soldierly man.

The girl seemed to wake from a reverie.

"Uncle Henry, this is Mr. Rodman. Mr. Rodman, my guardian, Colonel Carteret."

"Proud to meet you, sir," said the colonel, his honest blue eyes glowing as he fingered his short crisp moustache. "As fine a thing as I ever heard of, damme!"

"Yes, you are brave—brave," the girl whispered.

"I am wet—wet," said James, and went upstairs to change his clothes.

When he came down for lunch, he found to his relief that the girl had decided not to join them, and Colonel Carteret was silent and preoccupied. James, exerting himself in his capacity of host, tried him with the weather, golf, India, the Government, the high cost of living, first-class cricket, the modern dancing craze, and murderers he had met, but the other still preserved that strange, absent-minded silence. It was only when the meal was concluded and James had produced cigarettes that he came abruptly out of his trance.

"Rodman," he said, "I should like to speak to you."

"Yes?" said James, thinking it was about time.

"Rodman," said Colonel Carteret, "or rather, George—I may call you George?" he added, with a sort of wistful diffidence that had a singular charm.

"Certainly," replied James, "if you wish it. Though my name is James."

"James, eh? Well, well, it amounts to the same thing, eh, what, damme, by gad?" said the colonel with a momentary return of his bluff soldierly manner. "Well, then, James, I have something that I wish to say to you. Did Miss Maynard —did Rose happen to tell you anything about myself in—er—in connection with herself?"

"She mentioned that you and she were engaged to be married."

The colonel's tightly drawn lips quivered.

"No longer," he said.

"What?"

"No, John, my boy."

"James."

"No, James, my boy, no longer. While you were upstairs changing your clothes she told me—breaking down, poor child, as she spoke—that she wished our engagement to be at an end."

James half rose from the table, his cheeks blanched.

"You don't mean that!" he gasped.

Colonel Carteret nodded. He was staring out of the window, his fine eyes set in a look of pain.

"But this is nonsense!" cried James. "This is absurd! She—she mustn't be allowed to chop and change like this. I mean to say, it—it isn't fair——"

"Don't think of me, my boy."

"I'm not—I mean, did she give any reason?"

"Her eyes did."

"Her eyes did?"

"Her eyes, when she looked at you on the porch, as you stood there—young, heroic—having just saved the life of the dog she loves. It is you who have won that tender heart, my boy."

"Now, listen," protested James, "you aren't going to sit there and tell me that a girl falls in love with a man just because he saves her dog from drowning?"

"Why, surely," said Colonel Carteret, surprised. "What better reason could she have?" He sighed. "It is the old, old story, my boy. Youth to youth. I am an old man. I should have known—I should have foreseen—yes, youth to youth."

"You aren't a bit old."

"Yes, yes."

"No, no."

"Yes, yes."

"Don't keep on saying yes, yes!" cried James, clutching at his hair. "Besides, she wants a steady old buffer—a steady, sensible man of medium age—to look after her."

Colonel Carteret shook his head with a gentle smile.

"This is mere quixotry, my boy. It is splendid of you to take this attitude; but no, no."

"Yes, yes."

"No, no." He gripped James's hand for an instant, then rose and walked to the door. "That is all I wished to say, Tom."

"James."

"James. I just thought that you ought to know how matters stood. Go to her, my boy, go to her, and don't let any thought of an old man's broken dream keep you from pouring out what is in your heart. I am an old soldier, lad, an old soldier. I have learned to take the rough with the smooth. But I think—I think I will leave you now. I—I should—should like to be alone for a while. If you need me you will find me in the raspberry bushes."

He had scarcely gone when James also left the room. He took his hat and stick and walked blindly out of the garden, he knew not whither. His brain was numbed. Then, as his powers of reasoning returned, he told himself that he should have foreseen this ghastly thing. If there was one type of character over which Leila J. Pinckney had been wont to spread herself, it was the pathetic guardian who loves his ward but relinquishes her to the younger man. No wonder the girl had broken off the engagement. Any elderly guardian who allowed himself to come within a mile of Honeysuckle Cottage was simply asking for it. And then, as he turned to walk back, a dull defiance gripped James. Why, he asked, should he be put upon in this manner? If the girl liked to throw over this man, why should he be the goat?

He saw his way clearly now. He just wouldn't do it, that was all. And if they didn't like it they could lump it.

Full of a new fortitude, he strode in at the gate. A tall, soldierly figure emerged from the raspberry bushes and came to meet him.

"Well?" said Colonel Carteret.

"Well?" said James defiantly.

"Am I to congratulate you?"

James caught his keen blue eye and hesitated. It was not going to be so simple as he had supposed.

"Well—er——" he said.

Into the keen blue eyes there came a look that James had not seen there before. It was the stern, hard look which—probably—had caused men to bestow upon this old soldier the name of Cold-Steel Carteret.

"You have not asked Rose to marry you?"

"Er—no; not yet."

The keen blue eyes grew keener and bluer.

"Rodman," said Colonel Carteret in a strange, quiet voice, "I have known that little girl since she was a tiny child. For years she has been all in all to me. Her father died in my arms and with his last breath bade me see that no harm came to his darling. I have nursed her through mumps, measles—aye, and chicken-pox— and I live but for her happiness." He paused, with a significance that made James's toes curl. "Rodman," he said, "do you know what I would do to any man who trifled with that little girl's affections?" He reached in his hip pocket and an ugly-looking revolver glittered in the sunlight. "I would shoot him like a dog."

"Like a dog?" faltered James.

"Like a dog," said Colonel Carteret. He took James's arm and turned him towards the house. "She is on the porch. Go to her. And if——" He broke off. "But tut!" he said in a kindlier tone. "I am doing you an injustice, my boy. I know it."

"Oh, you are," said James fervently.

"Your heart is in the right place."

"Oh, absolutely," said James.

"Then go to her, my boy. Later on you may have something to tell me. You will find me in the strawberry beds."

It was very cool and fragrant on the porch. Overhead, little breezes played and laughed among the roses. Somewhere in the distance sheep bells tinkled, and in the shrubbery a thrush was singing its evensong.

Seated in her chair behind a wicker table laden with tea things, Rose Maynard watched James as he shambled up the path.

"Tea's ready," she called gaily. "Where is Uncle Henry?" A look of pity and distress flitted for a moment over her flower-like face. "Oh, I—I forgot," she whispered.

"He is in the strawberry beds," said James in a low voice.

She nodded unhappily.

"Of course, of course. Oh, why is life like this?" James heard her whisper.

He sat down. He looked at the girl. She was leaning back with closed eyes, and he thought he had never seen such a little squirt in his life. The idea of passing his remaining days in her society revolted him. He was stoutly opposed to the idea of marrying anyone; but if, as happens to the best of us, he ever were compelled to perform the wedding glide, he had always hoped it would be with some lady golf champion who would help him with his putting, and thus, by bringing his handicap down a notch or two, enable him to save something from the wreck, so to speak. But to link his lot with a girl who read his aunt's books and liked them; a girl who could tolerate the presence of the dog Toto; a girl who clapped her hands in pretty, childish joy when she saw a nasturtium in bloom—it was too much. Nevertheless, he took her hand and began to speak.

"Miss Maynard—Rose——"

She opened her eyes and cast them down. A flush had come into her cheeks. The dog Toto at her side sat up and begged for cake, disregarded.

"Let me tell you a story. Once upon a time there was a lonely man who lived in a cottage all by himself——"

He stopped. Was it James Rodman who was talking this bilge?

"Yes?" whispered the girl.

"——but one day there came to him out of nowhere a little fairy princess. She——"

He stopped again, but this time not because of the sheer shame of listening to his own voice. What caused him to interrupt his tale was the fact that at this moment the tea-table suddenly began to rise slowly in the air, tilting as it did so a considerable quantity of hot tea on to the knees of his trousers.

"Ouch!" cried James, leaping.

The table continued to rise, and then fell sideways, revealing the homely countenance of William, who, concealed by the cloth, had been taking a nap beneath it. He moved slowly forward, his eyes on Toto. For many a long day William had been desirous of putting to the test, once and for all, the problem of whether Toto was edible or not. Sometimes he thought yes, at other times no. Now seemed an admirable opportunity for a definite decision. He advanced on the object of his experiment, making a low whistling noise through his nostrils, not unlike a boiling kettle. And Toto, after one long look of incredulous horror, tucked his shapely tail between his legs and, turning, raced for safety. He had laid a course in a bee-line for the open garden gate, and William, shaking a dish of marmalade off his head a little petulantly, galloped ponderously after him. Rose Maynard staggered to her feet.

"Oh, save him!' she cried.

Without a word James added himself to the procession. His interest in Toto was but tepid. What he wanted was to get near enough to William to discuss with him that matter of the tea on his trousers. He reached the road and found that the order of the runners had not changed. For so small a dog, Toto was moving magnificently. A cloud of dust rose as he skidded round the corner. William followed. James followed William.

And so they passed Farmer Birkett's barn, Farmer Giles's cow shed, the place where Farmer Willetts's pigsty used to be before the big fire, and the Bunch of Grapes public house, Jno. Biggs propr., licensed to sell tobacco, wines and spirits. And it was as they were turning down the lane that leads past Farmer Robinson's chicken run that Toto, thinking swiftly, bolted abruptly into a small drain pipe.

"William!" roared James, coming up at a canter. He stopped to pluck a branch from the hedge and swooped darkly on.

William had been crouching before the pipe, making a noise like a bassoon into its interior; but now he rose and came beamingly to James. His eyes were aglow with chumminess and affection; and placing his forefeet on James's chest, he licked him three times on the face in rapid succession. And as he did so, something seemed to snap in James. The scales seemed to fall from James's eyes. For the first time he saw William as he really was, the authentic type of dog that saves his master from a frightful peril. A wave of emotion swept over him.

"William!" he muttered. "William!"

William was making an early supper off a half brick he had found in the road. James stooped and patted him fondly.

"William," he whispered, "you knew when the time had come to change the conversation, didn't you, old boy!" He straightened himself. "Come, William," he said. "Another four miles and we reach Meadowsweet Junction. Make it snappy and we shall just catch the up express, first stop London."

William looked up into his face and it seemed to James that he gave a brief nod of comprehension and approval. James turned. Through the trees to the east he could see the red roof of Honeysuckle Cottage, lurking like some evil dragon in ambush. Then, together, man and dog passed silently into the sunset.

That (concluded Mr. Mulliner) is the story of my distant cousin James Rodman. As to whether it is true, that, of course, is an open question. I, personally, am of the opinion that it is. There is no doubt that James did go to live at Honeysuckle Cottage and, while there, underwent some experience which has left an ineradicable mark upon him. His eyes today have that unmistakable look which is to be seen only in the eyes of confirmed bachelors whose feet have been dragged to the very brink of the pit and who have gazed at close range into the naked face of matrimony.

And, if further proof be needed, there is William. He is now James's inseparable companion. Would any man be habitually seen in public with a dog like William unless he had some solid cause to be grateful to him—unless they were linked together by some deep and imperishable memory? I think not. Myself, when I observe William coming along the street, I cross the road and look into a shop window till he has passed. I am not a snob, but I dare not risk my position in Society by being seen talking to that curious compound.

Nor is the precaution an unnecessary one. There is about William a shameless absence of appreciation of class distinctions which recalls the worst excesses of the French Revolution. I have seen him with these eyes chivvy a pomeranian belonging to a Baroness in her own right from near the Achilles Statue to within a few yards of the Marble Arch.

And yet James walks daily with him in Piccadilly. It is surely significant.

10

THE REVERENT WOOING OF ARCHIBALD

THE conversation in the bar-parlour of the Anglers' Rest, which always tends to get deepish towards closing-time, had turned to the subject of the Modern Girl; and a Gin-and-Ginger-Ale sitting in the corner by the window remarked that it was strange how types die out.

"I can remember the days," said the Gin-and-Ginger-Ale, "when every other girl you met stood about six feet two in her dancing-shoes, and had as many curves as a scenic railway. Now they are all five foot nothing and you can't see them side-ways. Why is this?"

The Draught Stout shook his head.

"Nobody can say. It's the same with dogs. One moment the world is full of pugs as far as the eye can reach; the next, not a pug in sight, only Pekes and Alsatians. Odd!"

The Small Bass and the Double-Whisky-and-Splash admitted that these things were very mysterious, and supposed we should never know the reason for them. Probably we were not meant to know.

"I cannot agree with you, gentlemen," said Mr. Mulliner. He had been sipping his hot Scotch and lemon with a rather abstracted air: but now he sat up alertly, prepared to deliver judgment. "The reason for the disappearance of the dignified, queenly type of girl is surely obvious. It is Nature's method of ensuring the continuance of the species. A world full of the sort of young woman that Meredith used to put into his novels and du Maurier into his pictures in *Punch* would be a world full of permanent spinsters. The modern young man would never be able to summon up the nerve to propose to them."

"Something in that," assented the Draught Stout.

"I speak with authority on that point," said Mr. Mulliner, "because my nephew, Archibald, made me his confidant when he fell in love with Aurelia Cammarleigh. He worshipped that girl with a fervour which threatened to unseat his reason, such as it was: but the mere idea of asking her to be his wife gave him, he informed me, such a feeling of sick faintness that only by means of a very stiff brandy and soda, or some similar restorative, was he able to pull himself together on the occasions when he contemplated it. Had it not been for . . . But perhaps you would care to hear the story from the beginning?"

People who enjoyed a merely superficial acquaintance with my nephew Archibald (said Mr. Mulliner) were accustomed to set him down as just an ordinary pinheaded young man. It was only when they came to know him better that they discovered their mistake. Then they realised that his pinheadedness, so far from being ordinary, was exceptional. Even at the Drones Club, where the average of intellect is not high, it was often said of Archibald that, had his brain been constructed of silk, he would have been hard put to it to find sufficient material to make a canary a pair of cami-knickers. He sauntered through life with a cheerful insouciance, and up to the age of twenty-five had only once been moved by anything in the nature of a really strong emotion—on the occasion when, in the heart of Bond Street and at the height of the London season, he discovered that his man, Meadowes, had carelessly sent him out with odd spats on.

And then he met Aurelia Cammarleigh.

The first encounter between these two has always seemed to me to bear an extraordinary resemblance to the famous meeting between the poet Dante and Beatrice Fortinari. Dante, if you remember, exchanged no remarks with Beatrice on that occasion. Nor did Archibald with Aurelia. Dante just goggled at the girl. So did Archibald. Like Archibald, Dante loved at first sight: and the poet's age at the time was, we are told, nine—which was almost exactly the mental age of Archibald Mulliner when he first set eyeglass on Aurelia Cammarleigh.

Only in the actual locale of the encounter do the two cases cease to be parallel. Dante, the story relates, was walking on the Ponte Vecchia, while Archibald Mulliner was having a thoughtful cocktail in the window of the Drones Club, looking out on Dover Street.

And he had just relaxed his lower jaw in order to examine Dover Street more comfortably when there swam into his line of vision something that looked like a Greek goddess. She came out of a shop opposite the club and stood on the pavement waiting for a taxi. And, as he saw her standing there, love at first sight seemed to go all over Archibald Mulliner like nettlerash.

It was strange that this should have been so, for she was not at all the sort of girl with whom Archibald had fallen in love at first sight in the past. I chanced, while in here the other day, to pick up a copy of one of the old yellowback novels of fifty years ago—the property, I believe, of Miss Postlethwaite, our courteous and erudite barmaid. It was entitled *Sir Ralph's Secret,* and its heroine, the Lady Elaine, was described as a superbly handsome girl, divinely tall, with a noble figure, the arched Montresor nose, haughty eyes beneath delicately pencilled brows, and that indefinable air of aristocratic aloofness which marks the daughter of a hundred Earls. And Aurelia Cammarleigh might have been this formidable creature's double.

Yet Archibald, sighting her, reeled as if the cocktail he had just consumed had been his tenth instead of his first.

"Golly!" said Archibald.

To save himself from falling, he had clutched at a passing fellow-member: and now, examining his catch, he saw that it was young Algy Wymondham-Wymondham. Just the fellow-member he would have preferred to clutch at, for Algy was a man who went everywhere and knew everybody and could doubtless give him the information he desired.

"Algy, old prune," said Archibald in a low, throaty voice, "a moment of your valuable time, if you don't mind."

He paused, for he had perceived the need for caution. Algy was a notorious babbler, and it would be the height of rashness to give him an inkling of the passion which blazed within his breast. With a strong effort, he donned the mask. When he spoke again, it was with a deceiving nonchalance.

"I was just wondering if you happened to know who that girl is, across the street there. I suppose you don't know what her name is in rough numbers? Seems to me I've met her somewhere or something, or seen her, or something. Or something, if you know what I mean."

Algy followed his pointing finger and was in time to observe Aurelia as she disappeared into the cab.

"That girl?"

"Yes," said Archibald, yawning. "Who is she, if any?"

"Girl named Cammarleigh."

"Ah?" said Archibald, yawning again. "Then I haven't met her."

"Introduce you if you like. She's sure to be at Ascot. Look out for us there."

Archibald yawned for the third time.

"All right," he said, "I'll try to remember. Tell me about her. I mean, has she any fathers or mothers or any rot of that description?"

"Only an aunt. She lives with her in Park Street. She's potty."

Archibald started, stung to the quick.

"Potty? That divine . . . I mean, that rather attractive-looking girl?"

"Not Aurelia. The aunt. She thinks Bacon wrote Shakespeare."

"Thinks who wrote what?" asked Archibald, puzzled, for the names were strange to him.

"You must have heard of Shakespeare. He's well known. Fellow who used to write plays. Only Aurelia's aunt says he didn't. She maintains that a bloke called Bacon wrote them for him."

"Dashed decent of him," said Archibald, approvingly. "Of course, he may have owed Shakespeare money."

"There's that, of course."

"What was the name again?"

"Bacon."

"Bacon," said Archibald, jotting it down on his cuff. "Right."

Algy moved on, and Archibald, his soul bubbling within him like a welsh rarebit at the height of its fever, sank into a chair and stared sightlessly at the ceiling. Then, rising, he went off to the Burlington Arcade to buy socks.

The process of buying socks eased for a while the turmoil that ran riot in Archibald's veins. But even socks with lavender clocks can only alleviate: they do not cure. Returning to his rooms, he found the anguish rather more overwhelming than ever. For at last he had leisure to think: and thinking always hurt his head.

Algy's careless words had confirmed his worst suspicions. A girl with an aunt who knew all about Shakespeare and Bacon must of necessity live in a mental atmosphere into which a lame-brained bird like himself could scarcely hope to soar. Even if he did meet her—even if she asked him to call—even if in due time their relations became positively cordial, what then? How could he aspire to such a goddess? What had he to offer her?

Money?

Plenty of that, yes, but what was money?

Socks?

Of these he had the finest collection in London, but socks are not everything.

A loving heart?

A fat lot of use that was.

No, a girl like Aurelia Cammarleigh would, he felt, demand from the man who aspired to her hand something in the nature of gifts, of accomplishments. He would have to be a man who Did Things.

And what, Archibald asked himself, could he do? Absolutely nothing except give an imitation of a hen laying an egg.

That he could do. At imitating a hen laying an egg he was admittedly a master. His fame in that one respect had spread all over the West End of London. "Others abide our question. Thou art free," was the verdict of London's gilded youth on Archibald Mulliner when considered purely in the light of a man who could imitate a hen laying an egg. "Mulliner," they said to one another, "may be a pretty minus quantity in many ways, but he can imitate a hen laying an egg."

And, so far from helping him, this one accomplishment of his would, reason told him, be a positive handicap. A girl like Aurelia Cammarleigh would simply be sickened by such coarse buffoonery. He blushed at the very thought of her ever learning that he was capable of sinking to such depths.

And so, when some weeks later he was introduced to her in the paddock at Ascot and she, gazing at him with what seemed to his sensitive mind contemptuous loathing, said:

"They tell me you give an imitation of a hen laying an egg, Mr. Mulliner."

He replied with extraordinary vehemence.

"It is a lie—a foul and contemptible lie which I shall track to its source and nail to the counter."

Brave words! But had they clicked? Had she believed him? He trusted so. But her haughty eyes were very penetrating. They seemed to pierce through to the depths of his soul and lay it bare for what it was—the soul of a hen-imitator.

However, she did ask him to call. With a sort of queenly, bored disdain and only after he had asked twice if he might—but she did it. And Archibald resolved that, no matter what the mental strain, he would show her that her first impression of him had been erroneous; that, trivial and vapid though he might seem, there were in his nature deeps whose existence she had not suspected.

For a young man who had been superannuated from Eton and believed everything he read in the Racing Expert's column in the morning paper, Archibald, I am bound to admit, exhibited in this crisis a sagacity for which few of his intimates would have given him credit. It may be that love stimulates the mind, or it may be that when the moment comes Blood will tell. Archibald, you must remember, was, after all, a Mulliner: and now the old canny strain of the Mulliners came out in him.

"Meadowes, my man," he said to Meadowes, his man.

"Sir," said Meadowes.

"It appears," said Archibald, "that there is—or was—a cove of the name of Shakespeare. Also a second cove of the name of Bacon. Bacon wrote plays, it seems, and Shakespeare went and put his own name on the programme and copped the credit."

"Indeed, sir?"

"If true, not right, Meadowes."

"Far from it, sir."

"Very well, then. I wish to go into this matter carefully. Kindly pop out and get me a book or two bearing on the business."

He had planned his campaign with infinite cunning. He knew that, before anything could be done in the direction of winning the heart of Aurelia Cammarleigh, he must first establish himself solidly with the aunt. He must court the aunt, ingratiate himself with her—always, of course, making it clear from the start that she was not the one. And, if reading about Shakespeare and Bacon could do it, he would, he told himself, have her eating out of his hand in a week.

Meadowes returned with a parcel of forbidding-looking volumes, and Archibald put in a fortnight's intensive study. Then, discarding the monocle which had up till then been his constant companion, and substituting for it a pair of horn-rimmed spectacles which gave him something of the look of an earnest sheep, he set out for Park Street to pay his first call. And within five minutes of his arrival he had declined a cigarette on the plea that he was a non-smoker, and had managed to say some rather caustic things about the practice, so prevalent among his contemporaries, of drinking cocktails.

Life, said Archibald, toying with his teacup, was surely given to us for some better purpose than the destruction of our brains and digestions with alcohol. Bacon, for instance, never took a cocktail in his life, and look at him.

At this, the aunt, who up till now had plainly been regarding him as just another of those unfortunate incidents, sprang to life.

"You admire Bacon, Mr. Mulliner?" she asked eagerly.

And, reaching out an arm like the tentacle of an octopus, she drew him into a corner and talked about Cryptograms for forty-seven minutes by the drawing-room clock. In short, to sum the thing up, my nephew Archibald, at his initial meeting with the only relative of the girl he loved, went like a sirocco. A Mulliner is always a Mulliner. Apply the acid test, and he will meet it.

It was not long after this that he informed me that he had sown the good seed to such an extent that Aurelia's aunt had invited him to pay a long visit to her country house, Brawstead Towers, in Sussex.

He was seated at the Savoy bar when he told me this, rather feverishly putting himself outside a Scotch and soda: and I was perplexed to note that his face was drawn and his eyes haggard.

"But you do not seem happy, my boy," I said.

"I'm not happy."

"But surely this should be an occasion for rejoicing. Thrown together as you will be in the pleasant surroundings of a country house, you ought easily to find an opportunity of asking this girl to marry you."

"And a lot of good that will be," said Archibald moodily. "Even if I do get a chance I shan't be able to make any use of it. I wouldn't have the nerve. You don't seem to realise what it means being in love with a girl like Aurelia. When I look into those clear, soulful eyes, or see that perfect profile bobbing about on the horizon, a sense of my unworthiness seems to slosh me amidships like some blunt instrument. My tongue gets entangled with my front teeth, and all I can do is stand there feeling like a piece of Gorgonzola that has been condemned by the local sanitary inspector. I'm going to Brawstead Towers, yes, but I don't expect anything to come of it. I know exactly what's going to happen to me. I shall just buzz along through life, pining dumbly, and in the end slide into the tomb a blasted, blighted bachelor. Another whisky, please, and jolly well make it a double."

Brawstead Towers, situated as it is in the pleasant Weald of Sussex, stands some fifty miles from London: and Archibald, taking the trip easily in his car, arrived there in time to dress comfortably for dinner. It was only when he reached the drawing-room at eight o'clock that he discovered that the younger members of the house-party had gone off in a body to dine and dance at a hospitable neighbour's, leaving him to waste the evening tie of a lifetime, to the composition of which he had devoted no less than twenty-two minutes, on Aurelia's aunt.

Dinner in these circumstances could hardly hope to be an unmixedly exhilarating function. Among the things which helped to differentiate it from a Babylonian orgy was the fact that, in deference to his known prejudices, no wine was served to Archibald. And, lacking artificial stimulus, he found the aunt even harder to endure philosophically than ever.

Archibald had long since come to a definite decision that what this woman needed was a fluid ounce of weed-killer, scientifically administered. With a good deal of adroitness he contrived to head her off from her favourite topic during the meal: but after the coffee had been disposed of she threw off all restraint. Scooping him up and bearing him off into the recesses of the west wing, she wedged him into a corner of a settee and began to tell him all about the remarkable discovery which had been made by applying the Plain Cipher to Milton's well-known Epitaph on Shakespeare.

"The one beginning 'What needs my Shakespeare for his honoured bones?' " said the aunt.

"Oh, that one?" said Archibald.

" 'What needs my Shakespeare for his honoured bones? The labour of an Age in piled stones? Or that his hallowed Reliques should be hid under a starry-pointing Pyramid?' " said the aunt.

Archibald, who was not good at riddles, said he didn't know.

"As in the Plays and Sonnets," said the aunt, "we substitute the name equivalents of the figure totals."

"We do what?"

"Substitute the name equivalents of the figure totals."

"The which?"

"The figure totals."

"All right," said Archibald. "Let it go. I daresay you know best."

The aunt inflated her lungs.

"These figure totals," she said, "are always taken out in the Plain Cipher, A equalling one to Z equals twenty-four. The names are counted in the same way. A capital letter with the figures indicates an occasional variation in the Name Count. For instance, A equals twenty-seven, B twenty-eight, until K equals ten is reached, when K, instead of ten, becomes one, and T instead of nineteen is one, and R or Reverse, and so on, until A equals twenty-four is reached. The short or single Digit is not used here. Reading the Epitaph in the light of this Cipher, it becomes: 'What need Verulam for Shakespeare? Francis Bacon England's King be hid under a W. Shakespeare? William Shakespeare. Fame, what needst Francis Tudor, King of England? Francis. Francis W. Shakespeare. For Francis thy William Shakespeare hath England's King took W. Shakespeare. Then thou our W. Shakespeare Francis Tudor bereaving Francis Bacon Francis Tudor such a tomb William Shakespeare.' "

The speech to which he had been listening was unusually lucid and simple for a Baconian, yet Archibald, his eye catching a battle-axe that hung on the wall, could not but stifle a wistful sigh. How simple it would have been, had he not been a Mulliner and a gentleman, to remove the weapon from its hook, spit on

his hands, and haul off and dot this doddering old ruin one just above the imitation pearl necklace. Placing his twitching hands underneath him and sitting on
them, he stayed where he was until, just as the clock on the mantelpiece chimed
the hour of midnight, a merciful fit of hiccoughs on the part of his hostess enabled
him to retire. As she reached the twenty-seventh "hic", his fingers found the door-
handle and a moment later he was outside, streaking up the stairs.

The room they had given Archibald was at the end of a corridor, a pleasant,
airy apartment with French windows opening upon a broad balcony. At any other
time he would have found it agreeable to hop out on to this balcony and revel in
the scents and sounds of the summer night, thinking the while long, lingering
thoughts of Aurelia. But what with all that Francis Tudor Francis Bacon such a
tomb William Shakespeare count seventeen drop one knit purl and set them up in
the other alley stuff, not even thoughts of Aurelia could keep him from his bed.

Moodily tearing off his clothes and donning his pyjamas, Archibald Mulliner
climbed in and instantaneously discovered that the bed was an apple-pie bed.
When and how it had happened he did not know, but at a point during the day
some loving hand had sewn up the sheets and put two hair-brushes and a branch
of some prickly shrub between them.

Himself from earliest boyhood an adept at the construction of booby-traps,
Archibald, had his frame of mind been sunnier, would doubtless have greeted this
really extremely sound effort with a cheery laugh. As it was, weighed down with
Verulams and Francis Tudors, he swore for a while with considerable fervour:
then, ripping off the sheets and tossing the prickly shrub wearily into a corner,
crawled between the blankets and was soon asleep.

His last waking thought was that if the aunt hoped to catch him on the morrow,
she would have to be considerably quicker on her pins than her physique indicated.

How long Archibald slept he could not have said. He woke some hours later
with a vague feeling that a thunderstorm of unusual violence had broken out in
his immediate neighbourhood. But this, he realised as the mists of slumber cleared
away, was an error. The noise which had disturbed him was not thunder but the
sound of someone snoring. Snoring like the dickens. The walls seemed to be
vibrating like the deck of an ocean liner.

Archibald Mulliner might have had a tough evening with the aunt, but his
spirit was not so completely broken as to make him lie supinely down beneath
that snoring. The sound filled him, as snoring fills every right-thinking man, with
a seething resentment and a passionate yearning for justice, and he climbed out
of bed with the intention of taking the proper steps through the recognised channels. It is the custom nowadays to disparage the educational methods of the English public-school and to maintain that they are not practical and of a kind to fit
the growing boy for the problems of after-life. But you do learn one thing at a

public-school, and that is how to act when somebody starts snoring.

You jolly well grab a cake of soap and pop in and stuff it down the blighter's throat. And this Archibald proposed—God willing—to do. It was the work of a moment with him to dash to the washstand and arm himself. Then he moved softly out through the French windows on to the balcony.

The snoring, he had ascertained, proceeded from the next room. Presumably this room also would have French windows; and presumably, as the night was warm, these would be open. It would be a simple task to oil in, insert the soap, and buzz back undetected.

It was a lovely night, but Archibald paid no attention to it. Clasping his cake of soap, he crept on and was pleased to discover, on arriving outside the snorer's room, that his surmise had been correct. The windows were open. Beyond them, screening the interior of the room, were heavy curtains. And he had just placed his hand upon these when from insde a voice spoke. At the same moment the light was turned on.

"Who's that?" said the voice.

And it was as if Brawstead Towers with all its stabling, outhouses and messuages had fallen on Archibald's head. A mist rose before his eyes. He gasped and tottered.

The voice was that of Aurelia Cammarleigh.

For an instant, for a single long, sickening instant, I am compelled to admit that Archibald's love, deep as the sea though it was, definitely wobbled. It had received a grievous blow. It was not simply the discovery that the girl he adored was a snorer that unmanned him: it was the thought that she could snore like that. There was something about those snores that had seemed to sin against his whole conception of womanly purity.

Then he recovered. Even though this girl's slumber was not, as the poet Milton so beautifully puts it, "airy light", but rather reminiscent of a lumber-camp when the wood-sawing is proceeding at its briskest, he loved her still.

He had just reached this conclusion when a second voice spoke inside the room.

"I say, Aurelia."

It was the voice of another girl. He perceived now that the question "Who's that?" had been addressed not to him but to this newcomer fumbling at the door-handle.

"I say, Aurelia," said the girl complainingly, "you've simply got to do something about that bally bulldog of yours. I can't possibly get to sleep with him snoring like that. He's making the plaster come down from the ceiling in my room."

"I'm sorry," said Aurelia. "I've got so used to it that I don't notice."

"Well, I do. Put a green-baize cloth over him or something."

Out on the moonlit balcony Archibald Mulliner stood shaking like a blancmange.

Although he had contrived to maintain his great love practically intact when he had supposed the snores to proceed from the girl he worshipped, it had been tough going, and for an instant, as I have said, a very near thing. The relief that swept over him at the discovery that Aurelia could still justifiably remain on her pinnacle was so profound that it made him feel filleted. He seemed for a moment in a daze. Then he was brought out of the ether by hearing his name spoken.

"Did Archie Mulliner arrive to-night?" asked Aurelia's friend.

"I suppose so," said Aurelia. "He wired that he was motoring down."

"Just between us girls," said Aurelia's friend, "what do you think of that bird?"

To listen to a private conversation—especially a private conversation between two modern girls when you never know what may come next—is rightly considered an action incompatible with the claim to be a gentleman. I regret to say, therefore, that Archibald, ignoring the fact that he belonged to a family whose code is as high as that of any in the land, instead of creeping away to his room edged at this point a step closer to the curtains and stood there with his ears flapping. It might be an ignoble thing to eavesdrop, but it was apparent that Aurelia Cammarleigh was about to reveal her candid opinion of him: and the prospect of getting the true facts—straight, as it were, from the horse's mouth—held him so fascinated that he could not move.

"Archie Mulliner?" said Aurelia meditatively.

"Yes. The betting at the Junior Lipstick is seven to two that you'll marry him."

"Why on earth?"

"Well, people have noticed he's always round at your place, and they seem to think it significant. Anyway, that's how the odds stood when I left London—seven to two."

"Get in on the short end," said Aurelia earnestly, "and you'll make a packet."

"Is that official?"

"Absolutely," said Aurelia.

Out in the moonlight, Archibald Mulliner uttered a low, bleak moan rather like the last bit of wind going out of a dying duck. True, he had always told himself that he hadn't a chance, but, however much a man may say that, he never in his heart really believes it. And now from an authoritative source he had learned that his romance was definitely blue round the edges. It was a shattering blow. He wondered dully how the trains ran to the Rocky Mountains. A spot of grizzly-bear shooting seemed indicated.

Inside the room, the other girl appeared perplexed.

"But you told me at Ascot," she said, "just after he had been introduced to you, that you rather thought you had at last met your ideal. When did the good thing begin to come unstuck?"

A silvery sigh came through the curtains.

"I did think so then," said Aurelia wistfully. "There was something about him. I liked the way his ears wiggled. And I had always heard he was such a perfectly genial, cheery, merry old soul. Algy Wymondham-Wymondham told me that his imitation of a hen laying an egg was alone enough to keep any reasonable girl happy through a long married life."

"Can he imitate a hen?"

"No. It was nothing but an idle rumour. I asked him, and he stoutly denied that he had ever done such a thing in his life. He was quite stuffy about it. I felt a little uneasy then, and the moment he started calling and hanging about the house I knew that my fears had been well-founded. The man is beyond question a flat tyre and a wet smack."

"As bad as that?"

"I'm not exaggerating a bit. Where people ever got the idea that Archie Mulliner is a bonhomous old bean beats me. He is the worlds worst monkey-wrench. He doesn't drink cocktails, he doesn't smoke cigarettes, and the thing he seems to enjoy most in the world is to sit for hours listening to the conversation of my aunt, who, as you know, is pure goof from the soles of the feet to the tortoiseshell comb and should long ago have been renting a padded cell in Earlswood. Believe me, Muriel, if you can really get seven to two, you are on to the best thing since Buttercup won the Lincolnshire."

"You don't say!"

"I do say. Apart from anything else, he's got a beastly habit of looking at me reverently. And if you knew how sick I am of being looked at reverently! They will do it, these lads. I suppose it's because I'm rather an out-size and modelled on the lines of Cleopatra."

"Tough!"

"You bet it's tough. A girl can't help her appearance. I may look as if my ideal man was the hero of a Viennese operetta, but I don't feel that way. What I want is some good sprightly sportsman who sets a neat booby-trap, and who'll rush up and grab me in his arms and say to me, 'Aurelia, old girl, you're the bee's roller-skates'!"

And Aurelia Cammarleigh emitted another sigh.

"Talking of booby-traps," said the other girl, "if Archie Mulliner has arrived he's in the next room, isn't he?"

"I suppose so. That's where he was to be. Why?"

"Because I made him an apple-pie bed."

"It was the right spirit," said Aurelia warmly. "I wish I'd thought of it myself."

"Too late now."

"Yes," said Aurelia. "But I'll tell you what I can and will do. You say you object to Lysander's snoring. Well, I'll go and pop him in at Archie Mulliner's window. That'll give him pause for thought."

"Splendid," agreed the girl Muriel. "Well, good night."

"Good night," said Aurelia.

There followed the sound of a door closing.

There was, as I have indicated, not much of my nephew Archibald's mind, but what there was of it was now in a whirl. He was stunned. Like every man who is abruptly called upon to revise his entire scheme of values, he felt as if he had been standing on top of the Eiffel Tower and some practical joker had suddenly drawn it away from under him. Tottering back to his room, he replaced the cake of soap in its dish and sat down on the bed to grapple with this amazing development.

Aurelia Cammarleigh had compared herself to Cleopatra. It is not too much to say that my nephew Archibald's emotions at this juncture were very similar to what Marc Antony's would have been had Egypt's queen risen from her throne at his entry and without a word of warning started to dance the Black Bottom.

He was roused from his thoughts by the sound of a light footstep on the balcony outside. At the same moment he heard a low woofly gruffle, the unmistakable note of a bulldog of regular habits who has been jerked out of his basket in the small hours and forced to take the night air.

> "She is coming, my own, my sweet!
>   Were it never so airy a tread,
> My heart would hear her and beat,
>   Were it earth in an earthly bed"

whispered Archibald's soul, or words to that effect. He rose from his seat and paused for an instant, irresolute. Then inspiration descended on him. He knew what to do, and he did it.

Yes, gentlemen, in that supreme crisis of his life, with his whole fate hanging, as you might say, in the balance, Archibald Mulliner, showing for almost the first time in his career a well-nigh human intelligence, began to give his celebrated imitation of a hen laying an egg.

Archibald's imitation of a hen laying an egg was conceived on broad and sympathetic lines. Less violent than Salvini's *Othello*, it had in it something of the poignant wistfulness of Mrs. Siddons in the sleep-walking scene of *Macbeth*. The rendition started quietly, almost inaudibly, with a sort of soft, liquid crooning— the joyful yet half-incredulous murmur of a mother who can scarcely believe as yet that her union has really been blessed, and that it is indeed she who is responsible for that oval mixture of chalk and albumen which she sees lying beside her in the straw.

Then, gradually, conviction comes.

"It looks like an egg," one seems to hear her say. "It feels like an egg. It's shaped like an egg. Damme, it *is* an egg!"

And at that, all doubting resolved, the crooning changes; takes on a firmer note; soars into the upper register; and finally swells into a maternal paean of joy—a "Charawk-chawk-chawk-chawk" of such a calibre that few had ever been able to listen to it dry-eyed. Following which, it was Archibald's custom to run round the room, flapping the sides of his coat, and then, leaping on to a sofa or some convenient chair, to stand there with his arms at right angles, crowing himself purple in the face.

All these things he had done many a time for the idle entertainment of fellow-members in the smoking-room of the Drones, but never with the gusto, the *brio,* with which he performed them now. Essentially a modest man, like all the Mulliners, he was compelled, nevertheless, to recognise that tonight he was surpassing himself. Every artist knows when the authentic divine fire is within him, and an inner voice told Archibald Mulliner that he was at the top of his form and giving the performance of a lifetime. Love thrilled through every "Brt-t't-t't" that he uttered, animated each flap of his arms. Indeed, so deeply did Love drive in its spur that he tells me that, instead of the customary once, he actually made the circle of the room three times before coming to rest on top of the chest of drawers.

When at length he did so he glanced towards the window and saw that through the curtains the loveliest face in the world was peering. And in Aurelia Cammarleigh's glorious eyes there was a look he had never seen before, the sort of look Kreisler or somebody like that beholds in the eyes of the front row as he lowers his violin and brushes his forehead with the back of his hand. A look of worship.

There was a long silence. Then she spoke.

"Do it again!" she said.

And Archibald did it again. He did it four times and could, he tells me, if he had pleased, have taken a fifth encore or at any rate a couple of bows. And then, leaping lightly to the floor, he advanced towards her. He felt conquering, dominant. It was his hour. He reached out and clasped her in his arms.

"Aurelia, old girl," said Archibald Mulliner in a clear, firm voice, "you are the bee's roller-skates."

And at that she seemed to melt into his embrace. Her lovely face was raised to his.

"Archibald!" she whispered.

There was another throbbing silence, broken only by the beating of two hearts and the wheezing of the bulldog, who seemed to suffer a good deal in his bronchial tubes. Then Archibald released her.

"Well, that's that," he said. "Glad everything's all settled and hotsy-totsy. Gosh, I wish I had a cigarette. This is the sort of moment a bloke needs one."

She looked at him, surprised.

"But I thought you didn't smoke."

"Oh yes, I do."

"And do you drink as well?"

"Quite as well," said Archibald. "In fact, rather better. Oh, by the way."

"Yes?"

"There's just one other thing. Suppose that aunt of yours wants to come and visit us when we are settled down in our little nest, what, dearest, would be your reaction to the scheme of socking her on the base of the skull with a stuffed eel-skin?"

"I should like it," said Aurelia warmly, "above all things."

"Twin souls," cried Archibald. "That's what we are, when you come right down to it. I suspected it all along, and now I know. Two jolly old twin souls." He embraced her ardently. "And now," he said, "let us pop downstairs and put this bulldog in the butler's pantry, where he will come upon him unexpectedly in the morning and doubtless get a shock which will do him as much good as a week at the seaside. Are you on?"

"I am," whispered Aurelia. "Oh, I am."

And hand in hand they wandered out together on to the broad staircase.

THE MAN WHO GAVE UP SMOKING

IN a mixed assemblage like the little group of serious thinkers which gathers nightly in the bar-parlour of the Anglers' Rest it is hardly to be expected that there will invariably prevail an unbroken harmony. We are all men of spirit: and when men of spirit, with opinions of their own, get together, disputes are bound to arise. Frequently, therefore, even in this peaceful haven, you will hear voices raised, tables banged, and tenor Permit-me-to-inform-you-sir's competing with baritone And-jolly-well-permit-me-to-inform-*you*'s. I have known fists to be shaken and on one occasion the word "fat-head" to be used.

Fortunately, Mr. Mulliner is always there, ready with the soothing magic of his personality to calm the storm before things have gone too far. To-night, as I entered the room, I found him in the act of intervening between a flushed Lemon Squash and a scowling Tankard of Ale who had fallen foul of one another in the corner by the window.

"Gentlemen, gentlemen," he was saying in his suave, ambassadorial way, "what is all the trouble about?"

The Tankard of Ale pointed the stem of his pipe accusingly at his adversary. One could see that he was deeply stirred.

"He's talking rot about smoking."

"I am talking sense."

"I didn't hear any."

"I said that smoking was dangerous to the health. And it is."

"It isn't.'

"It is. I can prove it from my own personal experience. I was once," said the Lemon Squash, "a smoker myself, and the vile habit reduced me to a physical wreck. My cheeks sagged, my eyes became bleary, my whole face gaunt, yellow and hideously lined. It was giving up smoking that brought about the change."

"What change?" asked the Tankard.

The Lemon Squash, who seemed to have taken offence at something, rose and, walking stiffly to the door, disappeared into the night. Mr. Mulliner gave a little sigh of relief.

"I am glad he has left us," he said. "Smoking is a subject on which I hold strong views. I look upon tobacco as life's outstanding boon, and it annoys me to hear these faddists abusing it. And how foolish their arguments are, how easily refuted.

They come to me and tell me that if they place two drops of nicotine on the tongue of a dog the animal instantly dies; and when I ask them if they have ever tried the childishly simple device of not placing nicotine on the dog's tongue, they have nothing to reply. They are nonplussed. They go away mumbling something about never having thought of that."

He puffed at his cigar in silence for a few moments. His genial face had grown grave.

"If you ask my opinion, gentlemen," he resumed, "I say it is not only foolish for a man to give up smoking—it is not safe. Such an action wakes the fiend that sleeps in all of us. To give up smoking is to become a menace to the community. I shall not readily forget what happened in the case of my nephew Ignatius. Mercifully, the thing had a happy ending, but . . ."

Those of you (said Mr. Mulliner) who move in artistic circles are possibly familiar with the name and work of my nephew Ignatius. He is a portrait-painter of steadily growing reputation. At the time of which I speak, however, he was not so well-known as he is today, and consequently had intervals of leisure between commissions. These he occupied in playing the ukulele and proposing marriage to Hermione, the beautiful daughter of Herbert J. Rossiter and Mrs. Rossiter, of 3 Scantlebury Square, Kensington. Scantlebury Square was only just round the corner from his studio, and it was his practice, when he had a moment to spare, to pop across, propose to Hermione, get rejected, pop back again, play a bar or two on the ukulele, and then light a pipe, put his feet on the mantelpiece, and wonder what it was about him that appeared to make him distasteful to this lovely girl.

It could not be that she scorned his honest poverty. His income was most satisfactory.

It could not be that she had heard something damaging about his past. His past was blameless.

It could not be that she objected to his looks for, like all the Mulliners, his personal appearance was engaging and even—from certain angles—fascinating. Besides, a girl who had been brought up in a home containing a father who was one of Kensington's leading gargoyles and a couple of sub-humans like her brother Cyprian and her brother George would scarcely be an exacting judge of male beauty. Cyprian was pale and thin and wrote art-criticism for the weekly papers, and George was stout and pink and did no work of any kind, having developed at an early age considerable skill in the way of touching friends and acquaintances for small loans.

The thought occurred to Ignatius that one of these two might be able to give him some inside information on the problem. They were often in Hermione's society, and it was quite likely that she might have happened to mention at one time or another what it was about him that caused her so repeatedly to hand the mitten to a good man's love. He called upon Cyprian at his flat and put the thing to him squarely. Cyprian listened attentively, stroking his left side-whisker with a lean hand.

"Ah?" said Cyprian. "One senses, does one, a reluctance on the girl's part to entertain one's suggestions of marriage?"

"One does," replied Ignatius.

"One wonders why one is unable to make progress?"

"One does."

"One asks oneself what is the reason?"

"One does—repeatedly."

"Well, if one really desires to hear the truth," said Cyprian, stroking his right whisker, "I happen to know that Hermione objects to you because you remind her of my brother George."

Ignatius staggered back, appalled, and an animal cry escaped his lips.

"Remind her of George?"

"That's what she says."

"But I can't be like George. It isn't humanly possible for anybody to be like George."

"One merely repeats what one has heard."

Ignatius staggered from the room and, tottering into the Fulham Road, made for the Goat and Bottle to purchase a restorative. And the first person he saw in the saloon-bar was George, taking his elevenses.

"What ho!" said George. "What ho, what ho, what ho!"

He looked pinker and stouter than ever, and the theory that he could possibly resemble this distressing object was so distasteful to Ignatius that he decided to get a second opinion.

"George," he said, "have you any idea why it is that your sister Hermione spurns my suit?"

"Certainly," said George.

"You have? Then why is it?"

George drained his glass.

"You ask me why?"

"Yes."

"You want to know the reason?"

"I do."

"Well, then, first and foremost," said George, "can you lend me a quid till Wednesday week without fail?"

"No, I can't."

"Nor ten bob?"

"Nor ten bob. Kindly stick to the subject and tell me why your sister will not look at me."

"I will," said George. "Not only have you a mean and parsimonious disposition, but she says you remind her of my brother Cyprian."

Ignatius staggered and would have fallen had he not placed a foot on the brass rail.

"I remind her of Cyprian?"

"That's what she says."

With bowed head Ignatius left the saloon-bar and returned to his studio to meditate. He was stricken to the core. He had asked for inside information and he had got it, but nobody was going to make him like it.

He was not only stricken to the core, but utterly bewildered. That a man—stretching the possibilities a little—might resemble George Rossiter was intelligible. He could also understand that a man—assuming that Nature had played a scurvy trick upon him—might conceivably be like Cyprian. But how could anyone be like both of them and live?

He took pencil and paper and devoted himself to making a list in parallel columns of the qualities and characteristics of the brothers. When he had finished, he scanned it carefully. This is what he found he had written:

GEORGE	CYPRIAN
Face like pig	Face like camel
Pimples	Whiskers
Confirmed sponger	Writes art-criticism
Says "What ho!"	Says "One senses"
Slaps backs	Has nasty, dry snigger
Eats too much	Fruitarian
Tells funny stories	Recites poetry
Clammy hands	Bony hands

He frowned. The mystery was still unsolved. And then he came to the last item.

GEORGE	CYPRIAN
Heavy smoker	Heavy smoker

A spasm ran through Ignatius Mulliner. Here, at last, was a common factor. Was it possible . . . ? Could it be . . . ?

It seemed the only solution, and yet Ignatius fought against it. His love for Hermione was the lodestar of his life, but next to it, beaten only by a short head, came his love for his pipe. Had he really to choose between the two?

Could he make such a sacrifice?

He wavered.

And then he saw the eleven photographs of Hermione Rossiter gazing at him from the mantelpiece, and it seemed to him that they smiled encouragingly. He hesitated no longer. With a soft sigh such as might have proceeded from some loving father on the Steppes of Russia when compelled, in order to ensure his own safety, to throw his children out of the back of the sleigh to the pursuing wolf-pack, he took the pipe from his mouth, collected his other pipes, his tobacco and his cigars, wrapped them in a neat parcel and, summoning the charwoman who cleaned his studio, gave her the consignment to take home to her husband, an estimable man of the name of Perkins who, being of straitened means, smoked, as a rule, only what he could pick up in the street.

Ignatius Mulliner had made the great decision.

As those of you have tried it are aware, the deadly effects of giving up smoking rarely make themselves felt immediately in their full virulence. The process is gradual. In the first stage, indeed, the patient not only suffers no discomfort but goes about inflated by a sort of gaseous spiritual pride. All through the morning of the following day, Ignatius, as he walked abroad, found himself regarding such fellow-members of the community as had pipes and cigarettes in their mouths with a pitying disdain. He felt like some saint purified and purged of the grosser emotions by a life of asceticism. He longed to tell these people all about pyridine and the intense irritation it causes to the throats and other mucous surfaces of those who inhale the tobacco smoke in which it lurks. He wanted to buttonhole men sucking at their cigars and inform them that tobacco contains an appreciable quantity of the gas known as carbon monoxide, which, entering into direct combination with the colouring matter of the blood, forms so staple a compound as to render the corpuscles incapable of carrying oxygen to the tissues. He yearned to make it clear to them that smoking was simply a habit which with a little exercise of the will-power a man could give up at a moment's notice, whenever he pleased.

It was only after he had returned to his studio to put the finishing touches to his Academy picture that the second stage set in.

Having consumed an artist's lunch consisting of two sardines, the remnants of a knuckle of ham, and a bottle of beer, he found stealing over him, as his stomach got on to the fact that the meal was not to be topped off by a soothing pipe, a kind of vague sense of emptiness and bereavement akin to that experienced by the historian Gibbon on completing his *Decline and Fall of the Roman Empire*. Its symptoms were an inability to work and a dim feeling of oppression, as if he had just lost some dear friend. Life seemed somehow to have been robbed of all motive. He wandered about the studio, haunted by a sensation that he was leaving undone something that he ought to be doing. From time to time he blew little bubbles, and once or twice his teeth clicked, as if he were trying to close them on something that was not there.

A twilight sadness had him in its grip. He took up his ukulele, an instrument to which, as I have said, he was greatly addicted, and played "Ol' Man River" for a while. But the melancholy still lingered. And now, it seemed to him, he had discovered its cause. What was wrong was the fact that he was not doing enough good in the world.

Look at it this way, he felt. The world is a sad, grey place, and we are put into it to promote as far as we can the happiness of others. If we concentrate on our own selfish pleasures, what do we find? We find that they speedily pall. We weary of gnawing knuckles of ham. The ukulele loses its fascination. Of course, if we could sit down and put our feet up and set a match to the good old pipe, that would be a different matter. But we no longer smoke, and so all that is left to us is the doing of good to others. By three o'clock, in short, Ignatius Mulliner had reached the third stage, the glutinously sentimental. It caused him to grab his hat, and sent him trotting round to Scantlebury Square.

But his object was not, as it usually was when he went to Scantlebury Square, to propose to Hermione Rossiter. He had a more unselfish motive. For some time past, by hints dropped and tentative remarks thrown out, he had been made aware that Mrs. Rossiter greatly desired him to paint her daughter's portrait: and until now he had always turned to these remarks and hints a deaf ear. Mrs. Rossiter's mother's heart wanted, he knew, to get the portrait for nothing: and, while love is love and all that, he had the artist's dislike for not collecting all that was coming to him. Ignatius Mulliner, the man, might entertain the idea of pleasing the girl he worshipped by painting her on the nod, but Ignatius Mulliner, the artist had his schedule of prices. And until today it was the second Ignatius Mulliner who had said the deciding word.

This afternoon, however, everything was changed. In a short but moving speech he informed Hermione's mother that the one wish of his life was to paint her daughter's portrait; that for so great a privilege he would not dream of charging a fee; and that if she would call at the studio on the morrow, bringing Hermione with her, he would put the job in hand right away.

In fact, he very nearly offered to paint another portrait of Mrs. Rossiter herself, in evening dress with her Belgian griffon. He contrived, however, to hold the fatal words back: and it was perhaps the recollection of this belated prudence which gave him, as he stood on the pavement outside the house after the interview, a sense of having failed to be as altruistic as he might have been.

Stricken with remorse, he decided to look up good old Cyprian and ask him to come to the studio tomorrow and criticise his Academy picture. After that, he would find dear old George and press a little money on him. Ten minutes later, he was in Cyprian's sitting-room.

"One wishes what?" asked Cyprian incredulously.

"One wishes," repeated Ignatius, "that you would come round tomorrow morning and have a look at one's Academy picture and give one a hint or two about it."

"Is one really serious?" cried Cyprian, his eyes beginning to gleam. It was seldom that he received invitations of this kind. He had, indeed, been thrown out of more studios for butting in and giving artists a hint or two about their pictures than any other art-critic in Chelsea.

"One is perfectly serious," Ignatius assured him. "One feels that an opinion from an expert will be invaluable."

"Then one will be there at eleven sharp," said Cyprian, "without fail."

Ignatius wrung his hand warmly, and hurried off to the Goat and Bottle to find George.

"George," he said, "George, my dear old chap, I passed a sleepless night last night, wondering if you had all the money you require. The fear that you might have run short seemed to go through me like a knife. Call on me for as much as you need."

George's face was partially obscured by a tankard. At these words, his eyes, bulging above the pewter, took on a sudden expression of acute horror. He lowered the tankard, ashen to the lips, and raised his right hand.

"This," he said in a shaking voice, "is the end. From this moment I go off the stuff. Yes, you have seen George Plimsoll Rossiter drink his last mild-and-bitter. I am not a nervous man, but I know when I'm licked. And when it comes to a fellow's ears going . . . '

Ignatius patted his arm affectionately.

"Your ears have not gone, George," he said. "They are still there."

And so, indeed, they were, as large and red as ever. But George was not to be comforted.

"I mean when a fellow thinks he hears things . . . I give you my honest word, old man—I solemnly assure you that I could have sworn I heard you voluntarily offer me money."

"But I did."

"You did?"

"Certainly."

"You mean you definitely—literally—without any sort of prompting on my part —without my so much as saying a word to indicate that I could do with a small loan till Friday week—absolutely, positively offered to lend me money?"

"I did."

George drew a deep breath and took up his tankard again.

"All this modern, advanced stuff you read about miracles not happening," he said severely, "is dashed poppycock. I disapprove of it. I resent it keenly. About how much?" he went on, pawing adoringly at Ignatius's sleeve. "To about what as it were, extent would you be prepared to go? A quid?"

Ignatius raised his eyebrows.

"A quid is not much, George," he said with quiet reproach.

George made little gurgling noises.

"A fiver?"

Ignatius shook his head. The movement was a silent rebuke.

"Correct this petty, cheese-paring spirit, George," he urged. "Be big and broad.

Think spaciously."

"Not a tenner?"

"I was about to suggest fifteen pounds," said Ignatius. "If you are sure that will be enough."

"What ho!"

"You're positive you can manage with that? I know how many expenses you have."

"What ho!"

"Very well, then. If you can get along with fifteen pounds, come round to my studio tomorrow morning and we'll fix it up."

And, glowing with fervour, Ignatius slapped George's back in a hearty sort of way and withdrew.

"Something attempted, something done," he said to himself, as he climbed into bed some hours later, "has earned a night's repose."

Like so many men who live intensely and work with their brains, my nephew Ignatius was a heavy sleeper. Generally, after waking to a new day, he spent a considerable time lying on his back in a sort of coma, not stirring till lured from his couch by the soft, appealing smell of frying bacon. On the following morning, however, he was conscious, directly he opened his eyes, of a strange alertness. He was keyed up to quite an extraordinary extent. He had, in short, reached the stage when the patient becomes a little nervous.

Yes, he felt, analysing his emotions, he was distinctly nervous. The noise of the cat stamping about in the passage outside caused him exquisite discomfort. He was just about to shout to Mrs. Perkins, his charwoman, to stop the creature, when she rapped suddenly on the panel to inform him that his shaving-water lay without: and at the sound he immediately shot straight up to the ceiling in a cocoon of sheets and blankets, turned three complete somersaults in mid-air, and came down, quivering like a frightened mustang, in the middle of the floor. His heart was entangled with his tonsils, his eyes had worked round to the back of their sockets, and he wondered dazedly how many human souls besides himself had survived the bomb-explosion.

Reason returning to her throne, his next impulse was to cry quietly. Remembering after a while that he was a Mulliner, he checked the unmanly tears and, creeping to the bathroom, took a cold shower and felt a little better. A hearty breakfast assisted the cure, and he was almost himself again, when the discovery that there was not a pipe or a shred of tobacco in the place plunged him once more into an inky gloom.

For a long time Ignatius Mulliner sat with his face in his hands, while all the sorrows of the world seemed to rise before him, And then, abruptly, his mood changed again. A moment before, he had been pitying the human race with an intensity that racked him almost unendurably. Now, the realisation surged over

him that he didn't care a hoot about the human race. The only emotion the human
race evoked in him was an intense dislike. He burned with an irritable loathing for
all created things. If the cat had been present, he would have kicked it. If Mrs.
Perkins had entered, he would have struck her with a mahl-stick. But the cat had
gone off to restore its tissues in the dust-bin, and Mrs. Perkins was in the kitchen,
singing hymns. Ignatius Mulliner boiled with baffled fury. Here he was, with all
this concentrated hatred stored up within him, and not a living thing in sight on
which to expend it. That, he told himself with a mirthless laugh, was the way
things happened.

And just then the door opened, and there, looking like a camel arriving at an
oasis, was Cyprian.

"Ah, my dear fellow," said Cyprian. "May one enter?"

"Come right in," said Ignatius.

At the sight of this art-critic, who not only wore short side-whiskers but also one
of those black stocks which go twice round the neck and add from forty to fifty per
cent to the loathsomeness of the wearer's appearance, a strange febrile excitement
had gripped Ignatius Mulliner. He felt like a tiger at the Zoo who sees the keeper
approaching with the luncheon-tray. He licked his lips slowly and gazed earnestly
at the visitor. From a hook on the wall beside him there hung a richly inlaid
Damascus dagger. He took it down and tested its point with the ball of his thumb.

Cyprian had turned his back, and was examining the Academy picture through
a black-rimmed monocle. He moved his head about and peered between his fingers
and made funny, art-critic noises.

"Ye-e-s," said Cyprian. "Myes. Ha! H'm. Hrrmph! The thing has rhythm
undoubted rhythm, and, to an extent, certain inevitable curves. And yet can one
conscientiously say that one altogether likes it? One fears one cannot."

"No?" said Ignatius,

"No," said Cyprian. He toyed with his left whisker. He seemed to be massaging
it for purposes of his own. "One quite inevitably senses at a glance that the patine
lacks vitality."

"Yes?" said Ignatius.

"Yes," said Cyprian. He toyed with the whisker again. It was too early to judge
whether he was improving it at all. He shut his eyes, opened them, half closed them
once more, drew back his head, fiddled with his fingers, and expelled his breath
with a hissing sound, as if he were grooming a horse. "Beyond a question one
senses in the patine a lack of vitality. And vitality must never be sacrificed. The
artist should use his palette as an orchestra. He should put on his colours as a
great conductor uses his instruments. There must be significant form. The colour
must have a flatness, a gravity, shall I say an aroma? The figure must be placed
on the canvas in a manner not only harmonious but awake. Only so can a picture
quite too exquisitely live. And, as regards the patine . . ."

He broke off. He had had more to say about the patine, but he had heard immediately behind him an odd, stealthy, shuffling sound not unlike that made by a leopard of the jungle when stalking its prey. Spinning round, he saw Ignatius Mulliner advancing upon him. The artist's lips were curled back over his teeth in a hideous set smile. His eyes glittered. And poised in his right hand he held a Damascus dagger, which, Cyprian noticed, was richly inlaid.

An art-critic who makes a habit of going round the studios of Chelsea and speaking his mind to men who are finishing their Academy pictures gets into the way of thinking swiftly. Otherwise, he would not quite too exquisitely live through a single visit. To cast a glance at the door and note that it was closed and that his host was between him and it was with Cyprian Rossiter the work of a moment; to dart behind the easel the work of another. And with the easel as a basis the two men for some tense minutes played a silent game of round-and-round-the-mulberry-bush. It was in the middle of the twelfth lap that Cyprian received a flesh wound in the upper arm.

On another man this might have had the effect of causing him to falter, lose his head, and become an easy prey to the pursuer. But Cyprian had the advantage of having been through this sort of thing before. Only a day or two ago, one of England's leading animal-painters had chivvied him for nearly an hour in a fruitless endeavour to get at him with a short bludgeon tipped with lead.

He kept cool. In the face of danger, his footwork, always impressive, took on a new agility. And finally, when Ignatius tripped over a loose mat, he seized his opportunity like the strategist which every art-critic has to be if he mixes with artists, and dodged nimbly into a small cupboard near the model-throne.

Ignatius recovered his balance just too late. By the time he had disentangled himself from the mat, leaped at the cupboard door and started to tug at the handle, Cyprian was tugging at it from the other side, and, strive though he might, Ignatius could not dislodge him.

Presently, he gave up the struggle and, moving moodily away, picked up his ukulele and played "Ol' Man River" for a while. He was just feeling his way cautiously through that rather tricky "He don't say nuffin', He must know somefin' " bit, when the door opened once more and there stood George.

"What ho!" said George.

"Ah!" said Ignatius.

"What do you mean, Ah?"

"Just 'Ah!'," said Ignatius.

"I've come for that money."

"Ah?"

"That twenty quid or whatever. it was that you very decently promised me yesterday. And, lying in bed this morning, the thought crossed my mind: Why not make it twenty-five? A nice, round sum," argued George.

"Ah!"

"You keep saying 'Ah!' " said George. "Why do you say 'Ah!'?"

Ignatius drew himself up haughtily.

"This is my studio, paid for with my own money, and I shall say 'Ah!' in it just as often as I please."

"Of course," agreed George hurriedly. "Of course, my dear old chap, of course, of course. Hullo!" He looked down. "Shoelace undone. Dangerous. Might trip a fellow. Excuse me a moment."

He stooped: and as Ignatius gazed at his spacious trouser-seat, the thought came to him that in the special circumstances there was but one thing to be done. He waggled his right leg for a moment to limber it up, backed a pace or two and crept forward.

Mrs. Rossiter, meanwhile, accompanied by her daughter Hermione, had left Scantlebury Square and, though a trifle short in the wind, had covered the distance between it and the studio in quite good time. But the effort had told upon her, and half-way up the stairs she was compelled to halt for a short rest. It was as she stood there, puffing slightly like a seal after diving for fish, that something seemed to shoot past her in the darkness.

"What was that?" she exclaimed.

"I thought I saw something, too," said Hermione.

"Some heavy, moving object."

"Yes," said Hermione. "Perhaps we had better go up and ask Mr. Mulliner if he has been dropping things downstairs."

They made their way to the studio. Ignatius was standing on one leg, rubbing the toes of his right foot. Your artist is proverbially a dreamy, absent-minded man, and he had realised too late that he was wearing bedroom slippers. Despite the fact, however, that he was in considerable pain, his expression was not unhappy. He had the air of a man who is conscious of having done the right thing.

"Good morning, Mr. Mulliner," said Mrs. Rossiter.

"Good morning, Mr. Mulliner," said Hermione.

"Good morning," said Ignatius, looking at them with deep loathing. It amazed him that he had ever felt attracted by this girl. Until this moment, his animosity had been directed wholly against the male members of her family: but now that she stood before him he realised that the real outstanding Rossiter gumboil was his Hermione. The brief flicker of *joie-de-vivre* which had followed his interview with George had died away, leaving his mood blacker than ever. One scarcely likes to think what might have happened had Hermione selected that moment to tie her shoelace.

"Well, here we are," said Mrs. Rossiter.

At this point, unseen by them, the cupboard door began to open noiselessly. A pale face peeped out. The next instant, there was a cloud of dust, a whirring noise, and the sound of footsteps descending the stairs three at a time.

Mrs. Rossiter put a hand to her heart and panted.

"What was that?"

"It was a little blurred," said Hermione, "but I think it was Cyprian."

Ignatius uttered a passionate cry and dashed to the head of the stairs.

"Gone!"

He came back, his face contorted, muttering to himself. Mrs. Rossiter looked at him keenly. It seemed plain to her that all that was wanted here was a couple of doctors with fountain-pens to sign the necessary certificate, but she was not dismayed. After all, as she reasoned with not a little shrewd sense, a gibbering artist is just as good as a sane artist, provided he makes no charge for painting portraits.

"Well, Mr. Mulliner," she said cheerily, dismissing from her mind the problem, which had been puzzling her a little, of why her son Cyprian had been in this studio behaving like the Scotch Express, "Hermione has nothing to do this morning, so, if you are free, now would be a good time for the first sitting."

Ignatius came out of his reverie.

"Sitting?"

"For the portrait."

"What portrait?"

"Hermione's portrait."

"You wish me to paint Miss Rossiter's portrait?"

"Why, you said you would—only last night."

"Did I?" Ignatius passed a hand across his forehead. "Perhaps I did. Very well. Kindly step to the desk and write out a cheque for fifty pounds. You have your book with you?"

"Fifty—what?"

"Guineas," said Ignatius. "A hundred guineas. I always require a deposit before I start work."

"But last night you said you would paint her for nothing."

"I said I would paint her for nothing?"

"Yes."

A dim recollection of having behaved in the fatuous manner described came to Ignatius.

"Well, and suppose I did," he said warmly. "Can't you women ever understand when a man is kidding you? Have you no sense of humour? Must you always take every light quip literally? If you want a portrait of Miss Rossiter, you will jolly well pay for it in the usual manner. The thing that beats me is why you do want a portrait of a girl who not only has most unattractive features but is also a dull yellow in colour. Furthermore, she flickers. As I look at her, she definitely flickers round the edges. Her face is sallow and unwholesome. Her eyes have no sparkle of intelligence. Her ears stick out and her chin goes in. To sum up, her whole appearance gives me an indefinable pain in the neck: and, if you hold me to my promise, I shall charge extra for moral and intellectual damage and wear and tear caused by having to sit opposite her and look at her."

With these words, Ignatius Mulliner turned and began to rummage in a drawer for his pipe. But the drawer contained no pipe.

"What!" cried Mrs. Rossiter.

"You heard," said Ignatius.

"My smelling-salts!" gasped Mrs. Rossiter.

Ignatius ran his hand along the mantelpiece. He opened two cupboards and looked under the settee. But he found no pipe.

The Mulliners are by nature a courteous family: and, seeing Mrs. Rossiter sniffing and gulping there, a belated sense of having been less tactful than he might have been came to Ignatius.

"It is possible," he said, "that my recent remarks may have caused you pain. If so, I am sorry. My excuse must be that they came from a full heart. I am fed to the tonsils with the human race and look on the entire Rossiter family as perhaps its darkest blots. I cannot see the Rossiter family. There seems to me to be no market for them. All I require of the Rossiters is their blood. I nearly got Cyprian with a dagger, but he was too quick for me. If he fails as a critic, there is always a future for him as a Russian dancer. However, I had decidedly better luck with George. I gave him the juiciest kick I have ever administered to human frame. If he had been shot from a gun he couldn't have gone out quicker. Probably he passed you on the stairs?"

"So *that* was what passed us!" said Hermione, interested. "I remember thinking at the time that there was a whiff of George."

Mrs. Rossiter was staring, aghast.

"You kicked my son!"

"As squarely in the seat of the pants, madam," said Ignatius with modest pride, "as if I had been practising for weeks."

"My stricken child!" cried Mrs. Rossiter. And, hastening from the room, she ran down the stairs in quest of the remains. A boy's best friend is his mother.

In the studio she had left, Hermione was gazing at Ignatius, in her eyes a look he had never seen there before.

"I had no idea you were so eloquent, Mr. Mulliner," she said, breaking the silence. "What a vivid description that was that you gave of me. Quite a prose poem."

Ignatius made a deprecating gesture.

"Oh, well," he said.

"Do you really think I am like that?"

"I do."

"Yellow?"

"Greeny yellow."

"And my eyes. . . .?" She hesitated for a word.

"They are not unlike blue oysters," said Ignatius, prompting her, "which have been dead some time."

"In fact, you don't admire my looks?"

"Far from it."

She was saying something, but he had ceased to listen. Quite suddenly he had remembered that about a couple of weeks ago, at a little party which he had given in the studio, he had dropped a half-smoked cigar behind the bureau. And as no charwoman is allowed by the rules of her union to sweep under bureaux, it might—nay, must—still be there. With feverish haste he dragged the bureau out. It was.

Ignatius Mulliner sighed an ecstatic sigh. Chewed and mangled, covered with dust and bitten by mice, this object between his fingers was nevertheless a cigar—a genuine, smokeable cigar, containing the regulation eight per cent of carbon monoxide. He struck a match and the next moment he had begun to puff.

And, as he did so, the milk of human kindness surged back into his soul like a vast tidal wave. As swiftly as a rabbit, handled by a competent conjurer, changes into a bouquet, a bowl of goldfish or the grand old flag, Ignatius Mulliner changed into a thing of sweetness and light, with charity towards all, with malice towards none. The pyridine played about his mucous surfaces, and he welcomed it like a long-lost brother. He felt gay, happy, exhilarated.

He looked at Hermione, standing there with her eyes sparkling and her beautiful face ashine, and he realised that he had been all wrong about her. So far from being a gumboil, she was the loveliest thing that had ever breathed the perfumed air of Kensington.

And then, chilling his ecstasy and stopping his heart in the middle of a beat, came the recollection of what he had said about her appearance. He felt pale and boneless. If ever a man had dished himself properly, that man, he felt, was Ignatius Mulliner. And he did not mean maybe.

She was looking at him, and the expression on her face seemed somehow to suggest that she was waiting for something.

"Well?" she said.

"I beg your pardon?" said Ignatius.

She pouted.

"Well, aren't you going to—er—?"

"What?"

"Well, fold me in your arms and all that sort of thing," said Hermione, blushing prettily.

Ignatius tottered.

"Who, me?"

"Yes, you."

"Fold you in my arms?"

"Yes."

"But—er—do you want me to?"

"Certainly."

"I mean . . . after all I said . . ."

She stared at him in amazement.

"Haven't you been listening to what I've been telling you?" she cried.

"I'm sorry." Ignatius stammered. "Good deal on my mind just now. Must have missed it. What did you say?"

"I said that, if you really think I look like that, you do not love me, as I had always supposed, for my beauty, but for my intellect. And if you knew how I have always longed to be loved for my intellect!"

Ignatius put down his cigar and breathed deeply.

"Let me get this right," he said. "Will you marry me?"

"Of course I will. You always attracted me strangely, Ignatius, but I thought you looked upon me as a mere doll."

He picked up his cigar, took a puff, laid it down again, took a step forward, extended his arms, and folded her in them. And for a space they stood there, clasped together, murmuring those broken words that lovers know so well. Then, gently disengaging her, he went back to the cigar and took another invigorating puff.

"Besides," she said, "how could a girl help but love a man who could lift my brother George right down a whole flight of stairs with a single kick?"

Ignatius's face clouded.

"George! That reminds me. Cyprian said you said I was like George."

"Oh! I didn't mean him to repeat that."

"Well, he did," said Ignatius moodily. "And the thought was agony."

"But I only meant that you and George were both always playing the ukulele. And I hate ukuleles."

Ignatius's face cleared.

"I will give mine to the poor this afternoon. And, touching Cyprian . . . George said you said I reminded you of him."

She hastened to soothe him.

"It's only the way you dress. You both wear such horrid sloppy clothes."

Ignatius folded her in his arms once more.

"You shall take me this very instant to the best tailor in London," he said. "Give me a minute to put on my boots, and I'll be with you. You don't mind if I just step in at my tobacconist's for a moment on the way? I have a large order for him."

12

THE STORY OF CEDRIC

I HAVE heard it said that the cosy peace which envelops the bar-parlour of the Anglers' Rest has a tendency to promote in the regular customers a certain callousness and indifference to human suffering. I fear there is something in the charge. We who have made the place our retreat sit sheltered in a backwater far removed from the rushing stream of Life. We may be dimly aware that out in the world there are hearts that ache and bleed: but we order another gin and ginger and forget about them. Tragedy, to us, has come to mean merely the occasional flatness of a bottle of beer.

Nevertheless, this crust of selfish detachment can be cracked. And when Mr. Mulliner entered on this Sunday evening and announced that Miss Postlethwaite, our gifted and popular barmaid, had severed her engagement to Alfred Lukyn, the courteous assistant at the Bon Ton Drapery Stores in the High Street, it is not too much to say that we were stunned.

"But it's only half an hour ago," we cried, "that she went off to meet him in her best black satin with the lovelight in her eyes. They were going to church together."

"They never reached the sacred edifice," said Mr. Mulliner sighing and taking a grave sip of hot Scotch and lemon. "The estrangement occurred directly they met. The rock on which the frail craft of Love split was the fact that Alfred Lukyn was wearing yellow shoes."

"Yellow shoes?"

"Yellow shoes," said Mr. Mulliner, "of a singular brightness. These came under immediate discussion. Miss Postlethwaite, a girl of exquisite sensibility and devoutness, argued that to attend evensong in shoes like that was disrespectful to the Vicar. The blood of the Lukyns is hot, and Alfred, stung, retorted that he had paid sixteen shillings and eightpence for them and that the Vicar could go and boil his head. The ring then changed hands and arrangements were put in train for the return of all gifts and correspondence."

"Just a lovers' tiff."

"Let us hope so."

A thoughtful silence fell upon the bar-parlour. Mr. Mulliner was the first to break it.

"Strange," he said, coming out of his reverie, "to what diverse ends Fate will employ the same instrument. Here we have two young loving hearts parted by a pair of yellow shoes. Yet in the case of my cousin Cedric it was a pair of yellow shoes that brought him a bride. These things work both ways."

To say that I ever genuinely liked my cousin Cedric (said Mr. Mulliner) would be paltering with the truth. He was not a man of whom many men were fond. Even as a boy he gave evidence of being about to become what eventually he did become—one of those neat, prim, fussy, precise, middle-aged bachelors who are so numerous in the neighbourhood of St. James's Street. It is a type I have never liked, and Cedric, in addition to being neat, prim, fussy and precise, was also one of London's leading snobs.

For the rest, he lived in comfortable rooms at the Albany, where between the hours of nine-thirty and twelve in the morning he would sit closeted with his efficient secretary, Miss Myrtle Watling, busy on some task the nature of which remained wrapped in mystery. Some said he was writing a monumental history of Spats, others that he was engaged upon his Memoirs. My private belief is that he was not working at anything, but entertained Miss Watling during those hours simply because he lacked the nerve to dismiss her. She was one of those calm, strong young women who look steadily out upon the world through spectacles with tortoiseshell rims. Her mouth was firm, her chin resolute. Mussolini might have fired her, if at the top of his form, but I think of nobody else capable of the feat.

So there you have my cousin Cedric. Forty-five years of age, forty-five inches round the waist, an established authority on the subject of dress, one of the six recognised bores at his club, and a man with the entree into all the best houses in London. That the peace of such a one could ever be shattered, that anything could ever occur seriously to disturb the orderly routine of such a man's life, might seem incredible. And yet this happened. How true it is that in this world we can never tell behind what corner Fate may not be lurking with the brass knuckles.

The day which was to prove so devastating to Cedric Mulliner's bachelor calm began, ironically, on a note of bright happiness. It was a Sunday, and he was always at his best on Sundays, for that was the day on which Miss Watling did not come to the Albany. For some little time back he had been finding himself more than usually ill at ease in Miss Watling's presence. She had developed a habit of looking at him with an odd, speculative expression in her eyes. It was an expression whose meaning he could not read, but it had disturbed him. He was glad to be relieved of her society for a whole day.

Then, again, his new morning-clothes had just arrived from the tailor's and, looking at himself in the mirror, he found his appearance flawless. The tie—quiet and admirable. The trousers—perfect. The gleaming black boots—just right. In the matter of dress, he was a man with a position to keep up. Younger men looked to him for guidance. Today, he felt, he would not fail them.

Finally, he was due at half-past one for luncheon at the house of Lord Knubble of Knopp in Grosvenor Square, and he knew that he could count on meeting there all that was best and fairest of England's aristocracy.

His anticipations were more than fulfilled. Except for a lout of a baronet who had managed to slip in somehow, there was nobody beside himself present at the luncheon table below the rank of Viscount: and, to complete his happiness, he found himself seated next to Lady Chloe Downblotton, the beautiful daughter of the seventh Earl of Choole, for whom he had long entertained a paternal and respectful fondness. And so capitally did they get on during the meal that, when the party broke up, she suggested that, if he were going in her direction, which was to the Achilles statue in the Park, they might stroll together.

"The fact is," said Lady Chloe, as they walked down Park Lane, "I feel I must confide in somebody. I've just got engaged."

"Engaged! Dear lady," breathed Cedric reverently, "I wish you every happiness. But I have seen no announcement in the *Morning Post*."

"No. And I shouldn't think the betting is more than fifteen to four that you ever will. It all depends on how the good old seventh Earl reacts when I bring Claude home this afternoon and lay him on the mat. I love Claude," sighed Lady Chloe, "with a passion too intense for words, but I'm quite aware that he isn't everybody's money. You see, he's an artist and, left to himself, he dresses more like a tramp cyclist than anything else on earth. Still, I'm hoping for the best. I dragged him off to Cohen Bros. yesterday and made him buy morning-clothes and a top hat. Thank goodness, he looked positively respectable, so . . ."

Her voice died away in a strangled rattle. They had entered the Park and were drawing near to the Achilles statue, and coming towards them, his top hat raised in a debonair manner, was a young man of pleasing appearance, correctly clad in morning-coat, grey tie, stiff collar, and an unimpeachable pair of sponge-bag trousers, nicely creased from north to south.

But he was, alas, not one hundred per cent correct. From neck to ankles beyond criticism, below that he went all to pieces. What had caused Lady Chloe to lose the thread of her remarks and Cedric Mulliner to utter a horrified moan was the fact that this young man was wearing bright yellow shoes.

"Claude!" Lady Chloe covered her eyes with a shaking hand. "Ye gods!" she cried. "The foot-joy! The banana specials! The yellow perils! Why? For what reason?"

The young man seemed taken aback.

"Don't you like them?" he said. "I thought they were rather natty. Just what the rig-out needed, in my opinion, a touch of colour. It seemed to me to help the composition."

"They're awful. Tell him how awful they are, Mr. Mulliner."

"Tan shoes are not worn with morning-clothes," said Cedric in a low, grave voice. He was deeply shaken.

"Why not?"

"Never mind why not," said Lady Chloe. "They aren't. Look at Mr. Mulliner's."

The young man did so.

"Tame," he said. "Colourless. Lacking in spirit and that indefinable something. I don't like them."

"Well, you've jolly well got to learn to like them," said Lady Chloe, "because you're going to change with Mr. Mulliner this very minute."

A shrill, bat-like, middle-aged bachelor squeak forced itself from Cedric's lips. He could hardly believe he had heard correctly.

"Come along, both of you," said Lady Chloe briskly. "You can do it over there behind those chairs. I'm sure you don't mind, Mr. Mulliner, do you?"

Cedric was still shuddering strongly.

"You ask me to put on yellow shoes with morning-clothes?" he whispered, the face beneath his shining silk hat pale and drawn.

"Yes."

"Here? In the Park? At the height of the Season?"

"Yes. Do hurry."

"But. . . ."

"Mr. Mulliner! Surely? To oblige me?"

She was gazing at him with pleading eyes, and from the confused welter of Cedric's thoughts there emerged, clear and crystal-like, the recollection of the all-important fact that this girl was the daughter of an Earl and related on her mother's side not only to the Somersetshire Meophams, but to the Brashmarleys of Bucks, the Widringtons of Wilts, and the Hilsbury-Hepworths of Hants. Could he refuse any request, however monstrous, proceeding from one so extremely well-connected?

He stood palsied. All his life he had prided himself on the unassailable ortho-doxy of his costume. As a young man he had never gone in for bright ties. His rigidity in the matter of turned-up trousers was a byword. And, though the fashion had been set by an Exalted Personage, he had always stood out against even such a venial lapse as the wearing of a white waistcoat with a dinner-jacket. How little this girl knew the magnitude of the thing she was asking of him. He blinked. His eyes watered and his ears twitched. Hyde Park seemed to whirl about him.

And then, like a voice from afar, something seemed to whisper in his ear that this girl's second cousin, Adelaide, had married Lord Slythe and Sayle and that among the branches of the family were the Sussex Booles and the .ffrench-ffarmiloes—not the Kent ffrench-ffarmiloes but the Dorsetshire lot. It just turned the scale.

"So be it!" said Cedric Mulliner.

For a few moments after he found himself alone, my cousin Cedric had all the appearance of a man at a loss for his next move. He stood rooted to the spot, staring spellbound at the saffron horrors which had blossomed on his hitherto blameless feet. Then, pulling himself together with a strong effort, he slunk to Hyde Park Corner, stopped a passing cab, and, having directed the driver to take him to the Albany, leaped hastily in.

The relief of being under cover was at first so exquisite that his mind had no room for other thoughts. Soon, he told himself, he would be safe in his cosy apartment, with the choice of thirty-seven pairs of black boots to take the place of these ghastly objects. It was only when the cab reached the Albany that he realised the difficulties which lay in his path.

How could he walk through the lobby of the Albany looking like a ship with yellow fever on board—he, Cedric Mulliner, the man whose advice on the niceties of dress had frequently been sought by young men in the Brigade of Guards and once by the second son of a Marquis? The thing was inconceivable. All his better nature recoiled from it. Then what to do?

It is characteristic of the Mulliners as a family that, however sore the straits in which they find themselves, they never wholly lose their presence of mind. Cedric leaned out of the window and addressed the driver of the cab.

"My man," he said, "how much do you want for your boots?"

The driver was not one of London's lightning thinkers. For a full minute he sat, looking like a red-nosed sheep, allowing the idea to penetrate.

"My boots?" he said at length.

"Your boots!"

"How much do I want for my boots?"

"Precisely. I am anxious to obtain your boots. How much for the boots?"

"How much for the boots?"

"Exactly. The boots. How much for them?"

"You want to buy my boots?"

"Precisely."

"Ah," said the driver, "but the whole thing is, you see, it's like this. I'm not wearing any boots. I suffer from corns, so I come out in a tennis shoe and a carpet slipper. I could do you them at ten bob the pair."

Cedric Mulliner sank dumbly back. The disappointment had been numbing. But the old Mulliner resourcefulness stood him in good stead. A moment later, his head was out of the window again.

"Take me," he said, "to Seven, Nasturtium Villas, Marigold Road, Valley Fields."

The driver thought this over for a while.

"Why?" he said.

"Never mind why."

"The Albany you told me," said the driver. "Take me to the Albany was what you said. And this here is the Albany. Ask anyone."

"Yes, yes, yes. But I now wish to go to Seven, Nasturtium Villas. . . ."

"How do you spell it?"

"One 'n'. Seven, Nasturtium Villas, Marigold Road. . . ."

"How do you spell *that*?"

"One 'g'."

"And it's in Valley Fields, you say?"

"Precisely."

"One 'v'?"

"One 'v' and one 'f'," said Cedric.

The driver sat silent for a while. The spelling-bee over, he seemed to be marshalling his thoughts.

"Now I'm beginning to get the whole thing," he said. "What you want to do is go to Seven, Nasturtium Villas, Marigold Road, Valley Fields."

"Precisely."

"Well, will you have the tennis-shoe and the carpet-slipper now, or wait till we get there?"

"I do not desire the tennis shoe. I have no wish for the carpet slipper. I am not in the market for them."

"I could do you them at half-a-crown apiece."

"No, thank you."

"Couple of bob, then."

"No, no, no. I do not want the tennis shoe. The carpet slipper makes no appeal to me."

"You don't want the shoe?"

"No."

"And you don't want the slipper?"

"No."

"But you do want," said the driver, assembling the facts and arranging them in an ordinary manner, "to go to Seven, Nasturtium Villas, Marigold Road, Valley Fields?"

"Precisely."

"Ah," said the driver, slipping in his clutch with an air of quiet rebuke. "Now we've got the thing straight. If you'd only told me that in the first place, we'd have been 'arf-way there by now."

The urge which had come upon Cedric Mulliner to visit Seven, Nasturtium Villas, Marigold Road, Valley Fields, that picturesque suburb in the south-eastern postal division of London, had been due to no idle whim. Nor was it prompted by a mere passion for travel and sightseeing. It was at that address that his secretary, Miss Myrtle Watling, lived: and the plan which Cedric had now formed was, in his opinion, the best to date. What he proposed to do was to seek out Miss Watling, give her his latch-key, and dispatch her to the Albany in the cab to fetch him one of his thirty-seven pairs of black boots. When she returned with them he could put them on and look the world in the face again.

He could see no flaw in the scheme, nor did any present itself during the long ride to Valley Fields. It was only when the cab had stopped outside the front garden of the neat little red-brick house and he had alighted and told the driver to wait ("Wait?" said the driver. "How do you mean, wait? Oh, you mean wait?") that doubts began to disturb him. Even as he raised his finger to press the door-bell, there crept over him a chilly feeling of mistrust, and he drew the finger back as sharply as if he had found it on the point of prodding a Dowager Duchess in the ribs.

Could he meet Miss Watling in morning-clothes and yellow shoes? Reluctantly he told himself that he could not. He remembered how often she had taken down at his dictation letters to *The Times* deploring modern laxity on matters of dress: and his brain reeled at the thought of how she would look if she saw him now. Those raised brows . . . those scornful lips . . . those clear, calm eyes registering disgust through their windshields. . . .

No, he could not face Miss Watling.

A sort of dull resignation came over Cedric Mulliner. It was useless, he saw, to struggle any longer. He was on the point of moving from the door and going back to the cab and embarking on the laborious task of explaining to the driver that he wished to return to the Albany ("But I took you there once, and you didn't like it," he could hear the man saying) when from somewhere close at hand there came to his ears a sudden, loud, gurgling noise, rather like that which might have proceeded from a pig suffocating in a vat of glue. It was the sound of someone snoring. He turned, and was aware of an open window at his elbow.

The afternoon, I should have mentioned before, was oppressively warm. It was the sort of afternoon when suburban householders, after keeping body and soul together with roast beef, Yorkshire pudding, mealy potatoes, apple tart, cheddar cheese and bottled beer, retire into sitting-rooms and take refreshing naps. Such a householder, enjoying such a nap, was the conspicuous feature of the room into which my cousin Cedric was now peering. He was a large, stout man, and he lay in an armchair with a handkerchief over his face and his feet on another chair. And those feet, Cedric saw, were clad merely in a pair of mauve socks. His boots lay beside him on the carpet.

With a sudden thrill as sharp as if he had backed into a hot radiator in his bathroom, Cedric perceived that they were black boots.

The next moment, as if impelled by some irresistible force, Cedric Mulliner had shot silently through the window and was crawling on all fours along the floor. His teeth were clenched, and his eyes gleamed with a strange light. If he had not been wearing a top hat, he would have been an almost exact replica of the hunting-cheetah of the Indian jungle stalking its prey.

Cedric crept stealthily on. For a man who had never done this sort of thing before, he showed astonishing proficiency and technique. Indeed, had the cheetah which he so closely resembled chanced to be present, it could undoubtedly have picked up a hint or two which it would have found useful in its business. Inch by inch he moved silently forward, and now his itching fingers were hovering over the nearer of the two boots. At this moment, however, the drowsy stillness of the summer afternoon was shattered by what sounded to his strained senses like G. K. Chesterton falling on a sheet of tin. It was, as a matter of fact, only his hat dropping to the floor, but in the highly nervous state of mind into which he had been plunged by recent events it nearly deafened him. With one noiseless, agile spring, remarkable in one of his waist-measurement, he dived for shelter behind the armchair.

A long moment passed. At first he thought that all was well. The sleeper had apparently not wakened. Then there was a gurgle, a heavy body sat up, and a large hand passed within an inch of Cedric's head and pressed the bell in the wall. And presently the door opened and a parlourmaid entered.

"Jane," said the man in the chair.

"Sir?"

"Something woke me up."

"Yes, sir?"

"I got the impression . . . Jane!"

"Sir?"

"What is that top-hat doing on the floor?"

"Top-hat, sir?"

"Yes, top-hat. This is a nice thing," said the man, speaking querulously. "I compose myself for a refreshing sleep, and almost before I can close my eyes the room becomes full of top-hats. I come in here for a quiet rest, and without the slightest warning I find myself knee-deep in top-hats. Why the top-hat, Jane? I demand a categorical answer."

"Perhaps Miss Myrtle put it there, sir."

"Why would Miss Myrtle strew top-hats about the place?"

"Yes, sir."

"What do you mean, Yes, sir?"

"No, sir."

"Very well. Another time, think before you speak. Remove the hat, Jane, and see to it that I am not disturbed again. It is imperative that I get my afternoon's rest."

"Miss Myrtle said that you were to weed the front garden, sir."

"I am aware of the fact, Jane," said the man with dignity. "In due course I shall proceed to the front garden and start weeding. But first I must have my afternoon's rest. This is a Sunday in June. The birds are sleeping in the trees. Master Willie is sleeping in his room, as ordered by the doctor. I, too, intend to sleep. Leave me, Jane, taking the top-hat with you."

The door closed. The man sank back in his chair with a satisfied grunt, and presently he had begun to snore again.

Cedric did not act hastily. Bitter experience was teaching him the caution which Boy Scouts learn in the cradle. For perhaps a quarter of an hour he remained where he was, crouching in his hiding place. Then the snoring rose to a crescendo. It had now become like something out of Wagner, and it seemed to Cedric that the moment had arrived when action could safely be taken. He removed his left boot and, creeping softly from his lair, seized one of the black boots and put it on. It was a nice fit, and for the first time something approaching contentment began to steal upon him. A minute more, one little minute, and all would be well.

This heartening thought had just crossed his mind when with an abruptness which caused his heart to loosen one of his front teeth the silence was again broken —this time by something that sounded like the Grand Fleet putting in a bit of gunnery-practice off the Nore. An instant later, he was back, quivering, in his niche behind the chair.

The sleeper sat up with a jerk.

"Save the women and children," he said.

Then the hand came out and pressed the bell again.

"Jane!"

"Sir?"

"Jane, that beastly window-sash has got loose again. I never saw anything like the sashes in this house. A fly settles on them and down they come. Prop it up with a book or something."

"Yes sir,"

"And I'll tell you one thing, Jane, and you can quote me as having said so. Next time I want a quiet afternoon's rest, I shall go to a boiler-factory."

The parlour-maid withdrew. The man heaved a sigh, and lowered himself into the chair again. And presently the room was echoing once more with the Ride of the Valkyries.

It was shortly after this that the bumps began on the ceiling.

They were good, hearty bumps. It sounded to Cedric as if a number of people with large feet were dancing Morris dances in the room above, and he chafed at the selfishness which could lead them to indulge in their pleasures at such a time. Already the man in the chair had begun to stir; and now he sat up and reached for the bell with the old familiar movement.

"Jane!"

"Sir?"

"Listen!"

"Yes, sir."

"What is it?"

"It is Master Willie, I think, sir, taking his Sunday sleep."

The man heaved himself out of the chair. It was plain that his emotions were too deep for speech. He yawned cavernously, and began to put on his boots.

"Jane!"

"Sir?"

"I have had enough of this. I shall now go and weed the front garden. Where is my hoe?"

"In the hall, sir."

"Persecution," said the man bitterly. "That's what it is, persecution. Top-hat . . . window-sashes . . . Master Willie. . . . You can argue as much as you like, Jane, but I shall speak out fearlessly. I insist—and the facts support me—that it is persecution. . . . Jane!"

A wordless gurgle proceeded from his lips. He seemed to be choking.

"Jane!"

"Yes, sir?"

"Look me in the face!"

"Yes, sir."

"Now, answer me Jane, and let us have no subterfuge or equivocation. Who turned this boot yellow?"

"Boot, sir?"

"Yes, boot."

"Yellow, sir?"

"Yes, yellow. Look at that boot. Inspect it. Run your eye over it in an unprejudiced spirit. When I took this boot off it was black. I close my eyes for a few brief moments and when I open them it is yellow. I am not a man tamely to submit to this sort of thing. Who did this?"

"Not me, sir."

"Somebody must have done it. Possibly it is the work of a gang. Sinister things are happening in this house. I tell you, Jane, that Seven, Nasturtium Villas has suddenly—on a Sunday, too, which makes it worse—become a house of mystery. I shall be vastly surprised if, before the day is out, clutching hands do not appear through the curtains and dead bodies drop out of the walls. I don't like it, Jane, and I tell you so frankly. Stand out of my way, woman, and let me get at those weeds."

The door banged, and there was peace in the sitting-room. But not in the heart of Cedric Mulliner. All the Mulliners are clear thinkers, and it did not take Cedric long to recognise the fact that his position had changed considerably for the worse. Yes, he had lost ground. He had come into this room with a top-hat and yellow boots. He would go out of it minus a top-hat and wearing one yellow boot and one black one.

A severe set-back.

And now, to complete his discomfiture, his line of communications had been cut. Between him and the cab in which he could find at least temporary safety there stood the man with the hoe. It was a situation to intimidate even a man with a taste for adventure. Douglas Fairbanks would not have liked it. Cedric himself found it intolerable.

There seemed but one course to pursue. This ghastly house presumably posessed a back garden with a door leading out into it. The only thing to do was to flit noiselessly along the passage—if in such a house noiselessness were possible—and find that door and get out into the garden and climb over the wall into the next garden and sneak out into the road and gallop to the cab and so home. He had almost ceased to care what the hall-porter at the Albany would think of him. Perhaps he could pass his appearance off with a light laugh and some story of a bet. Possibly a handsome bribe would close the man's mouth. At any rate, whatever might be the issue, upshot or outcome, back to the Albany he must go, and that with all possible speed. His spirit was broken.

Tiptoeing over the carpet, Cedric opened the door and peeped out. The passage was empty. He crept along it, and had nearly reached its end when he heard the sound of footsteps descending the stairs. There was a door to his left. It was ajar. He leaped through and found himself in a small room through the window of which he looked out on to a pleasant garden. The footsteps passed on and went down the kitchen stairs.

Cedric breathed again. It seemed to him that the danger was past and that he could now embark on the last portion of his perilous journey. The thought of the cab drew him like a magnet. Until this moment he had not been conscious of any marked fondness for the driver of the cab, but now he found himself yearning for his society. He panted for the driver as the hart pants after the water-brooks.

Cautiously, Cedric Mulliner opened the window. He put his head out to examine the terrain before proceeding farther. The sight encouraged him. The drop to the ground below was of the simplest. He had merely to wriggle through, and all would be well.

It was as he was preparing to do this that the window-sash descended on the back of his neck like a guillotine, and he found himself firmly pinned to the sill.

A thoughtful-looking ginger-coloured cat, which had risen from the mat at his entrance and had been scrutinising him with a pale eye, now moved forward and sniffed speculatively at his left ankle. The proceedings seemed to the cat irregular but full of human interest. It sat down and gave itself up to meditation.

Cedric, meanwhile, had done the same. There is, if you come to think of it, little else that a man in his position can do but meditate. And so for some considerable space of time Cedric Mulliner looked down upon the smiling garden and busied himself with his thoughts.

These, as may readily be imagined, were not of the most agreeable. In circumstances such as those in which he had been placed, it is but rarely that the sunny and genial side of a man's mind comes uppermost. He tends to be bitter, and it is inevitable that his rancour should be directed at those whom he considers responsible for his unpleasant situation.

In Cedric's case, there was no difficulty in fixing the responsibility. It was a woman—if one may apply the term to the only daughter of an Earl—who had caused his downfall. Nothing could be more significant of the revolution which circumstances had brought about in Cedric's mind than the fact that, regardless of her high position in Society, he now found himself thinking of Lady Chloe Downblotton in the harshest possible vein.

So moved, indeed, was he that, not content with thoroughly disliking Lady Chloe, he was soon extending his loathing—first to her nearer relations, and finally, incredible as it may seem, to the entire British aristocracy. Twenty-four hours ago—aye even a brief two hours ago—Cedric Mulliner had loved every occupant of Debrett's Peerage, from the premier Dukes right down to the people who scrape in at the bottom of the page under the heading "Collateral Branches", with a respectful fervour which it had seemed that nothing would ever be able to quench. And now there ran riot in his soul something that was little short of Red Republicanism.

Drones, he considered them, and—it might be severe, but he stuck to it—mere popinjays. Yes, mere thriftless popinjays. It so happened that he had never actually seen a popinjay, but he was convinced by some strange instinct that this was what the typical aristocrat of his native country resembled.

"How long?" groaned Cedric. "How long?"

He yearned for the day when the clean flame of Freedom, blazing from Moscow, should scorch these wastrels to a crisp, starting with Lady Chloe Downblotton and then taking the others in order of precedence.

It was at this point in his meditations that his attention was diverted from the Social Revolution by an agonising pain in his right calf.

To the more meditative type of cat there comes at irregular intervals a strange, dreamy urge to stand on its hind legs and sharpen its claws on the nearest perpendicular object. This is usually a tree, but in the present case, there being no tree to hand, the ginger-coloured cat inside the room had made shift with Cedric's right calf. Absently, its mind revolving who knows what abstruse subjects, it blinked once or twice; then, rising, got its claws well into the flesh and pulled them down with a slow, lingering motion.

From Cedric's lips there came a cry like that of some Indian peasant who, wandering on the banks of the Ganges, suddenly finds himself being bitten in half by a crocodile. It rang through the garden like a clarion, and, as the echoes died away, a girl came up the path. The sun glinted on her tortoiseshell-rimmed spectacles, and Cedric recognised his secretary, Miss Myrtle Watling.

"Good afternoon, Mr. Mulliner," said Miss Watling.

She spoke in her usual calm, controlled voice. If she was surprised to see her employer and, seeing him, to behold nothing of him except his head, there was little to show it. A private secretary learns at the outset of their association never to be astonished at anything her employer may do.

Yet Myrtle Watling was not altogether devoid of feminine curiosity.

"What are you doing there, Mr. Mulliner?" she asked.

"Something is biting me in the leg," cried Cedric.

"It is probably Mortal Error," said Miss Watling, who was a Christian Scientist. "Why are you standing there in that rather constrained attitude?"

"The sash came down as I was looking out of the window."

"Why were you looking out of the window?"

"To see how far there was to drop?"

"Why did you wish to drop?"

"I wanted to get away from here."

"Why did you come here?"

It became plain to Cedric that he must tell his story. He was loath to do so, but to refrain meant that Myrtle Watling would stand there till sunset, saying sentences beginning with "Why?" In a husky voice he told her all.

For some moments after he had finished, the girl remained silent. A pensive expression had come into her face.

"What you need," she said, "is someone to look after you."

She paused.

"Well, it's not everybody's job," she said reflectively, "but I don't mind taking it on."

A strange foreboding chilled Cedric.

"What do you mean?" he gasped.

"What you need," said Myrtle Watling, "is a wife. It is a matter which I have been turning over in my mind for some time, and now the thing is quite clear to me. You should be married. I will marry you, Mr. Mulliner."

Cedric uttered a low cry. This, then, was the meaning of that look which during the past few weeks he had happened to note from time to time in his secretary's glass-fringed eyes.

Footsteps sounded on the gravel path. A voice spoke, the voice of the man who had slept in the chair. He was plainly perturbed.

"Myrtle," he said, "I am not a man, as you know, to make a fuss about nothing. I take life as it comes, the rough with the smooth. But I feel it my duty to tell you that eerie influences are at work in this house. The atmosphere has become definitely sinister. Top-hats appear from nowhere. Black boots turn yellow. And now this cabby here, this cab-driver fellow. . . . I didn't get your name. Lanchester? Mr. Lanchester, my daughter Myrtle. . . . And now Mr. Lanchester here tells me that a fare of his entered our front garden some time back and instantly vanished off the face of the earth, and has never been seen again. I am convinced that some little-known Secret Society is at work and that Seven, Nasturtium Villas, is one of those houses you see in the mystery-plays where shrieks are heard from dark corners and mysterious Chinamen flit to and fro making significant gestures and. . . ." He broke off with a sharp howl of dismay, and stood staring. "Good God! What's that?"

"What father?"

"That. That bodiless head. That trunkless face. I give you my honest word that there is a severed head protruding from the side of the house. Come over where I'm standing. You can see it distinctly from here."

"Oh, that?" said Myrtle. "That is my fiancé."

"Your fiancé?"

"My fiancé, Mr. Cedric Mulliner."

"Is that all there is of him?" asked the cabman, surprised.

"There is more inside the house," said Myrtle.

Mr. Watling, his composure somewhat restored, was scrutinising Cedric narrowly.

"Mulliner? You're the fellow my daughter works for, aren't you?"

"I am," said Cedric.

"And you want to marry her?"

"Certainly he wants to marry me," said Myrtle, before Cedric could reply.

And suddenly something inside Cedric seemed to say "Why not?" It was true that he had never contemplated matrimony, except with that shrinking horror which all middle-aged bachelors feel when the thought of it comes into their minds in moments of depression. It was true, also, that if he had been asked to submit specifications for a bride, he would have sketched out something differing from Myrtle Watling in not a few respects. But, after all, he felt as he looked at her strong, capable face, with a wife like this girl he would at least be shielded and sheltered from the world, and never again exposed to the sort of thing he had been going through that afternoon. It seemed good enough.

And there was another thing. And to a man of Cedric's strong Republican views it was perhaps the most important of all. Whatever you might say against Myrtle Watling, she was not a member of the gay and heartless aristocracy. No Sussex Booles, no Hants Hilsbury-Hepworths in *her* family. She came of good, solid surburban stock, related on the male side to the Higginsons of Tangerine Road, Wandsworth, and through the female branch connected with the Browns of Bickley, the Perkinses of Peckham, and the Wodgers—the Winchmore Hill Wodgers, not the Ponder's End lot.

"It is my dearest wish," said Cedric in a low, steady voice. "And if somebody will kindly lift this window off my neck and kick this beastly cat or something which keeps clawing my leg, we can all get together and talk it over."

13

THE ORDEAL OF OSBERT MULLINER

THE unwonted gravity of Mr. Mulliner's demeanour had struck us all directly he entered the bar-parlour of the Anglers' Rest: and the silent, moody way in which he sipped his hot Scotch and lemon convinced us that something was wrong. We hastened to make sympathetic inquiries.

Our solicitude seemed to please him. He brightened a little.

"Well, gentlemen," he said, "I had not intended to intrude my private troubles on this happy gathering, but, if you must know, a young second cousin of mine has left his wife and is filing papers of divorce. It has upset me very much."

Miss Postlethwaite, our warm-hearted barmaid, who was polishing glasses, introduced a sort of bedside manner into her task.

"Some viper crept into his home?" she asked.

Mr. Mulliner shook his head.

"No," he said. "No vipers. The whole trouble appears to have been that, whenever my second cousin spoke to his wife, she would open her eyes to their fullest extent, put her head on one side like a canary, and say 'What?' He said he had stood it for eleven months and three days, which he believes to be a European record, and that the time had now come, in his opinion, to take steps."

Mr. Mulliner sighed.

"The fact of the matter is," he said, "marriage today is made much too simple for a man. He finds it so easy to go out and grab some sweet girl that when he has got her he does not value her. I am convinced that that is the real cause of this modern boom in divorce. What marriage needs, to make it a stable institution, is something in the nature of obstacles during the courtship period. I attribute the solid happiness of my nephew Osbert's union, to take but one instance, to the events which preceded it. If the thing had been a walk-over, he would have prized his wife far less highly."

"It took him a long time to teach her his true worth?" we asked.

"Love burgeoned slowly?" hazarded Miss Postlethwaite.

"On the contrary," said Mr. Mulliner, "she loved him at first sight. What made the wooing of Mabel Petherick-Soames so extraordinarily difficult for my nephew Osbert was not any coldness on her part, but the unfortunate mental attitude of J. Bashford Braddock. Does that name suggest anything to you, gentlemen?"

"No."

"You do not think that a man with such a name would be likely to be a toughish sort of egg?"

"He might be, now you mention it."

"He was. In Central Africa, where he spent a good deal of his time exploring, ostriches would bury their heads in the sand at Bashford Braddock's approach and even rhinoceroses, the most ferocious beasts in existence, frequently edged behind trees and hid till he had passed. And the moment he came into Osbert's life my nephew realised with a sickening clearness that those rhinoceroses had known their business."

Until the advent of this man Braddock (said Mr. Mulliner), Fortune seemed to have lavished her favours on my nephew Osbert in full and even overflowing measure. Handsome, like all the Mulliners, he possessed in addition to good looks the inestimable blessings of perfect health, a cheerful disposition, and so much money that Income-Tax assessors screamed with joy when forwarding Schedule D to his address. And, on top of all this, he had fallen deeply in love with a most charming girl and rather fancied that his passion was reciprocated.

For several peaceful, happy weeks all went well. Osbert advanced without a set-back of any description through the various stages of calling, sending flowers, asking after her father's lumbago, and patting her mother's Pomeranian to the point where he was able, with the family's full approval, to invite the girl out alone to dinner and a theatre. And it was on this night of nights, when all should have been joy and happiness, that the Braddock menace took shape.

Until Bashford Braddock made his appearance, no sort of hitch had occurred to mar the perfect tranquillity of the evening's proceedings. The dinner had been excellent, the play entertaining. Twice during the third act Osbert had ventured to squeeze the girl's hand in a warm, though of course gentlemanly, manner: and it seemed to him that the pressure had been returned. It is not surprising, therefore, that by the time they were parting on the steps of her house he had reached the conclusion that he was on to a good thing which should be pushed along.

Putting his fortune to the test, to win or lose it all, Osbert Mulliner reached forward, clasped Mabel Petherick-Soames to his bosom, and gave her a kiss so ardent that in the silent night it sounded like somebody letting off a Mills bomb.

And scarcely had the echoes died away, when he became aware that there was standing at his elbow a tall, broad-shouldered man in evening dress and an opera hat.

There was a pause. The girl was the first to speak.

"Hullo, Bashy," she said, and there was annoyance in her voice. "Where on earth did you spring from? I thought you were exploring on the Congo or somewhere."

The man removed his opera hat, squashed it flat, popped it out again, replaced it on his head and spoke in a deep, rumbling voice.

"I returned from the Congo this morning. I have been dining with your father and mother. They informed me that you had gone to the theatre with this gentleman."

"Mr. Mulliner. My cousin, Bashford Braddock."

"How do you do?" said Osbert.

There was another pause. Bashford Braddock again removed his opera hat, squashed it flat, popped it out and replaced it on his head. He seemed disappointed that he could not play a tune on it.

"Well, good night," said Mabel.

"Good night," said Osbert.

"Good night," said Bashford Braddock.

The door closed, and Osbert, looking from it to his companion, found that the other was staring at him with a peculiar expression in his eyes. They were hard, glittering eyes. Osbert did not like them.

"Mr. Mulliner," said Bashford Braddock.

"Hullo?" said Osbert.

"A word with you. I saw all."

"All?"

"All. Mr. Mulliner, you love that girl."

"I do."

"So do I."

"You do?"

"I do."

Osbert felt a little embarrassed. All he could think of to say was that it made them seem like one great big family.

"I have loved her since she was so high."

"How high?" asked Osbert, for the light was uncertain.

"About so high. And I have always sworn that if ever any man came between us, if ever any slinking, sneaking, pop-eyed, lop-eared son of a sea-cook attempted to rob me of that girl, I would. . . ."

"Er—what?" asked Osbert.

Bashford Braddock laughed a short, metallic laugh.

"Did you ever hear what I did to the King of Mgumbo-Mgumbo?"

"I didn't even know there was a King of Mgumbo-Mgumbo."

"There isn't—now," said Bashford Braddock.

Osbert was conscious of a clammy, creeping sensation in the region of his spine.

"What did you do to him?"

"Don't ask."

"But I want to know."

"Far better not. You will find out quite soon enough if you continue to hang round Mabel Petherick-Soames. That is all, Mr. Mulliner." Bashford Braddock looked up at the twinkling stars. "What delightful weather we are having," he said. "There was just the same quiet hush and peaceful starlight, I recollect, that time out in the Ngobi desert when I strangled the jaguar."

Osbert's Adam's Apple slipped a cog.

"W—what jaguar?"

"Oh, you wouldn't know it. Just one of the jaguars out there. I had a rather tricky five minutes of it at first, because my right arm was in a sling and I could only use my left. Well, good night, Mr. Mulliner, good night."

And Bashford Braddock, having removed his opera hat, squashed it flat, popped it out again and replaced it on his head, stalked off into the darkness.

For several minutes after he had disappeared Osbert Mulliner stood motionless, staring after him with unseeing eyes. Then, tottering round the corner, he made his way to his residence in South Audley Street, and, contriving after three false starts to unlock the front door, climbed the stairs to his cosy library. There, having mixed himself a strong brandy-and-soda, he sat down and gave himself up to meditation: and eventually, after one quick drink and another taken rather slower, was able to marshal his thoughts with a certain measure of coherence. And those thoughts, I regret to say, when marshalled, were of a nature which I shrink from revealing to you.

It is never pleasant, gentlemen, to have to display a relative in an unsympathetic light, but the truth is the truth and must be told. I am compelled, therefore, to confess that my nephew Osbert, forgetting that he was a Mulliner, writhed at this moment in an agony of craven fear.

It would be possible, of course, to find excuses for him. The thing had come upon him very suddenly, and even the stoutest are sometimes disconcerted by sudden peril. Then, again, his circumstances and upbringing had fitted him ill for such a crisis. A man who had been pampered by Fortune from birth becomes highly civilized: and the more highly civilized we are, the less adroitly do we cope with bounders of the Braddock type who seem to belong to an earlier and rougher age. Osbert Mulliner was simply unequal to the task of tackling cavemen. Apart from some slight skill at contract bridge, the only thing he was really good at was collecting old jade, and what a help that would be, he felt as he mixed himself a third brandy-and-soda, in a personal combat with a man who appeared to think it only sporting to give jaguars a chance by fighting them one-handed.

He could see but one way out of the delicate situation in which he had been placed. To give Mabel Petherick-Soames up would break his heart, but it seemed to be a straight issue between that and his neck, and in this black hour the voting in favour of the neck was a positive landslide. Trembling in every limb, my nephew Osbert went to the desk and began to compose a letter of farewell.

He was sorry, he wrote, that he would be unable to see Miss Petherick-Soames on the morrow, as they had planned, owing to his unfortunately being called away to Australia. He added that he was pleased to have made her acquaintance and that if, as seemed probable, they never saw each other again, he would always watch her future career with considerable interest.

Signing the letter. "Yrs. truly, O. Mulliner," Osbert addressed the envelope and, taking it up the street to the post-office, dropped it in the box. Then he returned home and went to bed.

The telephone, ringing by his bedside, woke Osbert at an early hour next morning. He did not answer it. A glance at his watch had told him that the time was half-past eight, when the first delivery of letters is made in London. It seemed only too likely that Mabel, having just received and read his communication, was endeavouring to discuss the matter with him over the wire. He rose, bathed, shaved and dressed, and had just finished a sombre breakfast when the door opened and Parker, his man, announced Major-General Sir Masterman Petherick-Soames.

An icy finger seemed to travel slowly down Osbert's backbone. He cursed the preoccupation which had made him omit to instruct Parker to inform all callers that he was not at home. With some difficulty, for the bones seemed to have been removed from his legs, he rose to receive the tall, upright, grizzled and formidable old man who entered, and rallied himself to play the host.

"Good morning," he said. "Will you have a poached egg?"

"I will not have a poached egg," replied Sir Masterman. "Poached egg, indeed! Poached egg, forsooth! Ha! Tcha! Bah!"

He spoke with such curt brusqueness that a stranger, had one been present, might have supposed him to belong to some league or society for the suppression of poached eggs. Osbert, however, with his special knowledge of the facts, was able to interpret this brusqueness correctly and was not surprised when his visitor, gazing at him keenly with a pair of steely blue eyes which must have got him very much disliked in military circles, plunged at once into the subject of the letter.

"Mr. Mulliner, my niece Mabel has received a strange communication from you."

"Oh, she got it all right?" said Osbert, with an attempt at ease.

"It arrived this morning. You had omitted to stamp it. There was threepence to pay."

"Oh, I say, I'm fearfully sorry. I must. . . ."

Major-General Sir Masterman Petherick-Soames waved down his apologies.

"It is not the monetary loss which has so distressed my niece, but the letter's contents. My niece is under the impression that last night she and you became engaged to be married, Mr. Mulliner."

Osbert coughed.

"Well—er—not exactly. Not altogether. Not, as it were. . . . I mean. . . . You see. . . ."

"I see very clearly. You have been trifling with my niece's affections, Mr. Mulliner. And I have always sworn that if ever a man trifled with the affections of any of my nieces, I would. . . ." He broke off and, taking a lump of sugar from the bowl, balanced it absently on the edge of a slice of toast. "Did you ever hear of a Captain Walkinshaw?"

"No."

"Captain J. G. Walkinshaw? Dark man with an eyeglass. Used to play the saxophone."

"No."

"Ah? I thought you might have met him. He trifled with the affections of my niece Hester. I horsewhipped him on the steps of the Drones Club. Is the name Blenkinsop-Bustard familiar to you?"

"No."

"Rupert Blenkinsop-Bustard trifled with the affections of my niece Gertrude. He was one of the Somersetshire Blenkinsop-Bustards. Wore a fair moustache and kept pigeons. I horsewhipped him on the steps of the Junior Bird-Fanciers. By the way, Mr. Mulliner, what is your club?"

"The United Jade-Collectors," quavered Osbert.

"Has it steps?"

"I—I believe so."

"Good. Good." A dreamy look came into the General's eyes. "Well, the announcement of your engagement to my niece Mabel will appear in tomorrow's *Morning Post*. If it is contradicted. . . . Well, good morning, Mr. Mulliner, good morning."

And, replacing in the dish the piece of bacon which he had been poising on a teaspoon, Major-General Sir Masterman Petherick-Soames left the room.

The meditation to which my nephew Osbert had given himself up on the previous night was as nothing to the meditation to which he gave himself up now. For fully an hour he must have sat, his head supported by his hands, frowning despairingly at the remains of the marmalade on the plate before him. Though, like all the Mulliners, a clear thinker, he had to confess himself completely nonplussed. The situation had become so complicated that after a while he went up to the library and tried to work it out on paper, letting X equal himself. But even this brought no solution, and he was still pondering deeply when Parker came up to announce lunch.

"Lunch?" said Osbert, amazed. "Is it lunch-time already?"

"Yes, sir. And might I be permitted to offer my respectful congratulations and good wishes, sir?"

"Eh?"

"On your engagement, sir. The General happened to mention to me as I let him out that a marriage had been arranged and would shortly take place between yourself and Miss Mabel Petherick-Soames. It was fortunate that he did so, as I was thus enabled to give the gentleman the information he required."

"Gentleman?"

"A Mr. Bashford Braddock, sir. He rang up about an hour after the General had left and said he had been informed of your engagement and wished to know if the news was well-founded. I assured him that it was, and he said he would be calling to see you later. He was very anxious to know when you would be at home. He seemed a nice, friendly gentleman, sir."

Osbert rose as if the chair in which he sat had suddenly become incandescent.

"Parker!"

"Sir?"

"I am unexpectedly obliged to leave London, Parker. I don't know where I am going—probably the Zambesi or Greenland—but I shall be away a long time. I shall close the house and give the staff an indefinite holiday. They will receive three months' wages in advance, and at the end of that period will communicate with my lawyers, Messrs. Peabody, Thrupp, Thrupp, Thrupp, Thrupp and Peabody of Lincoln's Inn. Inform them of this."

"Very good, sir."

"And, Parker."

"Sir?"

"I am thinking of appearing shortly in some amateur theatricals. Kindly step round the corner and get me a false wig, a false nose, some false whiskers and a good stout pair of blue spectacles."

Osbert's plans when, after a cautious glance up and down the street, he left the house an hour later and directed a taxi-cab to take him to an obscure hotel in the wildest and least-known part of the Cromwell Road were of the vaguest. It was only when he reached that haven and had thoroughly wigged, nosed, whiskered and blue-spectacled himself that he began to formulate a definite plan of campaign. He spent the rest of the day in his room, and shortly before lunch next morning set out for the Second-Hand Clothing establishment of the Bros. Cohen, near Covent Garden, to purchase a complete traveller's outfit. It was his intention to board the boat sailing on the morrow for India and to potter a while about the world, taking in *en route* Japan, South Africa, Peru, Mexico, China, Venezuela, the Fiji Islands and other beauty-spots.

All the Cohens seemed glad to see him when he arrived at the shop. They clustered about him in a body, as if guessing by instinct that here came one of those big orders. At this excellent emporium one may buy, in addition to second-hand clothing, practically anything that exists: and the difficulty—for the brothers are all thrustful salesmen—is to avoid doing so. At the end of five minutes, Osbert was mildly surprised to find himself in possession of a smoking-cap, three boxes of poker-chips, some polo sticks, a fishing-rod, a concertina, a ukulele, and a bowl of goldfish.

He clicked his tongue in annoyance. These men appeared to him to have got quite a wrong angle on the situation. They seemed to think that he proposed to make his travels one long round of pleasure. As clearly as he was able, he tried to tell them that in the few broken years that remained to him before a shark or jungle-fever put an end to his sorrows he would have little heart for polo, for poker, or for playing the concertina while watching the gambols of goldfish. They might just as well offer him, he said querulously, a cocked hat or just a sewing-machine.

Instant activity prevailed among the brothers.

"Fetch the gentleman his sewing-machine, Isadore."

"And, while you're getting him the cocked hat, Lou," said Irving, "ask the customer in the shoe department if he'll be kind enough to step this way. You're in luck," he assured Osbert. "If you're going travelling in foreign parts, he's the very man to advise you. You've heard of Mr. Braddock?"

There was very little of Osbert's face visible behind his whiskers, but that little paled beneath his tan.

"Mr. B-b-b. . . .?"

"That's right. Mr. Braddock, the explorer."

"Air!" said Osbert. "Give me air!"

He made rapidly for the door, and was about to charge through when it opened to admit a tall, distinguished-looking man of military appearance.

"Shop!" cried the newcomer in a clear, patrician voice, and Osbert reeled back against a pile of trousers. It was Major-General Sir Masterman Petherick-Soames.

A platoon of Cohens advanced upon him, Isadore hastily snatching up a fireman's helmet and Irving a microscope and a couple of jig-saw puzzles. The General waved them aside.

"Do you," he asked, "keep horsewhips?"

"Yes, sir. Plenty of horsewhips."

"I want a nice strong one with a medium-sized handle and lots of spring," said Major-General Sir Masterman Petherick-Soames

And at this moment Lou returned, followed by Bashford Braddock.

"Is this the gentleman?" said Bashford Braddock genially. "You're going abroad, sir, I understand. Delighted if I can be of any service."

"Bless my soul," said Major-General Sir Masterman Petherick-Soames. "Bashford? It's so confoundedly dark in here, I didn't recognize you."

"Switch on the light, Irving," said Isadore.

"No, don't," said Osbert. "My eyes are weak."

"If your eyes are weak you ought not to be going to the Tropics," said Bashford Braddock.

"This gentleman a friend of yours?" asked the General.

"Oh, no. I'm just going to help him to buy an outfit."

"The gentleman's already got a smoking-cap, poker chips, polo sticks, a fishing-rod, a concertina, a ukulele, a bowl of goldfish, a cocked hat and a sewing machine," said Isadore.

"Ah?" said Bashford Braddock. "Then all he will require now is a sun helmet, a pair of puttees, and a pot of ointment for relieving alligator-bites."

With the rapid decision of an explorer who is buying things for which somebody else is going to pay, he completed the selection of Osbert's outfit.

"And what brings you here, Bashford?" asked the General.

"Me? Oh, I looked in to buy a pair of spiked boots. I want to trample on a snake."

"An odd coincidence. I came here to buy a horsewhip to horsewhip a snake."

"A bad week-end for snakes," said Bashford Braddock.

The General nodded gravely.

"Of course, my snake," he said, "may prove not to be a snake. In classifying him as a snake I may have misjudged him. In that case I shall not require this horsewhip. Still, they're always useful to have about the house."

"Undoubtedly. Lunch with me, General?"

"Delighted, my dear fellow."

"Goodbye, sir," said Bashford Braddock, giving Osbert a friendly nod. "Glad I was able to be of some use. When do you sail?"

"Gentleman's sailing tomorrow morning on the *Rajputana*," said Isadore.

"What!" cried Major-General Sir Masterman Petherick-Soames. "Bless my soul! I didn't realize you were going to *India*. I was out there for years and can give you all sorts of useful hints. The old *Rajputana*? Why, I know the purser well. I'll come and see you off and have a chat with him. No doubt I shall be able to get you a number of little extra attentions. No, no, my dear fellow, don't thank me. I have a good deal on my mind at the moment, and it will be a relief to do somebody a kindness."

It seemed to Osbert, as he crawled back to the shelter of his Cromwell Road bedroom, that Fate was being altogether too rough with him. Obviously, if Sir Masterman Petherick-Soames intended to come down to the boat to see him off, it would be madness to attempt to sail. On the deck of a liner under the noonday sun the General must inevitably penetrate his disguise. His whole scheme of escape must be cancelled and another substituted. Osbert ordered two pots of black coffee, tied a wet handkerchief round his forehead, and plunged once more into thought.

It has been frequently said of the Mulliners that you may perplex but you cannot baffle them. It was getting on for dinner-time before Osbert finally decided upon a plan of action: but this plan, he perceived as he examined it, was far superior to the first one.

He had been wrong, he saw, in thinking of flying to foreign climes. For one who desired as fervently as he did never to see Major-General Sir Masterman

Petherick-Soames again in this world, the only real refuge was a London suburb. Any momentary whim might lead Sir Masterman to pack a suitcase and take the next boat to the Far East, but nothing would ever cause him to take a tram for Dulwich, Cricklewood, Winchmore Hill, Brixton, Balham or Surbiton. In those trackless wastes Osbert would be safe.

Osbert decided to wait till late at night; then go back to his house in South Audley Street, pack his collection of old jade and a few other necessaries, and vanish into the unknown.

It was getting on for midnight when, creeping warily to the familiar steps, he inserted his latchkey in the familiar key-hole. He had feared that Bashford Braddock might be watching the house, but there were no signs of him. He slipped swiftly into the dark hall and closed the front door softly behind him.

It was at this moment that he became aware that from under the door of the dining-room at the other end of the hall there was stealing a thin stream of light.

For an instant, this evidence that the house was not, as he had supposed, unoccupied startled Osbert considerably. Then, recovering himself, he understood what must have happened. Parker, his man, instead of leaving as he had been told to do, was taking advantage of his employer's presumed absence from London to stay on and do some informal entertaining. Osbert, thoroughly incensed, hurried to the dining-room and felt that his suspicion had been confirmed. On the table were set out all the materials, except food and drink, of a cosy little supper for two. The absence of food and drink was accounted for, no doubt, by the fact that Parker and—Osbert saw only too good reason to fear—his lady-friend were down in the larder, fetching them.

Osbert boiled from his false wig to the soles of his feet with a passionate fury. So this was the sort of thing that went on the moment his back was turned, was it? There were heavy curtains hiding the window, and behind these he crept. It was his intention to permit the feast to begin and then, stepping forth like some avenging Nemesis, to confront his erring man-servant and put it across him in no un-certain manner. Bashford Braddock and Major-General Sir Masterman Petherick-Soames, with their towering statue and whipcord muscles, might intimidate him, but with a shrimp like Parker he felt that he could do himself justice. Osbert had been through much in the last forty-eight hours, and unpleasantness with a man who, like Parker, stood a mere five feet five in his socks appeared to him rather in the nature of a tonic.

He had not been waiting long when there came to his ears the sound of foot-steps outside. He softly removed his wig, his nose, his whiskers and his blue spec-tacles. There must be no disguise to soften the shock when Parker found himself confronted. Then, peeping through the curtains, he prepared to spring.

Osbert did not spring. Instead, he shrank back like a more than ordinarily diffident tortoise into its shell, and tried to achieve the maximum of silence by breathing through his ears. For it was no Parker who had entered, no frivolous lady-friend, but a couple of plug-uglies of such outstanding physique that Bashford Braddock might have been the little brother of either of them.

Osbert stood petrified. He had never seen a burglar before, and he wished, now that he was seeing these, that it could have been arranged for him to do so through a telescope. At this close range, they gave him much the same feeling the prophet Daniel must have had on entering the lions' den, before his relations with the animals had been established on their subsequent basis of easy camaraderie. He was thankful that when the breath which he had been holding for some eighty seconds at length forced itself out in a loud gasp, the noise was drowned by the popping of a cork.

It was from a bottle of Osbert's best Bollinger that this cork had been removed. The marauders, he was able to see, were men who believed in doing themselves well. In these days when almost everybody is on some sort of diet it is rarely that one comes across the old-fashioned type of diner who does not worry about balanced meals and calories but just squares his shoulders and goes at it till his eyes bubble. Osbert's two guests plainly belonged to this nearly obsolete species. They were drinking out of tankards and eating three varieties of meat simultaneously, as if no such a thing as a high blood-pressure had ever been invented. A second pop announced the opening of another quart of champagne.

At the outset of the proceedings, there had been little or nothing in the way of supper-table conversation. But now, the first keen edge of his appetite satisfied by about three pounds of ham, beef and mutton, the burglar who sat nearest to Osbert was able to relax. He looked about him approvingly.

"Nice little crib, this, Ernest," he said.

"R!" replied his companion—a man of few words, and those somewhat impeded by cold potatoes and bread.

"Must have been some real swells in here one time and another."

"R!"

"Baronets and such, I wouldn't be surprised."

"R!" said the second burglar, helping himself to more champagne and mixing in a little port, sherry, Italian vermouth, old brandy and green Chartreuse to give it body.

The first burglar looked thoughtful.

"Talking of baronets," he said, "a thing I've often wondered is—well, suppose you're having a dinner, see?"

"R!"

"As it might be in this very room."

"R!"

"Well, would a baronet's sister go in before the daughter of the younger son of a peer? I've often wondered about that."

The second burglar finished his champagne, port, sherry, Italian vermouth, old brandy and green Chartreuse, and mixed himself another.

"Go in?"

"Go in to dinner."

"If she was quicker on her feet, she would," said the second burglar. "She'd get to the door first. Stands to reason."

The first burglar raised his eyebrows.

"Ernest," he said coldly, "you talk like an uneducated son of a what-not. Haven't you never been taught nothing about the rules and manners of good Society?"

The second burglar flushed. It was plain that the rebuke had touched a tender spot. There was a strained silence. The first burglar resumed his meal. The second burglar watched him with a hostile eye. He had the air of a man who is waiting for his chance, and it was not long before he found it.

"Harold," he said.

"Well?" said the first burglar.

"Don't gollup your food, Harold," said the second burglar.

The first burglar started. His eyes gleamed with sudden fury. His armour, like his companion's, had been pierced.

"Who's golluping his food?"

"You are."

"I am?"

"Yes, you."

"Who, me?"

"R!"

"Golluping my food?"

"R! Like a pig or something."

It was evident to Osbert, peeping warily through the curtains, that the generous fluids which these two men had been drinking so lavishly had begun to have their effect. They spoke thickly, and their eyes had become red and swollen.

"I may not know all about baronets' younger sisters," said the burglar Ernest, "but I don't gollup my food like pigs or somehting."

And, as if to drive home the reproach, he picked up the leg of mutton and began to gnaw it with an affected daintiness.

The next moment the battle had been joined. The spectacle of the other's priggish object-lesson was too much for the burglar Harold. He plainly resented tuition in the amenities from one on whom he had always looked as a social inferior. With a swift movement of the hand he grasped the bottle before him and bounced it smartly on his colleague's head.

Osbert Mulliner cowered behind the curtain. The sportsman in him whispered that he was missing something good, for ring-seats to view which many men would have paid large sums, but he could not nerve himself to look out. However, there was plenty of interest in the thing, even if you merely listened. The bumps and crashes seemed to indicate that the two principals were hitting one another with virtually everything in the room except the wall-paper and the large sideboard. Now they appeared to be grappling on the floor, anon fighting at long range with bottles. Words and combinations of whose existence he had till then been unaware floated to Osbert's ears: and more and more he asked himself, as the combat proceeded: What would the harvest be?

And then, with one titanic crash, the battle ceased as suddenly as it had begun.

It was some moments before Osbert Mulliner could bring himself to peep from behind the curtains. When he did so, he seemed to be gazing upon one of those Orgy scenes which have done so much to popularise the motion-pictures. Scenically, the thing was perfect. All that was needed to complete the resemblance was a few attractive-looking girls with hardly any clothes on.

He came out and gaped down at the ruins. The burglar Harold was lying with his head in the fireplace: the burglar Ernest was doubled up under the table: and it seemed to Osbert almost absurd to think that these were the same hearty fellows who had come into the room to take pot-luck so short a while before. Harold had the appearance of a man who has been passed through a wringer. Ernest gave the illusion of having recently become entangled in some powerful machinery. If, as was probable, they were known to the police, it would take a singularly keen-eyed contable to recognise them now.

The thought of the police reminded Osbert of his duty as a citizen. He went to the telephone and called up the nearest station and was informed that representatives of the Law would be round immediately to scoop up the remains. He went back to the dining-room to wait, but its atmosphere jarred upon him. He felt the need of fresh air: and, going to the front door, he opened it and stood upon the steps, breathing deeply.

And, as he stood there, a form loomed through the darkness and a heavy hand fell on his arm.

"Mr. Mulliner, I think? Mr. Mulliner, if I mistake not? Good evening, Mr. Mulliner," said the voice of Bashford Braddock. "A word with you, Mr. Mulliner."

Osbert returned his gaze without flinching. He was conscious of a strange, almost uncanny calm. The fact was that, everything in this world being relative, he was regarding Bashford Braddock at this moment as rather an undersized little pipsqueak, and wondering why he had ever worried about the man. To one who had come so recently from the society of Harold and Ernest, Bashford Braddock seemed like one of Singer's Midgets.

"Ah, Braddock?" said Osbert.

At this moment, with a grinding of brakes, a van stopped before the door and policemen began to emerge.

"Mr. Mulliner?" asked the sergeant.

Osbert greeted him affably.

"Come in," he said. "Come in. Go straight through. You will find them in the dining-room. I'm afraid I had to handle them a little roughly. You had better 'phone for a doctor."

"Bad are they?"

"A little the worse for wear."

"Well, they asked for it," said the sergeant.

"Exactly, sergeant," said Osbert. "*Rem acu tetigisti.*"

Bashford Braddock had been standing listening to this exchange of remarks with a somewhat perplexed air.

"What's all this?" he said.

Osbert came out of his thoughts with a start.

"You still here, my dear chap?"

"I am."

"Want to see me about anything, dear boy? Something on your mind?"

"I just want a quiet five minutes alone with you, Mr. Mulliner."

"Certainly, my dear old fellow," said Osbert. "Certainly, certainly, certainly. Just wait till these policemen have gone and I will be at your disposal. We have had a little burglary."

"Burg—" Bashford Braddock was beginning, when there came out on to the steps a couple of policemen. They were supporting the burglar Harold, and were followed by others assisting the burglar Ernest. The sergeant, coming last, shook his head at Osbert a little gravely.

"You ought to be careful, sir," he said. "I don't say these fellows didn't deserve all you gave them, but you want to watch yourself. One of these days . . ."

"Perhaps I did overdo it a little," admitted Osbert. "But I am rather apt to see red on these occasions. One's fighting blood, you know. Well, goodnight, Sergeant, good night. And now," he said, taking Bashford Braddock's arm in a genial grip, "what was it you wanted to talk to me about? Come into the house. We shall be all alone there. I gave the staff a holiday. There won't be a soul except ourselves."

Bashford Braddock released his arm. He seemed embarrassed. His face, as the light of the street lamp shone upon it, was strangely pale.

"Did you——" He gulped a little. "Was that really you?"

"Really me? Oh, you mean those two fellows. Oh, yes, I found them in my dining-room, eating my food and drinking my wine as cool as you please, and naturally I set about them. But the sergeant was quite right. I *do* get too rough when I lose my temper. I must remember," he said, taking out his handkerchief and tying a knot in it, "to cure myself of that. The fact is, I sometimes don't know my own strength. But you haven't told me what it is you want to see me about?"

Bashford Braddock swallowed twice in quick succession. He edged past Osbert to the foot of the steps. He seemed oddly uneasy. His face had now taken on a greenish tinge.

"Oh, nothing, nothing."

"But, my dear fellow," protested Osbert, "it must have been something important to bring you round at this time of night."

Bashford Braddock gulped.

"Well, it was like this. I—er—saw the announcement of your engagement in the paper this morning, and I thought—I—er—just thought I would look in and ask you what you would like for a wedding-present."

"My dear chap! Much too kind of you."

"So—er—so silly if I gave a fish-slice and found that everybody else had given fish-slices."

"That's true. Well, why not come inside and talk it over."

"No, I won't come in, thanks. I'd rather not come in. Perhaps you will write and let me know. *Poste Restante*, Bongo on the Congo, will find me. I am returning there immediately."

"Certainly," said Osbert. He looked down at his companion's feet. "My dear old lad, what on earth are you wearing those extraordinary boots for?"

"Corns," said Bashford Braddock.

"Why the spikes?"

"They relieve the pressure on the feet."

"I see, well, good night, Mr. Braddock."

"Good night, Mr. Mulliner."

"Good night," said Osbert.

"Good night," said Bashford Braddock.

14

UNPLEASANTNESS AT BLUDLEIGH COURT

THE poet who was spending the summer at the Anglers' Rest had just begun to read us his new sonnet-sequence when the door of the bar-parlour opened and there entered a young man in gaiters. He came quickly in and ordered beer. In one hand he was carrying a double-barrelled gun, in the other a posy of dead rabbits. These he dropped squashily to the floor: and the poet, stopping in mid-sentence, took one long, earnest look at the remains. Then, wincing painfully, he turned a light green and closed his eyes. It was not until the banging of the door announced the visitor's departure that he came to life again.

Mr. Mulliner regarded him sympathetically over his hot Scotch and lemon.

"You appear upset," he said.

"A little," admitted the poet. "A momentary malaise. It may be a purely personal prejudice, but I confess to preferring rabbits with rather more of their contents inside them."

"Many sensitive souls in your line of business hold similar views," Mr. Mulliner assured him. "My niece Charlotte did."

"It is my temperament," said the poet. "I dislike all dead things—particularly when, as in the case of the above rabbits, they have so obviously, so—shall I say? —blatantly made the Great Change. Give me," he went on, the greenish tinge fading from his face, "life and joy and beauty."

"Just what my niece Charlotte used to say."

"Oddly enough, that thought forms the theme of the second sonnet in my sequence—which, now that the young gentleman with the portable Morgue has left us, I will . . . ."

"My niece Charlotte," said Mr. Mulliner, with quiet firmness, "was one of those gentle, dreamy, wistful girls who take what I have sometimes felt to be a mean advantage of having an ample private income to write Vignettes in Verse for the artistic weeklies. Charlotte's Vignettes in Verse had a wide vogue among the editors of London's higher-browed but less prosperous periodicals. Directly these frugal men realised that she was willing to supply unstinted Vignettes gratis, for the mere pleasure of seeing herself in print, they were all over her. The consequence was that before long she had begun to move freely in the most refined literary circles: and one day, at a little luncheon at the Crushed Pansy (The Restaurant With A Soul), she found herself seated next to a godlike young man at the sight of whom something seemed to go off inside her like a spring."

"Talking of Spring . . ." said the poet.

"Cupid," proceeded Mr. Mulliner, "has always found the family to which I belong a ready mark for his bow. Our hearts are warm, our passions quick. It is not too much to say that my niece Charlotte was in love with this young man before she had finished spearing the first anchovy out of the hors-d'œuvres dish. He was intensely spiritual-looking, with a broad, white forehead and eyes that seemed to Charlotte not so much eyes as a couple of holes punched in the surface of a beautiful soul. He wrote, she learned, Pastels in Prose: and his name, if she had caught it correctly at the moment of their introduction, was Aubrey Trefusis.

Friendship ripens quickly at the Crushed Pansy. The *poulet roti au cresson* had scarcely been distributed before the young man was telling Charlotte his hopes, his fears, and the story of his boyhood. And she was amazed to find that he sprang— not from a long line of artists but from an ordinary, conventional county family of the type that cares for nothing except hunting and shooting.

"You can readily imagine," he said, helping her to Brussels sprouts, "how intensely such an environment jarred upon my unfolding spirit. My family are greatly respected in the neighbourhood, but I personally have always looked upon them as a gang of blood-imbrued plug-uglies. My views on kindness to animals are rigid. My impulse, on encountering a rabbit, is to offer it lettuce. To my family, on the other hand, a rabbit seems incomplete without a deposit of small shot in it. My father, I believe, has cut off more assorted birds in their prime than any other man in the Midlands. A whole morning was spoiled for me last week by the sight of a photograph of him in the *Tatler*, looking rather severely at a dying duck. My elder brother Reginald spreads destruction in every branch of the animal kingdom. And my younger brother Wilfred is, I understand, working his way up to the larger fauna by killing sparrows with an air-gun. Spiritually, one might just as well live in Chicago as at Bludleigh Court."

"Bludleigh Court?" cried Charlotte.

"The moment I was twenty-one and came into a modest but sufficient inheritance, I left the place and went to London to lead the life literary. The family, of course, were appalled. My uncle Francis, I remember, tried to reason with me for hours. Uncle Francis, you see, used to be a famous big-game hunter. They tell me he has shot more gnus than any other man who ever went to Africa. In fact, until recently he virtually never stopped shooting gnus. Now, I hear, he has developed lumbago and is down at Bludleigh treating it with Riggs's Superfine Emulsion and sunbaths."

"But is Bludleigh Court your home?"

"That's right. Bludleigh Court, Lesser Bludleigh, near Goresby-on-the-Ouse, Bedfordshire."

"But Bludleigh Court belongs to Sir Alexander Bassinger."

"My name is really Bassinger. I adopted the pen-name of Trefusis to spare the family's feelings. But how do you come to know of the place?"

"I'm going down there next week for a visit. My mother was an old friend of Lady Bassinger."

Aubrey was astonished. And, being, like all writers of Pastels in Prose, a neat phrase-maker, he said what a small world it was, after all.

"Well, well, well!" he said.

"From what you tell me," said Charlotte, "I'm afraid I shall not enjoy my visit. If there's one thing I loathe, it's anything connected with sport."

"Two minds with but a single thought," said Aubrey. "Look here, I'll tell you what. I haven't been near Bludleigh for years, but if you're going there, why, dash it, I'll come too—aye, even though it means meeting my uncle Francis."

"You will?"

"I certainly will. I don't consider it safe that a girl of your exquisite refinement and sensibility should be dumped down at an abattoir like Bludleigh Court without a kindred spirit to lend her moral stability."

"What do you mean?"

"I'll tell you." His voice was grave. "That house exercises a spell."

"A what?"

"A spell. A ghastly spell that saps the strongest humanitarian principles. Who knows what effect it might have upon you, should you go there without someone like me to stand by you and guide you in your hour of need?"

"What nonsense!"

"Well, all I can tell you is that once, when I was a boy, a high official of Our Dumb Brothers' League of Mercy arrived there lateish on a Friday night, and at two-fifteen on the Saturday afternoon he was the life and soul of an informal party got up for the purpose of drawing one of the local badgers out of an upturned barrel."

Charlotte laughed merrily.

"The spell will not affect me," she said.

"Nor me, of course," said Aubrey. "But all the same, I would prefer to be by your side, if you don't mind."

"Mind, Mr. Bassinger!" breathed Charlotte softly, and was thrilled to note that at the words and the look with which she accompanied them this man to whom—for, as I say, we Mulliners are quick workers—she had already given her heart, quivered violently. It seemed to her that in those soulful eyes of his she had seen the lovelight.

Bludleigh Court, when Charlotte reached it some days later, proved to be a noble old pile of Tudor architecture, situated in rolling parkland and flanked by pleasant gardens leading to a lake with a tree-fringed boathouse. Inside, it was comfortably furnished and decorated throughout with groves of glass cases containing the goggle-eyed remnants of birds and beasts assassinated at one time or another by Sir Alexander Bassinger and his son, Reginald. From every wall there peered down with an air of mild reproach selected portions of the gnus, moose, elks, zebus, antelopes, giraffes, mountain goats and wapiti which had had the misfortune to meet Colonel Sir Francis Pashley-Drake before lumbago spoiled him for the chase. The cemetery also included a few stuffed sparrows, which showed that little Wilfred was doing his bit.

The first two days of her visit Charlotte passed mostly in the society of Colonel Pashley-Drake, the uncle Francis to whom Aubrey had alluded. He seemed to have taken a paternal fancy to her: and, lithely though she dodged down back-stairs and passages, she generally found him breathing heavily at her side. He was a red-faced, almost circular man, with eyes like a prawns, and he spoke to her freely of lumbago, gnus and Aubrey.

"So you're a friend of my young nephew?" he said, snorting twice in a rather unpleasant manner. It was plain that he disapproved of the pastel-artist. "Shouldn't see too much of him, if I were you. Not the sort of fellow I'd like any daughter of mine to get friendly with."

"You are quite wrong," said Charlotte warmly. "You have only to gaze into Mr. Bassinger's eyes to see that his morals are above reproach."

"I never gaze into his eyes," replied Colonel Pashley-Drake. "Don't like his eyes. Wouldn't gaze into them if you paid me. I maintain his whole outlook on life is morbid and unwholesome. I like a man to be a clean, strong, upstanding Englishman who can look his gnu in the face and put an ounce of lead in it."

"Life," said Charlotte coldly, "is not all gnus."

"You imply that there are also wapiti, moose, zebus and mountain-goats?" said Sir Francis. "Well, maybe you're right. All the same, I'd give the fellow a wide berth, if I were you."

"So far from doing so," replied Charlotte proudly, "I am about to go for a stroll with him by the lake at this very moment."

And, turning away with a petulant toss of her head, she moved off to meet Aubrey, who was hurrying towards her across the terrace.

"I am so glad you came, Mr. Bassinger," she said to him as they walked together in the direction of the lake. "I was beginning to find your uncle Francis a little excessive."

Aubrey nodded sympathetically. He had observed her in conversation with his relative and his heart had gone out to her.

"Two minutes of my uncle Francis," he said, "is considered by the best judges a good medium dose for an adult. So you find him trying, eh? I was wondering what impression my family had made on you."

Charlotte was silent for a moment.

"How relative everything is in this world," she said pensively. "When I first met your father, I thought I had never seen anybody more completely loathsome. Then I was introduced to your brother Reginald, and I realised that, after all, your father might have been considerably worse. And, just as I was thinking that Reginald was the furthest point possible, along came your uncle Francis, and Reginald's quiet charm seemed to leap out at me like a beacon on a dark night. Tell me," she said, "has no one ever thought of doing anything about your uncle Francis?"

Aubrey shook his head gently.

"It is pretty generally recognised now that he is beyond the reach of human science. The only thing to do seems to be to let him go on till he eventually runs down."

They sat together on a rustic bench overlooking the water. It was a lovely morning. The sun shone on the little wavelets which the sighing breeze drove gently to the shore. A dreamy stillness had fallen on the world, broken only by the distant sound of Sir Alexander Bassinger murdering magpies, of Reginald Bassinger encouraging dogs to eviscerate a rabbit, of Wilfred busy among the sparrows, and a monotonous droning noise from the upper terrace, which was Colonel Sir Francis Pashley-Drake telling Lady Bassinger what to do with the dead gnu.

Aubrey was the first to break the silence.

"How lovely the world is, Miss Mulliner."

"Yes, isn't it?"

"How softly the breeze caresses yonder water."

"Yes, doesn't it?"

"How fragrant a scent of wild flowers it has."

"Yes, hasn't it?"

They were silent again.

"On such a day," said Aubrey, "the mind seems to turn irresistibly to Love."

"Love?" said Charlotte, her heart beginning to flutter.

"Love," said Aubrey. "Tell me, Miss Mulliner, have you ever thought of Love?"

He took her hand. Her head was bent, and with the toe of her dainty shoe she toyed with a passing snail.

"Life, Miss Mulliner," said Aubrey, "is a Sahara through which we all must pass. We start at the Cairo of the cradle and we travel on to the—er—well, we go travelling on."

"Yes, don't we?" said Charlotte.

"Afar we can see the distant goal . . . ."

"Yes, can't we?"

" . . . and would fain reach it."

"Yes, wouldn't we?"

"But the way is rough and weary. We have to battle through the sand-storms of Destiny, face with what courage we may the howling simooms of Fate. And very unpleasant it all is. But sometimes in the Sahara of Life, if we are fortunate, we come upon the Oasis of Love. That oasis, when I had all but lost hope, I reached at one-fifteen on the afternoon of Tuesday, the twenty-second of last month. There comes a time in the life of every man when he sees Happiness beckoning to him and must grasp it. Miss Mulliner, I have something to ask you which I have been trying to ask ever since the day when we two first met. Miss Mulliner . . . Charlotte . . . Will you be my . . . Gosh! Look at that whacking great rat! Loo-loo-loo-loo-loo-loo-loo-loo!" said Aubrey, changing the subject.

Once, in her childhood, a sportive playmate had secretly withdrawn the chair on which Charlotte Mulliner was preparing to seat herself. Years had passed, but the recollection of the incident remained green in her memory. In frosty weather she could still feel the old wound. And now, as Aubrey Bassinger suddenly behaved in this remarkable manner, she experienced the same sensation again. It was as though something blunt and heavy had hit her on the head at the exact moment when she was slipping on a banana-skin.

She stared round-eyed at Aubrey. He had released her hand, sprung to his feet, and now, armed with her parasol, was beating furiously in the lush grass at the waterside. And every little while his mouth would open, his head would go back, and uncouth sounds would proceed from his slavering jaws.

"Yoicks! Yoicks! Yoicks!" cried Aubrey.

And again,

"Tally-ho! Hard For'ard! Tally-ho!"

Presently the fever seemed to pass. He straightened himself and came back to where she stood.

"It must have got away into a hole or something," he said, removing a bead of perspiration from his forehead with the ferrule of the parasol. "The fact of the matter is, it's silly ever to go out in the country without a good dog. If only I'd had a nice, nippy terrier with me, I might have obtained some solid results. As it is, a fine rat—gone—just like that! Oh, well, that's Life, I suppose."

He paused. "Let me see," he said. "Where was I?"

And then it was as though he waked from a trance. His flushed face paled.

"I say," he stammered, "I'm afraid you must think me most awfully rude."

"Pray do not mention it," said Charlotte coldly.

"Oh, but you must. Dashing off like that."

"Not at all."

"What I was going to say, when I was interrupted, was, will you be my wife?"

"Oh?"

"Yes."

"Well, I won't."

"You won't?"

"No. Never." Charlotte's voice was tense with a scorn which she did not attempt to conceal. "So this is what you were all the time, Mr. Bassinger—a secret sportsman!"

Aubrey quivered from head to foot.

"I'm not! I'm not! It was the hideous spell of this ghastly house that overcame me."

"Pah!"

"What did you say?"

"I said 'Pah'?"

"Why did you say 'Pah'?"

"Because," said Charlotte, with flashing eyes, "I do not believe you. Your story is thin and fishy."

"But it's the truth. It was as if some hypnotic influence had gripped me, forcing me to act against all my higher inclinations. Can't you understand? Would you condemn me for a moment's passing weakness? Do you think," he cried passionately, "that the real Aubrey Bassinger would raise a hand to touch a rat, save in the way of kindness? I love rats, I tell you—love them. I used to keep them as a boy. White ones with pink eyes."

Charlotte shook her head. Her face was cold and hard.

"Goodbye, Mr. Bassinger," she said. "From this instant we meet as strangers."

She turned and was gone. And Aubrey Bassinger, covering his face with his hands, sank on the bench, feeling like a sand-bagged leper.

The mind of Charlotte Mulliner, in the days which followed the painful scene which I have just described, was torn, as you may well imagine, with conflicting emotions. For a time, as was natural, anger predominated. But after a while sadness overcame indignation. She mourned for her lost happiness.

And yet, she asked herself, how else could she have acted? She had worshipped Aubrey Bassinger. She had set him upon a pedestal, looked up to him as a great white soul. She had supposed him one who lived, far above this world's coarseness and grime, on a rarefied plane of his own, thinking beautiful thoughts. Instead of which, it now appeared, he went about the place chasing rats with parasols. What could she have done but spurn him?

That there lurked in the atmosphere of Bludleigh Court a sinister influence that sapped the principles of the most humanitarian and sent them ravening to and fro, seeking for prey, she declined to believe. The theory was pure banana-oil. If such an influence was in operation at Bludleigh, why had it not affected her?

No, if Aubrey Bassinger chased rates with parasols, it could only mean that he was one of Nature's rat-chasers. And to such a one, cost what it might to refuse, she could never confide her heart.

Few things are more embarrassing to a highly-strung girl than to be for any length of time in the same house with a man whose love she has been compelled to decline, and Charlotte would have given much to be able to leave Bludleigh Court. But there was, it seemed, to be a garden-party on the following Tuesday, and Lady Bassinger had urged her so strongly to stay on for it that departure was out of the question.

To fill the leaden moments, she immersed herself in her work. She had a long-standing commission to supply the *Animal-Lovers' Gazette* with a poem for its

Christmas number, and to the task of writing this she proceeded to devote herself. And gradually the ecstasy of literary composition eased her pain.

The days crept by. Old Sir Alexander continued to maltreat magpies. Reginald and the local rabbits fought a never-ceasing battle, they striving to keep up the birthrate, he to reduce it. Colonel Pashley-Drake maundered on about gnus he had met. And Aubrey dragged himself about the house, looking licked to a splinter. Eventually Tuesday came, and with it the garden-party.

Lady Bassinger's annual garden-party was one of the big events of the countryside. By four o'clock all that was bravest and fairest for miles around had assembled on the big lawn. But Charlotte, though she had stayed on specially to be present, was not one of the gay throng. At about the time when the first strawberry was being dipped in its cream, she was up in her room, staring with bewildered eyes at a letter which had arrived by the second post.

The *Animal-Lovers' Gazette* had turned her poem down!

Yes, turned it down flat, in spite of the fact that it had been commissioned and that she was not asking a penny for it. Accompanying the rejected manuscript was a curt note from the editor, in which he said that he feared its tone might offend his readers.

Charlotte was stunned. She was not accustomed to having her efforts rejected. This one, moreover, had seemed to her so particularly good. A hard judge of her own work, she had said to herself, as she licked the envelope, that this time, if never before, she had delivered the goods.

She unfolded the manuscript and re-read it.

It ran as follows:

GOOD GNUS

(A Vignette in Verse)

BY

CHARLOTTE MULLINER

When cares attack and life seems black,
How sweet it is to pot a yak,
   Or puncture hares and grizzly bears,
    And others I could mention:
But in my Animals "Who's Who"
No name stands higher than the Gnu;
   And each new gnu that comes in view
    Receives my prompt attention.

When Afric's sun is sinking low,
And shadows wander to and fro,
   And everywhere there's in the air
   A hush that's deep and solemn;
Then is the time good men and true
With View Halloo pursue the gnu:
   (The safest spot to put your shot
   Is through the spinal column).

To take the creature by surprise
We must adopt some rude disguise,
   Although deceit is never sweet,
   And falsehoods don't attract us:
So, as with gun in hand you wait,
Remember to impersonate
   A tuft of grass, a mountain-pass,
   A kopje or a cactus.

A brief suspense, and then at last
The waiting's o'er, the vigil past:
   A careful aim. A spurt of flame.
   It's done. You've pulled the trigger,
And one more gnu, so fair and frail.
Has handed in its dinner-pail:
   (The females all are rather small,
   The males are somewhat bigger).

Charlotte laid the manuscript down, frowning. She chafed at the imbecility of editors. Less than ever was she able to understand what anyone could find in it to cavil at. Tone likely to offend? What did the man mean about the tone being likely to offend? She had never heard such nonsense in her life. How could the tone possibly offend? It was unexceptionable. The whole poem breathed that clean, wholesome, healthy spirit of Sport which has made England what it is. And the thing was not only lyrically perfect, but educational as well. It told the young reader, anxious to shoot gnus but uncertain of the correct procedure, exactly what he wanted to know.

She bit her lip. Well, if this Animal-Lovers bird didn't know a red-hot contribution when he saw one, she would jolly well find somebody else who did—and quick, too. She . . . .

At this moment, something occurred to distract her thoughts. Down on the terrace below, little Wilfred, complete with airgun, had come into her line of vision. The boy was creeping along in a quiet, purposeful manner, obviously intent on the chase: and it suddenly came over Charlotte Mulliner in a wave that here she had been in this house all this time and never once had thought of borrowing the child's weapon and having a plug at something with it.

The sky was blue. The sun was shining. All Nature seemed to call to her to come out and kill things.

She left the room and ran quickly down the stairs.

And what of Aubrey, meanwhile? Grief having slowed him up on his feet, he had been cornered by his mother and marched off to hand cucumber sandwiches at the garden-party. After a brief spell of servitude, however, he had contrived to escape and was wandering on the terrace, musing mournfully, when he observed his brother Wilfred approaching. And at the same moment Charlotte Mulliner emerged from the house and came hurrying in their direction. In a flash, Aubrey perceived that here was a situation which, shrewdly handled, could be turned greatly to his advantage. Affecting to be unaware of Charlotte's approach, he stopped his brother and eyed the young thug sternly.

"Wilfred," he said, "where are you going with that gun?"

The boy appeared embarrassed.

"Just shooting."

Aubrey took the weapon from him and raised his voice slightly. Out of the corner of his eye he had seen that Charlotte was now well within hearing.

"Shooting, eh?" he said. "Shooting? I see. And have you never been taught, wretched child, that you should be kind to the animals that crave your compassion? Has no one ever told you that he prayeth best who loveth best all things both great and small? For shame, Wilfred, for shame!"

Charlotte had come up, and was standing there, looking at them inquiringly.

"What's all this about?" she asked.

Aubrey started dramatically.

"Miss Mulliner! I was not aware that you were there. All this? Oh, nothing. I found this lad here on his way to shoot sparrows with his airgun, and I am taking the thing from him. It may seem to you a high-handed action on my part. You may consider me hyper-sensitive. You may ask, Why all this fuss about a few birds? But that is Aubrey Bassinger. Aubrey Bassinger will not lightly allow even the merest sparrow to be placed in jeopardy. Tut, Wilfred!" he said. "Tut! Cannot you see now how wrong it is shoot the poor sparrows?"

"But I wasn't going to shoot sparrows," said the boy. "I was going to shoot Uncle Francis while he is having his sun-bath."

"It is also wrong," said Aubrey, after a slight hesitation, "to shoot Uncle Francis while he is having his sun-bath."

Charlotte Mulliner uttered an impatient exclamation. And Aubrey, looking at her, saw that her eyes were glittering with a strange light. She breathed quickly through her delicately-chiselled nose. She seemed feverish, and a medical man would have been concerned about her blood-pressure.

"Why?" she demanded vehemently. "Why is it wrong? Why shouldn't he shoot his Uncle Francis while he is having his sun-bath?"

Aubrey stood for a moment, pondering. Her razor-like feminine intelligence had cut cleanly to the core of the matter. After all, now that she put it like that, why not?

"Think how it would tickle him up."

"True," said Aubrey, nodding. "True."

"And his Uncle Francis is precisely the sort of man who ought to have been shot at with air-guns incessantly for the last thirty years. The moment I met him, I said to myself, 'That man ought to be shot at with air-guns.' "

Aubrey nodded again. Her girlish enthusiasm had begun to infect him.

"There is much in what you say," he admitted.

"Where is he?" asked Charlotte, turning to the boy.

"On the roof of the boathouse."

Charlotte's face clouded.

"H'm!" she said. "That's awkward. How is one to get at him?"

"I remember Uncle Francis telling me once," said Aubrey, "that, when you went shooting tigers, you climbed a tree. There are plenty of trees by the boat-house."

"Admirable!"

For an instant there came to disturb Aubrey's hearty joy in the chase a brief, faint flicker of prudence.

"But. . . . I say. . . . Do you really think. . . . Ought we. . . .?"

Charlotte's eyes flashed scornfully.

"Infirm of purpose," she said. "Give me the air-gun!"

"I was only thinking. . . ."

"Well?"

"I suppose you know he'll have practically nothing on?"

Charlotte Mulliner laughed lightly.

"He can't intimidate *me*," she said. "Come! Let us be going."

Up on the roof of the boathouse, the beneficent ultra-violet rays of the afternoon sun pouring down on his globular surface, Colonel Sir Francis Pashley-Drake lay in that pleasant half-waking, half-dreaming state that accompanies this particular form of lumbago-treatment. His mind flitted lightly from one soothing subject to another. He thought of elks he had shot in Canada, of moufflon he had shot in the Grecian Archipelago, of giraffes he had shot in Nigeria. He was just on the point of thinking of a hippopotamus which he had shot in Egypt, when the train of his meditations was interrupted by a soft popping, sound not far away. He smiled affectionately. So little Wilfred was out with his air-gun, eh?

A thrill of quiet pride passed through Colonel Pashley-Drake. He had trained the lad well, he felt. With a garden-party in progress, with all the opportunities it

offered for quiet gorging, how many boys of Wilfred's age would have neglected
their shooting to hang round the tea-table and stuff themselves with cakes. But
this fine lad. . . .

Ping! There it was again. The boy must be somewhere quite close at hand.
He wished he could be at his side, giving him kindly advice. Wilfred, he felt, was
a young fellow after his own heart. What destruction he would spread among the
really worthwhile animals when he grew up and put aside childish things and
exchanged his air-gun for a Winchester repeater.

Sir Francis Pashley-Drake started. Two inches from where he lay a splinter of
wood had sprung from the boathouse roof. He sat up, feeling a little less
affectionate.

"Wilfred!" There was no reply.

"Be careful, Wilfred, my boy. You nearly. . . ."

A sharp, agonizing twinge caused him to break off abruptly. He sprang to his
feet and began to address the surrounding landscape passionately in one of the
lesser-known dialects of the Congo basin. He no longer thought of Wilfred with
quiet pride. Few things so speedily modify an uncle's love as a nephew's air-gun
bullet in the fleshy part of the leg. Sir Francis Pashley-Drake's plans for this
boy's future had undergone in one brief instant a complete change. He no longer
desired to stand beside him through his formative years, teaching him the secrets
of shikari. All he wanted to do was to get close enough to him to teach him with
the flat of his right hand to be a bit more careful where he pointed his gun.

He was expressing a synopsis of these views in a mixture of Urdu and Cape
Dutch, when the words were swept from his lips by the sight of a woman's face,
peering from the branches of a near-by tree.

Colonel Pashley-Drake reeled where he stood. Like so many out-door men, he
was the soul of modesty. Once, in Bechuanaland, he had left a native witch-dance
in a marked manner because he considered the chief's third supplementary wife
insufficiently clad. An acute consciousness of the sketchiness of his costume overcame him. He blushed brightly.

"My dear young lady . . ." he stammered.

He had got thus far when he perceived that the young woman was aiming at
him something that looked remarkably like an air-gun. Her tongue protruding
thoughtfully from the corner of her mouth, she had closed one eye and with the
other was squinting tensely along the barrel.

Colonel Sir Francis Pashley-Drake did not linger. In all England there was
probably no man more enthusiastic about shooting: but the fascination of shooting
as a sport depends almost wholly on whether you are at the right or wrong end of
the gun. With an agility which no gnu, unless in the very pink of condition, could
have surpassed, he sprang to the side of the roof and leaped off. There was a
clump of reeds not far from the boathouse. He galloped across the turf and dived
into them.

Charlotte descended from her tree. Her expression was petulant. Girls nowadays are spoiled, and only too readily become peevish when baulked of their pleasures.

"I had no idea he was so nippy," she said.

"A quick mover," agreed Aubrey. "I imagine he got that way from dodging rhinoceroses."

"Why can't they make these silly guns with two barrels? A single barrel doesn't give a girl a chance."

Nestling among the reeds, Colonel Sir Francis Pashley-Drake, in spite of the indignation natural to a man in his position, could not help feeling a certain complacency. The old woodcraft of the hunter had stood him, he felt, in good stead. Not many men, he told himself, would have had the initiative and swift intelligence to act so promptly in the face of peril.

He was aware of voices close by.

"What do we do now?" he heard Charlotte Mulliner say.

"We must think," said the voice of his nephew Aubrey.

"He's in there somewhere."

"Yes."

"I hate to see a fine head like that get away," said Charlotte, and her voice was still querulous. "Especially after I winged him. The very next poem I write is going to be an appeal to air-gun manufacturers to use their intelligence, if they have any, and turn out a line with two barrels."

"I shall write a Pastel in Prose on the same subject," agreed Aubrey.

"Well, what shall we do?"

There was a short silence. An insect of unknown species crept up Colonel Pashley-Drake and bit him in the small of the back.

"I'll tell you what," said Aubrey. "I remember Uncle Francis mentioning to me once that when wounded zebus take cover by the reaches of the Lower Zambesi, the sportsman dispatches a native assistant to set fire to. . . ."

Sir Francis Pashley-Drake emitted a hollow groan. It was drowned by Charlotte's cry of delight.

"Why, of course! How clever you are, Mr. Bassinger!"

"Oh no," said Aubrey modestly.

"Have you matches?"

"I have a cigarette-lighter."

"Then would it be bothering you too much to go and set light to those reeds —about there would be a good place—and I'll wait here with the gun."

"I should be charmed."

"I hate to trouble you."

"No trouble, I assure you," said Aubrey. "A pleasure."

Three minutes later the revellers on the lawn were interested to observe a sight rare at the better class of English garden-party. Out of a clump of laurel-bushes that bordered the smoothly mown turf there came charging a stout, pink gentleman of middle age who hopped from side to side as he ran. He was wearing a loin-cloth, and seemed in a hurry. They had just time to recognise in this new-comer their hostess's brother, Colonel Sir Francis Pashley-Drake, when he snatched a cloth from the nearest table, draped it round him, and with a quick leap took refuge behind the portly form of the Bishop of Stortford, who was talking to the local Master of Hounds about the difficulty he had in keeping his vicars off the incense.

Charlotte and Aubrey had paused in the shelter of the laurels. Aubrey, peering through this zareba, clicked his tongue regretfully.

"He's taken cover again," he said. "I'm afraid we shall find it difficult to dig him out of there. He's gone to earth behind a bishop."

Receiving no reply, he turned.

"Miss Mulliner!" he exclaimed. "Charlotte! What is the matter?"

A strange change had come over the girl's beautiful face since he had last gazed at it. The fire had died out of those lovely eyes, leaving them looking like those of a newly awakened somnambulist. She was pale, and the tip of her nose quivered.

"Where am I?" she murmured.

"Bludleigh Manor, Lesser Bludleigh, Goresby-on-the-Ouse, Bedfordshire. Telephone 28 Goresby," said Aubrey quickly.

"Have I been dreaming? Or did I really. . . . Ah, yes, yes!" she moaned, shuddering violently. "It all comes back to me. I shot Sir Francis with the air-gun!"

"You certainly did," said Aubrey, and would have gone on to comment with warm approbation on the skill she had shown, a skill which—in an untrained novice— had struck him as really remarkable. But he checked himself. "Surely," he said, "you are not letting the fact disturb you? It's the sort of thing that might have happened to anyone."

She interrupted him.

"How right you were, Mr. Bassinger, to warn me against the spell of Bludleigh. And how wrong I was to blame you for borrowing my parasol to chase a rat. Can you ever forgive me?"

"Charlotte!"

"Aubrey!"

"Charlotte!"

"Hush!" she said. "Listen."

On the lawn, Sir Francis Pashley-Drake was telling his story to an enthralled audience. The sympathy of the meeting, it was only too plain, was entirely with him. This shooting of a sitting sun-bather had stirred the feelings of his hearers deeply. Indignant exclamations came faintly to the ears of the young couple in the laurels.

"Most irregular!"

"Not done!"

"Scarcely cricket!"

And then, from Sir Alexander Bassinger, a stern "I shall require a full explanation."

Charlotte turned to Aubrey.

"What shall we do?"

"Well," said Aubrey, reflecting, "I don't think we had better just go and join the party and behave as if nothing had happened. The atmosphere doesn't seem right. What I would propose is that we take a short cut through the fields to the station, hook up with the five-fifty express at Goresby, go to London, have a bit of dinner, get married and. . . ."

"Yes, yes," cried Charlotte. "Take me away from this awful house."

"To the ends of the world," said Aubrey fervently. He paused. "Look here," he said suddenly. "If you move over to where I'm standing, you get the old boy plumb spang against the sky-line. You wouldn't care for just one last. . . ."

"No, no!"

"Merely a suggestion," said Aubrey. "Ah well, perhaps you're right. Then let's be shifting."

15

THOSE IN PERIL ON THE TEE

I THINK the two young men in the chess-board knickerbockers were a little surprised when they looked up and perceived Mr. Mulliner brooding over their table like an affable Slave of the Lamp. Absorbed in their conversation, they had not noticed his approach. It was their first visit to the Anglers' Rest, and their first meeting with the Sage of its bar-parlour: and they were not yet aware that to Mr. Mulliner any assemblage of his fellow-men over and above the number of one constitutes an audience.

"Good evening, gentlemen," said Mr. Mulliner. "You have been playing golf, I see."

They said they had.

"You enjoy the game?"

They said they did.

"Perhaps you will allow me to request Miss Postlethwaite, princess of barmaids, to re-fill your glasses?"

They said they would.

"Golf," said Mr. Mulliner, drawing up a chair and sinking smoothly into it, "is a game which I myself have not played for some years. I was always an indifferent performer, and I gradually gave it up for the simpler and more straightforward pastime of fishing. It is a curious fact that, gifted though the Mulliners have been in virtually every branch of life and sport, few of us have ever taken kindly to golf. Indeed, the only member of the family I can think of who attained to any real proficiency with the clubs was the daughter of a distant cousin of mine—one of the Devonshire Mulliners who married a man named Flack. Agnes was the girl's name. Perhaps you have run across her? She is always playing in tournaments and competitions, I believe."

The young men said No, they didn't seem to know the name.

"Ah?" said Mr. Mulliner. "A pity. It would have made the story more interesting to you."

The two young men exchanged glances.

"Story?" said the one in the slightly more prismatic knickerbockers, speaking in a voice that betrayed agitation.

"Story?" said his companion, blenching a little.

"The story," said Mr. Mulliner, "of John Gooch, Frederick Pilcher, Sidney

McMurdo and Agnes Flack."

The first young man said he didn't know it was so late. The second young man said it was extraordinary how time went. They began to talk confusedly about trains.

"The story," repeated Mr. Mulliner, holding them with the effortless ease which makes this sort of thing such child's play to him, "of Agnes Flack, Sidney McMurdo, Frederick Pilcher and John Gooch."

It is an odd thing (said Mr. Mulliner) how often one finds those who practise the Arts are quiet, timid little men, shy in company and unable to express themselves except through the medium of the pencil or the pen. I have noticed it again and again. John Gooch was like that. So was Frederick Pilcher. Gooch was a writer and Pilcher was an artist, and they used to meet a good deal at Agnes Flack's house, where they were constant callers. And every time they met John Gooch would say to himself as he watched Pilcher balancing a cup of tea and smiling his weak, propitiatory smile, "I am fond of Frederick, but his best friend could not deny that he is a pretty dumb brick." And Pilcher, as he saw Gooch sitting on the edge of his chair and fingering his tie, would reflect, "Nice fellow as John is, he is certainly a total loss in mixed society."

Mark you, if ever men had an excuse for being ill at ease in the presence of the opposite sex, these two had. They were both eighteen-handicap men, and Agnes was exuberantly and dynamically scratch. Her physique was an asset to her, especially at the long game. She stood about five feet ten in her stockings, and had shoulders and forearms which would have excited the envious admiration of one of those muscular women on the music-halls, who good-naturedly allow six brothers, three sisters, and a cousin by marriage to pile themselves on her collar-bone while the orchestra plays a long-drawn chord and the audience hurries out to the bar. Her eye resembled the eye of one of the more imperious queens of history: and when she laughed, strong men clutched at their temples to keep the tops of their heads from breaking loose.

Even Sidney McMurdo was as a piece of damp blotting-paper in her presence. And he was a man who weighed two hundred and eleven pounds and had once been a semi-finalist in the Amateur championship. He loved Agnes Flack with an ox-like devotion. And yet—and this will show you what life is—when she laughed, it was nearly always at him. I am told by those in a position to know that, on the occasion when he first proposed to her—on the sixth green—distant rumblings of her mirth were plainly heard in the club-house locker-room, causing two men who were afraid of thunderstorms to scratch their match.

Such, then, was Agnes Flack. Such, also, was Sidney McMurdo. And such were Frederick Pilcher and John Gooch.

Now John Gooch, though, of course, they had exchanged a word from time to time, was in no sense an intimate of Sidney McMurdo. It was consequently a surprise to him when one night, as he sat polishing up the rough draft of a detective story—for his was the talent that found expression largely in blood, shots in the night, and millionaires who are found murdered in locked rooms with no possible means of access except a window forty feet above the ground—the vast bulk of McMurdo lumbered across his threshold and deposited itself in a chair.

The chair creaked. Gooch stared. McMurdo groaned.

"Are you ill?" said John Gooch.

"Ha!" said Sidney McMurdo.

He had been sitting with his face buried in his hands, but now he looked up; and there was a red glare in his eyes which sent a thrill of horror through John Gooch. The visitor reminded him of the Human Gorilla in his novel, *The Mystery of the Severed Ear.*

"For two pins," said Sidney McMurdo, displaying a more mercenary spirit than the Human Gorilla, who had required no cash payment for his crimes, "I would tear you into shreds."

"Me?" said John Gooch, blankly.

"Yes, you. And that fellow Pilcher, too." He rose; and, striding to the mantle-piece, broke off a corner of it and crumbled it in his fingers. "You have stolen her from me."

"Stolen? Whom?"

"My Agnes."

John Gooch stared at him, thoroughly bewildered. The idea of stealing Agnes Flack was rather like the notion of sneaking off with the Albert Hall. He could make nothing of it.

"She is going to marry you."

"What!" cried John Gooch, aghast.

"Either you or Pilcher." McMurdo paused. "Shall I tear you into little strips and tread you into the carpet?" he murmured, meditatively.

"No," said John Gooch. His mind was blurred, but he was clear on that point.

"Why did you come butting in?" groaned Sidney McMurdo, absently taking up the poker and tying it into a lover's knot. "I was getting along splendidly until you two pimples broke out. Slowly but surely I was teaching her to love me, and now it can never be. I have a message for you. From her. I proposed to her for the eleventh time tonight; and when she had finished laughing she told me that she could never marry a mere mass of brawn. She said she wanted brain. And she told me to tell you and the pest Pilcher that she had watched you closely and realised that you both loved her, but were too shy to speak, and that she under-stood and would marry one of you."

"Pilcher is a splendid fellow," said John Gooch. "She must marry Pilcher."

There was a long silence.

"She will, if he wins the match."

"What match?"

"The golf match. She read a story in a magazine the other day where two men played a match at golf to decide which was to win the heroine; and about a week later she read another story in another magazine where two men played a match at golf to decide which was to win the heroine. And a couple of days ago she read three more stories in three more magazines where exactly the same thing happened; and she has decided to accept it as an omen. So you and the hound Pilcher are to play eighteen holes, and the winner marries Agnes."

"The winner?"

"Certainly."

"I should have thought—I forget what I was going to say."

McMurdo eyed him keenly.

"Gooch," he said, "you are not one of those thoughtless butterflies, I hope, who go about breaking girls' hearts?"

"No, no," said John Gooch, learning for the first time that this was what butterflies did.

"You are not one of those men who win a good girl's love and then ride away with a light laugh?"

John Gooch said he certainly was not. He would not dream of laughing, even lightly, at any girl. Besides, he added, he could not ride. He had once had three lessons in the Park, but had not seemed to be able to get the knack.

"So much the better for you," said Sidney McMurdo heavily. "Because, if I thought that, I should know what steps to take. Even now. . . ." He paused, and looked at the poker in a rather yearning sort of way. "No, no," he said, with a sigh, "better not, better not." He flung the thing down with a gesture of resignation. "Better, perhaps, on the whole not." He rose, frowning. "Well, good night, weed," he said. "The match will be played on Friday morning. And may the better—or, rather, the less impossibly foul—man win."

He banged the door, and John Gooch was alone.

But not for long. Scarcely half an hour had passed when the door opened once more to admit Frederick Pilcher. The artist's face was pale, and he was breathing heavily. He sat down, and after a brief interval contrived to summon up a smile. He rose and patted John Gooch on the shoulder.

"John," he said, "I am a man who as a general rule hides his feelings. I mask my affections. But I want to say, straight out, here and now, that I like you, John."

"Yes?" said John Gooch.

Frederick Pilcher patted his other shoulder.

"I like you so much, John, old man, that I can read your thoughts, strive to conceal them though you may. I have been watching you closely of late, John, and I know your secret. You love Agnes Flack."

"I don't!"

"Yes, you do. Ah, John, John," said Frederick Pilcher, with a gentle smile, "why try to deceive an old friend? You love her, John. You love that girl. And I have good news for you, John—tidings of great joy. I happen to know that she will look favourably on your suit. Go in and win, my boy, go in and win. Take my advice and dash round and propose without a moment's delay."

John Gooch shook his head. He, too, smiled a gentle smile.

"Frederick," he said, "this is like you. Noble. That's what I call it. Noble. It's the sort of thing the hero does in act two. But it must not be, Frederick. It must not, shall not be. I also can read a friend's heart, and I know that you, too, love Agnes Flack. And I yield my claim. I am excessively fond of you, Frederick, and I give her up to you. God bless you, old fellow. God, in fact, bless both of you."

"Look here," said Frederick Pilcher, "have you been having a visit from Sidney McMurdo?"

"He did drop in for a minute."

There was a tense pause.

"What I can't understand," said Frederick Pilcher, at length, peevishly, "is why, if you don't love this infernal girl, you kept calling at her house practically every night and sitting goggling at her with obvious devotion."

"It wasn't devotion."

"It looked like it."

"Well, it wasn't. And, if it comes to that, why did you call on her practically every night and goggle just as much as I did?"

"I had a very good reason," said Frederick Pilcher. "I was studying her face. I am planning a series of humorous drawings on the lines of Felix the Cat, and I wanted her as a model. To goggle at a girl in the interests of one's Art, as I did, is a very different thing from goggling wantonly at her, like you."

"Is that so?" said John Gooch. "Well, let me tell you that I wasn't goggling wantonly. I was studying her psychology for a series of stories which I am preparing, entitled *Madeline Monk, Murderess*."

Frederick Pilcher held out his hand.

"I wronged you, John," he said. "However, be that as it may, the point is that we both appear to be up against it very hard. An extraordinarily well-developed man, that fellow McMurdo."

"A mass of muscle."

"And of a violent disposition."

"Dangerously so."

Frederick Pilcher drew out his handkerchief and dabbed at his forehead.

"You don't think, John, that you might ultimately come to love Agnes Flack?"

"I do not."

"Love frequently comes after marriage, I believe."

"So does suicide."

"Then it looks to me," said Frederick Pilcher, "as if one of us was for it. I see no way out of playing that match."

"Nor I."

"The growing tendency on the part of the modern girl to read trashy magazine stories," said Frederick Pilcher severely, "is one that I deplore. I view it with alarm. And I wish to goodness that you authors woudn't write tales about men who play golf matches for the hand of a woman."

"Authors must live," said John Gooch. "How is your game these days, Frederick?"

"Improved, unfortunately. I am putting better."

"I am steadier off the tee." John Gooch laughed bitterly. "When I think of the hours of practice I have put in, little knowing that a thing of this sort was in store for me, I appreciate the irony of life. If I had not bought Sandy McHoot's book last spring I might now be in a position to be beaten five and four."

"Instead of which, you will probably win the match on the twelfth."

John Gooch started.

"You can't be as bad as that!"

"I shall be on Friday."

"You mean to say you aren't going to try?"

"I do."

"You have sunk to such depths that you would deliberately play below your proper form?"

"I have."

"Pilcher," said John Gooch, coldly, "you are a hound, and I never liked you from the start."

You would have thought that, after the conversation which I have just related, no depth of low cunning on the part of Frederick Pilcher would have had the power to surprise John Gooch. And yet, as he saw the other come out of the club-house to join him on the first tee on the Friday morning, I am not exaggerating when I say that he was stunned.

John Gooch had arrived at the links early, wishing to get in a little practice. One of his outstanding defects as a golfer was a pronounced slice; and it seemed to him that, if he drove off a few balls before the match began, he might be able to analyse this slice and see just what was the best stance to take up in order that it might have full scope. He was teeing his third ball when Frederick Pilcher appeared.

"What—what—what——!" gasped John Gooch.

For Frederick Pilcher, discarding the baggy, mustard-coloured plus-fours in which it was his usual custom to infest the links, was dressed in a perfectly-fitting morning-coat, yellow waistcoat, striped trousers, spats, and patent-leather shoes.

He wore a high stiff collar, and on his head was the glossiest top-hat ever seen off the Stock Exchange. He looked intensely uncomfortable; and yet there was on his face a smirk which he made no attempt to conceal.

"What's the matter?" he asked.

"Why are you dressed like that?" John Gooch uttered an exclamation. "I see it all. You think it will put you off your game."

"Some idea of the kind did occur to me," replied Frederick Pilcher, airily.

"You fiend!"

"Tut, tut, John. These are hard words to use to a friend."

"You are no friend of mine."

"A pity," said Frederick Pilcher, "for I was hoping that you would ask me to be your best man at the wedding." He took a club from his bag and swung it. "Amazing what a difference clothes make. You would hardly believe how this coat cramps the shoulders. I feel as if I were a sardine trying to wriggle in its tin."

The world seemed to swim before John Gooch's eyes. Then the mist cleared, and he fixed Frederick Pilcher with a hypnotic gaze.

"You are going to play well," he said, speaking very slowly and distinctly. "You are going to play well. You are going to play well. You——"

"Stop it!" cried Frederick Pilcher.

"You are going to play well. You are going——"

A heavy hand descended on his shoulder. Sidney McMurdo was regarding him with a black scowl.

"We don't want any of your confounded chivalry," said Sidney McMurdo. "This match is going to be played in the strictest spirit of—— What the devil are you dressed like that for?" he demanded, wheeling on Frederick Pilcher.

"I—I have to go into the City immediately after the match," said Pilcher. "I shan't have time to change."

"H'm. Well, it's your own affair. Come along," said Sidney McMurdo, gritting his teeth. "I've been told to referee this match, and I don't want to stay here all day. Toss for the honour, worms."

John Gooch spun a coin. Frederick Pilcher called tails. The coin fell heads up.

"Drive off, reptile," said Sidney McMurdo.

As John Gooch addressed his ball, he was aware of a strange sensation which he could not immediately analyse. It was only when, after waggling two or three times, he started to draw his club back that it flashed upon him that this strange sensation was confidence. For the first time in his life he seemed to have no doubt that the ball, well and truly struck, would travel sweetly down the middle of the fairway. And then the hideous truth dawned on him. His subconscious self had totally misunderstood the purport of his recent remarks and had got the whole thing nicely muddled up.

Much has been written of the subconscious self, and all that has been written goes to show that of all the thick-headed, blundering chumps who take everything they hear literally, it is the worst. Anybody of any intelligence would have realised that when John Gooch said, "You are going to play well," he was speaking to Frederick Pilcher; but his subconscious self had missed the point completely. It had heard John Gooch say, "You are going to play well," and it was seeing that he did so.

The unfortunate man did what he could. Realising what had happened, he tried with a despairing jerk to throw his swing out of gear just as the club came above his shoulder. It was a fatal move. You may recall that when Arnaud Massy won the British Open Championship one of the features of his play was a sort of wiggly twiggle at the top of the swing, which seemed to have the effect of adding yards to his drive. This wiggly twiggle John Gooch, in his effort to wreck his shot, achieved to a nicety. The ball soared over the bunker in which he had hoped to waste at least three strokes; and fell so near the green that it was plain that only a miracle could save him from getting a four.

There was a sardonic smile on Frederick Pilcher's face as he stepped on to the tee. In a few moments he would be one down, and it would not be his fault if he failed to maintain the advantage. He drew back the head of his club. His coat, cut by a fashionable tailor who, like all fashionable tailors, resented it if the clothes he made permitted his customers to breathe, was so tight that he could not get the club-head more than half-way up. He brought it to this point, then brought it down in a lifeless semi-circle.

"Nice!" said Sidney McMurdo, involuntarily. He despised and disliked Frederick Pilcher, but he was a golfer. And a golfer cannot refrain from giving a good shot its meed of praise.

For the ball, instead of trickling down the hill as Frederick Pilcher had expected, was singing through the air like a shell. It fell near John Gooch's ball and, bounding past it, ran on to the green.

The explanation was, of course, simple. Frederick Pilcher was a man who, in his normal golfing costume, habitually over-swung. This fault the tightness of his coat had now rendered impossible. And his other pet failing, the raising of the head, had been checked by the fact that he was wearing a top-hat. It had been Pilcher's intention to jerk his head till his spine cracked; but the unseen influence of generations of ancestors who had devoted the whole of their intellect to the balancing of top-hats on windy days was too much for him.

A minute later the two men had halved the hole in four.

The next hole, the water-hole, they halved in three. The third, long and over the hill, they halved in five.

And it was as they moved to the fourth tee that a sort of madness came upon both Frederick Pilcher and John Gooch simultaneously.

These two, you must remember, were eighteen-handicap men. That is to say, they thought well of themselves if they could get sixes on the first, sevens on the third, and anything from fours to elevens on the second—according to the number of balls they sank in the water. And they had done these three holes in twelve. John Gooch looked at Frederick Pilcher and Frederick Pilcher looked at John Gooch. Their eyes were gleaming, and they breathed a little stertorously through their noses.

"Pretty work," said John Gooch.

"Nice stuff," said Frederick Pilcher.

"Get a move on, blisters," growled Sidney McMurdo.

It was at this point that the madness came upon these two men.

Picture to yourself their position. Each felt that by continuing to play in this form he was running a deadly risk of having to marry Agnes Flack. Each felt that his opponent could not possibly keep up so hot a pace much longer, and the prudent course, therefore, was for himself to ease off a bit before the crash came. And each, though fully aware of all this, felt that he was dashed if he wasn't going to have a stab at doing the round of his life. It might well be that, having started off at such a clip, he would find himself finishing somewhere in the eighties. And that, surely, would compensate for everything.

After all, felt John Gooch, suppose he did marry Agnes Flack, what of it? He had faith in his star, and it seemed to him that she might quite easily get run over by a truck or fall off a cliff during the honeymoon. Besides, with all the facilities for divorce which modern civilisation so beneficently provides, what was there to be afraid of in marriage, even with an Agnes Flack?

Frederick Pilcher's thoughts were equally optimistic. Agnes Flack, he reflected, was undeniably a pot of poison; but so much the better. Just the wife to keep an artist up to the mark. Hitherto he had had a tendency to be a little lazy. He had avoided his studio and loafed about the house. Married to Agnes Flack, his studio would see a lot more of him. He would spend all day in it—probably have a truckle bed put in and never leave it at all. A sensible man, felt Frederick Pilcher, can always make a success of marriage if he goes about it in the right spirit.

John Gooch's eyes gleamed. Frederick Pilcher's jaw protruded. And neck and neck, fighting grimly for their sixes and sometimes even achieving fives, they came to the ninth green, halved the hole, and were all square at the turn.

It was at this point that they perceived Agnes Flack standing on the club-house terrace.

"Yoo-hoo!" cried Agnes in a voice of thunder.

And John Gooch and Frederick Pilcher stopped dead in their tracks, blinking like abruptly-awakened somnambulists.

She made a singularly impressive picture, standing there with her tweed-clad form outlined against the white of the club-house wall. She had the appearance of one who is about to play Boadicea in a pageant; and John Gooch, as he gazed at her, was conscious of a chill that ran right down his back and oozed out at the soles of his feet.

"How's the match coming along?" she yelled, cheerily.

"All square," replied Sidney McMurdo, with a sullen scowl. "Wait where you are for a minute, germs," he said. "I wish to have a word with Miss Flack."

He drew Agnes aside and began to speak to her in a low rumbling voice. And presently it was made apparent to all within a radius of half a mile that he had been proposing to her once again, for suddenly she threw her head back and there went reverberating over the countryside that old familiar laugh.

"Ha, ha, ha, ha, ha, ha, HA!" laughed Agnes Flack.

John Gooch shot a glance at his opponent. The artist, pale to the lips, was removing his coat and hat and handing them to his caddie. And, even as John Gooch looked, he unfastened his braces and tied them round his waist. It was plain that from now on Frederick Pilcher intended to run no risk of not over-swinging.

John Gooch could appreciate his feelings. The thought of how that laugh would sound across the bacon and eggs on a rainy Monday morning turned the marrow in his spine to ice and curdled every red corpuscle in his veins. Gone was the exhilarating ferment which had caused him to skip like a young ram when a long putt had given him a forty-six for the first nine. How bitterly he regretted now those raking drives, those crisp flicks of the mashie-niblick of which he had been so proud ten minutes ago. If only he had not played such an infernally good game going out, he reflected, he might at this moment be eight or nine down and without a care in the world.

A shadow fell between him and the sun; and he turned to see Sidney McMurdo standing by his side, glaring with a singular intensity.

"Bah!" said Sidney McMurdo, having regarded him in silence for some moments.

He turned on his heel and made for the club-house.

"Where are you going, Sidney?" asked Agnes Flack.

"I am going home," replied Sidney McMurdo, "before I murder these two miserable harvest-bugs. I am only flesh and blood, and the temptation to grind them into powder and scatter them to the four winds will shortly become too strong. Good morning."

Agnes emitted another laugh like a steam-riveter at work.

"Isn't he funny?" she said, addressing John Gooch, who had clutched at his scalp and was holding it down as the vibrations died away. "Well, I suppose I shall have to referee the rest of the match myself. Whose honour? Yours? Then drive off and let's get at it."

The demoralising effects of his form on the first nine holes had not completely left John Gooch. He drove long and straight, and stepped back appalled. Only a similar blunder on the part of his opponent could undo the damage.

But Frederick Pilcher had his wits well about him. He overswung as he had never overswung before. His ball shot off into the long grass on the right of the course, and he uttered a pleased cry.

"Lost ball, I fancy," he said. "Too bad!"

"I marked it," said John Gooch, grimly. "I will come and help you find it."

"Don't trouble."

"It is no trouble."

"But it's your hole anyway. It will take me three or four to get out of there."

"It will take me four or five to get a yard from where I am."

"Gooch," said Frederick Pilcher, in a cautious whisper, "you are a cad."

"Pilcher," said John Gooch, in tones equally hushed, "you are a low bounder. And if I find you kicking that ball under a bush, there will be blood shed—and in large quantities."

"Ha, ha!"

"Ha, ha to you!" said John Gooch.

The ball was lying in a leathery tuft, and, as Pilcher had predicted, it took three strokes to move it back to the fairway. By the time Frederick Pilcher had reached the spot where John Gooch's drive had finished, he had played seven.

But there was good stuff in John Gooch. It is often in times of great peril that the artistic temperament shows up best. Missing the ball altogether with his next three swings, he topped it with his fourth, topped it again with his fifth, and, playing the like, sent a low, skimming shot well over the green into the bunker beyond. Frederick Pilcher, aiming for the same bunker, sliced and landed on the green. The six strokes which it took John Gooch to get out of the sand decided the issue. Frederick Pilcher was one up at the tenth.

But John Gooch's advantage was shortlived. On the right, as you approach the eleventh green, there is a deep chasm, spanned by a wooden bridge. Frederick Pilcher, playing twelve, just failed to put his ball into this, and it rolled on to within a few feet of the hole. It seemed to John Gooch that the day was his. An easy mashie-shot would take him well into the chasm, from which no eighteen-handicap player had ever emerged within the memory of man. This would put him two down—a winning lead. He swung jubilantly, and brought off a nicely-lofted shot which seemed to be making for the very centre of the pit.

And so, indeed, it was; and it was this fact that undid John Gooch's schemes. The ball, with all the rest of the chasm to choose from, capriciously decided to strike the one spot on the left-hand rail of the wooden bridge which would deflect it towards the flag. It bounded high in the air, fell on the green, and the next moment, while John Gooch stood watching with fallen jaw and starting eyes, it had trickled into the hole.

There was a throbbing silence. Then Agnes Flack spoke.

"Important, if true," she said. "All square again. I will say one thing for you two—you make this game very interesting."

And once more she sent the birds shooting out of the treetops with that hearty laugh of hers. John Gooch, coming slowly to after the shattering impact of it, found that he was clutching Frederick Pilcher's arm. He flung it from him as if it had been a loathsome snake.

A grimmer struggle than that which took place over the next six holes has probably never been seen on any links. First one, then the other seemed to be about to lose the hole, but always a well-judged slice or a timely top enabled his opponent to rally. At the eighteenth tee the game was still square; and John Gooch, taking advantage of the fact that Agnes had stopped to tie her shoe-lace, endeavoured to appeal to his one-time friend's better nature.

"Frederick," he said, "this is not like you."

What isn't like me?"

"Playing this low-down game. It is not like the old Frederick Pilcher."

"Well, what sort of a game do you think you are playing?"

"A little below my usual, it is true," admitted John Gooch. "But that is due to nervousness. You are deliberately trying to foozle, which is not only painting the lily but very dishonest. And I can't see what motive you have, either."

"You can't, can't you?"

John Gooch laid a hand persuasively on the other's shoulder.

"Agnes Flack is a most delightful girl."

"Who is?"

"Agnes Flack."

"A delightful girl?"

"Most delightful."

"Agnes Flack is a delightful girl?"

"Yes."

"Oh?"

"She would make you very happy."

"Who would?"

"Agnes Flack."

"Make me happy?"

"Very happy."

"Agnes Flack would make me happy?"

"Yes."

"Oh?"

John Gooch was conscious of a slight discouragement. He did not seem to be making headway.

"Well, then, look here," he said, "what we had better do is to have a gentlemen's agreement."

"Who are the gentlemen?"

"You and I."

"Oh?"

John Gooch did not like the other's manner, nor did he like the tone of voice in which he had spoken. But then there were so many things about Frederick Pilcher that he did not like that it seemed useless to try to do anything about it. Moreover, Agnes Flack had finished tying her shoe-lace, and was making for them across the turf like a mastodon striding over some prehistoric plain. It was no time for wasting words.

"A gentlemen's agreement to halve the match," he said hurriedly.

"What's the good of that? She would only make us play extra holes."

"We would halve those, too."

"Then we should have to play it off another day."

"But before that we could leave the neighbourhood."

"Sidney McMurdo would follow us to the ends of the earth."

"Ah, but suppose we didn't go there? Suppose we simply lay low in the city and grew beards?"

"There's something in it," said Frederick Pilcher, reflectively.

"You agree?"

"Very well."

"Splendid!"

"What's splendid?" asked Agnes Flack, thudding up.

"Oh—er—the match," said John Gooch. "I was saying to Pilcher that this was a splendid match."

Agnes Flack sniffed. She seemed quieter than she had been at the outset, as though something were on her mind.

"I'm glad you think so," she said. "Do you two always play like this?"

"Oh, yes. Yes. This is about our usual form."

"H'm! Well, push on."

It was with a light heart that John Gooch addressed his ball for the last drive of the match. A great weight had been lifted from his mind, and he told himself that now there was no objection to bringing off a real sweet one. He swung lustily; and the ball, struck on its extreme left side, shot off at right angles, hit the ladies' tee-box, and, whizzing back at a high rate of speed, would have mown Agnes Flack's ankles from under her, had she not at the psychological moment skipped in a manner extraordinarily reminiscent of the high hills mentioned in Sacred Writ.

"Sorry, old man," said John Gooch, hastily, flushing as he encountered Frederick Pilcher's cold look of suspicion. "Frightfully sorry, Frederick, old man. Absolutely unintentional."

"What are you apologising to *him* for?" demanded Agnes Flack with a good deal of heat. It had been a near thing, and the girl was ruffled.

Frederick Pilcher's suspicions had plainly not been allayed by John Gooch's words. He drove a cautious thirty yards, and waited with the air of one suspending judgment for his opponent to play his second. It was with a feeling of relief that John Gooch, smiting vigorously with his brassie, was enabled to establish his *bona fides* with a shot that rolled to within mashie-niblick distance of the green.

Frederick Pilcher seemed satisfied that all was well. He played his second to the edge of the green. John Gooch ran his third up into the neighbourhood of the pin.

Frederick Pilcher stooped and picked his ball up.

"Here!" cried Agnes Flack.

"Hey!" ejaculated John Gooch.

"What on earth do you think you're doing?" said Agnes Flack.

Frederick Pilcher looked at them with mild surprise.

"What's the matter?" he said. "There's a blob of mud on my ball. I just wanted to brush it off."

"Oh, my heavens!" thundered Agnes Flack. "Haven't you ever read the rules? You're disqualified."

"Disqualified?"

"Dis-jolly-well-qualified," said Agnes Flack, her eyes flashing scorn. "This cripple here wins the match."

Frederick Pilcher heaved a sigh.

"So be it," he said. "So be it."

"What do you mean, so be it? Of course it is."

"Exactly. Exactly. I quite understand. I have lost the match. So be it."

And, with drooping shoulders, Frederick Pilcher shuffled off in the direction of the bar.

John Gooch watched him go with a seething fury which for the moment robbed him of speech. He might, he told himself, have expected something like this. Frederick Pilcher, lost to every sense of good feeling and fair play, had double-crossed him. He shuddered as he realised how inky must be the hue of Frederick Pilcher's soul; and he wished in a frenzy of regret that he had thought of picking his own ball up. Too late! Too late!

For an instant the world had been blotted out for John Gooch by a sort of red mist. This mist clearing, he now saw Agnes Flack standing looking at him in a speculative sort of way, an odd expression in her eyes. And beyond her, leaning darkly against the club-house wall, his bulging muscles swelling beneath his coat and his powerful fingers tearing to pieces what appeared to be a section of lead piping, stood Sidney McMurdo.

John Gooch did not hesitate. Although McMurdo was some distance away, he could see him quite clearly; and with equal clearness he could remember every detail of that recent interview with him. He drew a step nearer to Agnes Flack, and having gulped once or twice, began to speak.

"Agnes," he said huskily, "there is something I want to say to you. Oh, Agnes, have you not guessed——"

"One moment," said Agnes Flack. "If you're trying to propose to me, sign off. There is nothing doing. The idea is all wet."

"All wet?"

"All absolutely wet. I admit that there was a time when I toyed with the idea of marrying a man with brains, but there are limits. I wouldn't marry a man who played golf as badly as you do if he were the last man in the world. Sid-nee!" she roared, turning and cupping her mouth with her hands; and a nervous golfer down by the lake-hole leaped three feet and got his mashie entangled between his legs.

"Hullo?"

"I'm going to marry you, after all."

"Me?"

"Yes, you."

"Three rousing cheers!" bellowed McMurdo.

Agnes Flack turned to John Gooch. There was something like commiseration in her eyes, for she was a woman. Rather on the large side, but still a woman.

"I'm sorry," she said.

"Don't mention it," said John Gooch.

"I hope this won't ruin your life."

"No, no."

"You still have your Art."

"Yes, I still have my Art."

"Are you working on anything just now?" asked Agnes Flack.

"I'm starting a new story to-night," said John Gooch. "It will be called *Saved From the Scaffold*."

16

SOMETHING SQUISHY

THERE had been a gap for a week or so in our little circle at the Anglers' Rest, and that gap the most serious that could have occurred. Mr. Mulliner's had been the vacant chair, and we had felt his absence acutely. Inquiry on his welcome return elicited the fact that he had been down in Hertfordshire, paying a visit to his cousin Lady Wickham at her historic residence, Skeldings Hall. He had left her well, he informed us, but somewhat worried.

"About her daughter Roberta," said Mr. Mulliner.

"Delicate girl?" we asked sympathetically.

"Not at all. Physically, most robust. What is troubling my cousin is the fact that she does not get married."

A tactless Mild-and-Bitter, who was a newcomer to the bar-parlour and so should not have spoken at all, said that that was often the way with these plain girls. The modern young man, he said, valued mere looks too highly, and instead of being patient, and carrying on pluckily till he was able to penetrate the unsightly exterior to the good womanly heart within. . . .

"My cousin's daughter Roberta," said Mr. Mulliner with some asperity, "is not plain. Like all the Mulliners on the female side, however distantly removed from the main branch, she is remarkably beautiful. And yet she does not get married."

"A mystery," we mused.

"One," said Mr. Mulliner, "that I have been able to solve. I was privileged to enjoy a good deal of Roberta's confidence during my visit, and I also met a young man named Algernon Crufts who appears to enjoy still more and also to be friendly with some of those of the male sex in whose society she has been moving lately. I am afraid that, like so many spirited girls of to-day, she is inclined to treat her suitors badly. They get discouraged, and I think with some excuse. There was young Attwater, for instance. . . ."

Mr. Mulliner broke off and sipped his hot Scotch and lemon He appeared to have fallen into a reverie. From time to time, as he paused in his sipping, a chuckle escaped him.

"Attwater?" we said.

"Yes, that was the name."

"What happened to him?"

"Oh, you wish to hear the story? Certainly, certainly, by all means."

He rapped gently on the table, eyed his re-charged glass with quiet satisfaction, and proceeded.

In the demeanour of Roland Moresby Attwater, that rising young essayist and literary critic, there appeared (said Mr. Mulliner), as he stood holding the door open to allow the ladies to leave his uncle Joseph's dining-room, no outward and visible sign of the irritation that seethed beneath his mudstained shirt-front. Well-bred and highly civilised, he knew how to wear the mask. The lofty forehead that shone above his rimless pince-nez was smooth and unruffled, and if he bared his teeth it was only in a polite smile. Nevertheless, Roland Attwater was fed to the eyebrows.

In the first place, he hated these family dinners. In the second place, he had been longing all the evening for a chance to explain that muddy shirt, and everybody had treated it with a silent tact which was simply maddening. In the third place, he knew that his uncle Joseph was only waiting for the women to go to bring up once again the infuriating topic of Lucy.

After a preliminary fluttering, not unlike that of hens disturbed in a barnyard, the female members of the party rustled past him in single file—his aunt Emily; his aunt Emily's friend, Mrs. Hughes Higham; his aunt Emily's companion and secretary, Miss Partlett; and his aunt Emily's adopted daughter, Lucy. The last-named brought up the rear of the procession. She was a gentle-looking girl with spaniel eyes and freckles, and as she passed she gave Roland a swift, shy glance of admiration and gratitude. It was the sort of look Ariadne might have given Theseus immediately after his turn-up with the Minotaur: and a casual observer, not knowing the facts, would have supposed that, instead of merely opening a door for her, Roland had rescued her at considerable bodily risk from some frightful doom.

Roland closed the door and returned to the table. His uncle, having pushed port towards him, coughed significantly and opened fire.

"How did you think Lucy was looking to-night, Roland?"

The young man winced, but the fine courtly spirit which is such a characteristic of the younger members of the intelligentsia did not fail him. Instead of banging the speaker over the head with the decanter, he replied with quiet civility:

"Splendid."

"Nice girl."

"Very."

"Wonderful disposition."

"Quite."

"And so sensible."

"Precisely."

"Very different from these shingled, cigarette-smoking young women who infest the place nowadays."

"Decidedly."

"Had one of 'em up before me this morning," said Uncle Joseph, frowning austerely over his port. Sir Joseph Moresby was by profession a metropolitan magistrate. "Charged with speeding. That's their idea of life."

"Girls," argued Roland, "will be girls."

"Not while I'm sitting at Bosher Street police-court, they won't," said his uncle, with decision. "Unless they want to pay five-pound fines and have their licences endorsed." He sipped thoughtfully. "Look here, Roland," he said, as one struck by a novel idea, "why the devil don't you marry Lucy?"

"Well, uncle——"

"You've got a bit of money, she's got a bit of money. Ideal. Besides, you want somebody to look after you."

"Do you suggest," inquired Roland, his eyebrows rising coldly, "that I am incapable of looking after myself?"

"Yes, I do. Why, dammit, you can't even dress for dinner, apparently, without getting mud all over your shirt-front."

Roland's cue had been long in coming, but it had arrived at a very acceptable moment.

"If you really want to know how that mud came to be on my shirt-front, Uncle Joseph," he said, with quiet dignity, "I got it saving a man's life."

"Eh? What? How?"

"A man slipped on the pavement as I was passing through Grosvenor Square on my way here. It was raining, you know, and I——"

"You walked here?"

"Yes. And just as I reached the corner of Duke Street——"

"Walked here in the rain? There you are! Lucy would never let you do a foolish thing like that."

"It began to rain after I had started."

"Lucy would never have let you start."

"Are you interested in my story, uncle," said Roland, stiffly, "or shall we go upstairs?"

"Eh? My dear boy, of course, of course. Most interested. Want to hear the whole thing from beginning to end. You say it was raining and this fellow slipped off the pavement. And then I suppose a car or a taxi or something came along suddenly and you pulled him out of danger. Yes, go on, my boy."

"How do you mean, go on?" said Roland, morosely. He felt like a public speaker whose chairman has appropriated the cream of his speech and inserted it in his own introductory remarks. "That's all there is."

"Well, who was the man? Did he ask you for your name and address?"

"He did."

"Good! A young fellow once did something very similar to what you did, and the man turned out to be a millionaire and left him his entire fortune. I remember reading about it."

"In the *Family Herald,* no doubt?"

"Did your man look like a millionaire?"

"He did not. He looked like what he actually was—the proprietor of a small bird-and-snake shop in the Seven Dials."

"Oh!" said Sir Joseph, a trifle dashed. "Well, I must tell Lucy about this," he said, brightening. "She will be tremendously excited. Just the sort of thing to appeal to a warm-hearted girl like her. Look, Roland, why don't you marry Lucy?"

Roland came to a swift decision. It had not been his intention to lay bare his secret dreams to this pertinacious old blighter, but there seemed no other way of stopping him. He drained a glass of port and spoke crisply.

"Uncle Joseph, I love somebody else."

"Eh? What's that? Who?"

"This is, of course, strictly between ourselves."

"Of course."

"Her name is Wickham. I expect you know the family? The Hertfordshire Wickhams."

"Hertfordshire Wickhams!" Sir Joseph snorted with extraordinary violence. "Bosher Street Wickhams, you mean. If it's Roberta Wickham, a red-headed hussy who ought to be smacked and sent to bed without her supper, that's the girl I fined this morning."

"You fined her!" gasped Roland.

"Five pounds," said his uncle, complacently. "Wish I could have given her five years. Menace to the public safety. How on earth did you get to know a girl like that?"

"I met her at a dance. I happened to mention that I was a critic of some small standing, and she told me that her mother wrote novels. I chanced to receive one of Lady Wickham's books for review shortly afterwards, and the—er—favourable tone of my notice apparently gave her some pleasure." Roland's voice trembled slightly, and he blushed. Only he knew what it had cost him to write eulogistically of that terrible book. "She has invited me down to Skeldings, their place in Hertfordshire, for the weekend tomorrow."

"Send her a telegram."

"Saying what?"

"That you can't go."

"But I am going." It is a pretty tough thing if a man of letters who has sold his critical soul is not to receive the reward of his crime. "I wouldn't miss it for anything."

"Don't you be a fool, my boy," said Sir Joseph. "I've known you all your life —know you better than you know yourself—and I tell you it's sheer insanity for a man like you to dream of marrying a girl like that. Forty miles an hour she was going, right down the middle of Piccadilly. The constable proved it up to the hilt. You're a quiet, sensible fellow, and you ought to marry a quiet, sensible girl. You're what I call a rabbit."

"A rabbit!"

"There is no stigma attached to being a rabbit," said Sir Joseph, pacifically. "Every man with a grain of sense is one. It simply means that you prefer a normal, wholesome life to gadding about like a—like a non-rabbit. You're going out of your class, my boy. You're trying to change your zoological species, and it can't be done. Half the divorces to-day are due to the fact that rabbits won't believe they're rabbits till it's too late. It is the peculiar nature of the rabbit——"

"I think we had better join the ladies, Uncle Joseph," said Roland frostily. "Aunt Emily will be wondering what has become of us."

In spite of the innate modesty of all heroes, it was with something closely resembling chagrin that Roland discovered, on going to his club in the morning, that the Press of London was unanimously silent on the subject of his last night's exploit. Not that one expected anything in the nature of publicity, of course, or even desired it. Still, if there had happened to be some small paragraph under some such title as "Gallant Behaviour of an Author" or "Critical Moment for a Critic", it would have done no harm to the sale of that little book of thoughtful essays which Blenkinsop's had just put on the market.

And the fellow had seemed so touchingly grateful at the time.

Pawing at Roland's chest with muddy hands he had told him that he would never forget this moment as long as he lived. And he had not bothered even to go and call at a newspaper office.

Well, well! He swallowed his disappointment and a light lunch and returned to his flat, where he found Bryce, his man-servant, completing the packing of his suitcase.

"Packing?" said Roland. "That's right. Did those socks arrive?"

"Yes, sir."

"Good!" said Roland. They were some rather special gents' half-hose from the Burlington Arcade, subtly passionate, and he was hoping much from them. He wandered to the table, and became aware that on it lay a large cardboard box. "Hullo, what's this?"

"A man left it a short while ago, sir. A somewhat shabbily-dressed person. The note accompanying it is on the mantelpiece, sir."

Roland went to the mantelpiece; and, having inspected the dirty envelope for a moment with fastidious distaste, opened it in a gingerly manner.

"The box appears to me, sir," continued Bryce, "to contain something alive. It seemed to me that I received the impression of something squirming."

"Good Lord!" exclaimed Roland, staring at the letter.

"Sir?"

"It's a snake. That fool has sent me a snake. Of all the——"

A hearty ringing at the front-door bell interrupted him. Bryce, rising from the suitcase, vanished silently. Roland continued to regard the unwelcome gift with a peevish frown.

"Miss Wickham, sir," said Bryce at the door.

The visitor, who walked springily into the room, was a girl of remarkable beauty. She resembled a particularly good-looking schoolboy who had dressed up in his sister's clothes.

"Ah!" she said, cocking a bright eye at the suitcase, "I'm glad you're bustling about. We ought to be starting soon. I'm going to drive you down in the two-seater." She began a restless tour of the room. "Hullo!" she said, arriving at the box. "What might this be?" She shook it experimentally. "I say! There's something squishy inside!"

"Yes, it's——"

"Roland," said Miss Wickham, having conducted further experiments, "immediate investigation is called for. Inside this box there is most certainly some living organism. When you shake it it definitely squishes."

"It's all right. It's only a snake."

"Snake!"

"Perfectly harmless," he hastened to assure her. "The fool expressly states that. Not that it matters, because I'm going to send it straight back, unopened."

Miss Wickham squeaked with pleased excitement.

"Who's been sending you snakes?"

Roland coughed diffidently.

"I happened to—er—save a man's life last night. I was coming along at the corner of Duke Street——"

"Now, isn't that an extraordinary thing?" said Miss Wickham, meditatively. "Here have I lived all these years and never thought of getting a snake!"

"——when a man——"

"The one thing every young girl should have."

"——slipped off the pavement——"

"There are the most tremendous possibilities in a snake. The diner-out's best friend. Pop it on the table after the soup and be Society's pet."

Roland, though nothing, of course, could shake his great love, was conscious of a passing feeling of annoyance.

"I'll tell Bryce to take the thing back to the man," he said, abandoning his story as a total loss.

"Take it back?" said Miss Wickham, amazed. "But, Roland, what frightful waste! Why, there are moments in life when knowing where to lay your hand on a snake means more than words can tell." She started. "Golly! Didn't you once say that old Sir Joseph What's-his-name—the beak, you know—was your uncle? He fined me five of the best yesterday for absolutely crawling along Piccadilly.

He needs a sharp lesson. He must be taught that he can't go about the place persecuting the innocent like that. I'll tell you what. Ask him to lunch here and hide the thing in his napkin! That'll make him think a bit!"

"No, no!" cried Roland, shuddering strongly.

"Roland! For my sake!"

"No, no, really!"

"And you said dozens of times that you would do anything in the world for me!" She mused. "Well, at least let me tie a string to it and dangle it out of the window in front of the next old lady that comes along."

"No, no, please! I must send it back to the man."

Miss Wickham's discontent was plain, but she seemed to accept defeat.

"Oh, all right if you're going to refuse me every little thing! But let me tell you, my lad, that you're throwing away the laugh of a lifetime. Wantonly and callously chucking it away. Where is Bryce? Gone to earth in the kitchen, I suppose. I'll go and give him the thing while you strap the suitcase. We ought to be starting, or we sha'n't get there by tea-time."

"Let me do it."

"No, I'll do it."

"You mustn't trouble."

"No trouble," said Miss Wickham, amiably.

In this world, as has been pointed out in various ways by a great many sages and philosophers, it is wiser for the man who shrinks from being disappointed not to look forward too keenly to moments that promise pleasure. Roland Attwater, who had anticipated considerable enjoyment from his drive down to Skeldings Hall, soon discovered, when the car had threaded its way through the London traffic and was out in the open country, that the conditions were not right for enjoyment. Miss Wickham did not appear to share the modern girl's distaste for her home. She plainly wanted to get there as quickly as possible. It seemed to Roland that from the time they left High Barnet to the moment when, with a grinding of brakes, they drew up at the door of Skeldings Hall the two-seater had only touched Hertfordshire at odd spots.

Yet, as they alighted, Roberta Wickham voiced a certain dissatisfaction with her work.

"Forty-three minutes," she said, frowning at her watch. "I can do better than that."

"Can you?" gulped Roland. "Can you, indeed?"

"Well, we're in time for tea, anyhow. Come in and meet the mater. Forgotten Sports of the Past—Number Three, Meeting the Mater."

Roland met the mater. The phrase, however, is too mild and inexpressive and does not give a true picture of the facts. He not merely met the mater; he was engulfed and swallowed up by the mater. Lady Wickham, that popular novelist

("Strikes a singularly fresh note."—R. Moresby Attwater in the *New Examiner*), was delighted to see her guest. Welcoming Roland to her side, she proceeded to strike so many singularly fresh notes that he was unable to tear himself away till it was time to dress for dinner. She was still talking with unimpaired volubility on the subject of her books, of which Roland had been kind enough to write so appreciatively, when the gong went.

"Is it as late as that?" she said, surprised, releasing Roland, who had thought it later. "We shall have to go on with our little talk after dinner. You know your room? No? Oh, well, Claude will show you. Claude, will you take Mr. Attwater up with you? His room is at the end of your corridor. By the way, you don't know each other, do you? Sir Claude Lynn—Mr. Attwater."

The two men bowed; but in Roland's bow there was not that heartiness which we like to see in our friends when we introduce them to fellow-guests. A considerable part of the agony which he had been enduring for the last two hours had been caused not so much by Lady Wickham's eloquence, though that had afflicted him sorely, as by the spectacle of this man Lynn, whoever he might be, monopolising the society of Bobbie Wickham in a distant corner. There had been to him something intolerably possessive about the back of Sir Claude's neck as he bent towards Miss Wickham. It was the neck of a man who is being much more intimate and devotional than a jealous rival cares about.

The close-up which he now received of this person did nothing to allay Roland's apprehension. The man was handsome, sickeningly handsome, with just that dark, dignified, clean-cut handsomeness which attracts impressionable girls. It was, indeed, his dignity that so oppressed Roland now. There was something about Sir Claude Lynn's calm and supercilious eye that made a fellow feel that he belonged to entirely the wrong set in London and that his trousers were bagging at the knees.

"A most delightful man," whispered Lady Wickham, as Sir Claude moved away to open the door for Bobbie. "Between ourselves, the original of Captain Mauleverer, D.S.O., in my *Blood Will Tell*. Very old family, ever so much money. Plays polo splendidly. And tennis. And golf. A superb shot. Member for East Bittlesham, and I hear on all sides that he may be in the Cabinet any day."

"Indeed?" said Roland, coldly.

It seemed to Lady Wickham, as she sat with him in her study after dinner— she had stated authoritatively that he would much prefer a quiet chat in that shrine of literature to any shallow revelry that might be going on elsewhere—that Roland was a trifle distrait. Nobody could have worked harder to entertain him than she. She read him the first seven chapters of the new novel on which she was engaged, and told him in gratifying detail the plot of the rest of it, but somehow all did not seem well. The young man, she noticed, had developed a habit of plucking at his hair; and once he gave a sharp, gulping cry which startled her. Lady Wickham began to feel disappointed in Roland, and was not sorry when he excused himself.

"I wonder," he said, in a rather overwrought sort of way, "if you would mind if I just went and had a word with Miss Wickham? I—I—there's something I wanted to ask her."

"Certainly," said Lady Wickham, without warmth. "You will probably find her in the billiards-room. She said something about having a game with Claude. Sir Claude is wonderful at billiards. Almost like a professional."

Bobbie was not in the billiards-room, but Sir Claude was, practising dignified cannons which never failed to come off. At Roland's entrance he looked up like an inquiring statue.

"Miss Wickham?" he said. "She left half an hour ago. I think she went to bed."

He surveyed Roland's flushed dishevelment for a moment with a touch of disapproval, then resumed his cannons. Roland, though he had that on his mind concerning which he desired Miss Wickham's counsel and sympathy, felt that it would have to stand over till the morning. Meanwhile, lest his hostess should pop out of the study and recapture him, he decided to go to bed himself.

He had just reached the passage where his haven lay, when a door which had apparently been standing ajar opened and Bobbie appeared, draped in a sea-green negligee of such a calibre that Roland's heart leaped convulsively and he clutched at the wall for support.

"Oh, there you are," she said, a little petulantly. "What a time you've been!"

"Your mother was——"

"Yes, I suppose she would be," said Miss Wickham, understandingly. "Well, I only wanted to tell you about Sidney."

"Sidney? Do you mean Claude?"

"No, Sidney. The snake. I was in your room just after dinner, to see if you had everything you wanted, and I noticed the box on your dressing-table".

"I've been trying to get hold of you all the evening to ask you what to do about that," said Roland, feverishly. "I was most awfully upset when I saw the beastly thing. How Bryce came to be such an idiot as to put it in the car——"

"He must have misunderstood me," said Bobbie, with a clear and childlike light shining in her hazel eyes. "I suppose he thought I said 'Put this in the back' instead of 'Take this back'. But what I wanted to say was that it's all right."

"All right?"

"Yes. That's why I've been waiting up to see you. I thought that, when you went to your room and found the box open, you might be a bit worried."

"The box open!"

"Yes. But it's all right. It was I who opened it."

"Oh, but I say—you—you oughtn't to have done that. The snake may be roaming about all over the house."

"Oh, no, it's all right. I know where it is."

"That's good."

"Yes, it's all right. I put it in Claude's bed."

Roland Attwater clutched at his hair as violently as if he had been listening to chapter six of Lady Wickham's new novel.

"You—you—you—what?"

"I put it in Claude's bed."

Roland uttered a little whinnying sound, like a very old horse a very long way away.

"Put it in Claude's bed!"

"Put it in Claude's bed."

"But—but—but why?"

"Why not?" asked Miss Wickham, reasonably.

"But—oh, my heavens!"

"Something on your mind?" inquired Miss Wickham, solicitously.

"It will give him an awful fright."

"Jolly good for him. I was reading an article in the evening paper about it. Did you know that fear increases the secretory activity of the thyroid, suprarenal, and pituitary glands? Well, it does. Bucks you up, you know. Regular tonic. It'll be like a day at the seaside for old Claude when he puts his bare foot on Sidney. Well, I must be turning in. Got that schoolgirl complexion to think about. Goodnight."

For some minutes after he had tottered to his room, Roland sat on the edge of the bed in deep meditation. At one time it seemed as if his reverie was going to take a pleasant turn. This was when the thought presented itself to him that he must have overestimated the power of Sir Claude's fascination. A girl could not, he felt, have fallen very deeply under a man's spell if she started filling his bed with snakes the moment she left him.

For an instant, as he toyed with this heartening reflection, something remotely resembling a smile played about Roland's sensitive mouth. Then another thought came to wipe the smile away—the realisation that, while the broad general principle of putting snakes in Sir Claude's bed was entirely admirable, the flaw in the present situation lay in the fact that this particular snake could be so easily traced to its source. The butler, or whoever had taken his luggage upstairs, would be sure to remember carrying up a mysterious box. Probably it had squished as he carried it and was already the subject of comment in the servants' hall. Discovery was practically certain.

Roland rose jerkily from his bed. There was only one thing to be done, and he must do it immediately. He must go to Sir Claude's room and retrieve his lost pet. He crept to the door and listened carefully. No sound came to disturb the stillness of the house. He stole out into the corridor.

It was at this precise moment that Sir Claude Lynn, surfeited with cannons, put on his coat, replaced his cue in the rack, and came out of the billiards-room.

If there is one thing in this world that should be done quickly or not at all, it is the removal of one's personal snake from the bed of a comparative stranger. Yet Roland, brooding over the snowy coverlet, hesitated. All his life he had had a horror of crawling and slippery things. At his private school, while other boys had fondled frogs and achieved terms of intimacy with slow-worms, he had not been able to bring himself even to keep white mice. The thought of plunging his hand between those sheets and groping for an object of such recognised squishiness as Sidney appalled him. And, even as he hesitated, there came from the corridor outside the sound of advancing footsteps.

Roland was not by nature a resourceful young man, but even a child would have known what to do in this crisis. There was a large cupboard on the other side of the room, and its door had been left invitingly open. In the rapidity with which he bolted into this his uncle Joseph would no doubt have seen further convincing evidence of his rabbit-hood. He reached it and burrowed behind a mass of hanging clothes just as Sir Claude entered the room.

It was some small comfort to Roland—and at the moment he needed what comfort he could get, however small—to find that there was plenty of space in the cupboard. And what was even better, seeing that he had had no time to close the door, it was generously filled with coats, overcoats, raincoats, and trousers. Sir Claude Lynn was evidently a man who believed in taking an extensive wardrobe with him on country-house visits; and, while he deplored the dandyism which this implied, Roland would not have had it otherwise. Nestling in the undergrowth, he peered out between a raincoat and a pair of golfing knickerbockers. A strange silence had fallen, and he was curious to know what his host was doing with himself.

At first he could not sight him; but, shifting slightly to the left, he brought him into focus, and discovered that in the interval that had passed Sir Claude had removed nearly all his clothes and was now standing before the open window, doing exercises.

It was not prudery that caused this spectacle to give Roland a sharp shock. What made him start so convulsively was the man's horrifying aspect as revealed in the nude. Downstairs, in the conventional dinner-costume of the well-dressed man, Sir Claude Lynn had seemed robust and soldierly, but nothing in his appearance then had prepared Roland for the ghastly physique which he exhibited now. He seemed twice his previous size as if the removal of constricting garments had caused him to bulge in every direction. When he inflated his chest, it looked like a barrel. And, though Roland in the circumstances would have preferred any other simile, there was only one thing to which his rippling muscles could be compared. They were like snakes, and nothing but snakes. They heaved and twisted beneath his skin just as Sidney was presumably even now heaving and twisting beneath the sheets.

If ever there was a man, in short, in whose bedroom one would rather not have been concealed in circumstances which might only too easily lead to a physical encounter, that man was Sir Claude Lynn; and Roland, seeing him, winced away with a shudder so violent that a coat-hanger which had been trembling on the edge of its peg fell with a disintegrating clatter.

There was a moment of complete silence: then the trousers behind which he cowered were snatched away, and a huge hand, groping like the tentacle of some dreadful marine monster, seized him painfully by the hair and started pulling.

"Ouch!" said Roland, and came out like a winkle at the end of a pin.

A modesty which Roland, who was modest himself, should have been the first to applaud had led the other to clothe himself hastily for this interview in a suit of pyjamas of a stupefying mauve. In all his life Roland had never seen such a colour-scheme; and in some curious way the brilliance of them seemed to complete his confusion. The result was that, instead of plunging at once into apologies and explanations, he remained staring with fallen jaw; and his expression, taken in conjunction with the fact that his hair, rumpled by the coats, appeared to be standing on end, supplied Sir Claude with a theory which seemed to cover the case. He remembered that Roland had had much the same cock-eyed look when he had come into the billiards-room. He recalled that immediately after dinner Roland had disappeared and had not joined the rest of the party in the drawing-room. Obviously the fellow must have been drinking like a fish in some secret part of the house for hours.

"Get out!" he said curtly, taking Roland by the arm with a look of disgust and leading him sternly to the door. An abstemious man himself, Sir Claude Lynn had a correct horror of excess in others. "Go and sleep it off. I suppose you can find your way to your room? It's the one at the end of the corridor, as you seem to have forgotten."

"But listen——."

"I cannot understand how a man of any decent upbringing can make such a beast of himself."

"Do listen!"

"Don't shout like that," snapped Sir Claude, severely. "Good heavens, man, do you want to wake the whole house? If you dare to open your mouth again, I'll break you into little bits."

Roland found himself out in the passage, staring at a closed door. Even as he stared it opened sharply, and the upper half of the mauve-clad Sir Claude popped out.

"No drunken singing in the corridor, mind!" said Sir Claude, sternly, and disappeared.

It was a little difficult to know what to do. Sir Claude had counselled slumber, but the suggestion was scarcely a practical one. On the other hand there seemed nothing to be gained by hanging about in the passage. With slow and lingering steps Roland moved towards his room, and had just reached it when the silence of the night was rent by a shattering scream; and the next moment there shot through the door he had left a large body. And, as Roland gazed dumbly, a voice was raised in deafening appeal.

"Shot-gun!" vociferated Sir Claude. "Help! Shot-gun! Bring a shot-gun, somebody!"

There was not the smallest room for doubt that the secretory activity of his thyroid, suprarenal, and pituitary glands had been increased to an almost painful extent.

It is only in the most modern and lively country houses that this sort of thing can happen without attracting attention. So quickly did the corridor fill that it seemed to Roland as if dressing-gowned figures had shot up through the carpet. Among those present he noticed Lady Wickham in blue, her daughter Roberta in green, three male guests in bath-robes, the under-housemaid in curl-papers, and Simmons, the butler, completely and correctly clad in full afternoon costume. They were all asking what was the matter, but, as Lady Wickham's penetrating voice o'ertopped the rest, it was to her that Sir Claude turned to tell his story.

"A snake?" said Lady Wickham, interested.

"A snake."

"In your bed?"

"In my bed."

"Most unusual," said Lady Wickham, with a touch of displeasure.

Sir Claude's rolling eye, wandering along the corridor, picked out Roland as he shrank among the shadows. He pointed at him with such swift suddenness that his hostess only saved herself from a nasty blow by means of some shifty footwork.

"That's the man!" he cried.

Lady Wickham, already ruffled, showed signs of peevishness.

"My dear Claude," she said, with a certain asperity, "do come to some definite decision. A moment ago you said there was a snake in your room; now you say it was a man. Besides, can't you see that that is Mr. Attwater? What would he be doing in your room?"

"I'll tell you what he was doing. He was putting that infernal snake in my bed. I found him there."

"Found him there? In your bed?"

"In my cupboard. Hiding. I hauled him out."

All eyes were turned upon Roland. His own he turned with a look of wistful entreaty upon Roberta Wickham. A cavalier of the nicest gallantry, nothing, of course, would induce him to betray the girl; but surely she would appreciate that the moment had come for her to step forward and clear a good man's name with a full explanation.

He had been too sanguine. A pretty astonishment lit up Miss Wickham's lovely eyes. But her equally lovely mouth did not open.

"But Mr. Attwater has no snake," argued Lady Wickham. "He is a well-known man-of-letters. Well-known men-of-letters," she said, stating a pretty generally recognised fact, "do not take snakes with them when they go on visits."

A new voice joined in the discussion.

"Begging your pardon, your ladyship."

It was the voice of Simmons, grave and respectful.

"Begging your pardon, your ladyship, it is my belief that Mr. Attwater did have a serpent in his possession. Thomas, who conveyed his baggage to his room, mentioned a cardboard box that seemed to contain something alive."

From the expression of the eyes that once more raked him in his retirement, it was plain that the assembled company were of the opinion that it was Roland's turn to speak. But speech was beyond him. He had been backing slowly for some little time, and now, as he backed another step, the handle of his bedroom door insinuated itself into the small of his back. It was almost as if the thing were hinting to him that refuge that lay beyond.

He did not resist the kindly suggestion. With one quick, emotional movement he turned, plunged into his room, and slammed the door behind him.

From the corridor without came the sound of voices in debate. He was unable to distinguish words, but the general trend of them was clear. Then silence fell.

Roland sat on his bed, staring before him. He was roused from his trance by a tap on the door.

"Who's that?" he cried, bounding up. His eye was wild. He was prepared to sell his life dearly.

"It is I, sir. Simmons."

"What do you want?"

The door opened a few inches. Through the gap there came a hand. In the hand was a silver salver. On the salver lay something squishy that writhed and wriggled.

"Your serpent, sir," said the voice of Simmons.

It was the opinion of Roland Attwater that he was now entitled to the remainder of the night in peace. The hostile forces outside must now, he felt, have fired their last shot. He sat on his bed, thinking deeply, if incoherently. From time to time the clock on the stables struck the quarters, but he did not move. And then into the silence it seemed to him that some sound intruded—a small tapping sound that might have been the first tentative efforts of a very young woodpecker just starting out in business for itself. It was only after this small noise had continued for some moments that he recognised it for what it was. Somebody was knocking softly on his door.

There are moods in which even the mildest man will turn to bay, and there gleamed in Roland Attwater's eyes as he strode to the door and flung it open a baleful light. And such was his militant condition that, even when he glared out and beheld Roberta Wickham, still in that green negligee, the light did not fade away. He regarded her malevolently.

"I thought I'd better come and have a word with you," whispered Miss Wickham.

"Indeed?" said Roland.

"I wanted to explain."

"Explain!"

"Well," said Miss Wickham, "you may not think there's any explanation due to you, but I really feel there is. Oh, yes, I do. You see, it was this way. Claude had asked me to marry him."

"And so you put a snake in his bed? Of course! Quite natural!"

"Well, you see, he was so frightfully perfect and immaculate and dignified and —oh, well, you've seen him for yourself, so you know what I mean. He was too darned overpowering—that's what I'm driving at—and it seemed to me that if I could only see him really human and undignified—just once—I might—well, you see what I mean?"

"And the experiment, I take it, was successful?"

Miss Wickham wriggled her small toes inside her slippers.

"It depends which way you look at it. I'm not going to marry him, if that's what you mean."

"I should have thought," said Roland, coldly, "that Sir Claude behaved in a manner sufficiently—shall I say human?—to satisfy even you."

Miss Wickham giggled reminiscently.

"He did leap, didn't he? But it's all off, just the same."

"Might I ask why?"

"Those pyjamas," said Miss Wickham, firmly. "The moment I caught a glimpse of them, I said to myself, 'No wedding bells for me!' No! I've seen too much of life to be optimistic about a man who wears mauve pyjamas." She plunged for a space into maiden meditation. When she spoke again, it was on another aspect of the affair. "I'm afraid mother is rather cross with you, Roland."

"You surprise me!"

"Never mind. You can slate her next novel."

"I intend to," said Roland, grimly, remembering what he had suffered in the study from chapters one to seven of it.

"But meanwhile I don't think you had better meet her again just yet. Do you know, I really think the best plan would be for you to go away to-night without saying goodbye. There is a very good milk-train which gets you into London at six-forty-five."

"When does it start?"

"At three-fifteen."

"I'll take it," said Roland.

There was a pause. Roberta Wickham drew a step closer.

"Roland," she said, softly, "you were a dear not to give me away. I do appreciate it so much."

"Not at all!"

"There would have been an awful row. I expect mother would have taken away my car."

"Ghastly!"

"I want to see you again quite soon, Roland. I'm coming up to London next week. Will you give me lunch? And then we might go and sit in Kensington Gardens or somewhere where it's quiet."

Roland eyed her fixedly.

"I'll drop you a line," he said.

Sir Joseph Moresby was an early breakfaster. The hands of the clock pointed to five minutes past eight as he entered his dining-room with a jaunty and hopeful step. There were, his senses told him, kidneys and bacon beyond that door. To his surprise he found that there was also his nephew Roland. The young man was pacing the carpet restlessly. He had a rumpled look as if he had slept poorly, and his eyes were pink about the rims.

"Roland!" exclaimed Sir Joseph. "Good gracious! What are you doing here? Didn't you go to Skeldings after all?"

"Yes, I went," said Roland, in a strange, toneless voice.

"Then what——?"

"Uncle Joseph," said Roland, "you remember what we were talking about at dinner? Do you really think Lucy would have me if I asked her to marry me?"

"What! My dear boy, she's been in love with you for years."

"Is she up yet?"

"No. She doesn't breakfast till nine."

"I'll wait."

Sir Joseph grasped his hand.

"Roland, my boy——" he began.

But there was that on Roland's mind that made him unwilling to listen to set speeches.

"Uncle Joseph," he said, "do you mind if I join you for a bite of breakfast?"

"My dear boy, of course——"

"Then I wish you would ask them to be frying two or three eggs and another rasher or so. While I'm waiting I'll be starting on a few kidneys."

It was ten minutes past nine when Sir Joseph happened to go into the morning-room. He had supposed it empty, but he perceived that the large armchair by the window was occupied by his nephew Roland. He was leaning back with the air of one whom the world is treating well. On the floor beside him sat Lucy, her eyes fixed adoringly on the young man's face.

"Yes, yes," she was saying. "How wonderful! Do go on, darling."

Sir Joseph tiptoed out, unnoticed. Roland was speaking as he softly closed the door.

"Well," Sir Joseph heard him say, "it was raining, you know, and just as I reached the corner of Duke Street——"

17

THE AWFUL GLADNESS OF THE MATER

"AND then," said Mr. Mulliner, "there was the case of Dudley Finch."

He looked inquiringly at his glass, found that it was three-parts full, and immediately proceeded to resume the Saga of his cousin's daughter, Roberta.

"At the moment at which I would introduce Dudley Finch to you," said Mr. Mulliner, "we find him sitting in the lobby of Claridge's Hotel, looking at his watch with the glazing eye of a starving man. Five minutes past two was the time it registered, and Roberta Wickham had promised to meet him for lunch at one-thirty sharp. He heaved a plaintive sigh, and a faint sense of grievance began to steal over him. Impious though it was to feel that that angelic girl had any faults, there was no denying, he told himself, that this tendency of hers to keep a fellow waiting for his grub amounted to something very like a flaw in an otherwise perfect nature. He rose from his chair and, having dragged his emaciated form to the door, tottered out into Brook Street and stood gazing up and down it like a male Lady of Shalott.

Standing there in the weak sunlight (said Mr. Mulliner), Dudley Finch made a singularly impressive picture. He was—sartorially—so absolutely right in every respect. From his brilliantined hair to his gleaming shoes, from his fawn-coloured spats to his Old Etonian tie, he left no loophole to the sternest critic. You felt as you saw him that if this was the sort of chap who lunched at Claridge's, old man Claridge was in luck.

It was not admiration, however, that caused the earnest-looking young man in the soft hat to stop as he hurried by. It was surprise. He stared wide-eyed at Dudley.

"Good heavens!" he exclaimed. "I thought you were on your way to Australia."

"No," said Dudley Finch, "not on my way to Australia." His smooth forehead wrinkled in a frown, "Rolie, old thing," he said, with gentle reproach, "you oughtn't to go about London in a hat like that." Roland Attwater was his cousin, and a man does not like to see his relatives careering all over the Metropolis looking as if cats had brought them in. "And your tie doesn't match your socks."

He shook his head sorrowfully. Roland was a literary man, and, worse, had been educated at an inferior school—Harrow, or some such name, Dudley understood that it was called; but even so he ought to have more proper feeling about the vital things of life.

"Never mind my hat," said Roland. "Why aren't you on your way to Australia?"

"Oh, that's all right. Broadhurst had a cable, and isn't sailing till the fifteenth."

Roland Attwater looked relieved. Like all the more serious-minded members of the family, he was deeply concerned about his cousin's future. With regard to this there had been for some time past a little friction, a little difficulty in reconciling two sharply conflicting points of view. The family had wanted Dudley to go into his Uncle John's business in the City; whereas what Dudley desired was that some broad-minded sportsman should slip him a few hundred quid and enable him to start a new dance-club. A compromise had been effected when his godfather, Mr. Sampson Broadhurst, arriving suddenly from Australia, had offered to take the young man back with him and teach him sheep-farming. It fortunately happening that he was a great reader of the type of novel in which everyone who goes to Australia automatically amasses a large fortune and leaves it to the hero, Dudley had formally announced at a family council that—taking it by and large—Australia seemed to him a pretty good egg, and that he had no objection to having a pop at it.

"Thank goodness," said Roland. "I thought you might have backed out of going at the last moment."

Dudley smiled.

"Funny you should have said that, old man. A coincidence, I mean. Because that's just exactly what I've made up my mind to do."

"What!"

"Absolutely. The fact is, Rolie," said Dudley, confidentially, "I've just met the most topping girl. And sometimes, when I think of buzzing off on the fifteenth and being separated from her by all those leagues of water, I could howl like a dog. I've a jolly good mind to let the old man sail by himself, and stick here on my native heath."

"This is appalling! You musn't dream——"

"She's the most wonderful girl. Knows you, too. Roberta Wickham's her name. She lets me call her Bobbie. She——"

He broke off abruptly. His eyes gazing past Roland, were shining with a holy light of devotion. His lips had parted in a brilliant smile.

"Yo-ho!" he cried.

Roland turned. A girl was crossing the road; a slim, boyish-looking girl, with shingled hair of a glorious red. She came tripping along with all the gay abandon of a woman who is forty minutes late for lunch and doesn't give a hoot.

"Yo-ho!" yowled young Mr. Finch. "Yo frightfully ho!"

The girl came up, smiling and debonair.

"I'm not late, am I?" she said.

"Rather not," cooed the love-sick Dudley. "Not a bit. Only just got here myself."

"That's good," said Miss Wickham. "How are you, Roland?"

"Very well, thanks," replied Roland Attwater, stiffly.

"I must congratulate you, mustn't I?"

"What on?" asked Dudley, puzzled.

"His engagement of course."

"Oh, that!" said Dudley. He knew that his cousin had recently become engaged to Lucy Moresby, and he had frequently marvelled at the lack of soul which could have led one acquainted with the divine Roberta to go and tack himself on to any inferior female. He put it down to Roland having been at Harrow.

"I hope you will be very happy."

"Thank you," said Roland, sedately. "Well, I must be going, Goodbye. Glad to have seen you."

He stalked off towards Grosvenor Square. It seemed to Dudley that his manner was peculiar.

"Not a very cordial bird, old Rolie," he said, returning to the point at the luncheon-table. "Biffed off a trifle abruptly, didn't it strike you?"

Miss Wickham sighed.

"I'm afraid Roland doesn't like me."

"Not like you!" Dudley swallowed a potato which, in a calmer moment, he would have realized was some eighty degrees Fahrenheit too warm for mastication. "Not like you!" he repeated, with watering eyes. "The man must be an ass."

"We were great friends at one time," said Roberta, sadly. "But ever since that snake business——"

"Snake business?"

"Roland had a snake, and I took it with me when he came down to Hertfordshire for the week-end. And I put it in a man's bed, and the mater got the impression that Roland had done it, and he had to sneak away on a milk-train. He's never quite forgiven me, I'm afraid."

"But what else could you have done?" demanded Dudley, warmly. "I mean to say, if a fellow's got a snake, naturally you put it in some other fellow's bed."

"That's just what I felt."

"Only once in a blue moon, I mean, you get hold of a snake. When you do, you can't be expected to waste it."

"Exactly. Roland couldn't see that, though. Nor, for the matter of that," continued Miss Wickham, dreamily, "could mother."

"I say," said Dudley, "that reminds me. I'd like to meet your mother."

"Well, I'm going down there this evening. Why don't you come, too?"

"No, I say, really? May I?"

"Of course."

"Rather short notice, though, isn't it?"

"Oh, that's all right. I'll send the mater a wire. She'll be awfully glad to see you."

"You're sure?"

"Oh, rather! Awfully glad."

"Well, that's fine. Thanks ever so much."

"I'll motor you down."

Dudley hesitated. Something of the brightness died out of his fair young face. He had had experience of Miss Wickham as a chauffeuse and had died half a dozen deaths in the extremely brief space of time which it had taken her to thread her way through half a mile of traffic.

"If it's all the same," he said, nervously, "I think I'll pop down by train."

"Just as you like. The best one's the six-fifteen. Gets you there in time for dinner."

"Six-fifteen? Right. Liverpool Street, of course? Just bring a suit-case, I suppose? Fine! I say, you're really sure your mother won't think I'm butting in?"

"Of course not. She'll be awfully glad to see you."

Splendid!" said Dudley.

The six-fifteen train was just about to draw out of Liverpool Street Station when Dudley flung himself and suit-case into it that evening. He had rather imprudently stepped in at the Drones Club on his way and, while having a brief refresher at the bar, had got into an interesting argument with a couple of the lads. There had only just been time for him to race to the cloak-room, retrieve his suit-case, and make a dash for the train. Fortunately, he had chanced upon an excellent taxi, and here he was, a little out of breath from the final sprint down the platform, but in every other respect absolutely all-righto. He leaned back against the cushions and gave himself up to thought.

From thinking of Bobbie he drifted shortly into meditation on her mother. If all went well, he felt this up-to-the-present-unmet mater was destined to be an important figure in his life. It was to her that he would have to go after Bobbie, hiding her face shyly on his waistcoat, had whispered that she had loved him from the moment they had met.

"Lady Wickham," he would say. "No, not Lady Wickham—mother!"

Yes, that was undoubtedly the way to start. After that it would be easy. Providing, of course, that the mater turned out to be one of the better class of maters and took to him from the beginning. He tried to picture Lady Wickham, and had evolved a mental portrait of a gentle, sweet-faced woman of lateish middle-age when the train pulled up at a station, and a lucky glimpse of a name on one of the lamps told Dudley that this was where he alighted.

Some twenty minutes later he was being relieved of his suit-case and shown into a room that looked like a study of sorts.

"The gentleman, m'lady," boomed the butler, and withdrew.

It was a rather a rummy way of announcing the handsome guest, felt Dudley, but he was not able to give much thought to the matter, for from a chair in front of the desk at which she had been writing there now rose a most formidable person, at the sight of whom his heart missed a beat. So vivid had been that image of sweet-faced womanhood which he had fashioned that his hostess in the flesh had the effect of being a changeling.

Beauty, as it has been well said, is largely in the eye of the beholder, and it may be stated at once that Lady Wickham's particular type did not appeal to Dudley. He preferred the female eye to be a good deal less like a combination of gimlet and X-ray, and his taste in chins was something a little softer and not quite so reminiscent of a battleship going into action. Bobbie's mater might, as Bobbie had predicted, be awfully glad to see him, but she did not look it. And suddenly there came over him like a wave the realization that the check suit which he had selected so carefully was much too bright. At the tailor's, and subsequently at the Drones Club, it had had a pleasing and cheery effect, but here in this grim study he felt that it made him look like an absconding bookmaker.

"You are very late," said Lady Wickham.

"Late?" quavered Dudley. The train had seemed to him to be making more or less good going.

"I supposed you would be here early in the afternoon. But perhaps you have brought a flashlight apparatus?"

"Flashlight apparatus?"

"Have you not brought a flashlight apparatus?"

Dudley shook his head. He prided himself on being something of an authority on what the young visitor should take with him on country-house visits, but this was a new one.

"No," he said, "no flashlight apparatus."

"Then how," demanded Lady Wickham, with some heat, "do you imagine that you can take photographs at this time of night?"

"Ah!" said Dudley, vaguely. "See what you mean, of course. Take a bit of doing, what?"

Lady Wickham seemed to become moderately resigned.

"Oh, well, I suppose they can send someone down tomorrow."

"That's right," said Dudley, brightening.

"In the meantime—this is where I work."

"No, really?"

"Yes. All my books have been written at this desk."

"Fancy that!" said Dudley. He remembered having heard Bobbie mention that Lady Wickham wrote novels.

"I get my inspirations, however, in the garden for the most part. Generally the rose-garden. I like to sit there in the mornings and think."

"And what," agreed Dudley, cordially, "could be sweeter?"

His hostess regarded him curiously. A sense of something wrong seemed to come upon her.

"You *are* from *Milady's Boudoir*?" she asked, suddenly.

"From what was that, once again?" asked Dudley.

"Are you that man the editor of *Milady's Boudoir* was sending down to interview me?"

Dudley could answer this one.

"No," he said.

"No?" echoed Lady Wickham.

"Most absolutely not-o," said Dudley, firmly.

"Then who," demanded Lady Wickham, "are you?"

"My name's Dudley Finch."

"And to what," asked his hostess in a manner so extraordinarily like that of his late grandmother that Dudley's toes curled in their shoes, "am I to attribute the honour of this visit?"

Dudley blinked.

"Why, I thought you knew all about it."

"I know nothing whatever about it."

"Didn't Bobbie send you a wire?"

"He did not. Nor do I know who Bobbie may be."

"Miss Wickham, I mean. Your daughter Roberta. She told me to buzz down here for the night, and said she would send you a wire paving the way, so to speak. Oh, I say, this is a bit thick. Fancy her forgetting!"

For the second time that day a disagreeable feeling that his idol was after all not entirely perfect stole upon Dudley. A girl, he meant, oughtn't to lure a bloke down to her mater's house and then forget to send a wire tipping the old girl off. No, he meant to say! Pretty dashed casual, he meant.

"Oh," said Lady Wickham, "you are a friend of my daughter?"

"Absolutely."

"I see. And where is Roberta?"

"She's tooling down in the car."

Lady Wickham clicked her tongue.

"Roberta is becoming too erratic for endurance," she said.

"I say, you know," said Dudley, awkwardly, "if I'm in the way, you know, just speak the word and I'll race off to the local pub. I mean to say, don't want to butt in, I mean."

"Not at all, Mr.——"

"Finch."

"Not at all, Mr. Finch. I am only too delighted," said Lady Wickham, looking at him as if he were a particularly loathsome slug which had interrupted some beautiful reverie of hers in the rose-garden, "that you were able to come." She touched the bell. "Oh, Simmons," she said, as the butler appeared, "in which room did you put Mr. Finch's luggage?"

"In the Blue Room, m'lady."

"Then perhaps you will show him the way there. He will wish to dress.

Dinner," she added to Dudley, "will be at eight o'clock."

"Righto!" said Dudley. He was feeling a little happier now. Formidable old bird as this old bird undoubtedly was, he was pretty confident that she would melt a bit when once he had got the good old dress-clothes draped about his person. He was prepared to stand or fall by his dress-clothes. There are a number of tailors in London who can hack up a bit of broadcloth and sew it together in some sort of shape, but there is only one who can construct a dress-suit so that it blends with the figure and seems as beautiful as a summer's dawn. It was this tailor who enjoyed the benefit of Dudley's patronage. Yes, Dudley felt as he entered the Blue Room, in about twenty minutes old Madame Lafarge was due to get her eye knocked out.

In the brief instant before he turned on the light he could dimly see that perfect suit laid out on the bed, and it was with something of the feeling of a wanderer returning home that he pressed the switch.

Light flooded the room, and Dudley stood their blinking.

But, no matter how much he blinked, the awful sight which had met his eyes refused to change itself in the slightest detail. What was laid out on the bed was not his dress-clothes, but the most ghastly collection of raiment he had ever beheld. He blinked once again as a forlorn hope, and then tottered forward.

He stood looking down at the foul things, his heart ice within him. Reading from left to right, the objects on the bed were as follows: A pair of short white woollen socks; a crimson made-up bow tie of enormous size; a sort of middy-blouse arrangement; a pair of blue velvet knickerbockers; and finally—and it was this that seemed to Dudley to make it all so sad and hopeless—a very small sailor-hat with a broad blue ribbon, across which in large white letters ran the legend *H.M.S. See-Sik.*

On the floor were a pair of brown shoes with strap-and-buckle attachment. They seemed to be roomy number twelves.

Dudley sprang· to the bell. A footman presented himself.

"Sir?" said the footman.

"What," demanded Dudley, wildly, "what is all this?"

"I found them in your suit-case, sir."

"But where are my dress-clothes?"

"No dress-clothes in the suit-case, sir."

A bright light shone upon Dudley. That argument with those two birds at the Drones had, he now recalled, been on the subject of fancy-dress. Both birds were dashing off to a fancy-dress ball that night, and one bird had appealed to Dudley to support him against the other bird in his contention that at these affairs the prudent man played for safety and went as a Pierrot. The second bird had said that he would sooner be dead in a ditch than don any such unimaginative costume. He was going as a small boy, he said, and with a pang Dudley remembered having laughed mockingly and prophesied that he would look the most priceless ass. And then he had sprinted off and collared the man's bag in mistake for his own.

"Look here," he said, "I can't possibly come down to dinner in those!"

"No, sir?" said the footman, respectfully, but with a really inhuman lack of interest and sympathy.

"You'd better leg it to the old girl's room——I mean," said Dudley, recollecting himself, "you had better go to Lady Wickham and inform her that Mr. Finch presents his compliments and I'm awfully sorry but he has mislaid his dress-clothes, so he will have to come down to dinner in what I've got on at present."

"Very good, sir."

"I say!" A horrid thought struck Dudley. "I say, we shall be alone, what? I mean to say, nobody else is coming to dinner?"

"Yes, sir," said the footman, brightly. "A number of guests are expected, sir."

It was a sagging and demoralized Dudley who crawled into the dining-room a quarter of an hour later. In spite of what moralists say, a good conscience is not enough in itself to enable a man to bear himself jauntily in every crisis of life. Dudley had had a good upbringing, and the fact that he was dining at a strange house in a bright check suit gave him a consciousness of sin which he strove vainly to overcome.

The irony of it was that in a normal frame of mind he woud have sneered loftily at the inferior garments which clothed the other male members of the party. On the left sleeve of the man opposite him was a disgraceful wrinkle. The fellow next to the girl in pink might have a good heart, but the waistcoat which covered it did not fit by a mile. And as for the tie of that other bloke down by Lady Wickham, it was not a tie at all in the deeper meaning of the word; it was just a deplorable occurrence. Yet, situated as he was, his heart ached with envy of all these tramps.

He ate but little. As a rule his appetite was of the heartiest, and many a novel had he condemned as untrue to life on the ground that his hero was stated to have pushed his food away untasted. Until tonight he had never supposed that such a feat was possible. But as course succeeded course he found himself taking almost no practical interest in the meal. All he asked was to get it over, so that he could edge away and be alone with his grief. There would doubtless be some sort of binge in the drawing-room after dinner, but it would not have the support of Dudley Finch. For Dudley Finch the quiet seclusion of the Blue Room.

It was as he was sitting there some two hours later that there drifted into his mind something Roberta had said about Roland Attwater leaving on the milk-train. At the time he had paid little attention to the remark, but now it began to be borne in upon him more and more strongly that this milk-train was going to be of great strategic importance in his life. This ghastly house was just the sort of house that fellows did naturally go away from on milk-trains, and it behoved him to be prepared.

He rang the bell once more.

"Sir?" said the footman.

"I say," said Dudley, "what time does the milk-train leave?"

"Milk-train, sir?"

"Yes. Train that takes the milk, you know."

"Do you wish for milk, sir?"

"No!" Dudley fought down a desire to stun this man with one of the number twelve shoes. "I just want to know what time the milk-train goes in the morning—in case—in—er—case I am called away unexpectedly, I mean to say."

"I will inquire, sir."

The footman made his way to the servants' hall, the bearer of great news.

"Guess what," said the footman.

"Well, Thomas?" asked Simmons, the butler, indulgently.

"That bloke—the Great What-is-it," said Thomas—for it was by this affectionate sobriquet that Dudley was now known below stairs—"is planning to go off on the milk-train!"

"What?" Simmons heaved his stout form out of his chair. His face did not reflect the gay mirth of his subordinate. "I must inform her ladyship. I must inform her ladyship at once."

The last guest had taken his departure, and Lady Wickham was preparing to go to a well-earned bed when there entered to her Simmons, grave and concerned.

"Might I speak to your ladyship?"

"Well, Simmons?"

"Might I first take the liberty of inquiring, m'lady, if the—er—the young gentleman in the tweed suit is a personal friend of your ladyship's?"

Lady Wickham was surprised. It was not like Simmons to stroll in and start chatting about her guests, and for a moment she was inclined to say as much; then something told her that by doing so she would miss information of interest.

"He says he is a friend of Miss Roberta, Simmons," she said graciously.

"Says!" said the butler, and there was no eluding the sinister meaning in his voice.

"What do you mean. Simmons?"

"Begging your pardon, m'lady, I am convinced that this person is here with some criminal intention. Thomas reports that his suit-case contained a complete disguise."

"Disguise! What sort of disguise?"

"Thomas did not convey that very clearly, your ladyship, but I understand that it was of a juvenile nature. And just now, m'lady, the man has been making inquiries as to the time of departure of the milk-train."

"Milk-train!"

"Thomas also states, m'lady, that the man was visibly took aback when he learned that there were guests expected here tonight. If you ask me, your ladyship, it was the man's intention to make what I might term a quick clean-up immediately after dinner and escape on the nine-fifty-seven. Foiled in that by the presence of the guests, he is going to endeavour to collect the swag in the small hours and get away on the milk-train."

"Simmons!"

"That is my opinion, your ladyship."

"Good gracious! He told me that Miss Roberta had said to him that she was coming down here tonight. She has not come!"

"A ruse, m'lady. To inspire confidence."

"Simmons, said Lady Wickham, rising to the crisis like the strong woman she was, "you must sit up tonight!"

"With a gun, m'lady," cried the butler, with a sportsman's enthusiasm.

"Yes, with a gun. And if you hear him prowling about you must come and wake me instantly."

"Very good, your ladyship."

"You must be very quiet, of course."

"Like a mouse, your ladyship," said Simmons.

Dudley, meanwhile, in his refuge in the Blue Room, had for some time past been regretting—every moment more keenly—that preoccupation with his troubles had led him to deal so sparingly with his food down there in the dining-room. The peace of the Blue Room had soothed his nervous system, and with calm had come the realisation that he was most confoundedly hungry. There was something uncanny in the way Fate had worked to do him out of his proper supply of proteins and carbohydrates today. Hungry as he had been when waiting at Claridge's for Bobbie, the moment she appeared love had taken his mind off the menu, and he had made a singularly light lunch. Since then he had had nothing but the few scattered mouthfuls which he had forced himself to swallow at the dinner-table.

He consulted his watch. It was later than he had supposed. Much too late to ring the bell and ask for sandwiches—even supposing that his standing in this poisonous house had been such as to justify the demand.

He flung himself back on the bed and tried to doze off. That footman had said that the milk-train left at three-fifteen, and he was firmly resolved to catch it. The sooner he was out of this place the better. Meanwhile, he craved food. Any sort of food. His entire interior organism was up on its feet, shouting wildly for sustenance.

A few minutes later, Lady Wickham, waiting tensely in her room, was informed by a knock on the door that the hour had arrived.

"Yes?" she whispered, turning the handle noiselessly and putting her head out.

"The man, m'lady" breathed the voice of Simmons in the darkness.

"Prowling?"

"Yes, m'lady."

Dudley Finch's unwilling hostess was a woman of character and decision. From girlhood up she had been accustomed to hunting and the other hardy sports of the aristocracy of the countryside. And though the pursuit of burglars had formed up to the present no part of her experience, she approached it without a qualm. Motioning the butler to follow, she wrapped her dressing-gown more closely about her and strode down the corridor.

There was plenty of noise to guide her to her goal. Dudley's progress from his bed-room to the dining-room, the fruit and biscuits on the sideboard of which formed his objective, had been far from quiet. Once he had tripped over a chair, and now, as his hostess and her attendant began to descend the stairs, he collided with and upset a large screen. He was endeavouring to remove the foot which he had inadvertently put through this when a quiet voice spoke from above.

"Can you see him, Simmons?"

"Yes, m'lady. Dimly but adequately."

"Then shoot if he moves a step."

"Very good, m'lady."

Dudley wrenched his foot free and peered upwards, appalled.

"I say!" he quavered. "It's only me, you know!"

Light flooded the hall.

"Only me!" repeated Dudley, feverishly. The sight of the enormous gun in the butler's hands had raised his temperature to a painful degree.

"What," demanded Lady Wickham, coldly, "are you doing here, Mr. Finch?"

An increased sense of the delicacy of his position flooded over Dudley. He was a young man with the nicest respect for the conventions, and he perceived that the situation required careful handling. It is not tactful, he realized, for a guest for whose benefit a hostess has only a few hours earlier provided a lavish banquet to announce to the said hostess that he has been compelled by hunger to rove the house in search of food. For a moment he stood there, licking his lips; then something like an inspiration came to him.

"The fact is," he said, "I couldn't sleep, you know."

"Possibly," said Lady Wickham, "you would have a better chance of doing so if you were to go to bed. Is it your intention to walk about the house all night?"

"No, no, absolutely not. I couldn't sleep, so I—er—I thought I would pop down and see if I could find something to read, don't you know."

"Oh, you want a book?"

"That's right. That's absolutely it. A book. You've put it in a nutshell."

"I will show you to the library."

In spite of her stern disapproval of this scoundrel who wormed his way into people's houses in quest of loot, a slight diminution of austerity came to Lady Wickham as the result of this introduction of the literary note. She ·was an indefatigable novelist, and it pleased her to place her works in the hands of even the vilest. Ushering Dudley into the library, she switched on the light and made her way without hesitation to the third shelf from the top nearest the fireplace. Selecting one from a row of brightly covered volumes, she offered it to him.

"Perhaps this will interest you," she said.

Dudley eyed it dubiously.

"Oh, I say," he protested, "I don't know, you know. This is one of that chap, George Masterman's."

"Well?" said Lady Wickham, frostily.

"He writes the most frightful bilge, I mean. Don't you think so?"

"I cannot say that I do. I am possibly biased, however, by the fact that George Masterman is the name I write under."

Dudley blinked.

"Oh, doy yuo?" he babbled. "Do you? You do, eh? Well, I mean——" An imperative desire to be elsewhere swept over him. "This'll do me," he said, grabbing wildly at the nearest shelf. "This will do me fine. Thanks awfully. Good night. I mean, thanks, thanks. I mean good night. Good night."

Two pairs of eyes followed him as he shot up the stairs. Lady Wickham's were cold and hard; the expression in those of Simmons was wistful. It was seldom that the butler's professional duties allowed him the opportunity of indulging the passion for sport which had been his since boyhood. A very occasional pop at a rabbit was about all the shooting he got nowadays, and the receding Dudley made his mouth water. He fought the craving down with a sigh.

"A nasty fellow, m'lady," he said.

"Quick-witted," Lady Wickham was forced to concede.

"Full of low cunning, m'lady," emended the butler. "All that about wanting a book. A ruse."

"You had better continue watching, Simmons."

"Most decidedly, your ladyship."

Dudley sat on his bed, panting. Nothing like this had ever happened to him before, and for a while the desire for food left him, overcome by a more spiritual misery. If there was one thing in the world that gave him the pip, it was looking like a silly idiot; and every nerve in his body told him that during the recent interview he must have looked the most perfect silly idiot. Staring bleakly before him, he re-lived every moment of the blighted scene, and the more he examined his own share in it the worse it looked. He quivered in an agony of shame. He seemed to be bathed from head to foot in a sort of prickly heat.

And then, faintly at first, but growing stronger every moment, hunger began to clamour once again.

Dudley clenched his teeth. Something must be done to combat this. Mind must somehow be enabled to triumph over matter. He glanced at the book which he had snatched from the shelf, and for the first time that night began to feel that Fate was with him. Out of a library which was probably congested with the most awful tosh, he had stumbled first pop upon Mark Twain's *Tramp Abroad*, a book which he had not read since he was a kid but had always been meaning to read again; just the sort of book, in fact, which would enable a fellow to forget the anguish of starvation until that milk-train went.

He opened it at random, and found with a shock that Fate had but been playing with him.

"It has now been many months, at the present writing" (read Dudley), *"since I have had a nourishing meal, but I shall soon have one—a modest, private affair all to myself. I have selected a few dishes, and made out a little bill of fare, which will go home in the steamer that precedes me and be hot when I arrive—as follows:—"*

Dudley quailed. Memories of his boyhood came to him, of the time when he had first read what came after those last two words. The passage had stamped itself on his mind, for he had happened upon it at school, at a time when he was permanently obsessed by a wolfish hunger and too impecunious to purchase anything at the school shop to keep him going till the next meal. It had tortured him then, and it would, he knew, torture him even more keenly now.

Nothing, he resolved, should induce him to go on reading. So he immediately went on.

"Radishes. Baked apples, with cream.
"Fried oysters; stewed oysters. Frogs.
"American coffee, with real cream.
"American butter.
"Fried chicken, Southern style.
"Porterhouse steak.
"Saratoga potatoes.
"Broiled chicken, American style."

A feeble moan escaped Dudley. He endeavoured to close the book, but it would not close. He tried to remove his eyes from the page, but they wandered back like homing pigeons.

"Brook trout, from Sierra Nevada.
"Lake trout, from Tahoe.
"Sheephead and croakers, from New Orleans.
"Black bass, from the Mississippi.
"American roast beef.
"Roast turkey, Thanksgiving style.
"Cranberry sauce. Celery.

"Roast wild turkey. Woodcock.
"Canvas-back duck, from Baltimore.
"Prairie hens, from Illinois.
"Missouri partridges, broiled.
"Possum. Coon.
"Boston bacon and beans.
"Bacon and greens, Southern style."

Dudley rose from the bed. He could endure no more. His previous experience as a prospector after food had not been such as to encourage further efforts in that direction, but there comes a time when a man recks not of possible discomfort. He removed his shoes and tip-toed out of the room. A familiar form advanced to meet him along the now brightly lit corridor.

"Well?" said Simmons, the butler, shifting his gun to the ready and massaging the trigger with a loving forefinger.

Dudley gazed upon him with a sinking heart.

"Oh, hullo!" he said.

"What do *you* want?"

"Oh—er—oh, nothing."

"You get back into that room."

"I say, listen, laddie," said Dudley, in desperation flinging reticence to the winds. "I'm starving. Absolutely starving. I wish, like a good old bird, you would just scud down to your pantry or somewhere and get me a sandwich or two."

"You get back into that room, you hound!" growled Simmons, with such intensity that sheer astonishment sent Dudley tottering back through the door. He had never heard a butler talk like that. He had not supposed that butlers could talk like that.

He put on his shoes again; and, lacing them up, brooded tensely on this matter. What, he asked himself, was the idea? What was the big thought that lay behind all this? That his hostess, alarmed by noises in the night, should have summoned the butler to bring firearms to her assistance was intelligible. But what was the blighter doing, camping outside his door? After all, they knew he was a friend of the daughter of the house.

He was still wrestling with this problem when a curious, sharp, tapping noise attracted his attention. It came at irregular intervals and seemed to proceed from the direction of the window. He sat up, listening. It came again. He crept to the window and looked out. As he did so, something with hard edges smote him painfully in the face.

"Oh, sorry!" said a voice.

Dudley started violently. Looking in the direction from which the voice had proceeded, he perceived that there ran out from the wall immediately to the left of his window a small balcony. On this balcony, bathed in silver moonlight, Roberta Wickham was standing. She was hauling in the slack of a length of string, to the end of which was attached a button-hook.

"Awfully sorry," she said. "I was trying to attract your attention."

"You did," said Dudley.

"I thought you might be asleep."

"Asleep!" Dudley's face contorted itself in a dreadful sneer. "Does anyone ever get any sleep in this house?" He leaned forward and lowered his voice. "I say, your bally butler has gone off his onion."

"What?"

"He's doing sentinel duty outside my door with a whacking great cannon. And when I put my head out just now he simply barked at me."

"I'm afraid," said Bobbie, gathering in the button-hook, "he thinks you're a burglar."

"A burglar? But I told your mother distinctly that I was a friend of yours."

Something akin to embarrassment seemed to come upon the not easily embarrassed Miss Wickham.

"Yes, I want to talk to you about that," she said. "It was like this."

"I say, when did you arrive, by the way?" asked Dudley, the question suddenly presenting itself to his disordered mind.

"About half an hour ago."

"What!"

"Yes. I sneaked in through the scullery window. And the first thing I met was mother in her dressing-gown." Miss Wickham shivered a little as at some unpleasing memory. "You've never seen mother in her dressing-gown," she said, in a small voice.

"Yes, I have," retorted Dudley. "And while it may be an experience which every chappie ought to have, let me tell you that once is sufficient."

"I had an accident coming down here," proceeded Miss Wickham, absorbed in her own story and paying small attention to his. "An idiot of a man driving a dray let me run into him. My car was all smashed up. I couldn't get away for hours, and then I had to come down on a train that stopped at every station."

It is proof, if such were needed, of the strain to which Dudley Finch had been subjected that night that the information that this girl had been in a motor-smash did not cause him that anguished concern which he would undoubtedly have felt twenty-four hours earlier. It left him almost cold.

"Well, when you saw your mother," he said, "didn't you tell her that I was a friend of yours?"

Miss Wickham hesitated.

"That's the part I want to explain," she said. "You see, it was like this. First I had to break it as gently as I could to her that the car wasn't insured. She wasn't frightfully pleased. And then she told me about you and——Dudley, old thing, whatever have you been doing since you got here? The mater seemed to think you had been behaving in the weirdest way."

"I'll admit that I brought the wrong bag and couldn't dress for dinner, but apart from that I'm dashed if I can see what I did that was weird."

"Well, she seems to have become frightfully suspicious of you almost from the start."

"If you had sent that wire, telling her I was coming——"

Miss Wickham clicked her tongue regretfully.

"I knew there was something I had forgotten. Oh, Dudley, I'm awfully sorry."

"Don't mention it," said Dudley, bitterly. "It's probably going to lead to my having my head blown off by a looney butler, but don't give it another thought. You were saying——"

"Oh, yes, when I met mother. You do see, Dudley dear, how terribly difficult it was for me, don't you? I mean, I had just broken it to her that the car was all smashed up and not insured, and then she suddenly asked me if it was true that I had invited you down here. I was just going to say I had, when she began to talk about you in such a bitter spirit that somehow the time didn't seem ripe. So when she asked me if you were a friend of mine, I——"

"You said I was?"

"Well, not in so many words."

"How do you mean?"

"I had to be awfully tactful, you see."

"Well?"

"So I told her I had never seen you in my life."

Dudley uttered a sound like the breeze sighing in the tree-tops.

"But it's all right," went on Miss Wickham, reassuringly.

"Yes, isn't it?" said Dudley. "I noticed that."

"I'm going to go and have a talk with Simmons and tell him he must let you escape. Then everything will be splendid. There's an excellent milk-train——"

"I know all about the milk-train, thanks."

"I'll go and see him now. So don't you worry, old thing."

"Worry?" said Dudley. "Me? What have I got to worry about?"

Bobbie disappeared. Dudley turned away from the window. Faint whispering made itself heard from the passage. Somebody tapped softly on the door. Dudley opened it and found the ambassadress standing on the mat. Farther down the corridor, tactfully withdrawn into the background, Simmons the butler stood grounding arms.

"Dudley," whispered Miss Wickham, "have you got any money on you?"

"Yes, a cetain amount."

"Five pounds? It's for Simmons."

Dudley felt the militant spirit of the Finches surging within him. His blood boiled.

"You don't mean to say that after what has happened the blighter has the crust to expect me to tip him?"

He glared past her at the man behind the gun, who simpered respectfully. Evidently Bobbie's explanations had convinced him that he had wronged Dudley, for the hostility which had been so marked a short while back had now gone out of his manner.

"Well, it's like this, you see," said Bobbie. "Poor Simmons is worried."

"I'm glad," said Dudley, vindictively. "I wish he would worry himself into a decline."

"He's afraid that mother may be angry with him when she finds that you have gone. He doesn't want to lose his place."

"A man who doesn't want to get out of a place like this must be an ass."

"And so, in case mother does cut up rough and dismiss him for not keeping a better watch over you, he wants to feel that he has something in hand. He started by asking for a tenner, but I got him down to five. So hand it over, Dudley, dear, and then we can get action."

Dudley produced a five-pound note and gazed at it with a long, lingering look of affection and regret.

"Here you are," he said. "I hope the man spends it on drink, gets tight, trips over his feet, and breaks his neck!"

"Thanks," said Bobbie. "There's just one other trifling condition he made, but you needn't worry about that."

"What was it?"

"Oh, just something very trifling. Nothing that you have to do. No need for you to worry at all. You had better start now tying knots in the sheets."

Dudley stared.

"Knots?" he said. "In the sheets?"

"To climb down by."

It was Dudley's guiding rule in life never, when once he had got it brushed and brilliantined and properly arranged in the fashionable back-sweep, to touch his hair; but on this fearful night all the rules of civilised life were going by the board. He clutched upwards, collected a handful and churned it about. No lesser gesture could have expressed his consternation.

"You aren't seriously suggesting that I climb out of window and shin down a knotted sheet?" he gasped.

"You must, I'm afraid. Simmons insists on it."

"Why?"

"Well——"

Dudley groaned.

"I know why," he said, bitterly. "He's been going to the movies. It's always the way. You give a butler an evening off and he sneaks out to a picture-house and comes back with a diseased mind, thinking he's playing a star part in *The*

Clutching Hand or something. Knotted sheets, indeed!" Such was his emotion that Dudley very nearly said "Forsooth"! "The man is simply a drivelling imbecile. Will you kindly inform me why, in the name of everything infernal, the poor, silly, dashed fish can't just let me out of the front door like an ordinary human being?"

"Why, don't you see?" reasoned Miss Wickham. "How could he explain to mother? She must be made to think that you escaped in spite of his vigilance."

Disordered though his faculties were, Dudley could dimly see that there was something in this. He made no further objections. Bobbie beckoned to the waiting Simmons. Money changed hands. The butler passed amiably into the room to lend assistance to the preparations.

"A little tighter, perhaps, sir," he suggested, obsequiously, casting a critical eye upon Dudley's knots. "It would never do for you to fall and kill yourself, sir, ha, ha!"

"Did you say 'ha, ha'?" said Dudley, in a pale voice.

"I did venture——"

"Don't do it again."

"Very good sir." The butler ambled to the window and looked out. "I fear the sheets will not reach quite to the ground, sir. You will have a drop of a few feet."

"But," added Bobbie, hastily, "you've got the most lovely, soft, squashy flower-bed to fall into."

It was not till some minutes later, when he had come to the end of the sheet and had at last nerved himself to let go and complete the journey after the fashion of a parachutist whose parachute has refused to open, that Dudley discovered that there was an error in Miss Wickham's description of the terrain. The lovely soft flower-bed of which she had spoken with such pretty girlish enthusiasm was certainly there, but what she had omitted to mention was that along it at regular intervals were planted large bushes of a hard and spiky nature. It was in one of these that Dudley, descending like a shooting star, found himself entangled: and he had never supposed that anything that was not actually a cactus plant could possibly have so many and such sharp thorns.

He scrambled out and stood in the moonlight soliloquising softly. A head protruded from the window above.

"Are you all right, sir?" inquired the voice of Simmons.

Dudley did not reply. With as much dignity as a man punctured in several hundred places could muster, he strode off.

He had reached the drive and was limping up it towards the gate which led to the road which led to the station which led to the milk-train which led to London, when the quiet of the night was suddenly shattered by the roar of a gun. Something infinitely more painful than all the thorns which had recently pierced him smote the fleshy part of his left leg. It seemed to be red-hot, and its effect on Dudley was almost miraculous. A moment before he had been slouching slowly along, a beaten and jaded man. He now appeared to become electrified. With one sharp yell he lowered the amateur record for the standing broad jump, and then, starting smartly off the mark, proceeded to try to beat the best professional time for the hundred-yard dash.

The telephone at the side of Dudley's bed had been ringing for some time before its noise woke him. Returning to his rooms in Jermyn Street shortly before seven a.m., he had quelled his great hunger with breakfast and then slipped with a groan between the sheets. It was, now, he saw from a glance at his watch, nearly five in the afternoon.

"Hullo?" he croaked.

"Dudley?"

It was a voice which twenty-four hours ago would have sent sharp thrills down the young man's spine. Twenty-four hours ago, if he had heard this voice on his telephone, he would have squealed with rapture. Hearing it now, he merely frowned. The heart beneath that rose-pink pyjama jacket was dead.

"Yes?" he said coldly.

"Oh, Dudley," purred Miss Wickham, "are you all right?"

"As far," replied Mr. Finch, frigidly, "as a bloke can be said to be all right whose hair has turned white to the roots and who has been starved and chucked out of windows into bushes with six-inch thorns, and chivvied and snootered and shot in the fleshy part of the leg——"

An exclamation of concern broke in upon his eloquence.

"Oh, Dudley, he didn't hit you?"

"He did hit me."

"But he promised that he wouldn't aim at you."

"Well, next time he goes shooting visitors, tell him to aim as carefully as he can. Then they may have a sporting chance."

"Is there anything I can do?"

"Outside of bringing me the blighter's head on a charger, nothing, thanks."

"He insisted on letting off the gun. That was the condition I said he had made. You remember?"

"I remember. The trifling condition I wasn't to worry about."

"It was to make the thing seem all right to mother."

"I hope your mother was pleased," said Dudley, politely.

"Dudley, I do wish there was something I could do for you. I'd like to come up and nurse you. But I'm in disgrace about the car, and I'm not allowed to come to London just yet. I'm 'phoning from the Wickham Arms. I believe I shall be able to get up, though, by Saturday week. Shall I come then?"

"Do," said Dudley, cordially.

"That's splendid! It's the seventeenth. All right, I'll try to get to London lateish in the morning. Where shall we meet?"

"We shan't meet," said Dudley. "At lunch-time on the seventeenth I shall be tooling off to Australia. Goodbye!"

He hung up the receiver and crawled back into bed, thinking imperially.

18

THE PASSING OF AMBROSE

"RIGHT HO," said Algy Crufts. "Then I shall go alone."

"Right ho," said Ambrose Wiffin. "Go alone."

"Right ho," said Algy Crufts. "I will."

"Right ho," said Ambrose Wiffin. "Do."

"Right ho, then," said Algy Crufts.

"Right ho," said Ambrose Wiffin.

"Right ho," said Algy Crufts.

Few things (said Mr. Mulliner) are more painful than an altercation between two boyhood friends. Nevertheless, when these occur, the conscientious narrator must record them.

It is also, no doubt, the duty of such a narrator to be impartial. In the present instance, however, it would be impossible to avoid bias. To realise that Algy Crufts was perfectly justified in taking an even stronger tone, one has only to learn the facts. It was the season of the year when there comes upon all right-thinking young men the urge to go off to Monte Carlo: and the plan had been that he and Ambrose should catch the ten o'clock boat-train on the morning of the sixteenth of February. All the arrangements had been made—the tickets bought; the trunks packed; the "One Hundred Systems of Winning At Roulette" studied from end to end: and here was Ambrose, on the afternoon of February the fourteenth, calmly saying that he proposed to remain in London for another fortnight.

Algy Crufts eyed him narrowly. Ambrose Wiffin was always a nattily-dressed young man, but to-day there had crept into his outer crust a sort of sinister effulgence which could have but one meaning. It shouted from his white carnation: it shrieked from his trouser-crease: and Algy read it in a flash.

"You're messing about after some beastly female," he said.

Ambrose Wiffin reddened and brushed his top-hat the wrong way.

"And I know who it is. It's that Wickham girl."

Ambrose reddened again, and brushed his top-hat once more—this time the right way, restoring the *status quo*.

"Well," he said, "you introduced me to her."

"I know I did. And, if you recollect, I drew you aside immediately afterwards and warned you to watch your step."

"If you have anything to say against Miss Wickham. . . ."

"I haven't anything to say against her. She's one of my best pals. I've known young Bobbie Wickham since she was a kid in arms, and I'm what you might call immune where she's concerned. But you can take it from me that every other fellow who comes in contact with Bobbie finds himself sooner or later up to the Adam's apple in some ghastly mess. She lets them down with a dull, sickening thud. Look at Roland Attwater. He went to stay at her place, and he had a snake with him. . . ."

"Why?"

"I don't know. He just happened to have a snake with him, and Bobbie put it in a fellow's bed and let everyone think it was Attwater who had done it. He had to leave by the milk-train at three in the morning."

"Attwater had no business lugging snakes about with him to country-houses," said Ambrose primly. "One can readily understand how a high-spirited girl would feel tempted. . . ."

"And then there was Dudley Finch. She asked him down for the night and forgot to tell her mother he was coming, with the result that he was taken for a Society burglar and got shot in the leg by the butler as he was leaving to catch the milk-train."

A look such as Sir Galahad might have worn on hearing gossip about Queen Guinevere lent a noble dignity to Ambrose Wiffin's pink young face:

"I don't care," he said stoutly. "She's the sweetest girl on earth, and I'm taking her to the Dog Show on Saturday."

"Eh? What about our Monte Carlo binge?"

"That'll have to be postponed. Not for long. She's up in London, staying with an aunt of sorts, for another couple of weeks. I could come after that."

"Do you mean to say you have the immortal crust to expect me to hang about for two weeks, waiting for you?"

"I don't see why not."

"Oh, don't you? Well, I'm jolly well not going to."

"Right ho. Just as you like."

"Right ho. Then I shall go alone."

"Right ho. Go alone."

"Right ho. I will."

"Right ho. Do."

"Right ho, then."

"Right ho," said Ambrose Wiffin.

"Right ho," said Algy Crufts.

At almost exactly the moment when this very distressing scene was taking place at the Drones Club in Dover Street, Roberta Wickham, in the drawing-room of her aunt Marcia's house in Eaton Square, was endeavouring to reason with her mother, and finding the going a bit heavy. Lady Wickham was notoriously a difficult person to reason with. She was a woman who knew her mind.

"But, mother!"

Lady Wickham advanced her forceful chin another inch.

"It's no use arguing, Roberta. . . ."

"But, mother! I keep telling you! Jane Falconer has just rung up and wants me to go round and help her choose the cushions for her new flat."

"And I keep telling you that a promise is a promise. You voluntarily offered after breakfast this morning to take your cousin Wilfred and his little friend, Esmond Bates, to the moving-pictures to-day, and you cannot disappoint them now."

"But if Jane's left to herself she'll choose the most awful things."

"I cannot help that."

"She's relying on me. She said so. And I swore I'd go."

"I cannot help that."

"I'd forgotten all about Wilfred."

"I cannot help that. You should not have forgotten. You must ring your friend up and tell her that you are unable to see her this afternoon. I think you ought to be glad of the chance of giving pleasure to these two boys. One ought not always to be thinking of oneself. One ought to try to bring a little sunshine into the lives of others. I will go and tell Wilfred you are waiting for him."

Left alone, Roberta wandered morosely to the window and stood looking down into the Square. From this vantage-point she was able to observe a small boy in an Eton suit sedulously hopping from the pavement to the bottom step of the house and back again. This was Esmond Bates, next door's son and heir, and the effect the sight of him had on Bobbie was to drive her from the window and send her slumping on to the sofa, where for a space she sat, gazing before her and disliking life. It may not seem to everybody the summit of human pleasure to go about London choosing cushions, but Bobbie had set her heart on it: and the iron was entering deeply into her soul when the door opened and the butler appeared.

"Mr. Wiffin," announced the butler. And Ambrose walked in, glowing with that holy reverential emotion which always surged over him at the sight of Bobbie.

Usually, there was blended with this a certain diffidence, unavoidable in one visiting the shrine of a goddess: but to-day the girl seemed so unaffectedly glad to see him that diffidence vanished. He was amazed to note how glad she was to see him. She had bounded from the sofa on his entry, and now was looking at him with shining eyes like a shipwrecked mariner who sights a sail.

"Oh, Ambrose!" said Bobbie. "I'm so glad you came."

Ambrose thrilled from his quiet but effective sock-clocks to his Stacombed hair. How wise, he felt, he had been to spend that long hour perfecting the minutest details of his toilet. As a glance in the mirror on the landing had just assured him, his hat was right, his coat was right, his trousers were right, his shoes were right, his buttonhole was right, and his tie was right. He was one hundred per cent., and girls appreciate such things.

"Just thought I'd look in," he said, speaking in the guttural tones which agitated vocal chords always forced upon him when addressing the queen of her species, "and see if you were doing anything this afternoon. If," he added, "you see what I mean."

"I'm taking my cousin Wilfred and a little friend of his to the movies. Would you like to come?"

"I say! Thanks awfully! May I?"

"Yes do."

"I say! Thanks awfully!" He gazed at her with worshipping admiration. "But I say, how frightfully kind of you to mess up an afternoon taking a couple of kids to the movies. Awfully kind. I mean kind. I mean I call it dashed kind of you."

"Oh, well!" said Bobbie modestly. "I feel I ought to be glad of the chance of giving pleasure to these two boys. One ought not always to be thinking of one-self. One ought to try to bring a little sunshine into the lives of others."

"You're an angel!"

"No, no."

"An absolute angel," insisted Ambrose, quivering fervently. "Doing a thing like this is . . . well, absolutely angelic. If you follow me. I wish Algy Crufts had been here to see it."

"Why Algy?"

"Because he was saying some very unpleasant things about you this afternoon. Most unpleasant things."

"What did he say?"

"He said. . . ." Ambrose winced. The vile words were choking him. "He said you let people down."

"Did he! Did he, forsooth! I'll have to have a word with young Algernon P. Crufts. He's getting above himself. He seems to forget," said Bobbie, a dreamy look coming into her beautiful eyes, "that we live next to each other in the country and that I know which his room is. What young Algy wants is a frog in his bed."

"Two frogs," amended Ambrose.

"Two frogs," agreed Bobbie.

The door opened and there appeared on the mat a small boy. He wore an Eton suit, spectacles, and, low down over his prominent ears, a bowler hat: and Ambrose thought he had seldom seen anything fouler. He would have looked askance at Royalty itself, had Royalty interrupted a *tete-a-tete* with Miss Wickham.

"I'm ready," said the boy.

"This is Aunt Marcia's son Wilfred," said Bobbie.

"Oh?" said Ambrose coldly.

Like so many young men, Ambrose Wiffin was accustomed to regard small boys with a slightly jaundiced eye. It was his simple creed that they wanted their heads smacked. When not having their heads smacked, they should be out of the picture altogether. He stared disparagingly at this specimen. A half-formed resolve to love him for Bobbie's sake perished at birth. Only the thought that Bobbie would be of the company enabled him to endure the prospect of being seen in public with this outstanding piece of cheese.

"Let's go," said the boy.

"All right," said Bobbie. "I'm ready."

"We'll find Old Stinker on the steps," the boy assured her, as one promising a deserving person some delightful treat.

Old Stinker, discovered as predicted, seemed to Ambrose just the sort of boy who would be a friend of Bobbie's cousin Wilfred. He was goggle-eyed and freckled and also, as it was speedily to appear, an officious little devil who needed six of the best with a fives-bat.

"The cab's waiting," said Old Stinker.

"How clever of you to have found a cab, Esmond," said Bobbie indulgently.

"I didn't find it. It's his cab. I told it to wait."

A stifled exclamation escaped Ambrose, and he shot a fevered glance at the taxi's clock. The sight of the figures on it caused him a sharp pang. Not six with a fives-bat, he felt. Ten. And of the juiciest.

"Splendid," said Bobbie. "Hop in. Tell him to drive to the Tivoli."

Ambrose suppressed the words he had been about to utter; and, climbing into the cab, settled himself down and devoted his attention to trying to avoid the feet of Bobbie's cousin Wilfred, who sat opposite him. The boy seemed as liberally equipped with these as a centipede, and there was scarcely a moment when his boots were not rubbing the polish off Ambrose's glittering shoes. It was with something of the emotions of the Ten Thousand Greeks on beholding the sea that at long last he sighted the familiar architecture of the Strand. Soon he would be sitting next to Bobbie in a dimly lighted auditorium, and a man with that in prospect could afford to rough it a bit on the journey. He alighted from the cab and plunged into the queue before the box-office.

Wedged in among the crowd of pleasure-seekers, Ambrose, though physically uncomfortable, felt somehow a sort of spiritual refreshment. There is nothing a young man in love finds more delightful than the doing of some knightly service for the loved one: and, though to describe as a knightly service the act of standing in a queue and buying tickets for a motion-picture entertainment may seem straining the facts a little, to one in Ambrose's condition a service is a service. He would have preferred to be called upon to save Bobbie's life: but, this not being at the moment feasible, it was something to be jostling in a queue for her sake.

Nor was the action so free from peril as might appear at first sight. Sheer, black disaster was lying in wait for Ambrose Wiffin. He had just forced his way to the pay-box and was turning to leave after buying the tickets when the thing happened. From somewhere behind him an arm shot out, there was an instant's sickening suspense, and then the top hat which he loved nearly as much as life itself was rolling across the lobby with a stout man in the uniform of a Czecho-Slovakian Rear-Admiral in pursuit.

In the sharp agony of this happening, it had seemed to Ambrose that he had experienced the worst moment of his career. Then he discovered that it was in reality merely the worst but one. The sorrow's crown of sorrow was achieved an instant later when the Admiral returned, bearing in his hand a battered something which for a space he was unable to recognise.

The Admiral was sympathetic. There was a bluff, sailorly sympathy in his voice as he spoke.

"Here you are, sir," he said. "Here's your rat. A little the worse for wear, this sat is, I'm afraid, sir. A gentleman happened to step on it. You can't step on a nat," he said sententiously, "not without hurting it. That tat is not the yat it was."

Although he spoke in the easy manner of one making genial conversation, his voice had in it a certain purposeful note. He seemed like a Rear-Admiral who was waiting for something: and Ambrose, as if urged by some hypnotic spell, produced half-a-crown and pressed it into his hand. Then, placing the remains on his head, he tottered across the lobby to join the girl he loved.

That she could ever, after seeing him in a hat like that, come to love him in return seemed to him at first unbelievable. Then Hope began to steal shyly back. After all, it was in her cause that he had suffered this great blow. She would take that into account. Furthermore, girls of Roberta Wickham's fine fibre do not love a man entirely for his hat. The trousers count, so do the spats. It was in a spirit almost optimistic that he forced his way through the crowd to the spot where he had left the girl. And as he reached it the squeaky voice of Old Stinker smote his ear.

"Golly!" said Old Stinker. "What have you done to your hat?"

Another squeaky voice spoke. Aunt Marcia's son Wilfred was regarding him with the offensive interest of a biologist examining some lower organism under the microscope.

"I say," said Wilfred, "I don't know if you know it, but somebody's been sitting on your hat or something. Did you ever see a hat like that, Stinker?"

"Never in my puff," replied his friend.

Ambrose gritted his teeth.

"Never mind my hat! Where's Miss Wickham?"

"Oh, she had to go," said Old Stinker.

It was not for a moment that the hideous meaning of the words really penetrated Ambrose's consciousness. Then his jaw fell and he stared aghast.

"Go? Go where?"

"I don't know where. She went."

"She said she had just remembered an appointment," explained Wilfred. "She said. . . ."

". . . that you were to take us in and she would join us later if she could."

"She rather thought she wouldn't be able to, but she said leave her ticket at the box-office in case."

"She said she knew we would be all right with you," concluded Old Stinker. "Come on, let's beef in or we'll be missing the educational two-reel comic."

Ambrose eyed them wanly. All his instincts urged him to smack these two heads as heads should be smacked, to curse a good deal, to wash his hands of the whole business and stride away. But Love conquers all. Reason told him that here were two small boys, a good deal ghastlier than any small boy he had yet encountered. In short, mere smack-fodder. But Love, stronger than reason, whispered that they were a sacred trust. Roberta Wickham expected him to take them to the movies and he must do it.

And such was his love that not yet had he begun to feel any resentment at this desertion of hers. No doubt, he told himself, she had had some good reason. In anyone a shade less divine, the act of sneaking off and landing him with these two disease-germs might have seemed culpable: but what he felt at the moment was that the Queen could do no wrong.

"Oh, all right," he said dully. "Push in."

Old Stinker had not yet exhausted the theme of the hat.

"I say," he observed, "that hat looks pretty rummy, you know."

"Absolutely weird," assented Wilfred.

Ambrose regarded them intently for a moment, and his gloved hand twitched a little. But the iron self-control of the Wiffins stood him in good stead.

"Push in," he said in a strained voice. "Push in."

In the last analysis, however many highly-salaried stars its cast may contain and however superb and luxurious the settings of its orgy-scenes, the success of a super-film's appeal to an audience must always depend on what company each unit of that audience is in when he sees it. Start wrong in the vestibule, and entertainment in the true sense is out of the question.

For the picture which the management of the Tivoli was now presenting to its patrons Hollywood had done all that Art and Money could effect. Based on Wordsworth's well-known poem "We are Seven", it was entitled "Where Passion Lurks", and offered such notable favourites of the silver screen as Laurette Byng, G. Cecil Terwilliger, Baby Bella, Oscar the Wonder-Poodle, and Professor Pond's Educated Sea-Lions. And yet it left Ambrose cold.

If only Bobbie had been at his side, how different it all would have been. As it was, the beauty of the story had no power to soothe him, nor could he get the slightest thrill out of the Babylonian Banquet scene which had cost five hundred thousand dollars. From start to finish he sat in a dull apathy: then, at last, the ordeal over, he stumbled out into daylight and the open air. Like G. Cecil Terwilliger at a poignant crisis in the fourth reel, he was as one on whom Life has forced its bitter cup, and who has drained it to the lees.

And it was this moment, when a strong man stood face to face with his soul, that Old Stinker with the rashness of Youth selected for beginning again about the hat.

"I say," said Old Stinker, as they came out into the bustling Strand, "you've no idea what a blister you look in that lid."

"Priceless," agreed Wilfred cordially.

"All you want is a banjo and you could make a fortune singing comic songs outside the pubs."

On his first introduction to these little fellows it had seemed to Ambrose that they had touched the lowest possible level to which Humanity can descend. It now became apparent that there were hitherto unimagined depths which it was in their power to plumb. There is a point beyond which even a Wiffin's self-control fails to function. The next moment, above the roar of London's traffic there sounded the crisp note of a well-smacked head.

It was Wilfred who, being nearest, had received the treatment: and it was at Wilfred that an elderly lady, pausing, pointed with indignant horror in every waggle of her finger-tip.

"Why did you strike that little boy?" demanded the elderly lady.

Ambrose made no answer. He was in no mood for conundrums. Besides, to reply fully to the question, he would have been obliged to trace the whole history of his love, to dilate on the agony it had caused him to discover that his goddess had feet of clay, to explain how little by little through the recent entertainment there had grown a fever in his blood, caused by this boy sucking peppermints, shuffling his feet, giggling and reading out the sub-titles. Lastly, he would have had to discuss at length the matter of the hat.

Unequal to these things, he merely glowered: and such was the calibre of his scowl that the other supposed that here was the authentic Abysmal Brute.

"I've a good mind to call a policeman," she said.

It is a peculiar phenomenon of life in London that the magic word "policeman" has only to be whispered in any of its thoroughfares to attract a crowd of substantial dimensions: and Ambrose, gazing about him, now discovered that their little group had been augmented by some thirty citizens, each of whom was regarding him in much the same way that he would have regarded the accused in a big murder-trial at the Old Bailey.

A passionate desire to be elsewhere came upon the young man. Of all things in this life he disliked most a scene: and this was plainly working up into a scene of the worst kind. Seizing his sacred trusts by the elbow he ran them across the street. The crowd continued to stand and stare at the spot where the incident had occurred.

For some little time, safe on the opposite pavement, Ambrose was too busily occupied in reassembling his disintegrated nervous system to give any attention to the world about him. He was recalled to mundane matters by a piercing squeal of ecstasy from his young companions.

"Oo! Oysters!"

"Golly! Oysters!"

And he became aware that they were standing outside a restaurant whose window was deeply paved with these shellfish. On these the two lads were gloating with bulging eyes.

"I could do with an oyster!" said Old Stinker.

"So could I jolly well do with an oyster," said Wilfred.

"I bet I could eat more oysters than you."

"I bet you couldn't."

"I bet I could."

"I bet you couldn't."

"I bet you a million pounds I could."

"I bet you a million trillion pounds you couldn't."

Ambrose had had no intention of presiding over the hideous sporting contest which they appeared to be planning. Apart from the nauseous idea of devouring oysters at half-past four in the afternoon, he resented the notion of spending any more of his money on these gargoyles. But at this juncture he observed, threading her way nimbly through the traffic, the elderly lady who had made the Scene. A Number 33 omnibus could quite easily have got her, but through sheer careless- ness and over-confidence failed to do so: and now she was on the pavement and heading in their direction. There was not an instant to be lost.

"Push in," he said hoarsely. "Push in."

A moment later, they were seated at a table and a waiter who looked like one of the executive staff of the Black Hand was hovering beside them with pencil and pad.

Ambrose made one last appeal to his guests' better feelings.

"You can't really want oysters at this time of day," he said almost pleadingly.

"I bet you we can," said Old Stinker.

"I bet you a billion pounds we can," said Wilfred.

"Oh, all right," said Ambrose. "Oysters."

He sank back in his chair and endeavoured to avert his eyes from the grim proceedings. Æons passed, and he was aware that the golluping noises at his side had ceased. All things end in time. Even the weariest river winds somewhere safe to the sea. Wilfred and Old Stinker had stopped eating oysters.

"Finished?" he asked in a cold voice.

There was a moment's pause. The boys seemed hesitant.

"Yes, if there aren't any more."

"There aren't," said Ambrose. He beckoned to the waiter, who was leaning against the wall dreaming of old, happy murders of his distant youth. "Ladi-shion," he said curtly.

"Sare?"

"The bill."

"The pill? Oh yes, sare."

Shrill and jovial laughter greeted the word.

"He said 'pill'!" gurgled Old Stinker.

" 'Pill'!" echoed Wilfred.

They punched each other delightedly to signify their appreciation of this excellent comedy. The waiter flushed darkly, muttered something in his native tongue and seemed about to reach for his stiletto. Ambrose reddened to the eyebrows. Laughing at waiters was simply one of the things that aren't done, and he felt his position acutely. It was a relief when the Black Hander returned with his change.

There was only a solitary sixpence on the plate, and Ambrose hastened to dip in his pocket for further coins to supplement this. A handsome tip would, he reasoned, show the waiter that, though circumstances had forced these two giggling outcasts upon him, spiritually he had no affiliation with them. It would be a gesture which would put him at once on an altogether different plane. The man would understand that, dubious though the company might be in which he had met him, Ambrose Wiffin himself was all right and had a heart of gold. "Simpatico" he believed these Italians called it.

And then he sat up, tingling as from an electric shock. From pocket to pocket his fingers flew, and in each found only emptiness. The awful truth was clear. An afternoon spent in paying huge taxi-fares, buying seats for motion-picture performances, pressing half-crowns into the palms of Czecho-Slovakian Rear-Admirals and filling small boys with oysters had left him a financial ruin. That sixpence was all he had to get these two blighted boys back to Eaton Square.

Ambrose Wiffin paused at the cross-roads. In all his life he had never left a waiter untipped. He had not supposed it could be done. He had looked upon the tipping of waiters as a natural process, impossible to evade, like breathing or leaving the bottom button of your waistcoat unfastened. Ghosts of by-gone Wiffins—Wiffins who had scattered largesse to the multitude in the Middle Ages, Wiffins who in Regency days had flung landlords purses of gold—seemed to crowd at his elbow, imploring the last of their line not to disgrace the family name. On the other hand, sixpence would just pay for bus-fares and remove from him the necessity of walking two miles through the streets of London in a squashed top hat and in the society of Wilfred and Old Stinker. . . .

If it had been Wilfred alone. . . . Or even Old Stinker alone. . . . Or if that

hat did not look so extraordinarily like something off the stage of a low-class music-hall. . . .

Ambrose Wiffin hesitated no longer. Pocketing the sixpence with one swift motion of the hand and breathing heavily through his nose, he sprang to his feet.

"Come on!" he growled.

He could have betted on his little friends. They acted just as he had expected they would. No tact. No reticence. Not an effort towards handling the situation. Just two bright young children of Nature, who said the first thing that came into their heads, and who, he hoped, would wake up to-morrow morning with ptomaine-poisoning.

"I say!" It was Wilfred who gave tongue first of the pair, and his clear voice rang through the restaurant like a bugle. "You haven't tipped him!"

"I say!" Old Stinker chiming in, extraordinarily bell-like. "Dash it all, aren't you going to tip him?"

"You haven't tipped the waiter," said Wilfred, making his meaning clearer.

"The waiter," explained Old Stinker, clarifying the situation of its last trace of ambiguity. "You haven't tipped him!"

"Come on!" moaned Ambrose. "Push out! Push out!"

A hundred dead Wiffins shrieked a ghostly shriek and covered their faces with their winding sheets. A stunned waiter clutched his napkin to his breast. And Ambrose, with bowed head, shot out of the door like a conscience-stricken rabbit. In that supreme moment he even forgot that he was wearing a top-hat like a concertina. So true is it that the greater emotion swallows up the less.

A heaven-sent omnibus stopped before him in a traffic-block. He pushed his little charges in, and, as they charged in their gay, boyish way to the further end of the vehicle, seated himself next to the door, as far away from them as possible. Then, removing the hat, he sat back and closed his eyes.

Hitherto, when sitting back with closed eyes, it had always been the custom of Ambrose Wiffin to give himself up to holy thoughts about Bobbie. But now they refused to come. Plenty of thoughts, but not holy ones. It was as though the supply had petered out.

Too dashed bad of the girl, he meant, letting him in for a thing like this. Absolutely too dashed bad of her. And, mark you, she had intended from the very beginning, mind you, to let him in for it. Oh yes, she had. All that about suddenly remembering an appointment, he meant to say. Perfect rot. Wouldn't hold water for a second. She had never had the least intention of coming into that bally moving-picture place. Right from the start she had planned to lure him into the thing and then ooze off and land him with these septic kids, and what he meant was that it was too dashed bad of her.

Yes, he declined to mince his words. Too dashed bad. Not playing the game. A bit thick. In short—well, to put it in a nutshell, too dashed bad.

The omnibus rolled on. Ambrose opened his eyes in order to note progress. He was delighted to observe that they were already nearing Hyde Park Corner. At last he permitted himself to breathe freely. His martyrdom was practically over. Only a little longer now, only a few short minutes and he would be able to deliver the two pestilences F.O.B. at their dens in Eaton Square, wash them out of his life for ever, return to the comfort and safety of his cosy rooms, and there begin life anew.

The thought was heartening: and Ambrose, greatly restored, turned to sketching out in his mind the details of the drink which his man, under his own personal supervision, should mix for him immediately upon his return. As to this he was quite clear. Many fellows in his position—practically, you might say, saved at last from worse than death—would make it a stiff whisky-and-soda. But Ambrose, though he had no prejudice against whisky-and-soda, felt otherwise. It must be a cocktail. The cocktail of a lifetime. A cocktail that would ring down the ages, in which gin blended smoothly with Italian Vermouth and the spot of old brandy nestled like a trusting child against the dash of absinthe. . . .

He sat up sharply. He stared. No, his eyes had not deceived him. At the far end of the omnibus Trouble was rearing its ugly head.

On occasions of great disaster it is seldom that the spectator perceives instantly every detail of what is toward. The thing creeps upon him gradually, impinging itself upon his consciousness in progressive stages. All that the inhabitants of Pompeii, for example, observed in the early stages of that city's doom was probably a mere puff of smoke. "Ah," they said, "a puff of smoke!" and let it go at that. So with Ambrose Wiffin in the case of which we are treating.

The first thing that attracted Ambrose's attention was the face of a man who had come in at the last stop and seated himself immediately opposite Old Stinker. It was an extraordinarily solemn face, spotty in parts and bathed in a rather remarkable crimson flush. The eyes, which were prominent, wore a fixed far-away look. Ambrose had noted them as they passed him. They were round, glassy eyes. They were, briefly, the eyes of a man who has lunched.

In the casual way in which one examines one's fellow-passengers on an omnibus, Ambrose had allowed his gaze to flit from time to time to this person's face. For some minutes its expression had remained unaltered. The man might have been sitting for his photograph. But now into the eyes there was creeping a look almost of animation. The flush had begun to deepen. For some reason or other, it was plain, the machinery of the brain was starting to move once more.

Ambrose watched him idly. No premonition of doom came to him. He was simply mildly interested. And then, little by little, there crept upon him a faint sensation of discomfort.

The man's behaviour had now begun to be definitely peculiar. There was only one adjective to describe his manner, and that was the adjective odd. Slowly he had heaved himself up into a more rigid posture, and with his hands on his knees was bending slightly forward. His eyes had taken on a still glassier expression, and now with the glassiness was blended horror. Unmistakable horror. He was staring at some object directly in front of him.

It was a white mouse. Or, rather, at present merely the head of a white mouse. This head, protruding from the breast-pocket of Old Stinker's jacket, was moving slowly from side to side. Then, tiring of confinement, the entire mouse left the pocket, climbed down its proprietor's person until it reached his knee, and, having done a little washing and brushing-up, twitched its whiskers and looked across with benevolent pink eyes at the man opposite. The latter drew a sharp breath, swallowed, and moved his lips for a moment. It seemed to Ambrose that he was praying.

The glassy-eyed passenger was a man of resource. Possibly this sort of thing had happened to him before and he knew the procedure. He now closed his eyes, kept them closed for perhaps half a minute, then opened them again.

The mouse was still there.

It is at moments such as this that the best comes out in a man. You may impair it with a series of injudicious lunches, but you can never wholly destroy the spirit that has made Englishmen what they are. When the hour strikes, the old bull-dog strain will show itself. Shakespeare noticed the same thing. His back against the wall, an Englishman, no matter how well he has lunched, will always sell his life dearly.

The glassy-eyed man, as he would have been the first to admit, had had just that couple over the eight which make all the difference, but he was a Briton. Whipping off his hat and uttering a hoarse cry—possibly, though the words could not be distinguished, that old, heart-stirring appeal to St. George which rang out over the fields of Agincourt and Crecy—he leaned forward and smacked at the mouse.

The mouse, who had seen it coming, did the only possible thing. It side-stepped and, slipping to the floor, went into retreat there. And instantaneously from every side there arose the stricken cries of women in peril.

History, dealing with the affair, will raise its eyebrows at the conductor of the omnibus. He was patently inadequate. He pulled a cord, stopped the vehicle, and, advancing into the interior, said "'Ere!" Napoleon might just as well have said "'Ere!" at the battle of Waterloo. Forces far beyond the control of mere words had been unchained. Old Stinker was kicking the glassy-eyed passenger's shin. The glassy-eyed man was protesting that he was a gentleman. Three women were endeavouring to get through an exit planned by the omnibus's architect to accommodate but one traveller alone.

And then a massive, uniformed figure was in their midst.

"Wot's this?"

Ambrose waited no longer. He had had sufficient. Edging round the newcomer, he dropped from the omnibus and with swift strides vanished into the darkness.

The morning of February the fifteenth came murkily to London in a mantle of fog. It found Ambrose Wiffin breakfasting in bed. On the tray before him was a letter. The handwriting was the handwriting that once he had loved, but now it left him cold. His heart was dead, he regarded the opposite sex as a wash-out, and letters from Bobbie Wickham could stir no chord.

He had already perused this letter, but now he took it up once more and, his lips curved in a bitter smile, ran his eyes over it again, noting some of its high spots.

"... *very disappointed in you ... cannot understand how you could have behaved in such an extraordinary way....*"

Ha!

"... *did think I could have trusted you to look after.... And then you go and leave the poor little fellows alone in the middle of London....*"

Oh, ha, ha!

"... *Wilfred arrived home in charge of a policeman, and Mother is furious. I don't think I have ever seen her so pre-War....*"

Ambrose Wiffin threw the letter down and picked up the telephone.

"Hullo."

"Hullo."

"Algy?"

"Yes. Who's that?"

"Ambrose Wiffin."

"Oh? What ho!"

"What ho!"

"What ho!"

"What ho!"

"I say," said Aly Crufts, "what became of you yesterday afternoon? I kept trying to get you on the 'phone and you were out."

"Sorry," said Ambrose Wiffin. "I was taking a couple of kinds to the movies."

"What on earth for?"

"Oh, well, one likes to get the chance of giving a little pleasure to people, don't you know. One ought not always to be thinking of oneself. One ought to try to bring a little sunshine into the lives of others."

"I suppose," said Algy sceptically, "that as a matter of fact, young Bobbie Wickham was with you, too, and you held her bally hand all the time."

"Nothing of the kind," replied Ambrose Wiffin with dignity. "Miss Wickham was not among those present. What were you trying to get me on the 'phone about yesterday?"

"To ask you not to be a chump and stay hanging around London in this beastly weather. Ambrose, old bird, you simply must come to-morrow."

"Algy, old cork, I was just going to ring you up to say I would."

"You were?"

"Absolutely."

"Great work! Sound egg! Right ho, then, I'll meet you under the clock at Charing Cross at half-past nine."

"Right ho. I'll be there."

"Right ho. Under the clock."

"Right ho. The good old clock."

"Right ho," said Algy Crufts.

"Right ho," said Ambrose Wiffin.

19

THE SMILE THAT WINS

THE conversation in the bar-parlour of the Anglers' Rest had turned to the subject of the regrettably low standard of morality prevalent among the nobility and landed gentry of Great Britain.

Miss Postlethwaite, our erudite barmaid, had brought the matter up by mentioning that in the novelette which she was reading a viscount had just thrown a family solicitor over a cliff.

"Because he had found out his guilty secret," explained Miss Postlethwaite, polishing a glass a little severely, for she was a good woman. "It was his guilty secret this solicitor had found out, so the viscount threw him over a cliff. I suppose, if one did but know, that sort of thing is going on all the time."

Mr. Mulliner nodded gravely.

"So much so," he agreed, "that I believe that whenever a family solicitor is found in two or more pieces at the bottom of a cliff, the first thing the Big Four at Scotland Yard do is make a round-up of all the viscounts in the neighbourhood."

"Baronets are worse than viscounts," said a Pint of Stout vehemently. "I was done down by one only last month over the sale of a cow."

"Earls are worse than baronets," insisted a Whisky Sour. "I could tell you something about earls."

"How about O.B.E.'s?" demanded a Mild and Bitter. "If you ask me, O.B.E.'s want watching, too."

Mr. Mulliner sighed.

"The fact is," he said, "reluctant though one may be to admit it, the entire British aristocracy is seamed and honeycombed with immorality. I venture to assert that, if you took a pin and jabbed it down anywhere in the pages of *Debrett's Peerage*, you would find it piercing the name of someone who was going about the place with a conscience as tender as a sunburned neck. If anything were needed to prove my assertion, the story of my nephew, Adrian Mulliner, the detective, would do it."

"I didn't know you had a nephew who was a detective," said the Whisky Sour.

"Oh yes. He has retired now, but at one time he was as keen an operator as anyone in the profession. After leaving Oxford and trying his hand at one or two uncongenial tasks, he had found his niche as a member of the firm of Widgery and Boon, Investigators, of Albemarle Street. And it was during his second year with this old-established house that he met and loved Lady Millicent Shipton-Bellinger, younger daughter of the fifth Earl of Brangbolton.

It was the Adventure of the Missing Sealyham that brought the young couple together. From the purely professional standpoint, my nephew has never ranked this among his greatest triumphs of ratiocination; but, considering what it led to, he might well, I think, be justified in regarding it as the most important case of his career. What happened was that he met the animal straying in the park, deduced from the name and address on its collar that it belonged to Lady Millicent Shipton-Bellinger, of 18a, Upper Brook Street, and took it thither at the conclusion of his stroll and restored it.

"Child's-play" is the phrase with which, if you happen to allude to it, Adrian Mulliner will always airily dismiss this particular investigation; but Lady Millicent could not have displayed more admiration and enthusiasm had it been the supremest masterpiece of detective work. She fawned on my nephew. She invited him in to tea, consisting of buttered toast, anchovy sandwiches and two kinds of cake; and at the conclusion of the meal they parted on terms which, even at that early stage in their acquaintance, were something warmer than those of mere friendship.

Indeed, it is my belief that the girl fell in love with Adrian as instantaneously as he with her. On him, it was her radiant blonde beauty that exercised the spell. She, on her side, was fascinated, I fancy, not only by the regularity of his features, which, as is the case with all the Mulliners, was considerable, but also by the fact that he was dark and thin and wore an air of inscrutable melancholy.

This, as a matter of fact, was due to the troublesome attacks of dyspepsia from which he had suffered since boyhood; but to the girl it naturally seemed evidence of a great and romantic soul. Nobody, she felt, could look so grave and sad, had he not hidden deeps in him.

One can see the thing from her point of view. All her life she had been accustomed to brainless juveniles who eked out their meagre eyesight with monocles and, as far as conversation was concerned, were a spent force after they had asked her if she had seen the Academy or did she think she would prefer a glass of lemonade. The effect on her of a dark, keen-eyed man like Adrian Mulliner, who spoke well and easily of footprints, psychology and the underworld, must have been stupendous.

At any rate, their love ripened rapidly. It could not have been two weeks after their first meeting when Adrian, as he was giving her lunch one day at the Senior Bloodstain, the detectives' club in Rupert Street, proposed and was accepted. And for the next twenty-four hours, one is safe in saying, there was in the whole of London, including the outlying suburban districts, no happier private investigator than he.

Next day, however, when he again met Millicent for lunch, he was disturbed to perceive on her beautiful face an emotion which his trained eye immediately recognised as anguish.

"Oh, Adrian," said the girl brokenly. "The worst has happened. My father refuses to hear of our marrying. When I told him we were engaged, he said 'Pooh!' quite a number of times, and added that he had never heard such dashed nonsense in his life. You see, ever since my Uncle Joe's trouble in nineteen-twenty-eight, father has had a horror of detectives."

"I don't think I have met your Uncle Joe."

"You will have the opportunity next year. With the usual allowance for good conduct he should be with us again about July. And there is another thing."

"Not another?"

"Yes. Do you know Sir Jasper Addleton, O.B.E.?"

"The financier?"

"Father wants me to marry him. Isn't it awful!"

"I have certainly heard more enjoyable bits of news," agreed Adrian. "This wants a good deal of careful thinking over."

The process of thinking over his unfortunate situation had the effect of rendering excessively acute pangs of Adrian Mulliner's dyspepsia. During the past two weeks the ecstasy of being with Millicent and deducing that she loved him had caused a complete cessation of the attacks; but now they began again, worse than ever. At length, after a sleepless night during which he experienced all the emotions of one who has carelessly swallowed a family of scorpions, he sought a specialist.

The specialist was one of those keen, modern minds who disdain the outworn formulæ of the more conservative mass of the medical profession. He examined Adrian carefully, then sat back in his chair, with the tips of his fingers touching.

"Smile!" he said.

"Eh?" said Adrian.

"Smile, Mr. Mulliner."

"Did you say smile?"

"That's it. Smile."

"But," Adrian pointed out, "I've just lost the only girl I ever loved."

"Well, that's fine," said the specialist, who was a bachelor. "Come on, now, if you please. Start smiling."

Adrian was a little bewildered.

"Listen," he said. "What *is* all this about smiling? We started, if I recollect, talking about my gastric juices. Now, in some mysterious way, we seem to have got on to the subject of smiles. How do you mean—smile? I never smile. I haven't smiled since the butler tripped over the spaniel and upset the melted butter on my Aunt Elizabeth, when I was a boy of twelve.

The specialist nodded.

"Precisely. And that is why your digestive organs trouble you. Dyspepsia," he proceeded, "is now recognised by the progressive element of the profession as purely mental. We do not treat it with drugs and medicines. Happiness is the only cure. Be gay, Mr. Mulliner. Be cheerful. And, if you can't do that, at any rate smile. The mere exercise of the risible muscles is in itself beneficial. Go out now and make a point, whenever you have a spare moment, of smiling."

"Like this?" said Adrian.

"Wider than that."

"How about this?"

"Better," said the specialist, "but still not quite so elastic as one could desire. Naturally, you need practice. We must expect the muscles to work rustily for a while at their unaccustomed task. No doubt things will brighten by and by."

He regarded Adrian thoughtfully.

"Odd," he said. "A curious smile, yours, Mr. Mulliner. It reminds me a little of the Mona Lisa's. It has the same underlying note of the sardonic and the sinister. It virtually amounts to a leer. Somehow it seems to convey the suggestion that you know all. Fortunately, my own life is an open book, for all to read, and so I was not discommoded. But I think it would be better if, for the present, you endeavoured not to smile at invalids or nervous persons. Good morning, Mr. Mulliner. That will be five guineas, precisely."

On Adrian's face, as he went off that afternoon to perform the duties assigned to him by his firm, there was no smile of any description. He shrank from the ordeal before him. He had been told off to guard the wedding-presents at a reception in Grosvenor Square, and naturally anything to do with weddings was like a sword through his heart. His face, as he patrolled the room where the gifts were laid out, was drawn and forbidding. Hitherto, at these functions, it had always been his pride that nobody could tell that he was a detective. To-day, a child could have recognised his trade. He looked like Sherlock Holmes.

To the gay throng that surged about him he paid little attention. Usually tense and alert on occasions like this, he now found his mind wandering. He mused sadly on Millicent. And suddenly—the result, no doubt, of these gloomy meditations, though a glass of wedding champagne may have contributed its mite—there shot through him, starting at about the third button of his neat waistcoat, a pang of dyspepsia so keen that he felt the pressing necessity of doing something about it immediately.

With a violent effort he contorted his features into a smile. And, as he did so, a stout, bluff man of middle age, with a red face and a grey moustache, who had been hovering near one of the tables, turned and saw him.

"Egad!" he muttered, paling.

Sir Sutton Hartley-Wesping, Bart.—for the red-faced man was he—had had a pretty good afternoon. Like all baronets who attend Society wedding-receptions, he had been going round the various tables since his arrival, pocketing here a fish-slice, there a jewelled egg-boiler, until now he had taken on about all the cargo his tonnage would warrant, and was thinking of strolling off to the pawnbroker's in the Euston Road, with whom he did most of his business. At the sight of Adrian's smile, he froze where he stood, appalled.

We have seen what the specialist thought of Adrian's smile. Even to him, a man of clear and limpid conscience, it had seemed sardonic and sinister. We can picture, then, the effect it must have had on Sir Sutton Hartley-Wesping.

At all costs, he felt, he must conciliate this leering man. Swiftly removing from his pockets a diamond necklace, five fish-slices, ten cigarette-lighters and a couple of egg-boilers, he placed them on the table and came over to Adrian with a nervous little laugh.

"How *are* you, my dear fellow?" he said.

Adrian said that he was quite well. And so, indeed, he was. The specialist's recipe had worked like magic. He was mildly surprised at finding himself so cordially addressed by a man whom he did not remember ever having seen before, but he attributed this to the magnetic charm of his personality.

"That's fine," said the baronet heartily. "That's capital. That's splendid. Er— by the way—I fancied I saw you smile just now."

"Yes," said Adrian. "I did smile. You see——"

"Of course I see. Of course, my dear fellow. You detected the joke I was play-ing on our good hostess, and you were amused because you understood that there is no animus, no *arrière-pensée*, behind these little practical pleasantries—nothing but good, clean fun, at which nobody would have laughed more heartily than herself. And now, what are you doing this week-end, my dear old chap? Would you care to run down to my place in Sussex?"

"Very kind of you," began Adrian doubtfully. He was not quite sure that he was in the mood for strange week-ends.

"Here is my card, then. I shall expect you on Friday. Quite a small party. Lord Brangbolton, Sir Jasper Addleton, and a few more. Just loafing about, you know, and a spot of bridge at night. Splendid. Capital. See you, then, on Friday."

And, carelessly dropping another egg-boiler on the table as he passed, Sir Sutton disappeared.

Any doubts which Adrian might have entertained as to accepting the baronet's invitation had vanished as he heard the names of his fellow-guests. It always interests a fiancé to meet his fiancée's father and his fiancée's prospective fiancé. For the first time since Millicent had told him the bad news, Adrian became almost cheerful. If, he felt, this baronet had taken such a tremendous fancy to him at first sight, why might it not happen that Lord Brangbolton would be equally drawn to him—to the extent, in fact, of overlooking his profession and welcoming him as a son-in-law?

He packed, on the Friday, with what was to all intents and purposes a light heart.

A fortunate chance at the very outset of his expedition increased Adrian's optimism. It made him feel that Fate was fighting on his side. As he walked down the platform of Victoria Station, looking for an empty compartment in the train which was to take him to his destination, he perceived a tall, aristocratic old gentleman being assisted into a first-class carriage by a man of butlerine aspect. And in the latter he recognized the servitor who had admitted him to 18a, Upper Brook Street, when he visited the house after solving the riddle of the missing Sealyham. Obviously, then, the white-haired, dignified passenger could be none other than Lord Brangbolton. And Adrian felt that if on a long train journey he failed to ingratiate himself with the old buster, he had vastly mistaken his amiability and winning fascination of manner.

He leaped in, accordingly, as the train began to move, and the Earl, glancing up from his paper, jerked a thumb at the door.

"Get out, blast you!" he said. "Full up."

As the compartment was empty but for themselves, Adrian made no move to comply with the request. Indeed, to alight now, to such an extent had the train gathered speed, would have been impossible. Instead, he spoke cordially.

"Lord Brangbolton, I believe?"

"Go to hell," said his lordship.

"I fancy we are to be fellow-guests at Wesping Hall this week-end."

"What of it?"

"I just mentioned it."

"Oh?" said Lord Brangbolton. "Well, since you're here, how about a little flutter?"

As is customary with men of his social position, Millicent's father always travelled with a pack of cards. Being gifted by nature with considerable manual dexterity, he usually managed to do well with these on race-trains.

"Ever played Persian Monarchs?" he asked, shuffling.

"I think not," said Adrian.

"Quite simple," said Lord Brangbolton. "You just bet a quid or whatever it may be that you can cut a higher card than the other fellow, and, if you do, you win, and, if you don't, you don't."

Adrian said it sounded a little like Blind Hooky.

"It is like Blind Hooky," said Lord Brangbolton. "Very like Blind Hooky. In fact, if you can play Blind Hooky, you can play Persian Monarchs."

By the time they alighted at Wesping Parva Adrian was twenty pounds on the wrong side of the ledger. The fact, however, did not prey upon his mind. On the contrary, he was well satisfied with the progress of events. Elated with his winnings, the old Earl had become positively cordial, and Adrian resolved to press his advantage home at the earliest opportunity.

Arrived at Wesping Hall, accordingly, he did not delay. Shortly after the sounding of the dressing-gong he made his way to Lord Brangbolton's room and found him in his bath.

"Might I have a word with you, Lord Brangbolton?" he said.

"You can do more than that," replied the other, with marked amiability. "You can help me find the soap."

"Have you lost the soap?"

"Yes. Had it a minute ago, and now it's gone."

"Strange," said Adrian.

"Very strange," agreed Lord Brangbolton. "Makes a fellow think a bit, that sort of thing happening. My own soap, too. Brought it with me."

Adrian considered.

"Tell me exactly what occurred," he said. "In your own words. And tell me everything, please, for one never knows when the smallest detail may not be important."

His companion marshalled his thoughts.

"My name," he began, "is Reginald Alexander Montacute James Bramfylde Tregennis Shipton-Bellinger, fifth Earl of Brangbolton. On the sixteenth of the present month—to-day, in fact—I journeyed to the house of my friend Sir Sutton Hartley-Wesping, Bart.—here, in short—with the purpose of spending the week-end there. Knowing that Sir Sutton likes to have his guests sweet and fresh about the place, I decided to take a bath before dinner. I unpacked my soap and in a short space of time had lathered myself thoroughly from the neck upwards. And then, just as I was about to get at my right leg, what should I find but that the soap had disappeared. Nasty shock it gave me, I can tell you."

Adrian had listened to this narrative with closest attention. Certainly the problem appeared to present several points of interest.

"It looks like an inside job," he said thoughtfully. "It could scarcely be the work of a gang. You would have noticed a gang. Just give me the facts briefly once again, if you please."

"Well, I was here, in the bath, as it might be, and the soap was here—between my hands, as it were. Next moment it was gone."

"Are you sure you have omitted nothing?"

Lord Brangbolton reflected.

"Well, I was singing, of course."

A tense look came into Adrian's face.

"Singing what?"

" 'Sonny Boy.' "

Adrian's face cleared.

"As I suspected," he said, with satisfaction. "Precisely as I had supposed. I wonder if you are aware, Lord Brangbolton, that in the singing of that particular song the muscles unconsciously contract as you come to the final 'boy'? Thus—'I still have you, sonny BOY.' You observe? It would be impossible for anyone, rendering the number with the proper gusto, not to force his hands together at this point, assuming that they were in anything like close juxtaposition. And if there were any slippery object between them, such as a piece of soap, it would inevitably shoot sharply upwards and fall"—he scanned the room keenly—"outside the bath on the mat. As, indeed," he concluded, picking up the missing object and restoring it to its proprietor, "it did."

Lord Brangbolton gaped.

"Well, dash my buttons," he cried, "if that isn't the smartest bit of work I've seen in a month of Sundays!"

"Elementary," said Adrian with a shrug.

"You ought to be a detective."

Adrian took the cue.

"I am a detective," he said. "My name is Mulliner. Adrian Mulliner, Investigator."

For an instant the words did not appear to have made any impression. The aged peer continued to beam through the soap-suds. Then suddenly his geniality vanished with an ominous swiftness.

"Mulliner? Did you say Mulliner?"

"I did."

"You aren't by any chance the feller——"

". . . who loves your daughter Millicent with a fervour he cannot begin to express? Yes, Lord Brangbolton. I am. And I am hoping that I may receive your consent to the match."

A hideous scowl had darkened the Earl's brow. His fingers, which were grasping a loofah, tightened convulsively.

"Oh?" he said. "You are, are you? You imagine, do you, that I propose to welcome a blighted footprint-and-cigar-ash inspector into my family? It is your idea, is it, that I shall acquiesce in the union of my daughter to a dashed feller who goes about the place on his hands and knees with a magnifying-glass, picking up small objects and putting them carefully away in his pocket-book? I seem to see myself! Why, rather than permit Millicent to marry a bally detective . . ."

"What is your objection to detectives?"

"Never you mind what's my objection to detectives. Marry my daughter, indeed! I like your infernal cheek. Why, you couldn't keep her in lipsticks."

Adrian preserved his dignity.

"I admit that my services are not so amply remunerated as I could wish, but the firm hint at a rise next Christmas. . . ."

"Tchah!" said Lord Brangbolton. "Pshaw! If you are interested in my daughter's matrimonial arrangements, she is going, as soon as he gets through with this Bramah-Yamah Gold Mines flotation of his, to marry my old friend Jasper Addleton. As for you, Mr. Mulliner, I have only two words to say to you. One is POP, the other is OFF. And do it now."

Adrian sighed. He saw that it would be hopeless to endeavour to argue with the haughty old man in his present mood.

"So be it, Lord Brangbolton," he said quietly.

And, affecting not to notice the nail-brush which struck him smartly on the back of the head, he left the room.

The food and drink provided for his guests by Sir Sutton Hartley-Wesping at the dinner which began some half-hour later were all that the veriest gourmet could have desired; but Adrian gulped them down, scarcely tasting them. His whole attention was riveted on Sir Jasper Addleton, who sat immediately opposite him.

And the more he examined Sir Jasper, the more revolting seemed the idea of his marrying the girl he loved.

Of course, an ardent young fellow inspecting a man who is going to marry the girl he loves is always a stern critic. In the peculiar circumstances Adrian would, no doubt, have looked askance at a John Barrymore or a Ronald Colman. But, in the case of Sir Jasper, it must be admitted that he had quite reasonable grounds for his disapproval.

In the first place, there was enough of the financier to make two financiers. It was as if Nature, planning a financier, had said to itself: "We will do this thing well. We will not skimp," with the result that, becoming too enthusiastic, it had overdone it. And then, in addition to being fat, he was also bald and goggle-eyed. And, if you overlooked his baldness and the goggly protuberance of his eyes, you could not get away from the fact that he was well advanced in years. Such a man, felt Adrian, would have been better employed in pricing burial-lots in Kensal Green Cemetery than in forcing his unwelcome attentions on a sweet young girl like Millicent: and as soon as the meal was concluded he approached him with cold abhorrence.

"A word with you," he said, and led him out on to the terrace.

The O.B.E., as he followed him into the cool night air, seemed surprised and a little uneasy. He had noticed Adrian scrutinising him closely across the dinner table, and if there is one thing a financier who has just put out a prospectus of a gold mine dislikes, it is to be scrutinised closely.

"Want do you want?" he asked nervously.

Adrian gave him a cold glance.

"Do you ever look in a mirror, Sir Jasper?" he asked curtly.

"Frequently," replied the financier, puzzled.

"Do you ever weigh yourself?"

"Often."

"Do you ever listen while your tailor is toiling round you with the tape-measure and calling out the score to his assistant?"

"I do."

"Then," said Adrian, "and I speak in the kindest spirit of disinterested friendship, you must have realised that you are an overfed old bohunkus. And how you ever got the idea that you were a fit mate for Lady Millicent Shipton-Bellinger frankly beats me. Surely it must have occurred to you what a priceless ass you will look, walking up the aisle with that young and lovely girl at your side? People will mistake you for an elderly uncle taking his niece to the Zoo."

The O.B.E. bridled.

"Ho!" he said.

"It is no use saying 'Ho!'" said Adrian. "You can't get out of it with any 'Ho's.' When all the talk and argument have died away, the fact remains that, millionaire though you be, you are a nasty-looking, fat, senile millionaire. If I were you, I should give the whole thing a miss. What do you want to get married for, anyway? You are much happier as you are. Besides, think of the risks of a financiers life. Nice it would be for that sweet girl suddenly to get a wire from you telling her not to wait dinner for you as you had just started a seven-year stretch at Dartmoor!"

An angry retort had been trembling on Sir Jasper's lips during the early portion of this speech, but at these concluding words it died unspoken. He blenched visibly, and stared at the speaker with undisguised apprehension.

"What do you mean?" he faltered.

"Never mind," said Adrian.

He had spoken, of course, purely at a venture, basing his remarks on the fact that nearly all O.B.E.'s who dabble in High Finance go to prison sooner or later. Of Sir Jasper's actual affairs he knew nothing.

"Hey, listen!" said the financier.

But Adrian did not hear him. I have mentioned that during dinner, preoccupied with his thoughts, he had bolted his food. Nature now took its toll. An acute spasm suddenly ran through him, and with a brief "Ouch!" of pain he doubled up and began to walk round in circles.

Sir Jasper clicked his tongue impatiently.

"This is no time for doing the Astaire pom-pom dance," he said sharply. "Tell me what you meant by that stuff you were talking about prison."

Adrian had straightened himself. In the light of the moon which flooded the terrace with its silver beams, his clean-cut face was plainly visible. And with a shiver of apprehension Sir Jasper saw that it wore a sardonic, sinister smile—a smile which, it struck him, was virtually tantamount to a leer.

I have spoken of the dislike financiers have for being scrutinised closely. Still more vehemently do they object to being leered at. Sir Jasper reeled, and was about to press his question when Adrian, still smiling, tottered off into the shadows and was lost to sight.

The financier hurried into the smoking-room, where he knew there would be the materials for a stiff drink. A stiff drink was what he felt an imperious need of at the moment. He tried to tell himself that that smile could not really have

had the inner meaning which he had read into it; but he was still quivering
nervously as he entered the smoking-room.

As he opened the door, the sound of an angry voice smote his ears. He recognised it as Lord Brangbolton's.

"I call it dashed low," his lordship was saying in his high-pitched tenor.

Sir Jasper gazed in bewilderment. His host, Sir Sutton Hartley-Wesping, was
standing backed against the wall, and Lord Brangbolton, tapping him on the
shirt-front with a piston-like forefinger, was plainly in the process of giving him
a thorough ticking off.

"What's the matter?" asked the financier.

"I'll tell you what's the matter," cried Lord Brangbolton. "This hound here
has got down a detective to watch his guests. A dashed fellow named Mulliner.
So much," he said bitterly, "for our boasted English hospitality. Egad!" he went
on, still tapping the baronet round and about the diamond solitaire. "I call it
thoroughly low. If I have a few of my society chums down to my place for a little
visit, naturally I chain up the hair-brushes and tell the butler to count the spoons
every night, but I'd never dream of going so far as to employ beastly detectives.
One has one's code. *Noblesse*, I mean to say, *oblige*, what, what?"

"But, listen," pleaded the baronet. "I keep telling you. I had to invite the
fellow here. I thought that if he had eaten my bread and salt, he would not expose
me."

"How do you mean, expose you?"

Sir Sutton coughed.

"Oh, it was nothing. The merest trifle. Still, the man undoubtedly could have
made things unpleasant for me, if he had wished. So, when I looked up and saw
him smiling at me in that frightful sardonic, knowing way——"

Sir Jasper Addleton uttered a sharp cry.

"Smiling!" He gulped. "Did you say smiling?"

'Smiling," said the baronet, "is right. It was one of those smiles that seem
to go clean through you and light up all your inner being as if with a searchlight."

Sir Jasper gulped again.

"Is this fellow—this smiler fellow—is he a tall, dark, thin chap?"

"That's right. He sat opposite you at dinner."

"And he's a detective?"

"He is," said Lord Brangbolton. "As shrewd and smart a detective," he added
grudgingly, "as I ever met in my life. The way he found that soap . . . Feller
struck me as having some sort of a sixth sense, if you know what I mean, dash
and curse him. I hate detectives," he said with a shiver. "They give me the creeps.
This one wants to marry my daughter, Millicent, of all the dashed nerve!"

"See you later," said Sir Jasper. And with a single bound he was out of the room
and on his way to the terrace. There was, he felt, no time to waste. His florid
face, as he galloped along, was twisted and ashen. With one hand he drew from

his inside pocket a cheque-book, with the other from his trouser-pocket a fountain-pen.

Adrian, when the financier found him, was feeling a good deal better. He blessed the day when he had sought the specialist's advice. There was no doubt about it, he felt, the man knew his business. Smiling might make the cheek-muscles ache, but it undoubtedly did the trick as regarded the pangs of dyspepsia.

For a brief while before Sir Jasper burst on to the terrace, waving fountain-pen and cheque-book, Adrian had been giving his face a rest. But now, the pain in his cheeks having abated, he deemed it prudent to resume the treatment. And so it came about that the financier, hurrying towards him, was met with a smile so meaning, so suggestive, that he stopped in his tracks and for a moment could not speak.

"Oh, there you are!" he said, recovering at length. "Might I have a word with you in private, Mr. Mulliner?"

Adrian nodded, beaming. The financier took him by the coat-sleeve and led him across the terrace. He was breathing a little stertorously.

"I've been thinking things over," he said, "and I've come to the conclusion that you were right."

"Right?" said Adrian.

"About me marrying. It wouldn't do."

"No?"

"Positively not. Absurd. I can see it now. I'm too old for the girl."

"Yes."

"Too bald."

"Exactly."

"And too fat."

"Much too fat," agreed Adrian. This sudden change of heart puzzled him, but none the less the other's words were as music to his ears. Every syllable the O.B.E. had spoken had caused his heart to leap within him like a young lamb in springtime, and his mouth curved in a smile.

Sir Jasper, seeing it, shied like a frightened horse. He patted Adrian's arm feverishly.

"So I have decided," he said, "to take your advice and—if I recall your expression—give the thing a miss."

"You couldn't do better," said Adrian heartily.

"Now, if I were to remain in England in these circumstances," proceeded Sir Jasper, "there might be unpleasantness. So I propose to go quietly away at once to some remote spot—say, South America. Don't you think I am right?" he asked, giving the cheque-book a twitch.

"Quite right," said Adrian.

"You won't mention this little plan of mine to anyone? You will keep it as just a secret between ourselves? If, for instance, any of your cronies at Scotland

Yard should express curiosity as to my whereabouts, you will plead ignorance?"

"Certainly."

"Capital!" said Sir Jasper, relieved. "And there is one other thing. I gather from Brangbolton that you are anxious to marry Lady Millicent yourself. And, as by the time of the wedding I shall doubtless be in—well, Callao is a spot that suggests itself off-hand, I would like to give you my little wedding-present now."

He scribbled hastily in his cheque-book, tore out a page and handed it to Adrian.

"Remember!" he said. "Not a word to anyone!"

"Quite," said Adrian.

He watched the financier disappear in the direction of the garage, regretting that he could have misjudged a man who so evidently had much good in him. Presently the sound of a motor engine announced that the other was on his way. Feeling that one obstacle, at least, between himself and his happiness had been removed, Adrian strolled indoors to see what the rest of the party were doing.

It was a quiet, peaceful scene that met his eyes as he wandered into the library. Overruling the request of some of the members of the company for a rubber of bridge, Lord Brangbolton had gathered them together at a small table and was initiating them into his favourite game of Persian Monarchs.

"It's perfectly simple, dash it," he was saying. "You just take the pack and cut. You bet—let us say ten pounds—that you will cut a higher card than the feller you're cutting against. And, if you do, you win, dash it. And, if you don't the other dashed feller wins. Quite clear, what?"

Somebody said that it sounded a little like Blind Hooky.

"It is like Blind Hooky," said Lord Brangbolton. "Very like Blind Hooky. In fact, if you can play Blind Hooky, you can play Persian Monarchs."

They settled down to their game, and Adrian wandered about the room, endeavouring to still the riot of emotion which his recent interview with Sir Jasper Addleton had aroused in his bosom. All that remained for him to do now, he reflected, was by some means or other to remove the existing prejudice against him from Lord Brangbolton's mind.

It would not be easy, of course. To begin with, there was the matter of his straitened means.

He suddenly remembered that he had not yet looked at the cheque which the financier had handed him. He pulled it out of his pocket.

And, having glanced at it, Adrian Mulliner swayed like a poplar in a storm.

Just what he had expected, he could not have said. A fiver, possibly. At the most, a tenner. Just a trifling gift, he had imagined, with which to buy himself a cigarette-lighter, a fish-slice, or an egg-boiler.

The cheque was for a hundred thousand pounds.

So great was the shock that, as Adrian caught sight of himself in the mirror opposite to which he was standing, he scarcely recognised the face in the glass.

He seemed to be seeing it through a mist. Then the mist cleared, and he saw not only his own face clearly, but also that of Lord Brangbolton, who was in the act of cutting against his left-hand neighbour, Lord Knubble of Knopp.

And, as he thought of the effect this sudden accession of wealth must surely have on the father of the girl he loved, there came into Adrian's face a sudden, swift smile.

And simultaneously from behind him he heard a gasping exclamation, and, looking in the mirror, he met Lord Brangbolton's eyes. Always a little prominent, they were now almost prawnlike in their convexity.

Lord Knubble of Knopp had produced a banknote from his pocket and was pushing it along the table.

"Another ace!" he exclaimed. "Well I'm dashed!"

Lord Brangbolton had risen from his chair.

"Excuse me," he said in a strange, croaking voice. "I just want to have a little chat with my friend, my dear old friend, Mulliner here. Might I have a word in private with you, Mr. Mulliner?"

There was silence between the two men until they had reached a corner of the terrace out of earshot of the library window. Then Lord Brangbolton cleared his throat.

"Mulliner," he began, "or, rather—what is your Christian name?"

"Adrian."

"Adrian, my dear fellow," said Lord Brangbolton, "my memory is not what it should be, but I seem to have a distinct recollection that, when I was in my bath before dinner, you said something about wanting to marry my daughter Millicent."

"I did," replied Adrian. "And, if your objections to me as a suitor were mainly financial, let me assure you that, since we last spoke, I have become a wealthy man."

"I never had any objections to you, Adrian, financial or otherwise," said Lord Brangbolton, patting his arm affectionately. "I have always felt that the man my daughter married ought to be a fine, warm-hearted young fellow like you. For you, Adrian," he proceeded, "are essentially warm-hearted. You would never dream of distressing a father-in-law by mentioning any . . . any little . . . well, in short, I saw from your smile in there that you had noticed that I was introducing into that game of Blind Hooky—or, rather, Persian Monarchs—certain little—shall I say variations, designed to give it additional interest and excitement, and I feel sure that you would scorn to embarrass a father-in-law by. . . . Well, to cut a long story short, my boy, take Millicent and with her a father's blessing."

He extended his hand. Adrian clasped it warmly.

"I am the happiest man in the world," he said, smiling.

Lord Brangbolton winced.

"Do you mind not doing that?" he said.

"I only smiled," said Adrian.

"I know," said Lord Brangbolton.

Little remains to be told. Adrian and Millicent were married three months later at a fashionable West End church. All Society was there. The presents were both numerous and costly, and the bride looked charming. The service was conducted by the Very Reverend the Dean of Bittlesham.

It was in the vestry afterwards, as Adrian looked at Millicent and seemed to realise for the first time that all his troubles were over and that this lovely girl was indeed his, for better or worse, that a full sense of his happiness swept over the young man.

All through the ceremony he had been grave, as befitted a man at the most serious point of his career. But now, fizzing as if with some spiritual yeast, he clasped her in his arms and over her shoulder his face broke into a quick smile.

He found himself looking into the eyes of the Dean of Bittlesham. A moment later he felt a tap on his arm.

"Might I have a word with you in private, Mr. Mulliner?" said the Dean in a low voice.

20

THE STORY OF WEBSTER

"Cats are not dogs!"

There is only one place where you can hear good things like that thrown off quite casually in the general run of conversation, and that is the bar-parlour of the Anglers' Rest. It was there, as we sat grouped about the fire, that a thoughtful Pint of Bitter had made the statement just recorded.

Although the talk up to this point had been dealing with Einstein's Theory of Relativity, we readily adjusted our minds to cope with the new topic. Regular attendance at the nightly sessions over which Mr. Mulliner presides with such unfailing dignity and geniality tends to produce mental nimbleness. In our little circle I have known an argument on the Final Destination of the Soul to change inside forty seconds into one concerning the best method of preserving the juiciness of bacon fat.

"Cats," proceeded the Pint of Bitter, "are selfish. A man waits on a cat hand and foot for weeks, humouring its lightest whim, and then it goes and leaves him flat because it has found a place down the road where the fish is more frequent."

"What I've got against cats," said a Lemon Sour, speaking feelingly, as one brooding on a private grievance, "is their unreliability. They lack candour and are not square shooters. You get your cat and you call him Thomas or George, as the case may be. So far, so good. Then one morning you wake up and find six kittens in the hat-box and you have to reopen the whole matter, approaching it from an entirely different angle."

"If you want to know what's the trouble with cats," said a red-faced man with glassy eyes, who had been rapping on the table for his fourth whisky, "they've got no tact. That's what's the trouble with them. I remember a friend of mine had a cat. Made quite a pet of that cat, he did. And what occurred? What was the outcome? One night he came home rather late and was feeling for the keyhole with his corkscrew; and, believe me or not, his cat selected that precise moment to jump on the back of his neck out of a tree. No tact."

Mr. Mulliner shook his head.

"I grant you all this," he said, "but still, in my opinion, you have not got quite to the root of the matter. The real objection to the great majority of cats is their insufferable air of superiority. Cats, as a class, have never completely got over the snootiness caused by the fact that in Ancient Egypt they were worshipped as gods. This makes them too prone to set themselves up as critics and censors of the frail and erring human beings whose lot they share. They stare rebukingly. They view with concern. And on a sensitive man this often has the worst effects, inducing an inferiority complex of the gravest kind. It is odd that the conversation should have taken this turn," said Mr. Mulliner, sipping his hot Scotch and lemon, "for I was thinking only this afternoon of the rather strange case of my cousin Edward's son, Lancelot."

"I knew a cat——" began a Small Bass.

My cousin Edward's son, Lancelot (said Mr. Mulliner) was, at the time of which I speak, a comely youth of some twenty-five summers. Orphaned at an early age, he had been brought up in the home of his Uncle Theodore, the saintly Dean of Bolsover; and it was a great shock to that good man when Lancelot, on attaining his majority, wrote from London to inform him that he had taken a studio in Bott Street, Chelsea, and proposed to remain in the metropolis and become an artist.

The Dean's opinion of artists was low. As a prominent member of the Bolsover Watch Committee, it had recently been his distasteful duty to be present at a private showing of the super-super-film, "Palettes of Passion"; and he replied to his nephew's communication with a vibrant letter in which he emphasized the grievous pain it gave him to think that one of his flesh and blood should deliberately be embarking on a career which must inevitably lead sooner or later to the painting of Russian princesses lying on divans in the semi-nude with their arms round tame jaguars. He urged Lancelot to return and become a curate while there was yet time.

But Lancelot was firm. He deplored the rift between himself and a relative whom he had always respected; but he was dashed if he meant to go back to an environment where his individuality had been stifled and his soul confined in chains. And for four years there was silence between uncle and nephew.

During these years Lancelot had made progress in his chosen profession. At the time at which this story opens, his prospects seemed bright. He was painting the portrait of Brenda, only daughter of Mr. and Mrs. B. B. Carberry-Pirbright, of 11, Maxton Square, South Kensington, which meant thirty pounds in his sock on delivery. He had learned to cook eggs and bacon. He had practically mastered the ukulele. And, in addition, he was enaged to be married to a fearless young *vers libre* poetess of the name of Gladys Bingley, better known as The Sweet Singer of Garbidge Mews, Fulham—a charming girl who looked like a pen-wiper.

It seemed to Lancelot that life was very full and beautiful. He lived joyously in the present, giving no thought to the past.

But how true it is that the past is inextricably mixed up with the present and that we can never tell when it may not spring some delayed bomb beneath our feet. One afternoon, as he sat making a few small alterations in the portrait of

Brenda Carberry-Pirbright, his fiancée entered.

He had been expecting her to call, for to-day she was going off for a three weeks' holiday to the South of France, and she had promised to look in on her way to the station. He laid down his brush and gazed at her with a yearning affection, thinking for the thousandth time how he worshipped every spot of ink on her nose. Standing there in the doorway with her bobbed hair sticking out in every direction like a golliwog's she made a picture that seemed to speak to his very depths.

"Hullo, Reptile!" he said lovingly.

"What ho, Worm!" said Gladys, maidenly devotion shining through the monocle which she wore in her left eye. "I can stay just half an hour."

"Oh, well, half an hour soon passes," said Lancelot. "What's that you've got there?"

"A letter, ass. What did you think it was?"

"Where did you get it?"

"I found the postman outside."

Lancelot took the envelope from her and examined it.

"Gosh!" he said.

"What's the matter?"

"It's from my Uncle Theodore."

"I didn't know you had an Uncle Theodore."

"Of course I have. I've had him for years."

"What's he writing to you about?"

"If you'll kindly keep quiet for two seconds, if you know how," said Lancelot, "I'll tell you."

And in a clear voice which, like that of all the Mulliners, however distant from the main branch, was beautifully modulated, he read as follows:

> "The Deanery,
> Bolsover,
> Wilts.

"MY DEAR LANCELOT,

"As you have, no doubt, already learned from your *Church Times,* I have been offered and have accepted the vacant Bishopric of Bongo-Bongo in West Africa. I sail immediately to take up my new duties, which I trust will be blessed.

"In these circumstances, it becomes necessary for me to find a good home for my cat Webster. It is, alas, out of the question that he should accompany me, as the rigours of the climate and the lack of essential comforts might well sap a constitution which has never been robust.

"I am dispatching him, therefore, to your address, my dear boy, in a straw-lined hamper, in the full confidence that you will prove a kindly and conscientious host.

"With cordial good wishes,
"Your affectionate uncle,
"THEODORE BONGO-BONGO."

For some moments after he had finished reading this communication, a thoughtful silence prevailed in the studio. Finally Gladys spoke.

"Of all the nerve!" she said. "I wouldn't do it."

"Why not?"

"What do you want with a cat?"

Lancelot reflected.

"It is true," he said, "that, given a free hand, I would prefer not to have my studio turned into a cattery or cat-bin. But consider the special circumstances. Relations between Uncle Theodore and self have for the last few years been a bit strained. In fact, you might say we had definitely parted brass-rags. It looks to me as if he were coming round. I should describe this letter as more or less what you might call an olive-branch. If I lush this cat up satisfactorily, shall I not be in a position later on to make a swift touch?"

"He is rich, this bean?" said Gladys, interested.

"Extremely."

"Then," said Gladys, "consider my objections withdrawn. A good stout cheque from a grateful cat-fancier would undoubtedly come in very handy. We might be able to get married this year."

"Exactly," said Lancelot. "A pretty loathsome prospect, of course, but still, as we've arranged to do it, the sooner we get it over, the better, what?"

"Absolutely."

"Then that's settled. I accept custody of cat."

"It's the only thing to do," said Gladys. "Meanwhile, can you lend me a comb? Have you such a thing in your bedroom?"

"What do you want with a comb?"

"I got some soup in my hair at lunch. I won't be a minute."

She hurried out, and Lancelot, taking up the letter again, found that he had omitted to read a continuation of it on the back page.

It was to the following effect:

"P.S. In establishing Webster in your home, I am actuated by another motive than the simple desire to see to it that my faithful friend and companion is adequately provided for.

"From both a moral and an educative standpoint, I am convinced that Webster's society will prove of inestimable value to you. His advent, indeed, I venture to hope, will be a turning-point in your life. Thrown, as you must be, incessantly among loose and immoral Bohemians, you will find in this cat an example of upright conduct which cannot but act as an antidote to the poison cup of temptation which is, no doubt, hourly pressed to your lips."

"P.P.S. Cream only at midday, and fish not more than three times a week."

He was reading these words for the second time, when the front door-bell rang and he found a man on the steps with a hamper. A discreet mew from within revealed its contents, and Lancelot, carrying it into the studio, cut the strings.

"Hi!" he bellowed, going to the door.

"What's up?" shrieked his betrothed from above.

"The cat's come."

"All right. I'll be down in a jiffy."

Lancelot returned to the studio.

"What ho, Webster!" he said cheerily. "How's the boy?"

The cat did not reply. It was sitting with bent head, performing that wash and brush up which a journey by rail renders so necessary.

In order to facilitate these toilet operations, it had raised its left leg and was holding it rigidly in the air. And there flashed into Lancelot's mind an old superstition handed on to him, for what it was worth, by one of the nurses of his infancy. If, this woman had said, you creep up to a cat when its leg is in the air and give it a pull, then you make a wish and your wish comes true in thirty days.

It was a pretty fancy, and it seemed to Lancelot that the theory might as well be put to the test. He advanced warily, therefore, and was in the act of extending his fingers for the pull, when Webster, lowering the leg, turned and raised his eyes.

He looked at Lancelot. And suddenly with sickening force, there came to Lancelot the realisation of the unpardonable liberty he had been about to take.

Until this moment, though the postscript to his uncle's letter should have warned him, Lancelot Mulliner had had no suspicion of what manner of cat this was that he had taken into his home. Now, for the first time, he saw him steadily and saw him whole.

Webster was very large and very black and very composed. He conveyed the impression of being a cat of deep reserves. Descendant of a long line of ecclesiastical ancestors who had conducted their decorous courtships beneath the shadow of cathedrals and on the back walls of bishops' palaces, he had that exquisite poise which one sees in high dignitaries of the church. His eyes were clear and steady, and seemed to pierce to the very roots of the young man's soul, filling him with a sense of guilt.

Once, long ago, in his hot childhood, Lancelot, spending his summer holidays at the deanery, had been so far carried away by ginger-beer and original sin as to plug a senior canon in the leg with his air-gun—only to discover, on turning, that a visiting archdeacon had been a spectator of the entire incident from his immediate rear. As he had felt then, when meeting the archdeacon's eye, so did he feel now as Webster's gaze played silently upon him.

Webster, it is true, had not actually raised his eyebrows. But this, Lancelot felt, was simply because he hadn't any.

He backed, blushing.

"Sorry!" he muttered.

There was a pause. Webster continued his steady scrutiny. Lancelot edged towards the door.

"Er—excuse me—just a moment . . ." he mumbled. And, sidling from the room, he ran distractedly upstairs.

"I say," said Lancelot.

"Now what?" asked Gladys.

"Have you finished with the mirror?"

"Why?"

"Well, I—er—I thought," said Lancelot, "that I might as well have a shave."

The girl looked at him, astonished.

"Shave? Why, you shaved only the day before yesterday."

"I know. But, all the same . . . I mean to say, it seems only respectful. That cat, I mean."

"What about him?"

"Well, he seems to expect it, somehow. Nothing actually said, don't you know, but you could tell by his manner. I thought a quick shave and perhaps change into my blue serge suit——"

"He's probably thirsty. Why don't you give him some milk?"

"Could one, do you think?" said Lancelot doubtfully. "I mean, I hardly seem to know him well enough." He paused. "I say, old girl," he went on, with a touch of hesitation.

"Hullo?"

"I know you won't mind my mentioning it, but you've got a few spots of ink on your nose."

"Of course I have. I always have spots of ink on my nose."

"Well . . . you don't think . . . a quick scrub with a bit of pumice-stone . . . I mean to say, you know how important first impressions are . . ."

The girl stared.

"Lancelot Mulliner," she said, "if you think I'm going to skin my nose to the bone just to please a mangy cat——"

"Sh!" cried Lancelot, in agony.

"Here, let me go down and look at him," said Gladys petulantly.

As they re-entered the studio, Webster was gazing with an air of quiet distaste at an illustration from *La Vie Parisienne* which adorned one of the walls. Lancelot tore it down hastily.

Gladys looked at Webster in an unfriendly way.

"So that's the blighter!"

"Sh!"

"If you want to know what I think," said Gladys. "that cat's been living too high. Doing himself a dashed sight too well. You'd better cut his rations down a bit."

In substance, her criticism was not unjustified. Certainly, there was about Webster more than a suspicion of *embonpoint*. He had that air of portly well-being which we associate with those who dwell in cathedral closes. But Lancelot winced uncomfortably. He had so hoped that Gladys would make a good impression, and here she was, starting right off by saying the tactless thing.

He longed to explain to Webster that it was only her way; that in the Bohemian circles of which she was such an ornament genial chaff of a personal order was accepted and, indeed, relished. But it was too late. The mischief had been done. Webster turned in a pointed manner and withdrew silently behind the chesterfield.

Gladys, all unconscious, was making preparations for departure.

"Well, bung-oh," she said lightly. "See you in three weeks. I suppose you and that cat'll both be out on the tiles the moment my back's turned."

"Please! Please!" moaned Lancelot. "Please!"

He had caught sight of the tip of a black tail protruding from behind the chesterfield. It was twitching slightly, and Lancelot could read it like a book. With a sickening sense of dismay, he knew that Webster had formed a snap judgment of his fiancée and condemned her as frivolous and unworthy.

It was some ten days later that Bernard Worple, the neo-Vorticist sculptor, lunching at the Puce Ptarmigan, ran into Rodney Scollop, the powerful young surrealist. And after talking for a while of their art——

"What's all this I hear about Lancelot Mulliner?" asked Worple. "There's a wild story going about that he was seen shaved in the middle of the week. Nothing in it, I suppose?"

Scollop looked grave. He had been on the point of mentioning Lancelot himself, for he loved the lad and was deeply exercised about him.

"It is perfectly true," he said.

"It sounds incredible."

Scollop leaned forward. His fine face was troubled.

"Shall I tell you something, Worple?"

"What?"

"I know for an absolute fact," said Scollop, "that Lancelot Mulliner now shaves every morning."

Worple pushed aside the spaghetti which he was wreathing about him and through the gap stared at his companion.

"Every morning?"

"Every single morning. I looked in on him myself the other day, and there he was, neatly dressed in blue serge and shaved to the core. And, what is more, I got the distinct impression that he had used talcum powder afterwards."

"You don't mean that!"

"I do. And shall I tell you something else? There was a book lying open on the table. He tried to hide it, but he wasn't quick enough. It was one of those etiquette books!"

"An etiquette book!"

" 'Polite Behaviour,' by Constance, Lady Bodbank."

Worple unwound a stray tendril of spaghetti from about his left ear. He was deeply agitated. Like Scollop, he loved Lancelot.

"He'll be dressing for dinner next!" he exclaimed.

"I have every reason to believe," said Scollop gravely, "that he does dress for dinner. At any rate, a man closely resembling him was seen furtively buying three stiff collars and a black tie at Hope Brothers in the King's Road last Tuesday."

Worple pushed his chair back, and rose. His manner was determined.

"Scollop," he said, "we are friends of Mulliner's, you and I. It is evident from what you tell me that subversive influences are at work and that never has he needed our friendship more. Shall we not go round and see him immediately?"

"It was what I was about to suggest myself," said Rodney Scollop.

Twenty minutes later they were in Lancelot's studio, and with a significant glance Scollop drew his companion's notice to their host's appearance. Lancelot Mulliner was neatly, even foppishly, dressed in blue serge with creases down the trouser-legs, and his chin, Worple saw with a pang, gleamed smoothly in the afternoon light.

At the sight of his friends' cigars, Lancelot exhibited unmistakable concern.

"You don't mind throwing those away, I'm sure," he said pleadingly.

Rodney Scollop drew himself up a little haughtily.

"And since when," he asked, "have the best fourpenny cigars in Chelsea not been good enough for you?"

Lancelot hastened to soothe him.

"It isn't me," he exclaimed. "It's Webster. My cat. I happen to know he objects to tobacco smoke. I had to give up my pipe in deference to his views."

Bernard Worple snorted.

"Are you trying to tell us," he sneered, "that Lancelot Mulliner allows himself to be dictated to by a blasted cat?"

"Hush!" cried Lancelot, trembling. "If you knew how he disapproves of strong language!"

"Where is this cat?" asked Rodney Scollop. "Is that the animal?" he said, pointing out of the window to where, in the yard, a tough-looking Tom with tattered ears stood mewing in a hardboiled way out of the corner of its mouth.

"Good heavens, no!" said Lancelot. "That is an alley cat which comes round here from time to time to lunch at the dust-bin. Webster is quite different. Webster has a natural dignity and repose of manner. Webster is a cat who prides himself on always being well turned out and whose high principles and lofty ideals shine from his eyes like beacon-fires . . ." And then suddenly, with an abrupt change of manner, Lancelot broke down and in a low voice added: "Curse him! Curse him! Curse him! Curse him!"

Worple looked at Scollop. Scollop looked at Worple.

"Come, old man," said Scollop, laying a gentle hand on Lancelot's bowed shoulder. "We are your friends. Confide in us."

"Tell us all," said Worple. "What's the matter?"

Lancelot uttered a bitter, mirthless laugh.

"You want to know what's the matter? Listen, then. I'm cat-pecked!"

"Cat-pecked?"

"You've heard of men being hen-pecked, haven't you?" said Lancelot with a touch of irritation. "Well, I'm cat-pecked."

And in broken accents he told his story. He sketched the history of his association with Webster from the latter's first entry into the studio. Confident now that the animal was not within earshot, he unbosomed himself without reserve.

"It's something in the beast's eye," he said in a shaking voice. "Something hypnotic. He casts a spell upon me. He gazes at me and disapproves. Little by little, bit by bit, I am degenerating under his influence from a wholesome, self-respecting artist into . . . well, I don't know what you would call it. Suffice it to say that I have given up smoking, that I have ceased to wear carpet slippers and go about without a collar, that I never dream of sitting down to my frugal evening meal without dressing, and"—he choked—"I have sold my ukulele."

"Not that!" said Worple, paling.

"Yes," said Lancelot. "I felt he considered it frivolous."

There was a long silence.

"Mulliner," said Scollop, "this is more serious than I had supposed. We must brood upon your case."

"It may be possible," said Worple, "to find a way out."

Lancelot shook his head hopelessly.

"There is no way out. I have explored every avenue. The only thing that could possibly free me from this intolerable bondage would be if once—just once—I could catch that cat unbending. If once—merely once—it would lapse in my presence from its austere dignity for but a single instant, I feel that the spell would be broken. But what hope is there of that?" cried Lancelot passionately. "You were pointing just now to that alley cat in the yard. There stands one who has strained every nerve and spared no effort to break down Webster's inhuman self-control. I have heard that animal say things to him which you would think no cat with red blood in its veins would suffer for an instant. And Webster merely looks at him like a Suffragan Bishop eyeing an erring choir-boy and turns his head and falls into a refreshing sleep."

He broke off with a dry sob. Worple, always an optimist, attempted in his kindly way to minimise the tragedy.

"Ah, well," he said. "It's bad, of course, but still, I suppose there is no actual

harm in shaving and dressing for dinner and so on. Many great artists . . .
Whistler, for example——"

"Wait!" cried Lancelot. "You have not heard the worst."

He rose feverishly, and, going to the easel, disclosed the portrait of Brenda
Carberry-Pirbright.

"Take a look at that," he said, "and tell me what you think of her."

His two friends surveyed the face before them in silence. Miss Carberry-
Pirbright was a young woman of prim and glacial aspect. One sought in vain for
her reasons for wanting to have her portrait painted. It would be a most unpleasant thing to have about any house.

Scollop broke the silence.

"Friend of yours?"

"I can't stand the sight of her," said Lancelot vehemently.

"Then," said Scollop, "I may speak frankly. I think she's a pill."

"A blister," said Worple.

"A boil and a disease," said Scollop, summing up.

Lancelot laughed hackingly.

"You have described her to a nicety. She stands for everything most alien to
my artist soul. She gives me a pain in the neck. I'm going to marry her."

"What!" cried Scollop.

"But you're going to marry Gladys Bingley," said Worple.

"Webster thinks not," said Lancelot bitterly. "At their first meeting he weighed
Gladys in the balance and found her wanting. And the moment he saw Brenda
Carberry-Pirbright he stuck his tail up at right angles, uttered a cordial gargle,
and rubbed his head against her leg. Then, turning, he looked at me. I could read
that glance. I knew what was in his mind. From that moment he has been doing
everything in his power to arrange the match."

"But, Mulliner," said Worple, always eager to point out the bright side, "why
should this girl want to marry a wretched, scrubby, hard-up footler like you?
Have courage, Mulliner. It is simply a question of time before you repel and
sicken her."

Lancelot shook his head.

"No," he said. "You speak like a true friend, Worple, but you do not understand. Old Ma Carberry-Pirbright, this exhibit's mother, who chaperons her at
the sittings, discovered at an early date my relationship to my Uncle Theodore,
who, as you know, has got it in gobs. She knows well enough that some day I
shall be a rich man. She used to know my Uncle Theodore when he was Vicar of
St. Botolph's in Knightsbridge, and from the very first she assumed towards me the
repellent chumminess of an old family friend. She was always trying to lure me
to her At Homes, her Sunday luncheons, her little dinners. Once she actually
suggested that I should escort her and her beastly daughter to the Royal
Academy."

He laughed bitterly. The mordant witticisms of Lancelot Mulliner at the expense of the Royal Academy were quoted from Tite Street in the south to Holland Park in the north and eastward as far as Bloomsbury.

"To all these overtures," resumed Lancelot, "I remained firmly unresponsive. My attitude was from the start one of frigid aloofness. I did not actually say in so many words that I would rather be dead in a ditch than at one of her At Homes, but my manner indicated it. And I was just beginning to think I had choked her off when in crashed Webster and upset everything. Do you know how many times I have been to that infernal house in the last week? Five. Webster seemed to wish it. I tell you, I am a lost man."

He buried his face in his hands. Scollop touched Worple on the arm, and together the two men stole silently out.

"Bad!" said Worple.

"Very bad," said Scollop.

"It seems incredible."

"Oh, no. Cases of this kind are, alas, by no means uncommon among those who, like Mulliner, possess to a marked degree the highly-strung, ultra-sensitive artistic temperament. A friend of mine, a rhythmical interior decorator, once rashly consented to put his aunt's parrot up at his studio while she was away visiting friends in the north of England. She was a woman of strong evangelical views, which the bird had imbibed from her. It had a way of putting its head on one side, making a noise like someone dawing a cork from a bottle, and asking my friend if he was saved. To cut a long story short, I happened to call on him a month later and he had installed a harmonium in his studio and was singing hymns, ancient and modern, in a rich tenor, while the parrot, standing on one leg on its perch, took the bass. A very sad affair. We were all much upset about it."

Worple shuddered.

"You appal me, Scollop! Is there nothing we can do?"

Rodney Scollop considered for a moment.

"We might wire Gladys Bingley to come home at once. She might possibly reason with the unhappy man. A woman's gentle influence . . . Yes, we could do that. Look in at the post office on your way home and send Gladys a telegram. I'll owe you for my half of it."

In the studio they had left, Lancelot Mulliner was staring dumbly at a black shape which had just entered the room. He had the appearance of a man with his back to the wall.

"No!" he was crying. "No! I'm dashed if I do!"

Webster continued to look at him.

"Why should I?" demanded Lancelot weakly.

Webster's gaze did not flicker.

"Oh, all right," said Lancelot sullenly.

He passed from the room with leaden feet, and, proceeding upstairs, changed into morning clothes and a top hat. Then, with a gardenia in his buttonhole, he made his way to 11, Maxton Square, where Mrs. Carberry-Pirbright was giving one of her intimate little teas ("just a few friends") to meet Clare Throckmorton Stooge, authoress of "A Strong Man's Kiss".

Gladys Bingley was lunching at her hotel in Antibes when Worple's telegram arrived. It occasioned her the gravest concern.

Exactly what it was all about, she was unable to gather, for emotion had made Bernard Worple rather incoherent. There were moments, reading it, when she fancied that Lancelot had met with a serious accident; others when the solution seemed to be that he had sprained his brain to such an extent that rival lunatic asylums were competing eagerly for his custom; others, again, when Worple appeared to be suggesting that he had gone into partnership with his cat to start a harem. But one fact emerged clearly. Her loved one was in serious trouble of some kind, and his best friends were agreed that only her immediate return could save him.

Gladys did not hesitate. Within half an hour of the receipt of the telegram she had packed her trunk, removed a piece of asparagus from her right eyebrow, and was negotiating for accommodation on the first train going north.

Arriving in London, her first impulse was to go straight to Lancelot. But a natural feminine curiosity urged her, before doing so, to call upon Bernard Worple and have light thrown on some of the more abstruse passages in the telegram.

Worple, in his capacity of author, may have tended towards obscurity, but, when confining himself to the spoken word, he told a plain story well and clearly. Five minutes of his society enabled Gladys to obtain a firm grasp on the salient facts, and there appeared on her face that grim, tight-lipped expression which is seen only on the faces of fiancées who have come back from a short holiday to discover that their dear one has been straying in their absence from the straight and narrow path.

"Brenda Carberry-Pirbright, eh?" said Gladys, with ominous calm. "I'll give him Brenda Carberry-Pirbright! My gosh, if one can't go off to Antibes for the merest breather without having one's betrothed getting it up his nose and starting to act like a Mormon Elder, it begins to look a pretty tough world for a girl."

Kind-hearted Bernard Worple did his best.

"I blame the cat," he said. "Lancelot, to my mind, is more sinned against than sinning. I consider him to be acting under undue influence or duress."

"How like a man!" said Gladys. "Shoving it all off on to an innocent cat!"

"Lancelot says it has a sort of something in its eye."

"Well, when I meet Lancelot," said Gladys, "he'll find that I have a sort of something in my eye."

She went out, breathing flame quietly through her nostrils. Worple, saddened, heaved a sigh and resumed his neo-Vorticist sculping.

It was some five minutes later that Gladys, passing through Maxton Square on her way to Bott Street, stopped suddenly in her tracks. The sight she had seen was enough to make any fiancée do so.

Along the pavement leading to Number Eleven two figures were advancing. Or three, if you counted a morose-looking dog of a semi-Dachshund nature which preceded them, attached to a leash. One of the figures was that of Lancelot Mulliner, natty in grey herring-bone tweed and a new Homburg hat. It was he who held the leash. The other Gladys recognised from the portrait which she had seen on Lancelot's easel as that modern Du Barry, that notorious wrecker of homes and breaker-up of love-nests, Brenda Carberry-Pirbright.

The next moment they had mounted the steps of Number Eleven, and had gone in to tea, possibly with a little music.

It was perhaps an hour and a half later that Lancelot, having wrenched himself with difficulty from the lair of the Philistines, sped homeward in a swift taxi. As always after an extended *tête-à-tête* with Miss Carberry-Pirbright, he felt dazed and bewildered, as if he had been swimming in a sea of glue and had swallowed a good deal of it. All he could think of clearly was that he wanted a drink and that the maerials for that drink were in the cupboard behind the chesterfield in his studio.

He paid the cab and charged in with his tongue rattling dryly against his front teeth. And there before him was Gladys Bingley, whom he had supposed far, far away.

"You!" exclaimed Lancelot.

"Yes, me!" said Gladys

Her long vigil had not helped to restore the girl's equanimity. Since arriving at the studio she had had leisure to tap her foot three thousand, one hundred and forty-two times on the carpet, and the number of bitter smiles which had flitted across her face was nine hundred and eleven. She was about ready for the battle of the century.

She rose and faced him, all the woman in her flashing from her eyes.

"Well, you Casanova!" she said.

"You who?" said Lancelot.

"Don't say 'Yoo-hoo!' to me!" cried Gladys. "Keep that for your Brenda Carberry-Pirbright. Yes, I know all about it, Lancelot Don Juan Henry the Eighth Mulliner! I saw you with her just now. I hear that you and she are inseparable. Bernard Worple says you said you were going to marry her."

"You mustn't believe everything a neo-Vorticist sculptor tells you," quavered Lancelot.

"I'll bet you're going back to dinner there to-night," said Gladys.

She had spoken at a venture, basing the charge purely on a possessive cock of the head which she had noticed in Brenda Carberry-Pirbright at their recent encounter. There, she had said to herself at the time, had gone a girl who was about to invite—or had just invited—Lancelot Mulliner to dine quietly and take her to the pictures afterwards. But the shot went home. Lancelot hung his head.

"There was some talk of it," he admitted.

"Ah!" exclaimed Gladys.

Lancelot's eyes were haggard.

"I don't want to go," he pleaded. "Honestly I don't. But Webster insists."

"Webster!"

"Yes, Webster. If I attempt to evade the appointment, he will sit in front of me and look at me."

"Tchah!"

"Well, he will. Ask him for yourself."

Gladys tapped her foot six times in rapid succession on the carpet, bringing the total to three thousand, one hundred and forty-eight. Her manner had changed and was now dangerously calm.

"Lancelot Mulliner," she said, "you have your choice. Me, on the one hand, Brenda Carberry-Pirbright on the other. I offer you a home where you will be able to smoke in bed, spill the ashes on the floor, wear pyjamas and carpet-slippers all day and shave only on Sunday mornings. From her, what have you to hope? A house in South Kensington—possibly the Brompton Road—probably with her mother living with you. A life that will be one long round of stiff collars and tight shoes, of morning-coats and top hats."

Lancelot quivered, but she went on remorselessly.

"You will be at home on alternate Thursdays, and will be expected to hand the cucumber sandwiches. Every day you will air the dog, till you become a confirmed dog-airer. You will dine out in Bayswater and go for the summer to Bournemouth or Dinard. Choose well, Lancelot Mulliner! I will leave you to think it over. But one last word. If by seven-thirty on the dot you have not presented yourself at 6A, Garbidge Mews ready to take me out to dinner at the Ham and Beef, I shall know what to think and shall act accordingly."

And brushing the cigarette ashes from her chin, the girl strode haughtily from the room.

"Gladys!" cried Lancelot.

But she had gone.

For some minutes Lancelot Mulliner remained where he was, stunned. Then, insistently, there came to him the recollection that he had not had that drink. He rushed to the cupboard and produced the bottle. He uncorked it, and was pouring out a lavish stream, when a movement on the floor below him attracted his attention.

Webster was standing there, looking up at him. And in his eyes was that familiar expression of quiet rebuke.

"Scarcely what I have been accustomed to at the Deanery," he seemed to be saying.

Lancelot stood paralysed. The feeling of being bound hand and foot, of being caught in a snare from which there was no escape, had become more poignant than ever. The bottle fell from his nerveless fingers and rolled across the floor, spilling its contents in an amber river, but he was too heavy in spirit to notice it. With a gesture such as Job might have made on discovering a new boil, he crossed to the window and stood looking moodily out.

Then, turning with a sigh, he looked at Webster again—and, looking, stood spellbound.

The spectacle which he beheld was of a kind to stun a stronger man than Lancelot Mulliner. At first, he shrank from believing his eyes. Then, slowly, came the realisation that what he saw was no mere figment of a disordered imagination. This unbelievable thing was actually happening.

Webster sat crouched upon the floor beside the widening pool of whisky. But it was not horror and disgust that had caused him to crouch. He was crouched because, crouching, he could get nearer to the stuff and obtain crisper action. His tongue was moving in and out like a piston.

And then abruptly, for one fleeting instant, he stopped lapping and glanced up at Lancelot, and across his face there flitted a quick smile—so genial, so intimate, so full of jovial camaraderie, that the young man found himself automatically smiling back, and not only smiling but winking. And in answer to that wink Webster winked, too—a wholehearted, roguish wink that said as plainly as if he had spoken the words:

"How long has this been going on?"

Then with a slight hiccough he turned back to the task of getting his quick before it soaked into the floor.

Into the murky soul of Lancelot Mulliner there poured a sudden flood of sunshine. It was as if a great burden had been lifted from his shoulders. The intolerable obsession of the last two weeks had ceased to oppress him, and he felt a free man. At the eleventh hour the reprieve had come. Webster, that seeming pillar of austere virtue, was one of the boys, after all. Never again would Lancelot quail beneath his eye. He had the goods on him.

Webster, like the stag at eve, had now drunk his fill. He had left the pool of alcohol and was walking round in slow, meditative circles. From time to time he mewed tentatively, as if he were trying to say "British Constitution". His failure to articulate the syllables appeared to tickle him, for at the end of each attempt he would utter a slow, amused chuckle. It was at about this moment that he suddenly broke into a rhythmic dance, not unlike the old Saraband.

It was an interesting spectacle, and at any other time Lancelot would have watched it raptly. But now he was busy at his desk, writing a brief note to Mrs. Carberry-Pirbright, the burden of which was that if she thought he was coming within a mile of her foul house that night or any other night she had vastly under-rated the dodging powers of Lancelot Mulliner.

And what of Webster? The Demon Rum now had him in an iron grip. A life-time of abstinence had rendered him a ready victim to the fatal fluid. He had now reached the stage when geniality gives way to belligerence. The rather foolish smile had gone from his face, and in its stead there lowered a fighting frown. For a few moments he stood on his hind legs, looking about him for a suitable adversary: then, losing all vestiges of self-control, he ran five times round the room at a high rate of speed and, falling foul of a small footstool, attacked it with the utmost ferocity, sparing neither tooth nor claw.

But Lancelot did not see him. Lancelot was not there. Lancelot was out in Bott Street, hailing a cab.

"6A, Garbidge Mews, Fulham," said Lancelot to the driver.

21

CATS WILL BE CATS

THERE had fallen upon the bar-parlour of the Anglers' Rest one of those soothing silences which from time to time punctuate the nightly feasts of Reason and flows of Soul in that cosy resort. It was broken by a Whisky and Splash.

"I've been thinking a lot," said the Whisky and Splash, addressing Mr. Mulliner, "about that cat of yours, that Webster,"

"Has Mr. Mulliner got a cat named Webster?" asked a Small Port who had rejoined our little circle after an absence of some days.

The Sage of the bar-parlour shook his head smilingly.

"Webster," he said, "did not belong to me. He was the property of the Dean of Bolsover who, on being raised to a bishopric and sailing from England to take up his episcopal duties at his See of Bongo-Bongo in West Africa, left the animal in the care of his nephew, my cousin Edward's son Lancelot, the artist. I was telling these gentlemen the other evening how Webster for a time completely revolutionised Lancelot's life. His early upbringing at the Deanery had made him austere and censorious, and he exerted on my cousin's son the full force of a powerful and bigoted personality. It was as if Savonarola or some minor prophet had suddenly been introduced into the carefree, Bohemian atmosphere of the studio."

"He stared at Lancelot and unnerved him," explained a Pint of Bitter.

"He made him shave daily and knock off smoking," added a Lemon Sour.

"He thought Lancelot's fiancée, Gladys Bingley, worldly," said a Rum and Milk, "and tried to arrange a match between him and a girl called Brenda Carberry-Pirbright."

"But one day," concluded Mr. Mulliner, "Lancelot discovered that the animal, for all its apparently rigid principles, had feet of clay and was no better than the rest of us. He happened to drop a bottle of alcoholic liquid and the cat drank deeply of its contents and made a sorry exhibition of itself, with the result that the spell was, of course, instantly broken. What aspect of the story of Webster," he asked the Whisky and Splash, "has been engaging your thoughts?"

"The psychological aspect," said the Whisky and Splash. "As I see it, there is a great psychological drama in this cat. I visualise his higher and lower selves warring. He has taken the first false step, and what will be the issue? Is this new, demoralising atmosphere into which he has been plunged to neutralise the pious teachings of early kittenhood at the Deanery? Or will sound churchmanship prevail and keep him the cat he used to be?"

"If," said Mr. Mulliner, "I am right in supposing that you want to know what happened to Webster at the conclusion of the story I related the other evening, I can tell you. There was nothing that you could really call a war between his higher and lower selves. The lower self won hands down. From the moment when he went on that first majestic toot this once saintly cat became a Bohemian of Bohemians. His days started early and finished late, and were a mere welter of brawling and loose gallantry. As early as the end of the second week his left ear had been reduced through incessant gang-warfare to a mere tattered scenario and his battle-cry had become as familiar to the denizens of Bott Street, Chelsea, as the yodel of the morning milkman."

The Whisky and Splash said it reminded him of some great Greek tragedy. Mr. Mulliner said yes, there were points of resemblance.

"And what," enquired the Rum and Milk, "did Lancelot think of all this?"

"Lancelot," said Mr. Mulliner, "had the easy live-and-let-live creed of the artist. He was indulgent towards the animal's excesses. As he said to Gladys Bingley one evening, when she was bathing Webster's right eye in a boric solution, cats will be cats. In fact, he would scarcely have given a thought to the matter had there not arrived one morning from his uncle a wireless message, dispatched in mid-ocean, announcing that he had resigned his bishopric for reasons of health and would shortly be back in England once more. The communication ended with the words: All my best to Webster.' "

If you recall the position of affairs between Lancelot and the Bishop of Bongo-Bongo, as I described them the other night (said Mr. Mulliner), you will not need to be told how deeply this news affected the young man. It was a bomb-shell. Lancelot, though earning enough by his brush to support himself, had been relying on touching his uncle for that extra bit which would enable him to marry Gladys Bingley. And when he had been placed *in loco parentis* to Webster, he had considered this touch a certainty. Surely, he told himself, the most ordinary gratitude would be sufficient to cause his uncle to unbelt.

But now what?

"You saw that wireless," said Lancelot, agitatedly discussing the matter with Gladys. "You remember the closing words: 'All my best to Webster.' Uncle Theodore's first act on landing in England will undoubtedly be to hurry here for a sacred reunion with this cat. And what will he find? A feline plug-ugly. A gangster. The Big Shot of Bott Street. Look at the animal now," said Lancelot, waving a distracted hand at the cushion where it lay. "Run your eye over him. I ask you!"

Certainly Webster was not a natty spectacle. Some tough cats from the public-house on the corner had recently been trying to muscle in on his personal dust-bin, and, though he had fought them off, the affair had left its mark upon him. A further section had been removed from his already abbreviated ear, and his once sleek flanks were short of several patches of hair. He looked like the late Legs Diamond after a social evening with a few old friends.

"What," proceeded Lancelot, writhing visibly, "will Uncle Theodore say on beholding that wreck? He will put the entire blame on me. He will insist that it was I who dragged that fine spirit down into the mire. And phut will go any chance I ever had of getting into his ribs for a few hundred quid for honeymoon expenses."

Gladys Bingley struggled with a growing hopelessness.

"You don't think a good wig-maker could do something?"

"A wig-maker might patch on a little extra fur," admitted Lancelot, "but how about that ear?"

"A facial surgeon?" suggested Gladys.

Lancelot shook his head.

"It isn't merely his appearance," he said. "It's his entire personality. The poorest reader of character, meeting Webster now, would recognise him for what he is— a hard egg and a bad citizen."

"When do you expect your uncle?" asked Gladys, after a pause.

"At any moment. He must have landed by this time. I can't understand why he has not turned up."

At this moment there sounded from the passage outside the *plop* of a letter falling into the box attached to the front door. Lancelot went listlessly out. A few moments later Gladys heard him utter a surprised exclamation, and he came hurrying back, a sheet of note-paper in his hand.

"Listen to this," he said. "From Uncle Theodore."

"Is he in London?"

"No. Down in Hampshire, at a place called Widdrington Manor. And the great point is that he does not want to see Webster yet."

"Why not?"

"I'll read you what he says."

And Lancelot proceeded to do so, as follows:

> Widdrington Manor,
> Bottleby-in-the-Vale,
> Hants.

"MY DEAR LANCELOT,

"You will doubtless be surprised that I have not hastened to greet you immediately upon my return to these shores. The explanation is that I am being entertained at the above address by Lady Widdrington, widow of the late Sir George Widdrington, C.B.E., an dher mother, Mrs. Pulteney-Banks, whose acquaintance I made on shipboard during my voyage home.

"I find our English countryside charming after the somewhat desolate environment of Bongo-Bongo, and am enjoying a pleasant and restful visit. Both Lady

Widdrington and her mother are kindness itself, especially the former, who is my constant companion on every country ramble. We have a strong bond in our mutual love of cats.

"And this, my dear boy, brings me to the subject of Webster. As you can readily imagine, I am keenly desirous of seeing him once more and noting all the evidences of the loving care which, I have no doubt, you have lavished upon him in my absence, but I do not wish you to forward him to me here. The fact is, Lady Widdrington, though a charming woman, seems entirely lacking in discrimination in the matter of cats. She owns and is devoted to a quite impossible orange-coloured animal of the name of Percy, whose society could not but prove distasteful to one of Webster's high principles. When I tell you that only last night this Percy was engaging in personal combat—quite obviously from the worst motives—with a large tortoiseshell beneath my very window, you will understand what I mean.

"My refusal to allow Webster to join me here is, I fear, puzzling my kind hostess, who knows how greatly I miss him, but I must be firm.

"Keep him, therefore, my dear Lancelot, until I call in person, when I shall remove him to the quiet rural retreat where I plan to spend the evening of my life.

"With every good wish to you both,

"Your affectionate uncle,

"THEODORE."

Gladys Bingley had listened intently to this letter, and as Lancelot came to the end of it she breathed a sigh of relief.

"Well, that gives us a bit of time," she said.

"Yes," agreed Lancelot. "Time to see if we can't awake in this animal some faint echo of its old self-respect. From to-day Webster goes into monastic seclusion. I shall take him round to the vet's, with instructions that he be forced to lead the simple life. In those pure surroundings, with no temptations, no late nights, plain food and a strict milk diet, he may become himself again."

" 'The Man who Came Back'," said Gladys.

"Exactly," said Lancelot.

And so for perhaps two weeks something approaching tranquillity reigned once more in my cousin Edward's son's studio in Bott Street, Chelsea. The veterinary surgeon issued encouraging reports. He claimed a distinct improvement in Webster's character and appearance, though he added that he would still not care to meet him at night in a lonely alley. And then one morning there arrived from his Uncle Theodore a telegram which caused the young man to knit his brows in bewilderment.

It ran thus:

"On receipt of this come immediately Widdrington Manor prepared for indefinite visit period Circumstances comma I regret to say comma necessitate

innocent deception semicolon so will you state on arrival that you are my legal
representative and have come to discuss important family matters with me
period Will explain fully when see you comma but rest assured comma my
dear boy comma that would not ask this were it not absolutely essential period
Do not fail me period Regards to Webster."

Lancelot finished reading this mysterious communication, and looked at Gladys
with raised eyebrows. There is unfortunately in most artists a material streak
which leads them to place an unpleasant interpretation on telegrams like this.
Lancelot was no exception to the rule.

"The old boy's been having a couple," was his verdict.

Gladys, a woman and therefore more spiritual, demurred.

"It sounds to me," she said, "more as if he had gone off his onion. Why should
he want you to pretend to be a lawyer?"

"He says he will explain fully."

"And how *do* you pretend to be a lawyer?"

Lancelot considered.

"Lawyers cough dryly, I know that," he said. "And then I suppose one would
put the tips of the fingers together a good deal and talk about Rex *v.* Biggs Ltd.
and torts and malfeasances and so forth. I think I could give a reasonably realistic
impersonation."

"Well, if you're going, you'd better start practising."

"Oh, I'm going all right," said Lancelot. "Uncle Theodore is evidently in
trouble of some kind, and my place is by his side. If all goes well, I might be able
to bite his ear before he sees Webster. About how much ought we to have in
order to get married comfortably?"

"At least five hundred."

"I will bear it in mind," said Lancelot, coughing dryly and putting the tips of
his fingers together.

Lancelot had hoped, on arriving at Widdrington Manor, that the first person he
met would be his Uncle Theodore, explaining fully. But when the butler ushered
him into the drawing-room only Lady Widdrington, her mother Mrs. Pulteney-
Banks, and her cat Percy were present. Lady Widdrington shook hands, Mrs.
Pulteney-Banks bowed from the arm-chair in which she sat swathed in shawls,
but when Lancelot advanced with the friendly intention of tickling the cat Percy
under the right ear, he gave the young man a cold, evil look out of the corner of
his eye, and backing a pace, took an inch of skin off his hand with one well-
judged swipe of a steel-pronged paw.

Lady Widdrington stiffened.

"I'm afraid Percy does not like you," she said in a distant voice.

"They know, they know!" said Mrs. Pulteney-Banks darkly. She knitted and
purled a moment, musing. "Cats are cleverer than we think," she added.

Lancelot's agony was too keen to permit him even to cough dryly. He sank into a chair and surveyed the little company with watering eyes.

They looked to him a hard bunch. Of Mrs. Pulteney-Banks he could see little but a cocoon of shawls, but Lady Widdrington was right out in the open, and Lancelot did not like her appearance. The chatelaine of Widdrington Manor was one of those agate-eyed, purposeful, tweed-clad women of whom rural England seems to have a monopoly. She was not unlike what he imagined Queen Elizabeth must have been in her day. A determined and vicious specimen. He marvelled that even a mutual affection for cats could have drawn his gentle uncle to such a one.

As for Percy, he was pure poison. Orange of body and inky-black of soul, he lay stretched out on the rug, exuding arrogance and hate. Lancelot, as I have said, was tolerant of toughness in cats, but there was about this animal none of Webster's jolly, whole-hearted, swashbuckling rowdiness. Webster was the sort of cat who would charge, roaring and ranting, to dispute with some rival the possession of a decaying sardine, but there was no more vice in him than in the late John L. Sullivan. Percy, on the other hand, for all his sleek exterior, was mean and bitter. He had no music in his soul, and was fit for treasons, stratagems and spoils. One could picture him stealing milk from a sick tabby.

Gradually the pain of Lancelot's wound began to abate, but it was succeeded by a more spiritual discomfort. It was plain to him that the recent episode had made a bad impression on the two women. They obviously regarded him with suspicion and dislike. The atmosphere was frigid, and conversation proceeded jerkily. Lancelot was glad when the dressing-gong sounded and he could escape to his room.

He was completing the tying of his tie when the door opened and the Bishop of Bongo-Bongo entered.

"Lancelot, my boy!" said the Bishop.

"Uncle!" cried Lancelot.

They clasped hands. More than four years had passed since these two had met, and Lancelot was shocked at the other's appearance. When last he had seen him, at the dear old deanery, his Uncle Theodore had been a genial, robust man who wore his gaiters with an air. Now, in some subtle way, he seemed to have shrunk. He looked haggard and hunted. He reminded Lancelot of a rabbit with a good deal on its mind.

The Bishop had moved to the door. He opened it and glanced along the passage. Then he closed it and tip-toeing back, spoke in a cautious undertone.

"It was good of you to come, my dear boy," he said.

"Why, of course I came," replied Lancelot heartily. "Are you in trouble of some kind, Uncle Theodore?"

"In the gravest trouble," said the Bishop, his voice a mere whisper. He paused for a moment. "You have met Lady Widdrington?"

"Yes."

"Then when I tell you that, unless ceaseless vigilance is exercised, I shall undoubtedly propose marriage to her, you will appreciate my concern."

Lancelot gaped.

"But why do you want to do a potty thing like that?"

The Bishop shivered.

"I do not want to do it, my boy," he said. "Nothing is further from my wishes. The salient point, however, is that Lady Widdrington and her mother want me to do it, and you must have seen for yourself that they are strong, determined women. I fear the worst."

He tottered to a chair and dropped into it, shaking. Lancelot regarded him with affectionate pity.

"When did this start?" he asked.

"On board ship," said the Bishop. "Have you ever made an ocean voyage, Lancelot?"

"I've been to America a couple of times."

"That can scarcely be the same thing," said the Bishop, musingly. "The transatlantic trip is so brief, and you do not get those nights of tropic moon. But even on your voyages to America you must have noticed the peculiar attitude towards the opposite sex induced by the salt air."

"They all look good to you at sea," agreed Lancelot.

"Precisely," said the Bishop. "And during a voyage, especially at night, one finds oneself expressing oneself with a certain warmth which even at the time one tells oneself is injudicious. I fear that on board the liner with Lady Widdrington, my dear boy, I rather let myself go."

Lancelot began to understand.

"You shouldn't have come to her house," he said.

"When I accepted the invitation, I was, if I may use a figure of speech, still under the influence. It was only after I had been here some ten days that I awoke to the realisation of my peril."

"Why didn't you leave?"

The Bishop groaned softly.

"They would not permit me to leave. They countered every excuse. I am virtually a prisoner in this house, Lancelot. The other day I said that I had urgent business with my legal adviser and that this made it imperative that I should proceed instantly to the metropolis."

"That should have worked," said Lancelot.

"It did not. It failed completely. They insisted that I invite my legal adviser down here where my business could be discussed in the calm atmosphere of the Hampshire countryside. I endeavoured to reason with them, but they were firm. You do not know how firm women can be," said the Bishop, shivering, "till you have placed yourself in my unhappy position. How well I appreciate now that powerful image of Shakespeare's—the one about grappling with hoops of steel. Every time I meet Lady Widdrington, I can feel those hoops drawing me ever closer to her. And the woman repels me even as that cat of hers repels me. Tell me, my boy, to turn for an instant to a pleasanter subject, how is my dear Webster?"

Lancelot hesitated.

"Full of beans," he said.

"He is on a diet?" asked the Bishop anxiously. "The doctor has ordered vegetarianism?"

"Just an expression," explained Lancelot, "to indicate robustness."

"Ah!" said the Bishop, relieved. "And what disposition have you made of him in your absence? He is in good hands, I trust?"

"The best," said Lancelot. "His host is the ablest veterinary in London—Doctor J. G. Robinson of 9 Bott Street, Chelsea, a man not only skilled in his profession but of the highest moral tone."

"I knew I could rely on you to see that all was well with him," said the Bishop emotionally. "Otherwise, I should have shrunk from asking you to leave London and come here—strong shield of defence though you will be to me in my peril."

"But what use can I be to you?" said Lancelot, puzzled.

"The greatest," the Bishop assured him. "Your presence will be invaluable. You must keep the closest eye upon Lady Widdrington and myself, and whenever you observe us wandering off together—she is assiduous in her efforts to induce me to visit the rose-garden in her company, for example—you must come hurrying up and detach me with the ostensible purpose of discussing legal matters. By these means we may avert what I had come to regard as the inevitable."

"I understand thoroughly," said Lancelot. "A jolly good scheme. Rely on me."

"The ruse I have outlined," said the Bishop regretfully, "involves, as I hinted in my telegram, a certain innocent deception, but at times iike this one cannot afford to be too nice in one's methods. By the way, under what name did you make your appearance here?"

"I used my own."

"I would have preferred Polkinghorne or Gooch or Withers," said the Bishop pensively. "They sound more legal. However, that is a small matter. The essential thing is that I may rely on you to—er—to——?"

"To stick around?"

"Exactly. To adhere. From now on, my boy, you must be my constant shadow. And if, as I trust, our efforts are rewarded, you will not find me ungrateful. In the course of a lifetime I have contrived to accumulate no small supply of this world's goods, and if there is any little venture or enterprise for which you require a certain amount of capital——"

"I am glad," said Lancelot, "that you brought this up, Uncle Theodore. As it so happens, I am badly in need of five hundred pounds—and could, indeed, do with a thousand."

The Bishop grasped his hand.

"See me through this ordeal, my dear boy," he said, "and you shall have it. For what purpose do you require this money?"

"I want to get married."

"Ugh!" said the Bishop, shuddering strongly. "Well, well," he went on, recovering himself, "it is no affair of mine. No doubt you know your own mind best. I must confess, however, that the mere mention of the holy stage occasions in me an indefinable sinking feeling. But then, of course, you are not proposing to marry Lady Widdrington."

"And nor," cried Lancelot heartily, "are you, uncle—not while I'm around. Tails up, Uncle Theodore, tails up!"

"Tails up!" repeated the Bishop dutifully, but he spoke the words without any real ring of conviction in his voice.

It was fortunate that, in the days which followed, my cousin Edward's son Lancelot was buoyed up not only by the prospect of collecting a thousand pounds, but also by a genuine sympathy and pity for a well-loved uncle. Otherwise, he must have faltered and weakened.

To a sensitive man—and all artists are sensitive—there are few things more painful than the realisation that he is an unwelcome guest. And not even if he had had the vanity of a Narcissus could Lancelot have persuaded himself that he was *persona grata* at Widdrington Manor.

The march of civilisation has done much to curb the natural ebullience of woman. It has brought to her the power of self-restraint. In emotional crises nowadays women seldom give physical expression to their feelings; and neither Lady Widdrington nor her mother, the aged Mrs. Pulteney-Banks, actually struck Lancelot or spiked him with a knitting-needle. But there were moments when they seemed only by a miracle of strong will to check themselves from such manifestations of dislike.

As the days went by, and each day the young man skilfully broke up a promising *tête-à-tête*, the atmosphere grew more tense and electric. Lady Widdrington spoke dreamily of the excellence of the train service between Bottleby-in-the-Vale and London, paying a particularly marked tribute to the 8.45 a.m. express. Mrs. Pulteney-Banks mumbled from among her shawls of great gowks—she did not specify more exactly, courteously refraining from naming names—who spent their time idling in the country (where they were not wanted) when their true duty and interest lay in the metropolis. The cat Percy, by word and look, continued to affirm his low opinion of Lancelot.

And, to make matters worse, the young man could see that his principal's *morale* was becoming steadily lowered. Despite the uniform success of their manœuvres, it was evident that the strain was proving too severe for the Bishop.

He was plainly cracking. A settled hopelessness had crept into his demeanour. More and more had he come to resemble a rabbit who, fleeing from a stoat, draws no cheer from the reflection that he is all right so far, but flings up his front paws in a gesture of despair, as if to ask what profit there can be in attempting to evade the inevitable.

And, at length, one night when Lancelot had switched off his light and composed himself for sleep, it was switched on again and he perceived his uncle standing by the bedside, with a haggard expression on his fine features.

At a glance Lancelot saw that the good old man had reached breaking-point.

"Something the matter, uncle?" he asked.

"My boy," said the Bishop, "we are undone."

"Oh, surely not?" said Lancelot, as cheerily as his sinking heart would permit.

"Undone," repeated the Bishop hollowly. "To-night Lady Widdrington specifically informed me that she wishes you to leave the house."

Lancelot drew in his breath sharply. Natural optimist though he was, he could not minimize the importance of this news.

"She has consented to allow you to remain for another two days, and then the butler has instructions to pack your belongings in time for the eight-forty-five express."

"H'm!" said Lancelot.

"H'm, indeed," said the Bishop. "This means that I shall be left alone and defenceless. And even with you sedulously watching over me it has been a very near thing once or twice. That afternoon in the summer-house!"

"And that day in the shrubbery," said Lancelot. There was a heavy silence for a moment.

"What are you going to do?" asked Lancelot.

"I must think . . . think," said the Bishop. "Well, good night, my boy."

He left the room with bowed head, and Lancelot, after a long period of wakeful meditation, fell into a fitful slumber.

From this he was aroused some two hours later by an extraordinary commotion somewhere outside his room. The noise appeared to proceed from the hall, and, donning a dressing-gown, he hurried out.

A strange spectacle met his eyes. The entire numerical strength of Widdrington Manor seemed to have assembled in the hall. There was Lady Widdrington in a mauve *négligé*, Mrs. Pulteney-Banks in a system of shawls, the butler in pyjamas, a footman or two, several maids, the odd-job man, and the boy who cleaned the shoes. They were gazing in manifest astonishment at the Bishop of Bongo-Bongo, who stood, fully clothed, near the front door, holding in one hand an umbrella, in the other a bulging suit-case.

In a corner sat the cat, Percy, swearing in a quiet undertone.

As Lancelot arrived the Bishop blinked and looked dazedly about him.

"Where am I?" he said.

Willing voices informed him that he was at Widdrington Manor, Bottleby-in-the-Vale, Hants, the butler going so far as to add the telephone number.

"I think," said the Bishop, "I must have been walking in my sleep."

"Indeed?" said Mrs. Pulteney-Banks, and Lancelot could detect the dryness in her tone.

"I am sorry to have been the cause of robbing the household of its well-earned slumber," said the Bishop nervously. "Perhaps it would be best if I now retired to my room."

"Quite," said Mrs. Pulteney-Banks, and once again her voice crackled dryly.

"I'll come and tuck you up," said Lancelot.

"Thank you, my boy," said the Bishop.

Safe from observation in his bedroom, the Bishop sank wearily on the bed, and allowed the umbrella to fall hopelessly to the floor.

"It is Fate," he said. "Why struggle further?"

"What happened?" asked Lancelot.

"I thought matters over," said the Bishop, "and decided that my best plan would be to escape quietly under cover of the night. I had intended to wire Lady Widdrington on the morrow that urgent matters of personal importance had necessitated a sudden visit to London. And just as I was getting the front door open I trod on that cat."

"Percy?"

"Percy," said the Bishop bitterly. "He was prowling about in the hall, on who knows what dark errand. It is some small satisfaction to me in my distress to recall that I must have flattened out his tail properly. I came down on it with my full weight, and I am not a slender man. Well," he said, sighing drearily, "this is the end. I give up. I yield."

"Oh, don't say that, uncle."

"I do say that," replied the Bishop, with some asperity. "What else is there to say?"

It was a question which Lancelot found himself unable to answer. Silently he pressed the other's hand, and walked out.

In Mrs. Pulteney-Bank's room, meanwhile, an earnest conference was taking place.

"Walking in his sleep, indeed!" said Mrs. Pulteney-Banks.

Lady Widdrington seemed to take exception to the older woman's tone.

"Why shouldn't he walk in his sleep?" she retorted.

"Why should he?"

"Because he was worrying."

"Worrying!" sniffed Mrs. Pulteney-Banks.

"Yes, worrying," said Lady Widdrington, with spirit. "And I know why. You don't understand Theodore as I do."

"As slippery as an eel," grumbled Mrs. Pulteney-Banks. "He was trying to sneak off to London."

"Exactly," said Lady Widdrington. "'To his cat. You don't understand what it means to Theodore to be separated from his cat. I have noticed for a long time that he was restless and ill at ease. The reason is obvious. He is pining for Webster. I know what it is myself. That time when Percy was lost for two days I nearly went off my head. Directly after breakfast to-morrow I shall wire to Doctor Robinson of Bott Street, Chelsea, in whose charge Webster now is, to send him down here by the first train. Apart from anything else, he will be nice company for Percy."

"Tchah!" said Mrs. Pulteney-Banks.

"What do you mean, Tchah?" demanded Lady Widdrington.

"I mean Tchah," said Mrs. Pulteney-Banks.

An atmosphere of constraint hung over Widdrington Manor throughout the following day. The natural embarrassment of the Bishop was increased by the attitude of Mrs. Pulteney-Banks, who had contracted a habit of looking at him over her zareba of shawls and sniffing meaningly. It was with relief that towards the middle of the afternoon he accepted Lancelot's suggestion that they should repair to the study and finish up what remained of their legal business.

The study was on the ground floor, looking out on pleasant lawns and shrubberies. Through the open window came the scent of summer flowers. It was a scene which should have soothed the most bruised soul, but the Bishop was plainly unable to draw refreshment from it. He sat with his head in his hands, refusing all Lancelot's well-meant attempts at consolation.

"Those sniffs!" he said, shuddering, as if they still rang in his ears. "What meaning they held! What a sinister significance!"

"She may just have got a cold in the head," urged Lancelot.

'No. The matter went deeper than that. They meant that that terrible old woman saw through my subterfuge last night. She read me like a book. From now on there will be added vigilance. I shall not be permitted out of their sight, and the end can be only a question of time. Lancelot, my boy," said the Bishop, extending a trembling hand pathetically towards his nephew, "you are a young man on the threshold of life. If you wish that life to be a happy one, always remember this: when on an ocean voyage, never visit the boat-deck after dinner. You will be tempted. You will say to yourself that the lounge is stuffy and that the cool breezes will correct that replete feeling which so many of us experience after the evening meal . . . you will think how pleasant it must be up there, with the rays of the moon turning the waves to molten silver . . . but don't go, my boy, don't go!"

"Right-ho, uncle," said Lancelot soothingly.

The Bishop fell into a moody silence.

"It is not merely," he resumed, evidently having followed some train of thought, "that, as one of Nature's bachelors, I regard the married state with alarm and concern. It is the peculiar conditions of my tragedy that render me distraught. My lot once linked to that of Lady Widdrington, I shall never see Webster again."

"Oh, come, uncle. This is morbid."

The Bishop shook his head.

"No," he said. "If this marriage takes place, my path and Webster's must divide. I could not subject that pure cat to life at Widdrington Manor, a life involving, as it would, the constant society of the animal Percy. He would be contaminated. You know Webster, Lancelot. He has been your companion—may I not almost say your mentor?—for months. You know the loftiness of his ideals."

For an instant, a picture shot through Lancelot's mind—the picture of Webster, as he had seen him only a brief while since—standing in the yard with the backbone of a herring in his mouth, crooning a war-song at the alley-cat from whom he had stolen the *bonne-bouche*. But he replied without hesitation.

"Oh, rather."

"They are very high."

"Extremely high."

"And his dignity," said the Bishop. "I deprecate a spirit of pride and self-esteem, but Webster's dignity was not tainted with those qualities. It rested on a clear conscience and the knowledge that, even as a kitten, he had never permitted his feet to stray. I wish you could have seen Webster as a kitten, Lancelot."

"I wish I could, uncle."

"He never played with balls of wool, preferring to sit in the shadow of the cathedral wall, listening to the clear singing of the choir as it melted on the sweet stillness of the summer day. Even then you could see that deep thoughts exercised his mind. I remember once . . ."

But the reminiscence, unless some day it made its appearance in the good old man's memoirs, was destined to be lost to the world. For at this moment the door opened and the butler entered. In his arms he bore a hamper, and from this hamper there proceeded the wrathful ejaculations of a cat who has had a long train-journey under constricted conditions and is beginning to ask what it is all about.

"Bless my soul!" cried the Bishop, startled.

A sickening sensation of doom darkened Lancelot's soul. He had recognised that voice. He knew what was in that hamper.

"Stop!" he exclaimed. "Uncle Theodore, don't open that hamper!"

But it was too late. Already the Bishop was cutting the strings with a hand that trembled with eagerness. Chirruping noises proceeded from him. In his eyes was the wild gleam seen only in the eyes of cat-lovers restored to their loved one.

"Webster!" he called in a shaking voice.

And out of the hamper shot Webster, full of strange oaths. For a moment he raced about the room, apparently searching for the man who had shut him up in the thing, for there was flame in his eye. Becoming calmer, he sat down and began to lick himself, and it was then for the first time that the Bishop was enabled to get a steady look at him.

Two week's residence at the vet.'s had done something for Webster, but not enough. Not, Lancelot felt agitatedly, nearly enough. A mere fortnight's seclusion cannot bring back fur to lacerated skin; it cannot restore to a chewed ear that extra inch which makes all the difference. Webster had gone to Doctor Robinson looking as if he just been caught in machinery of some kind, and that was how, though in a very slightly modified degree, he looked now. And at the sight of him the Bishop uttered a sharp, anguished cry. Then, turning on Lancelot, he spoke in a voice of thunder.

"So this, Lancelot Mulliner, is how you have fulfilled your sacred trust!"

Lancelot was shaken, but he contrived to reply.

"It wasn't my fault, uncle. There was no stopping him."

"Pshaw!"

"Well, there wasn't," said Lancelot. "Besides, what harm is there in an occasional healthy scrap with one of the neighbours? Cats will be cats."

"A sorry piece of reasoning," said the Bishop, breathing heavily.

"Personally," Lancelot went on, though speaking dully, for he realised how hopeless it all was, "if I owned Webster, I should be proud of him. Consider his record," said Lancelot, warming a little as he proceeded. "He comes to Bott Street without so much as a single fight under his belt, and, despite this inexperience, shows himself possessed of such genuine natural talent that in two weeks he has every cat for streets around jumping walls and climbing lamp-posts at the mere sight of him. I wish," said Lancelot, now carried away by this theme, "that you could have seen him clean up a puce-coloured Tom from Number Eleven. It was the finest sight I have ever witnessed. He was conceding pounds to this animal, who, in addition, had a reputation extending as far afield as the Fulham Road. The first round was even, with the exchanges perhaps a shade in favour of his opponent. But when the gong went for Round Two . . ."

The Bishop raised his hand. His face was drawn.

"Enough!" he cried. "I am inexpressibly grieved. I . . ."

He stopped. Someting had leaped upon the window-sill at his side, causing him to start violently. It was the cat Percy who, hearing a strange feline voice, had come to investigate.

There were days when Percy, mellowed by the influence of cream and the sunshine, could become, if not agreeable, at least free from active venom. Lancelot had once seen him actually playing with a ball of paper. But it was evident immediately that this was not one of those days. Percy was plainly in evil mood. His dark soul gleamed from his narrow eyes. He twitched his tail to and fro, and for a moment stood regarding Webster with a hard sneer.

Then, wiggling his whiskers, he said something in a low voice.

Until he spoke, Webster had apparently not observed his arrival. He was still cleaning himself after the journey. But hearing this remark, he started and looked up. And, as he saw Percy, his ears flattened and the battlelight came into his eye.

There was a moments pause. Cat stared at cat. Then, swishing his tail to and fro, Percy repeated his statement in a louder tone. And from this point, Lancelot tells me, he could follow the conversation word for word as easily as if he had studied cat-language for years.

This, he says, is how the dialogue ran:

WEBSTER: Who, me?
PERCY: Yes, you.
WEBSTER: A what?
PERCY: You heard.
WEBSTER: Is that so?
PERCY: Yeah.
WEBSTER: Yeah?
PERCY: Yeah. Come on up here and I'll bite the rest of your ear off.
WEBSTER: Yeah? You and who else?
PERCY: Come on up here. I dare you.
WEBSTER: (*flushing hotly*): You do, do you? Of all the nerve! Of all the crust! Why, I've eaten better cats than you before breakfast.
            (*to Lancelot*)
Here, hold my coat and stand to one side. Now, then!

And, with this, there was a whizzing sound and Webster had advanced in full battle-order. A moment later, a tangled mass that looked like seventeen cats in close communion fell from the window-sill into the room.

A cat-fight of major importance is always a spectacle worth watching, but Lancelot tells me that, vivid and stimulating though this one promised to be, his attention was riveted not upon it, but upon the Bishop of Bongo-Bongo.

In the first few instants of the encounter the prelate's features had betrayed no emotion beyond a grievous alarm and pain. "How art thou fallen from Heaven, oh Lucifer, Son of Morning," he seemed to be saying as he watched his once blameless pet countering Percy's onslaught with what had the appearance of being about sixteen simultaneous legs. And then, almost abruptly, there seemed to awake in him at the same instant a passionate pride in Webster's prowess and that sporting spirit which lies so near the surface in all of us. Crimson in the face, his eyes gleaming with partisan enthusiasm, he danced round the combatants, encouraging his nominee with word and gesture.

"Capital! Excellent! Ah, stoutly struck, Webster!"

"Hook him with your left Webster!" cried Lancelot.

"Precisely!" boomed the Bishop.

"Soak him, Webster!"

"Indubitably!" agreed the Bishop. "The expression is new to me, but I appreciate its pith and vigour. By all means, soak him, my dear Webster."

And it was at this moment that Lady Widdrington, attracted by the noise of battle, came hurrying into the room. She was just in time to see Percy run into a right swing and bound for the window-sill, closely pursued by his adversary. Long since Percy had begun to realise that, in inviting this encounter, he had gone out of his class and come up against something hot. All he wished for now was flight. But Webster's hat was still in the ring, and cries from without told that the battle had been joined once more on the lawn.

Lady Widdrington stood appalled. In the agony of beholding her pet so manifestly getting the loser's end she had forgotten her matrimonial plans. She was no longer the calm, purposeful woman who intended to lead the Bishop to the altar if she had to use chloroform; she was an outraged cat-lover, and she faced him with blazing eyes.

"What," she demanded, "is the meaning of this?"

The Bishop was still labouring under obvious excitement.

"That beastly animal of yours asked for it, and did Webster give it to him!"

"Did he!" said Lancelot. "That corkscrew punch with the left!"

"That sort of quick upper-cut with the right!" cried the Bishop.

"There isn't a cat in London that could beat him."

"In London?" said the Bishop warmly. "In the whole of England. O admirable Webster!"

Lady Widdrington stamped a furious foot.

"I insist that you destroy that cat!"

"Which cat?"

"That cat," said Lady Widdrington, pointing.

Webster was standing on the window-sill. He was panting slightly, and his ear was in worse repair than ever, but on his face was the satisfied smile of a victor. He moved his head from side to side, as if looking for the microphone through which his public expected him to speak a modest word or two.

"I demand that that savage animal be destroyed," said Lady Widdrington.

The Bishop met her eye steadily.

"Madam," he replied, "I shall sponsor no such scheme."

"You refuse?"

"Most certainly I refuse. Never have I esteemed Webster so highly as at this moment. I consider him a public benefactor, a selfless altruist. For years every right-thinking person must have yearned to handle that inexpressibly abominable cat of yours as Webster has just handled him, and I have no feelings towards him but those of gratitude and admiration. I intend, indeed, personally and with my own hands to give him a good plate of fish."

Lady Widdrington drew in her breath sharply.

"You will not do it here," she said.

She pressed the bell.

"Fotheringay," she said in a tense, cold voice, as the butler appeared, "the Bishop is leaving us to-night. Please see that his bags are packed for the six-forty-one."

She swept from the room. The Bishop turned to Lancelot with a benevolent smile.

"It will just give me nice time," he said, "to write you that cheque, my boy."

He stooped and gathered Webster into his arms, and Lancelot, after one quick look at them, stole silently out. This sacred moment was not for his eyes.

22

THE KNIGHTLY QUEST OF MERVYN

SOME sort of smoking-concert seemed to be in progress in the large room across the passage from the bar-parlour of the Angler's Rest, and a music-loving Stout and Mild had left the door open, the better to enjoy the entertainment. By this means we had been privileged to hear Kipling's "Mandalay", "I'll Sing Thee Songs of Araby", "The Midshipmite", and "Ho, Jolly Jenkin!; a..nd now the piano began to tinkle again and a voice broke into a less familiar number.

The words came to us faintly, but clearly:

> "The days of Chivalry are dead,
> Of which in stories I have read,
> When knights were bold and acted kind of scrappy;
> They used to take a lot of pains
> And fight all day to please the Janes,
> And if their dame was tickled they was happy.
> But now the men are mild and meek:
> They seem to have a yellow streak:
> They never lay for other guys, to flatten 'em:
> They think they've done a darned fine thing
> If they just buy the girl a ring
> Of imitation diamonds and platinum."

> "Oh, it makes me sort of sad
> To think about Sir Galahad
> And all the knights of that romantic day:
> To amuse a girl and charm her
> They would climb into their armour
> And jump into the fray:
> They called her "Lady love,"
> They used to wear her little glove,
> And everthing that she said went:
> For those were the days when a lady was a lady
> And a gent was a perfect gent."

A Ninepennyworth of Sherry sighed.

"True," he murmured. "Very true."

The singer continued:

> "Some night when they sat down to dine,
> Sir Claude would say: 'That girl of mine
> Makes every woman jealous when she sees her.'
> Then someone else would shout: 'Behave,
> Thou malapert and scurvy knave,
> Or I will smite thee one upon the beezer!'"
> And then next morning in the lists
> They'd take their lances in their fists
> And mount a pair of chargers, highly mettled:
> And when Sir Claude, so fair and young,
> Got punctured in the leg or lung,
> They looked upon the argument as settled."

The Ninepennyworth of Sherry sighed again.

"He's right," he said. "We live in degenerate days, gentlemen. Where now is the fine old tradition of derring-do? Where," demanded the Ninepennyworth of Sherry with modest fervour, "shall we find in these prosaic modern times the spirit that made the knights of old go through perilous adventures and brave dreadful dangers to do their lady's behest?"

"In the Mulliner family," said Mr. Mulliner, pausing for a moment from the sipping of his hot Scotch and lemon. "In the clan to which I have the honour to belong, the spirit to which you allude still flourishes in all its pristine vigour. I can scarcely exemplify this better than by relating the story of my cousin's son, Mervyn, and the strawberries."

"But I want to listen to the concert," pleaded a Rum and Milk. "I just heard the curate clear his throat. That always means 'Dangerous Dan McGrew.'"

"The story," repeated Mr. Mulliner with quiet firmness, as he closed the door, "of my cousin's son, Mervyn, and the strawberries."

In the circles in which the two moved (said Mr. Mulliner) it had often been debated whether my cousin's son, Mervyn, was a bigger chump than my nephew Archibald—the one who, if you recall, was so good at imitating a hen laying an egg. Some took one side, some the other; but, though the point still lies open, there is no doubt that young Mervyn was quite a big enough chump for everyday use. And it was this quality in him that deterred Clarice Mallaby from consenting to become his bride.

He discovered this one night when, as they were dancing at the Restless Cheese, he put the thing squarely up to her, not mincing his words.

"Tell me, Clarice," he said, "why is it that you spurn a fellow's suit? I can't for the life of me see why you won't consent to marry a chap. It isn't as if I hadn't asked you often enough. Playing fast and loose with a good man's love is the way I look at it."

And he gazed at her in a way that was partly melting and partly suggestive of the dominant male. And Clarice Mallaby gave one of those light, tinkling laughs and replied:

"Well, if you really want to know, you're such an ass."

Mervyn could make nothing of this.

"An ass? How do you mean an ass? Do you mean a silly ass?"

"I mean a goof," said the girl "A gump. A poop. A nitwit and a returned empty. Your name came up the other day in the course of conversation at home, and mother said you were a vapid and irreflective guffin, totally lacking in character and purpose."

"Oh?" said Mervyn. "She did, did she?"

"She did. And while it isn't often that I think along the same lines as mother, there—for once—I consider her to have hit the bull's-eye, rung the bell, and to be entitled to a cigar or coconut, according to choice. It seemed to me what they call the *mot juste*."

"Indeed?" said Mervyn, nettled. "Well, let me tell you something. When it comes to discussing brains, your mother, in my opinion, would do better to recede modestly into the background and not try to set herself up as an authority. I strongly suspect her of being the woman who was seen in Charing Cross Station the other day, asking a porter if he could direct her to Charing Cross Station. And, in the second place," said Mervyn, "I'll show you if I haven't got character and purpose. Set me some quest, like the knights of old, and see how quick I'll deliver the goods as per esteemed order."

"How do you mean—a quest?"

"Why, bid me do something for you, or get something for you, or biff somebody in the eye for you. You know the procedure."

Clarice thought for a moment. Then she said:

"All my life I've wanted to eat strawberries in the middle of winter. Get me a basket of strawberries before the end of the month and we'll take up this matrimonial proposition of yours in a spirit of serious research."

"Strawberries?" said Mervyn.

"Strawberries."

Mervyn gulped a little.

"Strawberries?"

"Strawberries."

"But, I say, dash it! *Strawberries*?"

"Strawberries," said Clarice.

And then at last Mervyn, reading between the lines, saw that what she wanted was strawberries. And how he was to get any in December was more than he could have told you.

"I could do you oranges," he said.

"Strawberries."

"Or nuts. You wouldn't prefer a nice nut?"

"Strawberries," said the girl firmly. "And you're jolly lucky, my lad, not to be sent off after the Holy Grail or something, or told to pluck me a sprig of edelweiss from the top of the Alps. Mind you, I'm not saying yes and I'm not saying no, but this I will say—that if you bring me that basket of strawberries in the stated time, I shall know that there's more in you than sawdust—which the casual observer wouldn't believe—and I will reopen your case and examine it thoroughly in the light of the fresh evidence. Whereas, if you fail to deliver the fruit, I shall know that mother was right, and you can jolly well make up your mind to doing without my society from now on."

Here she stopped to take in breath, and Mervyn, after a lengthy pause, braced himself up and managed to utter a brave laugh. It was a little roopy, if not actually hacking, but he did it.

"Right-ho," he said. "Right-ho. If that's the way you feel, well, to put it in a nutshell, right-ho."

My cousin's son Mervyn passed a restless night that night, tossing on the pillow not a little, and feverishly at that. If this girl had been a shade less attractive, he told himself, he would have sent her a telegram telling her to go to the dickens. But, as it so happened, she was not; so the only thing that remained for him to do was to pull up the old socks and take a stab at the programme, as outlined. And he was sipping his morning cup of tea, when something more or less resembling an idea came to him.

He reasoned thus. The wise man, finding himself in a dilemma, consults an expert. If, for example, some knotty point of the law has arisen, he will proceed immediately in search of a legal expert, bring out his eight-and-six, and put the problem up to him. If it is a cross-word puzzle and he is stuck for the word in three letters, beginning with E and ending with U and meaning "large Australian bird" he places the matter in the hands of the editor of the *Encyclopædia Britannica*.

And, similarly, when the question confronting him is how to collect strawberries in December, the best plan is obviously to seek out that one of his acquaintances who has the most established reputation for giving expensive parties.

This, Mervyn considered, was beyond a doubt Oofy Prosser. Thinking back, he could recall a dozen occasions when he had met chorus-girls groping their way along the street with a dazed look in their eyes, and when he had asked them what the matter was they had explained that they were merely living over again the exotic delights of the party Oofy Prosser had given last night. If anybody knew how to get strawberries in December, it would be Oofy.

He called, accordingly, at the latter's apartment, and found him in bed, staring at the ceiling and moaning in an undertone.

"Hullo!" said Mervyn. "You look a bit red-eyed, old corpse."

"I feel red-eyed," said Oofy. "And I wish, if it isn't absolutely necessary, that you wouldn't come charging in here early in the morning like this. By about ten o'clock to-night, I imagine, if I take great care of myself and keep quite quiet, I shall once more be in a position to look at gargoyles without wincing; but at the moment the mere sight of your horrible face gives me an indefinable shuddering feeling."

"Did you have a party last night?"

"I did."

"I wonder if by any chance you had strawberries?"

Oofy Prosser gave a sort of quiver and shut his eyes. He seemed to be wrestling with some powerful emotion. Then the spasm passed, and he spoke.

"Don't talk about the beastly things," he said. "I never want to see strawberries again in my life. Nor lobster, caviare, paté de fois gras, prawns in aspic, or anything remotely resembling Bronx cocktails, Martinis, Side-Cars, Lizard's Breaths, All Quiet on the Western Fronts, and any variety of champagne, whisky, brandy, chartreuse, benedictine, and curacao."

Mervyn nodded sympathetically.

"I know just how you feel, old man," he said. "And I hate to have to press the point. But I happen—for purposes which I will not reveal—to require about a dozen strawberries."

"Then go and buy them, blast you," said Oofy, turning his face to the wall.

"*Can* you buy strawberries in December?"

"Certainly. Bellamy's in Piccadilly have them."

"Are they frightfully expensive?" asked Mervyn, feeling in his pocket and fingering the one pound, two shillings and threepence which had got to last him to the end of the quarter when his allowance came in. "Do they cost a fearful lot?"

"Of course not. They're dirt cheap."

Mervyn heaved a relieved sigh.

"I don't suppose I pay more than a pound apiece—or at most, thirty shillings—for mine," said Oofy. "You can get quite a lot for fifty quid."

Mervyn utterd a hollow groan.

"Don't gargle," said Oofy. "Or, if you must gargle, gargle outside."

"Fifty quid?" said Mervyn.

"Fifty or a hundred, I forget which. My man attends to these things."

Mervyn looked at him in silence. He was trying to decide whether the moment had arrived to put Oofy into circulation.

In the matter of borrowing money, my cousin's son, Mervyn, was shrewd and level-headed. He had vision. At an early date he had come to the conclusion that it would be foolish to fritter away a fellow like Oofy in a series of ten bobs and quids. The prudent man, he felt, when he has an Oofy Prosser on his list, nurses him along till he feels the time is ripe for one of those quick Send-me-two-hundred-by-messenger-old-man-or-my-head-goes-in-the-gas-oven touches. For years, accordingly, he had been saving Oofy up for some really big emergency.

And the point he had to decide was: Would there ever be a bigger emergency than this? That was what he asked himself.

Then it came home to him that Oofy was not in the mood. The way it seemed to Mervyn was that, if Oofy's mother had crept to Oofy's bedside at this moment and tried to mace him for as much as five bob, Oofy would have risen and struck her with the bromo-seltzer bottle.

With a soft sigh, therefore, he gave up the idea and oozed out of the room and downstairs into Piccadilly.

Piccadilly looked pretty mouldy to Mervyn. It was full, he tells me, of people and other foul things. He wandered along for a while in a distrait way, and then suddenly out of the corner of his eye he became aware that he was in the presence of fruit. A shop on the starboard side was full of it, and he discovered that he was standing outside Bellamy's.

And what is more, there, nestling in a basket in the middle of a lot of cotton-wool and blue paper, was a platoon of strawberries.

And, as he gazed at them, Mervyn began to see how this thing could be worked with the minimum of discomfort and the maximum of profit to all concerned. He had just remembered that his maternal uncle Joseph had an account at Bellamy's.

The next moment he had bounded through the door and was in conference with one of the reduced duchesses who do the fruit-selling at this particular emporium. This one, Mervyn tells me, was about six feet high and looked down at him with large, haughty eyes in a derogatory manner—being, among other things, dressed from stem to stern in black satin. He was conscious of a slight chill, but he carried on according to plan.

"Good morning," he said, switching on a smile and then switching it off again as he caught her eye. "Do you sell fruit?"

If she had answered "No," he would, of course, have been nonplussed. But she did not. She inclined her head proudly.

"Quate," she said.

"That's fine," said Mervyn heartily. "Because fruit happens to be just what I'm after."

"Quate."

"I want that basket of strawberries in the window."

"Quate."

She reached for them and started to wrap them up. She did not seem to enjoy doing it. As she tied the string, her brooding look deepened. Mervyn thinks she may have had some great love tragedy in her life.

"Send them to the Earl of Blotsam, 66A, Berkeley Square," said Mervyn, alluding to his maternal uncle Joseph.

"Quate."

"On second thoughts," said Mervyn, "no. I'll take them with me. Save trouble. Hand them over, and send the bill to Lord Blotsam."

This, naturally, was the crux or nub of the whole enterprise. And to Mervyn's concern, his suggestion did not seem to have met with the ready acceptance for which he had hoped. He had looked for the bright smile, the courteous inclination of the head. Instead of which, the girl looked doubtful.

"You desi-ah to remove them in person?"

"Quate," said Mervyn.

"Podden me," said the girl, suddenly disappearing.

She was not away long. In fact, Mervyn, roaming hither and thither about the shop, had barely had time to eat three or four dates and a custard apple, when she was with him once more. And now she was wearing a look of definite disapproval, like a duchess who has found half a caterpillar in the castle salad.

"His lordship informs me that he desi-as no strawberries."

"Eh?"

"I have been in telephonic communication with his lordship and he states explicitly that he does not desi-ah strawberries."

Mervyn gave a little at the knees, but he came back stoutly.

"Don't you listen to what he says," he urged. "He's always kidding. That's the sort of fellow he is. Just a great big happy schoolboy. Of course, he desi-ahs strawberries. He told me so himself. I'm his nephew."

Good stuff, he felt, but it did not seem to be getting over. He caught a glimpse of the girl's face, and it was definitely cold and hard and proud. However, he gave a careless laugh, just to show that his heart was in the right place, and seized the basket.

"Ha, ha!" he tittered lightly, and started for the street at something midway between a saunter and a gallop.

And he had not more than reached the open spaces when he heard the girl give tongue behind him.

"EEEE—EEEE—EEEE—EEEE—EEEEEE————!" she said, in substance.

Now, you must remember that all this took place round about the hour of noon, when every young fellow is at his lowest and weakest and the need for the twelve o'clock bracer has begun to sap his morale pretty considerably. With a couple of quick cold ones under his vest, Mervyn would, no doubt, have faced the situation and carried it off with an air. He would have raised his eyebrows. He would have been nonchalant and lit a Murad. But, coming on him in his reduced condition, this fearful screech unnerved him completely.

The duchess had now begun to cry "Stop thief!" and Mervyn, most injudici-
ously, instead of keeping his head and leaping carelessly into a passing taxi, made
the grave strategic error of picking up his feet with a jerk and starting to run
along Piccadilly.

Well, naturally, that did him no good at all. Eight hundred people appeared
from nowhere, willing hands gripped his collar and the seat of his trousers, and
the next thing he knew he was cooling off in Vine Street Police Station.

After that, everything was more or less of a blur. The scene seemed suddenly
to change to a police-court, in which he was confronted by a magistrate who
looked like an owl with a dash of weasel blood in him.

A dialogue then took place, of which all he recalls is this:

POLICEMAN: 'Earing cries of. "Stop thief!" your worship, and observing the
accused running very 'earty. I apprehended 'im.

MAGISTRATE: How did he appear, when apprehended?

POLICEMAN: Very apprehensive, your worship.

MAGISTRATE: You mean he had a sort of pinched look?

(*Laughter in court.*)

POLICEMAN: It then transpired that 'e 'ad been attempting to purloin strawberries.

MAGISTRATE: He seems to have got the raspberry.

(*Laughter in court.*)

Well, what have you to say, young man?

MERVYN: Oh, ah!

MAGISTRATE: More "owe" than "ah," I fear.

(*Laughter in court, in which his worship joined.*)

Ten pounds or fourteen days.

Well, you can see how extremely unpleasant this must have been for my cousin's
son. Considered purely from the dramatic angle, the magistrate had played him
right off the stage, hogging all the comedy and getting the sympathy of the
audience from the start; and, apart from that, here he was, nearing the end of
the quarter, with all his allowance spent except one pound, two and threepence,
suddenly called upon to pay ten pounds or go to durance vile for a matter of two
weeks.

There was only one course before Him. His sensitive soul revolted at the thought
of languishing in a dungeon for a solid fortnight, so it was imperative that he
raise the cash somewhere. And the only way of raising it that he could think of
was to apply to his uncle, Lord Blotsam.

So he sent a messenger round to Berkeley Square, explaining that he was in
jail and hoping his uncle was the same, and presently a letter was brought back
by the butler, containing ten pounds in postal orders, the Curse of the Blotsams,

a third-class ticket to Blotsam Regis in Shropshire and instructions that, as soon as they smote the fetters from his wrists, he was to take the first train there and go and stay at Blotsam Castle till further notice.

Because at the castle, his uncle said in a powerful passage, even a blasted pimply pop-eyed good-for-nothing scallywag and nincompoop like his nephew couldn't get into mischief and disgrace the family name.

And in this, Mervyn tells me, there was a good deal of rugged sense. Blotsam Castle, a noble pile, is situated at least half a dozen miles from anywhere, and the only time anybody ever succeeded in disgracing the family name, while in residence, was back in the reign of Edward the Confessor, when the then Earl of Blotsam, having lured a number of neighbouring landowners into the banqueting hall on the specious pretence of standing them mulled sack, had proceeded to murder one and all with a battle-axe—subsequently cutting their heads off and—in rather loud taste—sticking them on spikes along the outer battlements.

So Mervyn went down to Blotsam Regis and started to camp at the castle, and it was not long, he tells me, before he began to find the time hanging a little heavy on his hands. For a couple of days he managed to endure the monotony, occupying himself in carving the girl's initials on the immemorial elms with a heart round them. But on the third morning, having broken his Boy Scout pocket-knife, he was at something of a loose end. And to fill in the time he started on a moody stroll through the messuages and pleasances, feeling a good deal cast down.

After pacing hither and thither for a while thinking of the girl Clarice, he came to a series of hothouses. And, it being extremely cold, with an east wind that went through his plus-fours like a javelin, he thought it would make an agreeable change if he were to go inside where it was warm and smoke two or perhaps three cigarettes.

And, scarcely had he got past the door, when he found he was almost entirely surrounded by strawberries. There they were, scores of them, all hot and juicy.

For a moment, he tells me, Mervyn had a sort of idea that a miracle had occurred. He seemed to remember a similar thing having happened to the Israelites in the desert—that time, he reminded me, when they were all saying to each other how well a spot of manna would go down and what a dashed shame it was they hadn't any manna and that was the slipshod way the commissariat department ran things and they wouldn't be surprised if it wasn't a case of graft in high places, and then suddenly out of a blue sky all the manna they could do with and enough over for breakfast next day.

Well, to be brief, that was the view which Mervyn took of the matter in the first flush of his astonishment.

Then he remembered that his uncle always opened the castle for the Christmas festivities, and these strawberries were, no doubt, intended for Exhibit A at some forthcoming rout or merry-making.

Well, after that, of course, everything was simple. A child would have known what to do. Hastening back to the house, Mervyn returned with a cardboard box and, keeping a keen eye out for the head-gardener, hurried in, selected about two dozen of the finest specimens, placed them in the box, ran back to the house again, reached for the railway guide, found that there was a train leaving for London in an hour, changed into town clothes, seized his top hat, borrowed the stable-boy's bicycle, pedalled to the station, and about four hours later was mounting the front-door steps of Clarice Mallaby's house in Eaton Square with the box tucked under his arm.

No, that is wrong. The box was not actually tucked under his arm, because he had left it in the train. Except for that, he had carried the thing through without a hitch.

Sturdy common sense is always a quality of the Mulliners, even of the less mentally gifted of the family. It was obvious to Mervyn that no useful end was to be gained by ringing the bell and rushing into the girl's presence, shouting "See what I've brought you!"

On the other hand, what to do? He was feeling somewhat unequal to the swirl of events.

Once, he tells me, some years ago, he got involved in some amateur theatricals, to play the role of a butler: and his part consisted of the following lines and business:

(*Enter* JORKINS, *carrying telegram on salver.*)
JORKINS: A telegram, m'lady.
                    (*Exit* JORKINS)

and on the night in he came, full of confidence, and, having said: "A telegram, m'lady," extended an empty salver towards the heroine, who, having been expecting on the strength of the telegram to clutch at her heart and say: "My God!" and tear open the envelope and crush it in nervous fingers and fall over in a swoon, was considerably taken aback, not to say perturbed.

He felt now as he had felt then.

Still, he had enough sense left to see the way out. After a couple of turns up and down the south side of Eaton Square, he came—rather shrewdly, I must confess—to the conclusion that the only person who could help him in this emergency was Oofy Prosser.

The way Mervyn sketched out the scenario in the rough, it all looked pretty plain sailing. He would go to Oofy, whom, as I told you, he had been saving up for years, and with one single impressive gesture get into his ribs for about twenty quid.

He would be losing money on the deal, of course, because he had always had

Oofy scheduled for at least fifty. But that could not be helped.

Then off to Bellamy's and buy strawberries. He did not exactly relish the prospect of meeting the black satin girl again, but when love is calling these things have to be done.

He found Oofy at home, and plunged into the agenda without delay.

"Hullo, Oofy, old man!" he said. "How are you, Oofy, old man? I say, Oofy, old man, I do like that tie you're wearing. What I call something like a tie. Quite the snappiest thing I've seen for years and years and years and years. I wish I could get ties like that. But then, of course, I haven't your exquisite taste. What I've always said about you, Oofy, old man, and what I always will say, is that you have the most extraordinary *flair*—it amounts to genius—in the selection of ties. But, then, one must bear in mind that anything would look well on you, because you have such a clean-cut, virile profile. I met a man the other day who said to me: 'I didn't know Ronald Colman was in England.' And I said 'He isn't.' And he said: 'But I saw you talking to him outside the Blotto Kitten.' And I said: 'That wasn't Ronald Colman. That was my pal—the best pal any man ever had—Oofy Prosser.' And he said: 'Well, I never saw such a remarkable resemblance.' And I said: 'Yes, there is a great resemblance, only, of course, Oofy is much the better-looking.' And this fellow said: 'Oofy Prosser? Is that *the* Oofy Prosser, the man whose name you hear everywhere?' And I said: 'Yes, and I'm proud to call him my friend. I don't suppose,' I said, 'there's another fellow in London in such demand. Duchesses clamour for him, and, if you ask a princess to dinner, you have to add: 'To meet Oofy Prosser,' or she won't come. 'This,' I explained, 'is because, in addition to being the handsomest and best-dressed man in Mayfair, he is famous for his sparkling wit and keen—but always kindly—repartee. And yet, in spite of all, he remains simple, unspoilt, unaffected.' Will you lend me twenty quid, Oofy, old man?"

"No," said Oofy Prosser.

Mervyn paled.

"What did you say?"

"I said No."

"No?"

"N—ruddy—o!" said Oofy firmly.

Mervyn clutched at the mantelpiece.

"But, Oofy, old man, I need the money—need it sorely."

"I don't care."

It seemed to Mervyn that the only thing to do was to tell all. Clearing his throat, he started in at the beginning. He sketched the course of his great love in burning words, and brought the story up to the point where the girl had placed her order for strawberries.

"She must be cuckoo," said Oofy Prosser. .

Mervyn was respectful, but firm.

"She isn't cuckoo," he said. "I have felt all along that the incident showed what a spiritual nature she has. I mean to say, reaching out yearningly for the unattainable and all that sort of thing, if you know what I mean. Anyway, the broad, basic point is that she wants strawberries, and I've got to collect enough money to get her them."

"Who is this half-wit?" asked Oofy.

Mervyn told him, and Oofy seemed rather impressed.

"I know her." He mused awhile. "Dashed pretty girl."

"Lovely," said Mervyn. "What eyes!"

"Yes."

"What hair!"

"Yes."

"What a figure!"

"Yes," said Oofy. "I always think she's one of the prettiest girls in London.

"Absolutely," said Mervyn. "Then, on second thoughts, old pal, you will lend me twenty quid to buy her strawberries?"

"No," said Oofy.

And Mervyn could not shift him. In the end he gave it up.

"Very well," he said. "Oh, very well. If you won't, you won't. But, Alexander Prosser," proceeded Mervyn, with a good deal of dignity, "just let me tell you this. I wouldn't be seen dead in a tie like that beastly thing you're wearing. I don't like your profile. Your hair is getting thin on top. And I heard a certain prominent society hostess say the other day that the great drawback to living in London was that a woman couldn't give so much as the simplest luncheon-party without suddenly finding that that appalling man Prosser—I quote her words—had wriggled out of the woodwork and was in her midst. Prosser, I wish you a very good afternoon!"

Brave words, of course, but, when you came right down to it, they could not be said to have got him anywhere. After the first thrill of telling Oofy what he thought of him had died away, Mervyn realised that his quandary was now greater than ever. Where was he to look for aid and comfort? He had friends, of course, but the best of them wasn't good for more than an occasional drink or possibly a couple of quid, and what use was that to a man who needed at least a dozen strawberries at a pound apiece?

Extremely bleak the world looked to my cousin's unfortunate son, and he was in sombre mood as he wandered along Piccadilly. As he surveyed the passing populace, he suddenly realised, he tells me, what these Bolshevist blokes were driving at. They had spotted—as he had spotted now—that what was wrong with the world was that all the cash seemed to be centred in the wrong hands and needed a lot of broadminded redistribution.

Where money was concerned, he perceived, merit counted for nothing. Money was too apt to be collared by some rotten bounder or bounders, while the good and deserving man was left standing on the outside, looking in. The sight of all those expensive cars rolling along, crammed to the bulwarks with overfed males and females with fur coats and double chins, made him feel, he tells me, that he wanted to buy a red tie and a couple of bombs and start the Social Revolution. If Stalin had come along at that moment, Mervyn would have shaken him by the hand.

Well, there is, of course, only one thing for a young man to do when he feels like that. Mervyn hurried along to the club and in rapid succession drank three Martini cocktails.

The treatment was effective, as it always is. Gradually the stern, censorious mood passed, and he began to feel an optimistic glow. As the revivers slid over the larynx, he saw that all was not lost. He perceived that he had been leaving out of his reckoning that sweet, angelic pity which is such a characteristic of woman.

Take the case of a knight of old, he meant to say. Was anyone going to tell him that if a knight of old had been sent off by a damsel on some fearfully tricky quest and had gone through all sorts of perils and privations for her sake, facing dragons in black satin and risking going to chokey and what not, the girl would have given him the bird when he got back, simply because—looking at the matter from a severely technical standpoint—he had failed to bring home the gravy?

Absolutely not, Mervyn considered. She would have been most awfully braced with him for putting up such a good show and would have comforted and cosseted him.

This girl Clarice, he felt, was bound to do the same, so obviously the move now was to toddle along to Eaton Square again and explain matters to her. So he gave his hat a brush, flicked a spot of dust from his coat-sleeve, and shot off in a taxi.

All during the drive he was rehearsing what he would say to her, and it sounded pretty good to him. In his mind's eye he could see the tears coming into her gentle eyes as he told her about the Arm of the Law gripping his trouser-seat. But, when he arrived, a hitch occurred. There was a stage wait. The butler at Eaton Square told him the girl was dressing.

"Say that Mr. Mulliner has called," said Mervyn.

So the butler went upstairs, and presently from aloft there came the clear penetrating voice of his loved one telling the butler to bung Mr. Mulliner into the drawing-room and lock up all the silver.

And Mervyn went into the drawing-room and settled down to wait.

It was one of those drawing-rooms where there is not a great deal to entertain and amuse the visitor. Mervyn tells me that he got a good laugh out of a photograph of the girl's late father on the mantelpiece—a heavily-whiskered old gentleman who reminded him of a burst horse-hair sofa—but the rest of the appointments were on the dull side. They consisted of an album of views of Italy and a copy of Indian Love Lyrics bound in limp cloth: and it was not long before he began to feel a touch of ennui.

He polished his shoes with one of the sofa-cushions, and took his hat from the table where he had placed it and gave it another brush: but after that there seemed to be nothing in the way of intellectual occupation offering itself, so he just leaned back in a chair and unhinged his lower jaw and let it droop, and sank into a sort of coma. And it was while he was still in this trance that he was delighted to hear a dog-fight in progress in the street. He went to the window and looked out, but the thing was apparently taking place somewhere near the front door, and the top of the porch hid it from him.

Now, Mervyn hated to miss a dog-fight. Many of his happiest hours had been spent at dog-fights. And this one appeared from the sound of it to be on a more or less major scale. He ran down the stairs and opened the front door.

As his trained senses had told him, the encounter was being staged at the foot of the steps. He stood in the open doorway and drank it in. He had always maintained that you got the best dog-fights down in the Eaton Square neighbourhood, because there tough animals from the King's Road, Chelsea, district were apt to wander in—dogs who had trained on gin and flat-irons at the local public-houses and could be relied on to give of their best.

The present encounter bore out this view. It was between a sort of *consommé* of mastiff and Irish terrier, on the one hand, and, on the other, a long-haired *macédoine* of about seven breeds of dog who had an indescribably raffish look, as if he had been mixing with the artist colony down by the river. For about five minutes it was as inspiring a contest as you could have wished to see; but at the end of that time it stopped suddenly, both principals simultaneously observing a cat at an area gate down the road and shaking hands hastily and woofing after her.

Mervyn was not a little disappointed at this abrupt conclusion to the entertainment, but it was no use repining. He started to go back into the house and was just closing the front door, when a messenger-boy appeared, carrying a parcel.

"Sign, please," said the messenger-boy.

The lad's mistake was a natural one. Finding Mervyn standing in the doorway without a hat, he had assumed him to be the butler. He pushed the parcel into his hand, made him sign a yellow paper, and went off, leaving Mervyn with the parcel.

And Mervyn, glancing at it, saw that it was addressed to the girl—Clarice.

But it was not this that made him reel where he stood. What made him reel where he stood was the fact that on the paper outside the thing was a label with "Bellamy & Co., Bespoke Fruitists" on it. And he was convinced, prodding it, that there was some squashy substance inside which certainly was not apples, oranges, nuts, bananas, or anything of that nature.

Mervyn lowered his shapely nose and gave a hard sniff at the parcel. And, having done so, he reeled where he stood once more.

A frightful suspicion had shot through him.

It was not that my cousin's son was gifted beyond the ordinary in the qualities that go to make a successful detective. You would not have found him deducing anything much from footprints or cigar-ash. In fact, if this parcel had contained cigar-ash, it would have meant nothing to him. But in the circumstances anybody with his special knowledge would have been suspicious.

For consider the facts. His sniff had told him that beneath the outward wrapping of paper lay strawberries. And the only person beside himself who knew that the girl wanted strawberries was Oofy Prosser. About the only man in London able to buy strawberries at that time of year was Oofy. And Oofy's manner, he recalled, when they were talking about the girl's beauty and physique generally, had been furtive and sinister.

To rip open the paper, therefore, and take a look at the enclosed card was with Mervyn Mulliner the work of a moment.

And, sure enough, it was as he had foreseen. "Alexander C. Prosser" was the name on the card, and Mervyn tells me he wouldn't be a bit surprised if the C. didn't stand for Clarence.

His first feeling, he tells me, as he stood there staring at that card, was one of righteous indignation at the thought that any such treacherous, double-crossing hound as Oofy Prosser should have been permitted to pollute the air of London, W.1, all these years. To refuse a fellow twenty quid with one hand, and then to go and send his girl strawberries with the other, struck Mervyn as about as low-down a bit of hornswoggling as you could want.

He burned with honest wrath. And he was still burning when the last cocktail he had had at the club, which had been lying low inside him all this while, suddenly came to life and got action. Quite unexpectedly, he tells me, it began to frisk about like a young lamb, until it leaped into his head and gave him the idea of a lifetime.

What, he asked himself, was the matter with suppressing this card, freezing on to the berries, and presenting them to the girl with a modest flourish as coming from M. Mulliner, Esq? And, he answered himself, there was abso-bally-nothing the matter with it. It was a jolly sound scheme and showed what three medium dry Martinis could do.

He quivered all over with joy and elation. Standing there in the hall, he felt that there was a Providence, after all, which kept an eye on good men and saw to it that they came out on top in the end. In fact, he felt so extremely elated that he burst into song. And he had not got much beyond the first high note when he heard Clarice Mallaby giving tongue from upstairs.

"Stop it!"

"What did you say?" said Mervyn.

"I said 'Stop it!' The cat's downstairs with a headache, trying to rest."

"I say," said Mervyn, "are you going to be long?"

"How do you mean—long?"

"Long dressing. Because I've something I want to show you."

"What?"

"Oh, nothing much," said Mervyn carelessly. "Nothing particular. Just a few assorted strawberries."

"Eek!" said the girl. "You don't mean you've really got them?"

"Got them?" said Mervyn. "Didn't I say I would?"

"I'll be down in just one minute," said the girl.

Well, you know what girls are. The minute stretched into five minutes, and the five minutes into a quarter of an hour, and Mervyn made the tour of the drawing-room, and looked at the photograph of her late father, and picked up the album of Views of Italy, and opened Indian Love Lyrics at page forty-three and shut it again, and took up the cushion and gave his shoes another rub, and brushed his hat once more, and still she didn't come.

And so, by way of something else to do, he started brooding on the strawberries for a space.

Considered purely as strawberries, he tells me, they were a pretty rickety collection, not to say spavined. They were an unhealthy whitish-pink in colour and looked as if they had just come through a lingering illness which had involved a good deal of blood-letting by means of leeches.

"They don't look much," said Mervyn to himself.

Not that it really mattered, of course, because all the girl had told him to do was to get her strawberries, and nobody could deny these were strawberries. C.3 though they might be, they were genuine strawberries, and from that fact there was no getting away.

Still, he did not want the dear little soul to be disappointed.

"I wonder if they have any flavour at all?" said Mervyn to himself.

Well, the first one had not. Nor had the second. The third was rather better. And the fourth was quite juicy. And the best of all, oddly enough, was the last one in the basket.

He was just finishing it when Clarice Mallaby came running in.

Well, Mervyn tried to pass it off, of course. But his efforts were not rewarded with any great measure of success. In fact, he tells me that he did not get beyond a tentative "Oh, I say . . ." And the upshot of the whole matter was that the girl threw him out into the winter evening without so much as giving him a chance to take his hat.

Nor had he the courage to go back and fetch it later, for Clarice Mallaby stated specifically that if he dared to show his ugly face at the house again the butler had instructions to knock him down and skin him, and the butler was looking forward to it, as he had never liked Mervyn.

So there the matter rests. The whole thing has been a great blow to my cousin's son, for he considers—and rightly, I suppose—that, if you really come down to it, he failed in his quest. Nevertheless, I think that we must give him credit for the possession of the old knightly spirit to which our friend here was alluding just now.

He meant well. He did his best. And even of a Mulliner more cannot be said than that.

23

THE VOICE FROM THE PAST

AT the ancient and historic public-school which stands a mile or two up the river from the Anglers' Rest there had recently been a change of headmasters, and our little group in the bar-parlour, naturally interested, was discussing the new appointment.

A grizzled Tankard of Stout frankly viewed it with concern.

"Benger!" he exclaimed. "Fancy making Benger a headmaster."

"He has a fine record."

"Yes, but, dash it, he was at school with me."

"One lives these things down in time," we urged.

The Tankard said we had missed his point, which was that he could remember young Scrubby Benger in an Eton collar with jam on it, getting properly cursed by the Mathematics beak for bringing white mice into the form-room.

"He was a small, fat kid with a pink face," proceeded the Tankard. "I met him again only last July, and he looked just the same. I can't see him as a headmaster. I thought they had to be a hundred years old and seven feet high, with eyes of flame, and long white beards. To me, a headmaster has always been a sort of blend of Epstein's Genesis and something out of the Book of Revelations."

Mr. Mulliner smiled tolerantly.

"You left school at an early age, I imagine?"

"Sixteen. I had to go into my uncle's business."

"Exactly," said Mr. Mulliner, nodding sagely. "You completed your school career, in other words, before the age at which a boy, coming into personal relationship with the man up top, learns to regard him as a guide, philosopher and friend. The result is that you are suffering from the well-know Headmaster Fixation or Phobia—precisely as my nephew Sacheverell did. A rather delicate youth, he was removed by his parents from Harborough College shortly after his fifteenth birthday and educated at home by a private tutor; and I have frequently heard him assert that the Rev. J. G. Smethurst, the ruling spirit of Harborough, was a man who chewed broken bottles and devoured his young."

"I strongly suspected my headmaster of conducting human sacrifices behind the fives-courts at the time of the full moon," said the Tankard.

"Men like yourself and my nephew Sacheverell who leave school early," said Mr. Mulliner, "never wholly lose these poetic boyish fancies. All their lives, the phobia persists. And sometimes this has curious results—as in the case of my nephew Sacheverell."

It was to the terror inspired by his old headmaster (said Mr. Mulliner) that I always attributed my nephew Sacheverell's extraordinary mildness and timidity. A nervous boy, the years seemed to bring him no store of self-confidence. By the time he arrived at man's estate, he belonged definitely to the class of humanity which never gets a seat on an underground train and is ill at ease in the presence of butlers, traffic policemen, and female assistants in post offices. He was the sort of young fellow at whom people laugh when the waiter speaks to them in French.

And this was particularly unfortunate, as he had recently become secretly affianced to Muriel, only daughter of Lieut.-Colonel Sir Redvers Branksome, one of the old-school type of squire and as tough an egg as ever said "Yoicks" to a fox-hound. He had met her while she was on a visit to an aunt in London, and had endeared himself to her partly by his modest and diffident demeanour and partly by doing tricks with a bit of string, an art at which he was highly proficient.

Muriel was one of those hearty, breezy girls who abound in the hunting counties of England. Brought up all her life among confident young men who wore gaiters and smacked them with riding-crops, she had always yearned subconsciously for something different: and Sacheverell's shy, mild, shrinking, personality seemed to wake the maternal in her. He was so weak, so helpless, that her heart went out to him. Friendship speedily ripened into love, with the result that one afternoon my nephew found himself definitely engaged and faced with the prospect of breaking the news to the old folks at home.

"And if you think you've got a picnic ahead of you," said Muriel, "forget it. Father's a gorilla. I remember when I was engaged to my cousin Bernard——"

"When you were what to your what?" gasped Sacheverell.

"Oh, yes," said the girl. "Didn't I tell you? I was engaged once to my cousin Bernard, but I broke it off because he tried to boss me. A little too much of the dominant male there was about old B., and I handed him his hat. Though we're still good friends. But what I was saying was that Bernard used to gulp like a seal and stand on one leg when father came along. And he's in the Guards. That just shows you. However, we'll start the thing going. I'll get you down to the Towers for a week-end, and we'll see what happens."

If Muriel had hoped that mutual esteem would spring up between her father and her betrothed during this week-end visit, she was doomed to disappointment. The thing was a failure from the start. Sacheverell's host did him extremely well, giving him the star guest-room, the Blue Suite, and bringing out the oldest port for his benefit, but it was plain that he thought little of the young man. The colonel's subjects were sheep (in sickness and in health), manure, wheat, mangold-wurzels, huntin', shootin' and fishin': while Sacheverell was at his best on Proust, the Russian Ballet, Japanese prints, and the Influence of James Joyce on the younger Bloomsbury novelists. There was no fusion between these men's souls. Colonel Branksome did not actually bite Sacheverell in the leg, but when you had said that you had said everything.

Muriel was deeply concerned.

"I'll tell you what it is, Dogface," she said, as she was seeing her loved one to his train on the Monday, "we've got off on the wrong foot. The male parent may have loved you at sight, but, if he did, he took another look and changed his mind."

"I fear we were not exactly *en rapport*," sighed Sacheverell. "Apart from the fact that the mere look of him gave me a strange, sinking feeling, my conversation seemed to bore him."

"You didn't talk about the right things."

"I couldn't. I know so little of mangold-wurzels. Manure is a sealed book to me."

"Just what I'm driving at," said Muriel. "And all that must be altered. Before you spring the tidings on father, there will have to be a lot of careful preliminary top-dressing of the soil, if you follow what I mean. By the time the bell goes for the second round and old Dangerous Dan McGrew comes out of his corner at you, breathing fire, you must have acquired a good working knowledge of Scientific Agriculture. That'll tickle him pink."

"But how?"

"I'll tell you how. I was reading a magazine the other day, and there was an advertisement in it of a Correspondence School which teaches practically everything. You put a cross against the course you want to take and clip out the coupon and bung it in, and they do the rest. I suppose they send you pamphlets and things. So the moment you get back to London, look up this advertisement—it was in the *Piccadilly Magazine*—and write to these people and tell them to shoot the works."

Sacheverell pondered this advice during the railway journey, and the more he pondered it the more clearly did he see how excellent it was. It offered the solution to all his troubles. There was no doubt whatever that the bad impression he had made on Colonel Branksome was due chiefly to his ignorance of the latter's pet subjects. If he were in a position to throw off a good thing from time to time on Guano or the Influence of Dip on the Younger Leicestershire Sheep, Muriel's father would unquestionably view him with a far kindlier eye.

He lost no time in clipping out the coupon and forwarding it with a covering cheque to the address given in the advertisement. And two days later a bulky package arrived, and he settled down to an intensive course of study.

By the time Sacheverell had mastered the first six lessons, a feeling of perplexity had begun to steal over him. He knew nothing, of course, of the methods of

Correspondence Schools and was prepared to put his trust blindly in his unseen tutor; but it did strike him as odd that a course on Scientific Agriculture should have absolutely no mention of Scientific Agriculture in it. Though admittedly a child in these matters, he had supposed that that was one of the first topics on which the thing would have touched.

But such was not the case. The lessons contained a great deal of advice about deep breathing and regular exercise and cold baths and Yogis and the training of the mind, but on the subject of Scientific Agriculture they were vague and elusive. They simply would not come to the point. They said nothing about sheep, nothing about manure, and from the way they avoided mangold-wurzels you might have thought they considered these wholesome vegetables almost improper.

At first, Sacheverell accepted this meekly, as he accepted everything in life. But gradually, as his reading progressed, a strange sensation of annoyance began to grip him. He found himself chafing a good deal, particularly in the mornings. And when the seventh lesson arrived and still there was this absurd coyness on the part of his instructors to come to grips with Scientific Agriculture, he decided to put up with it no longer, He was enraged. These people, he considered, were deliberately hornswoggling him. He resolved to go round and see them and put it to them straight that he was not the sort of man to be trifled with in this fashion.

The headquarters of the Leave-It-To-Us Correspondence School were in a large building off Kingsway. Sacheverell, passing through the front door like an east wind, found himself confronted by a small boy with a cold and supercilious eye.

"Yes?" said the boy, with deep suspicion. He seemed to be a lad who distrusted his fellowmen and attributed the worst motives to their actions.

Sacheverell pointed curtly to a door on which was the legend "Jno. B. Philbrick, Mgr."

"I wish to see Jno. B. Philbrick, Mgr.," he said.

The boy's lip curled contemptuously. He appeared to be on the point of treating the application with silent disdain. Then he vouchsafed a single, scornful word.

"Can'tseeMr.Philbrickwithoutanappointment," he said.

A few weeks before, a rebuff like this would have sent Sacheverell stumbling blushfully out of the place, tripping over his feet. But now he merely brushed the child aside like a feather, and strode to the inner office.

A bald-headed man with a walrus moustache was seated at the desk.

"Jno. Philbrick?" said Sacheverell brusquely.

"That is my name."

"Then listen to me, Philbrick," said Sacheverell. "I paid fifteen guineas in advance for a course on Scientific Agriculture. I have here the seven lessons which you have sent me to date, and if you can find a single word in them that has anything even remotely to do with Scientific Agriculture, I will eat my hat—and yours, too, Philbrick."

The manager had produced a pair of spectacles and through them was gazing at the mass of literature which Sacheverell had hurled before him. He raised his eyebrows and clicked his tongue.

"Stop clicking!" said Sacheverell. "I came here to be explained to, not clicked at."

"Dear me!" said the manager. "How very curious."

Sacheverell banged the desk forcefully.

"Philbrick," he shouted, "do not evade the issue. It is not curious. It is scandalous, monstrous, disgraceful, and I intend to take very strong steps. I shall give this outrage the widest and most pitiless publicity, and spare no effort to make a complete *exposé*."

The manager held up a deprecating hand.

"Please!" he begged. "I appreciate your indignation, Mr. . . Mulliner? Thank you . . . I appreciate your indignation, Mr. Mulliner. I sympathise with your concern. But I can assure you that there has been no desire to deceive. Merely an unfortunate blunder on the part of our clerical staff, who shall be severely reprimanded. What has happened is that the wrong course has been sent to you."

Sacheverell's righteous wrath cooled a little.

"Oh?" he said, somewhat mollified. "I see. The wrong course, eh?"

"The wrong course," said Mr. Philbrick. "And," he went on, with a sly glance at his visitor, "I think you will agree with me that such immediate results are a striking testimony to the efficacy of our system."

Sacheverell was puzzled.

"Results?" he said. "How do you mean, results?"

The manager smiled genially.

"What you have been studying for the past few weeks, Mr. Mulliner," he said, "is our course on How to Acquire Complete Self-Confidence and an Iron Will."

A strange elation filled Sacheverell Mulliner's bosom as he left the offices of the Correspondence School. It is always a relief to have a mystery solved which has been vexing one for any considerable time: and what Jno. Philbrick had told him made several puzzling things clear. For quite a little while he had been aware that a change had taken place in his relationship to the world about him. He recalled taxi-cabmen whom he had looked in the eye and made to wilt; intrusive pedestrians to whom he had refused to yield an inch of the pavement, where formerly he would have stepped meekly aside. These episodes had perplexed him at the time, but now everything was explained.

But what principally pleased him was the thought that he was now relieved of the tedious necessity of making a study of Scientific Agriculture, a subject from which his artist soul had always revolted. Obviously, a man with a will as iron as his would be merely wasting time boning up a lot of dull facts simply with the view of pleasing Sir Redvers Branksome. Sir Redvers Branksome, felt Sacheverell, would jolly well take him as he was, and like it.

He anticipated no trouble from that quarter. In his mind's eye he could see himself lolling at the dinner-table at the Towers and informing the Colonel over a glass of port that he proposed, at an early date, to marry his daughter. Possibly, purely out of courtesy, he would make the graceful gesture of affecting to seek the old buster's approval of the match: but at the slightest sign of obduracy he would know what to do about it.

Well pleased, Sacheverell was walking to the Carlton Hotel, where he intended to lunch, when, just as he entered the Haymarket, he stopped abruptly, and a dark frown came into his resolute face.

A cab had passed him, and in that cab was sitting his fiancée, Muriel Branksome. And beside her, with a grin on his beastly face, was a young man in a Brigade of Guards tie. They had the air of a couple on their way to enjoy a spot of lunch somewhere.

That Sacheverell should have deduced immediately that the young man was Muriel's cousin, Bernard, was due to the fact that, like all the Mulliners, he was keenly intuitive. That he should have stood, fists clenched and eyes blazing, staring after the cab, we may set down to the circumstance that the spectacle of these two, squashed together in carefree proximity on the seat of a taxi, had occasioned in him the utmost rancour and jealousy.

Muriel, as she had told him, had once been engaged to her cousin, and the thought that they were still on terms of such sickening intimacy acted like acid on Sacheverell's soul.

Hobnobbing in cabs, by Jove! Revelling *tête-à-tête* at luncheon-tables, forsooth! Just the sort of goings-on that got the Cities of the Plain so disliked. He saw clearly that Muriel was a girl who would have to be handled firmly. There was nothing of the possessive Victorian male about him—he flattered himself that he was essentially modern and broadminded in his outlook—but if Muriel supposed that he was going to stand by like a clam while she went on Babylonian orgies all over the place with pop-eyed, smirking, toothbrush-moustached Guardees, she was due for a rude awakening.

And Sacheverell Mulliner did not mean maybe.

For an instant, he toyed with the idea of hailing another cab and following them. Then he thought better of it. He was enraged, but still master of himself. When he ticked Muriel off, as he intended to do, he wished to tick her off alone. If she was in London, she was, no doubt, staying with her aunt in Ennismore Gardens. He would get a bit of food and go on there at his leisure.

The butler at Ennismore Gardens informed Sacheverell, when he arrived, that Muriel was, as he supposed, visiting the house, though for the moment out to lunch. Sacheverell waited, and presently the door of the drawing-room opened and the girl came in.

She seemed delighted to see him.

"Hullo, old steptococcus," she said. "Here you are, eh? I rang you up this morning to ask you to give me a bite of lunch, but you were out, so I roped in Bernard instead and we buzzed off to the Savoy in a taximeter."

"I saw you," said Sacheverell coldly.

"Did you? You poor chump, why didn't you yell?"

"I had no desire to meet your Cousin Bernard," said Sacheverell, still speaking in the same frigid voice. "And, while we are on this distasteful subject, I must request you not to see him again."

The girl stared.

"You must do how much?"

"I must request you not to see him again," repeated Sacheverell. "I do not wish you to continue your Cousin Bernard's acquaintance. I do not like his looks, nor do I approve of my fiancée lunching alone with young men."

Muriel seemed bewildered.

"You want me to tie a can to poor old Bernard?" she gasped.

"I insist upon it."

"But, you poor goop, we were children together."

Sacheverell shrugged his shoulders.

"If," he said, "you survived knowing Bernard as a child, why not be thankful and let it go at that? Why deliberately come up for more punishment by seeking him out now? Well, there it is," said Sacheverell crisply. "I have told you my wishes, and you will respect them."

Muriel appeared to be experiencing a difficulty in finding words. She was bubbling like a saucepan on the point of coming to the boil. Nor could any unprejudiced critic have blamed her for her emotion. The last time she had seen Sacheverell, it must be remembered, he had been the sort of man who made a shrinking violet look like a Chicago gangster. And here he was now, staring her in the eye and shooting off his head for all the world as if he were Mussolini informing the Italian Civil Service of a twelve per cent cut in their weekly salary.

"And now," said Sacheverell, "there is another matter of which I wish to speak. I am anxious to see your father as soon as possible, in order to announce our engagement to him. It is quite time that he learned what my plans are. I shall be glad, therefore, if you will make arrangements to put me up at the Towers this coming week-end. Well," concluded Sacheverell, glancing at his watch, "I must be going. I have several matters to attend to, and your luncheon with your cousin was so prolonged that the hour is already late. Good-bye. We shall meet on Saturday."

Sacheverell was feeling at the top of his form when he set out for Branksome Towers on the following Saturday. The eighth lesson of his course on how to develop an iron will had reached him by the morning post, and he studied it on the train. It was a pippin. It showed you exactly how Napoleon had got that way, and there was some technical stuff about narrowing the eyes and fixing them keenly on people which alone was worth the money. He alighted at Market Branksome Station in a glow of self-confidence. The only thing that troubled him was a fear lest Sir Redvers might madly attempt anything in the nature of opposition to his plans. He did not wish to be compelled to scorch the poor old man to a crisp at his own dinner-table.

He was meditating on this and resolving to remember to do his best to let the Colonel down as lightly as possible, when a voice spoke his name.

"Mr. Mulliner?"

He turned. He supposed he was obliged to believe his eyes. And, if he did believe his eyes, the man standing beside him was none other than Muriel's cousin Bernard.

"They sent me down to meet you," continued Bernard. "I'm the old boy's nephew. Shall we totter to the car?"

Sacheverell was beyond speech. The thought that, after what he had said, Muriel should have invited her cousin to the Towers had robbed him of utterance. He followed the other to the car in silence.

In the drawing-room of the Towers they found Muriel, already dressed for dinner, brightly shaking up cocktails.

"So you got here?" said Muriel.

At another time her manner might have struck Sacheverell as odd. There was an unwonted hardness in it. Her eye, though he was too preoccupied to notice it, had a dangerous gleam.

"Yes," he replied shortly. "I got here."

"The Bish. arrived yet?" asked Bernard.

"Not yet. Father had a telegram from him. He won't be along till late-ish. The Bishop of Bognor is coming to confirm a bevy of the local yokels," said Muriel, turning to Sacheverell.

"Oh?" said Sacheverell, He was not interested in Bishops. They left him cold. He was interested in nothing but her explanation of how her repellent cousin came to be here to-night in defiance of his own expressed wishes.

"Well," said Bernard, "I suppose I'd better be going up and disguising myself as a waiter."

"I, too," said Sacheverell. He turned to Muriel. "I take it I am in the Blue Suite, as before?"

"No," said Muriel. "You're in the Garden Room. You see——"

"I see perfectly," said Sacheverell curtly.

He turned on his heel and stalked to the door.

The indignation which Sacheverell had felt on seeing Bernard at the station was as nothing compared with that which seethed within him as he dressed for dinner. That Bernard should be at the Towers at all was monstrous. That he should have been given the star bedroom in preference to himself, Sacheverell Mulliner, was one of those things before which the brain reels.

As you are doubtless aware, the distribution of bedrooms in country houses is as much a matter of rigid precedence as the distribution of dressing-rooms at a theatre. The nibs get the best ones, the small fry squash in where they can. If Sacheverell had been a *prima donna* told off to dress with the second character-woman, he could not have been more mortified.

It was not simply that the Blue Suite was the only one in the house with a bathroom of its own: it was the principle of the thing. The fact that he was pigging it in the Garden Room, while Bernard wallowed in luxury in the Blue Suite was tantamount to a declaration on Muriel's part that she intended to get back at him for the attitude which he had taken over her luncheon-party. It was a slight, a deliberate snub, and Sacheverell came down to dinner coldly resolved to nip all this nonsense in the bud without delay.

Wrapped in his thoughts, he paid no attention to the conversation during the early part of dinner. He sipped a moody spoonful or two of soup and toyed with a morsel of salmon, but spiritually he was apart. It was only when the saddle of lamb had been distributed and the servitors had begun to come round with the vegetables that he was roused from his reverie by a sharp, barking noise from the head of the table, not unlike the note of a man-eating tiger catching sight of a Hindu peasant; and, glancing up, he perceived that it proceeded from Sir Redvers Branksom. His host was staring in an unpleasant manner at a dish which had just been placed under his nose by the butler.

It was in itself a commonplace enough occurrence—merely the old, old story of the head of the family kicking at the spinach; but for some reason it annoyed Sacheverell intensely. His strained nerves were jangled by the animal cries which had begun to fill the air, and he told himself that Sir Redvers, if he did not switch it off pretty quick, was going to be put through it in no uncertain fashion.

Sir Redvers, meanwhile, unconscious of impending doom, was glaring at the dish.

"What," he enquired in a hoarse, rasping voice, "is this dashed, sloppy, disgusting, slithery, gangrened mess?"

The butler did not reply. He had been through all this before. He merely increased in volume the detached expression which good butlers wear on these occasions. He looked like a prominent banker refusing to speak without advice of counsel. It was Muriel who supplied the necessary information.

"It's spinach, father."

"Then take it away and give it to the cat. You know I hate spinach."

"But it's so good for you."

"Who says it's good for me?"

"All the doctors. It bucks you up if you haven't enough hæmoglobins."

"I have plenty of hæmoglobins," said the Colonel testily. "More than I know what to do with."

"It's full of iron."

"Iron!" The Colonel's eyebrows had drawn themselves together into a single, formidable zareba of hair. He snorted fiercely. "Iron! Do you take me for a sword-swallower? Are you under the impression that I am an ostrich, that I should browse on iron? Perhaps you would like me to tuck away a few door-knobs and a couple of pairs of roller-skates? Or a small portion of tin-tacks? Iron, forsooth!"

Just, in short, the ordinary, conventional spinach-row of the better-class English home; but Sacheverell was in no mood for it. This bickering and wrangling irritated him and he decided that it must stop. He half rose from his chair.

"Branksome," he said in a quiet, level voice, "you will eat your spinach."

"Eh? What? What's that?"

"You will eat your nice spinach immediately, Branksome," said Sacheverell. And at the same time he narrowed his eyes and fixed them keenly on his host.

And suddenly the rich purple colour began to die out of the old man's cheeks. Gradually his eyebrows crept back into their normal position. For a brief while he met Sacheverell's eye; then he dropped his own and a weak smile came into his face.

"Well, well," he said, with a pathetic attempt at bluffness, as he reached over and grabbed the spoon. "What have we here? Spinach, eh? Capital, capital! Full of iron, I believe, and highly recommended by the medical profession."

And he dug in and scooped up a liberal portion.

A short silence followed, broken only by the sloshing sound of the Colonel eating spinach. Then Sacheverell spoke.

"I wish to see you in your study immediately after dinner, Branksome," he said curtly.

Muriel was playing the piano when Sacheverell came into the drawing-room some forty minutes after the conclusion of dinner. She was interpreting a work by one of those Russian composers who seem to have been provided by Nature especially with a view to soothing the nervous systems of young girls who are not feeling quite themselves. It was a piece from which the best results are obtained by hauling off and delivering a series of overhand swings which make the instrument wobble like the engine-room of a liner; and Muriel, who was a fine, sturdy girl, was putting a lot of beef into it.

The change in Sacheverell had distressed Muriel Branksome beyond measure. Contemplating him, she felt as she had sometimes felt at a dance when she had told her partner to bring her ice-cream and he had come frisking up with a bowl of mock-turtle soup. Cheated—that is what she felt she had been. She had given her heart to a mild, sweet-natured, lovable lamb; and the moment she had done so he had suddenly flung off his sheep's clothing and said: "April fool! I'm a wolf!"

Haughty by nature, Muriel Branksome was incapable of bearing anything in the shape of bossiness from the male. Her proud spirit revolted at it. And bossiness had become Sacheverell Mulliner's middle name.

The result was that, when Sacheverell entered the drawing-room, he found his loved one all set for the big explosion.

He suspected nothing. He was pleased with himself, and looked it.

"I put your father in his place all right at dinner, what?" said Sacheverell, buoyantly. "Put him right where he belonged, I think."

Muriel gnashed her teeth in a quiet undertone.

"He isn't so hot," said Sacheverell. "The way you used to talk about him, one would have thought he was the real ginger. Quite the reverse I found him. As nice a soft-spoken old bird as one could wish to meet. When I told him about our engagement, he just came and rubbed his head against my leg and rolled over with his paws in the air."

Muriel swallowed softly.

"Our what?" she said.

"Our engagement."

"Oh?" said Muriel. "You told him we were engaged, did you?"

"I certainly did."

"Then you can jolly well go back," said Muriel, blazing into sudden fury, "and tell him you were talking through your hat."

Sacheverell stared.

"That last remark once again, if you don't mind."

"A hundred times, if you wish it," said Muriel. "Get this well into your fat head. Memorise it carefully. If necessary, write it on your cuff. I am not going to marry you. I wouldn't marry you to win a substantial bet or to please an old school-friend. I wouldn't marry you if you offered me all the money in the world. So there!"

Sacheverell blinked. He was taken aback.

"This sounds like the bird," he said.

"It is the bird."

"You are really giving me the old raspberry?"

"I am."

"Don't you love your little Sacheverell?"

"No, I don't. I think my little Sacheverell is a mess."

There was a silence. Sacheverell regarded her with lowered brows. Then he uttered a short, bitter laugh.

"Oh, very well," he said.

Sacheverell Mulliner boiled with jealous rage. Of course, he saw what had happened. The girl had fallen once more under the glamorous spell of her cousin Bernard, and proposed to throw a Mulliner's heart aside like a soiled glove. But if she thought he was going to accept the situation meekly and say no more about it, she would soon discover her error.

Sacheverell loved this girl—not with the tepid preference which passes for love in these degenerate days, but with all the medieval fervour of a rich and passionate soul. And he intended to marry her. Yes, if the whole Brigade of Guards stood between, he was resolved to walk up the aisle with her arm in his and help her cut the cake at the subsequent breakfast.

Bernard . . . ! He would soon settle Bernard.

For all his inner ferment, Sacheverell retained undiminished the clearness of mind which characterises Mulliners in times of crisis. An hour's walk up and down the terrace had shown him what he must do. There was nothing to be gained by acting hastily. He must confront Bernard alone in the silent night, when they would be free from danger of interruption and he could set the full force of his iron personality playing over the fellow like a hose.

And so it came about that the hour of eleven, striking from the clock above the stables, found Sacheverell Mulliner sitting grimly in the Blue Suite, waiting for his victim to arrive.

His brain was like ice. He had matured his plan of campaign. He did not intend to hurt the man—merely to order him to leave the house instantly and never venture to see or speak to Muriel again.

So mused Sacheverell Mulliner, unaware that no Cousin Bernard would come within ten yards of the Blue Suite that night. Bernard had already retired to rest in the Pink Room on the third floor, which had been his roosting-place from the beginning of his visit. The Blue Suite, being the abode of the most honoured guest had, of course, been earmarked from the start for the Bishop of Bognor.

Carburettor trouble and a series of detours had delayed the Bishop in his journey to Branksome Towers. At first, he had hoped to make it in time for dinner. Then he had anticipated an arrival at about nine-thirty. Finally, he was exceedingly relieved to reach his destination shortly after eleven.

A quick sandwich and a small limejuice and soda were all that the prelate asked of his host at that advanced hour. These consumed, he announced himself ready for bed, and Colonel Branksome conducted him to the door of the Blue Suite.

"I hope you will find everything comfortable, my dear Bishop," he said.

"I am convinced of it, my dear Branksome," said the Bishop. "And to-morrow I trust I shall feel less fatigued and in a position to meet the rest of your guests."

"There is only one beside my nephew Bernard. A young fellow named Mulliner."

"Mulligan?"

"Mulliner."

"Ah, yes," said the Bishop. "Mulliner."

And simultaneously, inside the room, my nephew Sacheverell sprang from his chair, and stood frozen, like a statue.

In narrating this story, I have touched lightly upon Sacheverell's career at Harborough College. I shall not be digressing now if I relate briefly what had always been to him the high spot in it.

One sunny summer day, when a lad of fourteen and a half, my nephew had sought to relieve the tedium of school routine by taking a golf-ball and flinging it against the side of the building, his intention being to catch it as it rebounded. Unfortunately, when it came to the acid test, the ball did not rebound. Instead of going due north, it went nor'-nor'-east, with the result that it passed through the window of the headmaster's library at the precise moment when that high official was about to lean out for a breath of air. And the next moment, a voice, proceeding apparently from heaven, had spoken one word. The voice was like the deeper notes of a great organ, and the word was the single word:

"MULLINER ! ! !"

And, just as the word Sacheverell now heard was the same word, so was the voice the same voice.

To appreciate my nephew's concern, you must understand that the episode which I have just related had remained green in his memory right through the years. His pet nightmare, and the one which had had so depressing an effect on his *morale,* had always been the one where he found himself standing, quivering and helpless, while a voice uttered the single word "Mulliner!"

Little wonder, then, that he now remained for an instant paralysed. His only coherent thought was a bitter reflection that somebody might have had the sense to tell him that the Bishop of Bognor was his old headmaster, the Rev. J. G. Smethurst. Naturally, in that case, he would have been out of the place in two strides. But they had simply said the Bishop of Bognor, and it had meant nothing to him.

Now that it was too late, he seemed to recall having heard somebody somewhere say something about the Rev. J. G. Smethurst becoming a bishop; and even in this moment of collapse he was able to feel a thrill of justifiable indignation at the shabbiness of the act. It wasn't fair for headmasters to change their names like this and take people unawares. The Rev. J. G. Smethurst might argue as much as he liked, but he couldn't get away from the fact that he had played a shady trick on the community. The man was practically going about under an *alias.*

But this was no time for abstract meditations on the question of right and wrong. He must hide . . . hide.

Yet why, you are asking, should my nephew Sacheverell wish to hide? Had he not in eight easy lessons from the Leave-It-To-Us School of Correspondence acquired complete self-confidence and an iron will? He had, but in this awful moment all that he had learned had passed from him like a dream. The years had rolled back, and he was a fifteen-year-old jelly again, in the full grip of his Head-master Phobia.

To dive under the bed was with Sacheverell Mulliner the work of a moment. And there, as the door opened, he lay, holding his breath and trying to keep his ears from rustling in the draught.

Smethurst (*alias* Bognor) was a leisurely undresser. He doffed his gaiters, and then for some little time stood, apparently in a reverie, humming one of the song-hits from the psalms. Eventually, he resumed his disrobing, but even then the ordeal was not over. As far as Sacheverell could see, in the constrained position in which he was lying, the Bishop was doing a few setting-up exercises. Then he went into the bathroom and cleaned his teeth. It was only at the end of half an hour that he finally climbed between the sheets and switched off the light.

For a long while after he had done so, Sacheverell remained where he was, motionless. But presently a faint, rhythmical sound from the neighbourhood of the pillows assured him that the other was asleep, and he crawled cautiously from his lair. Then, stepping with infinite caution, he moved to the door, opened it, and passed through.

The relief which Sacheverell felt as he closed the door behind him would have been less intense, had he realised that through a slight mistake in his bearings he had not, as he supposed, reached the haven of the passage outside but had merely entered the bathroom. This fact was not brought home to him until he had collided with an unexpected chair, upset it, tripped over a bath-mat, clutched for support into the darkness and brushed from off the glass shelf above the basin a series of bottles, containing—in the order given—Scalpo ("It Fertilises the Fol-licles"), Soothine—for applying to the face after shaving, and Doctor Wilber-force's Golden Gargle in the large or seven-and-sixpenny size. These, crashing to the floor, would have revealed the truth to a far duller man than Sacheverell Mulliner.

He acted swiftly. From the room beyond, there had come to his ears the un-mistakable sound of a Bishop sitting up in bed, and he did not delay. Hastily groping for the switch, he turned on the light. He found the bolt and shot it. Only then did he sit down on the edge of the bath and attempt to pass the situation under careful review.

He was not allowed long for quiet thinking. Through the door came the sound of deep breathing. Then a voice spoke.

"Who is they-ah?"

As always in the dear old days of school, it caused Sacheverell to leap six inches. He had just descended again, when another voice spoke in the bedroom. It was that of Colonel Sir Redvers Branksome, who had heard the crashing of glass and had come, in the kindly spirit of a good host, to make enquiries.

"What is the matter, my dear Bishop?" he asked.

"It is a burglar, my dear Colonel," said the Bishop.

"A burglar?"

"A burglar. He has locked himself in the bathroom."

"Then how extremely fortunate," said the Colonel heartily, "that I should have brought along this battle-axe and shot-gun on the chance."

Sacheverell felt that it was time to join in the conversation. He went to the door and put his lips against the keyhole.

"It's all right," he said, quaveringly.

The Colonel uttered a surprised exclamation.

"He says it's all right," he reported.

"Why does he say it is all right?" asked the Bishop.

"I didn't ask him," replied the Colonel. "He just said it was all right."

The Bishop sniffed peevishly.

"It is not all right," he said, with a certain heat. "And I am at a loss to understand why the man should affect to assume that it is. I suggest, my dear Colonel, that our best method of procedure is as follows, you take the shotgun and stand in readiness, and I will hew down the door with this admirable battle-axe."

And it was at this undeniably critical point in the proceedings that something soft and clinging brushed against Sacheverell's right ear, causing him to leap again—this time a matter of eight inches and a quarter. And, spinning round, he discovered that what had touched his ear was the curtain of the bathroom window.

There now came a splintering crash, and the door shook on its hinges. The Bishop, with all the blood of a hundred Militant Churchmen ancestors afire within him, had started operations with the axe.

But Sacheverell scarcely heard the noise. The sight of the open window had claimed his entire attention. And now, moving nimbly, he clambered through it, alighting on what seemed to be leads.

For an instant he gazed wildly about him; then, animated, perhaps, by some subconscious memory of the boy who bore 'mid snow and ice the banner with the strange device "Excelsior!", he leaped quickly upwards and started to climb the roof.

Muriel Branksome, on retiring to her room on the floor above the Blue Suite, had not gone to bed. She was sitting at her open window, thinking, thinking.

Her thoughts were bitter ones. It was not that she felt remorseful. In giving Sacheverell the air at their recent interview, her conscience told her that she had acted rightly. He had behaved like a domineering sheik of the desert: and a dislike for domineering sheiks of the desert had always been an integral part of her spiritual make-up.

But the consciousness of having justice on her side is not always enough to sustain a girl at such a time: and an aching pain gripped Muriel as she thought of

the Sacheverell she had loved—the old, mild, sweet-natured Sacheverell who had
asked nothing better than to gaze at her with adoring eyes, removing them only
when he found it necessary to give his attention to the bit of string with which
he was doing tricks. She mourned for the vanished Sacheverell.

Obviously, after what had happened, he would leave the house early in the
morning—probably long before she came down, for she was a late riser. She
wondered if she would ever see him again.

At this moment, she did. He was climbing up the slope of the roof towards her
on his hands and knees—and, for one who was not a cat, doing it extremely well.
She had hardly risen to her feet before he was standing at the window, clutching
the sill.

Muriel choked. She stared at him with wide, tragic eyes.

"What do you want?" she asked harshly.

"Well, as a matter of fact," said Sacheverell, "I was wondering if you would
mind if I hid under your bed for bit."

And suddenly, in the dim light, the girl saw that his face was contorted with
a strange terror. And, at the spectacle, all her animosity seemed to be swept away
as if on a tidal wave, and back came the old love and esteem, piping hot and as
fresh as ever. An instant before, she had been wanting to beat him over the head
with a brick. Now, she ached to comfort and protect him. For here once more was
the Sacheverell she had worshipped—the poor, timid fluttering, helpless pipsqueak whose hair she had always wanted to stroke and to whom she had felt a
strange intermittent urge to offer lumps of sugar.

"Come right in," she said.

He threw her a hasty word of thanks and shot over the sill. Then abruptly he
stiffened, and the wild, hunted look was in his eyes again. From somewhere below
there had come the deep baying of a Bishop on the scent. He clutched at Muriel,
and she held him to her like a mother soothing a nightmare-ridden child.

"Listen!" he whispered.

"Who are they?" asked Muriel.

"Headmasters," panted Sacheverell. "Droves of headmasters. And colonels.
Coveys of colonels. With battle-axes and shot-guns. Save me, Muriel!"

"There, there!" said Muriel. "There, there, there!"

She directed him to the bed, and he disappeared beneath it like a diving duck.

"You will be quite safe there," said Muriel. "And now tell me what it is all
about."

Outside, they could hear the noise of the hue-and-cry. The original strength of
the company appeared to have been augmented by the butler and a few sporting
footmen. Brokenly, Sacheverell told her all.

"But what were you doing in the Blue Suite?" asked the girl, when he had
concluded his tale. "I don't understand."

"I went to interview your cousin Bernard, to tell him that he should marry you only over my dead body."

"What an unpleasant idea!" said Muriel, shivering a little. "And I don't see how it could have been done, anyway." She paused a moment, listening to the up-roar. Somewhere downstairs, footmen seemed to be falling over one another: and once there came the shrill cry of a Hunting Bishop stymied by a hat-stand. "But what on earth," she asked, resuming her remarks, "made you think that I was going to marry Bernard?"

"I thought that that was why you gave me the bird."

"Of course it wasn't. I gave you the bird because you had suddenly turned into a beastly, barking, bullying, overbearing blighter."

There was a pause before Sacheverell spoke.

"Had I?" he said at length. "Yes, I suppose I had. Tell me," he continued, "is there a good milk-train in the morning?"

"At three-forty, I believe."

"I'll catch it."

"Must you really go?"

"I must, indeed."

"Oh, well," said Muriel. "It won't be long before we meet again. I'll run up to London one of these days, and we'll have a bit of lunch together and get married and . . ."

A gasp came from beneath the bed.

"Married! Do you really mean that you will marry me, Muriel?"

"Of course I will. The past is dead. You are my own precious angel pet again, and I love you madly, passionately. What's been the matter with you these last few weeks I can't imagine, but I can see it's all over now, so don't let's talk any more about it. Hark!" she said, holding up a finger as a sonorous booming noise filled the night, accompanied by a flood of rich oaths in what appeared to be some foreign language, possibly Hindustani. "I think father has tripped over the dinner-gong."

Sacheverell did not answer. His heart was too full for words. He was thinking how deepy he loved this girl and how happy those few remarks of hers had made him.

And yet, mingled with his joy, there was something of sorrow. As the old Roman poet has it, *surgit amari aliquid*. He had just remembered that he had paid the Leave-It-To-Us Correspondence School fifteen guineas in advance for a course of twenty lessons. He was abandoning the course after taking eight. And the thought that stabbed him like a knife was that he no longer had enough self-confi-dence and iron will left to enable him to go to Jno. B. Philbrick, Mgr., and de-mand a refund.

OPEN HOUSE

MR. MULLINER put away the letter he had been reading, and beamed contentedly on the little group in the bar-parlour of the Anglers' Rest.

"Most gratifying," he murmured.

"Good news?" we asked.

"Excellent," said Mr. Mulliner. "The letter was from my nephew Eustace, who is attached to our Embassy in Switzerland. He has fully justified the family's hopes."

"Doing well, is he?"

"Capitally," said Mr. Mulliner.

He chuckled reflectively.

"Odd," he said, "now that the young fellow has made so signal a success, to think what a business we had getting him to undertake the job. At one time it seemed as if it would be hopeless to try to persuade him. Indeed, if Fate had not taken a hand . . ."

"Didn't he want to become attached to the Embassy?"

"The idea revolted him. Here was this splendid opening, dangled before his eyes through the influence of his godfather, Lord Knubble of Knopp, and he stoutly refused to avail himself of it. He wanted to stay in London, he said. He liked London, he insisted, and he jolly well wasn't going to stir from the good old place.

"To the rest of his relations this obduracy seemed mere capriciousness. But I, possessing the young fellow's confidence, knew that there were solid reasons behind his decision. In the first place, he knew himself to be the favourite nephew of his Aunt Georgiana, relict of the late Sir Cuthbert Beazley-Beazley, Bart., a woman of advanced years and more than ample means. And, secondly, he had recently fallen in love with a girl of the name of Marcella Tyrrwhitt.

"A nice sort of chump I should be, buzzing off to Switzerland," he said to me one day when I had been endeavouring to break down his resistance. "I've got to stay on the spot, haven't I, to give Aunt Georgiana the old oil from time to time? And if you suppose a fellow can woo a girl like Marcella Tyrrwhitt through the medium of the post, you are vastly mistaken. Something occurred this morning which makes me think she's weakening, and that's just the moment when the personal touch is so essential. Come one, come all, this rock shall fly from its firm base as soon as I," said Eustace, who, like so many of the Mulliners, had a strong vein of the poetic in him.

What had occurred that morning, I learned later, was that Marcella Tyrrwhitt had rung my nephew up on the telephone.

"Hullo!" she said. "Is that Eustace?"

"Yes," said Eustace, for it was.

"I say, Eustace," proceeded the girl, "I'm leaving for Paris tomorrow."

"You aren't!" said Eustace.

"Yes, I am, you silly ass," said the girl, "and I've got the tickets to prove it. Listen, Eustace. There's something I want you to do for me. You know my canary?"

"William?"

"William is right. And you know my Peke?"

"Reginald?"

"Reginald is correct. Well, I can't take them with me, because William hates travelling and Reginald would have to go into quarantine for six months when I got back, which would make him froth with fury. So will you give them a couple of beds at your flat while I'm away?"

"Absolutely," said Eustace. "We keep open house, we Mulliners."

"You won't find them any trouble. There's nothing of the athlete about Reginald. A brisk walk of twenty minutes in the park sets him up for the day, as regards exercise. And, as for food, give him whatever you're having yourself—raw meat, puppy biscuits and so on. Don't let him have cocktails. They unsettle him."

"Right-ho," said Eustace. "The scenario seems pretty smooth so far. How about William?"

"In *re* William, he's a bit of an eccentric in the food line. Heaven knows why, but he likes bird-seed and groundsel. Couldn't touch the stuff myself. You get bird-seed at a bird-seed shop."

"And groundsel, no doubt, at the groundsellers'?"

"Exactly. And you have to let William out of his cage once or twice a day, so that he can keep his waist-line down by fluttering about the room. He comes back all right as soon as he's had his bath. Do you follow all that?"

"Like a leopard," said Eustace.

"I bet you don't."

"Yes, I do. Brisk walk Reginald. Brisk flutter William."

"You've got it. All right, then. And remember that I set a high value on those two, so guard them with your very life."

"Absolutely," said Eustace. "Rather! You bet. I should say so. Positively."

Ironical, of course, it seems now, in the light of what occurred subsequently, but my nephew told me that that was the happiest moment of his life.

He loved this girl with very fibre of his being, and it seemed to him that, if she selected him out of all her circle for this intensely important trust, it must mean that she regarded him as a man of solid worth and one she could lean on.

"These others," she must have said to herself, running over the roster of her friends. "What are they, after all? Mere butterflies. But Eustace Mulliner—ah, that's different. Good stuff there. A young fellow of character."

He was delighted, also, for another reason. Much as he would miss Marcella Tyrrwhitt, he was glad that she was leaving London for awhile, because his love life at the moment had got into something of a tangle, and her absence would just give him nice time to do a little adjusting and unscrambling.

Until a week or so before he had been deeply in love with another girl—a certain Beatrice Watterson. And then, one night at a studio-party, he had met Marcella and had instantly discerned in her an infinitely superior object for his passion.

It is this sort of thing that so complicates life for the young man about town. He is too apt to make his choice before walking the whole length of the counter. He bestows a strong man's love on Girl A. and is just congratulating himself when along comes Girl B. whose very existence he had not suspected, and he finds that he has picked the wrong one and has to work like a beaver to make the switch.

What Eustace wanted to do at this point was to taper off with Beatrice, thus clearing the stage and leaving himself free to concentrate his whole soul on Marcella. And Marcella's departure from London would afford him the necessary leisure for the process.

So, by the way of tapering off with Beatrice, he took her to tea the day Marcella left, and at tea Beatrice happened to mention, as girls will, that it would be her birthday next Sunday, and Eustace said "Oh, I say, really? Come and have a bite of lunch at my flat," and Beatrice said that she would love it, and Eustace said that he must give her something tophole as a present, and Beatrice said "Oh, no, really, you mustn't," and Eustace said Yes, dash it, he was resolved. Which started the tapering process nicely, for Eustace knew that on the Sunday he was due down at his Aunt Georgiana's at Wittleford-cum-Bagsley-on-Sea for the week-end, so that when the girl arrived all eager for lunch and found not only that her host was not there but that there was not a birthday present in sight of any description, she would be deeply offended and would become cold and distant and aloof.

Tact, my nephew tells me, is what you need on these occasions. You want to gain the desired end without hurting anybody's feelings. And, no doubt, he is right.

After tea he came back to his flat and took Reginald for a brisk walk and gave William a flutter, and went to bed that night, feeling that God was in His heaven and all right with the world.

The next day was warm and sunny, and it struck Eustace that William would appreciate it if he put his cage out on the window-sill, so that he could get the actinic rays into his system. He did this, accordingly, and, having taken Reginald for his saunter, returned to the flat, feeling that he had earned the morning bracer. He instructed Blenkinsop, his man, to bring the materials, and soon peace was reigning in the home to a noticeable extent. William was trilling lustily on the window-sill, Reginald was resting from his exertions under the sofa, and Eustace had begun to sip his whisky-and-soda without a care in the world, when the door opened and Blenkinsop announced a visitor.

"Mr. Orlando Wotherspoon," said Blenkinsop, and withdrew, to go on with the motion-picture magazine which he had been reading in the pantry.

Eustace placed his glass on the table and rose to extend the courtesies in a somewhat puzzled, not to say befogged, state of mind. The name Wotherspoon had struck no chord, and he could not recollect ever having seen the man before in his life.

And Orlando Wotherspoon was not the sort of person who, once seen, is easily forgotten. He was built on large lines, and seemed to fill the room to overflowing. In physique, indeed, he was not unlike what Primo Carnera would have been, if Carnera had not stunted his growth by smoking cigarettes when a boy. He was preceded by a flowing moustache of the outsize soup-strainer kind, and his eyes were of the piercing type which one associates with owls, sergeant-majors, and Scotland Yard inspectors.

Eustace found himself not a little perturbed.

"Oh, hullo!" he said.

Orlando Wotherspoon scrutinised him keenly and, it appeared to Eustace, with hostility. If Eustace had been a rather more than ordinarily unpleasant black-beetle this man would have looked at him in much the same fashion. The expression in his eyes was that which comes into the eyes of suburban householders when they survey slugs among their lettuces.

"Mr. Mulliner?" he said.

"I shouldn't wonder," said Eustace, feeling that this might well be so.

"My name is Wotherspoon."

"Yes," said Eustace. "So Blenkinsop was saying, and he's a fellow I've found I can usually rely on."

"I live in the block of flats across the gardens."

"Yes?" said Eustace, still at a loss. "Have a pretty good time?"

"In answer to your question, my life is uniformly tranquil. This morning, however, I saw a sight which shattered my peace of mind and sent the blood racing hotly through my veins."

"Too bad when it's like that," said Eustace. "What made your blood carry on in the manner described?"

"I will tell you, Mr. Mulliner. I was seated in my window a few minutes ago, drafting out some notes for my forthcoming speech at the annual dinner of Our Dumb Chums' League, of which I am perpetual vice-president, when, to my horror, I observed a fiend torturing a helpless bird. For a while I gazed in appalled stupefaction, while my blood ran cold."

"Hot, you said."

"First hot, then cold. I seethed with indignation at this fiend."

"I don't blame you," said Eustace. "If there's one type of chap I bar, it's a fiend. Who was the fellow?"

"Mulliner," said Orlando Wotherspoon, pointing a finger that looked like a plantain or some unusually enlarged banana, "thou art the man!"

"What!"

"Yes," repeated the other, "you! Mulliner, the Bird-Bullier! Mulliner, the Scourge of Our Feathered Friends! What do you mean, you Torquemada, by placing that canary on the window-sill in the full force of the burning sun? How would you feel if some pop-eyed assassin left *you* out in the sun without a hat, to fry where you stood?" He went to the window and hauled the cage in. "It is men like you, Mulliner, who block the wheels of the world's progress and render societies like Our Dumb Chums' League necessary."

"I thought the bally bird enjoyed it," said Eustace feebly.

"Mulliner, you lie!" said Orlando Wotherspoon.

And he looked at Eustace in a way that convinced the latter, who had suspected it from the first, that he had not made a new friend.

"By the way," he said, hoping to ease the strain, "have a spot?"

"I will not have a spot!"

"Right-ho," said Eustace. "No spot. But, coming back to the agenda, you wrong me, Wotherspoon. Foolish, mistaken, I may have been, but, as God is my witness, I meant well. Honestly, I thought William would be tickled pink if I put his cage out in the sun."

"Tchah!" said Orlando Wotherspoon.

And, as he spoke, the dog Reginald, hearing voices, crawled out from under the sofa in the hope that something was going on which might possibly culminate in coffee-sugar.

At the sight of Reginald's honest face, Eustace brightened. A cordial friendship had sprung up between these two based on mutual respect. He extended a hand and chirruped.

Unfortunately, Reginald, suddenly getting a close-up of that moustache and being convinced by the sight of it that plots against his person were toward, uttered a piercing scream and dived back under the sofa, where he remained, calling urgently for assistance.

Orlando Wotherspoon put the worst construction on the incident.

"Ha, Mulliner!" he said. "This is vastly well! Not content with inflicting fiendish torments on canaries, it would seem that you also slake your inhuman fury on this innocent dog, so that he runs, howling, at the mere sight of you."

Eustace tried to put the thing right.

"I don't think it's the mere sight of me he objects to," he said. "In fact, I've frequently seen him take quite a long steady look at me without wincing."

"Then to what, pray, do you attribute the animal's visible emotion?"

"Well, the fact is," said Eustace, "I fancy the root of the trouble is that he doesn't much care for that moustache of yours."

His visitor began to roll up his left coat-sleeve in a meditative way.

"Are you venturing, Mulliner, to criticise my moustache?"

"No, no," said Eustace. "I admire it."

"I would be sorry," said Orlando Wotherspoon, "to think that you were aspersing my moustache, Mulliner. My grandmother has often described it as the handsomest in the West End of London. 'Leonine' is the adjective she applies to it. But perhaps you regard my grandmother as prejudiced? Possibly you consider her a foolish old woman whose judgments may be lightly set aside?"

"Absolutely not," said Eustace.

"I am glad," said Wotherspoon. "You would have been the third man I have thrashed within an inch of his life for insulting my grandmother. Or is it," he mused, "the fourth? I could consult my books and let you know."

"Don't bother," said Eustace.

There was a lull in the conversation.

"Well, Mulliner," said Orlando Wotherspoon at length, "I will leave you. But let me tell you this. You have not heard the last of me. You see this?" He produced a note-book. "I keep here a black list of fiends who must be closely watched. Your Christian name, if you please?"

"Eustace."

"Age?"

"Twenty-four."

"Height?"

"Five foot ten."

"Weight?"

"Well," said Eustace, "I was around ten stone eleven when you came in. I think I'm a bit lighter now."

"Let us say ten stone seven. Thank you, Mr. Mulliner. Everything is now in order. You have been entered on the list of suspects on whom I make a practice of paying surprise visits. From now on, you will never know when I may or may not knock upon your door."

"Any time you're passing," said Eustace.

"Our Dumb Chums' Leaue," said Orlando Wotherspoon, putting away his note-book, "is not unreasonable in these matters. We of the organisation have instructions to proceed in the matter of fiends with restraint and deliberation. For the first offence, we are content to warn. After that . . . I must remember, when I return home, to post you a copy of our latest booklet. It sets forth in detail what happened to J. B. Stokes, of 9 Manglesbury Mansions, West Kensington, on his ignoring our warning to him to refrain from throwing vegetables at his cat. Good morning, Mr. Mulliner. Do not trouble to see me to the door."

Young men of my nephew Eustace's type are essentially resilient. This interview had taken place on the Thursday. By Friday, at about one o'clock, he had practically forgotten the entire episode. And by noon on Saturday he was his own merry self once more.

It was on this Saturday, as you may remember, that Eustace was to go down to Wittleford-cum-Bagsley-on-Sea to spend the week-end with his aunt Georgiana.

Wittleford-cum-Bagsley-on-Sea, so I am informed by those who have visited it, is not a Paris or a pre-War Vienna. In fact, once the visitor has strolled along the pier and put pennies in the slot machines, he has shot his bolt as far as the hectic whirl of pleasure, for which the younger generation is so avid, is concerned.

Nevertheless, Eustace found himself quite looking forward to the trip. Apart from the fact that he would be getting himself in solid with a woman who combined the possession of a hundred thousand pounds in Home Rails with a hereditary tendency to rheumatic trouble of the heart, it was pleasant to reflect that in about twenty-four hours from the time he started the girl Beatrice would have called at the empty flat and gone away in a piqued and raised-eyebrow condition, leaving him free to express his individuality in the matter of the girl Marcella.

He whistled gaily as he watched Blenkinsop pack.

"You have thoroughly grasped the programme outlined for the period of my absence, Blenkinsop?" he said.

"Yes, sir."

"Take Master Reginald for the daily stroll."

"Yes, sir."

"See that Master William does his fluttering."

"Yes, sir."

"And don't get them mixed. I mean, don't let Reginald flutter and take William for a walk."

"No, sir."

"Right!" said Eustace. "And on Sunday, Blenkinsop—tomorrow, that is to say —a young lady will be turning up for lunch. Explain to her that I'm not here, and give her anything she wants."

"Very good, sir."

Eustace set out upon his journey with a light heart. Arrived at Wittleford-cum-Bagsley-on-Sea, he passed a restful week-end playing double patience with his aunt, tickling her cat under the left ear from time to time, and walking along the esplanade. On the Monday he caught the one-forty train back to London, his aunt cordial to the last.

"I shall be passing through London on my way to Harrogate next Friday," she said, as he was leaving. "Perhaps you will give me tea?"

"I shall be more than delighted, Aunt Georgiana," said Eustace. "It has often been a great grief to me that you allow me so few opportunities of entertaining you in my little home. At four-thirty next Friday. Right!"

Everything seemed to him to be shaping so satisfactorily that his spirits were at their highest. He sang in the train to quite a considerable extent.

"What ho, Blenkinsop!" he said, entering the flat in a very nearly rollicking manner. "Everything all right?"

"Yes, sir," said Blenkinsop. "I trust that you have enjoyed an agreeable week-end, sir?"

"Topping," said Eustace. "How are the dumb chums?"

"Master William is in robust health, sir."

"Splendid! And Reginald?"

"Of Master Reginald I cannot speak with the authority of first-hand knowledge, sir, as the young lady removed him yesterday."

Eustace clutched at a chair.

"Removed him?"

"Yes, sir. Took him away. If you recall your parting instructions, sir, you enjoined upon me that I should give the young lady anything she wanted. She selected Master Reginald. She desired me to inform you that she was sorry to have missed you but quite understood that you could not disappoint your aunt, and that, as you insisted on giving her a birthday present, she had taken Master Reginald."

Eustace pulled himself together with a strong effort. He saw that nothing was to be gained by upbraiding the man. Blenkinsop, he realised, had acted according to his lights. He told himself that he should have remembered that his valet was of a literal turn of mind, who always carried out instructions to the letter.

"Get her on the 'phone, quick," he said.

"Impossible, I fear, sir. The young lady informed me that she was leaving for Paris by the two o'clock train this afternoon,"

"Then, Blenkinsop," said Eustace, "give me a quick one."

"Very good, sir."

The restorative seemed to clear the young man's head.

"Blenkinsop," he said, "give me your attention. Don't let your mind wander. We've got to do some close thinking—some very close thinking."

"Yes, sir."

In simple words Eustace explained the position of affairs. Blenkinsop clicked his tongue. Eustace held up a restraining hand.

"Don't do that, Blenkinsop."

"No, sir."

"At any other moment I should be delighted to listen to you giving your imitation of a man drawing corks out of champagne bottles. But not now. Reserve it for the next party you attend."

"Very good, sir."

Eustace returned to the matter in hand.

"You see the position I am in? We must put our heads together, Blenkinsop. How can I account satisfactorily to Miss Tyrrwhitt for the loss of her dog?"

"Would it not be feasible to inform the young lady that you took the animal for a walk in the park and that it slipped its collar and ran away?"

"Very nearly right, Blenkinsop," said Eustace, "but not quite. What actually happened was that *you* took it for a walk and, like a perfect chump, went and lost it."

"Well, really, sir——"

"Blenkinsop," said Eustace, "if there is one drop of the old feudal spirit in your system, now is the time to show it. Stand by me in this crisis, and you will not be the loser."

"Very good, sir."

"You realise, of course, that when Miss Tyrrwhitt returns it will be necessary for me to curse you pretty freely in her presence, but you must read between the lines and take it all in a spirit of pure badinage."

"Very good, sir."

"Right-ho, then, Blenkinsop. Oh, by the way, my aunt will be coming to tea on Friday."

"Very good, sir."

These preliminaries settled, Eustace proceeded to pave the way. He wrote a long and well-phrased letter to Marcella, telling her that, as he was unfortunately confined to the house with one of his bronchial colds, he had been compelled to depute the walk-in-the-park-taking of Reginald to his man Blenkinsop, in whom he had every confidence. He went on to say that Reginald, thanks to his assiduous love and care, was in the enjoyment of excellent health and that he would always look back with wistful pleasure to the memory of their long, cosy evenings together. He drew a picture of Reginald and himself sitting side by side in silent communion—he deep in some good book, Reginald meditating on this and that—which almost brought the tears to his eyes.

Nevertheless, he was far from feeling easy in his mind. Women, he knew, in moments of mental stress, are always apt to spray the blame a good deal. And, while Blenkinsop would presumably get the main stream, there might well be a few drops left over which would come in his direction.

For, if this girl Marcella Tyrrwhitt had a defect, it was that the generous warmth of her womanly nature led her now and then to go off the deep end somewhat heartily. She was one of those tall, dark girls with flashing eyes who tend to a certain extent, in times of stress, to draw themselves to their full height and let their male *vis-à-vis* have it squarely in the neck. Time had done much to heal the wound, but he could still recall some of the things she had said to him the night when they had arrived late at the theatre, to discover that he had left the tickets on his sitting-room mantelpiece. In two minutes any competent biographer would have been able to gather material for a complete character-sketch. He had found out more about himself in that one brief interview than in all the rest of his life.

Naturally, therefore, he brooded a good deal during the next few days. His friends were annoyed at this period by his absent-mindedness. He developed a habit of saying "What?" with a glazed look in his eyes and then sinking back and draining his glass, all of which made him something of a dead weight in general conversation.

You would see him sitting hunched up in a corner with his jaw drooping, and a very unpleasant spectacle it was. His fellow members began to complain about it. They said the taxidermist had no right to leave him lying about the club after removing his insides, but ought to buckle to and finish stuffing him and make a job of it.

He was sitting like this one afternoon, when suddenly, as he raised his eyes to see if there was a waiter handy, he caught sight of the card on the wall which bore upon it the date and the day of the week. And the next moment a couple of fellow-members who had thought he was dead and were just going to ring to have him swept away were stunned to observe him leap to his feet and run swiftly from the room.

He had just discovered that it was Friday, the day his Aunt Georgiana was coming to tea at his flat. And he only had about three and a half minutes before the kick-off.

A speedy cab took him quickly home, and he was relieved, on entering the flat, to find that his aunt was not there. The tea-table had been set out, but the room was empty except for William, who was trying over a song in his cage. Greatly relieved, Eustace went to the cage and unhooked the door, and William, after jumping up and down for a few moments in the eccentric way canaries do, hopped out and started to flutter to and fro.

It was at this moment that Blenkinsop came in with a well-laden plate.

"Cucumber sandwiches, sir," said Blenkinsop. "Ladies are usually strongly addicted to them."

Eustace nodded. The man's instinct had not led him astray. Hhis aunt was passionately addicted to cucumber sandwiches. Many a time he had seen her fling herself on them like a starving wolf.

"Her ladyship not arrived?" he said.

"Yes, sir. She stepped down the street to dispatch a telegram. Would you desire me to serve cream, sir, or will the ordinary milk suffice?"

"Cream? Milk?"

"I have laid out an extra saucer."

"Blenkinsop," said Eustace, passing a rather feverish hand across his brow, for he had much to disturb him these days. "You appear to be talking of something, but it does not penetrate. What is all this babble of milk and cream? Why do you speak in riddles of extra saucers?"

"For the cat, sir."

"What cat?"

"Her ladyship was accompanied by her cat, Francis."

The strained look passed from Eustace's face.

"Oh? Her cat?"

"Yes, sir."

"Well, in regard to nourishment, it gets milk—the same as the rest of us—and likes it. But serve it in the kitchen, because of the canary."

"Master Francis is not in the kitchen, sir."

"Well, in the pantry or my bedroom or wherever he is."

"When last I saw Master Francis, sir, he was enjoying a cooling stroll on the window-sill."

And at this juncture there silhouetted itself against the evening sky a lissom form.

"Here! Hi! My gosh! I say! Dash it!" exclaimed Eustace, eyeing it with unconcealed apprehension.

"Yes, sir," said Blenkinsop. "Excuse me, sir. I fancy I heard the front door bell."

And he withdrew, leaving Eustace a prey to the liveliest agitation.

Eustace, you see, was still hoping, in spite of having been so remiss in the matter of the dog, to save his stake, if I may use the expression, on the canary. In other words, when Marcella Tyrrwhitt returned and began to be incisive on the subject of the vanished Reginald, he wished to be in a position to say: "True! True! In the matter of Reginald, I grant that I have failed you. But pause before you speak and take a look at that canary—fit as a fiddle and bursting with health. And why? Because of my unremitting care."

A most unpleasant position he would be in if, in addition to having to admit that he was one Peke down on the general score, he also had to reveal that William, his sheet-anchor, was inextricably mixed up with the gastric juices of a cat which the girl did not even know by sight.

And that this tragedy was imminent he was sickeningly aware from the expression on the animal's face. It was a sort of devout, ecstatic look. He had observed much the same kind of look on the face of his Aunt Georgiana when about to sail into the cucumber sandwiches. Francis was inside the room now, and was gazing up at the canary with a steady, purposeful eye. His tail was twitching at the tip.

The next moment, to the accompaniment of a moan of horror from Eustace, he had launched himself into the air in the bird's direction.

Well, William was no fool. Where many a canary would have blenched, he retained his *sang froid* unimpaired. He moved a little to the left, causing the cat to miss by a foot. And his beak, as he did so, was curved in a derisive smile. In fact, thinking it over later, Eustace realised that right from the beginning William had the situation absolutely under control and wanted nothing but to be left alone to enjoy a good laugh.

At the moment, however, this did not occur to Eustace. Shaken to the core, he supposed the bird to be in the gravest peril. He imagined it to stand in need of all the aid and comfort he could supply. And, springing quickly to the tea-table, he rummaged among its contents for something that would serve him as ammunition in the fray.

The first thing he put his hand on was the plate of cucumber sandwiches. These, with all the rapidity at his command, he discharged, one after the other. But, though a few found their mark, there was nothing in the way of substantial results. The very nature of a cucumber sandwich makes it poor throwing. He could have obtained direct hits on Francis all day without slowing him up. In fact, the very moment after the last sandwich had struck him in the ribs, he was up in the air again, clawing hopefully.

William side-stepped once more, and Francis returned to earth. And Eustace, emotion ruining his aim, missed him by inches with a sultana cake, three muffins, and a lump of sugar.

Then, desperate, he did what he should, of course, have done at the very outset. Grabbing the table-cloth, he edged round with extraordinary stealth till he was in the cat's immediate rear, and dropped it over him just as he was tensing his muscles for another leap. Then, flinging himself on the mixture of cat and table-cloth, he wound them up into a single convenient parcel.

Exceedingly pleased with himself Eustace felt at this point. It seemed to him that he had shown resource, intelligence, and an agility highly creditable in one who had not played Rugby football for years. A good deal of bitter criticism was filtering through the cloth, but he overlooked it. Francis, he knew, when he came to think the thing over calmly, would realise that he deserved all he was getting. He had always found Francis a fair-minded cat, when the cold sobriety of his judgment was not warped by the sight of canaries.

He was about to murmur a word or two to this effect, in the hope of inducing the animal to behave less like a gyroscope, when, looking round, he perceived that he was not alone.

Standing grouped about the doorway were his Aunt Georgiana, the girl Marcella Tyrrwhitt, and the well-remembered figure of Orlando Wotherspoon.

"Lady Beazley-Beazley, Miss Tyrrwhitt, Mr. Orlando Wotherspoon," announced Blenkinsop. "Tea is served, sir."

A wordless cry broke from Eustace's lips. The table-cloth fell from his nerveless fingers. And the cat, Francis, falling on his head on the carpet, shot straight up the side of the wall and entrenched himself on top of the curtains.

There was a pause. Eustace did not know quite what to say. He felt embarrassed. It was Orlando Wotherspoon who broke the silence.

"So!" said Orlando Wotherspoon. "At your old games, Mulliner, I perceive."

Eustace's Aunt Georgiana was pointing dramatically.

"He threw cucumber sandwiches at my cat!"

"So I observe," said Wotherspoon. He spoke in an unpleasant, quiet voice, and he was looking not unlike a high priest of one of the rougher religions who runs his eye over the human sacrifice preparatory to asking his caddy for the niblick. "Also, if I mistake not, sultana cake and muffins."

"Would you require fresh muffins, sir?" asked Blenkinsop.

"The case, in short, would appear to be on all fours," proceeded Wotherspoon, "with that of J. B. Stokes, of 9, Manglesbury Mansions, West Kensington."

"Listen!" said Eustace, backing towards the window. "I can explain everything."

"There is no need of explanations, Mulliner," said Orlando Wotherspoon. He had rolled up the left sleeve of his coat and was beginning to roll up the right. He twitched his biceps to limber it up. "The matter explains itself."

Eustace's Aunt Georgiana, who had been standing under the curtain making chirruping noises, came back to the group in no agreeable frame of mind. Overwrought by what had occurred, Francis had cut her dead, and she was feeling it a good deal.

"If I may use your telephone, Eustace," she said quietly, "I would like to ring up my lawyer and disinherit you. But first," she added to Wotherspoon, who was now inhaling and expelling the breath from his nostrils in rather a disturbing manner, "would you oblige me by thrashing him within an inch of his life?"

"I was about to do so, madam," replied Wotherspoon courteously. "If this young lady will kindly stand a little to one side—"

"Shall I prepare some more cucumber sandwiches, sir?" asked Blenkinsop.

"Wait!" cried Marcella Tyrrwhitt, who hitherto had not spoken.

Orlando Wotherspoon shook his head gently.

"If, deprecating scenes of violence, it is your intention, Miss Tyrrwhitt——Any relation of my old friend, Major-General George Tyrrwhitt of the Buffs, by the way?"

"My uncle."

"Well, well! I was dining with him only last night."

"It's a small world, after all," said Lady Beazley-Beazley.

"It is, indeed," said Orlando Wotherspoon. "So small that I feel there is scarcely room in it for both Mulliner the cat-slosher and myself. I shall, therefore, do my humble best to eliminate him. And, as I was about to say, if, deprecating scenes of violence, you were about to plead for the young man, it will, I fear, be useless. I can listen to no intercession. The regulations of Our Dumb Chums' League are very strict."

Marcella Tyrrwhitt uttered a hard, rasping laugh.

"Intercession?" she said. "What do you mean—intercession? I wasn't going to intercede for this wambling misfit. I was going to ask if I could have first whack."

"Indeed? Might I enquire why?"

Marcella's eyes flashed. Eustace became convinced, he tells me, that she had Spanish blood in her.

"Would you desire another sultana cake, sir?" asked Blenkinsop.

"I'll tell you why," cried Marcella. "Do you know what this man has done? I left my dog, Reginald, in his care, and he swore to guard and cherish him. And what occurred? My back was hardly turned when he went and gave him away as a birthday present to some foul female of the name of Beatrice Something."

Eustace uttered a strangled cry.

"Let me explain!"

"I was in Paris," proceeded Marcella, "walking along the Champs-Elysées, and I saw a girl coming towards me with a Peke, and I said to myself: 'Hullo, that Peke looks extraordinarily like my Reginald,' and then she came up and it was Reginald, and I said: 'Here! Hey! What are you doing with my Peke Reginald?' and this girl said: 'What do you mean, your Peke Reginald? It's my Peke Percival, and it was given to me as a birthday present by a friend of mine named Eustace Mulliner.' And I bounded on to the next aeroplane and came over here to tear him into little shreds. And what I say is, it's a shame if I'm not to be allowed a go at him after all the trouble and expense I've been put to."

And, burying her lovely face in her hands, she broke into uncontrollable sobs.

Orlando Wotherspoon looked at Lady Beazley-Beazley. Lady Beazley-Beazley looked at Orlando Wotherspoon. There was pity in their eyes.

"There, there!" said Lady Beazley-Beazley. "There, there, there, my dear!"

"Believe me, Miss Tyrrwhitt," said Orlando Wotherspoon, patting her shoulder paternally, "there are few things I would not do for the niece of my old friend, Major-General George of the Buffs, but this is an occasion when, much as it may distress me, I must be firm. I shall have to make my report at the annual committee-meeting of Our Dumb Chums' League, and how would I look, explaining that I had stepped aside and allowed a delicately nurtured girl to act for me in a matter so important as the one now on the agenda? Consider, Miss Tyrrwhitt! Reflect!"

"That's all very well," sobbed Marcella, "but all the way over, all during those long, weary hours in the aeroplane, I was buoying myself up with the thought of what I was going to do to Eustace Mulliner when we met. See! I picked out my heaviest parasol."

Orlando Wotherspoon eyed the dainty weapon with an indulgent smile.

"I fear that would hardly meet such a case as this," he said. "You had far better leave the conduct of this affair to me."

"Did you say more muffins, sir?" asked Blenkinsop.

"I do not wish to boast," said Wotherspoon, "but I have had considerable experience. I have been formally thanked by my committee on several occasions."

"So you see, dear," said Lady Beazley-Beazley soothingly, "it will be ever so much better to——"

"Any buttered toast, fancy cakes, or macaroons?" asked Blenkinsop.

"—leave the matter entirely in Mr. Wotherspoon's hands. I know just how you feel. I am feeling the same myself. But even in these modern days, my dear, it is the woman's part to efface herself and——"

"Oh, well!" said Marcella moodily.

Lady Beazley-Beazley folded her in her arms and over her shoulder nodded brightly at Orlando Wotherspoon.

"Please go on, Mr. Wotherspoon," she said.

Wotherspoon bowed, with a formal word of thanks. And, turning, was just in time to see Eustace disappearing through the window.

The fact is, as this dialogue progressed, Eustace had found himself more and more attracted by that open window. It had seemed to beckon to him. And at this juncture, dodging lightly round Blenkinsop, who had now lost his grip entirely and was suggesting things like watercress and fruit-salad, he precipitated himself into the depths and, making a good landing, raced for the open spaces at an excellent rate of speed.

That night, heavily cloaked and disguised in a false moustache, he called at my address, clamouring for tickets to Switzerland. He arrived there some few days later, and ever since has stuck to his duties with unremitting energy.

So much so that, in that letter which you saw me reading, he informs me that he has just been awarded the Order of the Crimson Edelweiss, Third Class, with crossed cuckoo-clocks, carrying with it the right to yodel in the presence of the Vice-President. A great honour for so young a man.

BEST SELLER

A SHARP snort, plainly emanating from a soul in anguish, broke the serene silence that brooded over the bar-parlour of the Anglers' Rest. And, looking up, we perceived Miss Postlethwaite, our sensitive barmaid, dabbing at her eyes with a dishcloth.

"Sorry you were troubled," said Miss Postlethwaite, in answer to our concerned gaze, "but he's just gone off to India, leaving her standing tight-lipped and dry-eyed in the moonlight outside the old Manor. And her little dog has crawled up and licked her hand, as if he understood and sympathised."

We stared at one another blankly. It was Mr. Mulliner who, with his usual clear insight, penetrated to the heart of the mystery.

"Ah," said Mr. Mulliner, "you have been reading 'Rue for Remembrance', I see. How did you like it?"

" 'Slovely," said Miss Postlethwaite. "It lays the soul of Woman bare as with a scalpel."

"You do not consider that there is any falling off from the standard of its predecessors? You find it as good as 'Parted Ways' ?"

"Better."

"Oh!" said a Stout and Bitter, enlightened. "You're reading a novel?"

"The latest work," said Mr. Mulliner, "from the pen of the authoress of 'Parted Ways', which, as no doubt you remember made so profound a sensation some years ago. I have a particular interest in this writer's work, as she is my niece."

"Your niece?"

"By marriage. In private life she is Mrs. Egbert Mulliner." He sipped his hot Scotch and lemon, and mused a while.

"I wonder," he said, "if you would care to hear the story of my nephew Egbert and his bride? It is a simple little story, just one of those poignant dramas of human interest which are going on in our midst every day. If Miss Postlethwaite is not too racked by emotion to replenish my glass, I shall be delighted to tell it to you."

I will ask you (said Mr. Mulliner) to picture my nephew Egbert standing at the end of the pier at the picturesque little resort of Burwash Bay one night in June, trying to nerve himself to ask Evangeline Pembury the question that was so near his heart. A hundred times he had tried to ask it, and a hundred times he had lacked the courage. But to-night he was feeling in particularly good form, and he cleared his throat and spoke.

"There is something," he said in a low, husky voice, "that I want to ask you."

He paused. He felt strangely breathless. The girl was looking out across the moonlit water. The night was very still. From far away in the distance came the faint strains of the town band, as it picked its way through the Star of Eve song from *Tannhauser*—somewhat impeded by the second trombone, who had got his music sheets mixed and was playing "The Wedding of the Painted Doll".

"Something," said Egbert, "that I want to ask you."

"Go on," she whispered.

Again he paused. He was afraid. Her answer meant so much to him.

Egbert Mulliner had come to this quiet seaside village for a rest cure. By profession he was an assistant editor, attached to the staff of *The Weekly Booklover;* and, as every statistician knows, assistant editors of literary weeklies are ranked high up among the Dangerous Trades. The strain of interviewing female novelists takes toll of the physique of all but the very hardiest.

For six months, week in and week out, Egbert Mulliner had been listening to female novelists talking about Art and their Ideals. He had seen them in cosy corners in their boudoirs, had watched them being kind to dogs and happiest when among their flowers. And one morning the proprietor of *The Booklover,* finding the young man sitting at his desk with little flecks of foam about his mouth and muttering over and over again in a dull, toneless voice the words, "Aurelia Mc-Goggin, she draws her inspiration from the scent of white lilies!" had taken him straight off to a specialist.

"Yes," the specialist had said, after listening at Egbert's chest for a while through a sort of telephone, "we are a little run down, are we not? We see floating spots, do we not, and are inclined occasionally to bark like a seal from pure depression of spirit? Precisely. What we need is to augment the red corpuscles in our bloodstream."

And this augmentation of red corpuscles had been effected by his first sight of Evangeline Pembury. They had met at a picnic. As Egbert rested for a moment from the task of trying to dredge the sand from a plateful of chicken salad, his eyes had fallen on a divine girl squashing a wasp with a teaspoon. And for the first time since he had tottered out of the offices of *The Weekly Booklover* he had ceased to feel like something which a cat, having dragged from an ash-can, has inspected and rejected with a shake of the head as unfit for feline consumption. In an instant his interior had become a sort of Jamboree of red corpuscles. Millions of them were splashing about and calling gaily to other millions, still hesitating on the bank: "Come on in! The blood's fine!"

Ten minutes later he had reached the conclusion that life without Evangeline Pembury would be a blank.

And yet he had hesitated before laying his heart at her feet. She looked all right. She seemed all right. Quite possibly she *was* all right. But before proposing he had to be sure. He had to make certain that there was no danger of her suddenly producing a manuscript fastened in the top left corner with pink silk and asking his candid opinion of it. Everyone has his pet aversion. Some dislike slugs, others cockroaches. Egbert Mulliner disliked female novelists.

And so now, as they stood together in the moonlight, he said:

"Tell me, have you ever written a novel?"

She seemed surprised.

"A novel? No."

"Short stories, perhaps?"

"No."

Egbert lowered his voice.

"Poems?" he whispered, hoarsely.

"No."

Egbert hesitated no longer. He produced his soul like a conjurer extracting a rabbit from a hat and slapped it down before her. He told her of his love, stressing its depth, purity, and lasting qualities. He begged, pleaded, rolled his eyes, and clasped her little hand in his. And when, pausing for a reply, he found that she had been doing a lot of thinking along the same lines and felt much about the same about him as he did about her, he nearly fell over backwards. It seemed to him that his cup of joy was full.

It is odd how love will affect different people. It caused Egbert next morning to go out on the links and do the first nine in one over bogey. Whereas Evangeline, finding herself filled with a strange ferment which demanded immediate outlet, sat down at a little near-Chippendale table, ate five marshmallows, and began to write a novel.

Three weeks of the sunshine and ozone of Burwash Bay had toned up Egbert's system to the point where his medical adviser felt that it would be safe for him to go back to London and resume his fearful trade. Evangeline followed him a month later. She arrived home at four-fifteen on a sunny afternoon, and at four-sixteen-and-a-half Egbert shot through the door with the lovelight in his eyes.

"Evangeline!"

"Egbert!"

But we will not dwell on the ecstasies of the reunited lovers. We will proceed to the point where Evangeline raised her head from Egbert's shoulder and uttered a little giggle. One would prefer to say that she gave a light laugh. But it was not a light laugh. It was a giggle—a furtive, sinister, shamefaced giggle, which froze Egbert's blood with a nameless fear. He stared at her, and she giggled again.

"Egbert," she said, "I want to tell you something."

"Yes?" said Egbert.

Evangeline giggled once more.

"I know it sounds too silly for words," she said, "but—"

"Yes? Yes?"

"I've written a novel, Egbert."

In the old Greek tragedies it was a recognised rule that any episode likely to excite the pity and terror of the audience to too great an extent must be enacted behind the scenes. Strictly speaking, therefore, this scene should be omitted. But the modern public can stand more than the ancient Greeks, so it had better remain on the records.

The room stopped swimming before Egbert Mulliner's tortured eyes. Gradually the piano, the chairs, the pictures, and the case of stuffed birds on the mantelpiece resumed their normal positions. He found speech.

"You've written a novel?" he said, dully.

"Well, I've got to chapter twenty-four."

"You've got to chapter twenty-four?"

"And the rest will be easy."

"The rest will be easy?"

Silence fell for a space—a silence broken only by Egbert's laboured breathing. Then Evangeline spoke impulsively.

"Oh, Egbert!" she cried. "I really do think some of it is rather good. I'll read it to you now."

How strange it is, when some great tragedy has come upon us, to look back at the comparatively mild beginnings of our misfortunes and remember how we thought then that Fate had done its worst. Egbert, that afternoon, fancied that he had plumbed the lowest depths of misery and anguish. Evangeline, he told himself, had fallen from the pedestal on which he had set her. She had revealed herself as a secret novel-writer. It was the limit, he felt, the extreme edge. It put the tin hat on things.

It was, alas! nothing of the kind. It bore the same resemblance to the limit that the first drop of rain bears to the thunderstorm.

The mistake was a pardonable one. The acute agony which he suffered that afternoon was more than sufficient excuse for Egbert Mulliner's blunder in supposing that he had drained the bitter cup to the dregs. He writhed, as he listened to this thing which she had entitled "Parted Ways", unceasingly. It tied his very soul in knots.

Evangeline's novel was a horrible, an indecent production. Not in the sense that it would be likely to bring a blush to any cheek but his, but because she had put on paper every detail of the only romance that had ever come under her notice—her own. There it was, his entire courtship, including the first holy kiss and not omitting the quarrel which they had had within two days of the engagement. In the novel she had elaborated this quarrel, which in fact had lasted twenty-three minutes, into a ten years' estrangement—thus justifying the title and preventing the story finishing in the first five thousand words. As for his proposal, that was inserted *verbatim;* and, as he listened, Egbert shuddered to think that he could have polluted the air with such frightful horse-radish.

He marvelled, as many a man has done before and will again, how women can do these things. Listening to "Parted Ways" made him, personally, feel as if he had suddenly lost his trousers while strolling along Piccadilly.

Something of these feelings he would have liked to put into words, but the Mulliners are famous for their chivalry. He would, he imagined, feel a certain shame if he ever hit Evangeline or walked on her face in thick shoes; but that shame would be as nothing to the shame he would feel if he spoke one millimetre of what he thought about "Parted Ways".

"Great!" he croaked.

Her eyes were shining.

"Do you really think so?"

"Fine!"

He found it easier to talk in monosyllables.

"I don't suppose any publisher would buy it," said Evangeline.

Egbert began to feel a little better. Nothing, of course, could alter the fact that she had written a novel; but it might be possible to hush it up.

"So what I am going to do is to pay the expenses of publication."

Egbert did not reply. He was staring into the middle distance and trying to light a fountain pen with an unlighted match.

And Fate chuckled grimly, knowing that it had only just begun having fun with Egbert.

Once in every few publishing seasons there is an Event. For no apparent reason, the great heart of the Public gives a startled jump, and the public's great purse is emptied to secure copies of some novel which has stolen into the world without advance advertising and whose only claim to recognition is that *The Licensed Victuallers' Gazette* has stated in a two-line review that it is "readable".

The rising firm of Mainprice and Peabody published a first edition of three hundred copies of "Parted Ways". And when they found, to their chagrin, that Evangeline was only going to buy twenty of these—somehow Mainprice, who was an optimist, had got the idea that she was good for a hundred ("You can sell them to your friends") their only interest in the matter was to keep an eye on the current quotations for waste paper. The book they were going to make their money on was Stultitia Bodwin's "Offal", in connection with which they had arranged in advance for a newspaper discussion on "The Growing Menace of the Sex Motive in Fiction: Is there to be no Limit?"

Within a month "Offal" was off the map. The newspaper discussion raged before an utterly indifferent public, which had made one of its quick changes and discovered that it had had enough of sex, and that what it wanted now was good, sweet, wholesome, tender tales of the pure love of a man for a maid, which you could leave lying about and didn't have to shove under the cushions of the chesterfield every time you heard your growing boys coming along. And the particular tale which it selected for its favour was Evangeline's "Parted Ways".

It is these swift, unheralded changes of the public mind which make publishers stick straws in their hair and powerful young novelists rush round to the wholesale grocery firms to ask if the berth of junior clerk is still open. Up to the very moment of the Great Switch, sex had been the one safe card. Publishers' lists were congested with scarlet tales of Men Who Did and Women Who Shouldn't Have Done But Who Took a Pop At It. And now the bottom had dropped out of the market without a word of warning, and practically the only way in which readers could gratify their new-born taste for the pure and simple was by fighting for copies of "Parted Ways".

They fought like tigers. The offices of Mainprice and Peabody hummed like a hive. Printing machines worked day and night. From the Butes of Kyle to the rock-bound coasts of Cornwall, a great cry went up for "Parted Ways". In every home in Ealing West "Parted Ways" was found on the whatnot, next to the aspidistra and the family album. Clergymen preached about it, parodists parodied it, stockbrokers stayed away from Cochran's Revue to sit at home and cry over it.

Numerous paragraphs appeared in the press concerning its probable adaptation into a play, a musical comedy, and a talking picture. Nigel Playfair was stated to have bought it for Sybil Thorndike, Sir Alfred Butt for Nellie Wallace. Laddie Cliff was reported to be planning a musical play based on it, starring Stanley Lupino and Leslie Henson. It was rumoured that Carnera was considering the part of "Percy", the hero.

And on the crest of this wave, breathless but happy, rode Evangeline.

And Egbert? Oh, that's Egbert, spluttering down in the trough there. We can't be bothered about Egbert now.

Egbert, however, found ample time to be bothered about himself. He passed the days in a frame of mind which it would be ridiculous to call bewilderment. He was stunned, overwhelmed, sandbagged. Dimly he realised that considerably more than a hundred thousand perfect strangers were gloating over the most sacred secrecies of his private life, and that the exact words of his proposal of marriage were engraven on considerably over a hundred thousand minds. But, except that it made him feel as if he were being tarred and feathered in front of a large and interested audience, he did not mind that so much. What really troubled him was the alteration in Evangeline.

The human mind adjusts itself readily to prosperity. Evangeline's first phase, when celebrity was new and bewildering, soon passed. The stammering reception of the first reporter became a memory. At the end of two weeks she was talking to the Press with the easy nonchalance of a prominent politician, and coming back at note-book-bearing young men with words which they had to look up in the office Webster. Her art, she told them, was rhythmical rather than architectural, and she inclined, if anything, to the school of the surrealists.

She had soared above Egbert's low-browed enthusiasms. When he suggested motoring out to Addington and putting in a few holes of golf, she excused herself. She had letters to answer. People would keep writing to her, saying how much "Parted Ways" had helped them, and one had to be civil to one's public. Autographs, too. She really could not spare a moment.

He asked her to come with him to the Amateur Championship. She shook her head. The date, she said, clashed with her lecture to the East Dulwich Daughters of Minerva Literary and Progress Club on "Some Tendencies of Modern Fiction".

All these things Egbert might have endured, for, despite the fact that she could speak so lightly of the Amateur Championship, he still loved her dealy. But at this point there suddenly floated into his life like a cloud of poison-gas the sinister figure of Jno. Henderson Banks.

"Who," he asked, suspiciously, one day, as she was giving him ten minutes before hurrying off to address the Amalgamated Mothers of Manchester on "The Novel: Should it Teach?"—"was that man I saw you coming down the street with?"

"That wasn't a man," replied Evangeline. "That was my literary agent."

And so it proved. Jno. Henderson Banks was now in control of Evangeline's affairs. This outstanding blot on the public weal was a sort of human *charlotte russe* with tortoiseshell-rimmed eye-glasses and a cooing, reverential manner towards his female clients. He had a dark, romantic face, a lissom figure, one of those beastly cravat things that go twice round the neck, and a habit of beginning his remarks with the words "Dear lady". The last man, in short, whom a fiancé would wish to have hanging about his betrothed. If Evangeline had to have a literary agent, the sort of literary agent Egbert would have selected for her would have been one of those stout, pie-faced literary agents who chew half-smoked cigars and wheeze as they enter the editorial sanctum.

A jealous frown flitted across his face.

"Looked a bit of a Gawd-help-us to me," he said, critically.

"Mr. Banks," retorted Evangeline, "is a superb man of business."

"Oh, yeah?" said Egbert, sneering visibly.

And there for a time the matter rested.

But not for long. On the following Monday morning Egbert called Evangeline up on the telephone and asked her to lunch.

"I am sorry," said Evangeline. "I am engaged to lunch with Mr. Banks."

"Oh?" said Egbert.

"Yes," said Evangeline.

"Ah!" said Egbert.

Two days later Egbert called Evangeline up on the telephone and invited her to dinner.

"I am sorry," said Evangeline. "I am dining with Mr. Banks."

"Ah!" said Egbert.

"Yes," said Evangeline.

"Oh!" said Egbert.

Three days after that Egbert arrived at Evangeline's flat with tickets for the theatre.

"I am sorry——" began Evangeline.

"Don't say it," said Egbert. "Let me guess. You are going to the theatre with Mr. Banks?"

"Yes, I am. He has tickets for the first night of Tchekov's 'Six Corpses in Search of an Undertaker.' "

"He has, has he?"

"Yes, he has."

"He *has*, eh?"

"Yes, he has."

Egbert took a couple of turns about the room, and for a space there was silence except for the sharp grinding of his teeth. Then he spoke.

"Touching lightly on this gumboil Banks," said Egbert, "I am the last man to stand in the way of your having a literary agent. If you must write novels, that is a matter between you and your God. And, if you do see fit to write novels, I suppose you must have a literary agent. But—and this is where I want you to follow me very closely—I cannot see the necessity of employing a literary agent who coos in your left ear, a literary agent who not only addresses you as 'Dear lady', but appears to find it essential to the conduct of his business to lunch, dine, and go to the theatre with you daily."

"I——"

Egbert held up a compelling hand.

"I have not finished," he said. "Nobody," he proceeded, "could call me a narrow-minded man. If Jno. Henderson Banks looked a shade less like one of the great lovers of history, I would have nothing to say. If, when he talked business to a client, Jno. Henderson Banks's mode of vocal delivery were even slightly less reminiscent of a nightingale trilling to its mate, I would remain silent. But he doesn't and it isn't. And such being the case, and taking into consideration the fact that you are engaged to me, I feel it my duty to instruct you to see this drooping flower far more infrequently. In fact, I would advocate expunging altogether. If he wishes to discuss business with you, let him do it over the telephone. And I hope he gets the wrong number."

Evangeline had risen, and was facing him with flashing eyes.

"Is that so?" she said.

"That," said Egbert, "is so."

"Am I a serf?" demanded Evangeline.

"A what?" said Egbert.

"A serf. A slave. A peon. A creature subservient to your lightest whim."

Egbert considered the point.

"No," he said. "I shouldn't think so."

"No," said Evangeline, "I am not. And I refuse to allow you to dictate to me in the choice of my friends."

Egbert stared blankly.

"You mean, after all I have said, that you intend to let this blighted chrysanthemum continue to frisk round?"

"I do."

"You seriously propose to continue chummy with this revolting piece of cheese?"

"I do."

"You absolutely and literally decline to give this mistake of Nature the push?"

"I do."

"Well!" said Egbert.

A pleading note came into his voice.

"But, Evangeline, it is your Egbert who speaks."

The haughty girl laughed a hard, bitter laugh.

"Is it?" she said. She laughed again. "Do you imagine that we are still engaged?"

"Aren't we?"

"We certainly aren't. You have insulted me, outraged my finest feelings, given an exhibition of malignant tyranny which makes me thankful that I have realised in time the sort of man you are. Goodbye, Mr. Mulliner!"

"But listen——" began Egbert.

"Go!" said Evangeline. "Here is your hat."

She pointed imperiously to the door. A moment later she had banged it behind him.

It was a grim-faced Egbert Mulliner who entered the elevator, and a grimmer-faced Egbert Mulliner who strode down Sloane Street. His dream, he realised, was over. He laughed harshly as he contemplated the fallen ruins of the castle which he had built in the air.

Well, he still had his work.

In the offices of *The Weekly Booklover* it was whispered that a strange change had come over Egbert Mulliner. He seemed a stronger, tougher man. His editor, who since Egbert's illness had behaved towards him with a touching humanity, allowing him to remain in the office and write paragraphs about Forthcoming Books while others, more robust, were sent off to interview the female novelists, now saw him a right-hand man on whom he could lean.

When a column on "Myrtle Bootle among her Books" was required, it was Egbert whom he sent out into the No Man's Land of Bloomsbury. When young Eustace Johnson, a novice who ought never to have been entrusted with such a dangerous commission, was found walking round in circles and bumping his head against the railings of Regent's Park after twenty minutes with Laura La Motte Grindlay, the great sex novelist, it was Egbert who was flung into the breach. And Egbert came through, wan but unscathed.

It was during this period that he interviewed Mabelle Grangerson and Mrs. Goole-Plank on the same afternoon—a feat which is still spoken of with bated breath in the offices of *The Weekly Booklover*. And not only in *The Booklover* offices. To this day "Remember Mulliner!" is the slogan with which every literary editor encourages the faint-hearted who are wincing and hanging back.

"Was Mulliner afraid?" they say. "Did Mulliner quail?"

And so it came about that when a "Chat with Evangeline Pembury" was needed for the big Christmas Special Number, it was of Egbert that his editor thought first. He sent for him.

"Ah, Mulliner!"

"Well, chief?"

"Stop me if you've heard this one before," said the editor, "but it seems there was once an Irishman, a Scotsman, and a Jew——"

Then, the formalities inseparable from an interview between editor and assistant concluded, he came down to business.

"Mulliner," he said, in that kind, fatherly way of his which endeared him to all his staff, "I am going to begin by saying that it is in your power to do a big thing for the dear old paper. But after that I must tell you that, if you wish, you can refuse to do it. You have been through a hard time lately, and if you feel yourself unequal to this task, I shall understand. But the fact is, we have got to have a 'Chat with Evangeline Pembury' for our Christmas Special."

He saw the young man wince, and nodded sympathetically.

"You think it would be too much for you? I feared as much. They say she is the worst of the lot. Rather haughty and talks about uplift. Well, never mind. I must see what I can do with young Johnson. I hear he has quite recovered now, and is anxious to re-establish himself. Quite. I will send Johnson."

Egbert Mulliner was himself again now.

"No, chief," he said. "I will go."

"You will?"

"I will."

"We shall need a column and a half."

"You shall have a column and a half."

The editor turned away, to hide a not unmanly emotion.

"Do it now, Mulliner," he said, "and get it over."

A strange riot of emotion seethed in Egbert Mulliner's soul as he pressed the familiar bell which he had thought never to press again. Since their estrangement he had seen Evangeline once or twice, but only in the distance. Now he was to meet her face to face. Was he glad or sorry? He could not say. He only knew he loved her still.

He was in the sitting-room. How cosy it looked, how impregnated with her presence. There was the sofa on which he had so often sat, his arm about her waist——

A footstep behind him warned him that the time had come to don the mask. Forcing his features into an interviewer's hard smile, he turned.

"Good afternoon," he said.

She was thinner. Either she had found success wearing, or she had been on the eighteen-day diet. Her beautiful face seemed drawn, and, unless he was mistaken, care-worn.

He fancied that for an instant her eyes had lit up at the sight of him, but he preserved the formal detachment of a stranger.

"Good afternoon, Miss Pembury," he said. "I represent *The Weekly Book-lover*. I understand that my editor has been in communication with you and that you have kindly consented to tell us a few things which may interest our readers regarding your art and aims."

She bit her lip.

"Will you take a seat, Mr. ——?"

"Mulliner," said Egbert.

"Mr. Mulliner," said Evangeline. "Do sit down. Yes, I shall be glad to tell you anything you wish."

Egbert sat down.

"Are you fond of dogs, Miss Pembury?" he asked.

"I adore them," said Evangeline.

"I should like, a little later, if I may," said Egbert, "to secure a snapshot of you being kind to a dog. Our readers appreciate these human touches, you understand."

"Oh, quite," said Evangeline. "I will send out for a dog. I love dogs—and flowers."

"You are happiest among your flowers, no doubt?"

"On the whole, yes."

"You sometimes think they are the souls of little children who have died in their innocence?"

"Frequently."

"And now," said Egbert, licking the tip of his pencil, "perhaps you would tell me something about your ideals. How are the ideals?"

Evangeline hesitated.

"Oh, they're fine," she said.

"The novel," said Egbert, "has been described as among this age's greatest instruments for uplift. How do you check up on *that*?"

"Oh, yes."

"Of course, there are novels and novels."

"Oh, yes."

"Are you contemplating a successor to 'Parted Ways'?"

"Oh, yes."

"Would it be indiscreet, Miss Pembury, to inquire to what extent it has progressed?"

"Oh, Egbert!" said Evangeline.

There are some speeches before which dignity melts like ice in August, resentment takes the full count, and the milk of human kindness surges back into the aching heart as if the dam had burst. Of these, "Oh, Egbert!", especially when accompanied by tears, is one of the most notable.

Evangeline's "Oh, Egbert!" had been accompanied by a Niagara of tears. She had flung herself on the sofa and was now chewing the cushion in an ecstasy of grief. She gulped like a bull-pup swallowing a chunk of steak. And, on the instant, Egbert Mulliner's adamantine reserve collapsed as if its legs had been knocked from under it. He dived for the sofa. He clasped her hand. He stroked her hair. He squeezed her waist. He patted her shoulder. He massaged her spine.

"Evangeline!"

"Oh, Egbert!"

The only flaw in Egbert Mulliner's happiness, as he knelt beside her, babbling comforting words, was the gloomy conviction that Evangeline would certainly lift the entire scene, dialogue and all, and use it in her next novel. And it was for this reason that, when he could manage it, he censored his remarks to some extent.

But, as he warmed to his work, he forgot caution altogether. She was clinging to him, whispering his name piteously. By the time he had finished, he had committed himself to about two thousand words of a nature calculated to send Mainprice and Peabody screaming with joy about their office.

He refused to allow himself to worry about it. What of it? He had done his stuff, and if it sold a hundred thousand copies—well, let it sell a hundred thousand copies. Holding Evangeline in his arms, he did not care if he was copyrighted in every language, including the Scandinavian.

"Oh, Egbert!" said Evangeline.

"My darling!"

"Oh, Egbert, I'm in such trouble."

"My angel! What is it?"

Evangeline sat up and tried to dry her eyes.

"It's Mr. Banks."

A savage frown darkened Egbert Mulliner's face. He told himself that he might have foreseen this. A man who wore a tie that went twice round the neck was sure,

sooner or later, to inflict some hideous insult on helpless womanhood. Add tortoiseshell-rimmed glasses, and you had what practically amounted to a fiend in
human shape.

"I'll murder him," he said. "I ought to have done it long ago, but one keeps
putting these things off. What has he done? Did he force his loathsome attentions
on you? Has that tortoiseshell-rimmed satyr been trying to kiss you, or something?"

"He has been fixing me up solid."

Egbert blinked.

"Doing what?"

"Fixing me up solid. With the magazines. He has arranged for me to write
three serials and I don't know how many short stories."

"Getting you contracts, you mean?"

Evangeline nodded tearfully.

"Yes. He seems to have fixed me up solid with almost everybody. And they've
been sending me cheques in advance, hundreds of them. What am I to do? Oh,
what am I to do?"

"Cash them," said Egbert.

"But afterwards?"

"Spend the money."

"But after that?"

Egbert reflected.

"Well, it's a nuisance, of course," he said, "but after that I suppose you'll have
to write the stuff."

Evangeline sobbed like a lost soul.

"But I can't! I've been trying for weeks, and I can't write anything. And I
never shall be able to write anything. I don't want to write anything. I hate
writing. I don't know what to write about. I wish I were dead."

She clung to him.

"I got a letter from him this morning. He has just fixed me up solid with two
more magazines."

Egbert kissed her tenderly. Before he had become an assistant editor, he, too,
had been an author, and he understood. It is not the being paid money in advance
that jars the sensitive artist: it is the having to work.

'What shall I do?" cried Evangeline.

"Drop the whole thing," said Egbert. "Evangeline, do you remember your first
drive at golf? I wasn't there, but I bet it travelled about five hundred yards and
you wondered what people meant when they talked about golf being a difficult
game. After that, for ages, you couldn't do anything right. And then, gradually,
after years of frightful toil, you began to get the knack of it. It is just the same
with writing. You've had your first drive, and it has been some smite. Now, if
you're going to stick to it, you've got to do the frightful toil. What's the use?

Drop it."

"And return the money?"

Egbert shook his head. "No," he said, firmly. "There you go too far. Stick to the money like glue. Clutch it with both hands. Bury it in the garden and mark the spot with a cross."

"But what about the stories? Who is going to write them?"

Egbert smiled a tender smile.

"I am," he said. "Before I saw the light, I, too, used to write stearine bilge just like 'Parted Ways'. When we are married, I shall say to you, if I remember the book of words correctly 'With all my worldly goods I thee endow'. They will include three novels I was never able to kid a publisher into printing, and at least twenty short stories no editor would accept. I give them to you freely. You can have the first of the novels to-night, and we will sit back and watch Mainprice and Peabody sell half a million copies."

"Oh, Egbert!" said Evangeline.

"Evangeline!" said Egbert.

STRYCHNINE IN THE SOUP

From the moment the Draught Stout entered the bar-parlour of the Anglers' Rest, it had been obvious that he was not his usual cheery self. His face was drawn and twisted, and he sat with bowed head in a distant corner by the window, contributing nothing to the conversation which, with Mr. Mulliner as its centre, was in progress around the fire. From time to time he heaved a hollow sigh.

A sympathetic Lemonade and Angostura, putting down his glass, went across and laid a kindly hand on the sufferer's shoulder.

"What is it, old man?" he asked. "Lost a friend?"

"Worse," said the Draught Stout. "A mystery novel. Got half-way through it on the journey down here, and left it in the train."

"My nephew Cyril, the interior decorator," said Mr. Mulliner, "once did the very same thing. These mental lapses are not infrequent."

"And now," proceeded the Draught Stout, "I'm going to have a sleepless night, wondering who poisoned Sir Geoffrey Tuttle, Bart."

"The Bart. Was poisoned, was he?"

"You never said a truer word. Personally, I think it was the Vicar who did him in. He was known to be interested in strange poisons."

Mr. Mulliner smiled indulgently.

"It was not the Vicar," he said. "I happen to have read 'The Murglow Manor Mystery'. The guilty man was the plumber."

"What plumber?"

"The one who comes in chapter two to mend the shower-bath. Sir Geoffrey had wronged his aunt in the year '96, so he fastened a snake in the nozzle of the shower-bath with glue; and when Sir Geoffrey turned on the stream the hot water melted the glue. This released the snake, which dropped through one of the holes, bit the Baronet in the leg, and disappeared down the waste-pipe."

"But that can't be right," said the Draught Stout. "Between chapter two and the murder there was an interval of several days."

"The plumber forgot his snake and had to go back for it," explained Mr. Mulliner. "I trust that this revelation will prove sedative."

"I feel a new man," said the Draught Stout. "I'd have lain awake worrying about that murder all night."

"I suppose you would. My nephew Cyril was just the same. Nothing in this modern life of ours," said Mr. Mulliner, taking a sip of his hot Scotch and lemon, "is more remarkable than the way in which the mystery novel has gripped the public. Your true enthusiast, deprived of his favourite reading, will stop at nothing in order to get it. He is like a victim of the drug habit when withheld from cocaine. My nephew Cyril——"

"Amazing the things people will leave in trains," said a Small Lager. "Bags . . . umbrellas . . . even stuffed chimpanzees, occasionally, I've been told. I heard a story the other day——"

My nephew Cyril (said Mr. Mulliner) had a greater passion for mystery stories than anyone I have ever met. I attribute this to the fact that, like so many interior decorators, he was a fragile, delicate young fellow, extraordinarily vulnerable to any ailment that happened to be going the rounds. Every time he caught mumps or influenza or German measles or the like, he occupied the period of convalescence in reading mystery stories. And, as the appetite grows by what it feeds on, he had become, at the time at which this narrative opens, a confirmed addict. Not only did he devour every volume of this type on which he could lay his hands, but he was also to be found at any theatre which was offering the kind of drama where skinny arms come unexpectedly out of the chiffonier and the audience feels a mild surprise if the lights stay on for ten consecutive minutes.

And it was during a performance of "The Grey Vampire" at the St. James's that he found himself sitting next to Amelia Bassett, the girl whom he was to love with all the stored-up fervour of a man who hitherto had been inclined rather to edge away when in the presence of the other sex.

He did not know her name was Amelia Bassett. He had never seen her before. All he knew was that at last he had met his fate, and for the whole of the first act he was pondering the problem of how he was to make her acquaintance.

It was as the lights went up for the first intermission that he was aroused from his thoughts by a sharp pain in the right leg. He was just wondering whether it was gout or sciatica when, glancing down, he perceived that what had happened was that his neighbour, absorbed by the drama, had absent-mindedly collected a handful of his flesh and was twisting it in an ecstasy of excitement.

It seemed to Cyril a good *point d'appui*.

"Excuse me," he said.

The girl turned. Her eyes were glowing, and the tip of her nose still quivered.

"I beg your pardon?"

"My leg," said Cyril. "Might I have it back, if you've finished with it?"

The girl looked down. She started visibly.

"I'm awfully sorry," she gasped.

"Not at all," said Cyril. "Only too glad to have been of assistance."

"I got carried away."

"You are evidently fond of mystery plays."

"I love them."

"So do I. And mystery novels?"

"Oh, yes!"

"Have you read 'Blood on the Banisters'?"

"Oh, *yes!* I thought it was better than 'Severed Throats'."

"So did I," said Cyril. "Much better. Brighter murders, subtler detectives, crisper clues . . . better in every way."

The two twin souls gazed into each other's eyes. There is no surer foundation for a beautiful friendship than a mutual taste in literature.

"My name is Amelia Bassett," said the girl.

"Mine is Cyril Mulliner. Bassett?" He frowned thoughtfully. "The name seems familiar."

"Perhaps you have heard of my mother. Lady Bassett. She's rather a well-known big-game hunter and explorer. She tramps through jungles and things. She's gone out to the lobby for a smoke. By the way"—she hesitated—"if she finds us talking, will you remember that we met at the Polterwoods'?"

"I quite understand."

"You see, mother doesn't like people who talk to me without a formal introduction. And, when mother doesn't like anyone, she is so apt to hit them over the head with some hard instrument."

"I see," said Cyril. "Like the Human Ape in 'Gore by the Gallon'."

"Exactly. Tell me," said the girl, changing the subject, "if you were a millionaire, would you rather be stabbed in the back with a paperknife or found dead without a mark on you, staring with blank eyes at some appalling sight?"

Cyril was about to reply when, looking past her, he found himself virtually in the latter position. A woman of extraordinary formidableness had lowered herself into the seat beyond and was scrutinising him keenly through a tortoiseshell lorgnette. She reminded Cyril of Wallace Beery.

"Friend of yours, Amelia?" she said.

"This is Mr. Mulliner, mother. We met at the Polterwoods'."

"Ah?" said Lady Bassett.

She inspected Cyril through her lorgnette.

"Mr. Mulliner," she said, "is a little like the chief of the Lower Issi—though, of course, he was darker and had a ring through his nose. A dear, good fellow," she continued reminiscently, "but inclined to become familiar under the influence of trade gin. I shot him in the leg."

"Er—why?" asked Cyril.

"He was not behaving like a gentleman," said Lady Bassett primly.

"After taking your treatment," said Cyril, awed, "I'll bet he could have written a Book of Etiquette."

"I believe he did," said Lady Bassett carelessly. "You must come and call on us some afternoon, Mr. Mulliner. I am in the telephone book. If you are interested in man-eating pumas, I can show you some nice heads."

The curtain rose on act two, and Cyril returned to his thoughts. Love, he felt joyously, had come into his life at last. But then, so he had to admit, had Lady Bassett. There is, he reflected, always something.

I will pass lightly over the period of Cyril's wooing. Suffice it to say that his progress was rapid. From the moment he told Amelia that he had once met Dorothy Sayers, he never looked back. And one afternoon, calling and finding that Lady Bassett was away in the country, he took the girl's hand in his and told his love.

For a while all was well. Amelia's reactions proved satisfactory to a degree. She checked up enthusiastically on his proposition. Falling into his arms, she admitted specifically that he was her Dream Man.

Then came the jarring note.

"But it's no use," she said, her lovely eyes filling with tears. "Mother will never give her consent."

"Why not?" said Cyril, stunned. "What is it she objects to about me?"

"I don't know. But she generally alludes to you as 'that pipsqueak'."

"Pipsqueak?" said Cyril. "What *is* a pipsqueak?"

"I'm not quite sure, but it's something mother doesn't like very much. It's a pity she ever found out that you are an interior decorator."

"An honourable profession," said Cyril, a little stiffly.

"I know; but what she admires are men who have to do with the great open spaces."

"Well, I also design ornamental gardens."

"Yes," said the girl doubtfully, "but still——"

"And, dash it," said Cyril indignantly, "this isn't the Victorian age. All that business of Mother's Consent went out twenty years ago."

"Yes, but no one told mother."

"It's preposterous!" cried Cyril. "I never heard such rot. Let's just slip off and get married quietly and send her a picture postcard from Venice or somewhere, with a cross and a 'This is our room. Wish you were with us' on it."

The girl shuddered.

"She would be with us," she said. "You don't know mother. The moment she got the picture postcard, she would come over to wherever we were and put you across her knee and spank you with a hair-brush. I don't think I could ever feel the same towards you if I saw you lying across mother's knee, being spanked with a hair-brush. It would spoil the honeymoon."

Cyril frowned. But a man who has spent most of his life trying out a series of patent medicines is always an optimist.

"There is only one thing to be done," he said. "I shall see your mother and try to make her listen to reason. Where is she now?"

"She left this morning for a visit to the Winghams in Sussex."

"Excellent! I know the Winghams. In fact, I have a standing invitation to go and stay with them whenever I like. I'll send them a wire and push down this evening. I will oil up to your mother sedulously and try to correct her present unfavourable impression of me. Then, choosing my moment, I will shoot her the news. It may work. It may not work. But at any rate I consider it a fair sporting venture."

"But you are so diffident, Cyril. So shrinking. So retiring and shy. How can you carry through such a task?"

"Love will nerve me."

"Enough, do you think? Remember what mother is. Wouldn't a good, strong drink be more help?"

Cyril looked doubtful.

"My doctor has always forbidden me alcoholic stimulants. He says they increase the blood pressure."

"Well, when you meet mother, you will need all the blood pressure you can get. I really do advise you to fuel up a little before you see her."

"Yes," agreed Cyril, nodding thoughtfully. "I think you're right. It shall be as you say. Good-bye, my angel one."

"Good-bye, Cyril, darling. You will think of me every minute while you're gone?"

"Every single minute. Well, practically every single minute. You see, I have just got Horatio Slingsby's latest book, 'Strychnine in the Soup', and I shall be dipping into that from time to time. But all the rest of the while . . . Have you read it, by the way?"

"Not yet. I had a copy, but mother took it with her."

"Ah? Well, if I am to catch a train that will get me to Barkley for dinner, I must be going. Good-bye, sweetheart, and never forget that Gilbert Glendale in 'The Missing Toe' won the girl he loved in spite of being up against two mysterious stranglers and the entire Black Moustache gang."

He kissed her fondly, and went off to pack.

Barkley Towers, the country seat of Sir Mortimer and Lady Wingham, was two hours from London by rail. Thinking of Amelia and reading the opening chapters of Horatio Slingsby's powerful story, Cyril found the journey pass rapidly. In fact, so preoccupied was he that it was only as the train started to draw out of Barkley Regis station that he realized where he was. He managed to hurl himself on to the platform just in time.

As he had taken the five-seven express, stopping only at Gluebury Peveril, he arrived at Barkley Towers at an hour which enabled him not only to be on hand for dinner but also to take part in the life-giving distribution of cocktails which preceded the meal.

The house-party, he perceived on entering the drawing-room, was a small one. Besides Lady Bassett and himself, the only visitors were a nondescript couple of the name of Simpson, and a tall, bronzed, handsome man with flashing eyes who, his hostess informed him in a whispered aside, was Lester Mapledurham (pronounced Mum), the explorer and big-game hunter.

Perhaps it was the oppressive sensation of being in the same room with two explorers and big-game hunters that brought home to Cyril the need for following Amelia's advice as quickly as possible. But probably the mere sight of Lady Bassett alone would have been enough to make him break a lifelong abstinence. To her normal resemblance to Wallace Beery she appeared now to have added a distinct suggestion of Victor McLaglen, and the spectacle was sufficient to send Cyril leaping toward the cocktail tray.

After three rapid glasses he felt a better and a braver man. And so lavishly did he irrigate the ensuing dinner with hock, sherry, champagne, old brandy and port, that at the conclusion of the meal he was pleased to find that his diffidence had completely vanished. He rose from the table feeling equal to asking a dozen Lady Bassetts for their consent to marry a dozen daughters.

In fact, as he confided to the butler, prodding him genially in the ribs as he spoke, if Lady Bassett attempted to put on any dog with *him*, he would know what to do about it. He made no threats, he explained to the butler, he simply stated that he would know what to do about it. The butler said "Very good, sir. Thank you, sir", and the incident closed.

It had been Cyril's intention—feeling, as he did, in this singularly uplifted and dominant frame of mind—to get hold of Amelia's mother and start oiling up to her immediately after dinner. But, what with falling into a doze in the smoking-room and then getting into an argument on theology with one of the under-footmen whom he met in the hall, he did not reach the drawing-room until nearly half-past ten. And he was annoyed, on walking in with a merry cry of "Lady Bassett! Call for Lady Bassett!" on his lips, to discover that she had retired to her room.

Had Cyril's mood been even slightly less elevated, this news might have acted as a check on his enthusiasm. So generous, however, had been Sir Mortimer's hospitality that he merely nodded eleven times, to indicate comprehension, and then, having ascertained that his quarry was roosting in the Blue Room, sped thither with a brief "Tally-ho!"

Arriving at the Blue Room, he banged heartily on the door and breezed in. He found Lady Bassett propped up with pillows. She was smoking a cigar and reading a book. And the book, Cyril saw with intense surprise and resentment, was none other than Horatio Slingsby's "Strychnine in the Soup".

The spectacle brought him to an abrupt halt.

"Well, I'm dashed!" he cried. "Well, I'm blowed! What do you mean by pinching my book?"

Lady Bassett had lowered her cigar. She now raised her eyebrows.

"What are you doing in my room, Mr. Mulliner?"

"It's a little hard," said Cyril, trembling with self-pity. "I go to enormous expense to buy detective stories, and no sooner is my back turned than people rush about the place sneaking them."

"This book belongs to my daughter Amelia."

"Good old Amelia!" said Cyril cordially. "One of the best."

"I borrowed it to read in the train. Now will you kindly tell me what you are doing in my room, Mr. Mulliner?"

Cyril smote his forehead.

"Of course. I remember now. It all comes back to me. She told me you had taken it. And, what's more, I've suddenly recollected something which clears you completely. I was hustled and bustled at the end of the journey. I sprang to my feet, hurled bags on to the platform—in a word, lost my head. And, like a chump, I went and left my copy of 'Strychnine in the Soup' in the train. Well, I can only apologise."

"You can not only apologise. You can also tell me what you are doing in my room."

"What I am doing in your room?"

"Exactly."

"Ah!" said Cyril, sitting down on the bed. "You may well ask."

"I *have* asked. Three times."

Cyril closed his eyes. For some reason, his mind seemed cloudy and not at its best.

"If you are proposing to go to sleep here, Mr. Mulliner," said Lady Bassett, "tell me, and I shall know what to do about it."

The phrase touched a chord in Cyril's memory. He recollected now his reasons for being where he was. Opening his eyes, he fixed them on her.

"Lady Bassett," he said, "you are, I believe, an explorer?"

"I am."

"In the course of your explorations, you have wandered through many a jungle in many a distant land?"

"I have."

"Tell me, Lady Bassett," said Cyril keenly, "while making a pest of yourself to the denizens of those jungles, did you notice one thing? I allude to the fact that Love is everywhere—aye, even in the jungle. Love, independent of bounds and frontiers, of nationality and species, works its spell on every living thing. So that, no matter whether an individual be a Congo native, an American song-writer, a jaguar, an armadillo, a bespoke tailor, or a tsetse-tsetse fly, he will infallibly seek his mate. So why shouldn't an interior decorator and designer of ornamental gardens? I put this to you Lady Bassett."

"Mr. Mulliner," said his room-mate, "you are blotto!"

Cyril waved his hand in a spacious gesture, and fell off the bed.

"Blotto I may be," he said, resuming his seat, "but, none the less, argue as you will, you can't get away from the fact that I love your daughter Amelia."

There was a tense pause.

"What did you say?" cried Lady Bassett.

"When?" said Cyril absently, for he had fallen into a day-dream and, as far as the intervening blankets would permit, was playing "This little pig went to market" with his companion's toes.

"Did I hear you say . . . my daughter Amelia?"

"Grey-eyed girl, medium height, sort of browny-red hair," said Cyril, to assist her memory. "Dash it, you *must* know Amelia. She goes everywhere. And let me tell you something, Mrs.—I've forgotten your name. We're going to be married, if I can obtain her foul mother's consent. Speaking as an old friend, what would you say the chances were?"

"Extremely slight."

"Eh?"

"Seeing that I *am* Amelia's mother . . ."

Cyril blinked, genuinely surprised.

"Why, so you are! I didn't recognise you. Have you been there all the time?"

"I have."

Suddenly Cyril's gaze hardened, He drew himself up stiffly.

"What are you doing in my bed?" he demanded.

"This is not your bed."

"Then whose is it?"

"Mine."

Cyril shrugged his shoulders helplessly.

"Well, it all looks very funny to me," he said. "I suppose I must believe your story, but, I repeat, I consider the whole thing odd, and I propose to institute very strict enquiries. I may tell you that I happen to know the ringleaders. I wish you a very hearty good night."

It was perhaps an hour later that Cyril, who had been walking on the terrace in deep thought, repaired once more to the Blue Room in quest of information. Running over the details of the recent interview in his head, he had suddenly discovered that there was a point which had not been satisfactorily cleared up.

"I say," he said.

Lady Bassett looked up from her book, plainly annoyed.

"Have you no bedroom of your own, Mr. Mulliner?"

"Oh, yes," said Cyril. "They've bedded me out in the Moat Room. But there was something I wanted you to tell me."

"Well?"

"Did you say I might or mightn't?"

"Might or mightn't what?"

"Marry Amelia?"

"No. You may not."

"No?"

"No!"

"Oh!" said Cyril. "Well, pip-pip once more."

It was a moody Cyril Mulliner who withdrew to the Moat Room. He now realised the position of affairs. The mother of the girl he loved refused to accept him as an eligible suitor. A dickens of a situation to be in, felt Cyril, sombrely unshoeing himself.

Then he brightened a little. His life, he reflected, might be wrecked, but he still had two-thirds of "Strychnine in the Soup" to read.

At the moment when the train reached Barkley Regis station, Cyril had just got to the bit where Detective Inspector Mould looks through the half-open cellar door and, drawing in his breath with a sharp, hissing sound, recoils in horror. It was obviously going to be good. He was just about to proceed to the dressing-table where, he presumed, the footman had placed the book on unpacking his bag, when an icy stream seemed to flow down the centre of his spine and the room and its contents danced before him.

Once more he had remembered that he had left the volume in the train.

He uttered an animal cry and tottered to a chair.

The subject of bereavement is one that has often been treated powerfully by poets, who have run the whole gamut of the emotions while laying bare for us the agony of those who have lost parents, wives, children, gazelles, money, fame, dogs, cats, doves, sweethearts, horses and even collar-studs. But no poet has yet treated of the most poignant bereavement of all—that of the man half-way through a detective-story who finds himself at bedtime without the book.

Cyril did not care to think of the night that lay before him. Already his brain was lashing itself from side to side like a wounded snake as it sought for some explanation of Inspector Mould's strange behaviour. Horatio Slingsby was an author who could be relied on to keep faith with his public. He was not the sort of man to fob the reader off in the next chapter with the statement that what had made Inspector Mould look horrified was the fact that he had suddenly remembered that he had forgotten all about the letter his wife had given him to post. If looking through cellar doors disturbed a Slingsby detective, it was because a dismembered corpse lay there, or at least a severed hand.

A soft moan, as of some thing in torment, escaped Cyril. What to do? What to do? Even a makeshift substitute for "Strychnine in the Soup" was beyond his reach. He knew so well what he would find if he went to the library in search of something to read. Sir Mortimer Wingham was heavy and country-squire-ish.

His wife affected strange religions. Their literature was in keeping with their tastes. In the library there would be books on Ba-ha-ism, volumes in old leather of the Rural Encyclopædia, "My Two Years in Sunny Ceylon", by the Rev. Orlo Waterbury . . . but of anything that would interest Scotland Yard, of anything with a bit of blood in it and a corpse or two into which a fellow could get his teeth, not a trace.

What, then, coming right back to it, to do?

And suddenly, as if in answer to the question, came the solution. Electrified, he saw the way out.

The hour was now well advanced. By this time Lady Bassett must surely be asleep. "Strychnine in the Soup" would be lying on the table beside her bed. All he had to do was to creep in and grab it.

The more he considered the idea, the better it looked. It was not as if he did not know the way to Lady Bassett's room or the topography of it when he got there. It seemed to him as if most of his later life had been spent in Lady Bassett's room. He could find his way about it with his eyes shut.

He hesitated no longer. Donning a dressing-gown, he left his room and hurried along the passage.

Pushing open the door of the Blue Room and closing it softly behind him, Cyril stood for a moment full of all those emotions which come to a man revisiting some long-familiar spot. There the dear old room was, just the same as ever. How it all came back to him! The place was in darkness, but that did not deter him. He knew where the bed-table was, and he made for it with stealthy steps.

In the manner in which Cyril Mulliner advanced towards the bed-table there was much which would have reminded Lady Bassett, had she been an eye-witness, of the furtive prowl of the Lesser Iguanodon tracking its prey. In only one respect did Cyril and this creature of the wild differ in their technique. Iguanodons—and this applies not only to the Lesser but to the Larger Iguanodon —seldom, if ever, trip over cords on the floor and bring the lamps to which they are attached crashing to the ground like a ton of bricks.

Cyril did. Scarcely had he snatched up the book and placed it in the pocket of his dressing-gown, when his foot became entangled in the trailing cord and the lamp on the table leaped nimbly into the air and, to the accompaniment of a sound not unlike that made by a hundred plates coming apart simultaneously in the hands of a hundred scullery-maids, nose-dived to the floor and became a total loss.

At the same moment, Lady Bassett, who had been chasing a bat out of the window, stepped in from the balcony and switched on the lights.

To say that Cyril Mulliner was taken aback would be to understate the facts. Nothing like his recent misadventure had happened to him since his eleventh year, when, going surreptitiously to his mother's cupboard for jam, he had jerked three shelves down on his head, containing milk, butter, home-made preserves, pickles, cheese, eggs, cakes, and potted-meat. His feelings on the present occasion closely paralleled that boyhood thrill.

Lady Bassett also appeared somewhat discomposed.

"You!" she said.

Cyril nodded, endeavouring the while to smile in a reassuring manner.

"Hullo!" he said.

His hostess's manner was now one of unmistakable displeasure.

"Am I not to have a moment of privacy, Mr. Mulliner?" she asked severely. "I am, I trust, a broad-minded woman, but I cannot approve of this idea of communal bedrooms."

Cyril made an effort to be conciliatory.

"I do keep coming in, don't I?" he said.

"You do," agreed Lady Bassett. "Sir Mortimer informed me, on learning that I had been given this room, that it was supposed to be haunted. Had I known that it was haunted by you, Mr. Mulliner, I should have packed up and gone to the local inn."

Cyril bowed his head. The censure, he could not but feel, was deserved.

"I admit" he said, "that my conduct has been open to criticism. In extenuation, I can but plead my great love. This is no idle social call, Lady Bassett. I looked in because I wished to take up again this matter of my marrying your daughter Amelia. You say I can't. Why can't I? Answer me that, Lady Bassett."

"I have other views for Amelia," said Lady Bassett stiffly. "When my daughter gets married it will not be to a spineless, invertebrate product of our modern hothouse civilisation, but to a strong, upstanding, keen-eyed, two-fisted he-man of the open spaces. I have no wish to hurt your feelings, Mr. Mulliner," she continued, more kindly, "but you must admit that you are, when all is said and done, a pipsqueak."

"I deny it," cried Cyril warmly. "I don't even know what a pipsqueak is."

"A pipsqueak is a man who has never seen the sun rise beyond the reaches of the Lower Zambezi; who would not know what to do if faced by a charging rhinoceros. What, pray, would you do if faced by a charging rhinoceros, Mr. Mulliner?"

"I am not likely," said Cyril, "to move in the same social circles as charging rhinoceri."

"Or take another simple case, such as happens every day. Suppose you are crossing a rude bridge over a stream in Equatorial Africa. You have been thinking of a hundred trifles and are in a reverie. From this you wake to discover that in the branches overhead a python is extending its fangs towards you. At the same time, you observe that at one end of the bridge is a crouching puma; at the other are two head hunters—call them Pat and Mike—with poisoned blowpipes to their lips. Below, half hidden in the stream, is an alligator. What would you do in such a case, Mr. Mulliner?"

Cyril weighed the point.

"I should feel embarrassed," he had to admit. "I shouldn't know where to look."

Lady Bassett laughed an amused, scornful little laugh.

"Precisely. Such a situation would not, however, disturb Lester Mapledurham."

"Lester Mapledurham!"

"The man who is to marry my daughter Amelia. He asked me for her hand shortly after dinner."

Cyril reeled. The blow, falling so suddenly and unexpectedly, had made him feel boneless. And yet, he felt, he might have expected this. These explorers and big-game hunters stick together.

"In a situation such as I have outlined, Lester Mapledurham would simply drop from the bridge, wait till the alligator made its rush, insert a stout stick between its jaws, and then hit it in the eye with a spear, being careful to avoid its lashing tail. He would then drift down-stream and land at some safer spot. That is the type of man I wish for as a son-in-law."

Cyril left the room without a word. Not even the fact that he now had "Strychnine in the Soup" in his possession could cheer his mood of unrelieved blackness. Back in his room, he tossed the book moodily on to the bed and began to pace the floor. And he had scarcely completed two laps when the door opened.

For an instant, when he heard the click of the latch, Cyril supposed that his visitor must be Lady Bassett, who, having put two and two together on discovering her loss, had come to demand her property back. And he cursed the rashness which had led him to fling it so carelessly upon the bed, in full view.

But it was not Lady Bassett. The intruder was Lester Mapledurham. Clad in a suit of pyjamas which in their general colour scheme reminded Cyril of a boudoir he had recently decorated for a Society poetess, he stood with folded arms, his keen eyes fixed menacingly on the young man.

"Give me those jewels!" said Lester Mapledurham.

Cyril was at a loss.

"Jewels?"

"Jewels!"

"What jewels?"

Lester Mapledurham tossed his head impatiently.

"I don't know what jewels. They may be the Wingham Pearls or the Bassett Diamonds or the Simpson Sapphires. I'm not sure which room it was I saw you coming out of."

Cyril began to understand.

"Oh, did you see me coming out of a room?"

"I did. I heard a crash and, when I looked out, you were hurrying along the corridor."

"I can explain everything," said Cyril. "I had just been having a chat with

Lady Bassett on a personal matter. Nothing to do with diamonds."

"You're sure?" said Mapledurham.

"Oh, rather," said Cyril. "We talked about rhinoceri and pythons and her daughter Amelia and alligators and all that sort of thing, and then I came away."

Lester Mapledurham seemed only half convinced.

"H'm!" he said. "Well, if anything is missing in the morning, I shall know what to do about it." His eyes fell on the bed. "Hullo!" he went on, with sudden animation. "Slingsby's latest? Well, well! I've been wanting to get hold of this. I hear it's good. The *Leeds Mercury* says: 'These gripping pages. . . .' "

He turned to the door, and with a hideous pang of agony Cyril perceived that it was plainly his intention to take the book with him. It was swinging lightly from a bronzed hand about the size of a medium ham.

"Here!" he cried, vehemently.

Lester Mapledurham turned.

"Well?"

"Oh, nothing," said Cyril. "Just good night."

He flung himself face downwards on the bed as the door closed, cursing himself for the craven cowardice which had kept him from snatching the book from the explorer. There had been a moment when he had almost nerved himself to the deed, but it was followed by another moment in which he had caught the other's eye. And it was as if he found himself exchanging glances with Lady Bassett's charging rhinoceros.

And now, thanks to this pusillanimity, he was once more "Strychnine in the Soup"-less.

How long Cyril lay there, a prey to the gloomiest thoughts, he could not have said. He was aroused from his meditations by the sound of the door opening again.

Lady Bassett stood before him. It was plain that she was very deeply moved. In addition to resembling both Wallace Beery and Victor McLaglen, she now had a distinct look of George Bancroft.

She pointed a quivering finger at Cyril.

"You hound!" she cried. "Give me that book!"

Cyril maintained his poise with a strong effort.

"What book?"

"The book you sneaked out of my room!"

"Has someone sneaked a book out of your room?" Cyril struck his forehead. "Great heavens!" he cried.

"Mr. Mulliner," said Lady Bassett coldly, "more book and less gibbering!"

Cyril raised a hand.

"I know who's got your book. Lester Mapledurham!"

"Don't be absurd."

"He has, I tell you. As I was on my way to your room just now, I saw him coming out, carrying something in a furtive manner. I remember wondering a bit at the time. He's in the Clock Room. If we pop along there now, we shall just catch him red-handed."

Lady Bassett reflected.

"It is impossible," she said at length. "He is incapable of such an act. Lester Mapledurham is a man who once killed a lion with a sardine-opener."

"The very worst sort," said Cyril. "Ask anyone."

"And he is engaged to my daughter." Lady Bassett paused. "Well, he won't be long, if I find that what you say is true. Come, Mr. Mulliner!"

Together the two passed down the silent passage. At the door of the Clock Room they paused. A light streamed from beneath it. Cyril pointed silently to this sinister evidence of reading in bed, and noted that his companion stiffened and said something to herself in an undertone in what appeared to be some sort of native dialect.

The next moment she had flung the door open and, with a spring like that of a crouching zebu, had leaped to the bed and wrenched the book from Lester Mapledurham's hands.

"So!" said Lady Bassett.

"So!" said Cyril, feeling that he could not do better than follow the lead of such a woman.

"Hullo!" said Lester Mapledurham, surprised. "Something the matter?"

"So it was you who stole my book!"

"Your book?" said Lester Mapledurham. "I borrowed this from Mr. Mulliner there."

"A likely story!" said Cyril. "Lady Bassett is aware that I left my copy of 'Strychnine in the Soup' in the train."

"Certainly," said Lady Bassett. "It's no use talking, young man, I have caught you with the goods. And let me tell you one thing that may be of interest. If you think that, after a dastardly act like this, you are going to marry Amelia, forget it!"

"Wipe it right out of your mind," said Cyril.

"But listen——!"

"I will not listen. Come, Mr. Mulliner."

She left the room, followed by Cyril. For some moments they walked in silence.

"A merciful escape," said Cyril.

"For whom?"

"For Amelia. My gosh, think of her tied to a man like that. Must be a relief to you to feel that she's going to marry a respectable interior decorator."

Lady Bassett halted. They were standing outside the Moat Room now. She looked at Cyril, her eyebrows raised.

"Are you under the impression, Mr. Mulliner," she said, "that, on the strength of what has happened, I intend to accept you as a son-in-law?"

Cyril reeled.

"Don't you?"

"Certainly not."

Something inside Cyril seemed to snap. Recklessness descended upon him. He became for a space a thing of courage and fire, like the African leopard in the mating season.

"Oh!" he said.

And, deftly whisking "Strychnine in the Soup" from his companion's hand, he darted into his room, banged the door, and bolted it.

"Mr. Mulliner!"

It was Lady Bassett's voice, coming pleadingly through the woodwork. It was plain that she was shaken to the core, and Cyril smiled sardonically. He was now in a position to dictate terms.

"Give me that book, Mr. Mulliner!"

"Certainly not," said Cyril. "I intend to read it myself. I hear good reports of it on every side. The *Peebles Intelligencer* says: 'Vigorous and absorbing.'"

A low wail from the other side of the door answered him.

"Of course," said Cyril, suggestively, "if it were my future mother-in-law who was speaking, her word would naturally be law."

There was a silence outside.

"Very well," said Lady Bassett.

"I may marry Amelia?"

"You may."

Cyril unbolted the door.

"Come—Mother," he said, in a soft, kindly voice. "We will read it together, down in the library."

Lady Bassett was still shaken.

"I hope I have acted for the best," she said.

"You have," said Cyril.

"You will make Amelia a good husband?"

"Grade A," Cyril assured her.

"Well, even if you don't," said Lady Bassett resignedly, "I can't go to bed without that book. I had just got to the bit where Inspector Mould is trapped in the underground den of the Faceless Fiend."

Cyril quivered.

"*Is* there a Faceless Fiend?" he cried.

"There are two Faceless Fiends," said Lady Bassett.

"My gosh!" said Cyril. "Let's hurry."

27

GALA NIGHT

The bar-parlour of the Anglers' Rest was fuller than usual. Our local race meeting had been held during the afternoon, and this always means a rush of custom. In addition to the *habitués*, that faithful little band of listeners which sits nightly at the feet of Mr. Mulliner, there were present some half a dozen strangers. One of these, a fair-haired young Stout and Mild, wore the unmistakable air of a man who has not been fortunate in his selections. He sat staring before him with dull eyes and a drooping jaw, and nothing that his compaions could do seemed able to cheer him up.

A genial Sherry and Bitters, one of the regular patrons, eyed the sufferer with bluff sympathy.

"What your friend appears to need, gentlemen," he said, "is a dose of Mulliner's Buck-U-Uppo."

"What's Mulliner's Buck-U-Uppo?" asked one of the strangers, a Whisky Sour, interested. "Never heard of it myself."

Mr. Mulliner smiled indulgently.

"He is referring," he explained, "to a tonic invented by my brother Wilfred, the well-known analytical chemist. It is not often administered to human beings, having been designed primarily to encourage elephants in India to conduct themselves with an easy nonchalance during the tiger-hunts which are so popular in that country. But occasionally human beings do partake of it, with impressive results. I was telling the company here not long ago of the remarkable effect it had on my nephew Augustine, the curate.'

"It bucked him up?"

"It bucked him up very considerably. It acted on his bishop, too, when he tried it, in a similar manner. It is undoubtedly a most efficient tonic, strong and invigorating."

"How is Augustine, by the way?" asked the Sherry and Bitters.

"Extremely well. I received a letter from him only this morning. I am not sure if I told you, but he is a vicar now, at Walsingford-below-Chiveney-on-Thames. A delightful resort, mostly honey-suckle and apple-cheeked villagers."

"Anything been happening to him lately?"

"It is strange that you should ask that," said Mr. Mulliner, finishing his hot Scotch and lemon and rapping gently on the table. "In this letter to which I allude he has quite an interesting story to relate. It deals with the loves of Ronald Bracy-Gascoigne and Hypatia Wace. Hypatia is a school-friend of my nephew's wife. She has been staying at the vicarage nursing her through a sharp attack of mumps. She is also the niece and ward of Augustine's superior of the Cloth, the Bishop of Stortford."

"Was that the bishop who took the Buck-U-Uppo?"

"The same," said Mr. Mulliner. "As for Ronald Bracy-Gascoigne, he is a young man of independent means who resides in the neighbourhood. He is, of course, one of the Berkshire Bracy-Gascoignes."

"Ronald," said a Lemonade and Angostura thoughtfully. "Now, there's a name I never cared for."

"In that respect," said Mr. Mulliner, "you differ from Hypatia Wace. She thought it swell. She loved Ronald Bracy-Gascoigne with all the fervour of a young girl's heart, and they were provisionally engaged to be married. Provisionally, I say, because, before the firing-squad could actually be assembled, it was necessary for the young couple to obtain the consent of the Bishop of Stortford. Mark that, gentlemen. Their engagement was subject to the Bishop of Stortford's consent. This was the snag that protruded jaggedly from the middle of the primrose path of their happiness, and for quite a while it seemed as if Cupid must inevitably stub his toe on it."

I will select as the point at which to begin my tale, said Mr. Mulliner, a lovely evening in June, when all Nature seemed to smile and the rays of the setting sun fell like molten gold upon the picturesque garden of the vicarage at Walsingford-below-Chiveney-on-Thames. On a rustic bench beneath a spreading elm, Hypatia Wace and Ronald Bracy-Gascoigne watched the shadows lengthening across the smooth lawn: and to the girl there appeared something symbolical and ominous about this creeping blackness. She shivered. To her, it was as if the sunbathed lawn represented her happiness and the shadows the doom that was creeping upon it.

"Are you doing anything at the moment, Ronnie?" she asked.

"Eh?" said Ronald Bracy-Gascoigne. "What? Doing anything? Oh, you mean doing anything? No, I'm not doing anything."

"Then kiss me," cried Hypatia.

"Right-ho," said the young man. "I see what you mean. Rather a scheme. I will."

He did so: and for some moments they clung together in a close embrace. Then Ronald, releasing her gently, began to slap himself between the shoulder-blades.

"Beetle or something down my back," he explained. "Probably fell off the tree."

"Kiss me again," whispered Hypatia.

"In one second, old girl," said Ronald. "The instant I've dealt with this beetle

or something. Would you mind just fetching me a whack on about the fourth knob
of the spine, reading from the top downwards. I fancy that would make it think
a bit."

Hypatia uttered a sharp exclamation.

"Is this a time," she cried passionately, "to talk of beetles?"

"Well, you know, don't you know," said Ronald, with a touch of apology in his
voice, "they seem rather to force themselves on your attention when they get down
your back. I dare say you've had the same experience yourself. I don't suppose in
the ordinary way I mention beetles half a dozen times a year, but . . . I should
say the fifth knob would be about the spot now. A good, sharp slosh with plenty
of follow-through ought to do the trick."

Hypatia clenched her hands. She was seething with that febrile exasperation
which, since the days of Eve, has come upon women who find themselves linked
to a cloth-head.

"You poor sap," she said tensely. "You keep babbling about beetles, and you
don't appear to realise that, if you want to kiss me, you'd better cram in all the
kissing you can now, while the going is good. It doesn't seem to have occurred to
you that after to-night you're going to fade out of the picture."

"Oh, I say, no! Why?"

"My Uncle Percy arrives this evening."

"The Bishop?"

"Yes. And my Aunt Priscilla."

"And you think they won't be any too frightfully keen on me?"

"I know they won't. I wrote and told them we were engaged, and I had a letter
this afternoon saying you wouldn't do."

"No, I say, really? Oh, I say, dash it!"

" 'Out of the question,' my uncle said. And underlined it."

"Not really? Not absolutely underlined it?"

"Yes. Twice. In very black ink."

A cloud darkened the young man's face. The beetle had begun to try out a few
tentative dancesteps on the small of his back, but he ignored it. A Tiller troupe of
beetles could not have engaged his attention now.

"But what's he got against me?"

"Well, for one thing he has heard that you were sent down from Oxford."

"But all the best men are. Look at What's-his-name. Chap who wrote poems.
Shellac, or some such name."

"And then he knows that you dance a lot."

"What's wrong with dancing? I'm not very well up in these things, but didn't
David dance before Saul? Or am I thinking of a couple of other fellows? Anyway,
I know that somebody danced before somebody and was extremely highly thought
of in consequence."

"David . . ."

"I'm not saying it *was* David, mind you. It may quite easily have been Samuel."

"David . . ."

"Or even Nimshi, the son of Bimshi, or somebody like that."

"David or Samuel, or Nimshi the son of Bimshi," said Hypatia, "did not dance at the Home From Home."

Her allusion was to the latest of those frivolous night-clubs which spring up from time to time on the reaches of the Thames which are within a comfortable distance from London. This one stood some half a mile from the vicarage gates.

"Is that what the Bish is beefing about?" demanded Ronald, genuinely astonished. "You don't mean to tell me he really objects to the Home From Home? Why, a cathedral couldn't be more rigidly respectable. Does he realise that the place has only been raided five times in the whole course of its existence? A few simple words of explanation will put all this right. I'll have a talk with the old boy."

Hypatia shook her head.

"No," she said. "It's no use talking. He has made his mind up. One of the things he said in his letter was that, rather than countenance my union to a worthless worldling like you, he would gladly see me turned into a pillar of salt like Lot's wife, Genesis 19, 26. And nothing could be fairer than that, could it? So what I would suggest is that you start in immediately to fold me in your arms and cover my face with kisses. It's the last chance you'll get."

The young man was about to follow her advice, for he could see that that there was much in what she said: but at this moment there came from the direction of the house the sound of a manly voice trolling the Psalm for the Second Sunday after Septuagesima. And an instant later their host, the Rev. Augustine Mulliner, appeared in sight. He saw them and came hurrying across the garden, leaping over the flower-beds with extraordinary lissomness.

"Amazing elasticity that bird has, both physical and mental," said Ronald Bracy-Gascoigne, eyeing Augustine, as he approached, with a gloomy envy. "How does he get that way?"

"He was telling me last night," said Hypatia. "He has a tonic which he takes regularly. It is called Mulliner's Buck-U-Uppo, and acts directly upon the red corpuscles."

"I wish he would give the Bish a swig of it," said Ronald moodily. A sudden light of hope came into his eyes. "I say, Hyp, old girl," he exclaimed. "That's rather a notion. Don't you think it's rather a notion? It looks to me like something of an idea. If the Bish were to dip his beak into the stuff, it might make him take a brighter view of me."

Hypatia, like all girls who intend to be good wives, made it a practice to look on any suggestions thrown out by her future lord and master as fatuous and futile.

"I never heard anything so silly," she said.

"Well, I wish you would try it. No harm in trying it, what?"

"Of course I shall do nothing of the kind."

Well, I do think you might try it," said Ronald. "I mean, try it, don't you know."

He could speak no further on the matter, for now they were no longer alone. Augustine had come up. His kindly face looked grave.

"I say, Ronnie, old bloke," said Augustine, "I don't want to hurry you, but I think I ought to inform you that the Bishes, male and female, are even now on their way up from the station. I should be popping, if I were you. The prudent man looketh well to his going. Proverbs, 14, 15."

"All right," said Ronald sombrely. "I suppose," he added, turning to the girl, "you wouldn't care to sneak out to-night and come and have one final spot of shoe-slithering at the Home From Home? It's a Gala Night. Might be fun, what? Give us a chance of saying good-bye properly, and all that."

"I never heard anything so silly," said Hypatia, mechanically. "Of course I'll come."

"Right-ho. Meet you down the road about twelve then," said Ronald Bracy-Gascoigne.

He walked swiftly away, and presently was lost to sight behind the shrubbery. Hypatia turned with a choking sob, and Augustine took her hand and squeezed it gently.

"Cheer up, old onion," he urged. "Don't lose hope. Remember, many waters cannot quench love. Song of Solomon, 8, 7."

"I don't see what quenching love has got to do with it," said Hypatia peevishly. "Our trouble is that I've got an uncle complete with gaiters and a hat with boot-laces on it who can't see Ronnie with a telescope."

"I know." Augustine nodded sympathetically. "And my heart bleeds for you. I've been through all this sort of thing myself. When I was trying to marry Jane, I was stymied by a father-in-law-to-be who had to be seen to be believed. A chap, I assure you, who combined chronic shortness of temper with the ability to bend pokers round his biceps. Tact was what won him over, and tact is what I propose to employ in your case. I have an idea at the back of my mind. I won't tell you what it is, but you may take it from me it's the real tabasco."

"How kind you are, Augustine!" sighed the girl.

"It comes from mixing with Boy Scouts. You may have noticed that the village is stiff with them. But don't you worry, old girl. I owe you a lot for the way you've looked after Jane these last weeks, and I'm going to see you through. If I can't fix up your little affair, I'll eat my Hymns Ancient and Modern. And uncooked at that."

And with these brave words Augustine Mulliner turned two hand-springs, vaulted over the rustic bench, and went about his duties in the parish.

Augustine was rather relieved, when he came down to dinner that night, to find that Hypatia was not to be among those present. The girl was taking her meal on a tray with Jane, his wife, in the invalid's bedroom, and he was consequently able to embark with freedom on the discussion of her affairs. As soon as the servants had left the room, accordingly he addressed himself to the task.

"Now listen, you two dear good souls," he said. "What I want to talk to you about, now that we are alone, is the business of Hypatia and Ronald Bracy-Gascoigne."

The Lady Bishopess pursed her lips, displeased. She was a woman of ample and majestic build. A friend of Augustine's, who had been attached to the Tank Corps during the War, had once said that he knew nothing that brought the old days back more vividly than the sight of her. All she needed, he maintained, was a steering-wheel and a couple of machine-guns, and you could have moved her up into any Front Line and no questions asked.

"Please, Mr. Mulliner!" she said coldly.

Augustine was not to be deterred. Like all the Mulliners, he was at heart a man of reckless courage.

"They tell me you are thinking of bunging a spanner into the works," he said. "Not true, I hope?"

"Quite true, Mr. Mulliner. Am I not right, Percy?"

"Quite," said the Bishop.

"We have made careful enquiries about the young man, and are satisfied that he is entirely unsuitable."

"Would you say that?" said Augustine. "A pretty good egg, I've always found him. What's your main objection to the poor lizard?"

The Lady Bishopess shivered.

"We learn that he is frequently to be seen dancing at an advanced hour, not only in gilded London night-clubs but even in what should be the purer atmosphere of Walsingford-below-Chiveney-on-Thames. There is a resort in this neighbourhood known, I believe, as the Home From Home."

"Yes, just down the road," said Augustine. "It's a Gala Night to-night, if you cared to look in. Fancy dress optional."

"I understand that he is to be seen there almost nightly. Now, against dancing *qua* dancing," proceeded the Lady Bishopess, "I have nothing to say. Properly conducted, it is a pleasing and innocuous pastime. In my own younger days I myself was no mean exponent of the polka, the schottische and the Roger de Coverley. Indeed, it was at a Dance in Aid of the Distressed Daughters of Clergymen of the Church of England Relief Fund that I first met my husband."

"Really?" said Augustine. "Well, cheerio!" he said, draining his glass of port.

"But dancing, as the term is understood nowadays, is another matter. I have no doubt that what you call a Gala Night would prove, on inspection, to be little less than one of those orgies where perfect strangers of both sexes unblushingly throw coloured celluloid balls at one another and in other ways behave in a manner more suitable to the Cities of the Plain than to our dear England. No, Mr. Mulliner, if this young man Ronald Bracy-Gascoigne is in the habit of frequenting places of the type of the Home From Home, he is not a fit mate for a pure young girl like my niece Hypatia. Am I not correct, Percy?"

"Perfectly correct, my dear."

"Oh, right-ho, then," said Augustine philosophically, and turned the conversation to the forthcoming Pan-Anglican synod.

Living in the country had given Augustine Mulliner the excellent habit of going early to bed. He had a sermon to compose on the morrow, and in order to be fresh and at his best in the morning he retired shortly before eleven. And, as he had anticipated an unbroken eight hours of refreshing sleep, it was with no little annoyance that he became aware, towards midnight, of a hand on his shoulder, shaking him. Opening his eyes, he found that the light had been switched on and that the Bishop of Stortford was standing at his bedside.

"Hullo!" said Augustine. "Anything wrong?"

The Bishop smiled genially, and hummed a bar or two of the hymn for those of riper years at sea. He was plainly in excellent spirits.

"Nothing, my dear fellow," he replied. "In fact, very much the reverse. How are you, Mulliner?"

"I feel fine, Bish."

"I'll bet you two chasubles to a hassock you don't feel as fine as I do," said the Bishop. "It must be something in the air of this place. I haven't felt like this since Boat Race Night of the year 1893. Wow!" he continued. "Whoopee! How goodly are thy tents, O Jacob, and thy tabernacles, O Israel! Numbers, 44, 5." And, gripping the rail of the bed, he endeavoured to balance himself on his hands with his feet in the air.

Augustine looked at him with growing concern. He could not rid himself of a curious feeling that there was something sinister behind this ebullience. Often before, he had seen his guest in a mood of dignified animation, for the robust cheerfulness of the other's outlook was famous in ecclesiastical circles. But here, surely, was something more than dignified animation.

"Yes," proceeded the Bishop, completing his gymnastics and sitting down on the bed, "I feel like a fighting-cock, Mulliner. I am full of beans. And the idea of wasting the golden hours of the night in bed seemed so silly that I had to get up and look in on you for a chat. Now, this is what I want to speak to you about, my dear fellow. I wonder if you recollect writing to me—round about Epiphany, it would have been—to tell me of the hit you made in the Boy Scouts pantomime here? You played Sindbad the Sailor, if I am not mistaken?"

"That's right."

"Well, what I came here to ask, my dear Mulliner, was this. Can you, by any chance, lay your hand on that Sindbad costume? I want to borrow it, if I may."

"What for?"

"Never mind what for, Mulliner. Sufficient for you to know that motives of the soundest churchmanship render it essential for me to have that suit."

"Very well, Bish. I'll find it for you to-morrow."

"To-morrow will not do. This dilatory spirit of putting things off, this sluggish attitude of *laissez-faire* and procrastination," said the Bishop, frowning, "are scarcely what I expected to find in you, Mulliner. But there," he added, more kindly, "let us say no more. Just dig up that Sindbad costume and look slippy about it, and we will forget the whole matter. What does it look like?"

"Just an ordinary sailor-suit, Bish."

"Excellent. Some species of head-gear goes with it, no doubt?"

"A cap with H.M.S. *Blotto* on the band."

"Admirable. Then, my dear fellow," said the Bishop, beaming, "if you will just let me have it, I will trouble you no further to-night. Your day's toil in the vineyard has earned repose. The sleep of the labouring man is sweet. Ecclesiastes, 5, 12."

As the door closed behind his guest, Augustine was conscious of a definite uneasiness. Only once before had he seen his spiritual superior in quite this exalted condition. That had been two years ago, when they had gone down to Harchester College to unveil the statue of Lord Hemel of Hempstead. On that occasion, he recollected, the Bishop, under the influence of an overdose of Buck-U-Uppo, had not been content with unveiling the statue. He had gone out in the small hours of the night and painted it pink. Augustine could still recall the surge of emotion which had come upon him when, leaning out of the window, he had observed the prelate climbing up the waterspout on his way back to his room. And he still remembered the sorrowful pity with which he had listened to the other's lame explanation that he was a cat belonging to the cook.

Sleep, in the present circumstances, was out of the question. With a pensive sigh, Augustine slipped on a dressing-gown and went downstairs to his study. It would ease his mind, he thought to do a little work on that sermon of his.

Augustine's study was on the ground floor, looking on to the garden. It was a lovely night, and he opened the French windows, the better to enjoy the soothing scents of the flowers beyond. Then, seating himself at his desk, he began to work.

The task of composing a sermon which should practically make sense and yet not be above the heads of his rustic flock was always one that caused Augustine Mulliner to concentrate tensely. Soon he was lost in his labour and oblivious to everything but the problem of how to find a word of one syllable that meant Supralapsarianism. A glaze of preoccupation had come over his eyes, and the tip of his tongue, protruding from the left corner of his mouth, revolved in slow circles.

From this waking trance he emerged slowly to the realisation that somebody was speaking his name and that he was no longer alone in the room.

Seated in his arm-chair, her lithe young body wrapped in a green dressing-gown, was Hypatia Wace.

"Hullo!" said Augustine, staring. "You here?"

"Hullo," said Hypatia. "Yes, I'm here."

"I thought you had gone to the Home From Home to meet Ronald."

Hypatia shook her head.

"We never made it," she said. "Ronnie rang up to say that he had had a private tip that the place was to be raided to-night. So we thought it wasn't safe to start anything."

"Quite right," said Augustine approvingly. "Prudence first. Whatsoever thou takest in hand, remember the end and thou shalt never do amiss. Ecclesiastes, 7, 36."

Hypatia dabbed at her eyes with her handkerchief.

"I couldn't sleep, and I saw the light, so I came down. I'm so miserable, Augustine."

"About this Ronnie business?"

"Yes."

"There, there. Everything's going to be hotsy-totsy."

"I don't see how you make that out. Have you heard Uncle Percy and Aunt Priscilla talk about Ronnie? They couldn't be more off the poor, unfortunate fish if he were the Scarlet Woman of Babylon."

"I know. I know. But, as I hinted this afternoon, I have a little plan. I have been giving your case a good deal of thought, and I think you will agree with me that it is your Aunt Priscilla who is the real trouble. Sweeten her, and the Bish will follow her lead. What she thinks to-day, he always thinks to-morrow. In other words, if we can win her over, he will give his consent in a minute. Am I wrong or am I right?"

Hypatia nodded.

"Yes," she said. "That's right, as far as it goes. Uncle Percy always does what Aunt Priscilla tells him to. But how are you going to sweeten her?"

"With Mulliner's Buck-U-Uppo. You remember how often I have spoken to you of the properties of that admirable tonic. It changes the whole mental outlook like magic. We have only to slip a few drops into your Aunt Priscilla's hot milk to-morrow night, and you will be amazed at the results."

"You really guarantee that?"

"Absolutely."

"Then that's fine," said the girl, brightening visibly, "because that's exactly what I did this evening. Ronnie was suggesting it when you came up this afternoon, and I thought I might as well try it. I found the bottle in the cupboard in here, and I put some in Aunt Priscilla's hot milk and, in order to make a good job of it, some in Uncle Percy's toddy, too."

An icy hand seemed to clutch at Augustine's heart. He began to understand the inwardness of the recent scene in his bedroom.

"How much?" he gasped.

"Oh, not much," said Hypatia. 'I didn't want to poison the dear old things. About a tablespoon apiece."

A shuddering groan came raspingly from Augustine's lips.

"Are you aware," he said in a low, toneless voice, "that the medium dose for an adult elephant is one teaspoonful?"

"No!"

"Yes. The most fearful consequences result from anything in the nature of an overdose." He groaned. "No wonder the Bishop seemed a little strange in his manner just now."

"Did he seem strange in his manner?"

Augustine nodded dully.

"He came into my room and did hand-springs on the end of the bed and went away in my Sindbad the Sailor suit."

"What did he want that for?"

Augustine shuddered.

"I scarcely dare to face the thought," he said, "but can he have been contemplating a visit to the Home From Home? It is Gala Night, remember."

"Why, of course," said Hypatia. "And that must have been why Aunt Priscilla came to me about an hour ago and asked me if I could lend her my Columbine costume."

"She did!" cried Augustine.

"Certainly she did. I couldn't think what she wanted it for. But now, of course, I see."

Augustine uttered a moan that seemed to come from the depths of his soul.

"Run up to her room and see if she is still there," he said. "If I'm not very much mistaken, we have sown the wind and we shall reap the whirlwind. Hosea, 8, 7."

The girl hurried away, and Augustine began to pace the floor feverishly. He had completed five laps and was beginning a sixth, when there was a noise outside the French windows and a sailorly form shot through and fell panting into the arm-chair.

"Bish!" cried Augustine.

The Bishop waved a hand, to indicate that he would be with him as soon as he had attended to this matter of taking in a fresh supply of breath, and continued to pant. Augustine watched him, deeply concerned. There was a shop-soiled look about the guest. Part of the Sindbad costume had been torn away as if by some irresistible force, and the hat was missing. His worst fears appeared to have been realised.

"Bish!" he cried. "What has been happening?"

The Bishop sat up. He was breathing more easily now, and a pleased, almost complacent, look had come into his face.

"Woof!" he said. "Some binge!"

"Tell me what happened," pleaded Augustine, agitated.

The Bishop reflected, arranging his facts in chronological order.

"Well," he said, "when I got to the Home From Home, everybody was dancing. Nice orchestra. Nice tune. Nice floor. So I danced, too."

"You danced?"

"Certainly I danced, Mulliner," replied the Bishop with a dignity that sat well upon him. "A hornpipe. I consider it the duty of the higher clergy on these occasions to set an example. You didn't suppose I would go to a place like the Home From Home to play solitaire? Harmless relaxation is not forbidden, I believe?"

"But can you dance?"

"*Can* I dance?" said the Bishop. "Can I *dance*, Mulliner? Have you ever heard of Nijinsky?"

"Yes."

"My stage name," said the Bishop.

Augustine swallowed tensely.

"Who did you dance with?" he asked.

"At first," said the Bishop, "I danced alone. But then, most fortunately, my dear wife arrived, looking perfectly charming in some sort of filmy material, and we danced together."

"But wasn't she surprised to see you there?"

"Not in the least. Why should she be?"

"Oh, I don't know."

"Then why did you put the question?"

"I wasn't thinking."

"Always think before you speak, Mulliner," said the Bishop reprovingly.

The door opened, and Hypatia hurried in.

"She's not——" She stopped. "Uncle!" she cried.

"Ah, my dear," said the Bishop. "But I was telling you, Mulliner. After we had been dancing for some time, a most annoying thing occurred. Just as we were enjoying ourselves—everybody cutting up and having a good time—who should come in but a lot of interfering policemen. A most brusque and unpleasant body of men. Inquisitive, too. One of them kept asking me my name and address. But I soon put a stop to all that sort of nonsense. I plugged him in the eye."

"You plugged him in the eye?"

"I plugged him in the eye, Mulliner. That's when I got this suit torn. The fellow was annoying me intensely. He ignored my repeated statement that I gave my name and address only to my oldest and closest friends, and had the audacity to clutch me by what I suppose a costumier would describe as the slack of my garment. Well, naturally I plugged him in the eye. I come of a fighting line, Mulliner. My ancestor, Bishop Odo, was famous in William the Conqueror's day for his work with the battle-axe. So I biffed this bird. And did he take a toss? Ask me!" said the Bishop, chuckling contentedly.

Augustine and Hypatia exchanged glances.

"But, uncle——" began Hypatia.

"Don't interrupt, my child," said the Bishop. "I cannot marshal my thoughts if you persist in interrupting. Where was I? Ah, yes. Well, then the already existing state of confusion grew intensified. The whole *tempo* of the proceedings became, as it were, quickened. Somebody turned out the lights, and somebody else upset a table and I decided to come away." A pensive look flitted over his face. "I trust," he said, "that my dear wife also contrived to leave without undue inconvenience. The last I saw of her, she was diving through one of the windows in a manner which, I thought, showed considerable lissomness and resource. Ah, here she is and looking none the worse for her adventures. Come in, my dear, I was just telling Hypatia and our good host here of our little evening from home."

The Lady Bishopess stood breathing heavily. She was not in the best of training. She had the appearance of a tank which is missing on one cylinder.

"Save me, Percy," she gasped.

"Certainly, my dear," said the Bishop cordially. "From what?"

In silence the Lady Bishopess pointed at the window. Through it, like some figure of doom, was striding a policeman. He, too, was breathing in a laboured manner, like one touched in the wind.

The Bishop drew himself up.

"And what, pray," he asked coldly, "is the meaning of this intrusion?"

"Ah!" said the policeman.

He closed the windows and stood with his back against them.

It seemed to Augustine that the moment had arrived for a man of tact to take the situation in hand.

"Good evening, constable," he said genially. "You appear to have been taking exercise. I have no doubt that you would enjoy a little refreshment."

The policeman licked his lips, but did not speak.

"I have an excellent tonic here in my cupboard," proceeded Augustine, "and I think you will find it most restorative. I will mix it with a little seltzer."

The policeman took the glass, but in a preoccupied manner. His attention was still riveted on the Bishop and his consort.

"Caught you, have I?" he said.

"I fail to understand you, officer," said the Bishop frigidly.

"I've been chasing her," said the policeman, pointing to the Lady Bishopess, "a good mile it must have been."

"Then you acted," said the Bishop severely, "in a most offensive and uncalled-for way. On her physician's recommendation, my dear wife takes a short cross-country run each night before retiring to rest. Things have come to a sorry pass if she cannot follow her doctor's orders without being pursued—I will use a stronger word—chivvied—by the constabulary."

"And it was by her doctor's orders that she went to the Home From Home, eh?" said the policeman keenly.

"I shall be vastly surprised to learn," said the Bishop, "that my dear wife has been anywhere near the resort you mention."

"And you were there, too. I saw you."

"Absurd!"

"I saw you punch Constable Booker in the eye."

"Ridiculous!"

"If you weren't there," said the policeman, "what are you doing wearing that sailor-suit?"

The Bishop raised his eyebrows.

"I cannot permit my choice of costume," he said, "arrived at—I need scarcely say—only after much reflection and meditation, to be criticised by a man who habitually goes about in public in a blue uniform and a helmet. What, may I enquire, is it that you object to in this sailor-suit? There is nothing wrong, I venture to believe, nothing degrading in a sailor-suit. Many of England's greatest men have worn sailor-suits. Nelson . . . Admiral Beatty——"

"And Arthur Prince," said Hypatia.

"And, as you say, Arthur Prince."

The policeman was scowling darkly. As a dialectician, he seemed to be feeling he was outmatched. And yet, he appeared to be telling himself, there must be some answer even to the apparently unanswerable logic to which he had just been listening. To assist thought, he raised the glass of Buck-U-Uppo and seltzer in his hand, and drained it at a draught.

And, as he did so, suddenly, abruptly, as breath fades from steel, the scowl passed from his face, and in its stead there appeared a smile of infinite kindliness and goodwill. He wiped his moustache, and began to chuckle to himself, as at some diverting memory.

"Made me laugh, that did," he said. "When old Booker went head over heels that time. Don't know when I've seen a nicer punch. Clean, crisp . . . Don't suppose it travelled more than six inches, did it? I reckon you've done a bit of boxing in your time, sir."

At the sight of the constable's smiling face, the Bishop had relaxed the austerity of his demeanour. He no longer looked like Savonarola rebuking the sins of the people. He was his old genial self once more.

"Quite true, officer," he said, beaming. "When I was a somewhat younger man than I am at present, I won the Curates' Open Heavy-weight Championship two years in succession. Some of the ancient skill still lingers, it would seem."

The policeman chuckled again.

"I should say it does, sir. But," he continued, a look of annoyance coming into his face, "what all the fuss was about is more than I can say. Our fat-headed Inspector says, 'You go and raid that Home From Home, chaps, see?' he says, and so we went and done it. But my heart wasn't in it, no more was any of the other fellers' hearts in it. What's wrong with a little rational enjoyment? That's what I say. What's wrong with it?"

"Precisely, officer."

"That's what I say. What's wrong with it? Let people enjoy themselves how they like is what I say. And if the police come interfering—well, punch them in the eye, I say, same as you did Constable Booker. That's what I say."

"Exactly," said the Bishop. He turned to his wife. "A fellow of considerable intelligence, this, my dear."

"I liked his face right from the beginning," said the Lady Bishopess. "What is your name, Officer?"

"Smith, lady. But call me Cyril."

"Certainly," said the Lady Bishopess. "It will be a pleasure to do so. I used to know some Smiths in Lincolnshire years ago, Cyril. I wonder if they were any relation."

"Maybe, lady. It's a small world."

"Though, now I come to think of it, their name was Robinson."

"Well, that's life, lady, isn't it?" said the policeman.

"That's just about what it is, Cyril," agreed the Bishop. "You never spoke a truer word."

Into this love-feast, which threatened to become more glutinous every moment, there cut the cold voice of Hypatia Wace.

"Well, I must say," said Hypatia, "that you're a nice lot!"

"Who's a nice lot, lady?" asked the policeman.

"Those two," said Hypatia. "Are you married, officer?"

"No, lady. I'm just a solitary chip drifting on the river of life."

"Well, anyway, I expect you know what it feels like to be in love."

"Too true, lady."

"Well, I'm in love with Mr. Bracy-Gascoigne. You've met him, probably. Wouldn't you say he was a person of the highest character?"

"The whitest man I know, lady."

"Well, I want to marry him, and my uncle and aunt here won't let me, because they say he's worldly. Just because he goes out dancing. And all the while they are dancing the soles of their shoes through. I don't call it fair."

She buried her face in her hands with a stifled sob. The Bishop and his wife looked at each other in blank astonishment.

"I don't understand," said the Bishop.

"Nor I," said the Lady Bishopess. "My dear child, what is all this about our not consenting to your marriage with Mr. Bracy-Gascoigne? However did you get that idea into your head? Certainly, as far as I am concerned, you may marry Mr. Bracy-Gascoigne. And I think I speak for my dear husband?"

"Quite," said the Bishop. "Most decidedly."

Hypatia uttered a cry of joy.

"Good egg! May I really?"

"Certainly you may. You have no objection, Cyril?"

"None whatever, lady."

Hypatia's face fell.

"Oh, dear!" she said.

"What's the matter?"

"It just struck me that I've got to wait hours and hours before I can tell him. Just think of having to wait hours and hours!"

The Bishop laughed his jolly laugh.

"Why wait hours and hours, my dear? No time like the present."

"But he's gone to bed."

"Well, rout him out," said the Bishop heartily. "Here is what I suggest that we should do. You and I and Priscilla—and you, Cyril?—will all go down to his house and stand under his window and shout."

"Or throw gravel at the window," suggested the Lady Bishopess.

"Certainly, my dear, if you prefer it."

"And when he sticks his head out," said the policeman, "how would it be to have the garden hose handy and squirt him? Cause a lot of fun and laughter, that would."

"My dear Cyril," said the Bishop, "you think of everything. I shall certainly use any influence I may possess with the authorities to have you promoted to a rank where your remarkable talents will enjoy greater scope. Come, let us be going. You will accompany us, my dear Mulliner?"

Augustine shook his head.

"Sermon to write, Bish."

"Just as you say, Mulliner. Then if you will be so good as to leave the window open, my dear fellow, we shall be able to return to our beds at the conclusion of our little errand of goodwill without disturbing the domestic staff."

"Right-ho, Bish."

"Then, for the present, pip-pip, Mulliner."

"Toodle-oo, Bish," said Augustine.

He took up his pen, and resumed his composition. Out in the sweet-scented night he could hear the four voices dying away in the distance. They seemed to be singing an old English part-song. He smiled benevolently.

"A merry heart doeth good like a medicine. Proverbs 17, 22," murmured Augustine.

28

MONKEY BUSINESS

A TANKARD of Stout had just squashed a wasp as it crawled on the arm of Miss Postlethwaite, our popular barmaid, and the conversation in the bar-parlour of the Anglers' Rest had turned to the subject of physical courage.

The Tankard himself was inclined to make light of the whole affair, urging modestly that his profession, that of a fruit-farmer, gave him perhaps a certain advantage over his fellow-men when it came to dealing with wasps.

"Why, sometimes in the picking season," said the Tankard, "I've had as many as six standing on each individual plum, rolling their eyes at me and daring me to come on."

Mr. Mulliner looked up from his hot Scotch and lemon.

"Suppose they had been gorillas?" he said.

The Tankard considered this. "There wouldn't be room," he argued, "not on an ordinary-sized plum."

"Gorillas?" said a Small Bass, puzzled.

"And I'm sure if it had been a gorilla Mr. Bunyan would have squashed it just the same," said Miss Postlethwaite, and she gazed at the Tankard with whole-hearted admiration in her eyes.

Mr. Mulliner smiled gently.

"Strange," he said, "how even in these orderly civilised days women still worship heroism in the male. Offer them wealth, brains, looks, amiability, skill at card-tricks or at playing the ukulele . . . unless these are accompanied by physical courage they will turn away in scorn."

"Why gorillas?" asked the Small Bass, who liked to get these things settled.

"I was thinking of a distant cousin of mine whose life became for a time considerably complicated owing to one of these animals. Indeed, it was the fact that this gorilla's path crossed his that nearly lost Montrose Mulliner the hand of Rosalie Beamish."

The Small Bass still appeared mystified.

"I shouldn't have thought anybody's path *would* have crossed a gorilla's. I'm forty-five next birthday, and I've never so much as seen a gorilla."

"Possibly Mr. Mulliner's cousin was a big-game hunter," said a Gin Fizz.

"No," said Mr. Mulliner. "He was an assistant-director in the employment of the Perfecto-Zizzbaum Motion Picture Corporation of Hollywood: and the gorilla of which I speak was one of the cast of the super-film 'Black Africa', a celluloid epic of the clashing of elemental passions in a land where might is right and the strong man comes into his own. Its capture in its native jungle was said to have cost the lives of seven half-dozen members of the expedition, and at the time when this story begins it was lodged in a stout cage on the Perfecto-Zizzbaum lot at a salary of seven hundred and fifty dollars a week, with billing guaranteed in letters not smaller than those of Edmund Wigham and Luella Benstead, the stars.

In ordinary circumstances (said Mr. Mulliner) this gorilla would have been to my distant cousin Montrose merely one of a thousand fellow-workers on the lot. If you had asked him, he would have said that he wished the animal every kind of success in its chosen profession, but that, for all the chance there was of them ever, as it were, getting together, they were just ships that pass in the night. It is doubtful, indeed, if he would even have bothered to go down to its cage and look at it, had not Rosalie Beamish asked him to do so. As he put it to himself, if a man's duties brought him into constant personal contact with Mr. Schnellenhamer, the President of the Corporation, where was the sense of wasting time looking at gorillas? *Blasé* about sums up his attitude.

But Rosalie was one of the extra girls in "Black Africa" and so had a natural interest in a brother-artist. And as she and Montrose were engaged to be married her word, of course, was law. Montrose had been planning to play draughts that afternoon with his friend, George Pybus, of the Press department, but he good-naturedly cancelled the fixture and accompanied Rosalie to the animal's headquarters.

He was more than ordinarily anxious to oblige her to-day, because they had recently been having a little tiff. Rosalie had been urging him to go to Mr. Schnellenhamer and ask for a rise of salary: and this Montrose, who was excessively timid by nature, was reluctant to do. There was something about being asked to pay out money that always aroused the head of the firm's worst passions.

When he met his betrothed outside the commissary, he was relieved to find her in a more amiable mood than she had been of late. She prattled merrily of this and that as they walked along, and Montrose was congratulating himself that there was not a cloud in the sky when, arriving at the cage, he found Captain Jack Fosdyke there, prodding at the gorilla with a natty cane.

This Captain Jack Fosdyke was a famous explorer who had been engaged to superintend the production of "Black Africa". And the fact that Rosalie's professional duties necessitated a rather close association with him had caused Montrose a good deal of uneasiness. It was not that he did not trust her, but love makes a man jealous and he knew the fascination of these lean, brown, hard-bitten adventurers of the wilds.

As they came up, the explorer turned, and Montrose did not like the chummy look in the eye which he cocked at the girl. Nor, for the matter of that, did he like the other's bold smile. And he wished that in addressing Rosalie Captain Fosdyke would not preface his remarks with the words "Ah, there, girlie."

"Ah, there, girlie," said the Captain. "Come to see the monk?"

Rosalie was staring open-mouthed through the bars.

"Doesn't he look fierce!" she cried.

Captain Jack Fosdyke laughed carelessly.

"Tchah!" he said, once more directing the ferrule of his cane at the animal's ribs. "If you had led the rough, tough, slam-bang, every-man-for-himself life I have, you wouldn't be frightened of gorillas. Bless my soul, I remember once in Equatorial Africa I was strolling along with my elephant gun and my trusty native bearer, 'Mlongi, and a couple of the brutes dropped out of a tree and started throwing their weight about and behaving as if the place belonged to them. I soon put a stop to that, I can tell you. Bang, bang, left and right, and two more skins for my collection. You have to be firm with gorillas. Dining anywhere to-night, girlie?"

"I am dining with Mr. Mulliner at the Brown Derby.

"Mr. who?"

"This is Mr. Mulliner."

"Oh, that?" said Captain Fosdyke, scrutinising Montrose in a supercilious sort of way as if he had just dropped out of a tree before him. "Well, some other time, eh?"

And, giving the gorilla a final prod, he sauntered away.

Rosalie was silent for a considerable part of the return journey. When at length she spoke it was in a vein that occasioned Montrose the gravest concern.

"Isn't he wonderful!" she breathed. "Captain Fosdyke, I mean."

"Yes?" said Montrose coldly.

"I think he's splendid. So strong, so intrepid. Have you asked Mr. Schnellenhamer for that raise yet?"

"Er—no," said Montrose. "I am—how shall I put it?—biding my time."

There was another silence.

"Captain Fosdyke isn't afraid of Mr. Schnellenhamer," said Rosalie pensively. "He slaps him on the back."

"Nor am I afraid of Mr. Schnellenhamer," replied Montrose, stung. "I would slap him on the back myself if I considered that it would serve any useful end. My delay in asking for that raise is simply due to the fact that in these matters of finance a certain tact and delicacy have to be observed. Mr. Schnellenhamer is a busy man, and I have enough consideration not to intrude my personal affairs on him at a time when he is occupied with other matters."

"I see," said Rosalie, and there the matter rested. But Montrose remained uneasy. There had been a gleam in her eyes and a rapt expression on her face as she spoke of Captain Fosdyke which he had viewed with concern. Could it be, he ask himself, that she was falling a victim to the man's undeniable magnetism? He decided to consult his friend, George Pybus, of the Press department, on the matter. George was a knowledgeable young fellow and would doubtless have something constructive to suggest.

George Pybus listened to his tale with interest and said it reminded him of a girl he had loved and lost in Des Moines, Iowa.

"She ditched me for a prizefighter," said George. "No getting away from it, girls do get fascinated by the strong, tough male."

Montrose's heart sank.

"You don't really think——?"

"It is difficult to say. One does not know how far this thing has gone. But I certainly feel that we must lose no time in drafting out some scheme whereby you shall acquire a glamour which will counteract the spell of this Fosdyke. I will devote a good deal of thought to the matter."

And it was on the very next afternoon, as he sat with Rosalie in the commissary sharing with her a Steak Pudding Marlene Dietrich, that Montrose noticed that the girl was in the grip of some strong excitement.

"Monty," she exclaimed, almost before she had dug out the first kidney, "do you know what Captain Fosdyke said this morning?"

Montrose choked.

"If that fellow has been insulting you," he cried, "I'll . . . Well, I shall be extremely annoyed," he concluded with a good deal of heat.

"Don't be silly. He wasn't talking to me. He was speaking to Luella Benstead. You know she's getting married again soon . . ."

"Odd how these habits persist."

". . . and Captain Fosdyke said why didn't she get married in the gorilla's cage. For the publicity."

"He did?"

Montrose laughed heartily. A quaint idea, he felt. Bizarre, even.

"She said she wouldn't dream of it. And then Mr. Pybus, who happened to be standing by, suddenly got the most wonderful idea. He came up to me and said why shouldn't you and I get married in the gorilla's cage."

Montrose's laughter died away. "You and I?"

"Yes."

"George Pybus suggested that?"

"Yes."

Montrose groaned in spirit. He was telling himself he might have known something like this would have been the result of urging a member of the Press department to exercise his intellect. The brains of members of the Press departments of motion-picture studios resemble soup at a cheap restaurant. It is wiser not to stir them.

"Think what a sensation it would make! No more extra work for me after that. I'd get parts, and good ones. A girl can't get anywhere in this business without publicity."

Montrose licked his lips. They had become very dry. He was thinking harshly of George Pybus. It was just loose talking like George Pybus's, he felt, that made half the trouble in this world.

"But don't you feel," he said, "that there is something a little undignified about publicity? In my opinion, a true artist ought to be above it. And I think you should not overlook another, extremely vital aspect of the matter. I refer to the deleterious effect which such an exhibition as Pybus suggests would have upon those who read about it in the papers. Speaking for myself," said Montrose, "there is nothing I should enjoy more than a quiet wedding in a gorilla's cage. But has one the right to pander to the morbid tastes of a sensation-avid-public? I am not a man who often speaks of these deeper things—on the surface, no doubt, I seem careless and happy-go-lucky—but I do hold very serious views on a citizen's duties in this fevered modern age. I consider that each one of us should do all that lies in his power to fight the ever-growing trend of the public mind towards the morbid and the hectic. I have a very real feeling that the body politic can never become healthy while this appetite for sensation persists. If America is not to go the way of Babylon and Rome, we must come back to normalcy and the sane outlook. It is not much that a man in my humble position can do to stem the tide, but at least I can refrain from adding fuel to its flames by getting married in gorillas' cages."

Rosalie was gazing at him incredulously.

"You don't mean you won't do it?"

"It would not be right."

"I believe you're scared."

"Nothing of the kind. It is purely a question of civic conscience."

"You *are* scared. To think," said Rosalie vehemently, "that I should have linked my lot with a man who's afraid of a teentsy-weentsy gorilla."

Montrose could not let this pass.

"It is not a teentsy-weentsy gorilla. I should describe the animal's muscular development as well above the average.

"And the keeper would be outside the cage with a spiked stick."

"*Outside* the cage!" said Montrose thoughtfully.

Rosalie sprang to her feet in sudden passion.

"Goodbye!"

"But you haven't finished your steak-pudding."

"Goodbye," she repeated. "I see now what your so-called love is worth. If you are going to start denying me every little thing before we're married, what would you be like after? I'm glad I have discovered your true character. Our engagement is at an end."

Montrose was pale to the lips, but he tried to reason with her.

"But, Rosalie," he urged, "surely a girl's wedding-day ought to be something for her to think of all her life—to recall with dreamily smiling lips as she knits the tiny garments or cooks the evening meal for the husband she adores. She ought to be able to look back and live again through the solemn hush in the church, savour once more the sweet scent of the lilies-of-the-valley, hear the rolling swell of the organ and the grave voice of the clergyman reading the service. What memories would you have if you carried out this plan that you suggest? One only—that of a smelly monkey. Have you reflected upon this, Rosalie?"

But she was obdurate.

"Either you marry me in the gorilla's cage, or you don't marry me at all. Mr. Pybus says it is certain to make the front page, with photographs and possibly even a short editorial on the right stuff being in the modern girl despite her surface irresponsibility."

"You will feel differently to-night, when we meet for dinner."

"We shall not meet for dinner. If you are interested, I may inform you that Captain Fosdyke invited me to dine with him and I intend to do so."

"Rosalie!"

"There is a man who really is a man. When he meets a gorilla, he laughs in its face."

"Very rude."

"A million gorillas couldn't frighten him. Goodbye, Mr. Mulliner. I must go and tell him that when I said this morning that I had a previous engagement I was mistaken."

She swept out, and Montrose went on with his steak-pudding like one in a dream.

It is possible (said Mr. Mulliner, taking a grave sip of his hot Scotch and lemon and surveying the company with a thoughtful eye) that what I have told you may have caused you to form a dubious opinion of my distant cousin Montrose. If so, I am not surprised. In the scene which I have just related, no one is better aware than myself that he has not shown up well. Reviewing his shallow arguments, we see through them, as Rosalie did: and, like Rosalie, we realise that he had feet of clay—and cold ones, to boot.

But I would urge in extenuation of his attitude that Montrose Mulliner, possibly through some constitutional defect such as an insufficiency of hormones, had been from childhood timorous in the extreme. And his work as an assistant director had served very noticeably to increase this innate pusillanimity.

It is one of the drawbacks to being an assistant director that virtually everything that happens to him is of a nature to create an inferiority-complex—or, if one already exists, to deepen it. He is habitually addressed as "Hey, you" and alluded to in the third person as "that fathead". If anything goes wrong on the set, he gets the blame and is ticked off not only by the producer but also by the director and all the principals involved. Finally, he has to be obsequious to so many people that it is little wonder that he comes in time to resemble one of the more shrinking and respectful breeds of rabbit. Five years of assistant-directing had so sapped Montrose's morale that nowadays he frequently found himself starting up and apologising in his sleep.

It is proof, then, of the great love which he had for Rosalie Beamish that, encountering Captain Jack Fosdyke a few days later, he should have assailed him with bitter reproaches. Only love could have impelled him to act in a manner so foreign to his temperament.

The fact was, he blamed the Captain for all that had occurred. He considered that he had deliberately unsettled Rosalie and influenced her mind with the set purpose of making her dissatisfied with the man to whom she had plighted her troth.

"If it wasn't for you," he concluded warmly, "I feel sure I could have reasoned her out of what is nothing but a passing girlish whim. But you have infatuated her, and now where do I get off?"

The Captain twirled his moustache airily.

"Don't blame me, my boy. All my life I have been cursed by this fatal attraction of mine for the sex. Poor little moths, they will beat their wings against the bright light of my personality. Remind me to tell you some time of an interesting episode which occurred in the harem of the King of the 'Mbongos. There is something about me which is—what shall I say?—hypnotic. It is not my fault that this girl has compared us. It was inevitable that she should compare us. And having compared us what does she see? On the one hand, a man with a soul of chilled steel who can look his gorilla in the eye and make it play ball. On the other—I use the term in the kindliest possible sense—a crawling worm. Well, goodbye, my boy, glad to have seen you and had this little chat," said Captain Fosdyke. "I like you young fellows to bring your troubles to me."

For some moments after he had gone, Montrose remained standing motionless, while all the repartees which he might have made surged through his mind in a glittering procession. Then his thoughts turned once more to the topic of gorillas.

It is possible that it was the innuendoes uttered by Captain Fosdyke that now awoke in Montrose something which bore a shadowy resemblance to fortitude. Certainly, until this conversation, he had not intended to revisit the gorilla's cage, one sight of its occupant having been ample for him. Now, stung by the other's slurs, he decided to go and have another look at the brute. It might be that further inspection would make it seem less formidable. He had known this to happen before. The first time he had seen Mr. Schnellenhamer, for example, he had had something not unlike a fit of what our grandparents used to call the "vapours". Now, he could bear him with at least an assumption of nonchalance.

He made his way to the cage, and was presently exchanging glances with the creature through the bars.

Alas, any hope he may have had that familiarity would breed contempt died as their eyes met. Those well-gnashed teeth, that hideous shagginess (a little reminiscent of a stockbroker motoring to Brighton in a fur coat) filled him with all the old familiar qualms. He tottered back and, with some dim idea of pulling himself together, he took a banana from the bag which he had bought at the commissary to see him through the long afternoon. And, as he did so, there suddenly flashed upon him the recollection of an old saw which he had heard in his infancy—The Gorilla Never Forgets. In other words, Do the square thing by gorillas, and they will do the square thing by you.

His heart leaped within him. He pushed the banana through the bars with a cordial smile, and was rejoiced to find it readily accepted. In rapid succession he passed over the others. A banana a day keeps the gorilla away, he felt jubilantly. By standing treat to this animal regardless of cost, he reasoned, he would so ingratiate himself with it as to render the process of geting married in its cage both harmless and agreeable. And it was only when his guest had finished the last of the fruit that he realised with a sickening sense of despair that he had got his facts wrong and that his whole argument, based on a false premise, fell to the ground and became null and void.

It was the elephant who never forgot—not the gorilla. It all came back to him now. He was practically sure that gorillas had never been mentioned in connection with the subject of mnemonics. Indeed, for all he knew, these creatures might be famous for the shortness of their memory—with the result that if later on he were to put on pin-striped trousers and a top-hat and enter this animal's cage with Rosalie on his arm and the studio band playing the Wedding March, all recollection of those bananas would probably have passed completely from its fat head, and it would totally fail to recognise its benefactor.

Moodily crumpling the bag, Montrose turned away. This, he felt, was the end.

I have a tender heart (said Mr. Mulliner), and I dislike to dwell on the spectacle of a human being groaning under the iron heel of Fate. Such morbid gloating, I consider, is better left to the Russians. I will spare you, therefore, a detailed analysis of my distant cousin Montrose's emotions as the long day wore on. Suffice it to say that by a few minutes to five o'clock he had become a mere toad beneath the harrow. He wandered aimlessly to and fro about the lot in the growing dusk, and it seemed to him that the falling shades of evening resembled the cloud that had settled upon his life.

He was roused from these meditations by a collision with some solid body and, coming to himself, discovered that he had been trying to walk through his old friend, George Pybus of the Press department. George was standing beside his car, apparently on the point of leaving for the day.

It is one more proof of Montrose Mulliner's gentle nature that he did not reproach George Pybus for the part he had taken in darkening his outlook. All he did was to gape and say:

"Hullo! You off?"

George Pybus climbed into the car and started the engine.

"Yes," he said, "and I'll tell you why. You know that gorilla?"

With a shudder which he could not repress Montrose said he knew the gorilla.

"Well, I'll tell you something," said George Pybus. "Its agent has been complaining that we've been throwing all the publicity to Luella Benstead and Edmund Wigham. So the boss sent out a hurry call for quick thinking. I told him that you and Rosalie Beamish were planning to get married in its cage, but I've seen Rosalie and she tells me you've backed out. Scarcely the spirit I should have expected in you, Montrose."

Montrose did his best to assume a dignity which he was far from feeling.

"One has one's code," he said. "One dislikes to pander to the morbidity of a sensation-avid . . ."

"Well, it doesn't matter, anyway," said George Pybus, "because I got another idea, and a better one. This one is a pippin. At five sharp this evening, Standard Pacific time, that gorilla's going to be let out of its cage and will menace hundreds. If that doesn't land him on the front page . . ."

Montrose was appalled.

"But you can't do that!" he gasped. "Once let that awful brute out of its cage and it may tear people to shreds."

George Pybus reassured him.

"Nobody of any consequence. The stars have all been notified and are off the lot. So are the directors. Also the executives, all except Mr. Schnellenhamer, who is cleaning up some work in his office. He will be quite safe there, of course. Nobody ever got into Mr. Schnellenhamer's office without waiting four hours in the ante-room. Well, I must be off," said George Pybus. "I've got to dress and get out to Malibu for dinner."

And, so speaking, he trod on the accelerator and was speedily lost to view in the gathering darkness.

It was a few moments later that Montrose, standing rooted to the spot, became aware of a sudden distant uproar: and, looking at his watch, he found that it was precisely five o'clock.

The spot to which Montrose had been standing rooted was in that distant part of the lot where the outdoor sets are kept permanently erected, so that a director with—let us suppose—a London street scene to shoot is able instantly to lay his hands on a back-alley in Algiers, a mediaeval castle, or a Parisian boulevard— none of which is any good to him but which make him feel that the studio is trying to be helpful.

As far as Montrose's eye could reach, Spanish patios, thatched cottages, tenement buildings, estaminets, Oriental bazaars, Kaffir kraals and the residences of licentious New York clubmen stood out against the evening sky: and the fact that he selected as his haven of refuge one of the tenement buildings was due to its being both tallest and nearest.

Like all outdoor sets, it consisted of a front just like the real thing and a back composed of steps and platforms. Up these steps he raced, and on the topmost of the platforms he halted and sat down. He was still unable to think very coherently, but in a dim sort of way he was rather proud of his agility and resource. He felt that he had met a grave crisis well. He did not know what the record was for climbing a flight of steps with a gorilla loose in the neighbourhood, but he would have felt surprise if informed that he had not lowered it.

The uproar which had had such a stimulating effect upon him was now increasing in volume: and, oddly, it appeared to have become stationary. He glanced down through the window of his tenement building, and was astonished to observe below him a dense crowd. And what perplexed him most about this crowd was that it was standing still and looking up.

Scarcely, felt Montrose, intelligent behaviour on the part of a crowd with a savage gorilla after it.

There was a good deal of shouting going on, but he found himself unable to distinguish any words. A woman who stood in the forefront of the throng appeared particularly animated. She was waving an umbrella in a rather neurotic manner.

The whole thing, as I say, perplexed Montrose. What these people thought they were doing, he was unable to say. He was still speculating on the matter when a noise came to his ears.

It was the crying of a baby.

Now, with all these mother-love pictures so popular, the presence of a baby on the lot was not in itself a thing to occasion surprise. It is a very unambitious mother in Hollywood who, the moment she finds herself and child doing well, does not dump the little stranger into a perambulator and wheel it round to the casting-office in the hope of cashing in. Ever since he had been with the Perfecto-Zissbaum, Montrose had seen a constant stream of offspring riding up and trying to break into the game. It was not, accordingly, the fact of a baby being among those present that surprised him. What puzzled him about this particular baby was that it seemed to be so close at hand. Unless the acoustics were playing odd tricks, the infant, he was convinced, was sharing this eyrie of his. And how a mere baby, handicapped probably by swaddling-clothes and a bottle, could have shinned up all those steps bewildered him to such an extent that he moved along the planks to investigate.

And he had not gone three paces when he paused, aghast. With its hairy back towards him, the gorilla was crouching over something that lay on the ground. And another bellow told him that this was the baby in person: and instantly Montrose saw what must have occurred. His reading of magazine stories had taught him once a gorilla gets loose, the first thing it does is to snatch a baby from a perambulator and climb to the nearest high place. It is pure routine.

This, then, was the position in which my distant cousin Montrose found himself at eight minutes past five on this misty evening. A position calculated to test the fortitude of the sternest.

Now, it has been well said that with nervous, highly-strung men like Montrose Mulliner, a sudden call upon their manhood is often enough to revolutionise their whole character. Psychologists have frequently commented on this. We are too ready, they say, to dismiss as cowards those who merely require the stimulus of the desperate emergency to bring out all their latent heroism. The crisis comes, and the craven turns magically into the paladin.

With Montrose, however, this was not the case. Ninety-nine out of a hundred of those who knew him would have scoffed at the idea of him interfering with an escaped gorilla to save the life of a child, and they would have been right. To tiptoe backwards, holding his breath, was with Montrose Mulliner the work of a moment. And it was the fact that he did it so quickly that wrecked his plans. Stubbing a heel on a loose board, in his haste, he fell backwards with a crash. And when the stars had ceased to obscure his vision, he found himself gazing up into the hideous face of the gorilla.

On the last occasion when the two had met, there had been iron bars between them: and even with this safeguard Montrose, as I have said, had shrunk from the creature's evil stare. Now, meeting the brute as it were socially, he experienced a thrill of horror such as had never come to him even in nightmares. Closing his eyes, he began to speculate as to which limb, when it started to tear him limb from limb, the animal would start with.

The one thing of which he was sure was that it would begin operations by uttering a fearful snarl: and when the next sound that came to his ears was a deprecating cough he was so astonished that he could keep his eyes closed no longer. Opening them, he found the gorilla looking at him with an odd, apologetic expression on its face.

"Excuse me, sir," said the gorilla, "but are you by any chance a family man?"

For an instant, on hearing the question, Montrose's astonishment deepened. Then he realised what must have happened. He must have been torn limb from limb without knowing it, and now he was in heaven. Though even this did not altogether satisfy him as an explanation, for he had never expected to find gorillas in heaven.

The animal now gave a sudden start.

"Why, it's you! I didn't recognise you at first. Before going any further, I should like to thank you for those bananas. They were delicious. A little something round about the middle of the afternoon picks one up quite a bit, doesn't it."

Montrose blinked. He could still hear the noise of the crowd below. His bewilderment increased.

"You speak very good English for a gorilla," was all he could find to say. And, indeed, the animal's diction had been remarkable for its purity.

The gorilla waved the compliment aside modestly.

"Oh, well, Balliol, you know. Dear old Balliol. One never quite forgets the lessons one learned at Alma Mater, don't you think? You are not an Oxford man, by any chance?"

"No."

"I came down in '26. Since then I have been knocking around a good deal, and a friend of mine in the circus business suggested to me that the gorilla field was not overcrowded. Plenty of room at the top, was his expression. And I must say," said the gorilla, "I've done pretty well at it. The initial expenditure comes high, of course . . . you don't get a skin like this for nothing . . . but there's virtually no overhead. Of course, to become a co-star in a big feature film, as I have done, you need a good agent. Mine, I am glad to say, is a capital man of business. Stands no nonsense from these motion-picture magnates."

Montrose was not a quick thinker, but he was gradually adjusting his mind to the facts.

"Then you're not a real gorilla?"

"No, no. Synthetic, merely."

"You wouldn't tear anyone limb from limb?"

"My dear chap! My idea of a nice time is to curl up with a good book. I am happiest among my books."

Montrose's last doubts were resolved. He extended his hand cordially.

"Pleased to meet you, Mr. . . . ."

"Waddesley-Davenport. Cyril Waddesley-Davenport. And I am extremely happy to meet you, Mr. . . . ."

"Mulliner. Montrose Mulliner."

They shook hands warmly. From down below came the hoarse uproar of the crowd. The gorilla started.

"The reason I asked you if you were a family man," it said, "was that I hoped you might be able to tell me what is the best method of procedure to adopt with a crying baby. I don't seem able to stop the child. And all my own silly fault, too. I see now I should never have snatched it from its perambulator. If you want to know what is the matter with me, I am too much the artist. I simply had to snatch that baby. It was how I saw the scene. I *felt* it . . . felt it *here*," said the gorilla, thumping the left side of his chest. "And now what?"

Montrose reflected. "Why don't you take it back?"

"To its mother?"

"Certainly."

"But . . ." The gorilla pulled doubtfully at its lower lip. "You have seen that crowd. Did you happen to observe a woman standing in the front row waving an umbrella?"

"The mother?"

"Precisely. Well, you know as well as I do, Mulliner, what an angry woman can do with an umbrella."

Montrose thought again. "It's all right," he said. "I have it. Why don't you sneak down the back steps? Nobody will see you. The crowd's in front, and it's almost dark."

The gorilla's eyes lit up. It slapped Montrose gratefully on the shoulder.

"My dear chap! The very thing. But as regards the baby . . ."

"I will restore it."

"Capital! I don't know how to thank you, dear fellow," said the gorilla. "By Jove, this is going to be a lesson to me in future not to give way to the artist in me. You don't know how I've been feeling about that umbrella. Well, then, in case we don't meet again, always remember that the Lotos Club finds me when I am in New York. Drop in any time you happen to be in that neighbourhood and we'll have a bite to eat and a good talk."

And what of Rosalie, meanwhile? Rosalie was standing beside the bereaved mother, using all her powers of cajolery to try to persuade Captain Jack Fosdyke to go to the rescue: and the Captain was pleading technical difficulties that stood in the way.

"Dash my buttons," he said, "if only I had my elephant gun and my trusty native bearer, 'Mlongi, here, I'd pretty soon know what to do about it. As it is, I'm handicapped."

"But you told me yesterday that you had often strangled gorillas with your bare hands."

"Not *gor*-illas, dear lady—*por*-illas. A species of South American wombat, and very good eating they make, too."

"You're afraid!"

"Afraid? Jack Fosdyke afraid? How they would laugh on the Lower Zambesi if they could hear you say that."

"You are! You, who advised me to have nothing to do with the man I love because he was of a mild and diffident nature."

Captain Jack Fosdyke twirled his moustache.

"Well, I don't notice," he sneered, "that he . . ." He broke off, and his jaw slowly fell. Round the corner of the building was walking Montrose Mulliner. His bearing was erect, even jaunty, and he carried the baby in his arms. Pausing for an instant to allow the busily-clicking cameras to focus him, he advanced towards the stupefied mother and thrust the child into her arms.

"That's that," he said carelessly, dusting his fingers. "No, no, please," he went on. "A mere nothing."

For the mother was kneeling before him, endeavouring to kiss his hand. It was not only maternal love that prompted the action. That morning she had signed up her child at seventy-five dollars a week for the forthcoming picture "Tiny Fingers", and all through these long, anxious minutes it had seemed as though the contract must be a total loss.

Rosalie was in Montrose's arms, sobbing.

"Oh, Monty!"

"There, there!"

"How I misjudged you!"

"We all make mistakes."

"I made a bad one when I listened to that man there," said Rosalie, darting a scornful look at Captain Jack Fosdyke. "Do you realise that, for all his boasting, he would not move a step to save that poor child?"

"Not a step?"

"Not a single step."

"Bad Fosdyke," said Montrose. "Rather bad. Not quite the straight bat, eh?"

"Tchah!" said the baffled man; he turned on his heel and strode away. He was still twirling his moustache, but a lot that got him.

Rosalie was clinging to Montrose.

"You aren't hurt? Was it a fearful struggle?"

"Struggle?" Montrose laughed. "Oh, dear no. There was no struggle. I very soon showed the animal that I was going to stand no nonsense. I generally find with gorillas that all one needs is the power of the human eye. By the way, I've been thinking it over and I realise that I may have been a little unreasonable about that idea of yours. I still would prefer to get married in some nice, quiet church, but if you feel you want the ceremony to take place in that animal's cage, I shall be delighted."

She shivered. "I couldn't do it. I'd be scared."

Montrose smiled understandingly.

"Ah, well," he said, "it is perhaps not unnatural that a delicately nurtured woman should be of less tough stuff than the more rugged male. Shall we be strolling along? I want to look in on Mr. Schnellenhamer, and arrange about that raise of mine. You won't mind waiting while I pop in at his office?"

"My hero!" whispered Rosalie.

29

THE NODDER

THE presentation of the super film, "Baby Boy", at the Bijou Dream in the High Street, had led to an animated discussion in the bar-parlour of the Angler's Rest. Several of our prominent first-nighters had dropped in there for much-needed restorative after the performance, and the conversation had turned to the subject of child stars in the motion-pictures.

"I understand they're all midgets, really," said a Rum and Milk.

"That's what I heard, too," said a Whisky and Splash. "Somebody told me that at every studio in Hollywood they have a special man who does nothing but go round the country, combing the circuses, and when he finds a good midget he signs him up."

Almost automatically we looked at Mr. Mulliner, as if seeking from that un-failing fount of wisdom an authoritative pronouncement on this difficult point. The Sage of the bar-parlour sipped his hot Scotch and lemon for a moment in thought-ful silence.

"The question you have raised," he said at length, "is one that has occupied the minds of thinking men ever since these little excrescences first became popular on the screen. Some argue that mere children could scarcely be so loathsome. Others maintain that a right-minded midget would hardly stoop to some of the things these child stars do. But, then, arising from that, we have to ask ourselves: Are midgets right-minded? The whole thing is very moot."

"Well, this kid we saw tonight," said the Rum and Milk. "This Johnny Bingley. Nobody's going to tell me he's only eight years old."

"In the case of Johnny Bingley," assented Mr. Mulliner, "your intuition has not led you astray. I believe he is in the early forties. I happen to know all about him because it was he who played so important a part in the affairs of my distant connection, Wilmot."

"Was your distant connection Wilmot a midget?"

"No. He was a Nodder."

"A what?"

Mr. Mulliner smiled.

"It is not easy to explain to the lay mind the extremely intricate ramifications of the personnel of a Hollywood motion-picture organisation. Putting is as briefly as possible, a Nodder is something like a Yes-Man, only lower in the social scale.

A Yes-Man's duty is to attend conferences and say 'Yes.' A Nodder's, as the name implies, is to nod. The chief executive throws out some statement of opinion, and looks about him expectantly. This is the cue for the senior Yes-Man to say yes. He is followed, in order of precedence, by the second Yes-Man—or Vice-Yesser, as he is sometimes called—and the junior Yes-Man. Only when all the Yes-Men have yessed, do the Nodders begin to function. They nod."

A Pint of Half-and-Half said it didn't sound much of a job.

"Not very exalted," agreed Mr. Mulliner. "It is a position which you might say, roughly, lies socially somewhere in between that of the man who works the wind-machine and that of a writer of additional dialogue. There is also a class of Untouchables who are known as Nodders' assistants, but this is a technicality with which I need not trouble you. At the time when my story begins, my distant connection Wilmot was a full Nodder. Yet, even so, there is no doubt that he was aiming a little high when he ventured to aspire to the hand of Mabel Potter, the private secretary of Mr. Schnellenhamer, the head of the Perfecto-Zizzbaum Corporation.

Indeed, between a girl so placed and a man in my distant connection's position there could in ordinary circumstances scarcely have been anything in the nature of friendly intercourse. Wilmot owed his entry to her good graces to a combination of two facts—the first, that in his youth he had been brought up on a farm and so was familiar with the customs and habits of birds; the second, that before coming to Hollywood, Miss Potter had been a bird-imitator in vaudeville.

Too little has been written of vaudeville bird-imitators and their passionate devotion to their art: but everybody knows the saying, Once a Bird-Imitator, Always a Bird-Imitator. The Mabel Potter of to-day might be a mere lovely machine for taking notes and tapping out her employer's correspondence, but within her there still burned the steady flame of those high ideals which always animate a girl who has once been accustomed to render to packed houses the liquid notes of the cuckoo, the whip-poor-will, and other songsters who are familiar to you all.

That this was so was revealed to Wilmot one morning when, wandering past an outlying set, he heard raised voices within and, recognizing the silver tones of his adored one, paused to listen. Mabel Potter seemed to be having some kind of an argument with a director.

"Considering," she was saying, "that I only did it to oblige and that it is in no sense a part of my regular duties for which I draw my salary, I must say . . ."

"All right, all right," said the director.

". . . that you have a nerve calling me down on the subject of cuckoos. Let me tell you, Mr. Murgatroyd, that I have made a life-long study of cuckoos and know them from soup to nuts. I have imitated cuckoos in every theatre on every circuit in the land. Not to mention urgent offers from England, Australia and . . ."

"I know, I know," said the director.

". . . South Africa, which I was compelled to turn down because my dear mother, then living, disliked ocean travel. My cuckoo is world-famous. Give me time to go home and fetch it and I'll show you the clipping from the *St. Louis Post-Democrat* which says. . ."

"I know, I know, I know," said the director, "but, all the same, I think I'll have somebody do it who'll do it my way."

The next moment Mabel Potter had swept out, and Wilmot addressed her with respectful tenderness.

"Is something the matter, Miss Potter? Is there anything I can do?"

Mabel Potter was shaking with dry sobs. Her self-esteem had been rudely bruised.

"Well, look," she said. "They ask me as a special favour to come and imitate the call of the cuckoo for this new picture, and when I do it Mr. Murgatroyd says I've done it wrong."

"The hound," breathed Wilmot.

"He says a cuckoo goes Cuckoo, Cuckoo, when everybody who has studied the question knows that what it really goes is Wuckoo, Wuckoo."

"Of course. Not a doubt about it. A distinct 'W' sound."

"As if it had got something wrong with the roof of its mouth."

"Or had omitted to have its adenoids treated."

"Wuckoo, Wuckoo . . . Like that."

"Exactly like that," said Wilmot.

The girl gazed at him with a new friendliness.

"I'll bet you've heard rafts of cuckoos."

"Millions. I was brought up on a farm."

"These know-it-all directors make me tired."

"Me, too," said Wilmot. Then, putting his fate to the touch, to win or lose it all, "I wonder, Miss Potter, if you would care to step round to the commissary and join me in a small coffee?"

She accepted gratefully, and from that moment their intimacy may be said to have begun. Day after day, in the weeks that followed, at such times as their duties would permit, you would see them sitting together either in the commissary or on the steps of some Oriental palace on the outskirts of the lot; he gazing silently up into her face; she, an artist's enthusiasm in her beautiful eyes, filling the air with the liquid note of the Baltimore oriole or possibly the more strident cry of the African buzzard. While ever and anon, by special request, she would hitch up the muscles of the larynx and go "Wuckoo, Wuckoo".

But when at length Wilmot, emboldened, asked her to be his wife, she shook her head.

"No," she said, "I like you, Wilmot. Sometimes I even think that I love you. But I can never marry a mere serf."

"A what was that?"

"A serf. A peon. A man who earns his living by nodding his head at Mr. Schnellenhamer. A Yes-man would be bad enough, but a Nodder!"

She paused, and Wilmot, from sheer force of habit, nodded.

"I am ambitious," proceeded Mabel. "The man I marry must be a king among men . . . well, what I mean, at least a supervisor. Rather than wed a Nodder, I would starve in the gutter."

The objection to this as a practical policy was, of course, that, owing to the weather being so uniformly fine all the year round, there are no gutters in Hollywood. But Wilmot was too distressed to point this out. He uttered a heart-stricken cry not unlike the mating-call of the Alaskan wild duck and began to plead with her. But she was not to be moved.

"We will always be friends," she said, "but marry a Nodder, no."

And with a brief "Wuckoo" she turned away.

There is not much scope or variety of action open to a man whose heart has been shattered and whose romance has proved an empty dream. Practically speaking, only two courses lie before him. He can go out West and begin a new life, or he can drown his sorrow in drink. In Wilmot's case, the former of these alternatives was rendered impossible by the fact that he was out West already. Little wonder, then, that as he sat in his lonely lodging that night his thoughts turned ever more and more insistently to the second.

Like all the Mulliners, my distant connection Wilmot had always been a scrupulously temperate man. Had his love-life but run smoothly, he would have been amply contented with a nut sundae or a malted milk after the day's work. But now, with desolation staring him in the face, he felt a fierce urge toward something with a bit more kick in it.

About half-way down Hollywood Boulevard, he knew, there was a place where, if you knocked twice and whistled "My Country, 'tis of thee," a grille opened and a whiskered face appeared. The Face said "Well?" and you said "Service and Co-operation", and then the door was unbarred and you saw before you the primrose path that led to perdition. And as this was precisely what, in his present mood, Wilmot most desired to locate, you will readily understand how it came about that, some hour and a half later, he was seated at a table in this establishment, feeling a good deal better.

How long it was before he realised that his table had another occupant he could not have said. But came a moment when, raising his glass, he found himself looking into the eyes of a small child in a Lord Fauntleroy costume, in whom he recognized none other than Little Johnny Bingley, the Idol of American Motherhood—the star of this picture, "Baby Boy", which you, gentlemen, have just been witnessing at the Bijou Dream in the High Street.

To say that Wilmot was astonished at seeing this infant in such surroundings would be to overstate the case. After half an hour at this home-from-home the customer is seldom in a condition to be astonished at anything—not even a gamboge elephant in golfing costume. He was, however, sufficiently interested to say "Hullo".

"Hullo," replied the child. "Listen," he went on, placing a cube of ice in his tumbler, "don't tell old Schnellenhamer you saw me here. There's a morality clause in my contract."

"Tell who?" said Wilmot.

"Schnellenhamer."

"How do you spell it?"

"I don't know."

"Nor do I," said Wilmot. "Nevertheless, be that as it may," he continued, holding out his hand impulsively, "he shall never learn from me."

"Who won't?" said the child.

"He won't" said Wilmot.

"Won't what?" asked the child.

"Learn from me," said Wilmot.

"Learn what?" inquired the child.

"I've forgotten," said Wilmot.

They sat for a space in silence, each busy with his own thoughts.

"You're Johnny Bingley, aren't you?" said Wilmot.

"Who is?" said the child.

"You are."

"I'm what?"

"Listen," said Wilmot. "My name's Mulliner. That's what it is. Mulliner. And let them make the most of it."

"Who?"

"I don't know," said Wilmot.

He gazed at his companion affectionately. It was a little difficult to focus him, because he kept flickering, but Wilmot could take the big, broad view about that. If the heart is in the right place, he reasoned, what does it matter if the body flickers?

"You're a good chap, Bingley."

"So are you, Mulliner."

"Both good chaps?"

"Both good chaps."

"Making two in all?" asked Wilmot, anxious to get this straight.

"That's how I work it out."

"Yes, two," agreed Wilmot, ceasing to twiddle his fingers. "In fact, you might say both gentlemen."

"Both gentlemen is correct."

"Then let us see what we have got. Yes," said Wilmot, as he laid down the pencil with which he had been writing figures on the table-cloth. "Here are the final returns, as I get them. Two good chaps, two gentlemen. And yet," he said, frowning in a puzzled way, "that seems to make four, and there are only two of us. However," he went on, "let that go. Immaterial. Not germane to the issue. The fact we have to face, Bingley, is that my heart is heavy."

"You don't say!"

"I do say. Heavy, Hearty. My bing is heavy."

"What's the trouble?"

Wilmot decided to confide in this singularly sympathetic infant. He felt he had never met a child he liked better.

"Well, it's like this."

"What is?"

"This is."

"Like what?"

"I'm telling you. The girl I love won't marry me."

"She won't?"

"So she says."

"Well, well," said the child star commiseratingly. "That's too bad. Spurned your love, did she?"

"You're dern tooting she spurned my love," said Wilmot. "Spurned it good and hard. Some spurning!"

"Well, that's how it goes," said the child star. "What a world!"

"You're right, what a world."

"I shouldn't wonder if it didn't make your heart heavy."

"You bet it makes my heart heavy," said Wilmot, crying softly. He dried his eyes on the edge of the table-cloth. "How can I shake off this awful depression?" he asked.

The child star reflected.

"Well, I'll tell you," he said. "I know a better place than this one. It's out Venice way. We might give it a try."

"We certainly might," said Wilmot.

"And then there's another one down at Santa Monica."

"We'll go there, too," said Wilmot. "The great thing is to keep moving about and seeing new scenes and fresh faces."

"The faces are always nice and fresh down at Venice."

"Then let's go," said Wilmot.

It was eleven o'clock on the following morning that Mr. Schnellenhamer burst in upon his fellow-executive, Mr. Levitsky, with agitation written on every feature of his expressive face. The cigar trembled between his lips.

"Listen!" he said. "Do you know what?"

"Listen!" said Mr. Levitsky. "What?"

"Johnny Bingley has just been in to see me."

"If he wants a raise of salary, talk about the Depression."

"Raise of salary? What's worrying me is how long is he going to be worth the salary he's getting."

"Worth it?" Mr. Levitsky stared. "Johnny Bingley? The Child With The Tear Behind The Smile? The Idol Of American Motherhood?"

"Yes, and how long is he going to be the idol of American Motherhood after American Motherhood finds out he's a midget from Connolly's Circus, and an elderly, hard-boiled midget, at that?"

"Well, nobody knows that but you and me."

"Is that so?" said Mr. Schnellenhamer. "Well, let me tell you, he was out on a toot last night with one of my Nodders, and he comes to me this morning and says he couldn't actually swear he told this guy he was a midget, but, on the other hand, he rather thinks he must have done. He says that between the time they were thrown out of Mike's Place and the time he stabbed the waiter with the pickle-fork there's a sort of gap in his memory, a kind of blur, and he thinks it may have been then, because by that time they had got pretty confidential and he doesn't think he would have had any secrets from him."

All Mr. Levitsky's nonchalance had vanished.

"But if this fellow—what's his name?"

"Mulliner."

"If this fellow Mulliner sells this story to the Press, Johnny Bingley won't be worth a nickel to us. And his contract calls for two more pictures at two hundred and fifty thousand each."

"That's right."

"But what are we to do?"

"You tell me."

Mr. Levitsky pondered.

"Well, first of all," he said, "we'll have to find out if this Mulliner really knows."

"We can't ask him."

"No, but we'll be able to tell by his manner. A fellow with a stranglehold on the Corporation like that isn't going to be able to go on acting same as he's always done. What sort of fellow is he?"

"The ideal Nodder," said Mr. Schnellenhamer regretfully. "I don't know when I've had a better. Always on his cues. Never tries to alibi himself by saying he had a stiff neck. Quiet . . . Respectful . . . What's that word that begins with a 'd'?"

"Damn?"

"Deferential. And what's the word beginning with an 'o'?"

"Oyster?"

"Obsequious. That's what he is. Quiet, respectful, deferential, and obsequious—that's Mulliner."

"Well, then it'll be easy to see. If we find him suddenly not being all what you said . . . if he suddenly ups and starts to throw his weight about, understand what I mean . . . why, then we'll know that he knows that Little Johhny Bingley is a midget."

"And then?"

"Why, then we'll have to square him. And do it right, too. No half-measures."

Mr. Schnellenhamer tore at his hair. He seemed disappointed that he had no straws to stick in it.

"Yes," he agreed, the brief spasm over, "I suppose it's the only way. Well, it won't be long before we know. There's a story-conference in my office at noon, and he'll be there to nod."

"We must watch him like a lynx."

"Like a what?"

"Lynx. Sort of wild-cat. It watches things."

"Ah," said Mr. Schnellenhamer, "I get you now. What confused me at first was that I thought you meant golf-links."

The fears of the two magnates, had they but known it, were quite without foundation. If Wilmot Mulliner had ever learned the fatal secret, he had certainly not remembered it next morning. He had woken that day with a confused sense of having passed through some soul-testing experience, but as regarded details his mind was a blank. His only thought as he entered Mr. Schnellenhamer's office for the conference was a rooted conviction that, unless he kept very still, his head would come apart in the middle.

Nevertheless, Mr. Schnellenhamer, alert for significant and sinister signs, plucked anxiously at Mr. Levitsky's sleeve.

"Look!"

"Eh?"

"Did you see that?"

"See what?"

"That fellow Mulliner. He sort of quivered when he caught my eye, as if with unholy glee."

"He did?"

"It seemed to me he did."

As a matter of fact, what had happened was that Wilmot, suddenly sighting his employer, had been unable to restrain a quick shudder of agony. It seemed to him that somebody had been painting Mr. Schnellenhamer yellow. Even at the best of times, the President of the Perfecto-Zizzbaum, considered as an object for the eye, was not everybody's money. Flickering at the rims and a dull orange in colour, as he appeared to be now, he had smitten Wilmot like a blow, causing him to wince like a salted snail.

Mr. Levitsky was regarding the young man thoughtfully.

"I don't like his looks," he said.

"Nor do I," said Mr. Schnellenhamer.

"There's a kind of horrid gloating in his manner."

"I noticed it, too."

"See how he's just buried his head in his hands, as if he were thinking out dreadful plots?"

"I believe he knows everything."

"I shouldn't wonder if you weren't right. Well, let's start the conference and see what he does when the time comes for him to nod. That's when he'll break out, if he's going to."

As a rule, these story-conferences were the part of his work which Wilmot most enjoyed. His own share in them was not exacting, and, as he often said, you met such interesting people.

To-day, however, though there were eleven of the studio's weirdest authors present, each well worth more than a cursory inspection, he found himself unable to overcome the dull listlessness which had been gripping him since he had first gone to the refrigerator that morning to put ice on his temples. As the poet Keats put it in his "Ode to a Nightingale", his head ached and a drowsy numbness pained his sense. And the sight of Mabel Potter, recalling to him those dreams of happiness which he had once dared to dream and which now could never come to fulfilment, plunged him still deeper into the despondency. If he had been a character in a Russian novel, he would have gone and hanged himself in the barn. As it was, he merely sat staring before him and keeping perfectly rigid.

Most people, eyeing him, would have been reminded of a corpse which had been several days in the water: but Mr. Schnellenhamer thought he looked like a leopard about to spring, and he mentioned this to Mr. Levitsky in an undertone.

"Bend down. I want to whisper."

"What's the matter?"

"He looks to me just like a crouching leopard."

"I beg your pardon," said Mabel Potter, who, her duty being to take notes of the proceedings, was seated at her employer's side. "Did you say 'crouching leopard' or 'grouchy shepherd'?"

Mr. Schnellenhamer started. He had forgotten the risk of being overheard. He felt that he had been incautious.

"Don't put that down," he said. "It wasn't part of the conference. Well, now, come on, come on," he proceeded, with a pitiful attempt at the bluffness which he used at conferences, "let's get at it. Where did we leave off yesterday, Miss Potter?"

Mabel consulted her notes.

"Cabot Delancy, a scion of an old Boston family, has gone to try to reach the North Pole in a submarine, and he's on an iceberg, and the scenes of his youth are passing before his eyes."

"What scenes?"

"You didn't get to what scenes."

"Then that's where we begin," said Mr. Schnellenhamer. "What scenes pass before this fellow's eyes?"

One of the authors, a weedy young man in spectacles, who had come to Hollywood to start a Gyffte Shoppe and had been scooped up in the studio's drag-net and forced into the writing-staff much against his will, said why not a scene where Cabot Delancy sees himself dressing his window with kewpie-dolls and fancy notepaper.

"Why kewpie-dolls?" asked Mr. Schnellenhamer testily.

The author said they were a good selling line.

"Listen!" said Mr. Schnellenhamer brusquely. "This Delancy never sold anything in his life. He's a millionaire. What we want is something romantic."

A diffident old gentleman suggested a polo-game.

"No good," said Mr. Schnellenhamer. "Who cares anything about polo? When you're working on a picture you've got to bear in mind the small-town population of the Middle West. Aren't I right?"

"Yes," said the senior Yes-man.

"Yes," said the Vice-Yesser.

"Yes," said the junior Yes-man.

And all the Nodders nodded. Wilmot, waking with a start to the realisation that duty called, hurriedly inclined his throbbing head. The movement made him feel as if a red-hot spike had been thrust through it, and he winced. Mr. Levitsky plucked at Mr. Schnellenhamer's sleeve.

"He scowled!"

"I thought he scowled, too."

"As it might be with sullen hate."

"That's the way it struck me. Keep watching him."

The conference proceeded. Each of the authors put forward a suggestion, but it was left for Mr. Schnellenhamer to solve what had begun to seem an insoluble problem.

"I've got it," said Mr. Schnellenhamer. "He sits on this iceberg and he seems to see himself—he's always been an athlete, you understand—he seems to see himself scoring the winning goal in one of these polo-games. Everybody's interested in polo nowadays. Aren't I right?"

"Yes," said the senior Yes-man.

"Yes," said the Vice-Yesser.

"Yes," said the junior Yes-man.

Wilmot was quicker off the mark this time. A conscientious employee, he did not intend mere physical pain to cause him to fall short in his duty. He nodded quickly, and returned to the "ready" a little surprised that his head was still attached to its moorings. He had felt so certain it was going to come off that time.

The effect of this quiet, respectful, deferential and obsequious nod on Mr. Schnellenhamer was stupendous. The anxious look had passed from his eyes. He was convinced now that Wilmot knew nothing. The magnate's confidence mounted high. He proceeded briskly. There was a new strength in his voice.

"Well," he said, "that's set for one of the visions. We want two, and the other's got to be something that'll pull in the women. Something touching and sweet and tender."

The young author in spectacles thought it would be kind of touching and sweet and tender if Cabot Delancy remembered the time he was in his Gyffte Shoppe and a beautiful girl came in and their eyes met as he wrapped up her order of Indian bead-work.

Mr. Schnellenhamer banged the desk.

"What is all this about Gyffte Shoppes and Indian bead-work? Don't I tell you this guy is a prominent clubman? Where would he get a Gyffte Shoppe? Bring a girl into it, yes—so far you're talking sense. And let him gaze into her eyes—certainly he can gaze into her eyes. But not in any Gyffte Shoppe. It's got to be a lovely, peaceful, old-world exterior set, with bees humming and doves cooing and trees waving in the breeze. Listen!" said Mr. Schnellenhamer. "It's spring, see, and all around is the beauty of Nature in the first shy sun-glow. The grass that waves. The buds that . . . what's the word?"

"Bud?" suggested Mr. Levitsky.

"No, it's two syllables," said Mr. Schnellenhamer, speaking a little self-consciously, for he was modestly proud of knowing words of two syllables.

"Burgeon?" hazarded an author who looked like a trained seal.

"I beg your pardon," said Mabel Potter. "A burgeon's a sort of fish."

"You're thinking of sturgeon," said the author.

"Excuse it, please," murmured Mabel. "I'm not strong on fishes. Birds are what I'm best at."

"We'll have birds, too," said Mr. Schnellenhamer jovially. "All the birds you want. Especially the cuckoo. And I'll tell you why. It gives us a nice little comedy touch. This fellow's with this girl in this old-world garden where everything's burgeoning . . . and when I say burgeoning I mean burgeoning. That burgeoning's got to be done *right*, or somebody'll get fired . . . and they're locked in a close embrace. Hold as long as the Philadelphia censors'll let you, and then comes your nice comedy touch. Just as these two young folks are kissing each other without a thought of anything else in the world, suddenly a cuckoo close by goes 'Cuckoo! Cuckoo!' Meaning how goofy they are. That's good for a laugh, isn't it?"

"Yes," said the senior Yes-man.

"Yes," said the Vice-Yesser.

"Yes," said the junior Yes-man.

And then, while the Nodders' heads—Wilmot's among them—were trembling

on their stalks preparatory to the downward swoop, there spoke abruptly a clear
female voice. It was the voice of Mabel Potter, and those nearest her were able to
see that her face was flushed and her eyes gleaming with an almost fanatic light.
All the bird-imitator in her had sprung to sudden life.

"I beg your pardon, Mr. Schnellenhamer, that's wrong."

A deadly stillness had fallen on the room. Eleven authors sat transfixed in their
chairs, as if wondering if they could believe their twenty-two ears. Mr. Schnellenhamer uttered a little gasp. Nothing like this had ever happened to him before in
his long experience.

"What did you say?" he asked incredulously. "Did you say that I . . . I . . .
was wrong?"

Mabel met his gaze steadily. So might Joan of Arc have faced her inquisitors.

"The cuckoo," she said, "does not go 'Cuckoo, cuckoo' . . . it goes 'Wuckoo,
wuckoo'. A distinct 'W' sound."

A gasp at the girl's temerity ran through the room. In the eyes of several of
those present there was something that was not far from a tear. She seemed so
young, so fragile.

Mr. Schnellenhamer's joviality had vanished. He breathed loudly through his
nose. He was plainly mastering himself with a strong effort.

"So I don't know the low-down on cuckoos?"

"Wuckoos," corrected Mabel.

"Cuckoos!"

"Wuckoos!"

"You're fired," said Mr. Schnellenhamer.

Mabel flushed to the roots of her hair.

"It's unfair and unjust," she cried. "I'm right, and anybody who's studied
cuckoos will tell you I'm right. When it was a matter of burgeons, I was mistaken,
and I admitted that I was mistaken, and apologised. But when it comes to cuckoos,
let me tell you you're talking to somebody who has imitated the call of the cuckoo
from the Palace, Portland, Oregon, to the Hippodrome, Sumquamset, Maine, and
taken three bows after every performance. Yes, sir, I know my cuckoos! And if
you don't believe me I'll put it up to Mr. Mulliner there, who was born and bred
on a farm and has heard more cuckoos in his time than a month of Sundays. Mr.
Mulliner, how about it? Does the cuckoo go 'Cuckoo'?"

Wilmot Mulliner was on his feet, and his eyes met hers with the love-light in
them. The spectacle of the girl he loved in distress and appealing to him for aid
had brought my distant connection's better self to the surface as if it had been
jerked up on the end of a pin. For one brief instant he had been about to seek
safety in a cowardly cringing to the side of those in power. He loved Mabel Potter
madly, desperately, he had told himself in that short, sickening moment of pol-
troonery, but Mr. Schnellenhamer was the man who signed the cheques: and the
thought of risking his displeasure and being summarily dismissed had appalled

him. For there is no spiritual anguish like that of the man who, grown accustomed to opening the crackling envelope each Saturday morning, reaches out for it one day and finds that it is not there. The thought of the Perfecto-Zizzbaum cashier ceasing to be a fount of gold and becoming just a man with a walrus moustache had turned Wilmot's spine to Jell-o. And for an instant, as I say, he had been on the point of betraying this sweet girl's trust.

But now, gazing into her eyes, he was strong again. Come what might, he would stand by her to the end.

"No!" he thundered, and his voice rang through the room like a trumpet blast. "No, it does not go 'Cuckoo'. You have fallen into a popular error, Mr. Schnellenhamer. The bird wooks, and, by heaven, I shall never cease to maintain that it wooks, no matter what offence I give to powerful vested interests. I endorse Miss Potter's view wholeheartedly and without compromise. I say the cuckoo does not cook. It wooks, so make the most of it!"

There was a sudden whirring noise. It was Mabel Potter shooting through the air into his arms.

"Oh, Wilmot!" she cried.

He glared over her back-hair at the magnate.

"'Wuckoo, wuckoo!" he shouted, almost savagely.

He was surprised to observe that Mr. Schnellenhamer and Mr. Levitsky were hurriedly clearing the room. Authors had begun to stream through the door in a foaming torrent. Presently, he and Mabel were alone with the two directors of the destinies of the Perfecto-Zizzbaum Corporation, and Mr. Levitsky was carefully closing the door, while Mr. Schnellenhamer came towards him, a winning, if nervous, smile upon his face.

"There, there, Mulliner," he said.

And Mr. Levitsky said "There, there," too.

"I can understand your warmth, Mulliner," said Mr. Schnellenhamer. "Nothing is more annoying to the man who knows than to have people making these silly mistakes. I consider the firm stand you have taken as striking evidence of loyalty to the Corporation."

"Me, too," said Mr. Levitsky. "I was admiring it myself."

"For you are loyal to the Corporation, Mulliner, I know. You would never do anything to prejudice its interests, would you?"

"Sure he wouldn't," said Mr. Levitsky.

"You would not reveal the Corporation's little secrets, thereby causing it alarm and despondency, would you, Mulliner?"

"Certainly he wouldn't," said Mr. Levitsky. "Especially now that we're going to make him an executive."

"An executive?" said Mr. Schnellenhamer, starting.

"An executive," repeated Mr. Levitsky firmly. "With brevet rank as a brother-in-law."

Mr. Schnellenhamer was silent for a moment. He seemed to be having a little trouble in adjusting his mind to this extremely drastic step. But he was a man of sterling sense, who realised that there are times when only the big gesture will suffice.

"That's right," he said. "I'll notify the legal department and have the contract drawn up right away."

"That will be agreeable to you, Mulliner?" inquired Mr. Levitsky anxiously. "You will consent to become an executive?"

Wilmot Mulliner drew himself up. It was his moment. His head was still aching, and he would have been the last person to claim that he knew what all this was about: but this he did know—that Mabel was nestling in his arms and that his future was secure.

"I . . ."

Then words failed him, and he nodded.

30

THE JUICE OF AN ORANGE

A SUDDEN cat shot in through the door of the bar-parlour of the Anglers' Rest, wearing the unmistakable air of a cat which has just been kicked by a powerful foot. At the same moment there came from without sounds indicative of a strong man's wrath: and recognising the voice of Ernest Biggs, the inn's popular landlord, we stared at one another in amazement. For Ernest had always been celebrated for the kindliness of his disposition. The last man, one would have thought, to raise a number eleven shoe against a faithful friend and good mouser.

It was a well-informed Rum and Milk who threw light on the mystery.

"He's on a diet," said the Rum and Milk. "On account of gout."

Mr. Mulliner sighed.

"A pity," he said, "that dieting, so excellent from a purely physical standpoint, should have this unfortunate effect on the temper. It seems to sap the self-control of the stoutest."

"Quite," said the Rum and Milk. "My stout Uncle Henry . . ."

"And yet," proceeded Mr. Mulliner, "I have known great happiness result from dieting. Take, for example, the case of my distant connection, Wilmot."

"Is that the Wilmot you were telling us about the other night?"

"Was I telling you about my distant connection Wilmot the other night?"

"The fellow I mean was a Nodder at Hollywood, and he found out that the company's child star, Little Johnny Bingley, was a midget, so to keep his mouth shut they made him an executive, and he married a girl named Mabel Potter."

"Yes, that was Wilmot. You are mistaken, however, in supposing that he married Mabel Potter at the conclusion of that story."

"But you distinctly said she fell into his arms."

"Many a girl has fallen into a man's arms," said Mr. Mulliner gravely, "only to wriggle out of them at a later date."

We left Wilmot, as you very rightly say (said Mr. Mulliner) in an extremely satisfactory position, both amatory and financial. The only cloud there had been ever between himself and Mabel Potter had been due, if you recollect, to the fact that she considered his attitude towards Mr. Schnellenhamer, the head of the Corporation, too obsequious and deferential. She resented his being a Nodder. Then he was promoted to the rank of executive, so there he was, reconciled to the girl he loved and in receipt of a most satisfactory salary. Little wonder that he felt that the happy ending had arrived.

One effect of his new-found happiness on my distant connection Wilmot was to fill him with the utmost benevolence and goodwill towards all humanity. His sunny smile was the talk of the studio, and even got a couple of lines in Louella Parsons' column in the *Los Angles Examiner*. Love, I believe, often has this effect on a young man. He went about the place positively seeking for ways of doing his fellow human beings good turns. And when one morning Mr. Schnellenhamer summoned him to his office Wilmot's chief thought was that he hoped that the magnate was going to ask some little favour of him, because it would be a real pleasure to him to oblige.

He found the head of the Perfecto-Zizzbaum Corporation looking grave.

"Times are hard, Mulliner," said Mr. Schnellenhamer.

"And yet," replied Wilmot cheerily, "there is still joy in the world; still the happy laughter of children and the singing of bluebirds."

"That's all right about bluebirds," said Mr. Schnellenhamer, "but we've got to cut down expenses. We'll have to do some salary-slicing."

Wilmot was concerned. This seemed to him morbid.

"Don't dream of cutting your salary, Chief," he urged. "You're worth every cent of it. Besides, reflect. If you reduce your salary, it will cause alarm. People will go about saying that things must be in a bad way. It is your duty to the community to be a man and bite the bullet and, no matter how much it may irk you, to stick to your eight hundred thousand dollars a year like glue."

"I wasn't thinking of cutting my salary so much," said Mr. Schnellenhamer. "Yours, more, if you see what I mean."

"Oh, mine?" cried Wilmot bouyantly. "Ah, that's different. That's another thing altogether. Yes, that's certainly an idea. If you think it will be of assistance and help to ease matters for all these dear chaps on the P-Z lot, by all means cut my salary. About how much were you thinking of?"

"Well, you're getting fifteen hundred a week."

"I know, I know," said Wilmot. "It's a lot of money."

"I thought if we said seven hundred and fifty from now on . . ."

"It's an awkward sort of sum," said Wilmot dubiously. "Not round, if you follow me. I would suggest five hundred."

"Or four?"

"Four, if you prefer it."

"Very well," said Mr. Schnellenhamer. "Then from now on we'll put you on the books as three. It's a more convenient sum than four," he explained. "Makes less book-keeping."

"Of course," said Wilmot. "Of course. What a perfectly lovely day it is, is it not? I was thinking as I came along here that I had never seen the sun shining more brightly. One just wanted to be out and about, doing lots of good on every side. Well, I'm delighted if I have been able to do anything in my humble way to make things easier for you, Chief. It has been a real pleasure."

And with a merry "Tra-la" he left the room and made his way to the commissary, where he had arranged to give Mabel Potter lunch.

She was a few minutes late in arriving, and he presumed that she had been detained on some matter by Mr. Schnellenhamer, whose private secretary, if you remember, she was. When she arrived, he was distressed to see that her lovely face was overcast, and he was just about to say something about bluebirds when she spoke abruptly.

"What is all this I hear from Mr. Schnellenhamer?"

"I don't quite understand," said Wilmot.

"About your taking a salary cut."

"Oh, that. I see. I suppose he drafted out a new agreement for you to take to the legal department. Yes," said Wilmot, "Mr. Schnellenhamer sent for me this morning, and I found him very worried, poor chap. There is a world-wide money shortage at the moment, you see, and industry is in a throttled state and so on. He was very upset about it. However, we talked things over, and fortunately we found a way out. I've reduced my salary. It has eased things all round."

Mabel's face was stony.

"Has it?" she said bitterly. "Well, let me tell you that, as far as I'm concerned, it has done nothing of the sort. You have failed me, Wilmot. You have forfeited my respect. You have proved to me that you are still the same cold-asparagus-backboned worm who used to cringe to Mr. Schnellenhamer. I thought, when you became an executive, that you would have the soul of an executive. I find that at heart you are still a Nodder. The man I used to think you—the strong, dominant man of my dreams—would have told Mr. Schnellenhamer to take a running jump up an alley at the mere hint of a cut in the weekly envelope. Ah, yes, how woefully I have been deceived in you. I think that we had better consider our engagement at an end."

Wilmot tottered.

"You are not taking up my option?" he gasped.

"No. You are at liberty to make arrangements elsewhere. I can never marry a poltroon."

"But, Mabel . . ."

"No. I mean it. Of course," she went on more gently, "if one day you should prove yourself worthy of my love, that is another matter. Give me evidence that you are a man among men, and then I'm not saying. But, meanwhile, the scenario reads as I have outlined."

And with a cold, averted face she passed on into the commissary alone.

The effect of this thunderbolt on Wilmot Mulliner may readily be imagined. It had never occurred to him that Mabel might take this attitude towards what

seemed to him an action of the purest altruism. Had he done wrong, he asked himself. Surely, to bring the light of happiness into the eyes of a motion-picture magnate was not a culpable thing. And yet Mabel thought otherwise, and, so thinking,
had given him the air. Life, felt Wilmot, was very difficult.

For some moments he debated within himself the possibility of going back to his
employer and telling him he had changed his mind. But no, he couldn't do that.
It would be like taking chocolate from an already chocolated child. There seemed
to Wilmot Mulliner nothing that he could do. It was just one of those things. He
went into the commissary, and, taking a solitary table at some distance from the
one where the haughty girl sat, ordered Hungarian goulash, salad, two kinds of
pie, ice-cream, cheese and coffee. For he had always been a good trencherman, and
sorrow seemed to sharpen his appetite.

And this was so during the days that followed. He found himself eating a good
deal more than usual, because food seemed to dull the pain at his heart. Unfortunately, in doing so, it substituted another in his stomach.

The advice all good doctors give to those who have been disappointed in love
is to eat lightly. Fail to do this, and the result is as inevitable as the climax of a
Greek tragedy. No man, however gifted his gastric juices, can go on indefinitely
brooding over a lost love and sailing into the starchy foods simultaneously. It was
not long before indigestion gripped Wilmot, and for almost the first time in his
life he was compelled to consult a physician. And the one he selected was a man
of drastic views.

"On rising," he told Wilmot, "take the juice of an orange. For luncheon, the
juice of an orange. And for dinner the juice—"—he paused a moment before
springing the big surprise—"of an orange. For the rest, I am not an advocate of
nourishment between meals, but I am inclined to think that, should you become
faint during the day—or possibly the night—there will be no harm in your taking
. . . well, yes, I really see no reason why you should not take the juice of—let us
say—an orange."

Wilmot stared. His manner resembled that of a wolf on the steppes of Russia
who, expecting a peasant, is fobbed off with a wafer biscuit.

"But aren't you leaving out something?"

"I beg your pardon?"

"How about steaks?"

"Most decidedly no steaks."

"Chops, then?"

"Absolutely no chops."

"But the way I figure it out—check my figures in case I'm wrong—you're
suggesting that I live solely on orange-juice."

"On the juice of an orange," corrected the doctor. "Precisely. Take your orange.
Divide it into two equal parts. Squeeze on a squeezer. Pour into a glass . . . or a
cup," he added, for he was not the man to be finicky about small details, "and

drink."

Put like that, it sounded a good and even amusing trick, but Wilmot left the consulting-room with his heart bowed down. He was a young man who all his life had been accustomed to take his meals in a proper spirit of seriousness, grabbing everything there was and, if there was no more, filling up with biscuits and butter. The vista which his doctor had opened up struck him as bleak to a degree, and I think that, had not a couple of wild cats at this moment suddenly started a rather ugly fight inside him, he would have abandoned the whole project.

The cats, however, decided him. He stopped at the nearest market and ordered a crate of oranges to be dispatched to his address. Then, having purchased a squeezer, he was ready to begin the new life.

It was some four days later that Mr. Schnellenhamer, as he sat in conference with his fellow-magnate, Mr. Levitsky—for these zealous men, when they had no one else to confer with, would confer with one another—was informed that Mr. Eustiss Vanderleigh desired to see him. A playwright, this Vanderleigh, of the Little Theatre school, recently shipped to Hollywood in a crate of twelve.

"What does he want?" asked Mr. Schnellenhamer.

"Probably got some grievance of some kind," said Mr. Levitsky. "These playwrights make me tired. One sometimes wishes the old silent days were back again."

"Ah," said Mr. Schnellenhamer wistfully. "Well, send him in."

Eustiss Vanderleigh was a dignified young man with tortoiseshell-rimmed spectacles and flowing front hair. His voice was high and plaintive.

"Mr. Schnellenhamer," he said. "I wish to know what rights I have in this studio."

"Listen . . ." began the magnate truculently.

Eustiss Vanderleigh held up a slender hand.

"I do not allude to my treatment as an artist and a craftsman. With regard to that I have already said my say. Though I have some slight reputation as a maker of plays, I have ceased to complain that my rarest scenes are found unsuitable for the medium of the screen. Nor do I dispute the right, however mistaken, of a director to assert that my subtlest lines are—to adopt his argot—'cheesy'. All this I accept as part of the give and take of Hollywood life. But there is a limit, and what I wish to ask you, Mr. Schnellenhamer, is this: Am I to be hit over the head with crusty rolls?"

"Who's been hitting you over the head with crusty rolls?"

"One of your executives. A man named Mulliner. The incident to which I allude occurred to-day at the luncheon hour in the commissary. I was entertaining a friend at the meal, and, as he seemed unable to make up his mind as to the precise nature of the refreshment which he desired, I began to read aloud to him the various items on the bill of fare. I had just mentioned roast pork with boiled potatoes and cabbage and was about to go on to Mutton Stew Joan Clarkson, when

I was conscious of a violent blow or buffet on the top of the head. And turning I perceived this man Mulliner with a shattered roll in his hand and on his face the look of a soul in torment. Upon my inquiring into his motives for the assault, he merely uttered something which I understood to be 'You and your roast pork!' and went on sipping his orange-juice—a beverage of which he appears to be inordinately fond, for I have seen him before in the commissary and he seems to take nothing else. However, that is neither here nor there. The question to which I desire an answer is this: How long is this going on? Must I expect, whenever I enter the studio's place of refreshment, to undergo furious assaults with crusty rolls, or are you prepared to exert your authority and prevent a repetition of the episode?"

Mr. Schnellenhamer stirred uneasily. "I'll look into it."

"If you would care to feel the bump or contusion . . .?"

"No, you run along. I'm busy now with Mr. Levitsky."

The playwright withdrew, and Mr. Schnellenhamer frowned thoughtfully.

"Something'll have to be done about this Mulliner," he said. "I don't like the way he's acting. Did you notice him at the conference yesterday?"

"Not specially. What did he do?"

"Well, listen," said Mr. Schnellenhamer, "he didn't give me the idea of willing service and selfless co-operation. Every time I said anything, it seemed to me he did something funny with the corner of his mouth. Drew it up in a twisted way that looked kind of . . . what's that word beginning with an 's'?"

"Cynical?"

"No, a snickle is a thing you cut corn with. Ah, I've got it. Sardinic. Every time I spoke he looked sardinic."

Mr. Levitsky was out of his depth.

"Like a sardine, do you mean?"

"No, not like a sardine. Sort of cold and sneering, like Glutz of the Medulla-Oblongata the other day on the golf-links when he asked me how many I'd taken in the rough and I said one."

"Maybe his nose was tickling."

"Well, I don't pay my staff to have tickling noses in the company's time. If they want tickling noses, they must have them after hours. Besides, it couldn't have been that, or he'd have scratched it. No, the way it looks to me, this Mulliner has got too big for his boots and is seething with rebellion. We've another story-conference this afternoon. You watch him and you'll see what I mean. Kind of tough and ugly he looks, like something out of a gangster film."

"I get you. Sardinic."

"That's the very word," said Mr. Schnellenhamer. "And if it goes on I'll know what to do about it. There's no room in this corporation for fellows who sit around drawing up the corners of their mouths and looking sardinical."

"Or hitting playwrights with crusty rolls."

"No, there you go too far," said Mr. Schnellenhamer. "Playwrights ought to be hit with crusty rolls."

Meanwhile, unaware that his bread-and-butter—or, as it would be more correct to say, his orange-juice—was in danger, Wilmot Mulliner was sitting in a corner of the commissary, glowering sullenly at the glass which had contained his midday meal. He had fallen into a reverie, and was musing on some of the characters in History whom he most admired . . . Genghis Khan . . . Jack the Ripper . . . Attila the Hun . . .

There was a chap, he was thinking. That Attila. Used to go about taking out people's eyeballs and piling them in neat heaps. The ideal way, felt Wilmot, of getting through the long afternoon. He was sorry Attila was no longer with us. He thought the man would have made a nice friend.

For the significance of the scene which I have just described will not have been lost on you. In the short space of four days, dieting had turned my distant connection Wilmot from a thing of almost excessive sweetness and light to a soured misanthrope.

It has sometimes seemed to me (said Mr. Mulliner, thoughtfully sipping his hot Scotch and lemon) that to the modern craze for dieting may be attributed all the unhappiness which is afflicting the world to-day. Women, of course, are chiefly responsible. They go in for these slimming systems, their sunny natures become warped, and they work off the resultant venom on their men-folk. These, looking about them for someone they can take it out of, pick on the males of the neighbouring country, who themselves are spoiling for a fight because their own wives are on a diet, and before you know where you are war has broken out with all its attendant horrors.

This is what happened in the case of China and Japan. It is this that lies at the root of all the unpleasantness in the Polish Corridor. And look at India. Why is there unrest in India? Because its inhabitants eat only an occasional handful of rice. The day when Mahatma Gandhi sits down to a good juicy steak and follows it up with roly-poly pudding and a spot of Stilton you will see the end of all this nonsense of Civil Disobedience.

Till then we must expect Trouble, Disorder . . . in a word, Chaos.

However, these are deep waters. Let us return to my distant connection, Wilmot.

In the brief address which he had made when prescribing, the doctor, as was his habit, had enlarged upon the spiritual uplift which might be expected to result from an orange-juice diet. The juice of an orange, according to him, was not only rich in the essential vitamins but contained also mysterious properties which strengthened and enlarged the soul. Indeed, the picture he had drawn of the soul squaring its elbows and throwing out its chest had done quite a good deal at the time to soothe the anguish that had afflicted Wilmot when receiving his sentence.

After all, the young man had felt, unpleasant though it might be to suffer the physical torments of a starving python, it was jolly to think that one was to become a sort of modern St. Francis of Assisi.

And now, as we have seen, the exact opposite had proved to be the case. Now that he had been called upon to convert himself into a mere vat or container for orange-juice, Wilmot Mulliner had begun to look on his fellow-man with a sullen loathing. His ready smile had become a tight-lipped sneer. And as for his eye, once so kindly, it could have been grafted on to the head of a man-eating shark and no questions asked.

The advent of a waitress, who came to clear away his glass, and the discovery that he was alone in the deserted commissary, awoke Wilmot to a sense of the passage of time. At two o'clock he was due in Mr. Schnellenhamer's office, to assist at the story-conference to which the latter had alluded in his talk with Mr. Levitsky. He glanced at his watch and saw that it was time to be moving.

His mood was one of sullen rebellion. He thought of Mr. Schnellenhamer with distaste. He was feeling that if Mr. Schnellenhamer started to throw his weight about, he, Wilmot Mulliner would know what to do about it.

In these circumstances, the fact that Mr. Schnellenhamer, having missed his lunch that day owing to the numerous calls upon him, had ordered a plateful of sandwiches to be placed upon his desk takes upon itself no little of the dramatic. A scenario-writer, informed of the facts of the case, would undoubtedly have thought of those sandwiches as Sandwiches of Fate.

It was not at once that Wilmot perceived the loathsome objects. For some minutes only the familiar features of a story-conference penetrated to his consciousness. Mr. Schnellenhamer was criticising a point that had arisen in connection with the scenario under advisement.

"This guy, as I see it," he was saying, alluding to the hero of the story, "is in a spot. He's seen his wife kissing a fellow and, not knowing it was really her brother, he's gone off to Africa, shooting big game, and here's this lion got him down and is starting to chew the face off him. He gazes into its hideous eyes, he hears its fearful snarls, and he knows the end is near. And where I think you're wrong, Levitsky, is in saying that that's the spot for our big cabaret sequence."

"A vision," explained Mr. Levitsky.

"That's all right about visions. I don't suppose there's a man in the business stronger for visions than I am. But only in their proper place. What I say is what we need here is for the United States Marines to arrive. Aren't I right?"

He paused and looked about him like a hostess collecting eyes at a dinner-party. The Yessers yessed. The Nodders' heads bent like poplars in a breeze.

"Sure I am," said Mr. Schnellenhamer. "Make a note, Miss Potter."

And with a satisfied air he reached out and started eating a sandwich.

Now, the head of the Perfecto-Zizzbaum Motion Picture Corporation was not one of those men who can eat sandwiches aloofly and, as it were, surreptitiously. When he ate a sandwich there was no concealment or evasion. He was patently, for all eyes to see, all ears to hear, a man eating a sandwich. There was a brio, a gusto, about the performance which stripped it of all disguise. His sandwich flew before him like a banner.

The effect on Wilmot Mulliner was stupendous. As I say, he had not been aware that there were sandwiches among those present, and the sudden and unexpected crunching went through him like a knife.

Poets have written feelingly of many a significant and compelling sound . . . the breeze in the trees; the roar of waves breaking on a stern and rockbound coast; the coo of doves in immemorial elms; and the song of the nightingale. But none of these can speak to the very depths of the soul like the steady champing of beef sandwiches when the listener is a man who for four days has been subsisting on the juice of an orange.

In the case of Wilmot Mulliner, it was as if the sound of those sandwiches had touched a spring, releasing all the dark forces within him. A tigerish light had come into his eyes, and he sat up in his chair, bristling.

The next moment those present were startled to observe him leap to his feet, his face working violently.

"Stop that!"

Mr. Schnellenhamer quivered. His jaw and sandwich fell. He caught Mr. Levitsky's eye. Mr. Levitsky's jaw had fallen, too.

"Stop it, I say!" thundered Wilmot. "Stop eating those sandwiches immediately!"

He paused, panting with emotion. Mr. Schnellenhamer had risen and was pointing a menacing finger. A deathly silence held the room.

And then, abruptly, into this silence there cut the shrill, sharp, wailing note of a syren. And the magnate stood spellbound, the words "You're fired!" frozen on his lips. He knew what that sound meant.

One of the things which have caused the making of motion pictures to be listed among the Dangerous Trades is the fact that it has been found impossible to dispense with the temperamental female star. There is a public demand for her, and the Public's word is law. The consequence is that in every studio you will find at least one gifted artiste, the mere mention of whose name causes the strongest to tremble like aspens. At the Perfecto-Zizzbaum this position was held by Hortensia Burwash, the Empress of Molten Passion.

Temperament is a thing that cuts both ways. It brings in the money, but it also leads to violent outbursts on the part of its possessor similar to those so common among the natives of the Malay States. Every Hortensia Burwash picture grossed five million, but in the making of them she was extremely apt, if thwarted in some whim, to run amuck, sparing neither age nor sex.

A procedure, accordingly, had been adopted not unlike that in use during air raids in the War. At the first sign that the strain had become too much for Miss Burwash, a syren sounded, warning all workers on the lot to take cover. Later, a bugler, blowing the "All Clear", would inform those in the danger zone that the star had now kissed the director and resumed work on the set.

It was this syren that had interrupted the tense scene which I have been describing.

For some moments after the last note had died away it seemed as though the splendid discipline on which the Perfecto-Zizzbaum organisation prided itself was to triumph. A few eyeballs rolled, and here and there you could hear the sharp intake of breath, but nobody moved. Then from without there came the sound of running footsteps, and the door burst open, revealing a haggard young assistant director with a blood-streaked face.

"Save yourselves!" he cried.

There was an uneasy stir.

"She's heading this way!"

Again that stir. Mr. Schnellenhamer rapped the desk sharply.

"Gentlemen! Are you afraid of an unarmed woman?"

The assistant director coughed.

"Not unarmed exactly," he corrected. "She's got a sword."

"A sword?"

"She borrowed it off one of the Roman soldiery in 'Hail, Caesar!' Seemed to want it for something. Well, goodbye, all," said the assistant director.

Panic set in. The stampede was started by a young Nodder, who, in fairness be it said, had got a hat-pin in the fleshy part of the leg that time when Miss Burwash was so worried over "Hearts Aflame". Reckless of all rules of precedence, he shot silently through the window. He was followed by the rest of those present, and in a few moments the room was empty save for Wilmot, brooding with folded arms; Mabel Potter, crouched on top of the filing cabinet; and Mr. Schnellenhamer himself, who, too stout to negotiate the window, was crawling into a convenient cupboard and softly closing the door after him.

To the scene which had just concluded Wilmot Mulliner had paid but scant attention. His whole mind was occupied with the hunger which was gnawing his vitals and that strange loathing for the human species which had been so much with him of late. He continued to stand where he was, as if in some dark trance.

From this he was aroused by the tempestuous entry of a woman with make-up on her face and a Roman sword in her hand.

"Ah-h-h-h-h!" she cried.

Wilmot was not interested. Briefly raising his eyebrows and baring his lips in an animal snarl, he returned to his meditations.

Hortensia Burwash was not accustomed to a reception like this. For a moment she stood irresolute; then, raising the sword, she brought it down with a powerful follow through on a handsome ink-pot which had been presented to Mr. Schnellenhamer by a few admirers and well-wishers on the occasion of the Perfecto-Zizzbaum's foundation.

"Ah-h-h-h-h!" she cried again.

Wilmot had had enough of this foolery. Like all the Mulliners, his attitude towards Woman had until recently been one of reverence and unfailing courtesy. But with four days' orange-juice under his belt, he was dashed if he was going to have females carrying on like this in his presence. A considerable quantity of the ink had got on his trousers, and he now faced Hortensia Burwash, pale with fury.

"What's the idea?" he demanded hotly. "What's the matter with you? Stop it immediately, and give me that sword."

The temperamental star emitted another "Ah-h-h-h-h!" but it was but a half-hearted one. The old pep had gone. She allowed the weapon to be snatched from her grasp. Her eyes met Wilmot's. And suddenly, as she gazed into those steel-hard orbs, the fire faded out of her, leaving her a mere weak woman face to face with what appeared to be the authentic caveman. It seemed to her for an instant, as she looked at him, that she had caught a glimpse of something evil. It was as if this man who stood before her had been a Fiend about to Seize Hatchet and Slay Six.

As a matter of fact, Wilmot's demeanour was simply the normal one of a man who every morning for four days has taken an orange, divided it into two equal parts, squeezed on a squeezer, poured into a glass or cup, and drunk; who has sipped the juice of an orange in the midst of rollicking lunchers doing themselves well among the roasts and hashes; and who, on returning to his modest flat in the evenfall, has got to work with the old squeezer once more. But Hortensia Burwash, eyeing him, trembled. Her spirit was broken.

"Messing about with ink," grumbled Wilmot, dabbing at his legs with blotting-paper. "Silly horseplay, I call it."

The star's lips quivered. She registered Distress.

"You needn't be so cross," she whimpered.

"Cross!" thundered Wilmot. He pointed wrathfully at his lower limbs. "The best ten-dollar trousers in Hollywood!"

"Well, I'm sorry."

"You'd better be. What did you do it for?"

"I don't know. Everything sort of went black."

"Like my trousers."

"I'm sorry about your trousers." She sniffed miserably. "You wouldn't be so unkind if you knew what it was like."

"What what was like?"

"This dieting. Fifteen days with nothing but orange-juice."

The effect of those words on William Mulliner was stunning. His animosity left him in a flash. He started. The stony look in his eyes melted, and he gazed at her

with a tender commiseration, mingled with remorse that he should have treated so
harshly a sister in distress.

"You don't mean you're dieting?"

"Yes."

Wilmot was deeply stirred. It was as if he had become once more the old,
kindly, gentle Wilmot, beloved by all.

"You poor little thing! No wonder you rush about smashing ink-pots. Fifteen
days of it! My gosh!"

"And I was upset, too, about the picture."

"What picture?"

"My new picture. I don't like the story."

"What a shame!"

"It isn't true to life."

"How rotten! Tell me all about it. Come on, tell Wilmot."

"Well, it's like this. I'm supposed to be starving in a garret, and they want me
with the last remnant of my strength to write a letter to my husband, forgiving him
and telling him I love him still. The idea is that I'm purified by hunger. And I
say it's all wrong."

"All wrong?" cried Wilmot. "You're right, it's all wrong. I never heard anything so silly in my life. A starving woman's heart wouldn't soften. And, as for
being purified by hunger, purified by hunger my hat! The only reason which
would make a woman in that position take pen in hand and write to her husband
would be if she could think of something nasty enough to say to make it worth
while."

"That's just how I feel."

"As a matter of fact, nobody but a female goof would be thinking of husbands
at all at a time like that. She would be thinking of roast pork . . ."

" . . . and steaks . . ."

". . . and chops . . ."

". . . and chicken casserole . . ."

". . . and kidneys *sautés* . . ."

". . . and mutton curry . . ."

". . . and doughnuts . . ."

". . . and layer-cake . . ."

". . . and peach pie, mince pie, apple pie, custard pie, and pie *á la mode*," said
Wilmot. "Of everything, in a word, but the juice of an orange. Tell me, who was
the half-wit who passed this story, so utterly alien to human psychology?"

"Mr. Schnellenhamer. I was coming to see him about it."

"I'll have a word or two with Mr. Schnellenhamer. We'll soon have that story
fixed. But what on earth do you want to diet for?"

"I don't want to. There's a weight clause in my contract. It says I mustn't weigh
more than a hundred and eight pounds. Mr. Schnellenhamer insisted on it."

A grim look came into Wilmot's face.

"Schnellenhamer again, eh? This shall be attended to."

He crossed to the cupboard and flung open the door. The magnate came out on all fours. Wilmot curtly directed him to the desk.

"Take paper and ink, Schnellenhamer, and write this lady out a new contract, with no weight clause."

"But listen . . ."

"Your sword, madam, I believe?" said Wilmot, extending the weapon.

"All right," said Mr. Schnellenhamer hastily. "All right. All right."

"And, while you're at it," said Wilmot, "I'll take one, too, restoring me to my former salary."

"What was your former salary?" asked Hortensia Burwash.

"Fifteen hundred."

"I'll double it. I've been looking for a business manager like you for years. I didn't think they made them nowadays. So firm. So decisive. So brave. So strong. You're the business manager of my dreams."

Wilmot's gaze, straying about the room, was attracted by a movement on top of the filing cabinet. He looked up, and his eyes met those of Mabel Potter. They yearned worshippingly at him, and in them there was something which he had no difficulty in diagnosing as the love-light. He turned to Hortensia Burwash.

"By the way, my fiancée, Miss Potter."

"How do you do?" said Hortensia Burwash.

"Pleased to meet you," said Mabel.

"What did you get up there for?" asked Miss Burwash, puzzled.

"Oh, I thought I would," said Mabel.

Wilmot, as became a man of affairs, was crisp and business-like.

"Miss Burwash wishes to make a contract with me to act as her manager," he said. "Take dictation, Miss Potter."

"Yes, sir," said Mabel.

At the desk, Mr. Schnellenhamer had paused for a moment in his writing. He was trying to remember if the word he wanted was spelled "clorse" or "clorze".

31

THE RISE OF MINNA NORDSTROM

THEY had been showing the latest Minna Nordstrom picture at the Bijou Dream in the High Street, and Miss Postlethwaite, our sensitive barmaid, who had attended the première, was still deeply affected. She snuffled audibly as she polished the glasses.

"It's really good, is it?" we asked, for in the bar-parlour of the Angler's Rest we lean heavily on Miss Postlethwaite's opinion where the silver screen is concerned. Her verdict can make or mar.

" 'Swonderful," she assured us. "It lays bare for all to view the soul of a woman who dared everything for love. A poignant and uplifting drama of life as it is lived to-day, purifying the emotions with pity and terror."

A Rum and Milk said that if it was as good as all that he didn't know but what he might not risk ninepence on it. A Sherry and Bitters wondered what they paid a woman like Minna Nordstrom. A Port from the Wood, raising the conversation from the rather sordid plane to which it threatened to sink, speculated on how motion-picture stars became stars.

"What I mean," said the Port from the Wood, "does a studio deliberately set out to create a star? Or does it suddenly say to itself 'Hullo, here's a star. What ho!' ?"

One of those cynical Dry Martinis who always know everything said that it was all a question of influence.

"If you looked into it, you would find this Nordstrom girl was married to one of the bosses."

Mr. Mulliner, who had been sipping his hot Scotch and lemon in a rather distrait way, glanced up.

"Did I hear you mention the name Minna Nordstrom?"

"We were arguing about how she became a star. I was saying that she must have had a pull of some kind."

"In a sense," said Mr. Mulliner, "you are right. She did have a pull. But it was one due solely to her own initiative and resource. I have relatives and connections in Hollywood, as you know, and I learn much of the inner history of the studio world through these channels. I happen to know that Minna Nordstrom raised herself to her present eminence by sheer enterprise and determination. If Miss Postlethwaite will mix me another hot Scotch and lemon, this time stressing the Scotch a little more vigorously, I shall be delighted to tell you the whole story."

When people talk with bated breath in Hollywood—and it is a place where there is always a certain amount of breath-bating going on—you will generally find, said Mr. Mulliner, that the subject of their conversation is Jacob Z. Schnellenhamer, the popular president of the Perfecto-Zizzbaum Corporation. For few names are more widely revered there than that of this Napoleonic man.

Ask for an instance of his financial acumen, and his admirers will point to the great merger for which he was responsible—that merger by means of which he combined his own company, the Colossal-Exquisite, with those two other vast concerns, the Perfecto-Fishbein and the Zizzbaum-Celluloid. Demand proof of his artistic genius, his flair for recognising talent in the raw, and it is given immediately. He was the man who discovered Minna Nordstrom.

To-day when interviewers bring up the name of the world-famous star in Mr. Schnellenhamer's presence, he smiles quietly.

"I had long had my eye on the little lady," he says, "but for one reason and another I did not consider the time ripe for her début. Then I brought about what you are good enough to call the epoch-making merger, and I was enabled to take the decisive step. My colleagues questioned the wisdom of elevating a totally unknown girl to stardom, but I was firm. I saw that it was the only thing to be done."

"You had vision?"

"I had vision."

All that Mr. Schnellenhamer had, however, on the evening when this story begins was a headache. As he returned from the day's work at the studio and sank wearily into an arm-chair in the sitting-room of his luxurious home in Beverly Hills, he was feeling that the life of the president of a motion-picture corporation was one that he would hesitate to force on any dog of which he was fond.

A morbid meditation, of course, but not wholly unjustified. The great drawback to being the man in control of a large studio is that everybody you meet starts acting at you. Hollywood is entirely populated by those who want to get into the pictures, and they naturally feel that the best way of accomplishing their object is to catch the boss's eye and do their stuff.

Since leaving home that morning Mr. Schnellenhamer had been acted at practically incessantly. First, it was the studio watchman who, having opened the gate to admit his car, proceeded to play a little scene designed to show what he would do in a heavy role. Then came his secretary, two book agents, the waitress who brought him his lunch, a life insurance man, a representative of a film weekly, and a barber. And, on leaving at the end of the day, he got the watchman again, this time in whimsical comedy.

Little wonder, then, that by the time he reached home the magnate was conscious of a throbbing sensation about the temples and an urgent desire for a restorative.

As a preliminary to obtaining the latter, he rang the bell and Vera Prebble, his parlourmaid, entered. For a moment he was surprised not to see his butler. Then he recalled that he had dismissed him just after breakfast for reciting Gunga Din in a meaning way while bringing the eggs and bacon.

"You rang, sir?"

"I want a drink."

"Very good, sir."

The girl withdrew, to return a few moments later with a decanter and siphon. The sight caused Mr. Schnellenhamer's gloom to lighten a little. He was proud of his cellar, and he knew that the decanter contained liquid balm. In a sudden gush of tenderness he eyed its bearer appreciatively, thinking what a nice girl she looked.

Until now he had never studied Vera Prebble's appearance to any great extent or thought about her much in any way. When she had entered his employment a few days before, he had noticed, of course, that she had a sort of ethereal beauty; but then every girl you see in Hollywood has either ethereal beauty or roguish gaminerie or a dark, slumbrous face that hints at hidden passion.

"Put it down there on the small table," said Mr. Schnellenhamer, passing his tongue over his lips.

The girl did so. Then, straightening herself, she suddenly threw her head back and clutched the sides of it in an ecstacy of hopeless anguish.

"Oh! Oh! Oh!" she cried.

"Eh?" said Mr. Schnellenhamer.

"Ah! Ah! Ah!"

"I don't get you at all," said Mr. Schnellenhamer.

She gazed at him with wide, despairing eyes.

"If you knew how sick and tired I am of it all! Tired . . . Tired . . . Tired. The lights . . . the glitter . . . the gaiety . . . It is so hollow, so fruitless. I want to get away from it all, ha-ha-ha-ha-ha!"

Mr. Schnellenhamer retreated behind the chesterfield. That laugh had had an unbalanced ring. He had not liked it. He was about to continue his backward progress in the direction of the door, when the girl, who had closed her eyes and was rocking to and fro as if suffering from some internal pain, became calmer.

"Just a little thing I knocked together with a view to showing myself in a dramatic role," she said. "Watch! I'm going to register."

She smiled. "Joy."

She closed her mouth. "Grief."

She wiggled her ears. "Horror."

She raised her eyebrows. "Hate."

Then, taking a parcel from the tray:

"Here," she said, "if you would care to glance at them, are a few stills of myself. This shows my face in repose. I call it 'Reverie'. This is me in a bathing suit . . . riding . . . walking . . . happy among my books . . . being kind to the dog. Here is one of which my friends have been good enough to speak in terms of praise—as Cleopatra, the warrior-queen of Egypt, at the Pasadena Gas-Fitters' Ball. It brings out what is generally considered my most effective feature—the nose, seen sideways."

During the course of these remarks, Mr. Schnellenhamer had been standing breathing heavily. For a while the discovery that this parlourmaid, of whom he had just been thinking so benevolently, was simply another snake in the grass had rendered him incapable of speech. Now his aphasia left him.

"Get out!" he said.

"Pardon?" said the girl.

"Get out this minute. You're fired."

There was a silence. Vera Prebble closed her mouth, wiggled her ears, and raised her eyebrows. It was plain that she was grieved, horror-stricken, and in the grip of a growing hate.

"What," she demanded passionately at length, "is the matter with all you movie magnates? Have you no hearts? Have you no compassion? No sympathy? No understanding? Do the ambitions of the struggling mean nothing to you?"

"No," replied Mr. Schnellenhamer in answer to all five questions.

Vera Prebble laughed bitterly.

"No is right!" she said. "For months I besieged the doors of the casting directors. They refused to cast me. Then I thought that if I could find a way into your homes I might succeed where I had failed before. I secured the post of parlourmaid to Mr. Fishbein of the Perfecto-Fishbein. Half-way through Rudyard Kipling's 'Boots' he brutally bade me begone. I obtained a similar position with Mr. Zizzbaum of the Zizzbaum-Celluloid. The opening lines of 'The Wreck of the *Hesperus*' had hardly passed my lips when he was upstairs helping me pack my trunk. And now you crush my hopes. It is cruel . . . cruel . . . Oh, ha-ha-ha-ha-ha!"

She rocked to and fro in an agony of grief. Then an idea seemed to strike her.

"I wonder if you would care to see me in light comedy? . . . No? . . . Oh, very well."

With a quick droop of the eyelids and a twitch of the muscles of the cheeks she registered resignation.

"Just as you please," she said. Then her nostrils quivered and she bared the left canine tooth to indicate Menace. "But one last word. Wait!"

"How do you mean, wait?"

"Just wait. That's all."

For an instant Mr. Schnellenhamer was conscious of a twinge of uneasiness. Like all motion-picture magnates, he had about forty-seven guilty secrets, many of them recorded on paper. Was it possible that . . .

Then he breathed again. All his private documents were secure in a safe-deposit box. It was absurd to imagine that this girl could have anything on him.

Relieved, he lay down on the chesterfield and gave himself up to day-dreams. And soon, as he remembered that that morning he had put through a deal which would enable him to trim the stuffing out of two hundred and seventy-three exhibitors, his lips curved in a contented smile and Vera Prebble was forgotten.

One of the advantages of life in Hollywood is that the Servant Problem is not a difficult one. Supply more than equals demand. Ten minutes after you have thrown a butler out of the back door his successor is bowling up in his sports-model car. And the same applies to parlourmaids. By the following afternoon all was well once more with the Schnellenhamer domestic machine. A new butler was cleaning the silver: a new parlourmaid was doing whatever parlourmaids do, which is very little. Peace reigned in the home.

But on the second evening, as Mr. Schnellenhamer, the day's tasks over, entered his sitting-room with nothing in his mind but bright thoughts of dinner, he was met by what had all the appearance of a human whirlwind. This was Mrs. Schnellenhamer. A graduate of the silent films, Mrs. Schnellenhamer had been known in her day as the Queen of Stormy Emotion, and she occasionally saw to it that her husband was reminded of this.

"Now see what!" cried Mrs. Schnellenhamer.

Mr. Schnellenhamer was perturbed.

"Is something wrong?" he asked nervously.

"Why did you fire that girl, Vera Prebble?"

"She went ha-ha-ha-ha-ha at me."

"Well, do you know what she has done? She has laid information with the police that we are harbouring alcoholic liquor on our premises, contrary to law, and this afternoon they came in a truck and took it all away."

Mr. Schnellenhamer reeled. The shock was severe. The good man loves his cellar.

"Not all?" he cried, almost pleadingly.

"All."

"The Scotch?"

"Every bottle."

"The gin?"

"Every drop."

Mr. Schnellenhamer supported himself against the chesterfield.

"Not the champagne?" he whispered.

"Every case. And here we are, with a hundred and fifty people coming to-night, including the Duke."

Her allusion was to the Duke of Wigan, who, as so many British dukes do, was at this time passing slowly through Hollywood.

"And you know how touchy dukes are," proceeded Mrs. Schnellenhamer. "I'm told that the Lulubelle Mahaffys invited the Duke of Kircudbrightshire for the week-end last year, and after he had been there two months he suddenly left in a huff because there was no brown sherry."

A motion-picture magnate has to be a quick thinker. Where a lesser man would have wasted time referring to the recent Miss Prebble as a serpent whom he had to all intents and purposes nurtured in his bosom, Mr. Schnellenhamer directed the whole force of his great brain on the vital problem of how to undo the evil she had wrought.

"Listen," he said. "It's all right. I'll get the bootlegger on the 'phone, and he'll have us stocked up again in no time."

But he had overlooked the something in the air of Hollywood which urges its every inhabitant irresistibly into the pictures. When he got his bootlegger's number, it was only to discover that that life-saving tradesman was away from home. They were shooting a scene in "Sundered Hearts" on the Outstanding Screen-Favourites lot, and the bootlegger was hard at work there, playing the role of an Anglican bishop. His secretary said he could not be disturbed, as it got him all upset to be interrupted when he was working.

Mr. Schnellenhamer tried another bootlegger, then another. They were out on location.

And it was just as he had begun to despair that he bethought him of his old friend, Isadore Fishbein; and into his darkness there shot a gleam of hope. By the greatest good fortune it so happened that he and the president of the Perfecto-Fishbein were at the moment on excellent terms, neither having slipped anything over on the other for several weeks. Mr. Fishbein, moreover, possessed as well-stocked a cellar as any man in California. It would be a simple matter to go round and borrow from him all he needed.

Patting Mrs. Schnellenhamer's hand and telling her that there were still blue-birds singing in the sunshine, he ran to his car and leaped into it.

The residence of Isadore Fishbein was only a few hundred yards away, and Mr. Schnellenhamer was soon whizzing in through the door. He found his friend beating his head against the wall of the sitting-room and moaning to himself in a quiet undertone.

"Is something the matter?" he asked, surprised.

"There is," said Mr. Fishbein, selecting a fresh spot on the tapestried wall and starting to beat his head against that. "The police came round this afternoon and took away everything I had."

"Everything?"

"Well, not Mrs. Fishbein," said the other, with a touch of regret in his voice. "She's up in the bedroom with eight cubes of ice on her forehead in a linen bag. But they took every drop of everything else. A serpent, that's what she is."

"Mrs. Fishbein?"

"Not Mrs. Fishbein. That parlourmaid. That Vera Prebble. Just because I stopped her when she got to 'boots, boots, boots, boots, marching over Africa' she ups and informs the police on me. And Mrs. Fishbein with a hundred and eighty people coming to-night, including the ex-King of Ruritania!"

And, crossing the room, the speaker began to bang his head against a statue of Genius Inspiring the Motion-Picture Industry.

A good man is always appalled when he is forced to contemplate the depths to which human nature can sink, and Mr. Schnellenhamer's initial reaction on hearing of this fresh outrage on the part of his late parlourmaid was a sort of sick horror. Then the brain which had built up the Colossal-Exquisite began to work once more.

"Well, the only thing for us to do," he said, "is to go round to Ben Zizzbaum and borrow some of his stock. How do you stand with Ben?"

"I stand fine with Ben," said Mr. Fishbein, cheering up. "I heard something about him last week which I'll bet he wouldn't care to have known."

"Where does he live?"

"Camden Drive."

"Then tally-ho!" said Mr. Schnellenhamer, who had once produced a drama in eight reels of two strong men battling for a woman's love in the English hunting district.

They were soon at Mr. Zizzbaum's address. Entering the sitting-room, they were shocked to observe a form rolling in circles round the floor with its head between its hands. It was travelling quickly, but not so quickly that they were unable to recognise it as that of the chief executive of the Zizzbaum-Celluloid Corporation. Stopped as he was completing his eleventh lap and pressed for an explanation, Mr. Zizzbaum revealed that a recent parlourmaid of his, Vera Prebble by name, piqued at having been dismissed for deliberate and calculated reciting of the works of Mrs. Hemans, had informed the police of his stock of wines and spirits and that the latter had gone off with the whole collection not half an hour since.

"And don't speak so loud," added the stricken man, "or you'll wake Mrs. Zizzbaum. She's in bed with ice on her head."

"How many cubes?' asked Mr. Fishbein.

"Six."

"Mrs. Fishbein needed eight," said that lady's husband a little proudly.

The situation was one that might well have unmanned the stoutest motion-picture executive and there were few motion-picture executives stouter than Jacob Schnellenhamer. But it was characteristic of this man that the tightest corner was always the one to bring out the full force of his intellect. He thought of Mrs. Schnellenhamer waiting for him at home, and it was as if an electric shock of high voltage had passed through him.

"I've got it," he said. "We must go to Glutz of the Medulla-Oblongata. He's never been a real friend of mine, but if you loan him Stella Svelte and I loan him Orlando Byng and Fishbein loans him Oscar the Wonder-Poodle on his own terms, I think he'll consent to give us enough to see us through to-night. I'll get him on the 'phone."

It was some moments before Mr. Schnellenhamer returned from the telephone booth. When he did so, his associates were surprised to observe in his eyes a happy gleam.

"Boys," he said, "Glutz is away with his family over the week-end. The butler and the rest of the help are out joy-riding. There's only a parlourmaid in the house. I've been talking to her. So there won't be any need for us to give him those stars, after all. We'll just run across in the car with a few axes and help ourselves. It won't cost us above a hundred dollars to square this girl. She can tell him she was upstairs when the burglars broke in and didn't hear anything. And there we'll be, with all the stuff we need and not a cent to pay outside of overhead connected with the maid."

There was an awed silence.

"Mrs. Fishbein will be pleased."

"Mrs. Zizzbaum will be pleased."

"And Mrs. Schnellenhamer will be pleased," said the leader of the expedition. "Where do you keep your axes, Zizzbaum?"

"In the cellar."

"Fetch 'em!" said Mr. Schnellenhamer in the voice a Crusader might have used in giving the signal to start against the Paynim.

In the ornate residence of Sigismund Glutz, meanwhile, Vera Prebble, who had entered the service of the head of the Medulla-Oblongata that morning and was already under sentence of dismissal for having informed him with appropriate gestures that a bunch of the boys were whooping it up in the Malemute saloon, was engaged in writing on a sheet of paper a short list of names, one of which she proposed as a *nom de théâtre* as soon as her screen career should begin.

For this girl was essentially an optimist, and not even all the rebuffs which she had suffered had been sufficient to quench the fire of ambition in her.

Wiggling her tongue as she shaped the letters, she wrote:

> *Ursuline Delmaine*
> *Theodora Trix*
> *Uvula Gladwyn*

None of them seemed to her quite what she wanted. She pondered. Possibly something a little more foreign and exotic . . .

Greta Garbo

No, that had been used . . .

And then suddenly inspiration descended upon her and, trembling a little with emotion, she inscribed on the paper the one name that was absolutely and indubitably right.

Minna Nordstrom

The more she looked at it, the better she liked it. And she was still regarding it proudly when there came the sound of a car stopping at the door and a few moments later in walked Mr. Schnellenhamer, Mr. Zizzbaum and Mr. Fishbein. They all wore Homburg hats and carried axes.

Vera Prebble drew herself up.

"All goods must be delivered in the rear," she had begun haughtily, when she recognised her former employers and paused, surprised.

The recognition was mutual. Mr. Fishbein started. So did Mr. Zizzbaum.

"Serpent!" said Mr. Fishbein.

"Viper!" said Mr. Zizzbaum.

Mr. Schnellenhamer was more diplomatic. Though as deeply moved as his colleagues by the sight of this traitoress, he realised that this was no time for invective.

"Well, well, well," he said, with a geniality which he strove to render frank and winning, "I never dreamed it was you on the 'phone, my dear. Well, this certainly makes everything nice and smooth—us all being, as you might say, old friends."

"Friends?" retorted Vera Prebble. "Let me tell you . . ."

"I know, I know. Quite, quite. But listen. I've got to have some liquor to-night . . ."

"What do you mean, *you* have?" said Mr. Fishbein.

"It's all right, it's all right," said Mr. Schnellenhamer soothingly. "I was coming to that. I wasn't forgetting you. We're all in this together. The good old spirit of co-operation. You see, my dear," he went on, "that little joke you played on us . . . oh, I'm not blaming you. Nobody laughed more heartily than myself . . ."

"Yes, they did," said Mr. Fishbein, alive now to the fact that this girl before him must be conciliated. "I did."

"So did I," said Mr. Zizzbaum.

"We all laughed very heartily," said Mr. Schnellenhamer. "You should have heard us. A girl of spirit, we said to ourselves. Still, the little pleasantry has left us in something of a difficulty, and it will be worth a hundred dollars to you, my dear, to go upstairs and put cotton-wool in your ears while we get at Mr. Glutz's cellar door with our axes."

Vera Prebble raised her eyebrows.

"What do you want to break down the cellar door for? I know the combination of the lock."

"You do?" said Mr. Schnellenhamer joyfully.

"I withdraw that expression 'Serpent'," said Mr. Fishbein.

"When I used the term 'Viper'," said Mr. Zizzbaum, "I was speaking thoughtlessly."

"And I will tell it you," said Vera Prebble, "at a price."

She drew back her head and extended an arm, twiddling the fingers at the end of it. She was plainly registering something, but they could not discern what it was.

"There is only one condition on which I will tell you the combination of Mr. Glutz's cellar, and that is this. One of you has got to give me a starring contract for five years."

The magnates started.

"Listen," said Mr. Zizzbaum, "you don't want to star."

"You wouldn't like it," said Mr. Fishbein.

"Of course you wouldn't," said Mr. Schnellenhamer. "You would look silly, starring—an inexperienced girl like you. Now, if you had said a nice small part . . ."

"Star."

"Or featured . . ."

"Star."

The three men drew back a pace or two and put their heads together.

"She means it," said Mr. Fishbein.

"Her eyes," said Mr. Zizzbaum. "Like stones."

"A dozen times I could have dropped something heavy on that girl's head from an upper landing, and I didn't do it," said Mr. Schnellenhamer remorsefully.

Mr. Fishbein threw up his hands.

"It's no use. I keep seeing that vision of Mrs. Fishbein floating before me with eight cubes of ice on her head. I'm going to star this girl."

"*You* are?" said Mr. Zizzbaum. "And get the stuff? And leave me to go home and tell Mrs. Zizzbaum there won't be anything to drink at her party to-night for a hundred and eleven guests including the Vice-President of Switzerland? No, sir! *I* am going to star her."

"I'll outbid you."

"You won't outbid *me*. Not till they bring me word that Mrs. Zizzbaum has lost the use of her vocal chords."

"Listen," said the other tensely. "When it comes to using vocal chords, Mrs. Fishbein begins where Mrs. Zizzbaum leaves off."

Mr. Schnellenhamer, that cool head, saw the peril that loomed.

"Boys," he said, "if we once start bidding against one another, there'll be no limit. There's only one thing to be done. We must merge."

His powerful personality carried the day. It was the President of the newly-formed Perfecto-Zizzbaum Corporation who a few moments later stepped forward and approached the girl.

"We agree."

And, as he spoke, there came the sound of some heavy vehicle stopping in the road outside. Vera Prebble uttered a stricken exclamation.

"Well, of all the silly girls!" she cried distractedly. "I've just remembered that an hour ago I telephoned the police, informing them of Mr. Glutz's cellar. And here they are!"

Mr. Fishbein uttered a cry, and began to look round for something to bang his head against. Mr. Zizzbaum gave a short, sharp moan, and started to lower himself to the floor. But Mr. Schnellenhamer was made of sterner stuff.

"Pull yourselves together, boys," he begged them. "Leave all this to me. Everything is going to be all right. Things have come to a pretty pass," he said, with a dignity as impressive as it was simple, "if a free-born American citizen cannot bribe the police of his native country."

"True," said Mr. Fishbein, arresting his head when within an inch and a quarter of a handsome Oriental vase.

"True, true," said Mr. Zizzbaum, getting up and dusting his knees.

"Just let me handle the whole affair," said Mr. Schnellenhamer. "Ah, boys!" he went on, genially.

Three policemen had entered the room—a sergeant, a patrolman, and another patrolman. Their faces wore a wooden, hard-boiled look.

"Mr. Glutz?" said the sergeant.

"Mr. Schnellenhamer," corrected the great man. "But Jacob to you, old friend."

The sergeant seemed in no wise mollified by this amiability.

"Prebble, Vera?" he asked, addressing the girl.

"Nordstrom, Minna," she replied.

"Got the name wrong, then. Anyway, it was you who 'phoned us that there was alcoholic liquor on the premises?"

Mr. Schnellenhamer laughed amusedly.

"You mustn't believe everything that girl tells you, sergeant. She's a great kidder. Always was. If she said that, it was just one of her little jokes. I know Glutz. I know his views. And many is the time I have heard him say that the laws of his country are good enough for him and that he would scorn not to obey them. You will find nothing here, sergeant."

"Well, we'll try," said the other. "Show us the way to the cellar," he added, turning to Vera Prebble.

Mr. Schnellenhamer smiled a winning smile.

"Now listen," he said. "I've just remembered I'm wrong. Silly mistake to make, and I don't know how I made it. There *is* a certain amount of the stuff in the house, but I'm sure you dear chaps don't want to cause any unpleasantness. You're broad-minded. Listen. Your name's Murphy, isn't it?"

"Donahue."

"I thought so. Well, you'll laugh at this. Only this morning I was saying to Mrs. Schnellenhamer that I must really slip down to headquarters and give my old friend Donahue that ten dollars I owed him."

"What ten dollars?"

"I didn't say ten. I said a hundred. One hundred dollars, Donny, old man, and I'm not saying there mightn't be a little over for these two gentlemen here. How about it?"

The sergeant drew himself up. There was no sign of softening in his glance.

"Jacob Schnellenhamer," he said coldly, "you can't square me. When I tried for a job at the Colossal-Exquisite last spring I was turned down on account you said I had no sex-appeal."

The first patrolman, who had hitherto taken no part in the conversation, started.

"Is that so, Chief?"

"Yessir. No sex-appeal."

"Well, can you tie that!" said the first patrolman. "When I tried to crash the Colossal-Exquisite, they said my voice wasn't right."

"Me," said the second patrolman, eyeing Mr. Schnellenhamer sourly, "they had the nerve to beef at my left profile. Lookut, boys," he said, turning, "can you see anything wrong with that profile?"

His companions studied him closely. The sergeant raised a hand and peered between his fingers with his head tilted back and his eyes half closed.

"Not a thing," he said.

"Why, Basil, it's a lovely profile," said the first patrolman.

"Well, that's how it goes," said the second patrolman moodily.

The sergeant had returned to his own grievance.

"No sex-appeal!" he said with a rasping laugh. "And me that had specially taken sex-appeal in the College of Eastern Iowa course of Motion Picture acting."

"Who says my voice ain't right?" demanded the first patrolman. "Listen. Mi-mi-mi-mi-mi."

"Swell," said the sergeant.

"Like a nightingale or something," said the second patrolman.

The sergeant flexed his muscles.

"Ready, boys?"

"Kayo, Chief."

"Wait!" cried Mr. Schnellenhamer. "Wait! Give me one more chance. I'm sure I can find parts for you all."

The sergeant shook his head.

"No. It's too late. You've got us mad now. You don't appreciate the sensitive-
ness of the artist. Does he, boys?"

"You're darned right he doesn't," said the first patrolman.

"I wouldn't work for the Colossal-Exquisite now," said the second patrolman
with a petulant twitch of his shoulder, "not if they wanted me to play Romeo
opposite Jean Harlow."

"Then let's go," said the sergeant. "Come along, lady, you show us where this
cellar is."

For some moments after the officers of the Law, preceded by Vera Prebble, had
left, nothing was to be heard in the silent sitting-room but the rhythmic beating
of Mr. Fishbein's head against the wall and the rustling sound of Mr. Zizzbaum
rolling round the floor. Mr. Schnellenhamer sat brooding with his chin in his
hands, merely moving his legs slightly each time Mr. Zizzbaum came round.
The failure of his diplomatic efforts had stunned him.

A vision rose before his eyes of Mrs. Schnellenhamer waiting in their sunlit
patio for his return. As clearly as if he had been there now, he could see her,
swooning, slipping into the goldfish pond, and blowing bubbles with her head
beneath the surface. And he was asking himself whether in such an event it would
be better to raise her gently or just leave Nature to take its course. She would, he
knew, be extremely full of that stormy emotion of which she had once been queen.

It was as he still debated this difficult point that a light step caught his ear.
Vera Prebble was standing in the doorway.

"Mr. Schnellenhamer."

The magnate waved a weary hand.

"Leave me," he said. "I am thinking."

"I thought you would like to know," said Vera Prebble, "that I've just locked
those cops in the coal-cellar."

As in the final reel of a super-super-film eyes brighten and faces light up at
the entry of the United States Marines, so at these words did Mr. Schnellenhamer, Mr. Fishbein and Mr. Zizzbaum perk up as if after a draught of some
magic elixir.

"In the coal-cellar?" gasped Mr. Schnellenhamer.

"In the coal-cellar."

"Then if we work quick . . ."

Vera Prebble coughed.

"One moment," she said. "Just one moment. Before you go, I have drawn up a
little letter covering our recent agreement. Perhaps you will all three just sign it."

Mr. Schnellenhamer clicked his tongue impatiently.

"No time for that now. Come to my office tomorrow. Where are you going?"
he asked, as the girl started to withdraw.

"Just to the coal-cellar," said Vera Prebble. "I think those fellows may want
to come out."

Mr. Schnellenhamer sighed. It had been worth trying, of course, but he had never really had much hope.

"Gimme," he said resignedly.

The girl watched as the three men attached their signatures. She took the document and folded it carefully.

"Would any of you like to hear me recite 'The Bells', by Edgar Allan Poe?" she asked.

"No!" said Mr. Fishbein.

"No!" said Mr. Zizzbaum.

"No!" said Mr. Schnellenhamer. "We have no desire to hear you recite 'The Bells', Miss Prebble."

The girl's eyes flashed haughtily.

"Miss Nordstrom," she corrected. "And just for that you'll get 'The Charge of the Light Brigade', and like it."

MONDAY night in the bar-parlour of the Angler's Rest is usually Book Night. This is due to the fact that on Sunday afternoon it is the practice of Miss Postlethwaite, our literature-loving barmaid, to retire to her room with a box of caramels and a novel from the circulating library and, having removed her shoes, to lie down on the bed and indulge in what she calls a good old read. On the following evening she places the results of her researches before us and invites our judgment.

This week-end it was one of those Desert Island stories which had claimed her attention.

"It's where this ship is sailing the Pacific Ocean," explained Miss Postlethwaite, "and it strikes a reef and the only survivors are Cyril Trevelyan and Eunice Westleigh, and they float ashore on a plank to this uninhabited island. And gradually they find the solitude and what I might call the loneliness drawing them strangely together, and in Chapter Nineteen, which is as far as I've got, they've just fallen into each other's arms and all around was the murmur of the surf and the cry of wheeling sea-birds. And why I don't see how it's all going to come out," said Miss Postlethwaite, "is because they don't like each other really and, what's more, Eunice is engaged to be married to a prominent banker in New York and Cyril to the daughter of the Duke of Rotherhithe. Looks like a mix-up to me."

A Sherry and Bitters shook his head.

"Far-fetched," he said disapprovingly. "Not the sort of thing that ever really happens."

"On the contrary," said Mr. Mulliner. "It is an almost exact parallel to the case of Genevieve Bootle and my brother Joseph's younger son, Bulstrode."

"Were they cast ashore on a desert island?"

"Practically," said Mr. Mulliner. "They were in Hollywood, writing dialogue for the talking pictures."

Miss Postlethwaite, who prides herself on her encyclopaedic knowledge of English Literature, bent her shapely eyebrows.

"Bulstrode Mulliner? Genevieve Bootle?" she murmured. "I never read anything by them. What did they write?"

"My nephew," Mr. Mulliner hastened to explain, "was not an author. Nor was Miss Bootle. Very few of those employed in writing motion-picture dialogue are.

The executives of the studios just haul in anyone they meet and make them sign contracts. Most of the mysterious disappearances you read about are due to this cause. Only the other day they found a plumber who had been missing for years. All the time he had been writing dialogue for the Mishkin Brothers. Once having reached Los Angeles, nobody is safe."

"Rather like the old Press Gang," said the Sherry and Bitters.

"Just like the old Press Gang," said Mr. Mulliner.

My nephew Bulstrode (said Mr. Mulliner), as is the case with so many English younger sons, had left his native land to seek his fortune abroad, and at the time when this story begins was living in New York, where he had recently become betrothed to a charming girl of the name of Mabelle Ridgway.

Although naturally eager to get married, the young couple were prudent. They agreed that before taking so serious a step they ought to have a little capital put by. And, after talking it over, they decided that the best plan would be for Bulstrode to go to California and try to strike oil.

So Bulstrode set out for Los Angeles, all eagerness and enthusiasm, and the first thing that happened to him was that somebody took his new hat, a parting gift from Mabelle, leaving in its place in the club car of the train a Fedora that was a size too small for him.

The train was running into the station when he discovered his loss, and he hurried out to scan his fellow-passengers, and presently there emerged a stout man with a face rather like that of a vulture which has been doing itself too well on the corpses. On this person's head was the missing hat.

And, just as Bulstrode was about to accost this stout man, there came up a mob of camera-men, who photographed him in various attitudes, and before Bulstrode could get a word in he was bowling off in a canary-coloured automobile bearing on its door in crimson letters the legend "Jacob Z. Schnellenhamer, President Perfecto-Zizzbaum Motion Picture Corp."

All the Mulliners are men of spirit, and Bulstrode did not propose to have his hats sneaked, even by the highest in the land, without lodging a protest. Next morning he called at the offices of the Perfecto-Zizzbaum, and after waiting four hours was admitted to the presence of Mr. Schnellenhamer.

The motion-picture magnate took a quick look at Bulstrode and thrust a paper and a fountain pen towards him.

"Sign here," he said.

A receipt for the hat, no doubt, thought Bulstrode. He scribbled his name at the bottom of the document, and Mr. Schnellenhamer pressed the bell.

"Miss Stern," he said, addressing his secretary, "what vacant offices have we on the lot?"

"There is Room 40 in the Leper Colony."

"I thought there was a song-writer there."

"He passed away Tuesday."

"Has the body been removed?"

"Yes, sir."

"Then Mr. Mulliner will occupy the room, starting from to-day. He has just signed a contract to write dialogue for us."

Bulstrode would have spoken, but Mr. Schnellenhamer silenced him with a gesture.

"Who are working on 'Scented Sinners' now?" he asked.

The secretary consulted a list.

"Mr. Doakes, Mr. Noakes, Miss Faversham, Miss Wilson, Mr. Fotheringay, Mr. Mendelsohn, Mr. Markey, Mrs. Cooper, Mr. Lennox and Mr. Dabney."

"That all?"

"There was a missionary who came in Thursday, wanting to convert the extra girls. He started a treatment, but he has escaped to Canada."

"Tchah!" said Mr. Schnellenhamer, annoyed. "We must have more vigilance, more vigilance. Give Mr. Mulliner a script of 'Scented Sinners' before he goes."

The secretary left the room. He turned to Bulstrode.

"Did you ever see 'Scented Sinners'?"

Bulstrode said he had not.

"Powerful drama of life as it is lived by the jazz-crazed, gin-crazed Younger Generation whose hollow laughter is but the mask for an aching heart," said Mr. Schnellenhamer. "It ran for a week in New York and lost a hundred thousand dollars, so we bought it. It has the mucus of a good story. See what you can do with it."

"But I don't want to write for the pictures," said Bulstrode.

"You've got to write for the pictures," said Mr. Schnellenhamer. "You've signed the contract."

"I want my hat."

"In the Perfecto-Zizzbaum Motion Picture Corporation," said Mr. Schnellenhamer coldly, "our slogan is Co-operation, not Hats."

The Leper Colony, to which Bulstrode had been assigned, proved to be a long, low building with small cells opening on a narrow corridor. It had been erected to take care of the overflow of the studio's writers, the majority of whom were located in what was known as the Ohio State Penitentiary. Bulstrode took possession of Room 40, and settled down to see what he could do with "Scented Sinners".

He was not unhappy. A good deal has been written about the hardships of life in motion-picture studios, but most of it, I am glad to say, is greatly exaggerated. The truth is that there is little or no actual ill-treatment of the writing staff, and the only thing that irked Bulstrode was the loneliness of the life.

Few who have not experienced it can realise the eerie solitude of a motion-picture studio. Human intercourse is virtually unknown. You are surrounded by writers, each in his or her little hutch, but if you attempt to establish communication with them you will find on every door a card with the words "Working. Do not disturb". And if you push open one of these doors you are greeted by a snarl so animal, so menacing, that you retire hastily lest nameless violence befall.

The world seems very far away. Outside, the sun beats down on the concrete, and occasionally you will see a man in shirt sleeves driving a truck to a distant set, while ever and anon the stillness is broken by the shrill cry of some wheeling supervisor. But for the most part a forlorn silence prevails.

The conditions, in short, are almost precisely those of such a desert island as Miss Postlethwaite was describing to us just now.

In these circumstances the sudden arrival of a companion, especially a companion of the opposite sex, can scarcely fail to have its effect on a gregarious young man. Entering his office one morning and finding a girl in it, Bulstrode Mulliner experienced much the same emotions as did Robinson Crusoe on meeting Friday. It is not too much to say that he was electrified.

She was not a beautiful girl. Tall, freckled and slab-featured, she had a distinct look of a halibut. To Bulstrode, however, she seemed a vision.

"My name is Bootle," she said. "Genevieve Bootle."

"Mine is Mulliner. Bulstrode Mulliner."

"They told me to come here."

"To see me about something?"

"To work with you on a thing called 'Scented Sinners'. I've just signed a contract to write dialogue for the company."

"Can you write dialogue?" asked Bulstrode. A foolish question, for, if she could, the Perfecto-Zizzbaum Corporation would scarcely have engaged her.

"No," said the girl despondently. "Except for letters to Ed., I've never written anything."

"Ed.?"

"Mr. Murgatroyd, my fiancé. He's a bootlegger in Chicago, and I came out here to try to work up his West Coast connection. And I went to see Mr. Schnellenhamer to ask if he would like a few cases of guaranteed pre-War Scotch, and I'd hardly begun to speak when he said 'Sign here.' So I signed, and now I find I can't leave till this 'Scented Sinners' thing is finished."

"I am in exactly the same position," said Bulstrode. "We must buckle to and make a quick job of it. You won't mind if I hold your hand from time to time? I fancy it will assist composition."

"But what would Ed. say?"

"Ed. won't know."

"No, there's that," agreed the girl.

"And when I tell you that I myself am engaged to a lovely girl in New York," Bulstrode pointed out, "you will readily understand that what I am suggesting is merely a purely mechanical device for obtaining the best results on this script of ours."

"Well, of course, if you put it like that . . ."

"I put it just like that," said Bulstrode, taking her hand in his and patting it.

Against hand-holding as a means of stimulating the creative faculties of the brain there is, of course, nothing to be said. All collaborators do it. The trouble is that it is too often but a first step to other things. Gradually, little by little, as the long days wore on and propinquity and solitude began to exercise their spell, Bulstrode could not disguise it from himself that he was becoming oddly drawn to this girl, Bootle. If she and he had been fishing for turtles on the same mid-Pacific isle, they could not have been in closer communion, and presently the realisation smote him like a blow that he loved her—and fervently, at that. For two pence, he told himself, had he not been a Mulliner and a gentleman, he could have crushed her in his arms and covered her face with burning kisses.

And, what was more, he could see by subtle signs that his love was returned. A quick glance from eyes that swiftly fell . . . the timid offer of a banana . . . a tremor in her voice as she asked if she might borrow his pencil-sharpener . . . These were little things, but they spoke volumes. If Genevieve Bootle was not crazy about him, he would eat his hat—or, rather, Mr. Schnellenhamer's hat.

He was appalled and horrified. All the Mulliners are the soul of honour, and as he thought of Mabelle Ridgway, waiting for him and trusting him in New York, Bulstrode burned with shame and remorse. In the hope of averting the catastrophe, he plunged with a fresh fury of energy into the picturisation of "Scented Sinners".

It was a fatal move. It simply meant that Genevieve Bootle had to work harder on the thing, too, and "Scented Sinners" was not the sort of production on which a frail girl could concentrate in warm weather without something cracking. Came a day with the thermometer in the nineties when, as he turned to refer to a point in Mr. Noakes's treatment, Bulstrode heard a sudden sharp snort at his side and, looking up, saw that Genevieve had begun to pace the room with feverish steps, her fingers entwined in her hair. And, as he stared at her in deep concern, she flung herself in a chair with a choking sob and buried her face in her hands.

And, seeing her weeping there, Bulstrode could restrain himself no longer. Something snapped in him. It was his collar-stud. His neck, normally a fifteen and an eighth, had suddenly swelled under the pressure of uncontrollable emotion into a large seventeen. For an instant he stood gurgling wordlessly like a bull-pup choking over a chicken-bone: then, darting forward, he clasped her in his arms and began to murmur all those words of love which until now he had kept pent up in his heart.

He spoke well and eloquently and at considerable length, but not at such length as he had planned. For at the end of perhaps two minutes and a quarter there rent the air in his immediate rear a sharp exclamation or cry: and, turning, he perceived in the doorway Mabelle Ridgway, his betrothed. With her was a dark young man with oiled hair and a saturnine expression, who looked like the sort of fellow the police are always spreading a drag-net for in connection with the recent robbery of Schoenstein's Bon Ton Delicatessen Store in Eighth Avenue.

There was a pause. It is never easy to know just what to say on these occasions: and Bulstrode, besides being embarrassed, was completely bewildered. He had supposed Mabelle three thousand miles away.

"Oh—hullo!" he said, untwining himself from Genevieve Bootle.

The dark young man was reaching in his hip-pocket, but Mabelle stopped him with a gesture.

"I can manage, thank you, Mr. Murgatroyd. There is no need for sawn-off shot-guns."

The young man had produced his weapon and was looking at it wistfully.

"I think you're wrong, lady," he demurred. "Do you know who that is that this necker is necking?" he asked, pointing an accusing finger at Genevieve Bootle, who was cowering against the ink-pot. "My girl. No less. In person. Not a picture."

Mabelle gasped.

"You don't say so!"

"I do say so."

"Well, it's a small world," said Mabelle. "Yes, sir, a small world, and you can't say it isn't. All the same, I think we had better not have any shooting. This is not Chicago. It might cause comment and remark."

"Maybe you're right," agreed Ed. Murgatroyd. He blew on his gun, polished it moodily with the sleeve of his coat, and restored it to his pocket. "But I'll give her a piece of my mind," he said, glowering at Genevieve, who had now retreated to the wall and was holding before her, as if in a piteous effort to shield herself from vengeance, an official communication from the Front Office notifying all writers that the expression "Polack mug" must no longer be used in dialogue.

"And I will give Mr. Mulliner a piece of *my* mind," said Mabelle. "You stay here and chat with Miss Bootle, while I interview the Great Lover in the passage."

Out in the corridor, Mabelle faced Bulstrode, tight-lipped. For a moment there was silence, broken only by the clicking of typewriters from the various hutches and the occasional despairing wail of a writer stuck for an adjective.

"Well, this is a surprise!" said Bulstrode, with a sickly smile. "How on earth do you come to be here, darling?"

"Miss Ridgway to you!" retorted Mabelle with flashing eyes. "I will tell you. I should have been in New York still if you had written, as you said you would. But all I've had since you left is one measly picture-postcard of the Grand

Canyon."

Bulstrode was stunned.

"You mean I've only written to you once?"

"Just once. And after waiting for three weeks, I decided to come here and see what was the matter. On the train I met Mr. Murgatroyd. We got into conversation, and I learned that he was in the same position as myself. His fiancée had disappeared into the No Man's Land of Hollywood, and she hadn't written at all. It was his idea that we should draw the studios. In the past two days we have visited seven, and to-day, flushing the Perfecto-Zizzbaum, we saw you coming out of a building . . ."

"The commissary. I had been having a small frosted malted milk. I felt sort of faint."

"You will feel sort of fainter," said Mabelle, her voice as frosted as any malted milk in California, "by the time I've done with you. So this is the kind of man you are, Bulstrode Mulliner! A traitor and a libertine!"

From inside the office came the sound of a girl's hysterics, blending with the deeper note of an upbraiding bootlegger and the rhythmic tapping on the wall of Mr. Dabney and Mr. Mendelsohn, who were trying to concentrate on "Scented Sinners". A lifetime in Chicago had given Mr. Murgatroyd the power of expressing his thoughts in terse, nervous English, and some of the words he was using, even when filtered through the door, were almost equivalent to pineapple bombs.

"A two-timing daddy and a trailing arbutus!" said Mabelle, piercing Bulstrode with her scornful eyes.

A messenger-boy came up with a communication from the Front Office notifying all writers that they must not smoke in the Exercise Yard. Bulstrode read it absently. The interruption had given him time to marshal his thoughts.

"You don't understand," he said. "You don't realise what it is like, being marooned in a motion-picture studio. What you have failed to appreciate is the awful yearning that comes over you for human society. There you sit for weeks and weeks, alone in the great silence, and then suddenly you find a girl in your office, washed up by the tide, and what happens? Instinctively you find yourself turning to her. As an individual, she may be distasteful to you, but she is—how shall I put it?—a symbol of the world without. I admit that I grabbed Miss Bootle. I own that I kissed her. But it meant nothing. It affected no vital issue. It was as if, locked in a dungeon cell, I had shown cordiality towards a pet mouse. You would not have censured me if you had come in and found me playing with a pet mouse. For all the kisses I showered on Miss Bootle, deep down in me I was true to you. It was simply that the awful loneliness . . . the deadly propinquity . . . Well, take the case," said Bulstrode, "of a couple on a raft in the Caribbean Sea . . ."

The stoniness of Mabelle's face did not soften.

"Never mind the Caribbean Sea," she interrupted. "I have nothing to say about the Caribbean Sea except that I wish somebody would throw you into it with a good, heavy brick round your neck. This is the end, Bulstrode Mulliner. I have done with you. If we meet on the street, don't bother to raise your hat."

"It is Mr. Schnellenhamer's hat."

"Well, don't bother to raise Mr. Schnellenhamer's hat, because I shall ignore you. I shall cut you dead." She looked past him at Ed. Murgatroyd, who was coming out of the office with a satisfied expression on his face. "Finished, Mr. Murgatroyd?"

"All washed up," said the bootlegger. "A nice clean job."

"Then perhaps you will escort me out of this Abode of Love."

"Oke, lady."

Mabelle glanced down with cold disdain at Bulstrode, who was clutching her despairingly.

"There is something clinging to my skirt, Mr. Murgatroyd," she said. "Might I trouble you to brush it off?"

A powerful hand fell on Bulstrode's shoulder. A powerful foot struck him on the trousers-seat. He flew through the open door of the office, tripping over Genevieve Bootle, who was now writhing on the floor.

Disentangling himself, he rose and dashed out. The corridor was empty. Mabelle Ridgway and Edward Murgatroyd had gone.

A good many of my relations, near and distant (proceeded Mr. Mulliner after a thoughtful sip at his hot Scotch and lemon), have found themselves in unpleasant situations in their time, but none, I am inclined to think, in any situation quite so unpleasant as that in which my nephew Bulstrode now found himself. It was as if he had stepped suddenly into one of those psychological modern novels where the hero's soul gets all tied up in knots as early as page 21 and never straightens itself out again.

To lose the girl one worships is bad enough in itself. But when, in addition, a man has got entangled with another girl, for whom he feels simultaneously and in equal proportions an overwhelming passion and a dull dislike—and when in addition to that he is obliged to spend his days working on a story like "Scented Sinners"—well, then he begins to realise how dark and sinister a thing this life of ours can be. Complex was the word that suggested itself to Bulstrode Mulliner.

He ached for Mabelle Ridgway. He also ached for Genevieve Bootle. And yet, even while he ached for Genevieve Bootle, some inner voice told him that if ever there was a pill it was she. Sometimes the urge to fold her in his arms and the urge to haul off and slap her over the nose with a piece of blotting paper came so close together that it was a mere flick of the coin which prevailed.

And then one afternoon when he had popped into the commissary for a frosted malted milk he tripped over the feet of a girl who was sitting by herself in a dark corner.

"I beg your pardon," he said courteously, for a Mulliner, even when his so l is racked, never forgets his manners.

"Don't mention it, Bulstrode," said the girl.

Bulstrode uttered a stunned cry.

"You!"

He stared at her, speechless. In his eyes there was nothing but amazement, but in those of Mabelle Ridgway there shone a soft and friendly light.

"How are you, Bulstrode?" she asked.

Bulstrode was still wrestling with his astonishment.

"But what are you doing here?" he cried.

"I am working on 'Scented Sinners'. Mr. Murgatroyd and I are doing a treatment together. It is quite simple," said Mabelle. "That day when I left you we started to walk to the studio gate, and it so happened that as we passed, Mr. Schnellenhamer was looking out of his window. A few moments later his secretary came running out and said he wished to see us. We went to his office, where he gave us contracts to sign. I think he must have extraordinary personal magnetism," said Mabelle pensively, "for we both signed immediately, though nothing was further from our plans than to join the writing staff of the Perfecto-Zizzbaum. I had intended to go back to New York, and Mr. Murgatroyd was complaining that his boot-legging business must be going all to pieces without him. It seems to be one of those businesses that need the individual touch." She paused. "What do you think of Mr. Murgatroyd, Bulstrode?"

"I dislike him intensely."

"You wouldn't say he had a certain strange, weird fascination?"

"No."

"Well, perhaps you're right," said Mabelle dubiously. "You were certainly right about it being lonely in this studio. I'm afraid I was a little cross, Bulstrode, when we last met. I understand now. You really don't think there is a curious, intangible glamour about Mr. Murgatroyd?"

"I do not."

"Well, you may be right, of course. Goodbye, Bulstrode, I must be going. I have already exceeded the seven and a quarter minutes which the Front Office allows female writers for the consumption of nut sundaes. If we do not meet again . . ."

"But surely we're going to meet all the time?"

Mabelle shook her head.

"The Front Office has just sent out a communication to all writers, forbidding inmates of the Ohio State Penitentiary to associate with those in the Leper Colony. They think it unsettles them. So unless we run into one another in the commissary . . . Well, goodbye, Bulstrode."

She bit her lip in sudden pain, and was gone.

It was some ten days later that the encounter at which Mabelle had hinted took place. The heaviness of a storm-tossed soul had brought Bulstrode to the commissary for a frosted malted milk once more, and there, toying with—repectively—a Surprise Gloria Swanson and a Cheese Sandwich Maurice Chevalier, were Mabelle Ridgway and Ed. Murgatroyd. They were looking into each other's eyes with a silent passion in which, an observer would have noted, there was a distinct admixture of dislike and repulsion.

Mabelle glanced up as Bulstrode reached the table.

"Good afternoon," she said, with a welcoming smile. "I think you know my fiancée, Mr. Murgatroyd?"

Bulstrode reeled.

"Your what did you say?" he exclaimed.

"We're engaged," said Mr. Murgatroyd sombrely.

"Since this morning," added Mabelle. "It was at exactly six minutes past eleven that we found ourselves linked in a close embrace."

Bulstrode endeavoured to conceal his despair.

"I hope you will be very happy," he said.

"A swell chance!" rejoined Mr. Murgatroyd. "I'm not saying this beasel here doesn't exert a strange fascination over me, but I think it only fair to inform her here and now—before witnesses—that at the same time the mere sight of her makes me sick."

"It is the same with me," said Mabelle. "When in Mr. Murgatroyd's presence, I feel like some woman wailing for her demon lover, and all the while I am shuddering at that awful stuff he puts on his hair."

"The best hair-oil in Chicago," said Mr. Murgatroyd, a little stiffly.

"It is as if I were under some terrible hypnotic influence which urged me against the promptings of my true self to love Mr. Murgatroyd," explained Mabelle.

"Make that double, sister," said the bootlegger. "It goes for me, too."

"Precisely," cried Bulstrode, "how I feel towards my fiancée, Miss Bootle."

"Are you engaged to that broad?" asked Mr. Murgatroyd.

"I am."

Ed. Murgatroyd paled and swallowed a mouthful of cheese sandwich. There was silence for a while.

"I see it all," said Mabelle. "We have fallen under the hideous spell of this place. It is as you said, Bulstrode, when you wanted me to take the case of a couple on a raft in the Caribbean Sea. There is a miasma in the atmosphere of the Perfecto-Zizzbaum lot which undoes all who come within its sphere of influence. And here I am, pledged to marry a gargoyle like Mr. Murgatroyd."

"And what about me?" demanded the bootlegger. "Do you think I enjoy being teamed up with a wren that doesn't know the first principles of needling beer? A swell helpmeet you're going to make for a man in my line of business!"

"And where do I get off?" cried Bulstrode passionately. "My blood races at the sight of Genevieve Bootle, and yet all the while I know that she is one of Nature's prunes. The mere thought of marrying her appals me. Apart from the fact that I worship you, Mabelle, with every fibre of my being."

"And I worship you, Bulstrode."

"And I'm that way about Genevieve," said Mr. Murgatroyd.

There was another silence.

"There is only one way out of this dreadful situation," said Mabelle. "We must go to Mr. Schnellenhamer and hand in our resignations. Once we are free from this noxious environment, everything will adjust itself nicely. Let us go and see him immediately."

They did not see Mr. Schnellenhamer immediately, for nobody ever did. But after a vigil of two hours in the reception-room, they were finally admitted to his presence, and they filed in and stated their case.

The effect on the President of the Perfecto-Zizzbaum Corporation of their request that they be allowed to resign was stupendous. If they had been Cossacks looking in at the office to start a pogrom, he could not have been more moved. His eyes bulged, and his nose drooped like the trunk of an elephant which has been refused a peanut.

"It can't be done," he said curtly. He reached in the drawer of his desk, produced a handful of documents and rapped them with an ominous decision. "Here are the contracts, duly signed by you, in which you engage to remain in the employment of the Perfecto-Zizzbaum Corporation until the completion of the picture entitled 'Scented Sinners'. Did you take a look at Para. 6, where it gives the penalties for breach of same? No, don't read them," he said, as Mabelle stretched out a hand. "You wouldn't sleep nights. But you can take it from me they're some penalties. We've had this thing before of writers wanting to run out on us, so we took steps to protect ourselves."

"Would we be taken for a ride?" asked Mr. Murgatroyd uneasily.

Mr. Schnellenhamer smiled quietly but did not reply. He replaced the contracts in the drawer, and his manner softened and became more appealing. This man knew well when to brandish the iron fist and when to display the velvet glove.

"And, anyway," he said, speaking now in almost a fatherly manner, "you wouldn't wan to quit till the picture was finished. Of course you wouldn't, not three nice, square-shooting folks like you. It wouldn't be right. It wouldn't be fair. It wouldn't be co-operation. You know what 'Scented Sinners' means to this organisation. It's the biggest proposition we have. Our whole programme is built around it. We are relying on it to be our big smash. It cost us a barrel of money to buy 'Scented Sinners', and naturally we aim to get it back."

He rose from his chair, and tears came into his eyes. It was as if he had been some emotional American football coach addressing a faint-hearted team.

"Stick to it!" he urged. "Stick to it, folks! You can do it if you like. Get back in there and fight. Think of the boys in the Front Office rooting for you, depending on you. You wouldn't let them down? No, no, not you. You wouldn't let me down? Of course you wouldn't. Get back in the game, then, and win—win—win . . . for dear old Perfecto-Zizzbaum and me."

He flung himself into his chair, gazing at them with appealing eyes.

"May I read Para. 6?" asked Mr. Murgatroyd after a pause.

"No, don't read Para. 6," urged Mr. Schnellenhamer. "Far, far better not read Para. 6."

Mabelle looked hopelessly at Bulstrode.

"Come," she said. "It is useless for us to remain here."

They left the office with dragging steps. Mr. Schnellenhamer, a grave expression on his face, pressed the bell for his secretary.

"I don't like the look of things, Miss Stern," he said. "There seems to be a spirit of unrest among the 'Scented Sinners' gang. Three of them have just been in wanting to quit. I shouldn't be surprised if rebellion isn't seething. Say, listen," he asked keenly, "nobody's been ill-treating them, have they?"

"Why, the idea, Mr. Schnellenhamer!"

"I thought I heard screams coming from their building yesterday."

"That was Mr. Doakes. He was working on his treatment, and he had some kind of a fit. Frothed at the mouth and kept shouting, 'No, no! It isn't possible!' If you ask me," said Miss Stern, "it's just the warm weather. We most generally always lose a few writers this time of year."

Mr. Schnellenhamer shook his head.

"This ain't the ordinary thing of authors going cuckoo. It's something deeper. It's the spirit of unrest, or rebellion seething, or something like that. What am I doing at five o'clock?"

"Conferencing with Mr. Levitsky."

"Cancel it. Send round notice to all writers on 'Scented Sinners' to meet me on Stage Four. I'll give them a pep-talk."

At a few minutes before five, accordingly, there debouched from the Leper Colony and from the Ohio State Penitentiary a motley collection of writers. There were young writers, old writers, middle-aged writers; writers with matted beards at which they plucked nervously, writers with horn-rimmed spectacles who muttered to themselves, writers with eyes that stared blankly or blinked in the unaccustomed light. On all of them 'Scented Sinners' had set its unmistakable seal. They shuffled listlessly along till they came to Stage Four, where they seated themselves on wooden benches, waiting for Mr. Schnellenhamer to arrive.

Bulstrode had found a place next to Mabelle Ridgway. The girl's face was drawn and despondent.

"Edward is breaking in a new quart of hair-oil for the wedding," she said, after a moment of silence.

Bulstrode shivered.

"Genevieve," he replied, "has bought one of those combination eyebrow tweezers and egg-scramblers. The advertisement said that no bride should be without them."

Mabelle drew her breath in sharply.

"Can nothing be done?" asked Bulstrode.

"Nothing," said Mabelle dully. "We cannot leave till 'Scented Sinners' is finished, and it never will be finished—never . . . never . . . never." Her spiritual face was contorted for a moment. "I hear there are writers who have been working on it for years and years. That grey-bearded gentleman over there, who is sticking straws in his hair," she said, pointing. "That is Mr. Markey. He has the office next to ours, and comes in occasionally to complain that there are spiders crawling up his wall. He has been doing treatments of 'Scented Sinners' since he was a young man."

In the tense instant during which they stared at each other with mournful, hopeless eyes, Mr. Schnellenhamer bustled in and mounted the platform. He surveyed the gathering authoritatively: then, clearing his throat, began to speak.

He spoke of Service and Ideals, of Co-operation and the Spirit That Wins to Success. He had just begun to touch on the glories of the Southern Californian climate, when the scent of a powerful cigar floated over the meeting, and a voice spoke.

"Hey!"

All eyes were turned in the intruder's direction. It was Mr. Isadore Levitsky, the chief business operative, who stood there, he with whom Mr. Schnellenhamer had had an appointment to conference.

"What's all this?" demanded Mr. Levitsky. "You had a date with me in my office."

Mr. Schnellenhamer hurried down from the platform and drew Mr. Levitsky aside.

"I'm sorry, I.G.," he said. "I had to break our date. There's all this spirit of unrest broke out among the 'Scented Sinners' gang, and I thought I'd better talk to them. You remember that time five years ago when we had to call out the State Militia."

Mr. Levitsky looked puzzled.

"The what gang?"

"The writers who are doing treatments on 'Scented Sinners'. You know 'Scented Sinners' that we bought."

"But we didn't," said Mr. Levitsky.

"We didn't?" said Mr. Schnellenhamer, surprised.

"Certainly we didn't. Don't you remember the Medulla-Oblongata-Glutz people outbid us?"

Mr. Schnellenhamer stood for a moment, musing.

"That's right, too," he said at length. "They did, didn't they?"

"Certainly they did."

"Then the story doesn't belong to us at all?"

"Certainly it doesn't. M-O-G has owned it for the last eleven years."

Mr. Schnellenhamer smote his forehead.

"Of course! It all comes back to me now. I had quite forgotten."

He mounted the platform once more.

"Ladies and gentlemen," he said, "all work on 'Scented Sinners' will cease immediately. The studio has discovered that it doesn't own it."

It was a merry gathering that took place in the commissary of the Perfecto-Zizzbaum Studios some half-hour later. Genevieve Bootle had broken her engagement to Bulstrode and was sitting with her hand linked in that of Ed. Murgatroyd. Mabelle Ridgway had broken her engagement to Ed. Murgatroyd and was stroking Bulstrode's arm. It would have been hard to find four happier people, unless you had stepped outside and searched among the horde of emancipated writers who were dancing the Carmagnole so blithely around the shoe-shining stand.

"And what are you two good folks going to do now?" asked Ed. Murgatroyd, surveying Bulstrode and Mabelle with kindly eyes. "Have you made any plans?"

"I came out here to strike oil," said Bulstrode. "I'll do it now."

He raised a cheery hand and brought it down with an affectionate smack on the bootlegger's gleaming head.

"Ha, ha!" chuckled Bulstrode.

"Ha, ha!" roared Mr. Murgatroyd.

"Ha, ha!" tittered Mabelle and Genevieve.

A perfect camaraderie prevailed among these four young people, delightful to see.

"No, but seriously," said Mr. Murgatroyd, wiping the tears from his eyes, "are you fixed all right? Have you got enough dough to get married on?"

Mabelle looked at Bulstrode. Bulstrode looked at Mabelle. For the first time a shadow seemed to fall over their happiness.

"We haven't," Bulstrode was forced to admit.

Ed. Murgatroyd slapped him on the shoulder.

"Then come and join my little outfit," he said heartily. "I've always room for a personal friend. Besides, we're muscling into the North Side beer industry next month, and I shall need willing helpers."

Bulstrode clasped his hand, deeply moved.

"Ed.," he exclaimed, "I call that square of you. I'll buy a machine-gun to-morrow."

With his other hand he sought Mabelle's hand and pressed it. Outside, the laughter of the mob had turned into wild cheering. A bonfire had been started, and Mr. Doakes, Mr. Noakes, Miss Faversham, Miss Wilson, Mr. Fotheringay, Mr. Mendelsohn, Mr. Markey and the others were feeding it with their scripts of 'Scented Sinners'.

In the Front Office, Mr. Schnellenhamer and Mr. Levitsky, suspending their seven hundred and forty-first conference for an instant, listened to the tumult.

"Makes you feel like Lincoln, doesn't it?" said Mr. Levitsky.

"Ah!" said Mr. Schnellenhamer.

They smiled indulgently. They were kindly men at heart and they liked the girls and boys to be happy.

33

ARCHIBALD AND THE MASSES

"THIS here Socialism," said a Pint of Bitter thoughtfully. "You see a lot of that about nowadays. Seems to be all the go."

Nothing in the previous conversation—we had been speaking of mangel-wurzels —had led up to the remark, but in the matter of debate we of the bar-parlour of the Anglers' Rest are quick movers. We range. We flit. We leap from point to point. As an erudite Gin and Angostura once put it, we are like Caesar's wife, ready for anything. Rapidly adjusting our minds, we prepared to deal with this new topic

"Ah," agreed a Small Bass, "you may well say that."

"You well may," said a Light Lager. "Spreading all the time, Socialism is. May be something in it, too. What I mean, it doesn't seem hardly right somehow that you and I should be living off the fat of the land, as the saying is, while there's others, in humbler circumstances, who don't know where to turn for their next half-pint."

Mr. Mulliner nodded.

"That," he said, "was precisely how my nephew Archibald felt."

"He was a Socialist, was he?"

"He became one temporarily."

The Small Bass wrinkled his forehead.

"Seems to me you've told us about your nephew Archibald before. Was he the one who had the trouble with the explorer?"

"That was Osbert."

"The one who stammered?"

"No. That was George."

"You seem to have so many nephews."

"I have been singularly blessed in that respect," agreed Mr. Mulliner. "But, as regards Archibald, it may serve to recall him to you if I mention that he was generally considered to be London's leading exponent of the art of imitating a hen laying an egg."

"Of course, yes. He got engaged to a girl named Aurelia Cammarleigh."

"At the time when my story begins, he was still engaged to her and possibly the happiest young man in the whole W.1. postal district. But the storm-clouds, I regret to say, were only just over the horizon. The tempest which was so nearly to wreck the bark of Love had already begun to gather."

Few fashionable engagements (said Mr. Mulliner) have ever started with fairer prospects of success than that of my nephew Archibald and Aurelia Cammerleigh. Even cynical Mayfair had to admit that for once a really happy and enduring marriage appeared to be indicated. For such a union there is no surer basis than a community of taste, and this the young couple possessed in full measure. Archibald liked imitating hens, and Aurelia liked listening to him. She used to say she could listen to him all day, and she sometimes did.

It was after one of these sessions—when, hoarse but happy, he was walking back to his rooms to dress for dinner, that he found his progress impeded by a man of seedy aspect who, without any preamble but a short hiccough, said that he had not been able to taste bread for three days.

It puzzled Archibald a little that a complete stranger should be making him the recipient of confidences which might more reasonably have been bestowed upon his medical adviser: but it so happened that only recently he himself had not been able to taste even Stilton cheese. So he replied as one having knowledge.

"Don't you worry, old thing," he said. "That often happens when you get a cold in the head. It passes off."

"I have not got a cold in the head, sir," said the man. "I have got pains in the back, weak lungs, a sick wife, stiff joints, five children, internal swellings, and no pension after seven years in His Majesty's army owing to jealousy in high quarters, but not a cold in the head. Why I can't taste bread is because I have no money to buy it. I wish, sir, you could hear my children crying for bread."

"I'd love to," said Archibald civilly. "I must come up and see you some time. But tell me about bread. Does it cost much?"

"Well, sir, it's this way. If you buy it by the bottle, that's expensive. What I always say it, best to get in a cask. But then, again, that needs capital."

"If I slipped you a fiver, could you manage?"

"I'd try, sir."

"Right ho," said Archibald.

This episode had a singular effect on Archibald Mulliner. I will not say that it made him think deeply, for he was incapable of thinking deeply. But it engendered a curious gravity, an odd sense that life was stern and life was earnest, and he was still in the grip of this new mood when he reached his rooms and Meadowes, his man, brought him a tray with a decanter and syphon upon it.

"Meadowes," said Archibald, "are you busy for the moment?"

"No, sir."

"Then let us speak for a while on the subject of bread. Do you realise, Meadowes, that there are blokes who can't get bread? They want it, their wives want it, their children are all for it, but in spite of this unanimity what is the upshot? No bread. I'll bet you didn't know that, Meadowes."

"Yes, sir. There is a great deal of poverty in London."

"Not really?"

"Oh, yes, indeed, sir. You should go down to a place like Bottleton East. That is where you hear the Voice of the People."

"What people?"

"The masses, sir. The martyred proletariat. If you are interested in the martyred proletariat, I could supply you with some well-written pamphlets. I nave been a member of the League for the Dawn of Freedom for many years, sir. Our object, as the name implies, is to hasten the coming revolution."

"Like in Russia, do you mean?"

"Yes, sir."

"Massacres and all that?"

"Yes, sir."

"Now, listen, Meadowes," said Archibald firmly. "Fun's fun, but no rot about stabbing me with a dripping knife. I won't have it, do you understand?"

"Very good, sir."

"That being clear, you may bring me those pamphlets. I'd like to have a look at them."

Knowing Archibald as I do (said Mr. Mulliner), I find it difficult to believe that the remarkable change which at this point took place in what for want of a better term one may call his mental outlook could have come entirely from reading pamphlets. Indeed, I cannot bring myself to think that he ever read one of those compositions in its entirety. You know what pamphlets are. They ramble. They go into sections and sub-sections. If they can think of a phrase like "the basic fundamentals of the principles governing distribution", they shove it in. It seems far more likely that he was influenced by hearing Meadowes speak in the Park. Meadowes, on his days off, had the third rostrum from the left as you enter by the Marble Arch gate, and in addition to an impressive delivery enjoyed a considerable gift of invective.

However, of one thing there is no doubt. Before the end of the second week Archibald had become completely converted to the gospel of the Brotherhood of Man: and, as this made him a graver, deeper Archibald, it was not long, of course, before Aurelia noticed the change. And one night, when they were dancing at the Mottled Earwig, she took him to task in her forthright way, accusing him in set terms of going about the place looking like an uncooked haddock.

"I'm sorry, old girl," replied Archibald apologetically. "The fact is, I'm brooding a bit at the moment on the situation in Bottleton East."

Aurelia stared at him.

"Archibald," she said, for she was a girl of swift intuitions, "you've had one over the eight."

"No, I haven't, honestly. It's simply that I'm brooding. And I was wondering if you would mind if I toddled home fairly shortly. All this sort of thing jars on me a goodish bit. All this dancing and so forth, I mean. I mean to say, so different from the home-life of Bottleton East. I don't think a chap ought to be dancing at a time when the fundamental distribution of whatever-it-is is so dashed what-d'you-call-it. You don't find Stalin dancing. Nor Maxton. Nor, for the matter of that, Sidney, Lord Passfield."

Aurelia refused to be mollified.

"I don't know what's come over you," she said petulantly. "You seem absolutely to have changed this last couple of weeks. You used to be one of the cheeriest old bounders that ever donned a spat, and now you're a sort of emperor of the Glooms. You don't even do your hen-imitation any more."

"Well, the thing is, you can't imitate a hen laying an egg properly if your heart's bleeding for the martyred proletariat."

"The what?"

"The martyred proletariat."

"What's that?"

"Well . . . er . . . it's—how shall I put it? . . . it's the martyred proletariat."

"You wouldn't know a martyred proletariat if they brought it to you on a skewer with Béarnaise sauce."

"Oh, yes, I should. Meadowes has been giving me all the inside stuff. What it all boils down to, if you follow me, is that certain blokes—me, for example—have got much too much of the ready, while certain blokes—the martyred proletariat, for instance—haven't got enough. This makes it fairly foul for the m.p., if you see what I mean."

"I don't see what you mean at all. Oh, well, let's hope you'll have slept all this off by tomorrow. By the way, where are you taking me to dine tomorrow?"

Archibald looked embarrassed.

"I'm awfully sorry, old prune, but I had rather planned to buzz down to Bottleton East tomorrow, to take a dekko at the martyred p."

"Listen," said Aurelia tensely, "do you know what you're really going to do tomorrow? You're coming round to my house and you're going to render that hen-imitation of yours . . ."

"But it seems so shallow. Sir Stafford Cripps doesn't imitate hens."

". . . and render it," continued Aurelia, "with even more than ordinary brio, gusto and zip. Otherwise, everything is over."

"But don't you realise that one four four oh point oh oh six families in Bottleton East . . ."

"That will be all about Bottleton East," said Aurelia coldly. "I've said all I am going to say. You understand the position. If, by closing-time tomorrow, you are not round at Number 36A, Park Street, imitating hens till your eyes bubble, you may seek elsewhere for a mate. Because, as far as I am concerned, my nomination will be cancelled. I don't think anybody could call me an unreasonable girl. I am not capricious, not exacting. But I'm positively dashed if I'm going to marry a man who is beginning to be hailed on all sides as London's leading living corpse."

It was a thoughtful Archibald Mulliner who rose towards evening of the following day and rang the bell for Meadowes, his man. This expedition to Bottleton East was very near his heart. What he felt, he meant to say, was that it's not much good a chap loving the Masses if he never goes near them. He wanted to dash about and fraternise, and show the Masses that in Archibald Mulliner they had a bird whose heart bled for them. And unless he went and looked them up every now and then, they couldn't know that there was an Archibald Mulliner in existence.

No, come what might, he could not forgo this trip. He put it to Meadowes when he entered, explaining all the circumstances, and Meadowes felt the same.

"There must always be martyrs to the Cause, Comrade Mulliner," said Meadowes.

"Yes, I suppose there must, when you come right down to it," agreed Archibald moodily. "Though I'd a dashed sight rather it was a couple of other fellows. All right, then, I'll go. And if that's a drink you've got there, my dear old Third Internationalist, pour it out. There are moments when a chap needs a stiff one."

"Say when, Comrade Mulliner."

"Not all the soda, Comrade Meadowes," said Archibald.

My nephew Archibald, like all the Mulliners, is of an honest and candid disposition, incapable of subterfuge, and there is no doubt that if you had asked him his opinion of Bottleton East as he pased its streets that night he would have confessed frankly that he was just a bit disappointed in the place. Too bright, would have been his verdict, too bally jovial. Arriving in the expectation of finding a sort of grey inferno, he appeared to have been plunged into a perfect maelstrom of gaiety.

On every side, merry matrons sat calling each other names on doorsteps. Cheery cats fought among the garbage-pails. From the busy public-houses came the sound of mouth-organ and song. While, as for the children, who were present in enormous quantities, so far from crying for bread, as he had been led to expect, they were playing hop-scotch all over the pavements. The whole atmosphere, in a word, was, he tells me, more like that of Guest Night at the National Liberal Club than anything he had ever encountered.

But a Mulliner is not easily discouraged. Archibald had come to Bottleton East to relieve the sufferings of the tortured Masses, and he intended to do so if it took all night. Surely, he felt, somewhere among these teeming, pleasure-seeking children there must be one who could do with a bit of bread. And presently it seemed to him that he had found such a one. He had turned down a side-street, and there, coming towards him, kicking a tin can in a preoccupied manner was a small boy who looked just about in the right vein for a slice or two. His face was grave, his manner sombre and introspective. If he was not actually crying for the stuff at the moment, it was simply, Archibald felt, because he was taking time off.

To seize this child by the hand and drag him to the nearest confectioner and baker was with Archibald Mulliner the work of a moment. He pulled out his note-case and was soon in possession of a fine quartern loaf. He thrust it into the child's hands.

"Bread," he said cordially.

The child recoiled. The look of pain on his face had deepened.

"It's all right," Archibald assured him. "Nothing to pay. This is on me. A free gift. One loaf, with comps. of A. Mulliner."

Gently patting the stripling's head, he turned away, modestly anxious to be spared any tearful gratitude, and he had hardly gone a couple of steps when something solid struck him a violent blow on the nape of the neck. For an instant, he thought of thunderbolts, falling roofs, and explosions which kill ten. Then, looking down, he perceived the quartern loaf rolling away along the gutter.

The fact was, the child had been a little vexed. At first, when Archibald had started steering him towards the shop, he had supposed my nephew unbalanced. Then, observing that among the objects for sale at the emporium were chocolate bars, jujubes, and all-day suckers, he had brightened a little. Still dubious as to his companion's sanity, he had told himself that an all-day sucker tastes just as good, even if it proceeds from a dotty donor. And then, just as hope had begun to rise high, this man had fobbed him off with a loaf of bread.

Little wonder that he had chafed. His mood was bitter. And when moods are bitter in Bottleton East direct action follows automatically.

Well, Archibald did what he could. Stooping and picking up the loaf, he darted after the child with bared teeth and flaming eyes. It was his intention to overtake him and fill him up with bread, regardless of his struggles and protests. The thing seemed to him a straight issue. This child needed bread, and he was jolly well going to get it—even if it meant holding him with one hand and shoving the stuff down his throat with the other. In all the history of social work in London's East End there can seldom have been an instance of one of the philanthropic rich being more firmly bent on doing good and giving of his abundance.

His efforts, however, were fruitless. Life in Bottleton East tends to make the young citizen nippy on his feet. Archibald cut out quite a nice pace, but a knowledge of the terrain stood the little fellow in good stead. Presently he had vanished into the night from which he had come, and Archibald, for the weather was sultry and the going had been fast, was left standing—all other emotions swept away in an imperious desire for a cool drink.

There is something about the atmosphere of the tap-room of a public-house that never fails to act like magic on ruffled feelings. The rich smell of mixed liquors, the gay clamour of carefree men arguing about the weather, the Government, the Royal Family, greyhound racing, the tax on beer, pugilism, religion, and the price of bananas—these things are medicine to the bruised soul. Standing in the doorway of the Goose and Gherkin, Archibald became immediately conscious of a restored benevolence.

He had been wrong, he saw, to allow the unpleasant personality of a single child to colour his views on the Masses. Probably that blighted kid had been in no sense representative of the Masses. If one did but know, he told himself, the little beast was very likely thoroughly unpopular in the neighbourhood, if not actually cut by the Bottleton East equivalent of the County. Judging the martyred proletariat by that child was like coming to Mayfair and forming your opinion of the West End of London after meeting somebody like Clarence ("Pot of Poison") Greaseley.

No, the Masses were all right. Once more his heart bled for them, and it seemed to him that the least he could do was to stand them drinks all round. With this humane object in view, he advanced to the counter and, with recollections of old Western films in his mind, addressed the shirt-sleeved man behind it.

"Set 'em up!" he said.

"What's that?" asked the shirt-sleeved man.

"Set 'em up. Ask these gentlemen to name their poison."

"I don't follow you at all," said the shirt-sleeved man.

"Dash it," said Archibald, a little nettled, "it's quite simple, isn't it? I want these martyred chaps to join me in a spot. Serve out noggins to the multitude and chalk it up to me."

"Ah!" said the shirt-sleeved man. "Now I see. Now I understand."

The information, rapidly flashed about the room that a human drinking-fountain was in their midst, had the usual effect on the gathering. Their already marked geniality became intensified, and Archibald, as the founder of the feast, was soon the centre of a loving group. They all seemed to look to him for guidance on the various topics of discussion, and with each minute his favourable opinion of the Masses grew. A young man who, when among his peers, generally experienced a certain difficulty in obtaining an audience for his views—his fellow-members of the Drones Club being too prone, whenever he opened his mouth, to urge him to put a sock in it—he found this novel deference enchanting. In the Masses, it seemed to him, he had found his spiritual mates.

Madame Récamier or any other of the hostesses of the old-time *salon* would have recognised and understood his emotions. They knew how agreeable it is to be the focal point of a brilliant gathering. His first half-hour in the tap-room of the Goose and Gherkin was, I should imagine, the happiest of my nephew Archibald's life.

They seemed so anxious to make it plain to him, these honest fellows, that in him they recognised not only the life and soul of the party but the Master Mind.

Draining and refilling their glasses at his expense, they hung on his words and made him the unquestioned arbiter of their little disputes. Scarcely had he reassured one as to the chances of the rain holding off, when he was informing another that the Government, though fat-headed, on the whole meant well. He told a man in a cloth cap how to address a Duchess at an informal lunch. He put a man with a broken nose right on the subject of the Apostolic Claims of the Church of Abyssinia.

Each dictum that he uttered was received with murmurs of assent and approval, while at intervals some hearty soul would have his glass recharged and the expense debited to Archibald's account in order that he might drink Archibald's health. I have heard my nephew describe the scene again and again, and each time he described it I could see more clearly how closely the whole affair must have approximated to a love-feast.

But the pleasantest of functions must come to an end, and it seemed to Archibald that the time had come to be pushing along. Much as he liked these tortured bimbos, there were other tortured bimbos in Bottleton East and it was only fair that he should give those, too, a little happiness. So, having ordered a final round, he asked for his account and, thrusting a hand into his pocket, brought it out empty. His note-case was not there. Presumably, when paying for the loaf of bread, he must have left it on the counter of the baker's shop, and the baker, one of those strong, silent men who give the Englishman his reputation for reticence the world over, had not thought it worth while to call his attention to the lapse.

As a psychologist, I found it interesting when Archibald told me that his immediate reaction to this discovery was not dismay. So uplifted was he by the atmosphere of adulation in which he had been basking for the past half-hour that all he felt for the moment was a sort of humorous self-reproach. The laugh, he recognised, was on him. He would have to be prepared, he foresaw, to become the butt of a certain amount of good-natured chaff. With a deprecatory titter he informed the shirt-sleeved man of the position of affairs, and he was just about to add his name and address, in order to facilitate the forwarding of the bill by post, when there broke out something which in its general aspect, he felt dimly, closely paralleled that social revolution of which Meadowes had often spoken so feelingly. And through a sort of mist he saw the shirt-sleeved man vaulting over the counter, moistening the palms of his hands in a purposeful manner.

One can see the situation through the eyes of this shirt-sleeved man. From boyhood up, his views on bilking had been hard and bigoted. Even a mere snitched half-pint had been, in the past, enough to rouse his worst passions. And here before him he saw a man who had bilked on a scale so stupendous, so—as one might say—epic, that history had been made that night in Bottleton East.

Archibald's assertion that the shirt-sleeved man had six arms I discount as due to his not unnatural perturbation at the moment. He bases it on the fact that someone—he assumes it to have been the shirt-sleeved man—seized him by the collar, the right arm, the left arm, the right leg, the left leg, and the seat of the trousers simultaneously. However, be that as it may, my nephew passed the next few moments of his career being shaken like some patent medicine until he could feel his contents frothing within him. Then, just as he had begun to realise that, if this continued, he must reluctantly come unstuck, something seemed to give and he was shooting through the night air—to hit the pavement, bounce, hit it again, bounce for the second time, ricochet along the polished surface for a considerable distance, and eventually come to a halt in the gutter with his head resting against what in its prime must have been part of a good-sized fish. A halibut, Archibald thinks, or a cod.

He did not remain there long. In relating to you these little family reminiscences of mine, I have often been struck by a curious thing. I refer to the manner in which a Mulliner, when the crisis arrives, always proves himself a Mulliner—a man, that is to say, of sagacity, resource and initiative. It would be paltering with the truth to say that my nephew Archibald was one of the most quick-witted of the clan, but even he, on observing the shirt-sleeved man heading in his direction, followed by an incensed mob of his recent guests, knew enough to jump to his feet and disappear into the darkness like a hare. Panic lent him wings. There was a moment or two when he heard footsteps clattering in his rear, and once a hard-boiled egg missed him by a hair's-breadth, but eventually he won to a clear lead, and presently was at leisure to halt and give himself up to his meditations.

These, as you may readily imagine, were not of the kindliest. Sir Stafford Cripps would not have liked them. Stalin, could he have been aware of them, would have pursed his lips. For they were definitely hostile to the Masses. All his pitying love for the martyred proletariat had vanished. He has specifically inform-ed me since that in those black moments he wished the martyred proletariat would choke. And the·same went for the tortured Masses. He tells me that when he reflected how he had, to all intents and purposes, spurned Aurelia's love and broken her gentle heart just for the sake of doing a bit of good to these tortured bounders he could have laid his head against a lamp-post and wept.

At length, rested and refreshed by his halt, he resumed his progress. He desired above all else to find a way out of this ghastly locality, to return to the civilised amenities of Mayfair, W.1., where men are men and where, if one of those men finds himself short of cash in a place of refreshment, he can simply call for a pencil and sign the bill. Imagine, he meant to say, Ferraro at the Berkeley taking a fellow by the seat of the trousers and playing quoits with him along Piccadilly.

Yes, as I say, my nephew Archibald yearned for Mayfair as the hart pants for cooling streams when heated in the chase. But the problem was: How to get there. He had steeled himself to the prospect of having to walk. All he wanted to know was in what direction to walk. He asked a policeman the way to Piccadilly Circus, but you cannot ask a question like that in Bottleton East without exciting unpleasant suspicions. The policeman merely gave Archibald a narrow look and told him to pass along. Upon which, Archibald passed along and the episode concluded.

It was possibly some twenty minutes after this that he became conscious of a great hunger.

It had been his intention, on setting out for Bottleton East, to take his evening meal there. He had not supposed that the place would run to anything luxurious, but he rather enjoyed the prospect of roughing it as a sort of graceful gesture towards the Masses. And, after all, he was no hog. A little clear soup, with possibly a touch of smoked salmon or a bit of melon in front of it, followed by—say—*truite bleue* and the wing of a chicken and some sort of *soufflé* would do him nicely. And he had been about to look around him for a suitable restaurant when the affair of the anti-bread child had distracted his thoughts. And after that there had been all the *salon* stuff and then the race for life. The consequence was that he was now extremely peckish.

And it was at this moment that he found himself outside one of the myriad public-houses of the locality, staring through an open window into a room with two oilcloth-covered tables in it. At one there sat a dishevelled man, asleep with his head on his arms. The other was unoccupied, except for a knife and fork which gave promise of rich entertainment.

For a while he stood, staring wolfishly. As he had no money, the situation seemed an *impasse*. But, as I said before, the crisis always brings out the Mulliner in a member of my family. Suddenly, like a flash, there shot into Archibald's mind the recollection that round his neck, carefully adjusted so that it should lie exactly over his heart, he always wore a miniature of Aurelia Cammarleigh in a neat little platinum case.

He hesitated. His spiritual side told him that it would be sacrilege to hand over the outer covering of that sweet girl's miniature in exchange for a meal. But his material self wanted steak and beer, and had him charging through the doorway like a mustang before the hesitation had lasted ten seconds.

Half an hour later, Archibald Mulliner was pushing back his plate and uttering a deep sigh.

It was a sigh of repletion, not of regret. And yet in it there was, perhaps, something of regret as well—for, his hunger now satisfied, kindlier feelings had once more begun to burgeon within him, and he was feeling a little remorseful that he should have allowed himself to think such hard thoughts about the Masses.

After all, reasoned Archibald, sipping his beer and glowing with the broad-minded charity of repletion, you had to admit that at the time of all that unpleasantness there had been something to be said for the view-point of the Masses. He meant to say, a nasty jar it must have been for those poor old proletarians, after having been martyred like the dickens since they were slips of boys, to suck down what they had been led to suppose were free drinks and then suddenly to realise that, owing to donor having no money, they were in ghastly danger of having to pay for them themselves.

And the shirt-sleeved man. Yes, he could follow the shirt-sleeved man's thought-processes. Perfect stranger comes in and starts strewing drinks all over the place. . . . Can't pay for them. . . . What to do? What to do? . . . Yes, attitude of shirt-sleeved man quite intelligible. Whole episode, Archibald considered, well calculated to cause a spot of alarm and despondency.

In fact, he had reached at this juncture such a pitch of sweetness and light that, had he been able at that moment to transport himself to his cosy rooms in Cork Street, W.1., it is highly probable that he would still be the same lover of the Masses who had set out that night with such benevolence for Bottleton East.

But more was to happen to my nephew Archibald in Bottleton East that night, and that which happened ruined the Masses' chances of winning his esteem finally.

I have mentioned, I think, that at the other table in this eating-room there was seated—or, rather, reclining—a dishevelled man who slept. He now awoke with a start and, hoisting himself up, blinked beerily at Archibald. He had been doing himself well that night, and the process known as sleeping it off was not yet quite completed. It was, therefore, a rather fishy and inflamed eye that now rested on my nephew. And as the dishevelled man was one of those people who are always a little cross on waking, there was in this eye nothing of the genial, the kindly, or the beaming. He looked at Archibald as if he disliked him, and it is extremely probable that he did. For one thing, Archibald was wearing a collar—slightly soiled after the experiences through which he had passed, but nevertheless a collar—and a sturdy distaste for collars was part of this awakened sleeper's spiritual make-up.

"Wot you doin' there?" he demanded.

Archibald replied cordially enough that he had just been enjoying a medium-grilled steak and fried.

"R!" said the other. "And took it out of the mouth of the widow and the orphan, like as not."

"Absolutely no," replied Archibald. "The waitress brought it on a tray."

"So you say."

"I give you my solemn word," said Archibald. "I wouldn't dream of eating a steak that had been in the mouth of a widow or an orphan. I mean to say, in any case, what a beastly idea."

"And flaunting a collar," grumbled the man.

"Oh, no, dash it," objected Archibald. "Would you say flaunting?"

"Flaunting," insisted the other.

Archibald was embarrassed.

"Well, I'm awfully sorry," he said. "If I'd only known we were going to meet and you would take it like this, I wouldn't have worn a collar. It isn't a stiff collar," he added, more hopefully. "Just flannel, soft, gent's one. But, if you like, I'll take it off."

"Wear it while yo ucan," advised the dishevelled man. "The day's coming when collars'll run in streams down Park Lane."

This puzzled Archibald.

"You don't mean collars, do you? Blood, surely?"

"Blood, too. Blood *and* collars."

"We'll be able to play boats," suggested Archibald brightly.

"*You* won't," said the man. "And why? Because you'll be inside one of them collars and outside all that blood. Rivers of blood there'll be. Great flowing, bubbling rivers of spouting blood."

"I say, old lad," begged Archibald, who was a little squeamish, "not quite so soon after dinner, if you don't mind."

"Eh?"

"I say I've just finished dinner, and . . ."

"Dinner! And took it out of the mouth of the widow and the . . ."

"No, no. We went into all that before."

"Well, get on with it," said the man, with a moody gesture. Archibald was perplexed.

"Get on with it?"

"Your dinner. You ain't got much time. Because soon you'll be flowing down Park Lane."

"But I've finished my dinner."

"No, you ain't."

"Yes, I have."

"No, you ain't. That's just where you make your ruddy error. If you've finished your dinner, what's all that fat doing there on the side of the plate?"

"I never eat fat."

The man had risen. He was now scowling menacingly at Archibald.

"You don't eat fat?"

"No, never."

The man banged the table.

"You eat that fat," he bellowed. "That's what you do. I was taught when I was a nipper to always eat my fat."

"But, I say . . ."

"You eat that fat!"

"No, but listen, laddie . . ."

"You eat that FAT!"

It was a difficult situation, and my nephew Archibald recognised it as such. It was not easy to see how two individuals of such conflicting views as this dishevelled man and himself could ever find a formula. Where he liked collars and disliked fat, the other had this powerful anti-collar complex and, apparently, an equally strong fat-urge. He was glad when, presumably attracted by the voice of his companion, who for the last minute and a half had been shouting "Fat! Fat! Fat!" at the extreme limit of his lungs, somebody came hurrying along the corridor outside and burst into the room.

I say he was glad, but I must add that his gladness was of very brief duration. For the newcomer was none other than his old acquaintance, the shirt-sleeved man.

Yes, gentlemen, like all travellers lost in strange, desert lands, my nephew Archibald, after leaving the Goose and Gherkin, had been wandering round in a circle. And at long last his footsteps had taken him back to the Goose and Gherkin once more. And here he was, face to face again with the one man who, he had hoped, had passed permanently out of his life.

"Wot's all this?" demanded the shirt-sleeved man.

The dishevelled customer had undergone a sudden change of mood. No longer menacing, he was now crying quietly into an ash-tray.

"He won't eat his fat," he sobbed. "His fat, that's what he won't eat, and it's breakin' his poor father's heart." He gulped. "Wears a blinkin' collar, goes runnin' in streams down Park Lane, and won't eat his fat. Make him eat his fat," he begged, brushing away with a piece of potato the tears that coursed over his face.

"Don't you pay no attention to him . . ." the shirt-sleeved man had begun to say to Archibald. And then the ingratiating note of host to customer faded from his voice. He stopped, stared, uttered a strangled gulp, stared again.

"Gor-blimey!" he whispered, awed. "*You* again?"

He raised a hand, moistened it slightly: raised the other, and moistened that.

"I say, listen . . ." begged Archibald.

"I'm listenin'," said the dishevelled man. He was now in his old position, with head sunk on arms. "I'm listenin'. That's right," he said, as a fearful crashing resounded through the room. "Make him eat his fat."

It was as the hands of such clocks as were right by Greenwich time were pointing to five minutes past three on the following morning that an at first faint, then swelling "Charawk-chawk-chawk" made itself heard beneath the window of Aurelia Cammarleigh's bedroom at Number 36A, Park Street. Weary, footsore, remorseful, emptied of his love for the Masses, but full once more of passion for the girl he adored, Archibald Mulliner was fulfilling her behest and imitating for her the hen laying an egg. She had ordered him to come round to her house and give of his best, and here he was, doing it.

For a while, physical fatigue had rendered the performance a poor one. But gradually, as, artist-like, he became absorbed in his task, Archibald's voice gained in volume, in expression, and in all those qualities which make a hen-imitation a thing of beauty. Soon windows all along the street were opening, heads were being thrust out, and complaining voices calling for the police. All the world loves a lover, but not when imitating hens outside their bedroom windows at three in the morning.

The force manifested itself in the person of Constable C-44.

"What," he asked, "is all this?"

"Charawk," cried Archibald.

"Pardon?" said the constable.

"Charawk," fluted Archibald. "Charawk."

And now, having reached the point where it was necessary for the purposes of his art to run round in a circle, holding the sides of his coat, and finding the officer's hand on his shoulder an impediment, he punched the latter smartly in the wind and freed himself. And it was at this moment that Aurelia's window flew open. The lovely girl was a sound sleeper, and, at first, even when the mellow clucking had reached her ears, she had thought it but a dream.

But now she was awake, and her heart was filled with an ecstasy of relief and love.

"Archibald!" she cried. "Is that really you, you old leper?"

"In person," replied Archibald, suspending his rendition for an instant.

"Come in and have a spot."

"Thanks. I'd like to. No, sorry," added Archibald, as the hand of the Law fell on his shoulder once more. "I'm afraid I can't."

"Why not?"

"I've just been pinched by a bally policeman."

"And you'll stay pinched," said Officer C-44 in a none too genial voice. His abdomen was still paining him.

"And he says I'll stay pinched," added Archibald. "Indeed, it looks very much as if I were even now off to chokey . . . for about how long would you say, Officer?"

"For about fourteen days without the op.", replied the other, rubbing his waistband with his disengaged hand. "Charged with resisting and assaulting the police in the execution of their duty, that's what you'll be."

"Fourteen days or two weeks, it begins to look like," shouted Archibald, as he was dragged away. "Call it a fortnight."

"I will be waiting for you when you come out," cried Aurelia.

"You'll be what?" asked Archibald. His voice was barely audible to her now, for the officer was cutting out a good pace.

"Waiting for you . . . When you come out," shrieked Aurelia.

"Then you love me still?"

"Yes."

"What?"

"Yes!!"

"Sorry. I didn't get it."

"YES ! ! !" roared Aurelia.

And, as she stopped to ease her tortured throat, from round the corner there came to her ears a faint, barely audible "Charawk", and she knew that he understood.

Park Street closed its windows and went to sleep again.

34

THE CODE OF THE MULLINERS

OUR little group of serious thinkers in the bar-parlour of the Anglers' Rest had been discussing a breach of promise case to which the papers were giving a good deal of prominence at the moment: and a Whisky Sour had raised the question of how these fellows did it.

"Tell a girl it's all off, I mean," said the Whisky Sour. "It must take the courage of a lion. I was a daring sort of young chap in my prime, but if you had told me to go to my dear wife—Miss Bootle she was then, one of the East Balham Bootles—and cast her aside like a soiled glove, I'd never have had the nerve. Yet apparently it's happening every day. Odd."

A thoughtful Eggnogg said that he understood that the telephone was a great help on these occasions. A Gin and Ginger preferred what he called the good old false beard method.

"It solves the whole problem," said the Gin and Ginger. "You get your false beard, then you write the girl a letter, then you slap on the beard and go to Nova Scotia."

A Half of Stout said that wasn't British. The Gin and Ginger said: Yes, it was, very British. The Half of Stout appealed to Mr. Mulliner.

"Would you do that, Mr. M.? If you were engaged to a girl and wanted to break it off, would you buy a false beard?"

Mr. Mulliner smiled indulgently.

"In my case, as in that of any member of my family," he said, sipping his hot Scotch and lemon, "the question of how to break off an engagement could never arise. We may be wrong, we may be foolishly jealous of the *noblesse oblige* of an ancient name, but the code of the Mulliners is that an engagement cannot be broken off by the male contracting party. When a Mulliner plights his troth, it stays plighted. It was this scrupulous sense of chivalry, handed down to him by a long line of ancestors, that so complicated matters for my nephew Archibald when he wished to be free of his honourable obligations to Aurelia Cammarleigh."

We were stunned.

"Archibald?" we cried. "Your nephew Archibald? The one who imitated hens? But we thought he worshipped the girl with the utmost fervour."

"He did."

"Then why did he want to break the engagement?"

"I need scarcely say that his motives, as the motives of any nephew of mine could not fail to be, were in the last degree praiseworthy and altruistic. He conceived himself to be acting entirely in Aurelia's best interests. But perhaps you would care to hear the story?"

You remarked just now (said Mr. Mulliner) that my nephew Archibald worshipped Aurelia Cammarleigh with the utmost fervour, and that is precisely what he did worship her with. Her lightest word was law to him. A smile from her made his day. When I tell you that not once but on three separate occasions he sent his man, Meadowes, out into the Park with instructions to carve his, Archibald's, initials and those of Miss Cammarleigh on the nearest convenient tree with a heart round them, you will understand something of the depths of his feelings. And you will also understand why, when after they had been betrothed some six weeks he found her manner towards him growing definitely cold, he was shaken to the core.

Now, mere temporary and fleeting demonstrations of frigidity on the part of the adored object are, of course, not unusual. Girls affect them simply in order to enjoy the luxury of melting again. But this was different. This had all the earmarks of the real stuff. He would call her the lodestar of his life, and she would say "Ho-hum." He would enquire of her if she loved her little Archibald, and she would say "Hi-ho." He would speak of their coming wedding-day, and she would ask him if he had read any good books lately. Trifles, you may say . . . Nothing tangible, I grant. . . . But, nevertheless, taking this with that and weighing all the evidence, Archibald Mulliner became convinced that for some mysterious reason his Aurelia had gone off the boil. And at length, as every young man should do when his heart is aching, he decided to go and ask advice of his mother.

Archibald's mother, since her widowhood, had taken up her abode in the neighbourhood of Kew. Between her and Aurelia there had sprung up a warm friendship, and it occurred to Archibald that in the course of one of their chats together the girl might possibly have let fall some remark which would provide a clue to the mystery. At any rate, it seemed a good speculative venture to pop round and enquire, so he unleashed his two-seater and presently was making his way through the little garden to the sunlit room at the back of the house where his mother liked to sit of an afternoon. And he was just about to step through the open french windows with a filial "Pip-pip," when a sudden sight sent him back on his heels and he stood gaping—his eyeglass, cast adrift in his emotion, bobbing like some live thing on the end of its cord.

For there, gentlemen, in that sunlit room, stood Lady (Wilhelmina) Mulliner, relict of the late Sir Sholto Mulliner, M.V.O., with her tongue out like a dog's, panting in deep gasps with a sort of horrible "ha-ha-ha-ha-ha" sound that turned the blood in Archibald's veins to ice. And then, as he watched, she suddenly stopped panting and began to utter a remark which, even by Archibald's not too exacting standards, seemed noticeably goofy. It consisted of the letters "QX", repeated over and over again. And, as Archibald has often told me, it was the way she said them that got right in amongst a fellow.

The "Q", he tells me, was an almost inaudible murmur, produced through pouting lips. That, he says, he could have endured. What made everything seem so sad and hopeless was the "X". As she emitted this, she drew her mouth back in a ghastly grin till the muscles of her neck stood out like ropes. And she went on and on and on. She refrained from Q-ing the "Q" only to X the "X", and when she wasn't X-ing to beat the band she was Q-ing away like a two-year-old. That was how my nephew Archibald described the scene to me, and I must admit that it conjures up a vivid picture.

Well, of course, Archibald understood now why Aurelia's manner towards him had changed of late. Obviously, she must have come upon the poor old parent unexpectedly in the middle of one of these spells of hers and perceived, as he did, that she was as loony as a coot. Enough to make any girl think a bit.

He turned away and staggered out of the garden with blind steps. One can, of course, appreciate his agony, poor lad. Few things are less pleasant for a young man in the spring-time of life than to have a well-loved mother suddenly go off her rocker: and when such a tragedy involves also the breaking off of his engagement to the girl he worships, you have got something that Somerset Maugham could make a three-act play out of without conscious cerebration.

For he realised, of course, that his engagement would have to be broken off. A man of nice scruples like Archibald Mulliner could have no option. A chap, he meant to say, can't go lugging girls off to the altar if there is insanity in his family. Apart from anything else, this pottiness was probably catching. Quite likely it would be coming out in himself, too, before he knew where he was. And a nice thing it would be for Aurelia if, as they stood side by side in the sacred edifice and the clergyman said "Wilt thou, Archibald?" he were to reply "QX" or, worse, pant like a dog with his tongue out. All sorts of remarks it would cause. A girl in such circumstances could scarcely help but feel pretty silly.

No, he must break the engagement at once. . . .

And then, suddenly, even as he framed the thought, there rose up before him the recollection of the code of the Mulliners, and he saw that the whole affair was going to be a good deal more difficult and complex than he had supposed. He could not break the engagement. He would have to do something to make Aurelia take that step. And what it now boiled down to was What?

He mused. What girls of his acquaintance had broken off their engagements? And why?

There was Jane Todmarsh. Her betrothed, taking her out for a spin in the old Pommery Seven, had driven it, her, and himself into a duck-pond out Hitchin way. She had given the young man his freedom within two seconds of spitting the first newt out of her mouth.

Suppose he were to take Aurelia for a drive and . . . No. He shrank from it. He couldn't say why exactly, but he shrank from it.

Milly Salt had returned her fiancé to store because of his habit of uttering a short, dry, nasty snigger every time she missed a shot in the mixed doubles. No help for Archibald here. Aurelia did not play tennis. Besides, he knew that in no circumstances could he bring himself to snigger dryly and nastily at one who to him was more like some sort of a goddess than anything.

The case of Hypatia Sloggett was different. A former flame of the future lord and master had turned up in the middle of dinner one night at the Savoy and made a row.

This, Archibald felt, was the best bet yet. There was the difficulty that he had no former flames, but a moment's thought told him that he could easily go round to some theatrical agency and engage one. There were probably a hundred out-of-work actresses in the Strand neighbourhood who would be delighted to come in on the deal for a fiver.

And yet once again he found himself shrinking. That sort of thing happening in a crowded restaurant could not fail to make a fellow feel pretty dashed conspicuous, and he hated feeling conspicuous. If there was any other alternative, he would vastly prefer to take it.

And it was then that he remembered Dora Trevis. On the eve of becoming Mrs. Aubrey Rochester-Wapshott, she had notified the *Morning Post* that the fixture was off, and the whole trouble, Archibald recalled, had been caused by poor old Aubrey getting a bit pie-eyed at the family dinner table and insulting her father.

There was the solution. He would insult old Cammarleigh and leave the rest to Aurelia.

Not but what, felt Archibald, it was going to take some doing. This father of Aurelia's was not one of those mild old men who make nice easy insulting. He was a tough, hard-bitten retired Colonial Governor of the type which comes back to England to spend the evening of its days barking at club waiters, and until now it had been Archibald's prudent policy to conciliate him to the utmost. With sedulous assiduity he had always bent himself to the task of giving Sir Rackstraw Cammarleigh the old oil. He had deferred to his opinions. He had smirked meekly, infusing into his manner a rather revolting reverence. Above all, he had listened raptly to his stories, caring little that a certain eccentricity of memory sometimes led the ex-proconsul to tell the same one four evenings in succession.

By these means, he had so succeeded in ingratiating himself with the old blighter that a sudden reversal of policy would have all the greater effect. One bold effort, and it seemed to Archibald that the whole subject of wedding-bells must inevitably be removed from the agenda-paper.

Pale but resolute, my nephew dressed himself with his usual care and set off to dine *en famille* at his loved one's home.

I do not know if any of you gentlemen have ever watched a retired Colonial Governor at his evening meal. I have not had the experience myself, but Archibald tells me it is one fraught with interest. He begins, it seems, in a spirit rather similar to that of the lion of the jungle at feeding-time, growling fiercely over his soup, absorbing his fish to the accompaniment of a series of muffled snarls. It is only with the entrée that a softer mood starts to manifest itself. Then, and onward through the joint and sweet, one is aware of a growing geniality. The first animal hunger has abated. Repletion has done its kindly work.

With the dessert and port, the now mellow subject leans back and starts to tell stories.

It was so that it happened tonight. Bagshot, the butler, filled his employer's glass and stepped back into the shadows: and Sir Rackstraw, grunting not un-amiably, fixed Archibald with a bulging eye. Had he been a man to take notice of such phenomena, he would have seen that the young man was white and tense and wore a strung-up look. But if there was one thing in this world that did not interest Sir Rackstraw Cammarleigh it was the play of expression on the face of Archibald Mulliner. He was regarding him now purely in the light of a recipient of his story of old George Bates and the rhinoceros.

"What you say about there being a full moon tonight," he began, for it was on this subject that Archibald had just hazarded a remark, "reminds me of a curious thing that happened to an old friend of mine out in Bongo-Bongo. Old George Bates."

He paused to sip at his glass, and Archibald saw that Aurelia's face had grown tired and hard. Her mother, too, a pale, worn woman, uttered a stifled little sigh. Somewhere in the background he could hear Bagshot stirring uneasily.

"At the time of the full moon," resumed Sir Rackstraw, "it is the custom in Bongo-Bongo to hunt the rhinoceros, and this friend of mine . . . George Bates his name was . . . by the way, stop me if I've told you this before . . ."

"Stop!" said Archibald.

There was a tense silence. Sir Rackstraw was quivering as if the word had been a bullet and he the rhinoceros which in his less cordial moods he somewhat resembled.

"What did you say?" he rasped.

"I said 'Stop!'" replied Archibald. Though quaking inwardly, he preserved an outward firmness, even a sort of truculence. "You told me to stop you if I had heard it before and I stopped you. I have heard that story six times before. Even if it were good, I wouldn't like it. But it is not good. It is rotten. And I shall be extremely obliged, Cammarleigh, if you will refrain from inflicting it upon me either now or at any other time when you may feel the urge. I never wish to hear of Bates and his rhinoceros again. And I couple with the name of this rhinoceros the names of any other rhinoceri you or your friends may have encountered in your exceptionally tedious past. You understand me, Cammarleigh? Enough is enough."

He stopped and helped himself to port. At the same moment, he pushed his chair back a little, prepared, should events so shape themselves as to render such a course advisable, to slide under the table and there defend himself with tooth and claw. A stoutish ex-Colonial Governor, he reasoned, would find it pretty hard to get at a fellow who had dug himself well in under a table.

It was as he reached this decision that Lady Cammarleigh spoke.

"Thank you, Archibald," she said, and there were tears in her faded voice. "It was about time some tough bimbo came along and spoke those brave words. You have said just what I have been wanting to say for years. This would have made the hundred and twenty-seventh time I have heard the story of George Bates and the rhinoceros."

Aurelia's eyes were shining.

"I've heard it forty-three times," she said.

There was a decorous cough in the shadows.

"And I," said Bagshot, the butler, "eighty-six. May I take the liberty of adding my humble tribute of gratitude to Mr. Mulliner for the firm stand he has taken. I sometimes think that gentlemen do not realise how distressing it is for a butler to have to listen to their after-dinner stories. His official position, involving, as it does, the necessity of standing with his back against the sideboard, renders escape impossible. It makes a butler's life very wearing, very wearing. Thank you, Mr. Mulliner."

"Not at all," said Archibald.

"Thank you, Archibald," said Lady Cammarleigh.

"Don't mention it," said Archibald.

"Thank you, dear," said Aurelia.

"Only too pleased," said Archibald.

"You see now, Father," said Aurelia, turning to Sir Rackstraw, "why you are shunned at the club."

The proconsul started.

"I am not shunned at the club!"

"You are shunned at the club. It's all over London."

"Well, upon my word, do you know, I believe you're right," said Sir Rackstraw thoughtfully. "Now you mention it, fellows have shunned me at the club. I see it all now. I was degenerating into a club bore. And, thanks to the fearless candour of this fine young fellow here, my eyes have been opened. I see the light. Bagshot, charge the glasses. My dear, have you port? Aurelia, you? Then I give you my future son-in-law, Archibald Mulliner, who has rendered me a service this night which I can never sufficiently repay. And now, Aurelia, my dear, as we have finished our simple evening meal, perhaps you and our young friend here would care to take a stroll round the square. As he so justly observed a moment ago," chuckled Sir Rackstraw, "there is a full moon."

Out in the moonlit square, Aurelia was all remorse and worshipping admiration.

"Oh, Archibald," she cried, as she pressed against his arm, "I feel so awful. You must have noticed how cold I have been of late. It was because you were so meek and wormlike with Father. I recognised, of course, that he is a man who chews tenpenny nails and swallows broken bottles, but it revolted me to think that you should be afraid of him. You were my wonder-man, and it seemed during those awful days that I had been mistaken in you; that you had failed me. And all the while you were simply biding your time, preparatory to slipping it across him properly. I really do think, darling that you are the most marvellous man on earth."

Well, Archibald said "No, I say, really, thanks awfully," but it was in a dull, toneless voice that he said it. The hideous irony of his position was weighing sorely on the young man. Here he was, adored—one might say fawned upon—by this lovely girl, and simple decency made it impossible that he should marry her. And if you could tie that, even in a Russian novel, he would like to know how.

"Tomorrow," said Aurelia, "you shall take me to dine at the Savoy, and we'll celebrate."

"Right-ho," said Archibald absently.

He was wondering where the best theatrical agency was.

It was at eleven-thirty next morning that Archibald stood with reluctant feet half-way up the dark staircase that leads to the offices of Isadore McCallum, the well-known agent who has told more people that he will write and let them know if anything turns up than any other man of his profession in London. His mood was Hamlet-like—wavering, irresolute. Reason told him that this thing had got to be done: but, as he told Reason, nobody was going to make him like it.

And so he hesitated. And it was while he was still hesitating that there came from above the sound of a slammed door and the noise of rushing feet. A moment later, a solid body had struck him, and in its company, inextricably entwined, he fell the half-flight of stairs that ended in the street door. It was only when this frail barrier had given way before their combined weights and he was sorting himself out upon the pavement that he perceived that what had caused all this activity was a stout young woman in pink with peroxide hair.

For a few moments she stood there panting, her demeanour that of one who has recently passed through some great ordeal. Then she spoke.

"Did I bump you, dearie? I'm sorry."

"Not at all," said Archibald courteously, straightening with his right hand a rib that seemed to have got a little bent

"I wasn't looking where I was going."

"It's quite all right."

"And who would have been looking where they were going after being insulted by a worm?" demanded the woman.

Archibald, ever sympathetic, clicked his tongue.

"Did a worm insult you?"

"You bet a worm insulted me."

"Worms will be worms," suggested Archibald.

This tolerant view-point seemed to give offence.

"Not while I have my strength, they won't," said the woman. "Listen! What do you think that man up there said to me? Said I was too stout to play heroines in the Number Two towns!" She sniffed bitterly. "Why, you can't be too stout for the Number Two towns. The thing isn't possible. They like their heroines stout. It makes them feel they've had their money's worth. 'This buxom beauty'— *Leicester Argus*."

"I beg your pardon?"

"I was saying what the *Leicester Argus* said about me. My 'Geraldine' in *Twisted Lives*."

Archibald's intellect, such as it was, began to assert itself. He had been a little shaken by his fall.

"Do you play heroines in melodramas?" he asked eagerly.

"Do *I* play heroines in melodramas?" she echoed. "Do I play *heroines* in melodramas? Do I play heroines in *melodramas*? Why . . ."

Archibald saw that she did.

"I say," he said, "how about stepping up to the Bodega for a small port? I've a little business proposition I should like to put to you."

She seemed suspicious. Her gaze, unlike her waist-measurement, was narrow.

"Business?"

"Strictly business."

"You don't want to cover me with jewels?"

"Absolutely not."

"Well, then, I don't mind if I do," she said, relieved. "You've no notion how careful a girl has got to be these days," she added. "I've had men in places like Huddersfield offer me guilty splendour on the strength of my having accepted a Bath bun and a small cocoa at their hands."

"Baronets?" asked Archibald, for he had heard that there was a good deal of moral laxness among that class.

"I think so," said his companion. "Disguised."

And so, chatting amiably, they passed into the fragrant coolness of the Bodega.

I have little or no acquaintance among the pure and beefy ladies who play heroines in our Number Two towns (said Mr. Mulliner), so I am unable to say whether Miss Yvonne Maltravers—for such was the name on the professional card which she had handed to my nephew—was exceptionally gifted, or whether intelligence like hers is the rule or norm in those circles. Suffice it to say that she not only grasped his position, as he explained it, with lightning celerity, but seemed to find nothing unusual in a young man being in such a position. And Archibald, who had anticipated a good deal of tedious explanation, was enchanted by her quickness at the uptake.

"Then you follow the scenario?" he said. "You see what I'm driving at? You really will breeze along to the Savoy tonight and play the role of a betrayed girl?"

Miss Maltravers coughed with a touch of rebuke.

"Not betrayed, dearie. I've always kept my Art clean and always shall. You don't read the *Bexhill Gazette*, do you? 'She is purity personified,' it said. I put it in my professional ads. for a time. That was when I was 'Myrtle' in *The Hand of Doom*. If you will allow me to make a suggestion—we're all working for the good of the show—I'd say let me be someone unspotted who's bringing a breach of promise action against you."

"That's just as good, you think?"

"It's better," said Miss Maltravers firmly. "It's the duty of all of us in these licentious post-war days to put our hands to the plough and quench the flame of this rising tide of unwholesome suggestiveness."

"I've thought that a hundred times," said Archibald.

"I've thought it a couple of hundred," said Miss Maltravers.

"Then that's fine," said Archibald, rising. "I'll expect you at the Savoy Grill round about nine-fifteen. You come in——"

"Enter," corrected Miss Maltravers.

"That's right."

"Left. I always enter left. It shows up my best profile."

"And you accuse me of having trifled with your affections——"

"In a nice way."

"In a perfectly nice way . . . at . . . where would you say?"

"Middlesbrough," said Miss Maltravers with decision. "And I'll tell you why. My affections actually were trifled with in Middlesbrough once, so it'll help me give colour and movement to the scene. When I remember Bertram, I mean to say. That was his name—Bertram Lushington. I put him over my knee and gave him a good spanking."

"That won't be necessary tonight, will it?" asked Archibald, a little anxiously. "Of course, I don't want to interfere with your conception of the role or whatever you call it——"

"It's how I *see* the part."

"Dress trousers are dashed thin, you know."

"Very well," said Miss Maltravers regretfully. "Just as you like. Cut business. Lines only."

"Thanks awfully."

"I'll tell you one thing that's going to be a great help," said Miss Maltravers, brightening. "The whole scene's very like my big second-act smash in *His Forgotten Bride*, except that that was at the altar rails. You wouldn't prefer to postpone production till we can get an altar-rail set?"

"No, I think we'd better rush the thing through tonight."

"Just as you say. It'll mean making a few line cuts, but most of the speeches will fit in. You won't mind if I call you a heartless cur who should blush to think that he sullies the grand old name of Englishman?"

"Not at all."

"It got a round at Eastbourne. All right, then. Nine-fifteen tonight."

"Nine-fifteen on the dot," said Archibald.

It might be supposed that, now that everything had been so satisfactorily arranged, my nephew Archibald would have felt relieved. But such was not the case. As he sat toying with his food at the Savoy that night, the reflection that he had done his duty like a Mulliner was not enough to keep him from experiencing a hideous depression and apprehension.

One paid dearly, he mused, for the traditions of his race. How simple it would have been for one who was not a Mulliner to write Aurelia a letter severing their relations and then go abroad somewhere and lie low till the thing had blown over. Instead of which, here he was, faced with the prospect of disgrace and shame in a restaurant filled with his friends and acquaintances.

He had always been so proud of his reputation. He had liked to think that, as he walked about London, people pointed him out and whispered "That's Mulliner, the chap who imitates hens." From tonight the formula would be changed. It would be "Look! See that bird? Mulliner. The fellow who was mixed up in that priceless scene at the Savoy Grill." A bitter reflection, rendered none the more pleasant by the thought that it was quite possible that, carried away by her art, his accomplice might forget their gentleman's agreement and spank him after all.

It was with a distrait ear, therefore, that he listened to Aurelia's conversation. She was in a lively mood, and her silvery laugh often rang out over the din and chatter. And every time it did so it seemed to go right through Archibald like an electric drill.

He looked about him, and shuddered at what he saw. Somehow, when he had first conceived this masquerade, he had visualised it as taking place in what Miss Maltravers would have described as a "set" occupied only by himself and Aurelia. But tonight the whole muster-roll of his acquaintance seemed to be present. Over there sat the young Marquis of Hampshire, who did the Gossip for the *Daily Tribune*. Two tables beyond, he saw the young Duke of Datchet, who did the Gossip for the *Daily Post*. And, besides these, at least half a dozen more Earls, Barons, Viscounts, and Baronets, who did the Gossip for a half-dozen more journals. He would be sure of an extended, if not a good, Press.

And then suddenly there occurred something which seemed to him positively to put the saucepan cover on it. Through the door, accompanied by an elderly gentleman of military aspect, came his mother.

Archibald had reached the sardines-on-toast stage by this time, and he tells me that he distinctly felt those sardines turn to ashes in his mouth. He had always loved and respected his mother, even after circumstances had so arranged themselves as to convince him that she was leaky in the overhead valves, and the thought that she was to be a witness of tonight's scene gashed him like a knife.

Dimly, he realised that Aurelia was saying something to him.

"Eh?" he said.

"I said 'There's your mother'."

"I saw her."

"She's looking ever so much better, don't you think?"

"Better?"

"She was worried," explained Aurelia, "because she was getting a double chin. I found her in floods of tears one afternoon, trying to work it off with a squeegee. Absolutely no good, of course, and I told her so. There's only one thing for a double chin, and that's this new method everybody's going in for these days. First, you stand and pant like a dog for twenty minutes. This hardens the throat muscles. Then you breathe deeply and keep saying 'QX', 'QX' over and over again. The 'Q' isn't so important, but the 'X' is the goods. It works directly on the chin and neck, tightening them up and breaking down the fatty tissues."

The room seemed to be rocking about Archibald.

"What!"

"Absolutely," said Aurelia. "You've got to be careful, of course, at first, otherwise you're extremely apt to dislocate your neck, or something."

"Do you mean to tell me," demanded Archibald, choking, "that all that 'QX' stuff I saw her doing was simply one of these bally modern beauty-drill things?"

"Oh, did you see her? It must have given you rather a shock, I should think. The first time I saw my aunt doing it, I was on the phone, ringing up doctors to come on the run and certify her, before you could say 'What ho.' "

Archibald leaned back in his chair, breathing heavily. For a moment, all he could feel was a sullen resentment against the Fate that wrecks our lives—as far as one can see, in a spirit of pure whimsicality. A fat lot of good it was, he felt, acting from the best motives in this world.

Then his resentment extended itself to Woman. Women, he felt, simply ought not to be allowed loose. You never knew what they were going to do next.

And then, correcting himself, he realised that he knew quite well what one woman, at least, was going to do next. Miss Yvonne Maltravers was going to come entering left and telling him that he was sullying the grand old name of Middlesbrough or whatever it was.

He looked at his watch. The hands pointed to fourteen minutes past nine.

"Of course, if it's a question of reducing the tummy," said Aurelia, "that's different. You have to go down on all fours and crawl round the room, saying 'Oofa-oofa.' I say," she broke off, and her silvery laugh rang through the room once more, "you do get all sorts in these eating-houses nowadays. Look at that weird female by the door."

Archibald followed her gaze, and his heart did two double hand-springs. It was Miss Maltravers who stood on the threshold or, as she would no doubt have preferred to put it herself, in the down-stage O.P. entrance. She was peering about her at the tables.

"Seems to be looking for someone," said Aurelia.

If some sportive hand had suddenly introduced a bradawl into the seat of my nephew Archibald's trousers, he could not have risen with more celerity. There was, he told himself, just one hope. It might lead to a certain amount of talk, but if he were to place one hand over Miss Maltravers's mouth and, seizing the slack of her dress with the other, rush her out the way she had come, dump her into a cab, tell that cab to drive to Shepherd's Bush, and on the way thither drop the talented artiste out of window into a convenient basement, he might yet be saved.

The policy, as I say, might excite comment. Aurelia, no doubt, would raise her eyebrows in a mute demand for an explanation. But he could always say that it was one of these new slimming exercises, designed to strengthen the triceps muscles and remove superfluous fat from the upper chest.

More like a puma of the African hinterlands than a Mulliner, Archibald sped across the room. And Miss Maltravers, sighting him, spoke.

"Oh, Mr. Mulliner, I was looking for you."

To Archibald's surprise, she spoke in a whisper. At their previous meeting, in the Bodega, her voice had been full and robust—so much so that nervous fellow-customers had twice complained. But now she was more like a leaky gas-pipe than anything Archibald could think of. And even this novel method of delivery seemed to cause her pain. She winced distinctly.

"I wanted to tell you, dearie," she proceeded, still in that same strange, hushed voice, "that there's been a sort of hitch, if you know what I mean. The fact is, like a silly girl, taking those harsh words of Mr. McCallum's too much to heart, I started trying one of these new exercises for reducing the chin this afternoon, that a lady friend happened to tell me of. You may have heard of it—it's the one where you say 'QX,' and it was all right for the first three 'Qs' and the first two 'Xs,' but I wasn't more than half-way through the third 'X' when something suddenly seemed to go crack in my throat, and now I can't speak except in a whisper without feeling as if I was being torn asunder with pincers. So there it is, dearie, I hate to disappoint my public, a thing I've never done in my life before—'This loyal artist.'—*Wolverhampton Express*—so I'll go on, if you like, but I warn you it won't be the same thing. I shan't be able to do myself what you might call justice. That part wants playing, and a girl can't give of her best in a whisper. Why, once in Peebles I cracked a couple of footlights. Still, as I say, if you'd like me to walk the scene, I will."

For a moment, Archibald could not speak. It was not so much that his mouth was still full of sardines on toast as that he was overpowered, unmanned by a rush of emotion such as he had not experienced since the day when Aurelia Cammarleigh had promised to be his.

"Don't dream of it," he urged. "It won't be necessary. Owing to unforeseen circumstances, the production is off. You go straight home, old soul, and rub liniment on yourself. I'll send you a cheque in the morning."

"It's just about here that it seems to catch me."

"I'll bet it does," said Archibald. "Well, pip-pip, toodle-oo, cheerio, and God bless you. I shall watch your future career with considerable interest."

With feet that hardly seemed to touch the floor he returned to his table. Aurelia was puzzled and curious.

"Did you know her?" she asked.

"Oh yes," said Archibald. "Old nurse of mine."

"What did she want?"

"Just came to wish me many happy returns of the day."

"But it isn't your birthday."

"No, but you know what these old nurses are. Now, tell me, my precious angel dream-rabbit," said Archibald, "this wedding of ours. My idea is to rope in a couple of Bishops and do the thing right. Not one Bishop, if you see what I mean —two Bishops. Because, if you have a spare, nothing can go wrong. And nowadays, when you see people straining their throats on all sides, you can't afford to take any chances."

35

THE FIERY WOOING OF MORDRED

THE Pint of Lager breathed heavily through his nose.

"Silly fathead!" he said. "Ashtrays in every nook and cranny of the room—ashtrays staring you in the eye wherever you look—and he has to go and do a fool thing like that."

He was alluding to a young gentleman with a vacant, fish-like face who, leaving the bar-parlour of the Anglers' Rest a few moments before, had thrown his cigarette into the wastepaper basket, causing it to burst into a cheerful blaze. Not one of the little company of amateur fire-fighters but was ruffled. A Small Bass with a high blood pressure had had to have his collar loosened, and the satin-clad bosom of Miss Postlethwaite, our emotional barmaid, was still heaving.

Only Mr. Mulliner seemed disposed to take a tolerant view of what had occurred.

"In fairness to the lad," he pointed out, sipping his hot Scotch and lemon, "we must remember that our bar-parlour contains no grand piano or priceless old walnut table, which to the younger generation are the normal and natural repositories for lighted cigarette-ends. Failing these, he, of course, selected the wastepaper basket. Like Mordred."

"Like who?" asked a Whisky and Splash.

"Whom," corrected Miss Postlethwaite.

The Whisky and Splash apologised.

"A nephew of mine. Mordred Mulliner, the poet."

"Mordred," murmured Miss Postlethwaite pensively. "A sweet name."

"And one," said Mr. Mulliner, "that fitted him admirably, for he was a comely lovable sensitive youth with large, faun-like eyes, delicately chiselled features and excellent teeth. I mention these teeth, because it was owing to them that the train of events started which I am about to describe."

"He bit somebody?" queried Miss Postlethwaite, groping.

"No. But if he had had no teeth he would not have gone to the dentist's that day, and if he had not gone to the dentist's he would not have met Annabelle."

"Annabelle whom?"

"Who," corrected Miss Postlethwaite.

"Oh, shoot," said the Whisky and Splash.

Annabelle Sprockett-Sprockett, the only daughter of Sir Murgatroyd and Lady Sprockett-Sprockett of Smattering Hall, Worcestershire. Impractical in many ways, (said Mr. Mulliner), Mordred never failed to visit his dentist every six months, and on the morning on which my story opens he had just seated himself in the empty waiting-room and was turning the pages of a three-months-old copy of the *Tatler* when the door opened and there entered a girl at the sight of whom —or who, if our friend here prefers it—something seemed to explode on the left side of his chest like a bomb. The *Tatler* swam before his eyes, and when it solidified again he realised that love had come to him at last.

Most of the Mulliners have fallen in love at first sight, but few with so good an excuse as Mordred. She was a singularly beautiful girl, and for a while it was this beauty of hers that enchained my nephew's attention to the exclusion of all else. It was only after he had sat gulping for some minutes like a dog with a chicken bone in its throat that he detected the sadness in her face. He could see now that her eyes, as she listlessly perused her four-months-old copy of *Punch*, were heavy with pain.

His heart ached for her, and as there is something about the atmosphere of a dentist's waiting-room which breaks down the barriers of conventional etiquette he was emboldened to speak.

"Courage!" he said. "It may not be so bad, after all. He may just fool about with that little mirror thing of his, and decide that there is nothing that needs to be done."

For the first time she smiled—faintly, but with sufficient breadth to give Mordred another powerful jolt.

"I'm not worrying about the dentist," she explained. "My trouble is that I live miles away in the country and only get a chance of coming to London about twice a year for about a couple of hours. I was hoping that I should be able to put in a long spell of window-shopping in Bond Street, but now I've got to wait goodness knows how long I don't suppose I shall have time to do a thing. My train goes at one-fifteen."

All the chivalry in Mordred came to the surface like a leaping trout.

"If you would care to take my place——"

"Oh, I couldn't."

"Please. I shall enjoy waiting. It will give me an opportunity of catching up with my reading."

"Well, if you really wouldn't mind——"

Considering that Mordred by this time was in the market to tackle dragons on her behalf or to climb the loftiest peak of the Alps to supply her with edelweiss, he was able to assure her that he did not mind. So in she went, flashing at him a shy glance of gratitude which nearly doubled him up, and he lit a cigarette and fell into a reverie. And presently she came out and he sprang to his feet, courteously throwing his cigarette into the waste-paper basket.

She uttered a cry. Mordred recovered the cigarette.

"Silly of me," he said, with a deprecating laugh. "I'm always doing that. Absent-minded. I've burned two flats already this year."

She caught her breath.

"Burned them to the ground?"

"Well, not to the ground. They were on the top floor."

"But you burned them?"

"Oh, yes. I burned them."

"Well, well!" She seemed to muse. "Well, goodbye, Mr.——"

"Mulliner. Mordred Mulliner."

"Goodbye, Mr. Mulliner, and thank you so much."

"Not at all, Miss——"

"Sprockett-Sprockett."

"Not at all, Miss Sprockett-Sprockett. A pleasure."

She passed from the room, and a few minutes later he was lying back in the dentist's chair, filled with an infinite sadness. This was not due to any activity on the part of the dentist, who had just said with a rueful sigh that there didn't seem to be anything to do this time, but to the fact that his life was now a blank. He loved this beautiful girl, and he would never see her more. It was just another case of ships that pass in the waiting-room.

Conceive his astonishment, therefore, when by the afternoon post next day he received a letter which ran as follows:

> Smattering Hall,
> Lower Smattering-on-the-Wissel,
> Worcestershire.

Dear Mr. Mulliner,

My little girl has told me how very kind you were to her at the dentist's today. I cannot tell you how grateful she was. She does so love to walk down Bond Street and breathe on the jewellers' windows, and but for you she would have had to go another six months without her little treat.

I suppose you are a very busy man, like everybody in London, but if you can spare the time it would give my husband and myself so much pleasure if you could run down and stay with us for a few days—a long week-end, or even longer if you can manage it.

> With best wishes,
> Yours sincerely,
> Aurelia Sprockett-Sprockett.

Mordred read this communication six times in a minute and a quarter and then seventeen times rather more slowly in order to savour any *nuance* of it that he might have overlooked. He took it that the girl must have got his address from the dentist's secretary on her way out, and he was doubly thrilled—first, by this evidence that one so lovely was as intelligent as she was beautiful, and secondly because the whole thing seemed to him so frightfully significant. A girl, he meant to say, does not get her mother to invite fellows to her country home for long week-ends (or even longer if they can manage it unless such fellows have made a pretty substantial hit with her. This, he contended, stood to reason.

He hastened to the nearest post-office, despatched a telegram to Lady Sprockett-Sprockett assuring her that he would be with her on the morrow, and returned to his flat to pack his effects. His heart was singing within him. Apart from anything else, the invitation could not have come at a more fortunate moment, for what with musing on his great love while smoking cigarettes he had practically gutted his little nest on the previous evening, and while it was still habitable in a sense there was no gainsaying the fact that all those charred sofas and things struck a rather melancholy note and he would be glad to be away from it all for a few days.

It seemed to Mordred, as he travelled down on the following afternoon, that the wheels of the train, clattering over the metals, were singing "Sprockett-Sprockett"—not "Annabelle", of course, for he did not yet know her name—and it was with a whispered "Sprockett-Sprockett" on his lips that he alighted at the little station of Smattering-cum-Blimpstead-in-the-Vale, which, as his hostess's notepaper had informed him, was where you got off for the Hall. And when he perceived that the girl herself had come to meet him in a two-seater car the whisper nearly became a shout.

For perhaps three minutes, as he sat beside her, Mordred remained in this condition of ecstatic bliss. Here he was, he reflected, and here she was—here, in fact, they both were—together, and he was just about to point out how jolly this was and—if he could work it without seeming to rush things too much—to drop a hint to the effect that he could wish this state of affairs to continue through all eternity, when the girl drew up outside a tobacconist's.

"I won't be a minute," she said. "I promised Biffy I would bring him back some cigarettes."

A cold hand seemed to lay itself on Mordred's heart.

"Biffy?"

"Captain Biffing, one of the men at the Hall. And Guffy wants some pipe-cleaners."

"Guffy?"

"Jack Cuffington. I expect you know his name, if you are interested in racing. He was third in last year's Grand National."

"Is he staying at the Hall, too?"

"Yes."

"You have a large house-party?"

"Oh, not so very. Let me see. There's Billy Biffing, Jack Guffington, Ted Prosser, Freddie Boot—he's the tennis champion of the county, Tommy Mainprice, and—oh, yes, Algy Fripp—the big-game hunter, you know."

The hand on Mordred's heart, now definitely iced, tightened its grip. With a lover's sanguine optimism, he had supposed that this visit of his was going to be just three days of jolly sylvan solitude with Annabelle Sprockett-Sprockett. And now it appeared that the place was unwholesomely crowded with his fellow men. And what fellow men! Big-game hunters . . . Tennis champions . . . Chaps who rode in Grand Nationals . . . He could see them in his mind's eye—lean, wiry, riding-breeched and flannel-trousered young Apollos, any one of them capable of cutting out his weight in Clark Gables.

A faint hope stirred within him.

"You have also, of course, with you Mrs. Biffing, Mrs. Guffington, Mrs. Prosser, Mrs. Boot, Mrs. Mainprice and Mrs. Algernon Fripp?"

"Oh, no, they aren't married."

"None of them?"

"No."

The faint hope coughed quietly and died.

"Ah," said Mordred.

While the girl was in the shop, he remained brooding. The fact that none of these blisters should be married filled him with an austere disapproval. If they had had the least spark of civic sense, he felt, they would have taken on the duties and responsibilities of matrimony years ago. But no. Intent upon their selfish pleasures, they had callously remained bachelors. It was this spirit of *laissez-faire* Mordred considered, that was eating like a canker into the soul of England.

He was aware of Annabelle standing beside him.

"Eh?" he said, starting.

"I was saying: 'Have you plenty of cigarettes?' "

"Plenty, thank you."

"Good. And of course there will be a box in your room. Men always like to smoke in their bedrooms, don't they? As a matter of fact, two boxes—Turkish and Virginian. Father put them there specially."

"Very kind of him," said Mordred mechanically.

He relapsed into a moody silence and they drove off.

It would be agreeable (said Mr. Mulliner) if, having shown you my nephew so gloomy, so apprehensive, so tortured with dark forebodings at this juncture, I were able now to state that the hearty English welcome of Sir Murgatroyd and Lady Sprockett-Sprockett on his arrival at the Hall cheered him up and put new life into him. Nothing, too, would give me greater pleasure than to say that he found, on encountering the dreaded Biffies and Guffies, that they were negligible little runts with faces incapable of inspiring affection in any good woman.

But I must adhere rigidly to the facts. Genial, even effusive, though his host and hostess showed themselves, their cordiality left him cold. And, so far from his rivals being weeds, they were one and all models of manly beauty, and the spectacle of their obvious worship of Annabelle cut my nephew like a knife.

And on top of all this there was Smattering Hall itself.

Smattering Hall destroyed Mordred's last hope. It was one of those vast edifices, so common throughout the countryside of England, whose original founders seem to have budgeted for families of twenty-five or so and a domestic staff of not less than a hundred. "Home isn't home," one can picture them saying to themselves, "unless you have plenty of elbow room." And so this huge, majestic pile had come into being. Romantic persons, confronted with it, thought of knights in armour riding forth to the Crusades. More earthy individuals felt that it must cost a packet to keep up. Mordred's reaction on passing through the front door was a sort of sick sensation, a kind of settled despair.

How, he asked himself, even assuming that by some miracle he succeeded in fighting his way to her heart through all these Biffies and Guffies, could he ever dare to take Annabelle from a home like this? He had quite satisfactory private means, of course, and would be able, when married, to give up the bachelor flat and spread himself to something on a bigger scale—possibly, if sufficiently *bijou*, even a desirable residence in the Mayfair district. But after Smattering Hall would not Annabelle feel like a sardine in the largest of London houses?

Such were the dark thoughts that raced through Mordred's brain before, during and after dinner. At eleven o'clock he pleaded fatigue after his journey, and Sir Murgatroyd accompanied him to his room, anxious, like a good host, to see that everything was comfortable.

"Very sensible of you to turn in early," he said, in his bluff, genial way. "So many young men ruin their health with late hours. Now you, I imagine, will just get into a dressing-gown and smoke a cigarette or two and have the light out by twelve. You have plenty of cigarettes? I told them to see that you were well supplied. I always think the bedroom smoke is the best one of the day. Nobody to disturb you, and all that. If you want to write letters or anything, there is lots of paper, and here is the waste-paper basket, which is always so necessary. Well, good night, my boy, good night."

The door closed, and Mordred, as foreshadowed, got into a dressing-gown and lit a cigarette. But though, having done this, he made his way to the writing-table, it was not with any idea of getting abreast of his correspondence. It was his purpose to compose a poem to Annabelle Sprockett-Sprockett. He had felt it seething within him all the evening, and sleep would be impossible until it was out of his system.

Hitherto, I should mention, my nephew's poetry, for he belonged to the modern fearless school, had always been stark and rhymeless and had dealt principally with corpses and the smell of cooking cabbage. But now, with the moonlight silvering the balcony outside, he found that his mind had become full of words like "love" and "dove" and "eyes" and "summer skies".

> *Blue eyes*, wrote Mordred . . .
> *Sweet lips*, wrote Mordred . . .
> *Oh, eyes like skies of summer blue* . . .
> *Oh, love* . . .
> *Oh, dove* . . .
> *Oh, lips* . . .

With a muttered ejaculation of chagrin he tore the sheet across and threw it into the wastepaper basket.

Blue eyes that burn into my soul,
   Sweet lips that smile my heart away,
Pom-pom, pom-pom, pom something whole (Goal?)
   And tiddly-iddly-umpty-ay (Gay? Say? Happy-day?)

Blue eyes into my soul that burn,
   Sweet lips that smile away my heart,
Oh, something something turn or yearn
   And something something something part.

You burn into my soul, blue eyes,
   You smile my heart away, sweet lips,
Short long short long of summer skies
   And something something something trips. (Hips? Ships? Pips?)

He threw the sheet into the waste-paper basket and rose with a stifled oath. The wastepaper basket was nearly full now, and still his poet's sense told him that he had not achieved perfection. He thought he saw the reason for this. You can't just sit in a chair and expect inspiration to flow—you want to walk about and clutch your hair and snap your fingers. It had been his intention to pace the room, but the moonlight pouring in through the open window called to him. He went out on to the balcony. It was but a short distance to the dim, mysterious lawn. Impulsively he dropped from the stone balustrade.

The effect was magical. Stimulated by the improved conditions, his Muse gave quick service, and this time he saw at once that she had rung the bell and delivered the goods. One turn up and down the lawn, and he was reciting as follows:

TO ANNABELLE
Oh, lips that smile! Oh, eyes that shine

Like summer skies, or stars above!
Your beauty maddens me like wine,
Oh, umpty-pumpty-tumty love!

And he was just wondering, for he was a severe critic of his own work, whether that last line couldn't be polished up a bit, when his eye was attracted by something that shone like summer skies or stars above and, looking more closely, he perceived that his bedroom curtains were on fire.

Now, I will not pretend that my nephew Mordred was in every respect that cool-headed man of action, but this happened to be a situation with which use had familiarised him. He knew the procedure.

"Fire!" he shouted.

A head appeared in an upstairs window. He recognised it as that of Captain Biffing.

"Eh?" said Captain Biffing.

"Fire!"

"What?"

"Fire!" vociferated Mordred. "F for Francis, I for Isabel . . ."

"Oh, fire?" said Captain Biffing. "Right ho."

And presently the house began to discharge its occupants.

In the proceedings which followed, Mordred, I fear, did not appear to the greatest advantage. This is an age of specialisation, and if you take the specialist off his own particular ground he is at a loss. Mordred's genius, as we have seen, lay in the direction of starting fires. Putting them out called for quite different qualities, and these he did not possess. On the various occasions of holocausts at his series of flats, he had never attempted to play an active part, contenting himself with going downstairs and asking the janitor to step up and see what he could do about it. So now, though under the bright eyes of Annabelle Sprockett-Sprockett he would have given much to be able to dominate the scene, the truth is that the Biffies and Guffies simply played him off the stage.

His heart sank as he noted the hideous efficiency of these young men. They called for buckets. They formed a line. Freddie Boot leaped lissomely on to the balcony, and Algy Fripp, mounted on a wheel-barrow, handed up to him the necessary supplies. And after Mordred, trying to do his bit, had tripped up Jack Guffington and upset two buckets over Ted Prosser, he was advised in set terms to withdraw into the background and stay there.

It was a black ten minutes for the unfortunate young man. One glance at Sir Murgatroyd's twisted face as he watched the operations was enough to tell him how desperately anxious the fine old man was for the safety of his ancestral home and how bitter would be his resentment against the person who had endangered it. And the same applied to Lady Sprockett-Sprockett and Annabelle. Mordred could see the anxiety in their eyes, and the thought that ere long those eyes must be turned accusingly on him chilled him to the marrow.

Presently Freddie Boot emerged from the bedroom to announce that all was well.

"It's out," he said, jumping lightly down. "Anybody know whose room it was?"

Mordred felt a sickening qualm, but the splendid Mulliner courage sustained him. He stepped forward, white and tense.

"Mine," he said.

He became the instant centre of attention. The six young men looked at him.

"Yours?"

"Oh, yours, was it?"

"What happened?"

"How did it start?"

"Yes, how did it start?"

"Must have started somehow, I mean," said Captain Biffing, who was a clear thinker. "I mean to say, must have, don't you know, what?"

Mordred mastered his voice.

"I was smoking, and I suppose I threw my cigarette into the wastepaper basket, and as it was full of paper . . ."

"Full of paper? Why was it full of paper?"

"I had been writing a poem."

There was a stir of bewilderment.

"A what?" said Ted Prosser.

"Writing a what?" said Jack Guffington.

"Writing a *poem*?" asked Captain Biffing of Tommy Mainprice.

"That's how I got the story," said Tommy Mainprice, plainly shaken.

"Chap was writing a poem," Freddie Boot informed Algy Fripp.

"You mean the chap writes poems?"

"That's right. Poems."

"Well, I'm dashed!"

"Well, I'm blowed!"

Their now unconcealed scorn was hard to bear. Mordred chafed beneath it. The word "poem" was flitting from lip to lip, and it was only too evident that, had there been an "s" in the word, those present would have hissed it. Reason told him that these men were mere clods, Philistines, fatheads who would not recognise the rare and the beautiful if you handed it to them on a skewer, but that did not seem to make it any better. He knew that he should be scorning them, but it is not easy to go about scorning people in a dressing-gown, especially if you have no socks on and the night breeze is cool around the ankles. So, as I say, he chafed. And finally, when he saw the butler bend down with pursed lips to the ear of the cook, who was a little hard of hearing, and after a contemptuous glance in his direction speak into it, spacing his syllables carefully, something within him seemed to snap.

"I regret, Sir Murgatroyd," he said, "that urgent family business compels me to return to London immediately. I shall be obliged to take the first train in the morning."

Without another word he went into the house.

In the matter of camping out in devastated areas my nephew had, of course, become by this time an old hand. It was rarely nowadays that a few ashes and cinders about the place disturbed him. But when he had returned to his bedroom one look was enough to assure him that nothing practical in the way of sleep was to be achieved here. Apart from the unpleasant, acrid smell of burned poetry, the apartment, thanks to the efforts of Freddie Boot, had been converted into a kind of inland sea. The carpet was awash, and on the bed only a duck could have made itself at home.

And so it came about that some ten minutes later Mordred Mulliner lay stretched upon a high-backed couch in the library, endeavouring by means of counting sheep jumping through a gap in a hedge to lull himself into unconsciousness.

But sleep refused to come. Nor in his heart had he really thought that it would. When the human soul is on the rack, it cannot just curl up and close its eyes and expect to get its eight hours as if nothing had happened. It was all very well for Mordred to count sheep, but what did this profit him when each sheep in turn assumed the features and lineaments of Annabelle Sprockett-Sprockett and, what was more, gave him a reproachful glance as it drew itself together for the spring?

Remorse gnawed him. He was tortured by a wild regret for what might have been. He was not saying that with all these Biffies and Guffies in the field he had ever had more than a hundred to eight chance of winning that lovely girl, but at least his hat had been in the ring. Now it was definitely out. Dreamy Mordred may have been—romantic—impractical—but he had enough sense to see that the very worst thing you can do when you are trying to make a favourable impression on the adored object is to set fire to her childhood home, every stick and stone of which she has no doubt worshipped since they put her into rompers.

He had reached this point in his meditations, and was about to send his two hundred and thirty-second sheep at the gap, when with a suddenness which affected him much as an explosion of gelignite would have done, the lights flashed on. For an instant, he lay quivering, then, cautiously poking his head round the corner of the couch, he looked to see who his visitors were.

It was a little party of three that had entered the room. First came Sir Murgatroyd, carrying a tray of sandwiches. He was followed by Lady Sprockett-Sprockett with a syphon and glasses. The rear was brought up by Annabelle, who was bearing a bottle of whisky and two dry ginger ales.

So evident was it that they were assembling here for purposes of a family council that, but for one circumstance, Mordred, to whom anything in the nature of eavesdropping was as repugnant as it has always been to all the Mulliners, would have sprung up with a polite "Excuse me" and taken his blanket elsewhere. This circumstance was the fact that on lying down he had kicked his slippers under the couch, well out of reach. The soul of modesty, he could not affront Annabelle with the spectacle of his bare toes.

So he lay there in silence, and silence, broken only by the swishing of soda-water and the *whoosh* of opened ginger-ale bottles, reigned in the room beyond.

Then Sir Murgatroyd spoke.

"Well, that's that," he said, bleakly.

There was a gurgle as Lady Sprockett-Sprockett drank ginger ale. Then her quiet well-bred voice broke the pause.

"Yes," she said, "it is the end."

"The end," agreed Sir Murgatroyd heavily. "No good trying to struggle on against luck like ours. Here we are and here we have got to stay, mouldering on in this blasted barrack of a place which eats up every penny of my income when, but for the fussy interference of that gang of officious, ugly nitwits, there would have been nothing left of it but a pile of ashes, with a man from the Insurance Company standing on it with his fountain-pen, writing cheques. Curse those imbeciles! Did you see that young Fripp with those buckets?"

"I did, indeed," sighed Lady Sprockett-Sprockett.

"Annabelle," said Sir Murgatroyd sharply.

"Yes, Father?"

"It has seemed to me lately, watching you with a father's eye, that you have shown signs of being attracted by young Algernon Fripp. Let me tell you that if ever you allow yourself to be ensared by his insidious wiles, or by those of William Biffing, John Guffington, Edward Prosser, Thomas Mainprice or Frederick Boot, you will do so over my dead body. After what occurred tonight, those young men shall never darken my door again. They and their buckets! To think that we could have gone and lived in London . . ."

"In a nice little flat . . ." said Lady Sprockett-Sprockett.

"Handy for my club . . ."

"Convenient for the shops . . ."

"Within a stone's throw of the theatres . . ."

"Seeing all our friends . . ."

"Had it not been," said Sir Murgatroyd, summing up, "for the pestilential activities of these Guffingtons, these Biffings, these insufferable Fripps, men who ought never to be trusted near a bucket of water when a mortgaged country-house has got nicely alight. I did think," proceeded the stricken man, helping himself to a sandwich, "that when Annabelle, with a ready intelligence which I cannot overpraise, realised this young Mulliner's splendid gifts and made us ask him down here, the happy ending was in sight. What Smattering Hall has needed for generations has been a man who throws his cigarette-ends into wastepaper baskets.

I was convinced that here at last was the angel of mercy we required."

"He did his best, Father."

"No man could have done more," agreed Sir Murgatroyd cordially. "The way he upset those buckets and kept getting entangled in people's legs. Very shrewd. It thrilled me to see him. I don't know when I've met a young fellow I liked and respected more. And what if he is a poet? Poets are all right. Why, dash it, I'm a poet myself. At the last dinner of the Loyal Sons of Worcestershire I composed a poem which, let me tell you, was pretty generally admired. I read it out to the boys over the port, and they cheered me to the echo. It was about a young lady of Bewdley, who sometimes behaved rather rudely . . ."

"Not before Mother, Father."

"Perhaps you're right. Well, I'm off to bed. Come along, Aurelia. You coming, Annabelle?"

"Not yet, Father. I want to stay and think."

"Do what?"

"Think."

"Oh, think? Well, all right."

"But, Murgatroyd," said Lady Sprockett-Sprockett, "is there no hope? After all, there are plenty of cigarettes in the house, and we could always give Mr. Mulliner another wastepaper basket . . ."

"No good. You heard him say he was leaving by the first train tomorrow. When I think that we shall never see that splendid young man again . . . Why, hullo, hullo, hullo, what's this? Crying, Annabelle?"

"Oh, Mother!"

"My darling, what is it?"

A choking sob escaped the girl.

"Mother, I love him! Directly I saw him in the dentist's waiting-room, something seemed to go all over me, and I knew that there could be no other man for me. And now . . ."

"Hi!" cried Mordred, popping up over the side of the couch like a jack-in-the-box.

He had listened with growing understanding to the conversation which I have related, but had shrunk from revealing his presence because, as I say, his toes were bare. But this was too much. Toes or no toes, he felt that he must be in this.

"You love me Annabelle?" he cried.

His sudden advent had occasioned, I need scarcely say, a certain reaction in those present. Sir Murgatroyd had leaped like a jumping bean. Lady Sprockett-Sprockett had quivered like a jelly. As for Annabelle, her lovely mouth was open to the extent of perhaps three inches, and she was staring like one who sees a vision.

"You really love me, Annabelle?"

"Yes, Mordred."

"Sir Murgatroyd," said Mordred formally, "I have the honour to ask you for your daughter's hand. I am only a poor poet . . ."

"How poor?" asked the other, keenly.

"I was referring to my Art," explained Mordred. "Financially, I am nicely fixed. I could support Annabelle in modest comfort."

"Then take her, my boy, take her. You will live, of course"—the old man winced—"in London?"

"Yes. And so shall you."

Sir Murgatroyd shook his head.

"No, no, that dream is ended. It is true that in certain circumstances I had hoped to do so, for the insurance, I may mention, amounts to as much as a hundred thousand pounds, but I am resigned now to spending the rest of my life in this infernal family vault. I see no reprieve."

"I understand," said Mordred, nodding. "You mean you have no paraffin in the house?"

Sir Murgatroyd started.

"Paraffin?"

"If," said Mordred, and his voice was very gentle and winning, "there had been paraffin on the premises, I think it possible that tonight's conflagration, doubtless imperfectly quenched, might have broken out again, this time with more serious results. It is often this way with fires. You pour buckets of water on them and think they are extinguished, but all the time they have been smouldering unnoticed, to break out once more in—well, in here, for example."

"Or the billiard-room," said Lady Sprockett-Sprockett.

"*And* the billiard-room," corrected Sir Murgatroyd.

"And the billiard-room," said Mordred. "And possibly—who knows?—in the drawing-room, dining-room, kitchen, servants' hall, butler's pantry, and the usual domestic offices, as well. Still, as you say you have no paraffin . . ."

"My boy," said Sir Murgatroyd, in a shaking voice, "what gave you the idea that we have no paraffin? How did you fall into this odd error? We have gallons of paraffin. The cellar is full of it."

"And Annabelle will show you the way to the cellar—in case you thought of going there," said Lady Sprockett-Sprockett. "Won't you, dear?"

"Of course, Mother. You will like the cellar, Mordred, darling. Most picturesque. Possibly, if you are interested in paraffin, you might also care to take a look at our little store of paper and shavings, too."

"My angel," said Mordred, tenderly, "you think of everything."

He found his slippers, and hand in hand they passed down the stairs. Above them, they could see the head of Sir Murgatroyd, as he leaned over the banisters. A box of matches fell at their feet like a father's benediction.

36

BURIED TREASURE

THE situation in Germany had come up for discussion in the bar parlour of the Anglers' Rest, and it was generally agreed that Hitler was standing at the crossroads and would soon be compelled to do something definite. His present policy, said a Whisky and Splash, was mere shilly-shallying.

"He'll have to let it grow or shave it off," said the Whisky and Splash. "He can't go on sitting on the fence like this. Either a man has a moustache or he has not. There can be no middle course."

The thoughtful pause which followed these words was broken by a Small Bass.

"Talking of moustaches," he said, "you don't seem to see any nowadays, not what I call moustaches. What's become of them?"

"I've often asked myself the same question," said a Gin and Italian Vermouth. "Where, I've often asked myself, are the great sweeping moustaches of our boyhood? I've got a photograph of my grandfather as a young man in the album at home, and he's just a pair of eyes staring over a sort of quickset hedge."

"Special cups they used to have," said the Small Bass, "to keep the vegetation out of their coffee. Ah, well, those days are gone for ever."

Mr. Mulliner shook his head.

"Not entirely," he said, stirring his hot Scotch and lemon. "I admit that they are rarer than they used to be, but in the remoter rural districts you will still find these curious growths flourishing. What causes them to survive is partly boredom and partly the good, clean spirit of amateur sport which has made us Englishmen what we are."

The Small Bass said he did not quite get that.

"What I mean," said Mr. Mulliner, "is that life has not much to offer in the way of excitement to men who are buried in the country all the year round, so for want of anything better to do they grow moustaches at one another."

"Sort of competitively, as it were?"

"Exactly. One landowner will start to try to surpass his neighbour in luxuriance of moustache, and the neighbour, inflamed, fights back at him. There is often a great deal of very intense feeling about these contests, with not a little wagering on the side. So, at least, my nephew Brancepeth, the artist, tells me. And he should know, for his present affluence and happiness are directly due to one of them."

"Did he grow a moustache?"

"No. He was merely caught up in the whirlwind of the struggle for supremacy between Lord Bromborough, of Rumpling Hall, Lower Rumpling, Norfolk, and Sir Preston Potter, Bart., of Wapleigh Towers in the same county. Most of the vintage moustaches nowadays are to be found in Norfolk and Suffolk. I suppose the keen, moist sea air brings them on. Certainly it, or some equally stimulating agency, had brought on those of Lord Bromborough and Sir Preston Potter, for in the whole of England at that time there were probably no two finer specimens than the former's Joy use and the latter's Love in Idleness.

It was Lord Bromborough's daughter Muriel (said Mr. Mulliner) who had entitled these two moustaches in this manner. A poetic, imaginative girl, much addicted to reading old sagas and romances, she had adapted to modern conditions the practice of the ancient heroes of bestowing names on their favourite swords. King Arthur, you will remember, had his Excalibur, Charlemagne his Flamberge, Doolin of Mayence the famous Merveilleuse: and Muriel saw no reason why this custom should be allowed to die out. A pretty idea, she thought, and I thought it a pretty idea when my nephew Brancepeth told me of it, and he thought it a pretty idea when told of it by Muriel.

For Muriel and Brancepeth had made one another's acquaintance some time before this story opens. The girl, unlike her father, who never left the ancestral acres, came often to London, and on one of these visits my nephew was introduced to her.

With Brancepeth it seems to have been a case of love at first sight and it was not long before Muriel admitted to returning his passion. She had been favourably attracted to him from the moment when she found that their dance steps fitted, and when some little while later he offered to paint her portrait for nothing there was a look in her eyes which it was impossible to mistake. As early as the middle of the first sitting, he folded her in his arms, and she nestled against his waistcoat with a low, cooing gurgle. Both knew that in the other they had found a soul-mate.

Such, then, was the relationship of the young couple, when one summer morning Brancepeth's telephone rang and, removing the receiver, he heard the voice of the girl he loved.

"Hey, cocky," she was saying.

"What ho, reptile," responded Brancepeth. "Where are you speaking from?"

"Rumpling. Listen, I've got a job for you."

"What sort of job?"

"A commission. Father wants his portrait painted."

"Oh yes?"

"Yes. His sinister design is to present it to the local Men's Club. I don't know what he's got against them. A nasty jar it'll be for the poor fellows when they learn of it."

"Why, is the old dad a bit of a gargoyle?"

"You never spoke a truer word. All moustache and eyebrows. The former has to be seen to be believed."

"Pretty septic?"

"My dear! Suppurating. Well, are you on? I've told Father you're the coming man."

"So I am," said Brancepeth. "I'm coming this afternoon."

He was as good as his word. He caught the 3.15 train from Liverpool Street and at 7.20 alighted at the little station of Lower Rumpling, arriving at the Hall just in time to dress for dinner.

Always a rapid dresser, tonight Brancepeth excelled himself, for he yearned to see Muriel once more after their extended separation. Racing down to the drawing-room, however, tying his tie as he went, he found that his impetuosity had brought him there too early. The only occupant of the room at the moment of his entrance was a portly man whom, from the evidence submitted, he took to be his host. Except for a few outlying ears and the tip of a nose, the fellow was entirely moustache, and until he set eyes upon it, Brancepeth tells me, he had never really appreciated the full significance of those opening words of Longfellow's Evangeline, "This is the forest primeval."

He introduced himself courteously.

"How do you do, Lord Bromborough? My name is Mulliner."

The other regarded him—over the zareba—with displeasure, it seemed to Brancepeth.

"What do you mean—Lord Bromborough?" he snapped curtly.

Brancepeth said he had meant Lord Bromborough.

"I'm not Lord Bromborough," said the man.

Brancepeth was taken aback.

"Oh, aren't you?" he said. "I'm sorry."

"I'm glad," said the man. "Whatever gave you the silly idea that I was old Bromborough?"

"I was told that he had a very fine moustache."

"Who told you that?"

"His daughter."

The other snorted.

"You can't go by what a man's daughter says. She's biased. Prejudiced. Blinded by filial love, and all that sort of thing. If I wanted an opinion on a moustache, I wouldn't go to a man's daughter. I'd go to somebody who knew about moustaches. 'Mr. Walkinshaw,' I'd say, or whatever the name might be. . . . Bromborough's moustache a very fine moustache, indeed! Pshaw! Bromborough *has* a moustache —of a sort. He is not clean-shaven—I concede that . . . but fine? Pooh. Absurd. Ridiculous. Preposterous. Never heard of such nonsense in my life."

He turned pettishly away, and so hurt and offended was his manner that Brancepeth had no heart to continue the conversation. Muttering something about having forgotten his handkerchief, he sidled from the room and hung about on the landing outside. And presently Muriel came tripping down the stairs, looking more beautiful than ever.

She seemed delighted to see him.

"Hullo, Brancepeth, you old bounder," she said cordially. "So you got here? What are you doing parked on the stairs? Why aren't you in the drawing room?"

Brancepeth shot a glance at the closed door and lowered his voice.

"There's a hairy bird in there who wasn't any too matey. I thought it must be your father and accosted him as such, and he got extraordinarily peevish. He seemed to resent my saying that I had heard your father had a fine moustache."

The girl laughed.

"Golly! You put your foot in it properly. Old Potter's madly jealous of Father's moustache. That was Sir Preston Potter, of Wapleigh Towers, one of our better-known local Barts. He and his son are staying here." She broke off to address the butler, a kindly, silver-haired old man who at this moment mounted the stairs. "Hullo, Phipps, are you ambling up to announce the tea and shrimps? You're a bit early. I don't think Father and Mr. Potter are down yet. Ah, here's Father," she said, as a brilliantly moustached man of middle age appeared. "Father, this is Mr. Mulliner."

Brancepeth eyed his host keenly as he shook hands, and his heart sank a little. He saw that the task of committing this man to canvas was going to be a difficult one. The recent slurs of Sir Preston Potter had been entirely without justification. Lord Bromborough's moustache was an extraordinarily fine one, fully as lush as that which barred the public from getting a square view of the Baronet. It seemed to Brancepeth, indeed, that the job before him was more one for a landscape artist than a portrait painter.

Sir Preston Potter, however, who now emerged from the drawing-room, clung stoutly to his opinion. He looked sneeringly at his rival.

"You been clipping your moustache, Bromborough?"

"Of course I have not been clipping my moustache," replied Lord Bromborough shortly. It was only too plain that there was bad blood between the two men. "What the dooce would I clip my moustache for? What makes you think I've been clipping my moustache?"

"I thought it had shrunk," said Sir Preston Potter. "It looks very small to me, very small. Perhaps the moth's been at it."

Lord Bromborough quivered beneath the coarse insult, but his patrician breeding checked the hot reply which rose to his lips. He was a host. Controlling himself with a strong effort, he turned the conversation to the subject of early mangold-wurzels; and it was while he was speaking of these with eloquence and even fire that a young man with butter-coloured hair came hurrying down the stairs.

"Buck up, Edwin," said Muriel impatiently. "What's the idea of keeping us all waiting like this?"

"Oh, sorry," said the young man.

"So you ought to be. Well, now you're here, I'd like to introduce you to Mr. Mulliner. He's come to paint Father's portrait. Mr. Mulliner . . . Mr. Edwin Potter, my *fiancé*."

"Dinner is served," said Phipps the butler.

It was in a sort of trance that my nephew Brancepeth sat through the meal which followed. He toyed listlessly with his food and contributed so little to the conversation that a casual observer entering the room would have supposed him to be a deaf-mute who was on a diet. Nor can we fairly blame him for this, for he had had a severe shock. Few things are more calculated to jar an ardent lover and upset his poise than the sudden announcement by the girl he loves that she is engaged to somebody else, and Muriel's words had been like a kick in the stomach from an army mule. And in addition to suffering the keenest mental anguish, Brancepeth was completely bewildered.

It was not as if this Edwin Potter had been Clark Gable or somebody. Studying him closely, Brancepeth was unable to discern in him any of those qualities which win girl's hearts. He had an ordinary, meaningless face, disfigured by an eyeglass, and was plainly a boob of the first water. Brancepeth could make nothing of it. He resolved at the earliest possible moment to get hold of Muriel and institute a probe.

It was not until the next day before luncheon that he found an opportunity of doing so. His morning had been spent in making preliminary sketches of her father. This task concluded, he came out into the garden and saw her reclining in a hammock slung between two trees at the edge of the large lawn.

He made his way towards her with quick, nervous strides. He was feeling jaded and irritated. His first impressions of Lord Bromborough had not misled him. Painting his portrait, he saw, was going to prove, as he had feared it would prove, a severe test of his courage and strength. There seemed so little about Lord Bromborough's face for an artist to get hold of. It was as if he had been commissioned to depict a client who, for reasons of his own, insisted on lying hid behind a haystack.

His emotions lent acerbity to his voice. It was with a sharp intonation that he uttered the preliminary "Hoy!"

The girl sat up.

"Oh, hullo," she said.

"Oh, hullo, yourself, with knobs on," retorted Brancepeth. "Never mind the 'Oh, hullo.' I want an explanation."

"What's puzzling you?"

"This engagement of yours."

"Oh, that?"

"Yes, that. A nice surprise that was to spring on a chap, was it not? A jolly way of saying 'Welcome to Rumpling Hall,' I don't think." Brancepeth choked. "I came here thinking that you loved me . . . "

"So I do."

"What!"

"Madly. Devotedly."

"Then why the dickens do I find you betrothed to this blighted Potter?"

Muriel sighed.

"It's the old, old story."

"What's the old, old story?"

"This is. It's all so simple, if you'd only understand. I don't suppose any girl ever worshipped a man as I worship you, Brancepeth, but Father hasn't a bean . . . you know what it's like owning land nowadays. Between ourselves, while we're on the subject, I'd stipulate for a bit down in advance on that portrait if I were you . . ."

Brancepeth understood.

"Is this Potter rotter rich?"

"Rolling. Sir Preston was Potter's Potted Table Delicacies."

There was a silence.

"H'm," said Brancepeth.

"Exactly. You see now. Oh, Brancepeth," said the girl, her voice trembling, "why haven't you money? If you only had the merest pittance—enough for a flat in Mayfair and a little weekend place in the country somewhere and a couple of good cars and a villa in the South of France and a bit of trout fishing on some decent river, I would risk all for love. But as it is . . ."

Another silence fell.

"What you ought to do," said Muriel, "is invent some good animal for the movies. That's where the money is. Look at Walt Disney."

Brancepeth started. It was as if she had read his thoughts. Like all young artists nowadays, he had always held before him as the goal of his ambition the invention of some new comic animal for the motion pictures. What he burned to do, as Velasquez would have burned to do if he had lived today, was to think of another Mickey Mouse and then give up work and just sit back and watch the money roll in.

"It isn't so easy," he said sadly.

"Have you tried?"

"Of course I've tried. For years I have followed the gleam. I thought I had something with Hilda the Hen and Bertie the Bandicoot, but nobody would look at them. I see now that they were lifeless, uninspired. I am a man who needs the direct inspiration."

"Doesn't Father suggest anything to you?"

Brancepeth shook his head.

"No. I have studied your father, alert for the slightest hint . . ."

"Walter the Walrus?"

"No. Lord Bromborough looks like a walrus, yes, but unfortunately not a funny walrus. That moustache of his is majestic rather than diverting. It arouses in the beholder a feeling of awe, such as one gets on first seeing the pyramids. One senses the terrific effort behind it. I suppose it must have taken a lifetime of incessant toil to produce a cascade like that?"

"Oh, no. Father hadn't a moustache at all a few years ago. It was only when Sir Preston began to grow one and rather flaunt it at him at District Council meetings that he buckled down to it. But why," demanded the girl passionately, "are we wasting time talking about moustaches? Kiss me, Brancepeth. We have just time before lunch."

Brancepeth did as directed, and the incident closed.

I do not propose (resumed Mr. Mulliner, who had broken off his narrative at this point to request Miss Postlethwaite, our able barmaid, to give him another hot Scotch and lemon) to dwell in detail on the agony of spirit endured by my nephew Brancepeth in the days that followed this poignant conversation. The spectacle of a sensitive artist soul on the rack is never a pleasant one. Suffice it to say that as each day came and went it left behind it an increased despair.

What with brooding on his shattered romance and trying to paint Lord Bromborough's portrait and having his nerves afflicted by the incessant bickering that went on between Lord Bromborough and Sir Preston Potter and watching Edwin Potter bleating round Muriel and not being able to think of a funny animal for the movies, it is little wonder that his normally healthy complexion began to shade off to a sallow pallor and that his eyes took on a haunted look. Before the end of the first week he had become an object to excite the pity of the tender-hearted.

Phipps the butler was tender-hearted, and had been since a boy. Brancepeth excited his pity, and he yearned to do something to emeliorate the young man's lot. The method that suggested itself to him was to take a bottle of champagne to his room. It might prove a palliative rather than a cure, but he was convinced that it would, if only temporarily, bring the roses back to Brancepeth's cheeks. So he took a bottle of champagne to his room on the fifth night of my nephew's visit and found him lying on his bed in striped pyjamas and a watered silk dressing-gown, staring at the ceiling.

The day that was now drawing to a close had been a particularly bad one for Brancepeth. The weather was unusually warm, and this had increased his despondency, so that he had found himself chafing beneath Lord Bromborough's moustache in a spirit of sullen rebellion. Before the afternoon sitting was over, he had become conscious of a vivid feeling of hatred for the thing. He longed for the courage to get at it with a hatchet after the manner of a pioneer in some wild country hewing a clearing in the surrounding jungle. When Phipps found him, his fists were clenched and he was biting his lower lip.

"I have brought you a little champagne, sir," said Phipps, in his kindly, silver-haired way. "It occurred to me that you might be in need of a restorative."

Brancepeth was touched. He sat up, the hard glare in his eyes softening.

"That's awfully good of you," he said. "You are quite right. I could do with a drop or two from the old bin. I am feeling rather fagged. The weather, I suppose."

A gentle smile played over the butler's face as he watched the young man put away a couple, quick.

"No, sir. I do not think it is the weather. You may be quite frank with me, sir. I understand. It must be a very wearing task, painting his lordship. Several artists have had to give it up. There was a young fellow here in the spring of last year who had to be removed to the cottage hospital. His manner had been strange and moody for some days, and one night we found him on a ladder, in the nude, tearing and tearing away at the ivy on the west wall. His lordship's moustache had been too much for him."

Brancepeth groaned and refilled his glass. He knew just how his brother brush must have felt.

"The ironical thing," continued the butler, "is that conditions would be just as bad, were the moustache non-existent. I have been in service at the Hall for a number of years, and I can assure you that his lordship was fully as hard on the eye when he was clean-shaven. Well, sir, when I tell you that I was actually relieved when he began to grow a moustache, you will understand."

"Why, what was the matter with him?"

"He had a face like a fish, sir."

"A fish?"

"Yes, sir."

Something resembling an electric shock shot through Brancepeth, causing him to quiver in every limb.

"A funny fish?" he asked in a choking voice.

"Yes, sir. Extremely droll."

Brancepeth was trembling like a saucepan of boiling milk at the height of its fever. A strange, wild thought had come into his mind. A funny fish . . .

There had never been a funny fish on the screen. Funny mice, funny cats, funny dogs . . . but not a funny fish. He stared before him with glowing eyes.

"Yes, sir, when his lordship began to grow a moustache, I was relieved. It seemed to me that it must be a change for the better. And so it was at first. But now . . . you know how it is, sir . . . I often find myself wishing those old, happy days were back again. We never know when we are well off, sir, do we?"

"You would be glad to see the last of Lord Bromborough's moustache?"

"Yes, sir. Very glad."

"Right," said Brancepeth. "Then I'll shave it off."

In private life, butlers relax that impassive gravity which the rules of their union compel them to maintain in public. Spring something sensational on a butler when he is chatting with you in your bedroom, and he will leap and goggle like any ordinary man. Phipps did so now.

"Shave it off, sir?" he gasped, quaveringly.

"Shave it off," said Brancepeth, pouring out the last of the champagne.

"Shave off his lordship's moustache?"

"This very night. Leaving not a wrack behind."

"But, sir . . ."

"Well?"

"The thought that crossed my mind, sir, was—how?"

Brancepeth clicked his tongue impatiently.

"Quite easy. I suppose he likes a little something last thing at night? Whisky or what not?"

"I always bring his lordship a glass of warm milk to the smoking-room."

"Have you taken it to him yet?"

"Not yet, sir. I was about to do so when I left you."

"And is there anything in the nature of a sleeping draught in the house?"

"Yes, sir. His lordship is a poor sleeper in the hot weather and generally takes a tablet of Slumberola in his milk."

"Then, Phipps, if you are the pal I think you are, you will slip into his milk tonight not one tablet but four tablets."

"But, sir . . ."

"I know, I know. What you are trying to say, I presume, is—What is there in it for you? I will tell you, Phipps. There is a packet in it for you. If Lord Bromborough's face in its stark fundamentals is as you describe it, I can guarantee that in less than no time I shall be bounding about the place trying to evade super-tax. In which event, rest assured that you will get your cut. You are sure of your facts? If I make a clearing in the tangled wildwood, I shall come down eventually to a face like a fish?"

"Yes, sir."

"A fish with good comedy values?"

"Oh, yes, sir. Till it began to get me down, many is the laugh I have had at the sight of it."

"That is all I wish to know. Right. Well, Phipps, can I count on your co-operation? I may add, before you speak, that this means my life's happiness. Sit in, and I shall be able to marry the girl I adore. Refuse to do your bit, and I drift through the remainder of my life a soured, blighted bachelor."

The butler was plainly moved. Always kindly and silver-haired, he looked kindlier and more silver-haired than ever before.

"It's like that, is it, sir?"

"It is."

"Well, sir, I wouldn't wish to come between a young gentleman and his life's happiness. I know what it means to love."

"You do?"

"I do indeed, sir. It is not for me to boast, but there was a time when the girls used to call me Saucy George."

"And so——?"

"I will do as you request, sir."

"I knew it, Phipps," said Brancepeth with emotion. "I knew that I could rely on you. All that remains, then, is for you to show me which is Lord Bromborough's room." He paused. A disturbing thought had struck him. "I say! Suppose he locks his door?"

"It is quite all right, sir," the butler reassured him. "In the later summer months, when the nights are sultry, his lordship does not sleep in his room. He reposes in a hammock slung between two trees on the large lawn."

"I know the hammock," said Brancepeth tenderly. "Well that's fine, then. The thing's in the bag. Phipps," said Brancepeth, grasping his hand, "I don't know how to express my gratitude. If everything develops as I expect it to; if Lord Bromborough's face gives me the inspiration which I antipicate and I clean up big, you, I repeat, shall share my riches. In due season there will call at your pantry elephants laden with gold, and camels bearing precious stones and rare spices. Also apes, ivory and peacocks. And . . . you say your name is George?"

"Yes, sir."

"Then my eldest child shall be christened George. Or, if female, Georgiana."

"Thank you very much, sir."

"Not at all," said Brancepeth. "A pleasure."

Brancepeth's first impression on waking next morning was that he had had a strange and beautiful dream. It was a vivid, lovely thing, all about stealing out of the house in striped pyjamas and a watered silk dressing-gown with a pair of scissors, and stooping over the hammock where Lord Bromborough lay and razing his great moustache Joyeuse to its foundations. And he was just heaving a wistful sigh and wishing it were true, when he found that it was. It all came back to him—the furtive sneak downstairs, the wary passage of the lawn, the snip-snip-snip of the scissors blending with a strong man's snores in the silent night. It was no dream. The thing had actually occurred. His host's upper lip had become a devastated area.

It was not Brancepeth's custom, as a rule, to spring from his bed at the beginning of a new day, but he did so now. He was consumed with a burning eagerness to gaze upon his handiwork, for the first time to see Lord Bromborough steadily and see him whole. Scarcely ten minutes had elapsed before he was in his clothes and on his way to the breakfast-room. The other, he knew, was an early riser, and even so great a bereavement as he had suffered would not deter him from getting at the coffee and kippers directly he caught a whiff of them.

Only Phipps, however, was in the breakfast-room. He was lighting wicks under the hot dishes on the sideboard. Brancepeth greeted him jovially.

"Good morning, Phipps. What ho, what ho, with a hey nonny nonny and a hot cha-cha."

The butler was looking nervous, like Macbeth interviewing Lady Macbeth after one of her visits to the spare room.

"Good morning, sir. Er—might I ask, sir . . ."

"Oh, yes," said Brancepeth. "The operation was a complete success. Everything went according to plan."

"I am very glad to hear it, sir."

"Not a hitch from start to finish. Tell me, Phipps," said Brancepeth, helping himself buoyantly to a fried egg and a bit of bacon and seating himself at the table, "what sort of a fish did Lord Bromborough look like before he had a moustache?"

The butler reflected.

"Well, sir, I don't know if you have seen Sidney the Sturgeon?"

"Eh?"

"On the pictures, sir. I recently attended a cinematographic performance at Norwich—it was on my afternoon off last week—and," said Phipps, chuckling gently at the recollection, "they were showing a most entertaining new feature, 'The Adventures of Sidney the Sturgeon'. It came on before the big picture, and was all I could do to keep a straight face. This sturgeon looked extremely like his lordship in the the old days."

He drifted from the room and Brancepeth stared after him, stunned. His air castles had fallen about him in ruins. Fame, fortune, and married bliss were as far away as ever. All his labour had been in vain. If there was already a funny fish functioning on the silver screen, it was obvious that it would be mere waste of time to do another. He clasped his head in his hands and groaned over his fried egg. And, as he did so, the door opened.

"Ha!" said Lord Bromborough's voice. "Good morning, good morning."

Brancepeth spun round with a sharp jerk which sent a piece of bacon flying off his fork as if it had been shot from a catapult. Although his host's appearance could not affect his professional future now, he was consumed with curiosity to see what he looked like. And, having spun round, he sat transfixed. There before him stood Lord Bromborough, but not a hair of his moustache was missing. It flew before him like a banner in all its pristine luxuriance.

"Eh, what?" said Lord Bromborough, sniffing. "Kedgeree? Capital, capital."

He headed purposefully for the sideboard. The door opened again, and Edwin Potter came in, looking more of a boob than ever.

In addition to looking like a boob, Edwin Potter seemed worried.

"I say," he said, "My father's missing."

"On how many cylinders?" asked Lord Bromborough. He was a man who liked his joke of a morning.

"I mean to say," continued Edwin Potter, "I can't find him. I went to speak to him about something just now, and his room was empty and his bed had not been slept in."

Lord Bromborough was dishing out kedgeree on to a plate.

"That's all right," he said. "He wanted to try my hammock last night, so I let him. If he slept as soundly as I did, he slept well. I came over all drowsy as I was finishing my glass of hot milk and I woke this morning in an arm-chair in the smoking-room. Ah, my dear," he went on, as Muriel entered, "come along and try this kedgeree. It smells excellent. I was just telling our young friend here that his father slept in my hammock last night."

Muriel's face was wearing a look of perplexity.

"Out in the garden, do you mean?"

"Of course I mean out in the garden. You know where my hammock is. I've seen you lying in it."

"Then there must be a goat in the garden."

"Goat?" said Lord Bromborough, who had now taken his place at the table and was shovelling kedgeree into himself like a stevedore loading a grain ship. "What do you mean, goat? There's no goat in the garden. Why should there be a goat in the garden?"

"Because something has eaten off Sir Preston's moustache."

"What!"

"Yes. I met him outside, and the shrubbery had completely disappeared. Here he is. Look."

What seemed at first to Brancepeth a total stranger was standing in the doorway. It was only when the newcomer folded his arms and began to speak in a familiar rasping voice that he recognised Sir Preston Potter, Bart., of Wapleigh Towers.

"So!" said Sir Preston, directing at Lord Bromborough a fiery glance full of deleterious animal magnetism.

Lord Bromborough finished his kedgeree and looked up.

"Ah, Potter," he said. "Shaved your moustache, have you? Very sensible. It would never have amounted to anything, and you will be happier without it."

Flame shot from Sir Preston Potter's eyes. The man was plainly stirred to his foundations.

"Bromborough," he snarled, "I have only five things to say to you. The first is that you are the lowest, foulest fiend that ever disgraced the pure pages of Debrett; the second that your dastardly act in clipping off my moustache shows you a craven, who knew that defeat stared him in the eye and that only thus he could hope to triumph; the third that I intend to approach my lawyer immediately with a view to taking legal action; the fourth is goodbye for ever; and the fifth——"

"Have an egg," said Lord Bromborough.

"I will not have an egg. This is not a matter which can be lightly passed off with eggs. The fifth thing I wish to say——"

"But, my dear fellow, you seem to be suggesting that I had something to do with this. I approve of what has happened, yes. I approve of it heartily. Norfolk will be a sweeter and better place to live in now that this has occurred. But it was none of my doing. I was asleep in the smoking-room all night."

"The fifth thing I wish to say——" '

"In an arm-chair. If you doubt me, I can show you the arm-chair."

"The fifth thing I wish to say is that the engagement between my son and your daughter is at an end."

"Like your moustache. Ha, ha!" said Lord Bromborough, who had many good qualities but was not tactful.

"Oh, but, Father!" cried Edwin Potter. "I mean, dash it!"

"And *I* mean," thundered Sir Preston, "that your engagement is at an end. You have my five points quite clear, Bromborough?"

"I think so," said Lord Bromborough, ticking them off on his fingers. "I am a foul fiend, I'm a craven, you are going to institute legal proceedings, you bid me goodbye for ever, and my daughter shall never marry your son. Yes, five in all."

"Add a sixth. I shall see that you are expelled from all your clubs."

"I haven't got any."

"Oh?" said Sir Preston, a little taken aback. "Well, if ever you make a speech in the House of Lords, beware. I shall be in the gallery, booing."

He turned and strode from the room, followed by Edwin, protesting bleatingly. Lord Bromborough took a cigarette from his case.

"Silly old ass," he said. "I expect that moustache of his was clipped off by a body of public-spirited citizens. Like the Vigilantes they have in America. It is absurd to suppose that a man could grow a beastly, weedy caricature of a moustache like Potter's without inflaming popular feeling. No doubt they have been lying in wait for him for months. Lurking. Watching their opportunity. Well, my dear, so your wedding's off. A nuisance in a way, of course, for I'd just bought a new pair of trousers to give you away in. Still, it can't be helped."

"No, it can't be helped," said Muriel. "Besides, there will be another one along in a minute."

She shot a tender smile at Brancepeth, but on his lips there was no answering simper. He sat in silence, crouched over his fried egg.

What did it profit him, he was asking himself bitterly, that the wedding was off? He himself could never marry Muriel. He was a penniless artist without prospects. He would never invent a comic animal for the movies now. There had been an instant when he had hoped that Sir Preston's uncovered face might suggest one, but the hope had died at birth. Sir Preston Potter, without his moustache, had merely looked like a man without a moustache.

He became aware that his host was addressing him.

"I beg your pardon?"

"I said, 'Got a light?' "

"Oh, sorry," said Brancepeth.

He took out his lighter and gave it a twiddle. Then, absently, he put the flame to the cigarette between his host's lips.

Or, rather, for preoccupation had temporarily destroyed his judgment of distance, to the moustache that billowed above and around it. And the next moment there was a great sheet of flame and a cloud of acrid smoke. When this had cleared away, only a smouldering stubble was left of what had once been one of Norfolk's two most outstanding eyesores.

A barely human cry rent the air, but Brancepeth hardly heard it. He was staring like one in a trance at the face that confronted him through the shrouding mists, fascinated by the short, broad nose, the bulging eyes, the mouth that gaped and twitched. It was only when his host had made a swift dive across the table with bared teeth and clutching hands that Prudence returned to its throne. He slid under the table and came out on the other side.

"Catch him!" cried the infuriated peer. "Trip him up! Sit on his head!"

"Certainly not," said Muriel. "He's the man I love."

"Is he!" said Lord Bromborough, breathing heavily as he crouched for another spring. "Well, he's the man I am going to disembowel with my bare hands—when I catch him."

"I think I should nip through the window, darling," said Muriel gently.

Brancepeth weighed the advice hastily and found it good. The window, giving on to the gravel drive, was, he perceived, open at the bottom. The sweet summer air floated in, and an instant later he was floating out. As he rose from the gravel, something solid struck him on the back of the head. It was a coffee-pot.

But coffee-pots, however shrewdly aimed, mattered little to Brancepeth now. This one had raised a painful contusion, and he had in addition skinned both hands and one of his knees. His trousers, moreover, a favourite pair, had a large hole in them. Nevertheless, his heart was singing within him.

For Phipps had been wrong. Phipps was an ass. Phipps did not know a fish when he saw one. Lord Bromborough's face did not resemble a fish at all. It suggested something much finer, much fuller of screen possibilities, much more box-office than a fish. In that one blinding instant of illumination before he had dived under the table, Brancepeth had seen Lord Bromborough for what he was—Ferdinand Frog.

He turned, to perceive his host in the act of hurling a cottage loaf.

"Muriel!" he cried.

"Hullo?" said the girl, who had joined her father at the window and was watching the scene with great interest.

"I love you, Muriel."

"Same here."

"But for the moment I must leave you."

"I would," said Muriel. She glanced over her shoulder. "He's gone to get the kedgeree." And Brancepeth saw that Lord Bromborough had left his butt. "He is now," she added, "coming back."

"Will you wait for me, Muriel?"

"To all eternity."

"It will not be necessary," said Brancepeth. "Call in six months or a year. By that time I shall have won fame and fortune."

He would have spoken further, but at this moment Lord Bromborough reappeared, poising the kedgeree. With a loving smile and a wave of the hand, Brancepeth leaped smartly to one side. Then, turning, he made his way down the drive, gazing raptly into a future of Rolls-Royces, caviare, and silk underclothing made to measure.

37
ANSELM GETS HIS CHANCE

THE Summer Sunday was drawing to a close. Twilight had fallen on the little garden of the Anglers' Rest, and the air was fragrant with the sweet scent of jasmine and tobacco plant. Stars were peeping out. Blackbirds sang drowsily in the shrubberies. Bats wheeled through the shadows, and a gentle breeze played fitfully among the hollyhocks. It was, in short, as a customer who had looked in for a gin and tonic rather happily put it, a nice evening.

Nevertheless, to Mr. Mulliner and the group assembled in the bar parlour of the inn there was a sense of something missing. It was due to the fact that Miss Postlethwaite, the efficient barmaid, was absent. Some forty minutes had elapsed before she arrived and took over from the pot-boy. When she did so, the quiet splendour of her costume and the devout manner in which she pulled the beer-handle told their own story.

"You've been to church," said a penetrating Sherry and Angostura.

Miss Postlethwaite said Yes, she had, and it had been lovely.

"Beautiful in every sense of the word," said Miss Postlethwaite, filling an order for a pint of bitter. "I do adore evening service in the summer. It sort of does something to you, what I mean. All that stilly hush and what not."

The vicar preached the sermon, I suppose?" said Mr. Mulliner.

"Yes," said Miss Postlethwaite, adding that it had been extremely moving.

Mr. Mulliner took a thoughtful sip of his hot Scotch and lemon.

"The old old story," he said, a touch of sadness in his voice. "I do not know if you gentlemen were aware of it, but in the rural districts of England vicars always preach the evening sermon during the summer months, and this causes a great deal of discontent to seethe among curates. It exasperates the young fellows, and one can understand their feelings. As Miss Postlethwaite rightly says, there is something about the atmosphere of evensong in a village church that induces a receptive frame of mind in a congregation, and a preacher, preaching under such conditions, can scarcely fail to grip and stir. The curates, withheld from so preaching, naturally feel that they are being ground beneath the heel of an iron monopoly and chiselled out of their big chance."

A Whisky and Splash said he had never thought of that.

"In that respect," said Mr. Mulliner, "you differ from my cousin Rupert's younger son, Anselm. He thought of it a great deal. He was the curate of the

parish of Rising Mattock in Hampshire, and when he was not dreaming fondly of
Myrtle Jellaby, niece of Sir Leopold Jellaby, O.B.E., the local squire, you would
generally find him chafing at his vicar's high-handed selfishness in always hogging the evening sermon from late in April till well on in September. He told me
once that it made him feel like a caged skylark."

"Why did he dream fondly of Myrtle Jellaby?" asked a Stout and Mild, who
was not very quick at the uptake.

"Because he loved her. And she loved him. She had, indeed, consented to
become his wife."

"They were engaged?" said the Stout and Mild, beginning to get it.

"Secretly. Anselm did not dare to inform her uncle of the position of affairs,
because all he had to marry on was his meagre stipend. He feared the wrath of
that millionaire philatelist."

"Millionaire what?" asked a Small Bass.

"Sir Leopold," explained Mr. Mulliner, "collected stamps."

The Small Bass said that he had always thought that a philatelist was a man
who was kind to animals.

"No," said Mr. Mulliner, "a stamp collector. Though many philatelists are,
I believe, also kind to animals. Sir Leopold Jellaby had been devoted to this
hobby for many years, ever since he had retired from business as a promoter of
companies in the City of London. His collection was famous."

"And Anselm didn't like to tell him about Myrtle," said the Stout and Mild.

"No. As I say, he lacked the courage. He pursued instead the cautious policy
of lying low and hoping for the best. And one bright summer day the happy
ending seemed to have arrived. Myrtle, calling at the vicarage at breakfast-time,
found Anselm dancing round the table, in one hand a half-consumed piece of
toast, in the other a letter, and learned from him that under the will of his late
godfather, the recently deceased Mr. J. G. Beenstock, he had benefited by an
unexpected legacy—to wit, the stout stamp album which now lay beside the
marmalade dish.

The information caused the girl's face to light up (continued Mr. Mulliner). A
philatelist's niece, she knew how valuable these things could be.

"What's it worth?" she asked eagerly.

"It is insured, I understand, for no less a sum than five thousand pounds."

"Golly!"

"Golly, indeed," assented Anselm.

"Nice sugar!" said Myrtle.

"Exceedingly nice," agreed Anselm.

"You must take care of it. Don't leave it lying about. We don't want somebody
pinching it."

A look of pain passed over Anselm's spiritual face.

"You are not suggesting that the vicar would stoop to such an act?"

"I was thinking more," said Myrtle, "of Joe Beamish."

She was alluding to a member of her loved one's little flock who had at one time been a fairly prosperous burglar. Seeing the light after about sixteen prison sentences, he had given up his life-work and now raised vegetables and sang in the choir.

"Old Joe is supposed to have reformed and got away from it all, but, if you ask me, there's a lot of life in the old dog yet. If he gets to hear that there's a five-thousand-pound stamp collection lying around . . ."

"I think you wrong our worthy Joe, darling. However, I will take precautions. I shall place the album in a drawer in the desk in the vicar's study. It is provided with a stout lock. But before doing so, I thought I might take it round and show it to your uncle. It is possible that he may feel disposed to make an offer for the collection."

"That's a thought," agreed Myrtle. "Soak him good."

"I will assuredly omit no effort to that end," said Anselm.

And, kissing Myrtle fondly, he went about his parochial duties.

It was towards evening that he called upon Sir Leopold, and the kindly old squire, learning the nature of his errand and realising that he had not come to make a touch on behalf of the Church Organ Fund, lost the rather strained look which he had worn when his name was announced and greeted him warmly.

"Stamps?" he said. "Yes, I am always ready to add to my collection, provided that what I am offered is of value and the price reasonable. Had you any figure in mind for these of yours, my dear Mulliner?"

Anselm said that he had been thinking of something in the neighbourhood of five thousand pounds, and Sir Leopold shook from stem to stern like a cat that had received half a brick in the short ribs. All his life the suggestion that he should part with large sums of money had shocked him.

"Oh?" he said. Then, seeming to master himself with a strong effort. "Well, let me look at them."

Ten minutes later, he had closed the volume and was eyeing Anselm compassionately.

"I am afraid you must be prepared for bad news, my boy," he said.

A sickening feeling of apprehension gripped Anselm.

"You don't mean they are not valuable?"

Sir Leopold put the tips of his fingers together and leaned back in his chair in the rather pontifical manner which he had been accustomed to assume in the old days when addressing meetings of shareholders.

"The term 'valuable,' my dear fellow, is a relative one. To some people five pounds would be a large sum."

"Five pounds!"

"That is what I am prepared to offer. Or, seeing that you are a personal friend, shall we say ten?"

"But they are insured for five thousand."

Sir Leopold shook his head with a half-smile.

"My dear Mulliner, if you knew as much as I do about the vanity of stamp collectors, you would not set great store by that. Well, as I say, I don't mind giving you ten pounds for the lot. Think it over and let me know."

On leaden feet Anselm left the room. His hopes were shattered. He felt like a man who, chasing rainbows, has had one of them suddenly turn and bite him in the leg.

"Well?" said Myrtle, who had been awaiting the result of the conference in the passage.

Anselm broke the sad news. The girl was astounded.

"But you told me the thing was insured for——"

Anselm sighed.

"Your uncle appeared to attribute little or no importance to that. It seems that stamp collectors are in the habit of insuring their collections for fantastic sums, out of a spirit of vanity. I intend," said Anselm broodingly, "to preach a very strong sermon shortly on the subject of Vanity."

There was a silence.

"Ah, well," said Anselm, "these things are no doubt sent to try us. It is by accepting such blows in a meek and chastened spirit. . ."

"Meek and chastened spirit my left eyeball," cried Myrtle, who, like so many girls to-day, was apt to be unguarded in her speech. "We've got to do something about this."

"But what? I am not denying," said Anselm, "that the shock has been a severe one, and I regret to confess that there was a moment when I was sorely tempted to utter one or two of the observations which I once heard the coach of my college boat at Oxford make to Number Five when he persisted in obtruding his abdomen as he swung his oar. It would have been wrong, but it would unquestionably have relieved my . . ."

"I know!" cried Myrtle. "Joe Beamish!"

Anselm stared at her.

"Joe Beamish? I do not understand you, dear."

"Use your bean, boy, use your bean. You remember what I told you. All we've got to do is let old Joe know where those stamps are, and he will take over from there. And there we shall be with our nice little claim for five thousand of the best on the insurance company."

"Myrtle!"

"It would be money for jam," the enthusiastic girl continued. "Just so much velvet. Go and see Joe at once."

"Myrtle! I beg you, desist. You shock me inexpressibly."

She gazed at him incredulously. "You mean you won't do it?"

"I could not even contemplate such a course."

"You won't unleash old Joe and set him acting for the best?"

"Certainly not. Most decidedly not. A thousand times, no."

"But what's wrong with the idea?"

"The whole project is ethically unsound."

There was a pause. For a moment it seemed as if the girl was about to express her chagrin in an angry outburst. A frown darkened her brow, and she kicked petulantly at a passing beetle. Then she appeared to get the better of her emotion. Her face cleared, and she smiled at him tenderly, like a mother at her fractious child.

"Oh, all right. Just as you say. Where are you off to now?"

"I have a Mothers' Meeting at six."

"And I," said Myrtle, "have got to take a few pints of soup to the deserving poor. I'd better set about it. Amazing the way these bimbos absorb soup. Like sponges."

They walked together as far as the Village Hall. Anselm went in to meet the Mothers. Myrtle, as soon as he was out of sight, turned and made her way to Joe Beamish's cosy cottage. The crooning of a hymn from within showing that its owner was at home, she walked through its honeysuckle-covered porch.

"Well, Joe, old top," she said, "how's everything?"

Joe Beamish was knitting a sock in the tiny living-room which smelled in equal proportions of mice, ex-burglars and shag tobacco, and Myrtle, as her gaze fell upon his rugged features, felt her heart leap within her like that of the poet Wordsworth when beholding a rainbow in the sky. His altered circumstances had not changed the erstwhile porch-climber's outward appearance. It remained that of one of those men for whom the police are always spreading drag-nets; and Myrtle, eyeing him, had the feeling that in supposing that in this pre-eminent plugugly there still lurked something of the Old Adam, she had called her shots correctly.

For some minutes after her entry, the conversation was confined to neutral topics—the weather, the sock and the mice behind the wainscoting. It was only when it turned to the decorations of the church for the forthcoming Harvest Festival—to which, she learned, her host would be in a position to contribute two cabbages and a pumpkin—that Myrtle saw her opportunity of approaching a more intimate subject.

"Mr. Mulliner will be pleased about that," she said. "He's nuts on the Harvest Festival."

"R," said Joe Beamish. "He's a good man, Mr. Mulliner."

"He's a lucky man," said Myrtle. "Have you heard what's just happened to him? Some sort of deceased Beenstock has gone and left him five thousand quid."

"Coo! Is that right?"

"Well, it comes to the same thing. An album of stamps that's worth five thousand. You know how valuable stamps are. Why, my uncle's collection is worth ten times that. That's why we've got all those burglar alarms up at the Hall."

A rather twisted expression came into Joe Beamish's face.

"I've heard there's a lot of burglar alarms up at the Hall," he said.

"But there aren't any at the vicarage, and, between you and me, Joe, it's worrying me rather. Because, you see, that's where Mr. Mulliner is keeping his stamps."

"R," said Joe Beamish, speaking now with a thoughtful intonation.

"I told him he ought to keep them at his bank."

Joe Beamish started.

"Wot ever did you go and say a silly thing like that for?" he asked.

"It wasn't at all silly," said Myrtle warmly. "It was just ordinary common sense. I don't consider those stamps are safe, left lying in a drawer in the desk in the vicar's study, that little room on the ground floor to the right of the front door with its flimsy French windows that could so easily be forced with a chisel or something. They are locked up, of course, but what good are locks? I've seen these, and anybody could open them with a hairpin. I tell you, Joe, I'm worried."

Joe Beamish bent over his socks, knitting and purling for a while in silence. When he spoke again, it was to talk of pumpkins and cabbages, and after that, for he was a man of limited ideas, of cabbages and pumpkins.

Anselm Mulliner, meanwhile, was passing through a day of no little spiritual anguish. At the moment when it had been made, Myrtle's proposal had shaken him to his foundations. He had not felt so utterly unmanned since the evening when he had been giving young Willie Purvis a boxing lesson at the Lads' Club, and Willie, by a happy accident, had got home squarely on the button.

This revelation of the character of the girl to whom he had given a curate's unspotted heart had stunned him. Myrtle, it seemed to him, appeared to have no notion whatsoever of the distinction between right and wrong. And while this would not have mattered, of course, had he been a gun-man and she his prospective moll, it made a great deal of difference to one who hoped later on to become a vicar and, in such event, would want his wife to look after the parish funds. He wondered what the prophet Isaiah would have had to say about it, had he been informed of her views on strategy and tactics.

All through the afternoon and evening he continued to brood on the thing. At supper that night he was distrait and preoccupied. Busy with his own reflections, he scarcely listened to the conversation of the Rev. Sidney Gooch, his vicar. And this was perhaps fortunate, for it was a Saturday and the vicar, as was his custom at Saturday suppers, harped a good deal on the subject of the sermon which he was proposing to deliver at evensong on the morrow. He said, not once but many times, that he confidently expected, if the fine weather held up, to knock his little flock cockeyed. The Rev. Sidney was a fine, upstanding specimen of the muscular Christian, but somewhat deficient in tact.

Towards nightfall, however, Anselm found a kindlier, mellower note creeping into his meditations. Possibly it was the excellent round of beef of which he had partaken, and the wholesome ale with which he had washed it down, that caused this softer mood. As he smoked his after-supper cigarette, he found himself beginning to relax in his austere attitude towards Myrtle's feminine weakness. He reminded himself that it must be placed to her credit that she had not been obdurate. On the contrary, the moment he had made plain his disapproval of her financial methods, conscience had awakened, her better self had prevailed and she had abandoned her dubious schemes. That was much.

Happy once more, he went to bed and, after dipping into a good book for half an hour, switched off the light and fell into a restful sleep.

But it seemed to him that he had scarcely done so when he was awakened by loud noises. He sat up, listening. Something in the nature of a free-for-all appeared to be in progress in the lower part of the house. His knowledge of the vicarage's topography suggested to him that the noises were proceeding from the study and, hastily donning a dressing-gown, he made his way thither.

The room was in darkness, but he found the switch and, turning on the light, perceived that the odd, groaning sound which had greeted him as he approached the door proceeded from the Rev. Sidney Gooch. The vicar was sitting on the floor, a hand pressed to his left eye.

"A burglar!" he said, rising. "A beastly bounder of a burglar."

"He has injured you, I fear," said Anselm commiseratingly.

"Of course he has injured me," said the Rev. Sidney, with some testiness. "Can a man take fire in his bosom and his clothes not be burned? Proverbs, six, twenty-seven. I heard a sound and came down and seized the fellow, and he struck me so violently that I was compelled to loosen my grip, and he made his escape through the window. Be so kind, Mulliner, as to look about and see if he has taken anything. There were some manuscript sermons which I should not care to lose."

Anselm was standing beside the desk. He had to pause for a moment in order to control his voice.

"The only object that appears to have been removed," he said, "is an album of stamps belonging to myself."

"The sermons are there?"

"Still there."

"Bitter," said the vicar. "Bitter."

"I beg your pardon?" said Anselm.

He turned. His superior of the cloth was standing before the mirror, regarding himself in it with a rueful stare.

"Bitter!" he repeated. "I was thinking," he explained, "of the one I had

568   THE WORLD OF MR. MULLINER

planned to deliver at evensong to-morrow. A pippin, Mulliner, in the deepest and truest sense a pippin. I am not exaggerating when I say that I would have had them tearing up the pews. And now that dream is ended. I cannot possibly appear in the pulpit with a shiner like this. It would put wrong ideas into the heads of the congregation—always, in these rural communities, so prone to place the worst construction on such disfigurements. To-morrow, Mulliner, I shall be confined to my bed with a slight chill, and you will conduct both matins and evensong. Bitter!" said the Rev. Sidney Gooch. "Bitter!"

Anselm did not speak. His heart was too full for words.

In Anselm's deportment and behaviour on the following morning there was nothing to indicate that his soul was a maelstrom of seething emotions. Most curates who find themselves unexpectedly allowed to preach on Sunday evening in the summer time are like dogs let off the chain. They leap. They bound. They sing snatches of the more rollicking psalms. They rush about saying "Good morning, good morning," to everybody and patting children on the head. Not so Anselm. He knew that only by conserving his nervous energies would he be able to give of his best when the great moment came.

To those of the congregation who were still awake in the later stages of the service his sermon at Matins seemed dull and colourless. And so it was. He had no intention of frittering away eloquence on a morning sermon. He deliberately held himself back, concentrating every fibre of his being on the address which he was to deliver in the evening.

He had had it by him for months. Every curate throughout the English country-side keeps tucked away among his effects a special sermon designed to prevent him being caught short, if suddenly called upon to preach at evensong. And all through the afternoon he remained closeted in his room, working upon it. He pruned. He polished. He searched the Thesaurus for the telling adjective. By the time the church bells began to ring out over the fields and spinneys of Rising Mattock in the quiet gloaming, his masterpiece was perfected to the last comma.

Feeling more like a volcano than a curate, Anselm Mulliner pinned together the sheets of manuscript and set forth.

The conditions could not have been happier. By the end of the pre-sermon hymn the twilight was far advanced, and through the door of the little church there poured the scent of trees and flowers. All was still, save for the distant tinkling of sheep bells and the drowsy calling of rooks among the elms. With quiet confidence Anselm mounted the pulpit steps. He had been sucking throat pastilles all day and saying "Mi-mi" to himself in an undertone throughout the service, and he knew that he would be in good voice.

For an instant he paused and gazed about him. He was rejoiced to see that he was playing to absolute capacity. Every pew was full. There, in the squire's high-backed stall, was Sir Leopold Jellaby, O.B.E., with Myrtle at his side. There, among the choir, looking indescribably foul in a surplice, sat Joe Beamish. There, in their respective places, were the butcher, the baker, the candlestick-maker and all the others who made up the personnel of the congregation. With a little sigh of rapture, Anselm cleared his throat and gave out the simple text of Brotherly Love.

I have been privileged (said Mr. Mulliner) to read the script of this sermon of Anselm's, and it must, I can see, have been extremely powerful. Even in manuscript form, without the added attraction of the young man's beautifully modulated tenor voice, one can clearly sense its magic.

Beginning with a thoughtful excursus on Brotherly Love among the Hivites and Hittites, it came down through the Early Britons, the Middle Ages and the spacious days of Queen Elizabeth to these modern times of ours, and it was here that Anselm Mulliner really let himself go. It was at this point, if one may employ the phrase, that he—in the best and most reverent spirit of the words—reached for the accelerator and stepped on it.

Earnestly, in accents throbbing with emotion, he spoke of our duty to one another; of the task that lies clear before all of us to make this a better and a sweeter world for our fellows; of the joy that waits those who give no thought to self but strain every nerve to do the square thing by one and all. And with each golden phrase he held his audience in an ever-tightening grip. Tradesmen who had been nodding somnolently woke up and sat with parted lips. Women dabbed at their eyes with handkerchiefs. Choir-boys who had been sucking acid drops swallowed them remorsefully and stopped shuffling their feet.

Even at a morning service, such a sermon would have been a smash hit. Delivered in the gloaming, with all its adventitious aids to success, it was a riot.

It was not immediately after the conclusion of the proceedings that Anselm was able to tear himself away from the crowd of admirers that surged round him in the vestry. There were churchwardens who wanted to shake his hand, other churchwardens who insisted on smacking him on the back. One even asked for his autograph. But eventually he laughingly shook himself free and made his way back to the vicarage. And scarcely had he passed through the garden gate when something shot out at him from the scented darkness, and he found Myrtle Jellaby in his arms.

"Anselm!" she cried. "My wonder-man! However did you do it? I never heard such a sermon in my life!"

"It got across, I think?" said Anselm modestly.

"It was terrific. Golly! When you admonish a congregation, it stays admonished. How you think of all these things beats me."

"Oh, they come to one."

"And another thing I can't understand is how you came to be preaching at all in the evening. I thought you told me the vicar always did."

"The vicar," began Anselm, "has met with a slight . . ."

And then it suddenly occurred to him that in the excitement of being allowed to preach at evensong he had quite forgotten to inform Myrtle of that other important happening, the theft of the stamp album.

"A rather extraordinary thing occurred last night, darling," he said. "The vicarage was burgled."

Myrtle was amazed.

"Not really?"

"Yes. A marauder broke in through the study window."

"Well, fancy that! Did he take anything?"

"He took my collection of stamps."

Myrtle uttered a cry of ecstasy.

"Then we collect!"

Anselm did not speak for a moment.

"I wonder."

"What do you mean, you wonder? Of course we collect. Shoot the claim in to the insurance people without a moment's delay."

"But have you reflected, dearest? Am I justified in doing as you suggest?"

"Of course. Why ever not?"

"It seems to me a moot point. The collection, we know, is worthless. Can I justly demand of this firm—The London and Midland Counties Aid and Benefit Association is its name—that they pay me five thousand pounds for an album of stamps that is without value?"

"Of course you can. Old Beenstock paid the premiums, didn't he?"

"That is true. Yes. I had forgotten that."

"It doesn't matter whether a thing's valuable or not. The point is what you insure it for. And it isn't as if it's going to hurt these Mutual Aid and Benefit birds to brass up. It's sinful the amount of money those insurance companies have. Must be jolly bad for them, if you ask me."

Anselm had not thought of that. Examining the point now, it seemed to him that Myrtle, with her woman's intuition, had rather gone to the root of the matter and touched the spot.

Was there not, he asked himself, a great deal to be said for this theory of hers that insurance companies had much too much money and would be better, finer, more spiritual insurance companies if somebody came along occasionally and took a bit of the stuff off them? Unquestionably there was. His doubts were removed. He saw now that it was not only a pleasure, but a duty, to nick the London and Midland Counties Mutual Aid and Benefit Association for five thousand. It might prove the turning-point in the lives of its Board of Directors.

"Very well," he said. "I will send in the claim."

"At-a-boy! And the instant we touch, we'll get married."

"Myrtle!"

"Anselm!"

"Guv'nor," said the voice of Joe Beamish at their side, "could I 'ave a word with you?"

They drew apart with a start, and stared dumbly at the man.

"Guv'nor," said Joe Beamish, and it was plain from the thickness of his utterance that he was in the grip of some strong emotion, "I want to thank you, guv'nor, for that there sermon of ycurs. That there wonderful sermon."

Anselm smiled. He had recovered from the shock of hearing this sudden voice in the night. It was a nuisance, of course, to be interrupted like this at such a moment, but one must, he felt, be courteous to the fans. No doubt he would have to expect a lot of this sort of thing from now on.

"I am rejoiced that my poor effort should have elicited so striking an encomium."

"Wot say?"

"He says he's glad you liked it." said Myrtle, a little irritably, for she was not feeling her most amiable. A young girl who is nestling in the arms of the man she loves resents having cracksmen popping up through traps at her elbow.

"R," said Joe Beamish, enlightened. "Yes, guv'nor, that was a sermon, that was. That was what I call a blinking sermon."

"Thank you, Joe, thank you. It is nice to feel that you were pleased."

"You're right, I was pleased, guv'nor. I've 'eard sermons in Pentonville, and I've 'eard sermons in Wormwood Scrubs, and I've 'eard sermons in Dartmoor, and very good sermons they were, but of all the sermons I've 'eard I never 'eard a sermon that could touch this 'ere sermon for class and pep and . . ."

"Joe," said Myrtle.

"Yes, lady?"

"Scram!"

"Pardon, lady?"

"Get out. Pop off. Buzz along. Can't you see you're not wanted? We're busy."

"My dear," said Anselm, with gentle reproach, "is not your manner a little peremptory? I would not have the honest fellow feel . . ."

"R," interrupted Joe Beamish, and there was a suggestion of unshed tears in his voice, "but I'm not an honest feller, guv'nor. There, if you don't mind me saying so, no offence meant and none, I 'ope, taken, is where you make your bloomin' error. I'm a pore sinner and backslider and evildoer and . . ."

"Joe," said Myrtle, with a certain menacing calm, "if you get a thick ear, always remember that you asked for it. The same applies to a lump the size of an egg on top of your ugly head through coming into violent contact with the knob of my parasol. Will you or will you not," she said, taking a firmer grip of the handle of the weapon to which she had alluded, "push off?"

"Lady," said Joe Beamish, not without a rough dignity, "as soon as I've done what I come to do, I will withdraw. But first I got to do what I come to do. And

what I come to do is 'and back in a meek and contrite spirit this 'ere album of
stamps what I snitched last night, never thinking that I was to 'ear that there
wonderful sermon and see the light. But 'avin' 'eard that there wonderful sermon
and seen the light, I now 'ave great pleasure in doing what I come to do, namely,"
said Joe Beamish, thrusting the late J. G. Beenstock's stamp collection into
Anselm's hand, "this 'ere. Lady . . . Guv'nor . . . With these few words, 'opin'
that you are in the pink as it leaves me at present, I will now withdraw."

"Stop!" cried Anselm.

"R?"

Anselm's face was strangely contorted. He spoke with difficulty.

"Joe. . . ."

"Yes, guv'nor?"

"Joe . . . I would like . . . I would prefer . . . In a very real sense I do so feel
. . . In short, I would like you to keep this stamp album, Joe."

The burglar shook his head.

"No, guv'nor. It can't be done. When I think of that there wonderful sermon
and all those beautiful things you said in that there wonderful sermon about the
'Ivites and the 'Ittites and doing the right thing by the neighbours and 'elping so
far as in you lies to spread sweetness and light throughout the world, I can't keep
no albums which 'ave come into my possession through gettin' in at other folks'
french winders on account of not 'avin' seen the light. It don't belong to me, not
that album don't, and I now take much pleasure in 'anding' it back with these few
words. Goo' night, guv'nor. Goo' night, lady. Goo' night all. I will now withdraw."

His footsteps died away, and there was silence in the quiet garden. Both Anselm
and Myrtle were busy with their thoughts. Once more through Anselm's mind
there was racing that pithy address which the coach of his college boat had
delivered when trying to do justice to the spectacle of Number Five's obtrusive
stomach: while Myrtle, on her side, was endeavouring not to give utterance to a
rough translation of something she had once heard a French taxi-driver say to a
gendarme during her finishing-school days in Paris.

Anselm was the first to speak.

"This, dearest," he said, "calls for discussion. One does so feel that little or
nothing can be accomplished without earnest thought and a frank round-table
conference. Let us go indoors and thresh the whole matter out in as calm a spirit
as we can achieve."

He led the way to the study and seated himself moodily, his chin in his hands,
his brow furrowed. A deep sigh escaped him.

"I understand now," he said, "why it is that curates are not permitted to preach
on Sunday evenings during the summer months. It is not safe. It is like exploding
a bomb in a public place. It upsets existing conditions too violently. When I reflect
that, had our good vicar but been able to take evensong to-night, this distressing
thing would not have occurred, I find myself saying in the words of the prophet

Hosea to the children of Adullam . . ."

"Putting the prophet Hosea to one side for the moment and temporarily pigeon-holing the children of Adullum," interrupted Myrtle, "what are we going to do about this?"

Anselm sighed again.

"Alas, dearest, there you have me. I assume that it is no longer feasible to submit a claim to the London and Midland Counties Mutual Aid and Benefit Association."

"So we lose five thousand of the best and brightest?"

Anselm winced. The lines deepened on his careworn face.

"It is not an agreeable thing to contemplate, I agree. One had been looking on the sum as one's little nest-egg. One did so want to see it safely in the bank, to be invested later in sound, income-bearing securities. I confess to feeling a little vexed with Joe Beamish."

"I hope he chokes."

"I would not go so far as that, darling," said Anselm, with loving rebuke. "But I must admit that if I heard that he had tripped over a loose shoelace and sprained his ankle, it would—in the deepest and truest sense—be all right with me. I deplore the man's tactless impulsiveness. 'Officious' is the word that springs to the lips."

Myrtle was musing.

"Listen," she said. "Why not play a little joke on these London and Midland bozos? Why tell them you've got the stamps back? Why not just sit tight and send in the claim and pouch their cheque? That would be a lot of fun."

Again, for the second time in two days, Anselm found himself looking a little askance at his loved one. Then he reminded himself that she was scarcely to be blamed for her somewhat unconventional outlook. The niece of a prominent financier, she was perhaps entitled to be somewhat eccentric in her views. No doubt, her earliest childhood memories were of coming down to dessert and hearing her elders discuss over the nuts and wine some burgeoning scheme for trimming the investors.

He shook his head.

"I could hardly countenance such a policy, I fear. To me there seems something—I do not wish to hurt your feelings, dearest—something almost dishonest about what you suggest. Besides," he added meditatively, "when Joe Beamish handed back that album, he did it in the presence of witnesses."

"Witnesses?"

"Yes, dearest. As we came into the house, I observed a shadowy figure. Whose it was, I cannot say, but of this I feel convinced—that this person, whoever he may have been, heard all."

"You're sure?"

"Quite sure. He was standing beneath the cedar-tree, within easy earshot. And, as you know, our worthy Beamish's voice is of a robust and carrying timbre."

He broke off. Unable to restrain her pent-up feelings any longer, Myrtle Jellaby had uttered the words which the taxi-driver had said to the gendarme, and there was that about them which might well have rendered a tougher curate than Anselm temporarily incapable of speech. A throbbing silence followed the ejaculation. And during this silence there came to their ears from the garden without a curious sound.

"Hark," said Myrtle.

They listened. What they heard was unmistakably a human being sobbing.

"Some fellow creature in trouble," said Anselm.

"Thank goodness," said Myrtle.

"Should we go and ascertain the sufferer's identity?"

"Let's," said Myrtle. "I have an idea it may be Joe Beamish. In which case, what I am going to do to him with my parasol will be nobody's business."

But the mourner was not Joe Beamish, who had long since gone off to the Goose and Grasshopper. To Anselm, who was short-sighted, the figure leaning against the cedar-tree, shaking with uncontrollable sobs, was indistinct and unrecognisable, but Myrtle, keener-eyed, uttered a cry of surprise.

"Uncle!"

"Uncle?" said Anselm, astonished.

"It is Uncle Leopold."

"Yes," said the O.B.E., choking down a groan and moving away from the tree, "it is I. Is that Mulliner standing beside you, Myrtle?"

"Yes."

"Mulliner," said Sir Leopold Jellaby, "you find me in tears. And why am I in tears? Because, my dear Mulliner, I am still overwhelmed by that wonderful sermon of yours on Brotherly Love and our duty to our neighbours."

Anselm began to wonder if ever a curate had had notices like these.

"Oh, thanks," he said, shuffling a foot. "Awfully glad you liked it."

" 'Liked it', Mulliner, is a weak term. That sermon has revolutionised my entire outlook. It has made me a different man. I wonder, Mulliner, if you can find me pen and ink inside the house?"

"Pen and ink?"

"Precisely. I wish to write you a cheque for ten thousand pounds for that stamp collection of yours."

"Ten thousand!"

"Come inside," said Myrtle. "Come right in."

"You see," said Sir Leopold, as they led him to the study and plied him with many an eager query as to whether he preferred a thick nib or a thin, "when you showed me those stamps yesterday, I recognised their value immediately—they would fetch five thousand pounds anywhere—so I naturally told you they were worthless. It was one of those ordinary, routine business precautions which a man is bound to take. One of the first things I remember my dear father saying to me, when he sent me out to battle with the world, was 'Never give a sucker an even break', and until now I have always striven not to do so. But your sermon to-night has made me see that there is something higher and nobler than a code of business ethics. Shall I cross the cheque?"

"If you please."

"No," said Myrtle. "Make it open."

"Just as you say, my dear. You appear," said the kind old squire, smiling archly through his tears, "to be showing considerable interest in the matter. Am I to infer——?"

"I love Anselm. We are engaged."

"Mulliner! Is this so?"

"Er—yes," said Anselm. "I was meaning to tell you about that."

Sir Leopold patted him on the shoulder.

"I could wish her no better husband. There. There is your cheque, Mulliner. The collection, as I say, is worth five thousand pounds, but after that sermon, I give ten freely—freely!"

Anselm, like one in a dream, took the oblong slip of paper and put it in his pocket. Silently, he handed the album to Sir Leopold.

"Thank you," said the latter. "And now, my dear fellow, I think I shall have to ask you for the loan of a clean pocket handkerchief. My own, as you see, is completely saturated."

It was while Anselm was in his room, rummaging in the chest of drawers, that a light footstep caused him to turn. Myrtle was standing in the doorway, a finger on her lip.

"Anselm," she whispered, "have you a fountain pen?"

"Certainly, dearest. There should be one in this drawer. Yes, here it is. You wish to write something?"

"I wish you to write something. Endorse that cheque here and now, and give it to me, and I will motor to London to-night in my two-seater, so as to be at the bank the moment it opens and deposit it. You see, I know Uncle Leopold. He might take it into his head, after he had slept on it and that sermon had worn off a bit, to 'phone and stop payment. You know how he feels about business precautions. This way we shall avoid all rannygazoo."

Anselm kissed her fondly.

"You think of everything, dearest," he said. "How right you are. One does so wish, does one not, to avoid rannygazoo."

38

THE RIGHT APPROACH

THE subject of magazine stories came up quite suddenly in the bar parlour of the Anglers' Rest, as subjects are wont to do there, for in the way the minds of our little group flit from this topic to that there is always a suggestion of the chamois of the Alps springing from crag to crag. We were, if I remember rightly, discussing supralapsarianism, when a Whisky-and-Splash, who had been turning the pages of the Saturday Evening Post, the property of our courteous and popular barmaid Miss Postlethwaite, uttered a snort.

"Gesundheit," said a Draught Ale.

"I wasn't sneezing, I was snorting," said the Whisky-and-Splash. Disgustedly, he added. "Why do they publish these things?"

"What things would that be?"

"These stories, illustrated in glorious technicolour, where the fellow meets the girl on the beach, and they start kidding back and forth, and twenty minutes after they've seen each other for the first time, they're engaged to be married."

Mr. Mulliner took a sip from his hot Scotch and lemon.

"You find that unconvincing?"

"Yes, I do. I am a married man, and it took me two years and more boxes of chocolates than I care to think of to persuade the lady who is now my wife to sign on the dotted line. And though it is not for me to say so, I was a pretty fascinating chap in those days. Ask anybody."

Mr. Mulliner nodded.

"Your point is well taken. But you must make allowances for the editor of the Saturday Evening Post. He lives in a world of his own, and really does think that two complete strangers can meet in bathing suits on the beach and conclude their initial conversation by becoming betrothed. However, as you say, it seldom happens in ordinary life. Even the Mulliners, most of whom have fallen in love at first sight, have not found the going quite so smooth and simple as that. They have been compelled to pull up their socks and put in not a little preliminary spadework. The case of my nephew Augustus is one that springs to the mind."

"Did he meet girls in bathing suits on beaches?"

"Frequently. But it was at a charity bazaar at a house called Balmoral on Wimbledon Common that love came to him, for it was there that he saw Hermione Brimble and fell with a thud that could have been heard as far off as Putney Hill."

It was owing to his godmother's fondness for bazaars (said Mr. Mulliner) that Augustus found himself in the garden of Balmoral, and it is ironical to reflect that when she ordered him to escort her there, he was considerably annoyed, for he had been planning to go to Kempton Park and with word and gesture encourage in the two-thirty race a horse in whose fortunes he was interested. But his chagrin was not long-lasting. What caused it to vanish was the sight of a girl so divine that, as his gaze rested upon her, the top hat rocked on his head and only a sudden snatch at the last moment prevented his umbrella from falling from his grip.

"Well, well," he said to himself, as he drank her in, "this certainly opens up a new line of thought."

She was presiding over a stall in the shade of a large cedar at the edge of the lawn, and as soon as he could get his limbs to function he hastened up and began buying everything in sight. And when a tea-cosy, two Teddy bears, a penwiper, a bowl of wax flowers and a fretwork pipe-rack had changed hands he felt that he was entitled to regard himself as a member of the club and get friendly.

"Lovely day," he said.

"Beautiful," said the girl.

"The sun," said Augustus, pointing it out with his umbrella.

The girl said Yes, she had noticed the sun.

"I always think it seems to make everything so much brighter, if you know what I mean, when the sun's shining," said Augustus. "Well, it's been awfully jolly, meeting you. My name, in case you're interested, is Mulliner."

The girl said hers was Hermione Brimble, and further enquiry elicited the fact that she lived there with her aunt, Mrs. Willoughby Gudgeon. And Augustus was wondering if he could start calling her Hermione right away, or whether it would be better to wait for a few minutes, when a formidable woman of the heavy-battle-cruiser class came rolling up.

"Well, dear," she said. "How are you doing?"

The girl, addressing the newcomer as Aunt Beatrice, replied that the market had opened easy, but that sales had recently been stepped up by the arrival of a big-time operator. "Mr. Mulliner," she said, indicating Augustus, who was standing on one leg, looking ingratiating.

"Mulliner?" said Mrs. Gudgeon. "Are you related to the Bishop of Bognor? He was the Rev. Theophilus Mulliner. We were great friends when I was a girl."

It was the first time that Augustus had heard of this prelate, but he was not going to pass up the smallest chance of furthering his interests.

"Oh, rather. A cousin. But I always call him Uncle Phil."

"I have not seen him for some time. How is he these days?"

"Oh, fine. Full of yeast "

"I am relieved to hear it. He used to be troubled a good deal by clergyman's sore throat, like my niece Hermione's father, the late Bishop of Stortford," said Mrs. Gudgeon, and it was at this moment that Augustus came to the decision which was to plunge him into what Shakespeare calls a sea of troubles.

This girl, he told himself, was the daughter of a bishop and looked like something out of a stained-glass window, a pure white soul if he ever saw one. Her aunt was the sort of woman who went around with gangs of the higher clergy. Obviously, then, what would establish him as a desirable suitor was saintly rectitude. His until now had been a somewhat rackety life, including no fewer than three fines for disorderly conduct on Boat Race Night, but he resolved from even date to be so saintly and so rectitudinous that both the girl and her aunt would draw in their breath with an awed "What ho!" as he did his stuff.

Taking as his cue a statement on the part of the latter that this bazaar was in aid of the Wimbledon Social Purity League, he hitched up his diaphragm and let himself go. He said he was glad they were giving Social Purity a break because he was strong for it and always had been. There was a type of young man, he went on, who would not recognise Social Purity if you handed it to him on a skewer, and it was a type he had always avoided. Give him fine weather and a spot of Social Purity, he said, and you need not worry about him any further. You could just leave him, he said, confident that he was having the time of his life. And it was not long before he was receiving from Mrs. Willoughby Gudgeon a cordial invitation to haunt the house, an invitation of which he was determined to avail himself freely.

Into the events of the next few weeks it is not necessary for me to go in detail. Suffice it to say that at his every visit to Balmoral Augustus displayed an all-in saintliness which would have caused comment at a Pan-Anglican Synod. He brought the girl serious books. He spoke of his ideals. On several occasions at luncheon he declined a second go at the roast duck and peas or whatever it might be, indicating by his manner that all that sort of thing seemed to him a little gross and unspiritual. And it was clear to him that in supposing that this was the stuff to give them he had not been mistaken. He would sometimes catch the girl looking at him in a strange, thoughtful way, as if she were asking herself if he could really be true, and he was convinced that love was burgeoning.

At the outset of his wooing he had had some anxious moments owing to the constant presence at Balmoral of Mrs. Gudgeon's stepson, Oswald Stoker, a young man who wrote novels and, differing in this respect from the great majority of novelists, looked not like something brought in by a not too fastidious cat but was extremely personable. He was also gay and debonair. He did not live at Balmoral, but he was frequently there, and every time his visits coincided with those of Augustus the latter was pained to observe the cordiality of his relations with Hermione.

Of course, they were sort of cousins, and you have to allow sort of cousins a bit of leeway, but still he did not like it, and it was with profound relief that he learned one day that Oswald was earmarked elsewhere, being betrothed to a girl named Yvonne something who was connected with the television industry. It changed his whole view of the man. He could see now that Oswald Stoker was a charming chap, with whom he might easily form a beautiful friendship, and when one afternoon arriving at Balmoral for the day's haunting, he found him in the drawing-room with Hermione, he greeted him warmly and enquired solicitously after his health.

"My health," said Oswald Stoker, having thanked him for asking, "is at present excellent, but who can predict how I shall be feeling this time tomorrow? I have stern work before me this night, Mulliner. Russell Clutterbuck, my American publisher, is in London, and I am dining with him. Have you ever dined with Russell Clutterbuck?"

Augustus said that he had not the pleasure of Mr. Clutterbuck's acquaintance.

"It's an experience," said Oswald Stoker moodily, and left the room shaking his head.

His new affection for the novelist made Augustus feel concerned. He said he was afraid Oswald was worried, and Hermione sighed.

"He is thinking of the last time he dined with Mr. Clutterbuck."

"What happened?"

"He is vague on the subject. He says his memory is blurred. All he can recall is waking next morning on the floor of his bedroom and shooting up to the ceiling when a sparrow on the window-sill chirped unexpectedly. Gave his head a nasty bump, he tells me."

"You mean that on the previous night he had over-indulged?"

"The evidence would seem to point that way."

"Tck, tck!"

"It shocks you?"

"It does a little, I confess. I have never been able to understand what pleasure men can find in spirituous liquors. Lemonade is so much more refreshing. I drink nothing else myself."

"But you're different."

"I suppose so."

"You are so good and steady," said Hermione, giving him that strange, thoughtful look of hers.

It seemed to Augustus that he could scarcely want a better cue than this. He tried, but failed, to take her little hand in his.

"Hermione," he said, "I love you."

"Oh, yes?" said Hermione.

"Will you marry me?"

"No," said Hermione.

Augustus stared, amazed.

"No?"

"No."

"You mean you won't marry me?"

Hermione said that that put in a nutshell exactly what she was trying to convey. She then gazed at him, gave a little shudder, and left the room.

All through the day and far into the night Augustus sat in his rooms brooding on the girl's extraordinary attitude, and the more he brooded on it, the more baffling did it apear. She had bewildered him. He reviewed his behaviour of the last few weeks, and if ever there was behaviour calculated to make the daughter of a bishop feel that here was her destined mate, this behaviour, he considered, was that behaviour. If she was not satisfied with the Augustus Mulliner of his Wimbledon period, all one could say was that she must be holding out for something pretty super.

It was towards one in the morning that he came to the conclusion that she had not meant what she said, maidenly modesty having caused her to fluff her lines, and he decided that this theory must be tested immediately. The hour was a little advanced, but your impetuous lover does not keep his eye on the clock. Augustus, like all the Mulliners, was a man of action. He sprang from his chair, sprang for his hat, sprang into the street, sprang into a passing taxi, and some forty minutes later was ringing the front door bell of Balmoral.

After a considerable interval the door was opened by Staniforth, the butler, in pyjamas and a dressing gown. His manner seemed a little short, Augustus was unable to think why, and it was almost curtly that he informed my nephew that Mrs. Gudgeon and Hermione were attending the Social Purity Ball at the Town Hall and would not be back for some time.

"I'll come in and wait," said Augustus.

He was in error. Even as he spoke, the door slammed, leaving him alone in the silent night.

An ardent swain who is left alone in the silent night in the garden of the aunt of the girl he loves does not say to himself "Ho, hum. Well, better call it a day, I suppose" and go home to bed. He backs away from the house and stands gazing reverently up at her window. And if, like Augustus, he does not know which her window is, he gazes reverently at all the windows, taking them in rotation. Augustus was doing this, and had just shifted his eye from the top left second window to the top left third window, when a voice spoke behind him, causing him to break the European record for the standing high jump.

"Ah, Mulliner, old friend," said Oswald Stoker, for the voice was his, "I thought I should find you here. Gazing at her window, eh? Very natural. In my courting days I used to do a lot of window-gazing. There is no healthier pursuit. Keeps you out in the open and fills your lungs with fresh air. Harley Street physicians recommend it. But is window-gazing enough? That is what we must ask ourselves. I say no. You need a better approach. In this matter of wooing, everything, I contend, turns on getting the right approach, and this, my dear Mulliner, you have not yet got. I have watched with a fatherly eye your passion for my step-cousin or whatever the hell she is, and it has amazed me that you have overlooked the one essential factor in winning a girl's heart. I allude to the serenade. Have you ever stood beneath her window and to the accompaniment of a banjo begged her to throw you down one little rose from her hair? To the best of my knowledge, no. You should iron out this bug in the production at the earliest possible moment, Mulliner, if you want the thing to be a success."

Augustus did not at all like having his great love subjected to analysis by one who, after all, was a comparative stranger, but his mind at the moment was occupied with another aspect of the matter. The visibility was too poor for him to see his companion's face, but there was that in the timbre of his voice which enabled him to form a swift diagnosis. He had had countless opportunities of studying the symptoms, and it was plain to him that the man, if not yet actually ossified, was indubitably plastered. Yielding to the dictates of his lower nature, he must for some hours have been mopping up the stuff like a suction pump.

Oswald Stoker seemed to sense the silent criticism, for it was on this that he now touched.

"It has probably not escaped you, Mulliner, that I am a trifle under the influence of the sauce. As who would not be after spending the evening with Russell Clutterbuck, of the firm of Winch and Clutterbuck, Madison Avenue, New York, publishers of the book beautiful. I suppose there is no wilder Indian than an American publisher, when he gets off the reservation. Relieved for the nonce of the nauseous daily task of interviewing American authors, most of them wearing horn-rimmed spectacles, he has an exhilarating sense of freedom. He expands. He lets himself go. Well, when I tell you that in a few short hours Russell Clutterbuck got self and guest thrown out of three grillrooms and a milk bar, you will appreciate what I mean. Rightly or wrongly, he feels that electric fans are placed there to have eggs thrown at them, and he saw to it that before we started making the rounds he was well supplied with these. He kept showing me how a baseball pitcher winds up and propels the ball. Speed and control, he told me, are what you have to have."

"You must be glad to have seen the last of him."

"I haven't seen the last of him. I brought him here to show him the spot where I played as a child. I didn't really play here as a child, because we lived at Cheltenham, but he won't know the difference. He's out there somewhere, exercising the dog."

"The dog?"

"He bought a dog earlier in the evening. He generally makes some such purchase on these occasions. I have known him to buy an ostrich. I suppose I had better be going and looking for him," said Oswald Stoker, and vanished into the darkness.

It was perhaps two minutes later that the dog to which he had alluded suddenly entered Augustus's life.

It was a large, uncouth dog, in its physique and deportment not unlike the hound of the Baskervilles, though of course not covered with phosphorus, and it seemed to be cross about something. Its air was that of a dog which has discovered plots against its person, and it appeared to be under the impression that in Augustus it had found one of the ringleaders, for the menace in its manner, as it now advanced on him, was unmistakable. A few words of explanation might have convinced the animal of my nephew's innocence, but Augustus deemed it wisest not to linger and deliver them. To climb the nearest tree was the work of an instant. It happened, oddly enough, to be the very cedar in the shade of which in happier days Hermione Brimble had sold him a tea-cosy, two Teddy bears, a penwiper, a bowl of wax fruit and a fretwork pipe-rack.

He crouched there in the upper branches while the dog, seeming puzzled, as if unused to having members of the underworld take to themselves the wings of a dove, paced to and fro like a man looking for a dropped collar-stud. Presently it abandoned the search and trotted off with a muffled oath, and some little time after that Augustus, peering down from his eyrie, saw Oswald Stoker returning, accompanied by a very stout man holding a bottle of champagne by the neck and singing the Star-Spangled Banner. They halted beneath the tree.

It would have been possible for Augustus at this juncture to have made his presence known, but something told him that the less he had to do with Oswald Stoker in his present unbalanced condition, the better. He continued crouching, therefore, in silence, and Oswald Stoker spoke.

"Well, well," he said, "my young friend Mulliner, of whom I was speaking to you just now, appears to have left us. I was telling you, if you remember, of his great love for my step-cousin Hermione and of my wish to do all that lies in my power to promote his interests. Your singing reminds me that the first step, the serenade, has yet to be taken. No doubt you are about to draw to my attention the fact that he can't serenade her, if he isn't here. Very true. But what happens in the theatre when the star is absent? You put on an understudy. I propose to step into the breach and take his place. It would be more effective, of course, had I some musical instrument such as a clavichord or sackbut on which to accompany myself, but if you would hum the bass, I think the performance should be adequate. I beg your pardon?"

Mr. Clutterbuck had muttered something about launching the ship. He shook his head, as if demurring.

"Gotta launch ship first," he said. "Customary ceremony," and raising the bottle he held he flung it adroitly through the pane of one of the upper windows.

"Good luck to all who sail in you," he said.

It was Oswald Stoker's turn to shake his head.

"Now there, my dear fellow, if you don't mind me saying so, I think you deviated from the usual programme. It is surely the bottle, not the ship, that should be broken. However," he went on, as the upper slopes of Staniforth the butler thrust themselves out of the window, "it has produced results. We have assembled an audience. You were saying?" he said, addressing Staniforth.

The butler, like the dog, seemed to be cross about something.

"Who," he demanded, "is there?"

"Augustus Mulliner speaking. Or, rather," said Oswald Stoker, starting to do so, "singing."

The sight of the protruding head had had the effect of stirring Mr. Clutterbuck to give of his best. Once more Oswald Stoker was privileged to witness his impersonation of a baseball pitcher winding up, which in its essentials rather closely resembles the first stages of an epileptic fit. The next moment an egg, unerringly aimed, had found its target.

"Right in the groove," said Mr. Clutterbuck contentedly. He wandered off, conscious of a good night's work done, and Oswald Stoker had scarcely had time to light a cigarette and enjoy a few refreshing puffs when he was joined by Mrs. Gudgeon's major-domo, carrying a shotgun.

"Ah, Staniforth," he said genially. "Out for a day with the birds?"

"Good evening, Mr. Stoker. I am looking for Mr. Mulliner," said the butler with cold menace.

"Mulliner, eh? He was here a moment ago. I remember noticing. You want him for some special reason?"

"I think he should be overpowered and placed under restraint before the ladies return."

"Why, what has he been doing?"

"He sang beneath my window."

"Rather a compliment. What was the burden of his song?"

"As far as I could understand him, he was requesting me to throw him a rose from my hair."

"You didn't?"

"No, sir."

"Quite right. Roses cost money."

"He also threw an egg at me."

"So that is why you have so much yolk on your face. I thought it might be one of those beauty treatments, like the mud-pack. Ah well, young blood, Staniforth."

"Sir?"

"At Mulliner's age one has these ebullitions of high spirits. Much must be excused in the young."

"Not singing under windows and throwing eggs at three in the morning."

"No, there perhaps he went too far. He has been a little over-excited all the evening. We dined together, and he got us bounced in rapid succession from three grill-rooms and a milk bar. Would keep throwing eggs at the electric fan. Hullo!" said Oswald Stoker, as a distant splash sounded in the night. "I think a friend of mine has fallen in the pond. I will go and investigate. He may need a helping hand."

He hurried off, and Augustus was glad to see him go. But his pleasure was rendered imperfect by the fact that the butler did not follow his example. Staniforth had plainly decided to make a night of it. He remained *in statu quo*, and presently there was the sound of a vehicle stopping at the gate, and Mrs. Gudgeon and Hermione came walking down the drive.

"Staniforth!" the former cried. It was a novel experience for her to find the domestic staff prowling the grounds in the small hours, and Augustus received the impression that if she had been less carefully brought up and had known fewer bishops, she would have said "Gorblimey!".

"Good evening, madam."

"What are you doing out here at this time?"

"I am pursuing Mr. Mulliner, madam."

"Pursuing *what*?"

The butler, having paused for a moment, as if asking himself if "whom" would not have been more correct, repeated his statement.

"But Mr. Mulliner is not here?"

"Yes, madam."

"At three o'clock in the morning?"

"Yes, madam. He called shortly before two, and rang the front-door bell. I informed him that you were not at home, and supposed that he had left the premises. Such, however, was not the case. Ten minutes ago he flung a bottle of champagne through my window, and when I looked out expressed a wish that I would throw him a rose from my hair. He then hit me in the left eye with an egg."

It seemed to Augustus that he heard Hermione utter a startled cry, but it was lost in Mrs. Gudgeon's snort of amazement.

"Mr. *Mulliner* did this?"

"Yes, madam. I gather from Mr. Stoker, with whom I was conversing a short while ago, that his behaviour throughout the evening has been on similar lines. He was a member of the dinner party which Mr. Stoker attended, and Mr. Stoker tells me that he was instrumental in getting himself and friends ejected from three grillrooms and a milk bar. Mr. Stoker attributed his exuberance to youthful high spirits, and advanced the suggestion that such conduct should be excused in the young. I must confess that I am unable to take so liberal a view."

Mrs. Gudgeon was silent for some moments. She appeared to be trying to adjust her mind to these revelations. It is never easy for a woman to realise that she has been nursing in her bosom, which is practically what she had been doing to my nephew Augustus, a viper. But presently the adjusting process seemed to be complete. She spoke grimly.

"Next time Mr. Mulliner calls, Staniforth, I am not at home . . . What was that?"

"Madam?"

"I thought I heard a moan."

"The breeze sighing in the trees, no doubt, madam."

"Perhaps you are right. The breeze does sigh in trees, frequently. Did you hear it, Hermione?"

"I thought I heard something."

"A moan?"

"A groan, I should have said."

"A moan or groan," said Mrs. Gudgeon, conceding the point. "As if wrenched from the lips of some soul in agony." She broke off as a figure came out of the shadows. "Oswald!"

Oswald Stoker waved a genial hand.

"Hullo there. Hullo, hullo, hullo, hullo."

"What are you doing here?"

"Just winding up the evening. Oh, before I forget, my publisher fell into the pond and is now in the hothouse, drying out. So if you go there and see a nude publisher, pretend not to notice."

"Oswald, you are intoxicated!"

"It is virtually impossible not to be," said Oswald Stoker gravely, "when you have been entertained at dinner by Russell Clutterbuck of Clutterbuck and Winch, publishers of the book beautiful, and your fellow guest is Augustus Mulliner. I'm looking for him, by the way. I want to warn him that there is a herd of purple rhinoceroses down by the pond. Very dangerous things, purple rhinoceroses, especially in the mating season. Bite you in the leg as soon as look at you."

Hermione spoke. Her voice shook.

"Oswald!"

"Hullo?"

"Is this true what Staniforth has been saying about Mr. Mulliner?"

"What did he say?"

"That Mr. Mulliner sang under his window and threw eggs at him?"

"Perfectly correct. I was an eyewitness."

Mrs. Gudgeon swelled formidably.

"I shall write Mr. Mulliner a very strong letter tomorrow. In the third person. He shall never enter this house again . . . There! I'm sure that was a moan. I wonder if the garden is haunted."

She turned away, and Oswald Stoker regarded her anxiously.

"You aren't going to the hothouse?"

"I am going to my room. Bring me a glass of warm milk there, Staniforth."

"Very good, madam."

She moved off toward the house, followed by the butler, and Oswald Stoker, turning to Hermione, was concerned to find her shaking with uncontrollable sobs.

"Hullo!" he said. "Something wrong?"

The girl gulped like a leaky radiator.

"You bet your Old Etonian sock suspenders there's something wrong. I have lost the man I love."

"Where did you see him last?"

"How was I to know," Hermione went on, her voice vibrating with pain, "that —that was the sort of ball of fire Augustus Mulliner really was? I thought him a wet smack and a total loss, and all the time he was a sportsman who throws eggs at butlers and breaks windows with champagne bottles. I never dreamed that there was this deeper side to him. When first we met, I was strangely attracted to him, but as I came to know him, he appeared to have all the earmarks of a Grade A hammerhead. I wrote him off as a bohunkus. Romantically considered, he seemed to me strictly a cigar-store Indian, all wood from the neck up. And now I see that for some reason he was hiding his light beneath a bushel, as father used to say. Oh, what shall I do? I love him, I love him, I love him!"

"Well, he loves you, which makes it all square."

"Yes, but this afternoon he asked me to be his wife, and I turned him down like a bedspread."

"Send him a civil note, saying you have changed your mind."

"Too late. A man as fascinating as that is sure to have been snapped up by some other girl by this time. Oh, what . . .?"

She would have spoken further, probably adding the words "shall I do?", but at this moment speech was wiped from her lips as if with a wet sponge. From the tree in whose shade she stood a passionate voice had shouted "Hoy!" and looking up she saw the face of my nephew.

"Au-us-us!" she cried. His sudden advent had caused her to bite her tongue rather severely.

"Ah, Mulliner," said Oswald Stoker. "Birds-nesting?"

"I say," bellowed Augustus, "I heard what you were saying. Did you mean it?"

"Yek, yek, a 'ousand 'imes yek!"

"You really love me?"

"Of course I love you."

"You will be my wife?"

"You couldn't stop me with an injunction."

"Then . . . just getting it straightened out, if you don't mind . . . it will be in order if I nip down and cover your upturned face with burning kisses?"

"Perfectly in order."

"Right ho. Be with you in a moment."

As they fell into an embrace which, had it occurred in a motion picture, would have made the Johnston office purse its lips and suggest the cutting of several hundred feet of film, Oswald Stoker heaved a sentimental little sigh. A fiancé himself, he liked to see sundered hearts coming together.

"Well, well!" he said. "So you're getting married, eh? Starting out on the new life, are you, you two young things? Then take this simple toad," said Oswald Stoker, pressing the reptile into Augustus's hand. "A wedding present," he explained. "A poor gift, but one that comes straight from the heart. And, after all, it's the thought behind the gift that counts, don't you think? Goodnight. God bless you. I must be getting along and finding how Russell Clutterbuck is making out. Have you ever seen an American publisher sitting in a hothouse with nothing on except horn-rimmed spectacles? It is a sight well worth seeing, but not one that I would recommend to nervous people and invalids."

He passed into the darkness, leaving Augustus looking at the toad a little dubiously. He did not really want it, but it might be ungracious to throw it away.

An idea struck him.

"Darling!"

"Yes, Angel?"

"I wonder, my queen, if you know which is that butler's room?"

"Of course, my king. Why?"

"I thought if you were to put this toad in his bed some night, shortly before he retired to rest. . . . Just a suggestion, of course."

"An admirable suggestion. Come, my dream man," said Hermione, "and let us hunt around and see if we can't find a few frogs, too."

39

BIG BUSINESS

In a corner of the bar parlour of the Anglers' Rest a rather heated dispute had arisen between a Small Bass and a Light Lager. Their voices rose angrily.

"Old," said the Small Bass.

"Ol'," said the Light Lager.

"Bet you a million pounds it's Old."

"Bet you a million trillion pounds it's Ol'."

Mr. Mulliner looked up indulgently from his hot Scotch and lemon. On occasions like this he is usually called in to arbitrate.

"What is the argument, gentlemen?"

"It's about that song Old Man River," said the Small Bass.

"Ol' Man River," insisted the Light Lager. "He says it's Old Man River, I say its Ol' Man River. Who's right?"

"In my opinion," said Mr. Mulliner, "both of you. Mr. Oscar Hammerstein, who wrote that best of all lyrics, preferred Ol', but I believe the two readings are considered equally correct. My nephew sometimes employed one, sometimes the other, according to the whim of the moment."

"Which nephew was that?"

"Reginald, the son of my late brother. He sang the song repeatedly, and at the time of that sudden change in his fortunes was billed to render it at the annual village concert at Lower-Smattering-on-the-Wissel in Worcestershire, where he maintained a modest establishment."

"His fortunes changed, did they?"

"Quite remarkably. He was rehearsing the number in an undertone over the breakfast eggs and bacon one morning, when he heard the postman's knock and went to the door.

"Oh, hullo, Bagshot," he said. "Shift that trunk."

"Sir?"

"Lift that bale."

"To what bale do you refer, sir?"

"Get a little drunk and you . . . Oh, sorry," said Reginald, "I was thinking of something else. Forget I spoke. Is that a letter for me?"

"Yes, sir. Registered."

Reginald signed for the letter and, turning it over, saw that the name and address on the back of the envelope were those of Watson, Watson, Watson, Watson and Watson of Lincoln's Inn Fields. He opened it, and found within a communication requesting him to call on the gang at his earliest convenience, when he would hear of something to his advantage.

Something to his advantage being always what he was glad to hear of, he took train to London, called at Lincoln's Inn Fields, and you could have knocked him down with a toothpick when Watson—or Watson or Watson or Watson, or it may have been Watson—informed him that under the will of a cousin in the Argentine, whom he had not seen for years, he had benefited to the extent of fifty thousand pounds. It is not surprising that on receipt of this news he reeled and would have fallen, had he not clutched at a passing Watson. It was enough to stagger anyone, especially someone who, like Reginald, had never been strong in the head. Apart from his ability to sing Old Man River, probably instinctive, he was not a very gifted young man. Amanda Biffen, the girl he loved, though she admired his looks—for, like all the Mulliners, he was extraordinarily handsome—had never wavered in her view that if men were dominoes, he would have been the double blank.

His first act on leaving the Watson office was, of course, to put in a trunk call to Lower Smattering and tell Amanda of this signal bit of luck that had befallen him, for it was going to make all the difference to their love lives. Theirs till now had had to be a secret engagement, neither wishing to disturb the peace of mind of Amanda's uncle and guardian, Sir Jasper Todd, the retired financier. Reginald had one of those nice little bachelor incomes which allow a man to get his three square meals a day and do a certain amount of huntin', shootin' and fishin', but before the descent of these pennies from heaven he had been in no sense a matrimonial prize, and Amanda's theory that Sir Jasper, if informed of the betrothal, would have fifty-seven conniption fits was undoubtedly a correct one.

"Who was that, my dear?" Sir Jasper asked as Amanda came back from the telephone, and Amanda said that it was Reginald Mulliner, speaking from London.

"The most wonderful news. He has been left fifty thousand pounds."

"He has?" said Sir Jasper. "Well, well! Just fancy!"

Now when a financier, even a retired one, learns that a young fellow of the mental calibre of Reginald Mulliner has come into possession of fifty thousand pounds, he does not merely say "Just fancy!" and leave it at that. He withdraws to his study, ties a wet towel about his forehead, has lots of black coffee sent in, and starts to ponder on schemes for getting the stuff away from him. Sir Jasper had many expenses, and the circumstance of his young friend having acquired this large sum of money seemed to him, for he was a pious man, a direct answer to prayer. He had often felt how bitterly ironical it was that a super-mug like Reginald, so plainly designed by Nature to be chiselled out of his cash, had had no cash to be chiselled out of.

He rang Reginald up at his bungalow a few days later.

"Good morning, Mulliner, my boy."

"Oh, what ho, Sir Jasper."

"Amanda . . . I beg your pardon?"

"Eh?"

"I understood you to say 'He don't plant taters, he don't plant cotton.' Who does not plant potatoes, and how have they and cotton crept into the conversation?"

"Oh, frightfully sorry. I'm singing Old Man River at the village concert tonight, and I must have been rehearsing unconsciously, as it were."

"I see. A comic song?"

"Well, more poignant, I think you'd call it. Or possibly stark. It's about a Negro on the Mississippi who trembles a bit when he sees a job of work."

"Quite. I believe many Negroes do. Well, be that as it may, Amanda has been telling me of your good fortune. My heartiest congratulations. I wonder if you could spare the time to come and see me this morning. I would enjoy a chat."

"Oh, rather."

"Don't come immediately, if you don't mind, as I have a man from the insurance company calling in a few minutes about increasing the insurance on my house. Suppose we say an hour from now? Excellent."

And at the appointed time Reginald alighted from his new motor-cycle at the door of Sir Jasper's residence, Wissel Hall, and found Sir Jasper on the front steps, bidding farewell to a man in a bowler hat. The bowler-hatted one took his departure, and the financier regarded the motor-cycle with what seemed to Reginald disapproval.

"A recent purchase, is it not?"

"I got it a couple of days ago."

Sir Jasper shook his head.

"A costly toy. I hope, Mulliner, you are not one of those young men who, when suddenly enriched, get it up their noses and start squandering their substance on frivolities and gew-gaws?"

"Good Lord, no," said Reginald. "I plan to freeze on to my little bit of lolly like a porous plaster. The lawyer bloke from whom I heard of something to my advantage was recommending me to put it into a thing called Funding Loan. Don't ask me what it is, because I haven't the foggiest, but it's something run by the Government, and you buy a chunk of it and get back so much twice a year, just like finding it in the street. They pay four and a half per centum per annum, whatever that means, with the net result, according to this legal eagle, that my fifty thousand will bring me in rather more than two thousand a year. Fairly whizzo, I call it, and one wonders how long this has been going on."

To his surprise, Sir Jasper did not appear to share his enthusiasm. It would be too much, perhaps, to say that he sneered, but he came very close to sneering.

"Two thousand is not much."

"Oh, isn't it?"

"In these days of inflation and rising costs, a mere pittance. Would you not prefer twenty-five thousand?"

"Yes, that would be nice."

"Then it can be quite simply arranged. Have you made a study of the oil market?"

"I don't think there is a special market for oil. I get mine at the garage."

"But you know how vital oil is to our industries?"

"Oh, rather. Sardines and all that."

"Just so. There is no sounder investment. Now there happens to be among my effects a block of Smelly River Ordinaries, probably the most valuable share on the market, and I think I could let you have fifty thousand pounds worth of them, as you are—may I say?—a personal friend. They would bring you in a safe fifty per centum."

"Per annum?"

"Exactly."

"Per person?"

"Precisely. The annual yield would be, I imagine, somewhere in the neighbourhood of twenty-five or thirty thousand pounds."

"I say! That sounds smashing! But are you sure you can spare them? Won't you be losing money?"

Sir Jasper smiled.

"When you get to my age, my boy, you will realise that money is not everything in life. As somebody once said, 'I expect to pass through this world but once. Any good thing, therefore, that I can do, or any kindness that I can show to a fellow creature, let me do it now, for I shall not pass this way again.' Sign here," said Sir Jasper, producing from an inner pocket a number of stock certificates, a blank cheque, a fountain pen and a piece of blotting paper.

It was with uplifted heart that Reginald went in search of Amanda. He found her, dressed for tennis, about to start off in her car for a neighbouring house, and told her the great news. His income, he said, from now on would be twenty-five thousand pounds or thereabouts each calendar year, which you couldn't say wasn't a bit of a good egg, and this desirable state of things was entirely due to the benevolence of her Uncle Jasper. He had no hesitation, he said, in asking Heaven to bless Sir Jasper Todd.

To his concern, the girl, instead of running about clapping her little hands, shot straight up into the air like a cat which has rashly sat on a too hot radiator.

"You mean to say," she cried, coming back to earth and fixing him with a burning eye, "that you gave him the whole fifty thousand?"

"Not 'gave', old crumpet," said Reginald, amused. Women understand so little of finance. "What happens on these occasions is that one chap, as it might be me, slips another chap, as it might be your uncle, a spot of cash, and in return receives what are called shares. And such shares, for some reason which I haven't quite grasped yet, are the source of wealth beyond the dreams of avarice. These Smelly River Ordinaries, for instance——"

Amanda uttered a snort which ran through the quiet garden like a pistol shot.

"Let me tell you something," she said, speaking from between clenched teeth. "One of my earliest recollections as a child is of sitting on Uncle Jasper's knee and listening, round-eyed, while he told me how, at a moment when he was not feeling quite himself, having been hit on the head with a bottle by a disgruntled shareholder at a general meeting, he had allowed some hornswoggling highbinder to stick him with these dud Smelly River Ordinaries. I can still remember the light that shone in his eyes as he spoke of his resolve some day, somewhere, to find a mug on whom he could unload them. He realised that such a mug would have to be the Mug Supreme, the sort of mug that happens only once in a lifetime, but that was the gleam which he was following patiently through the years, never deviating from his purpose, and he was confident of eventual success. He related the story to illustrate what Tennyson had meant when he wrote about rising on stepping stones of our dead selves to higher things."

It was not easy to depress Reginald Mulliner, but this *conte* had done it. Her words, it seemed to him, could have but one meaning.

"Are you telling me that these ruddy shares are no ruddy good?"

"As wall paper, perhaps, they might lend a tasteful note to a study or rumpus room, but otherwise I should describe their value as non-existent."

"Well, I'm blowed!"

"You are also bust."

"Then how are we going to get married?"

"We aren't. I do not propose," said Amanda coldly, "to link my lot with that of a man who on the evidence would seem to be a member in good standing of the Jukes family. If you are interested in my future plans, I will sketch them out for you. I am now going off to play tennis with Lord Knubble of Knopp at Knubble Towers. Between the sets or possibly while standing me a gin and tonic at the end of the game he will, I imagine, ask me to be his wife. He always has so far. On this occasion my reply will be in the affirmative. Goodbye, Reginald. It has been nice knowing you. If you follow the path to the right, you will find your way out."

Reginald was not a quickwitted man, but, reading between the lines, he seemed to sense what she was trying to say.

"This sounds like the raspberry."

"It is."

"You mean all is over?"

"I do."

"You are casting me aside like a . . . what are those things people cast aside?"

" 'Worn-out glove' is, I presume, the expression for which you are groping."

"Do you know," said Reginald, struck by a thought, "I don't believe I've ever cast aside a worn-out glove. I always give mine to the Salvation Army. However, that is not the point at issue. The point at issue is that you have broken my bally heart."

"A girl with less self-control," said Amanda, switching her tennis racquet, "would have broken your bally head."

Such then was the situation in which Reginald Mulliner found himself on this sunny summer day, and it was one that seemed to him to present few redeeming features. He was down fifty thousand pounds, he had lost the girl he loved, his heart was broken, and he had a small pimple coming on the back of his neck—a combination which in his opinion gave him a full hand. The only thing that could possibly be regarded as an entry on the credit side was that his spiritual anguish had put him in rare shape for singing Old Man River at the village concert.

Too little attention has been given by our greatest minds to the subject of Old Man River-singing, though such a subject is of absorbing interest. It has never, as far as one knows, been pointed out that this song is virtually impossible of proper rendition by a vocalist who is feeling boomps-a-daisy and on top of the world. The full flavour can be obtained and the last drop of juice squeezed out only by the man who is down among the wines and spirits and brooding gloomily on life in general. Hamlet would have sung it superbly. So would Schopenhauer and J. B. Priestley. And so, at eight o'clock that night, up on the platform at the village hall with the Union Jack behind him and Miss Frisby, the music teacher, playing the accompaniment at his side, did Reginald Mulliner.

He had not been feeling any too happy to begin with, and the sight of Amanda in the front row in close proximity to a horse-faced young man with large ears and no chin, in whom he recognised Lord Knubble of Knopp, set the seal on his sombre mood, lending to each low note something of the quality of the *obiter dicta* of Hamlet's father's ghost. By the time he had reached that "He must know somefin', he don't say nuffin', he jest keeps rollin' along" bit there was not a dry eye in the house—or very few—and the applause that broke out from the two-bob seats, the one-bob seats, the sixpenny seats and the three-penny standees at the back can only be described as thunderous. He took three encores and six bows and, had not the curtain been lowered for the intermission, might have stolen a seventh. That organ of the theatre world, *Variety*, does not cover amateur concerts at places like Lower-Smattering-on-the-Wissel, but if it did its headline for Reginald Mulliner's performance that night would have been

MULL SWEET SOCKO

The effect on Reginald of this tornado of enthusiasm was rather remarkable. It was as though he had passed through some great spiritual experience which left him a changed man. Normally diffident, he was conscious now of a strange new sense of power. He felt masterful and dominant and for the first time capable of seeking out Sir Jasper Todd, who until now had always overawed him, and telling him just what he thought of him. Before he had even emerged into the open air, six excellent descriptions of Sir Jasper had occurred to him, the mildest of which was "pot-bellied old swindler". He resolved to lose no time in sharing these with the financier face to face.

He had not seen Sir Jasper among the audience. In the seat in which he should have been sitting, on Amanda's right, the eye had rested on what looked like a woman of good family who kept cats. The inference, therefore, was that he had given the concert a miss and was having a quiet evening at home, and it was to his home, accordingly, that Reginald now made his way.

Wissel Hall was a vast Tudor mansion, one of those colossal edifices which retired financiers so often buy on settling in the country and the purchase of which, when they realise what it is going to cost to keep them up, they almost invariably regret. Built in the days when a householder thought home was not home unless one had accommodation for sixty guests and a corresponding number of attendant scurvy knaves and varlets, it towered to the skies rather in the manner of Windsor Castle, and in conversation with other retired financiers Sir Jasper usually referred to it as a white elephant and a pain in the neck.

When Reginald reached the massive front door, the fact that repeated ringing of the bell produced no response suggested that the domestic staff had been given the night off to attend the concert. But he was convinced that the man he sought was somewhere inside, and as he had now thought of five more names to call him, bringing the total to eleven, he had no intention of being foiled by a closed front door. As Napoleon would have done in his place, he hunted around till he had found a ladder. Bringing this back and propping it up against the balcony of one of the rooms on the first floor, he climbed up. He had now thought of a twelfth name, and it was the best of the lot.

Windows of country houses are seldom fastened at night, and he had no difficulty in opening the one outside of which he stood. He found himself in an ornate guest room, and passing through this and down the corridor outside came to a broad gallery looking down on the main hall.

This was at the moment empty, but presently Sir Jasper appeared through a door at the far end. He had presumably been down in the cellar, for he was carrying a large container from which he now proceeded to sprinkle about the floor what from its aroma was evidently paraffin. As he did so, he sang in a soft undertone the hymn which runs "We plough the fields and scatter the good seed o'er the land". The floor, Reginald observed, was liberally strewn with paper and shavings.

Odd, he felt. No doubt one of the newfangled methods of removing stains from carpets. Probably very effective, but had their relations been more cordial, he would have shouted down to the financier, warning him that he was running a grave risk of starting a fire. One cannot be too careful with paraffin.

But he was in no mood to give this man kindly warnings. All he wanted to do was start calling him the names, now fourteen in number, which were bubbling in the boiling cauldron of his soul. And he was about to do so, when he chanced to look down at his hand as it rested on the rail, and the sight gave him pause.

I have carelessly omitted to mention—one gets carried away by one's story and tends to overlook small details—that in order to perfect his rendering of Old Man River Reginald had smeared his face and hands with burnt cork. The artist in him had told him that it would be too silly, a chap coming out in faultless evening dress, with a carnation in his buttonhole and a pink face protruding from a high collar, and trying to persuade an intelligent audience that he was an Afro-American in reduced circumstances who wanted to be taken away from the Mississippi.

This, of course, radically altered the run of the scenario. Though, as has been shown, not very intelligent, he could see that a bimbo—call him Bimbo A—who wants to dominate another bimbo—Bimbo B, as it might be—starts at a serious disadvantage if he is blacked up. The wrong note is struck from the outset. It would be necessary, if he was to render so tough an old bounder as Sir Jasper Todd less than the dust beneath his chariot wheels, to go home and wash.

Tut-tutting, for this hitch made him feel frustrated and disappointed, he returned to the ladder and climbed down it. And his foot was leaving the last rung, when a heavy hand descended on his shoulder and a voice gruesomely official in its intonation observed "Ho!" It was Police Constable Popjoy, the sleepless guardian of the peace of Lower Smattering-On-The-Wissel, who had made this remark. He was one of the few inhabitants of the village who had not attended the concert. Concerts meant nothing to P. C. Popjoy. Duty, stern daughter of the voice of God, told him, concert or no concert, to walk his beat at night, and he walked it.

His task involved keeping an eye on the home of Sir Jasper Todd, and the eye he had been keeping had detected a negroid burglar coming down a ladder from a first-floor balcony. It had struck him from the very first as suspicious. Nice goings-on, thought P. C. Popjoy, and he gripped him, as stated, by the shoulder.

"Ho!" he said again. He was a man of few words, and those mostly of one syllable.

And what, meanwhile, of Amanda?

All through Reginald's deeply moving performance she had sat breathless, her mind in a whirl and her soul stirred to her very depths. With each low note that he pulled up from the soles of his shoes she could feel the old affection and esteem surging back into her with a whoosh, and long before he had taken his sixth bow she knew that he was, if one may coin a phrase, the only onion in the stew and that it would be madness to try to seek happiness elsewhere, particularly as the wife of a man with large ears and no chin, who looked as if he were about to start in the two-thirty race at Kempton Park.

"I love you, I love you!" she murmured, and when Lord Knubble, over-hearing the words, beamed and said "At-a-girl, that's the spirit", she had turned on him with a cold "Not you, you poor fish", and broken their engagement. And now she was driving home, thinking long, sad thoughts of the man she adored, the man lost to her, she feared, for ever.

Could he ever forgive those harsh words she had spoken?

Extremely doubtful.

Would she ever see him again?

Against this second question one can pencil in the word "Yes", for at this moment, having freed himself from his custodian's grasp with a shrewd kick on the left ankle, he came galloping round the corner at 40 m.p.h., and even as she braked her car, speculating on his motives in running along the high road at this brisk speed, along came Police Constable Popjoy, doing approximately 55 m.p.h.

When a man doing 55 m.p.h. pursues a man capable of only 40, the end is merely a question of time. On the present occasion it came somewhat sooner than might have been expected owing to Reginald tripping on a loose pebble and falling like a sack of coals. The constable, coming up, bestrode him like a colossus.

"Ho!" he said, for, as has been indicated, he was a man of limited conver-sational resources, and all the woman in Amanda sprang into sudden life. She would have been the last person to affect to know what all this was about, but it was abundantly plain that the man to whom she had given her heart was in the process of getting pinched by the police and only a helpmeet's gentle hand could save him. Reaching in the tool box, she produced a serviceable spanner and, not letting a twig snap beneath her feet, advanced on the officer from behind. There was a dull, chunky sound as he sank to earth, and Reginald, looking up, saw who it was that had popped up through a trap to his aid. A surge of emotion filled him.

"Oh, hullo," he said. "So there you are."

"That's right."

"Nice evening."

"Beautiful. How's everything, Reggie?"

"Smashing, thanks, now that you've socked the flatty."

"I noticed he was in your hair a bit."

"He was, rather. You don't think he'll suddenly recover and make a spring, do you?"

"He will be out of circulation for some little time, I imagine. In which respect he differs from me, because I'm back in circulation."

"Eh?"

"I've broken my engagement to Percy Knubble."

"Oh, fine."

"You are the man I love."

"Oh, finer."

"And now," said Amanda, "let's have the gen. How did you happen to get snarled up with the constabulary?"

She listened with a thoughtful frown as Reginald related the events of the evening. She found herself particularly intrigued by his account of the activities of her Uncle Jasper.

"You say he was sprinkling paraffin hither and thither?"

"Freely."

"And there were paper and shavings on the floor?"

"In considerable abundance. Rather risky, it seemed to me. You never know when that sort of thing won't start a fire."

"You're quite right. If he had happened to drop a lighted match. . . . Look," said Amanda. "You go home and de-black yourself. I'll stay here and lend the rozzer a helping hand when he comes to."

It was some minutes later that Police Constable Popjoy opened his eyes and said: "Where am I?"

"Right here," said Amanda. "Did you see what hit you?"

"No, I didn't."

"It was that Russian Sputnik thing you've probably read about in the papers."

"Coo!"

"Coo is correct. They raise a nasty bump, these Sputniks, do they not? That head of yours wants a beefsteak or something slapped on it. Jump into my car and come along with me, and we'll see what the larder of Wissel Hall has to offer."

Sir Jasper, having used up all the paraffin in the cellar, had left the house to go to the garage for petrol and was approaching the front steps when Amanda drove up. His emotion on beholding her was marked.

"Amanda! I was not expecting you for another two hours."

The girl alighted from the car and drew him aside.

"So," she said, "I rather gathered when Reggie Mulliner told me a few moments ago that he had seen you strewing the floor of the hall with paper and shavings and sprinkling paraffin on them."

Sir Jasper had not presided over a hundred general meetings for nothing. He preserved his composure. The closest observer, eyeing his face, could not have known that his heart, leaping into his mouth, had just loosened two front teeth. He spoke with the dignified calm which had so often quelled unruly shareholders.

"Absurd! There are no shavings and paper on the floor."

"Reggie said he saw them."

"An optical illusion, no doubt."

"Perhaps you're right. Still, just for fun, I'll go in and look. And I'll take Constable Popjoy with me. I'm sure he will be interested."

Sir Jasper's heart did another *entrechat*.

"Constable Popjoy?" he quavered.

"He's in my car. I thought it would be a sound move to bring him along."

Sir Jasper clutched her arm.

"No, do not go in, particularly in the company of P. C. Popjoy. The fact is, my dear, that there is a certain amount of substance in what young Mulliner told you. I did happen to drop a few shavings and a little paper which I was carrying about with me—I cannot remember for what reason—and I carelessly tripped and upset a container of paraffin. It was the sort of thing that might have happened to anyone, but it is possible that a man like Popjoy would draw a wrong conclusion."

"He might think you were planning to do down the insurance company for a substantial sum."

"It is conceivable. These policemen are so prone to think the worst."

"You wouldn't dream of doing a thing like that?"

"Certainly not."

"Or of sticking poor trusting halfwitted baa-lambs with dud oil stock. Oh, that reminds me, Uncle Jasper. I knew there was something I wanted to talk to you about. Reggie's changed his mind about those Smelly River Ordinaries. He doesn't want them. True," said Amanda in response to Sir Jasper's remark that he had jolly well got them. "But he would like you to buy them back."

"He would, would he?"

"I told him you would be delighted."

"You did, did you?"

"Won't you be delighted?"

"No, I won't."

"Too bad. Oh, Popjoy."

"Miss?"

"Kindly step this way."

"Please!" cried Sir Jasper. "Please, please, please!"

"One moment, Popjoy. You were saying, Uncle Jasper?"

"If young Mulliner really prefers to sell me back those shares . . . "

"He does. This is official. He has taken one of those strange unaccountable dislikes for them."

There was silence for a space. Then from Sir Jasper's interior there proceeded a groan not unlike one of the lower notes of Old Man River.

"Very well. I agree."

"Splendid. Popjoy!"

"Miss?"

"Don't step this way."

"Very good, miss."

"And now," said Amanda, "ho for your study, where I shall require you to write out a cheque, payable to Reginald Mulliner, for a hundred thousand pounds."

Sir Jasper reeled.

"A hundred thousand? He only paid me fifty thousand."

"The stock has gone up. Surely no one understands better than you these market fluctuations. Close the deal at once, is my advice, before it hits a new high. Or would you prefer that I once more asked Constable Popjoy to navigate in this direction?"

"No, no, no, on no account."

"Just as you say. Popjoy."

"Miss?"

"Continue not to step this way."

"Very good, miss."

Another groan escaped Sir Jasper. He looked at his niece with infinite reproach.

"So this is how you repay my unremitting kindness! For years I have bestowed on you an uncle's love . . ."

"And now you're going to bestow on Reggie an uncle's hundred thousand pounds."

A thought struck Sir Jasper.

"I wonder," he said, "if instead of a cheque for that sum young Mulliner would not prefer a block of Deep Blue Atlantic stock of equivalent value? It is a company formed for the purpose of extracting gold from sea water, and its possibilities are boundless. I should be surprised—nay, astounded—if anyone investing in it did not secure a return of ninety per centum on his . . ." Sir Jasper broke off as the girl began to speak. "Yes, yes," he said, when she had finished. "Quite, quite. I see what you mean." He heaved a little sigh. "It was merely a suggestion."

40

GEORGE AND ALFRED

THE little group of serious thinkers in the bar parlour of the Anglers' Rest were talking about twins. A Gin and Tonic had brought the subject up, a cousin of his having recently acquired a couple, and the discussion had not proceeded far when it was seen that Mr. Mulliner, the Sage of the bar parlour, was smiling as if amused by some memory.

"I was thinking of my brother's sons George and Alfred," he explained. "They were twins."

"Identical?" asked a Scotch on the Rocks.

"In every respect."

"Always getting mistaken for each other, I suppose?"

"They would have been, no doubt, if they had moved in the same circles, but their walks in life kept them widely separated. Alfred was a professional conjuror and spent most of his time in London, while George some years previously had gone to seek his fortune in Hollywood, where after various vicissitudes he had become a writer of additional dialogue on the staff of Jacob Schnellenhamer of the Colossal-Exquisite corporation.

The lot of a writer of additional dialogue in a Hollywood studio is not an exalted one—he ranks, I believe, just above a script girl and just below the man who works the wind machine—but any pity I might have felt for George for being one of the dregs was mitigated by the fact that I knew his position was only temporary, for on his thirtieth birthday, which would be occurring very shortly, he would be coming into possession of a large fortune left to him in trust by his godmother.

It was on Mr. Schnellenhamer's yacht that I met George again after an interval of several years. I had become friendly with Mr. Schnellenhamer on one of his previous visits to England, and when I ran into him one day in Piccadilly he told me he was just off to Monte Carlo to discuss some business matters with Sam Glutz of the Perfecto-Wonderful, who was wintering there, and asked me if I would care to come along. I accepted the invitation gratefully, and the first person I saw when I came on board was George.

I found him in excellent spirits, and I was not surprised, for he said he had reached the age of thirty a few days ago and would be collecting his legacy directly we arrived in Monaco.

"Your trustee is meeting you there?"

"He lives there. An old boy of the name of Bassinger."

"Well, I certainly congratulate you, George. Have you made any plans?"

"Plenty. And the first is to stop being a Yes man."

"I thought you were a writer of additional dialogue."

"It's the same thing. I've been saying Yes to Schnellenhamer for three years, but no longer. A radical change of policy there's going to be. In the privacy of my chamber I've been practising saying No for days. No, Mr. Schnellenhamer!" said George. "No, no, no! You're wrong, Mr. Schnellenhamer. You're quite mistaken, Mr. Schnellenhamer. You're talking through your hat, Mr. Schnellenhamer. Would it be going too far if I told him he ought to have his head examined?"

"A little, I think."

"Perhaps you're right."

"You don't want to hurt his feelings."

"I don't think he has any. Still, I see what you mean."

We arrived in Monte Carlo after a pleasant voyage, and as soon as we had anchored in Monaco harbour I went ashore to see the sights and buy the papers, and I was thinking of returning to the yacht, when I saw George coming along, seeming to be in a hurry. I hailed him, and to my astonishment he turned out to be not George but Alfred, the last person I would have expected to find in Monte Carlo. I had always supposed that conjurors never left London except to appear at children's parties in the provinces.

He was delighted to see me. We had always been very close to one another. Many a time as a boy he had borrowed my top hat in order to take rabbits out of it, for even then he was acquiring the rudiments of his art and the skill which had enabled him to bill himself as The Great Alfredo. There was genuine affection in his manner as he now produced a hardboiled egg from my breast pocket.

"But how in the world do you come to be here, Alfred?" I asked.

His explanation was simple.

"I'm appearing at the Casino. I have a couple of spots in the revue there, and I don't mind telling you that I'm rolling the customers in the aisles nightly," he said, and I recalled that he had always interspersed his feats with humorous dialogue. "How do you happen to be in Monte Carlo? Not on a gambling caper, I trust?"

"I am a guest on Mr. Schnellenhamer's yacht."

He started at the mention of the name.

"Schnellenhamer? The movie man? The one who's doing the great Bible epic Solomon And The Queen Of Sheba?"

"Yes. We are anchored in the harbour."

"Well, well," said Alfred. His air was pensive. My words had apparently started a train of thought. Then he looked at his watch and uttered an exclamation.

"Good Lord," he said, "I must rush, or I'll be late for rehearsal."

And before I could tell him that his brother George was also on Mr. Schnellenhamer's yacht he had bounded off.

Mr. Schnellenhamer was on the deck when I reached the yacht, concluding a conversation with a young man whom I presumed to be a reporter, come to interview him. The young man left, and Mr. Schnellenhamer jerked a thumb at his retreating back.

"Listen," he said. "Do you know what that fellow's been telling me? You remember I was coming here to meet Sam Glutz? Well, it seems that somebody mugged Sam last night."

"You don't say!"

"Yessir, laid him out cold. Are those the papers you've got there? Lemme look. It's probably on the front page."

He was perfectly correct. Even George would have had to say 'Yes, Mr. Schnellenhamer.' The story was there under big headlines. On the previous n'ght, it appeared, Mr. Glutz had been returning from the Casino to his hotel, when some person unknown had waylaid him and left him lying in the street in a considerably battered condition. He had been found by a passer-by and taken to the hospital to be stitched together.

"And not a hope of catching the fellow," said Mr. Schnellenhamer.

I pointed out that the paper said that the police had a clue, and he snorted contemptuously.

"Police!"

"At your service," said a voice, and turning I saw what I thought for a moment was General De Gaulle. Then I realised that he was some inches shorter than the General and had a yard or so less nose. But not even General De Gaulle could have looked sterner and more intimidating. "Sergeant Brichoux of the Monaco police force," he said. "I have come to see a Mr. Mulliner, who I understand is a member of your entourage."

This surprised me. I was also surprised that he should be speaking English so fluently, but the explanation soon occurred to me. A sergeant of police in a place like Monte Carlo, constantly having to question international spies, heavily veiled adventuresses and the like, would soon pick it up.

"I am Mr. Mulliner," I said.

"Mr. George Mulliner?"

"Oh, George? No, he is my nephew. You want to see him?"

"I do."

"Why?" asked Mr. Schnellenhamer.

"In connection with last night's assault on Mr. Glutz. The police have reason to believe that he can assist them in their enquiries."

"How?"

"They would like him to explain how his wallet came to be lying on the spot where Mr. Glutz was attacked. One feels, does one not, that the fact is significant. Can I see him, if you please?" said Sergeant Brichoux, and a sailor was despatched to find George. He returned with the information that he did not appear to be on board.

"Probably gone for a stroll ashore," said Mr. Schnellenhamer.

"Then with your permission," said the sergeant, looking more sinister than ever, "I will await his return."

"And I'll go and look for him," I said.

It was imperative, I felt, that George be intercepted and warned of what was waiting for him on the yacht. It was, of course, absurd to suppose that he had been associated in any way with last night's outrage, but if his wallet had been discovered on the scene of the crime, it was obvious that he would have a good deal of explaining to do. As I saw it, he was in the position the hero is always getting into in novels of suspense—forced by circumstances, though innocent, into the role of Suspect Number One and having a thoroughly sticky time till everything comes right in the last chapter.

It was on a bench near the harbour that I found him. He was sitting with his head between his hands, probably feeling that if he let go of it it would come in half, for when I spoke his name and he looked up, it was plain to see that he was in the grip of a severe hangover. I am told by those who know that there are six varieties of hangover—the Broken Compass, the Sewing Machine, the Comet, the Atomic, the Cement Mixer and the Gremlin Boogie, and his aspect suggested that he had got them all.

I was not really surprised. He had told me after dinner on the previous night that he was just off to call on his trustee and collect his inheritance, and it was natural to suppose that after doing so he would celebrate. But when I asked him if this was so, he uttered one of those hollow rasping laughs that are so unpleasant.

"Celebrate!" he said. "No, I wasn't celebrating. Shall I tell you what happened last night? I went to Bassinger's hotel and gave my name and asked if he was in, and they told me he had checked out a week or two ago and had left a letter for me. I took the letter. I opened it. I read it. And having read it . . . Have you ever been slapped in the eye with a wet fish?"

"Oddly enough, no."

"I was once when I got into an argument with an angler down at Santa Monica, and the sensation now was very similar. For this letter, this *billet doux* from that offspring of unmarried parents P. P. Bassinger, informed me that he had been gambling for years with the trust money and was deeply sorry to say that there was now no trust. It had gone. So, he added, had he. By the time I read this, he said, he would be in one of those broadminded South American countries where they don't believe in extradition. He apologised profusely, but places the blame on some man he had met in a bar who had given him an infallible system for winning at the tables. And why my godmother gave the trusteeship to someone living in Monte Carlo within easy walking distance of the Casino we shall never know. Just asking for it is the way it looks to me."

My heart bled for him. By no stretch of optimism could I regard this as his lucky day. All this and Sergeant Brichoux, too. There was a quaver in my voice as I spoke.

"My poor boy!"

"Poor is right."

"It must have been a terrible shock."

"It was."

"What did you do?"

"What would you have done? I went out and got pie-eyed. And here's a funny thing. I had the most extraordinary nightmare. Do you ever have nightmares?"

"Sometimes."

"Bad ones?"

"Occasionally."

"I'll bet they aren't as bad as the one I had. I dreamed that I had done a murder. And that dream is still lingering with me. I keep seeing myself engaged in a terrific brawl with someone and laying him out. It's a most unpleasant sensation. Why are you looking at me like a sheep with something on its mind?"

I had to tell him.

"It wasn't a nightmare, George."

He seemed annoyed.

"Don't be an ass. Do you think I don't know a nightmare when I see one?"

"I repeat, it was no nightmare."

He looked at me incredulously, his jaw beginning to droop like a badly set souffle.

"You don't mean it actually happened?"

"I fear so. The papers have featured it."

"I really slugged somebody?"

"Not just somebody. The president of a motion picture corporation, which makes your offence virtually *lese majesté*."

"Then how very fortunate," said George, looking on the bright side after a moment of intense thought, "that nobody can possibly know it was me. That certainly takes a weight off my mind. You're still goggling at me like a careworn sheep. Why is that?"

"I was thinking what a pity it was that you should have dropped your wallet—containing your name and address—on the spot of the crime."

"Did I do that?"

"You did."

"Hell's bells!"

"Hell's bells is correct. There's a sergeant of police on board the yacht now, waiting for your return. He has reason to believe that you can assist him in his enquiries."

"Death and despair!"

"You may well say so. There is only one thing to be done. You must escape while there is yet time. Get over the frontier into Italy."

"But my passport's on the yacht."

"I could bring it to you."

"You'd never find it."

"Then I don't know what to suggest. Of course, you might——"

"That's no good."

"Or you could——"

"That's no good, either. No," said George, "this is the end. I'm a rat in a trap. I'm for it. Well-meaning, not to be blamed, the victim of the sort of accident that might have happened to anyone when lit up as I was lit, but nevertheless for it. That's Life. You come to Monte Carlo to collect a large fortune, all pepped up with the thought that at last you're going to be able to say No to old Schnellenhamer, and what do you get? No fortune, a headache, and to top it all off the guillotine or whatever they have in these parts. That's Life, I repeat. Just a bowl of cherries. You can't win."

Twin! I uttered a cry, electrified.

"I have it, George!"

"Well?"

"You want to get on the yacht."

"Well?"

"To secure your passport."

"Well?"

"Then go there."

He gave me a reproachful look.

"If," he said, "you think this is the sort of stuff to spring on a man with a morning head who is extremely worried because the bloodhounds of the law are sniffing on his trail and he's liable to be guillotined at any moment, I am afraid I cannot agree with you. On your own showing that yacht is congested with sergeants of police, polishing the handcuffs and waiting eagerly for my return. I'd look pretty silly sauntering in and saying 'Well, boys, here I am'. Or don't you think so?"

"I omitted to mention that you would say you were Alfred."

He blinked.

"Alfred?"

"Yes."

"My brother Alfred?"

"Your twin brother Alfred," I said, emphasising the second word in the sentence, and I saw the light of intelligence creep slowly into his haggard face. "I will go there ahead of you and sow the good seed by telling them that you have a twin brother who is your exact double. Then you make your appearance. Have no fear that your story will not be believed. Alfred is at this moment in Monte Carlo, performing nightly in the revue at the Casino and is, I imagine, a familiar figure in local circles. He is probably known to the police—not, I need scarcely say, in any derogatory sense but because they have caught his act and may even have been asked by him to take a card—*any* card—and memorise it before returning it to the pack, his aim being to produce it later from the inside of a lemon. There will be no question of the innocent deception failing to succeed. Once on board it will be a simple matter to make some excuse to go below. An urgent need for bicarbonate of soda suggests itself. And once below you can find your passport, say a few graceful words of farewell and leave."

"But suppose Schnellenhamer asks me to do conjuring tricks?"

"Most unlikely. He is not one of those men who are avid for entertainment. It is his aim in life to avoid it. He has told me that it is the motion picture magnate's cross that everybody he meets starts acting at him in the hope of getting on the payroll. He says that on a good morning in Hollywood he has sometimes been acted at by a secretary, two book agents, a life insurance man, a masseur, the man with the benzedrine, the studio watchman, a shoe-shine boy and a barber, all before lunch. No need to worry about him wanting you to entertain him."

"But what would be Alfred's reason for coming aboard?"

"Simple. He has heard that Mr. Schnellenhamer has arrived. It would be in the Society Jottings column. He knows that I am with Mr. Schnellenhamer——"

"How?"

"I told him so when I met him yesterday. So he has come to see me."

The light of intelligence had now spread over George's face from ear to ear. He chuckled hoarsely.

"Do you know, I really believe it would work."

"Of course it will work. It can't fail. I'll go now and start paving the way. And as your raiment is somewhat disordered, you had better get a change of clothes, and a shave and a wash and brush-up would not hurt. Here is some money," I said, and with an encouraging pat on the back I left him.

Brichoux was still at his post when I reached the yacht, inflexible determination written on every line of his unattractive face. Mr. Schnellenhamer sat beside him looking as if he were feeling that what the world needed to make it a sweeter and better place was a complete absence of police sergeants. He had never been fond of policemen since one of them, while giving him a parking ticket, had recited Hamlet's To be or not to be speech to give him some idea of what he could do in a dramatic role. I proceeded to my mission without delay.

"Any sign of my nephew?" I asked.

"None," said the sergeant.

"He has not been back?"

"He has not."

"Very odd."

"Very suspicious."

An idea struck me.

"I wonder if by any chance he has gone to see his brother."

"Has he a brother?"

"Yes. They are twins. His name is Alfred. You have probably seen him sergeant. He is playing in the revue at the Casino. Does a conjuring act."

"The Great Alfredo?"

"That is his stage name You have witnessed his performance?"

"I have."

"Amazing the resemblance between him and George. Even I can hardly tell them apart. Same face, same figure, same way of walking, same coloured hair and eyes. When you meet George, you will be astounded at the resemblance."

"I am looking forward to meeting Mr. George Mulliner."

"Well, Alfred will probably be here this morning to have a chat with me, for he is bound to have read in the paper that I am Mr. Schnellenhamer's guest. Ah, here he comes now," I said, as George appeared on the gangway. "Ah, Alfred."

"Hullo, uncle."

"So you found your way here?"

"That's right."

"My host, Mr. Schnellenhamer."

"How do you do?"

"And Sergeant Brichoux of the Monaco police."

"How do *you* do? Good morning, Mr. Schnellenhamer, I have been wanting very much to meet you. This is a great pleasure."

I was proud of George. I had been expecting a show of at least some nervousness on his part, for the task he had undertaken was a stern one, but I could see no trace of it. He seemed completely at his ease, and he continued to address himself to Mr. Schnellenhamer without so much as a tremor in his voice.

"I have a proposition I would like to put up to you in connection with your forthcoming Bible epic Solomon And The Queen Of Sheba. You have probably realised for yourself that the trouble with all these ancient history super-pictures is that they lack comedy. Colossal scenery, battle sequences of ten thousand a side, more semi-nude dancing girls than you could shake a stick at, but where are the belly laughs? Take *Cleopatra*. Was there anything funny in that? Not a thing. And what occurred to me the moment I read your advance publicity was that what Solomon And The Queen Of Sheba needs, if it is really to gross grosses, is a comedy conjuror, and I decided to offer my services. You can scarcely require to be told how admirably an act like mine would fit into the scheme of things. There is nothing like a conjuror to keep a monarch amused through the long winter evenings, and King Solomon is bound to have had one at his court. So what happens? The Queen of Sheba arrives. The magnificence of her surroundings stuns her. 'The half was not told unto me" she says. 'You like my little place?' says the King. 'Well, it's a home. But wait, you ain't seen nothing yet. Send for the Great Alfredo.' And on I come. 'Well, folks,' I say, 'a funny thing happened to me on my way to the throne room,' and then I tell a story and then a few gags and then I go into my routine, and I would like just to run through it now. For my first trick——"

I was aghast. Long before the half-way mark of this speech the awful truth had flashed upon me. It was not George whom I saw before me—through a flickering mist—but Alfred, and I blamed myself bitterly for having been so mad as to mention Mr. Schnellenhamer to him, for I might have known that he would be inflamed by the news that the motion-picture magnate was within his reach and that here was his chance of getting signed up for a lucrative engagement. And George due to appear at any moment! No wonder that I reeled and had to support myself on what I believe is called a bollard.

"For my first trick," said Alfred, "I shall require a pound of butter, two bananas and a bowl of goldfish. Excuse me. Won't keep you long."

He went below, presumably in quest of these necessaries, and as he did so George came up the gangway.

There was none of that breezy self-confidence in George which had so impressed me in Alfred. He was patently suffering from stage fright. His legs wobbled and I could see his adam's apple going up and down as if pulled by an invisible string. He looked like a nervous speaker at a public banquet who on rising to his feet to propose the toast of Our Guests realises that he has completely forgotten the story of the two Irishmen Pat and Mike, with which he had been hoping to convulse his audience.

Nor did I blame him, for Sergeant Brichoux had taken a pair of handcuffs from his pocket and was breathing on them and polishing them on his sleeve, while Mr. Schnellenhamer subjected him to the stony glare which had so often caused employees of his on the Colossal-Exquisite lot to totter off to the commissary to restore themselves with frosted malted milk shakes. There was an ominous calm in the motion picture magnate's manner such as one finds in volcanoes just before they erupt and make householders in the neighbourhood wish they had settled elsewhere. He was plainly holding himself in with a powerful effort, having decided to toy with my unhappy nephew before unmasking him. For George's opening words had been "Good morning. I—er—that is to say—I—er—my name is Alfred Mulliner", and I could see that neither on the part of Mr. Schnellenhamer or of Sergeant Brichoux was there that willing suspension of disbelief which dramatic critics are always writing about.

"Good morning," said the former. "Nice weather."

"Yes, Mr. Schnellenhamer."

"Good for the crops."

"Yes, Mr. Schnellenhamer."

"Though bad for the umbrella trade."

"Yes, Mr. Schnellenhamer."

"Come along and join the party. Alfred Mulliner did you say the name was?"

"Yes, Mr. Schnellenhamer."

"You lie!" thundered Mr. Schnellenhamer, unmasking his batteries with horrifying abruptness. "You're no more Alfred Mulliner than I am, which isn't much. You're George Mulliner, and you're facing a murder rap or the next thing to it. Send for the police," he said to Sergeant Brichoux.

"I *am* the police," the sergeant reminded him, rather coldly it seemed to me.

"So you are. I was forgetting. Then arrest this man."

"I will do so immediately."

Sergeant Brichoux advanced on George handcuffs in hand, but before he could adjust them to his wrists an interruption occurred.

Intent though I had been on the scene taking place on the deck of the yacht, I had been able during these exchanges to observe out of the corner of my eye that a heavily bandaged man of middle age was approaching us along the quay, and he now mounted the gangway and hailed Mr. Schnellenhamer with a feeble "Hi, Jake."

So profuse were his bandages that one would hardly have expected his own mother to have recognised him, but Mr. Schnellenhamer did.

"Sam Glutz!" he cried. "Well, I'll be darned. I thought you were in the hospital."

"They let me out."

"You look like Tutunkhamen's mummy, Sam."

"So would you if you'd been belted by a hoodlum like I was. Did you read about it in the papers?"

"Sure. You made the front page."

"Well, that's something. But I wouldn't care to go through an experience like that again. I thought it was the end. My whole past life flashed before me."

"You can't have liked that."

"I didn't."

"Well, you'll be glad to hear, Sam, that we've got the fellow who slugged you."

"You have? Where is he?"

"Right there. Standing by the gentleman with the handcuffs."

George's head had been bowed, but now he happened to raise it, and Mr. Glutz uttered a cry.

"*You!*"

"That's him. George Mulliner. Used to work for the Colossal-Exquisite, but of course I've fired him. Take him to the cooler, sergeant."

Every bandage on Mr. Glutz's body rippled like wheat beneath a west wind, and his next words showed that what had caused this was horror and indignation at the programme Mr. Schnellenhamer had outlined.

"Over my dead body!" he cried. "Why, that's the splendid young man who saved my life last night."

"What!"

"Sure. The hood was beating the tar out of me when he came galloping up and knocked him for a loop, and after a terrific struggle the hood called it a day and irised out. Proud and happy to meet you, Mr. Mulliner. I think I heard Jake say he'd fired you. Well, come and work for the Perfecto-Wonderful, and I shall be deeply offended if you don't skin me for a salary beyond the dreams of avarice. I'll pencil you in as vice-president with brevet rank as a cousin by marriage."

I stepped forward. George was still incapable of speech.

"One moment, Mr. Glutz," I said.

"Who are you?"

"George's agent. And there is just one clause in the contract which strikes me as requiring revision. Reflect, Mr. Glutz. Surely cousin by marriage is a poor reward for the man who saved your life?"

Mr. Glutz was visibly affected. Groping among the bandages, he wiped away a tear.

"You're right," he said. "We'll make it brother-in-law. And now let's go and get a bite of lunch. You, too," he said to me, and I said I would be delighted. We left the boat in single file—first Mr. Glutz, then myself, then George, who was still dazed. The last thing I saw was Alfred coming on deck with his pound of butter and his two bananas. I seemed to detect on his face a slight touch of chagrin, caused no doubt by his inability to locate the bowl of goldfish so necessary to his first trick.

41

ANOTHER CHRISTMAS CAROL

THE subject of dieting had come up in the bar parlour of the Anglers' Rest, and a thoughtful Gin and Tonic said he wondered how fellows who were on a diet managed at Christmas.

"Precisely the problem which presented itself to my cousin Egbert," said Mr. Mulliner.

"Was he on a diet?" a Scotch on the Rocks asked.

"Very much the reverse until one day he felt a funny feeling in the upper left side of his chest and went to see a medical friend of his, a Doctor Potter."

"And what can I do for you, L. Nero Wolfe?" said Dr. Potter.

It was a sobriquet which had been bestowed on my cousin at their mutual school, for even then his ample frame had invited criticism. Egbert had started life as a bouncing baby, had grown into a bulbous boy, and was now, in his forty-second year, a man beneath whom weighing machines quivered like aspens. In common with all his ancestors he had a passionate love of food, but while they had worked off their superfluous tissue by jousting, fighting the Patnim, dancing old English dances and what not, on him it had accumulated.

"I don't think it's anything much, Bill," he replied, "but I thought I had better get a medical opinion. It's a sort of pain . . . well, not a pain exactly, more of a kind of funny feeling up here on the left side of my chest. It catches me when I breathe."

"Don't breathe," said Dr. Potter, for it was Christmas time, when even Harley Street physicians like their little joke. "All right, let's have a look at you. H'm," he said, the examination concluded. "Ha," he added, and threw in another "H'm" for good measure. "Yes, just as I supposed. You're too fat."

This surprised Egbert. He had sometimes thought that he might be an ounce or two overweight, but he would never have applied such an adjective to himself.

"Would you call me fat?"

"I'd go further. I'd call you grossly obese, and the fat's accumulating round your heart. We'll have to get at least a stone off you. If we don't—."

"What happens if we don't?"

"All that fuss and bother of buying wreaths and turning out for your funeral."

"Good heavens, Bill!"

"It's no use saying 'Good heavens'. For a year you've got to knock off all starchy foods, all rich foods. In fact it wouldn't be a bad idea if you knocked off food altogether."

It was a crushing blow, but there was good stuff in Egbert Mulliner. Though nothing could make such a régime agreeable, he was confident that he could go through with it. It was not as if he were not used to roughing it. He had often been at cocktail parties where the supply of sausages on those little wooden sticks had given out, and a sort of reserve strength had pulled him through.

His upper lip was stiff as he left the consulting room. It remained so till he was in the street, when all the stiffening suddenly went out of it. He had remembered his Aunt Serena, with whom as usual he would be taking dinner on the night of Christmas Day.

As Egbert from boyhood up had shown no signs of possessing any intelligence whatsoever, a place had been found for him in the Civil Service. But though he could drink tea at four o'clock as well as the next man, he had not really liked being in his country's service, however civil. What he wanted was to buy a partnership in a friend's interior decorating and antique selling firm, and this could be done only if his Aunt Serena, who was extraordinarily rich, put up the money. He had often asked her to do so and she had refused because she thought that haggling with customers about prices would bruise his gentle spirit. He had planned to make one last appeal on Christmas night when she would be mellowed by food and drink.

But in what frame of mind would a touchy hostess, who prided herself on the lavishness of her hospitality, be to finance a nephew who refused every course of the dinner she had taken such pains to assemble?

Two minutes later he was back in Dr. Potter's consulting room.

"Listen, Bill," he said. "You were only kidding just now about that diet, weren't you?"

"I was not."

"What would happen if I ate caviar, turtle soup, turkey, plum pudding, mince pies, biscuit tortoni, hot rolls with butter and crystallised fruit and drank hock, champagne, port and liquers? Would I die?"

"Of course. But what a jolly death. Were you thinking of doing that?"

"It's what I shall have to do when I have Christmas dinner at my aunt's. If I skip a single course, she will never speak to me again, and bang will go my interior decorator partnership," said Egbert, and in the clear concise way civil servants have he explained the delicate position in which he found himself.

Dr. Potter listened attentively and at the conclusion of the narrative said "H'm," added "Ha," and then said "H'm" again.

"You're sure that abstinence on your part would offend this aunt of whom you speak?"

"She would never forgive me."

"Then you must get out of it."

"I can't get out of it."

"You could if you had a good excuse. She could hardly blame you if, for instance, you had bubonic plague. I could inject a serum into you which would give you all the bubonic plague a heart could desire."

Egbert weighed the suggestion. He appreciated its ingenuity, but nevertheless he hesitated.

"What's bubonic plague like?"

"I don't know that it's like anything. Except, of course, bubonic plague."

"Is it painful?"

"I've never had it myself, but I'm told it gives you a sort of funny feeling."

"Don't you come out in spots?"

"I believe that is the usual procedure."

Egbert shook his head.

"I don't think I'll have it."

"Then have an accident."

"What sort of accident?"

"The choice is wide, but perhaps the simplest thing would be to get run over by a taxi cab."

"Have you ever been run over by a taxi cab?"

"Dozens of times."

"Did it hurt?"

"Just a kind of tickling sensation."

Egbert mused awhile.

"That does seem the best thing to do."

"Much the best."

"And there's no need to get actually run over. I can just step off into the road and stick a leg out."

"Exactly. The charioteer will do the rest."

Christmas Day dawned with its sprinkling of snow, its robin redbreasts and all the things one has always been led to expect, and as it progressed Egbert's determination to follow the doctor's advice became solidified. He was not altogether persuaded of the accuracy of the latter's statement that getting together with a taxi cab caused merely a kind of tickling sensation, but even if the results were far worse, they must be faced. As he walked up to his aunt's house, he was encouraged to see there was no stint of the necessary vehicles. They whizzed to and fro in dozens, and to extend a leg in front of one of them would be a task well within the scope of the least gifted man. It was simply a matter of making one's selection.

He rejected the first that came along because he disliked the driver's moustache, the second because the cab was the wrong colour, and he was just about to step in front of a third which met all his qualifications, when he paused with leg in air. He had suddenly remembered that his aunt's birthday was on February the eleventh, by which time he would be out of hospital and expected as a guest at the banquet with which she always celebrated her natal day. And her birthday dinners, as he knew full well, were just as stupendous as those at Christmas.

Of course, it would be open to him to get knocked down by another taxi cab on February 10, but if he yielded to this temptation, how would his superiors at the office react? Would they not shake their heads and say to one another "Mulliner has got into a rut" and feel that the services of an employee so accident prone were better dispensed with?

It was a possibility that froze his feet and caused both his chins to tremble. The salary the taxpayers paid him for drinking tea at four o'clock was not as generous as he could have wished, but it was all he had. Bereft of it, he would be penniless. And he would not even be able to beg his bread in the streets, for his medical adviser had expressly forbidden him all starchy foods.

Only one course lay before him. Whatever the price involved, he must continue on his way to his aunt's residence and there tuck, though with a heavy heart, into the caviar, the turtle soup, the turkey, the plum pudding, the mince pies, the biscuit tortoni, the hot rolls with butter and the crystallised fruit, washing them down with hock, champagne, port and liqueurs. If the worst happened, he reflected, for he was a philosophical man, it would be just one more grave among the hills.

Nevertheless, though philosophical, it was in no buoyant mood that he came to journey's end and exchanged Christmas greetings with his aunt in her ornate drawing-room. There was, he noted, even more of her than when they had last met. She, too, had started life as a bouncing baby and from there had grown into a globular girl, finishing up as one of the three stoutest women in the W.1 postal division of London.

He delivered his Christmas gift, and in return she pressed into his hand an oblong slip of paper.

"The money for your partnership, dear," she said.

It would have seemed incredible to anyone, seeing Egbert, that he was capable of swelling with ecstasy any more than he was swelling already, but at these words he seemed to expand like one of those odd circular fish you get down in Florida, which when hauled to the surface puff themselves out like balloons. His nose quivered, his ears wiggled, his eyes, usually devoid of any expression whatsoever, shone like twin stars. He had not felt such a gush of elation since his seventh birthday, when somebody had given him a box of chocolates and he had devoured the top layer and supposed that that was the end and then had found that there was a second layer lurking underneath. He put his arm round his aunt's waist as far as it would go, and kissed her fondly.

"How can I thank you?" he murmured brokenly.

"I thonght you would be pleased, dear," she said. "But now I am afraid I have a little disappointment for you. Do you read a magazine called *Pure Diet And World Redemption*?"

"Is that the one that has all those pictures of girls without any clothes on?"

"No, that is *Playboy*. I subscribe to that regularly. This one is all about vegetarianism. A copy was left here by mistake last week. I glanced at it idly, and my whole outlook became changed. It said vegetarianism was an absolute vital essential prerequisite to a new order of civilisation in which humanity will have become truly humane."

Egbert, as far as was possible for one of his stoutness, leapt in his chair. A wild thought had flashed into his mind, such as it was. Not even if he had been a victim of bubonic plague could the feeling he was feeling have been funnier.

"Do you mean—?"

"It said that only thus can there come peace on earth with a cessation of wars, the abolition of crime, diseases, insanity, poverty and oppression. And you can't say that wouldn't be nice, can you dear?"

As a rule, Egbert when speaking had the beautifully clear enunciation found only in the Civil Service, but now emotion made him stutter.

"Do you mean," he cried, inserting five or six m's into the last word, "that you have become a vegetarian?"

"Yes, dear."

"There won't be any turkey tonight?"

"I'm afraid not."

"No turtle soup? No mince pies?"

"I know how disappointed you must be."

Egbert, who had leapt in his chair, sprang from it like some lissom adagio dancer, a feat against the performance of which any knowledgeable bookmaker would have given odds of at least a hundred to eight.

"Disappointed?" he thundered. "Disappointed? I couldn't be more pleased. I've just become a vegetarian myself. Well, practically. I wouldn't touch a turkey with a ten-foot pole. What shall we be having for dinner?"

"To start with, seaweed soup."

"Most nutritious."

"Then mock salmon. It is vegetable marrow coloured pink."

"Splendid!"

"Followed by nut cutlets with spinach."

"Capital!"

"And an orange."

"We split one?"

"No, one each."

"A positive banquet. God bless us, every one," said Egbert.

He had a feeling that he had heard that before somewhere, but we cannot all be original, and it seemed to him to sum up the situation about as neatly as a situation could be summed up.

42

FROM A DETECTIVE'S NOTEBOOK

WE were sitting round the club fire, old General Malpus, Driscoll the Q.C., young Freddie ffinch-ffinch and myself, when Adrian Mulliner, the private investigator, gave a soft chuckle. This was, of course, in the smoking room where soft chuckling is permitted.

"I wonder," he said, "if it would interest you chaps to hear the story of what I always look upon as the greatest triumph of my career?"

We said, "No, it wouldn't," and he began.

"Looking back over my years as a detective, I recall many problems the solution of which made me modestly proud, but though all of them undoubtedly presented certain features of interest and tested my powers to the utmost, I can think of none of my feats of ratiocination that gave me more pleasure than the unmasking of the man Sherlock Holmes, now better known as The Fiend Of Baker Street."

Here General Malpus looked at his watch, said, "Bless my soul," and hurried out, no doubt to keep some appointment which had temporarily slipped his mind.

"I had at first so little to go on," Adrian Mulliner proceeded. "But just as a brief sniff at a handkerchief or shoe will start one of Mr. Thurber's bloodhounds giving quick service, so is the merest suggestion of anything that I might call fishy enough to set me off on the trail, and what first aroused my suspicions of this sinister character was his peculiar financial position.

"Here we had a man who evidently was obliged to watch the pennies closely, for when we are introduced to him he is, according to Doctor Watson's friend Stamford, 'bemoaning himself because he could not find someone to go halves with him in some nice rooms which he had found and which were too much for his purse.' Watson offers himself as a fellow lodger, and they settle down in— I quote—a couple of comfortable bedrooms and a large sitting room at 221-B Baker Street.

"Now, I never lived in Baker Street at the turn of the century, but I knew old gentlemen who had done so, and they assured me that in those days you could get a bedroom and sitting room and three meals a day for a pound a week. An extra bedroom no doubt made the thing come higher, but thirty shillings must have covered the rent, and there was never a question of a man as honest as Doctor Watson failing to come up with his fifteen each Saturday. It followed, then, that even allowing for expenditure in the way of Persian slippers, tobacco, disguises, revolver cartridges, cocaine and spare fiddle strings, Holmes would have been getting by on a couple of pounds or so weekly. And with this modest state of life he appeared to be perfectly content. In a position where you or I would have spared no effort to add to our resources, he simply did not bother about the financial side of his profession. Let us take a few instances at random and see what he made as a 'consulting detective'. Where are you going, Driscoll?"

"Out," said the Q.C., suiting action to the word.

Adrian Mulliner resumed his tale.

"In the early days of their association Watson speaks of being constantly bundled off into his bedroom because Holmes needed the sitting room for interviewing callers. 'I have to use this room as a place of business,' he said, 'and these people are my clients.' And who were these clients? 'A grey-headed, seedy visitor, who was closely followed by a slipshod elderly woman' and after these came 'a railway porter in his velveteen uniform'. Not much cash in that lot, and things did not noticeably improve later, for we find his services engaged by a stenographer, an average commonplace British tradesman, a commissionaire, a city clerk, a Greek interpreter, a landlady ('You arranged an affair for a lodger of mine last year') and a Cambridge undergraduate.

"So, far from making money as a consulting detective, he must have been a good deal out of pocket most of the time. In *A Study In Scarlet,* Inspector Gregson says there has been a bad business during the night at 3 Lauriston Gardens off the Brixton Road and he would esteem it a great kindness if Holmes would favour him with his opinions. Off goes Holmes in a hansom from Baker Street to Brixton, a fare of several shillings, dispatches a long telegram (another two or three bob to the bad), summons 'half a dozen of the dirtiest and most ragged street Arabs that ever I clapped eyes on' and gives each of them a shilling, and, finally, calling on Police Constable Bunce, the officer who discovered the body, takes half a sovereign from his pocket and after 'playing with it pensively' presents it to the constable. The whole affair must have cost him considerably more than a week's rent at Baker Street, and no hope of getting it back from Inspector Gregson, for Gregson, according to Holmes himself, was one of the smartest of all of the Scotland Yarders.

"Inspector Gregson! Inspector Lestrade! These clients! I found myself thinking a good deal about them, and it was not long before the truth dawned upon me that they were merely cheap actors, hired to deceive Doctor Watson. For what would the ordinary private investigator have said to himself when starting out in business? He would have said, 'Before I take on work for a client I must be sure that that client has the stuff. The daily sweetener and the little something down in advance are of the essence' and would have had those landladies and those Greek interpreters out of that sitting room before you could say 'blood-stain'. Yet Holmes, who could not afford a pound a week for lodgings, never bothered. Significant!"

On what seemed to me the somewhat shallow pretext that he had to see a man about a dog, Freddie ffinch-ffinch now excused himself and left the room.

"Later," Adrian Mulliner went on, "the thing became absolutely farcical, for all pretence that he was engaged in a gainful occupation was dropped by himself and the clients. I quote Doctor Watson:

" 'He tossed a crumpled letter across to me. It was dated from Montague Place upon the preceding evening and ran thus:

Dear Mr. Holmes,
    I am anxious to consult you as to whether or not I should accept a situation which has been offered me as a governess. I shall call at half past ten tomorrow if I do not inconvenience you. Yours faithfully,
                                                                Violet Hunter.'

"Now, the fee an investigator could expect from a governess, even one in full employment, could scarcely be more than a few shillings, yet when two weeks later Miss Hunter wired 'Please be at the Black Swan Hotel at Winchester at mid-day tomorrow,' Holmes dropped everything and sprang into the 9.30 train."

Adrian Mulliner chuckled softly. "You see where all this is heading?"

I said, "No, I don't." I was the only one there, and I had to say something.

"Tut, tut, man, you know my methods. Apply them. Why is a man casual about money?"

"Because he has a lot of it."

"Precisely."

"But you said Holmes hadn't."

"I said nothing of the sort. That was merely the illusion he was trying to create, because he needed a front for his true activities. He was pulling in the stuff from another source. Where is the big money? Where has it always been? In crime. Bags of it, and no income tax. If you want to salt away a few million for a rainy day, you don't spring into 9.30 trains to go and see governesses, you become a Master Criminal, sitting like a spider in the centre of its web and egging your corps of assistants on to steal jewels and Naval Treaties. It was not long before I saw daylight and all the pieces of the jigsaw puzzle fell into place. Holmes was Professor Moriarty."

"What was that name again?"

"Professor Moriarty."

"The bird who was forever slowly oscillating his face from side to side in a curiously reptilian fashion?"

"That's the chap."

"But Holmes's face didn't forever oscillate slowly from side to side in a curiously reptilian fashion."

"Nor did Professor Moriarty's."

"Holmes said it did."

"And to whom? To Doctor Watson. Purely in order to ensure that the misleading description got publicity. Watson never saw Moriarty. All he knew about him was what Holmes told him on the evening of April 24th, 1891. And he made a little slip on that occasion."

"Watson?"

"Holmes. When he said that on his way to Watson's he had been attacked by a rough with a bludgeon. A Napoleon of Crime, anxious to eliminate someone he disliked, would have thought up something better than roughs with bludgeons. Dropping cobras down the chimney is the mildest thing that would have occurred to him. It was that little slip that first put me on Holmes's track. Well, that's the story, old man."

"The whole story?"

"Yes."

"There isn't any more?"

"No."

I chuckled softly.